QUEEN
ORCA
& THE PIGS
AN ALASKAN ADVENTURE

R.V. Bailey

INDIE CRAWLERS

Queen Orca & the Pigs
An Alaskan Adventure

Indie Crawlers is a vanity press imprint. Mother Spider Publishing is not responsible for the content, editing, or images within this work.

Indie Crawlers books may be ordered through booksellers or by contacting:

Indie Crawlers
www.MotherSpider.com
(239) 693-DRAW (3729)

ISBN: 978-1-942728-28-3 (Print)
ISBN: 978-1-942728-29-0 (Digital)

LCCN: 2016909255

Printed in the United States of America

Editor: R.V. Bailey
Cover concept: R.V. Bailey
Cover design: Bernard John Dollison
Book design: Jennifer FitzGerald

Any people depicted in stock imagery are models, and such images are being used for illustrative purposes only. Images copyright: stock.adobe.com

WARNING: This book contains adult themes which some readers may find objectionable and/or offensive, including sexual intercourse.

CONTENTS

Acknowledgements   5
Chapter One: 7
 Disappearance

Chapter Two   21
 Orcas Described

Chapter Three   47
 Halibut

Chapter four   65
 Champ

Chapter Five   79
 Rocky Bay

Chapter six   115
 The mini-pigs

Chapter Seven   137
 Plans

Chapter eight   153
 Placer Gold

Chapter Nine   169
 Reed arrives

Chapter Ten   173
 Finding The Pack

Chapter Eleven   203
 Hunters

Chapter twelve   219
 Theory

Chapter Thirteen   225
 Kids and orcas

Chapter Fourteen   237
 Interview

Chapter Fifthteen   243
   Research
Chapter Sixteen   257
   Hunting sea lions
Chapter Seventeen   265
   OCS - Orca
   Communication Society
Chapter Eighteen   273
   Blind Justice
Chapter Nineteen   287
   The Pharoah
Chapter Twenty   299
   Shipping plan
Chapter Twenty one   323
   Knight Island.
Chapter Twenty two   335
   Kennelsto Herring Bay
Chapter Twenty Three   361
   Training
Chapter Twenty Four   395
   Contact attempt
Chapter Twenty five   415
   Close look
Chapter Twenty Six   433
   Aircraft
Chapter Twenty Seven   439
   A-T found
Chapter Twenty Eight   457
   Follow
Chapter Twenty Nine   467
   Kennels over water
Chapter 30   493
   Corralled
End.   517

Acknowledgements

Thanks to author Erich Hoyt for his excellent observations of killer whale activity as expressed in his 1981 book Orca – The Whale Called Killer. His excellent reporting of killer whale activities over time in waters off British Columbia is very educational and inspiring.

Work on this novel took place in southern Alaska, Castle Rock, Colorado, Port of the Islands near Naples, Florida, and in Casper, Wyoming. In Casper my daughter, Diane and her husband Greg Waldron were very hospitable and my son in Casper, Steve Bailey and his wife Susan were supportive and helpful. Mary Baune in Casper provided some computer guidance.

CHAPTER ONE:

Disappearance

J im Tubbs maneuvered the small rented boat along the eastern shore
of the island. He and Brooke Adams looked forward to some rest
and warmth at a protected cove where the boat could be beached
on sand or at least away from sharp rocks. The cool breeze from the
west had died somewhat after blowing since early morning, but, overall,
it had been a long, enjoyable, early June, 1989 day in Prince William
Sound. Their legs had become increasingly cramped and their aching
posterior muscles were yearning for an opportunity to stretch into a
different position. This was the third day of a planned four day boating
trip across a small part of this sound in what many considered to be the
most beautiful part of southern Alaska. The Exxon Valdez oil spill had
come and gone, and the abundant marine life they observed, including
the much publicized sea otter, demonstrated the overreaction to the spill.
They had observed no oil on any of the beaches they had visited. Given
time, nature itself had performed the cleanup.

Brooke had begun to wonder if their mini-vacation would prove to
be more than she cared to handle. Her posterior was tired of the small
bench seats and she longed for a hot shower and food other than the freeze-
dried rations Jim had promised would taste so good in the wild. She was
beginning to hope that the boat which dropped them off would arrive early
to return them to the small port of Whittier on the western edge of Prince
William Sound.

As one of the small number of dancers in the US who attained the
privilege of becoming a Reno showgirl, Brooke was no stranger to physical
exertion. But the strenuous dance routines of the shows had done little to

harden her to the unaccustomed and difficult positions in the boat. Her main reason for being on the trip was to be with Jim, an up and coming assistant manager for Reno's Peppermill Hotel and Casino.

They motored north toward a rocky island which might offer some shelter. The only sounds were an occasional sea gull, the sound of the small outboard and the slap of waves against the turquoise boat. As they rounded an offshore boulder Jim smiled, "there's a good spot on that small beach in the cove. There's some firewood there, too."

"Looks wonderful," Brooke responded with eagerness as she leaned forward to stretch her back. In a few minutes the boat skidded up onto the coarse black sand of the beach and Jim stepped out of the craft into the cold water and pushed it up onto the hard-packed sand. Brooke slowly stretched up and out of the boat, her muscles stiff. Jim pulled the boat further up the beach and completely out of the water. It felt good to be on land again and to stand upright. They both stretched and moaned as the tired muscles rejoiced in new positions. The complex smell of evergreens, flowers, grass and humus added to their welcome. As Jim began removing the tent and provisions from the small forward storage area of the boat, Brooke continued stretching and began looking closer at the beautiful small cove. The sandy beach was only 50 feet wide with large boulders on the north side of the east-facing beach. Water depth increased quickly and just a stone's throw offshore the bottom could not be seen. A linear stand of spruce and aspen formed a two-toned green backdrop resembling a curtain to the west, ending against a steep rock face. In a way the setting reminded Brooke of the huge stage at the Ziegfeld Theatre in Bally's Hotel and Casino in Reno.

"If we're lucky, in the morning we may have some nice early sun to wake up to," she sighed, but she knew there was little hope. The sun had shone briefly only twice in the three days since she and Jim were dropped off at the southern end of this chain of islands by the charter boat from Whittier. As she looked upward into the tops of a couple of tall trees she suddenly recognized the chocolate brown body and stark white head of a bald eagle, watching them from a gnarled, bare upper limb 100 feet above the rocks.

"Jim, there's a bald eagle," she whispered to him as she took the binoculars from the case and focussed on the silent, regal-looking turkey-sized bird. The handsome brown plumage of the body, the dark yellow beak, and the piercing eyes set in brilliant white head feathers were gorgeous against the cloudy sky. Jim stopped unrolling the tent to study the bird through the binoculars. It seemed to regard them with a mixture of disdain and curiosity.

"It's nice to have some company, I hope he stays for a while. Can you believe they used to have a bounty on bald eagles in Alaska?"

"Why would they want to kill eagles?"

"I can only assume it was another crazy idea of the commercial fishermen on the theory that the eagles were some sort of competition. Remember that article in the *Anchorage Times* last week describing the opposition by commercial fishermen to fish farming in Alaska? Those people have alot of ideas that don't make sense; the gutless politicians often go along with them."

They turned back to their work and in a few minutes their tent was up and the sleeping bag, mini-duffle bags and the few other items they had brought were stashed inside should the rains once again come. Pine needles, small sticks and wood were gathered and the fire, started with a small amount of charcoal lighter fluid, crackled as it grew in size. The eagle watched, undisturbed, occasionally turning its head from side to side and observing all the action below. w

Brooke took off her blue knitted wool cap, revealing her long braided brown hair wrapped in a bun on her head. "Jim, I know the water's cold, but we haven't had a shower for days. Don't you think this might be a good time to use some of that detergent we brought that's supposed to make suds in salt water?" Jim stared out at the surface reflections on the slightly rippling water. To the north 500 feet away a small group of sea gulls huddled on the rocks as if watching to see if he had the nerve to get in.

"I was hoping we might find a fresh water pond with water warmed to at least 50 or 60 degrees. This sea water is likely in the 40's but it feels closer to freezing. You're right, a bath would feel good, but why not wait until the day after tomorrow and take a hot one in Whittier?"

Brooke persisted, "I don't mean to overdo it, let's just wade out and suds off. It won't be that bad, and the fire is really getting warm to help dry us off. Besides, Jim, after the last three night's activities my dignity hinges on bathing; we really need a wash."

"Well, OK, but let's have a toddy first." He retrieved a pint bottle of vodka from his pack along with a small bottle of tonic. Generous portions were poured into plastic cups and he handed one to Brooke. "Cheers" he smiled at her as they both took a drink. The alcohol generated an internal warmth as the fire grew larger and brighter.

Jim nodded approvingly and stepped over to place more wood on the fire. When he turned again, Brooke was down to her panties and bra. It was nice to look at the beautifully sculpted body which had been beside him either in bed or in the double sleeping bag since leaving Reno a week ago. The bikini marks still showed from the tan she had gotten when they spent ten days in Mexico in March.

Brooke moved closer to the fire to take off her panties and bra. She remembered reading about Finnish saunas and how the Finns would overheat their bodies and then run outside to dive into ice water; she wondered if she could similarly absorb some of the fire's warmth before getting into the frigid waters of Prince William Sound. Jim stripped down to his underwear as Brooke, now feeling warmer and in happier spirits, trotted over to the water's edge. High tide was in, and the water gently drew a line along the upper part of the beach. Jim threw the small plastic bottle of detergent to her as she caught her breath and turned and began wading out into the water. The eagle watched with more interest.

———— ◆◆◆ ————

The resident pack of the top predator species of the world's oceans had spent three hours in the afternoon sleeping and cruising slowly westward in the island-dotted southwest part of Prince William Sound. It had been a good quiet rest, and as evening approached the entire pack of nineteen orcas began to vocalize, whistle and more closely scan the surroundings with sonar. The oceans, covering 80% of the earth's surface, were their domain and they loved the cold water and the almost limitless variety of organisms they encountered in their travels.

The succulent pink salmon consumed earlier that morning were mostly digested and, despite the rich fare, hunger was again creeping into their consciousness. Two of the juveniles began to play by rapidly gliding through the icy water, like cleverly guided torpedoes, in rotation around the others. Through highly accurate sonar scanning, the rocky bottom ahead and below, as well as various sizes and varieties of fish on and near the bottom, was revealed to the entire pack.

Although visibility in the slightly cloudy water was only 70 or so feet, the scene was read as easily as a soaring falcon scans a patchy forest below.

With their acute hearing they knew a second, smaller resident pack was 20 miles to the northwest and could detect croakers, shrimp and other noisemaking fish on the sea floor. To these large brained creatures the ocean scene, observed mostly through sound and sonar rather than visually, was always interesting.

One of the male juveniles, ranging ahead of the pack, detected through his sonar, an object floating on the surface about 100 yards from shore 300 yards ahead. A click train from a highly focused sonar beam identified the object as a 3 foot long sea otter, a length less than half the width of a mature whale's tail flukes. This would be fun, he thought. He signaled the find to the others in the pack and another juvenile and one adult female, as a sort of nanny, joined him. The three black and white torpedoes, 30 feet below the surface and undetected by the dimwitted otter, quickly closed the distance to the otter floating on its back. The male juvenile, 14 feet long and weighing 3,000 pounds, got there first and, at half it's top speed of 35 miles per hour, grabbed the otter by the upper body with its sharp teeth. It took the otter to the bottom in 40 feet of water in a few seconds and then released it. The other two killer whales, close behind, broadcast focussed squeals and whistles intended to scare the otter.

They would have more fun if the otter would try to escape by swimming, but instinct told the otter its best tactic was to play dead. Its natural buoyancy, created by air within dense, brown fur, carried it in a spiral to the surface. The second youngster seized the otter at the surface and dove with it, with the other two in pursuit. Again the otter was released and this time the adult female powerfully stroked near it with her tail flukes causing it to tumble as it again floated to the surface. The young male again grabbed the otter by the upper body and swam about with it at the surface. The otter looked helplessly about, certain it was going to be eaten. But not this time. The whales were simply playing, and though they were capable of cutting the otter to pieces with a few bites, the skin of the terrified animal had not even been punctured. The thick coat of luxurious fur on the otter placed it well down on the desirable eating list of the whales, although they could skin it through the use of their teeth and dexterous tongue if they chose to do so. They would not eat the otter this day.

The three broke off the harassment and rejoined the pack, now a quarter of a mile away and moving northwest toward one of the small islands in Prince William Sound. Their speed had picked up to 6 knots and they surfaced in unison every two minutes to blow. Play time was over. The pack was getting increasingly hungry and it was time to hunt. As a welcome change from the salmon, herring, cod and miscellaneous fish they had been eating for the past several days, they would hunt mammals tonight: most likely harbor seals and harbor porpoise. But any animal in the water could be fair and perhaps interesting game, including such prey as blacktailed deer which might be caught swimming from island to island. Chasing and catching mammals, especially the fast swimmers, was a great delight to the females and to the youngsters. The older bulls seldom got excited, but enjoyed the warm, red meat when a catch was made. The brightness of the June Alaska sky belied the fact that it was approaching 7 pm.

The undisputed leader of this pack was a mature female whale known to the others as Tinga. She was strong, agile, highly intelligent and aggressive. The group of whales which she now headed had adopted her several years ago and two years previously she had borne a calf fathered by the large bull in this group. But Tinga's family tree lay not in this "*resident*" Prince William Sound pack but in a "*transient*" group which patrolled the shoreline and open ocean along the north margin of the Gulf of Alaska and as far southeast as British Columbia, Canada. While the resident whale groups were relatively docile and fed mostly on fish, the transients were aggressive meat eaters known for their vicious attacks on almost any animal in the water, including other whales more than twice their size.

Tinga had been two years old and was learning the predatory ways of the transient group when her mother, the leader of the pack, was turned on by other transient pack members for a reason Tinga never understood. Her mother would have been killed by the other orcas had she not taken her youngster and fled into a rock-strewn cove where she nearly beached herself and her calf to escape the attack. Several hours passed before Tinga's mother would leave the protection of the cove and then she swam north with her calf.

Several days later they reached Prince William Sound and found good food there although they preferred red meat to the fish diet. In time they had joined one of the resident packs of orcas and, for three years before she died, Tinga's mother taught the pack how to effectively hunt, kill and eat more mammals as a fun and nutritious variation from fish. Tinga herself was a good learner and soon was leading the pack on hunting forays and was making many of the kills. By the age of twelve she was the acknowledged pack leader.

Noisy communication within the pack ceased and the pack split into one group of ten and another group of nine whales. The chances of success in making a find and kill were better by splitting up and hunting as two closely coordinated groups. The quick, agile females would take the lead of each group. Joining Tinga in the lead group were nine other whales including Kee, another mature female and Zirgo, a nearly mature bull. The two juveniles, now silent but eager to hunt, were side by side 50 feet behind Tinga. Three hundred feet behind Tinga and her group were the other nine whales including Ming, a mature female, Targa, a mature female with a four month old infant, and Zinda, a sub-adult female. Kray, the large mature bull, would be at the rear and on the outside when they approached a shoreline.

The positioning was wisely maintained; if Tinga slowed, the pack slowed, if she accelerated, the entire pack accelerated. In order not to alert seals, porpoises or other mammal prey of their approach, communications between the intelligent orcas ceased almost entirely when they were hunting. Though underwater visibility was no more than 40 feet, their highly sensitive sonar, even when used at extremely low intensity, allowed each to know precisely where the others were and the course they were following. The en echelon positions, like one side of a spearhead of migrating geese, allowed orcas in the front of the line to have unrestricted sonar scanning ahead. Tinga, the sleek mature female, 22 feet long and weighing 6,000 pounds, was leading her group of ten as they approached the first island. She was the point of the blade.

The whales were cruising almost silently at 6 knots 20 feet below the surface and moving toward the rocky shore, rising to blow and inhale in close unison at two minute intervals. Simultaneous surfacing allowed all to transmit and receive sonar and detect other sounds below the surface without disturbances which would be caused by any uncoordinated whale surfacing. Occasional sonar clicks gave them all the information they needed concerning water depth, bottom configuration, and distance to the island.

Leading her group, Tinga approached the island in 20 feet of water and within 30 feet of the steep, rocky shoreline. Her black dorsal fin and upper body could not be detected at the surface until she rose every two minutes to blow. The fat, spotted, gray and silver female harbor seal had been foraging on the rocky bottom of the bay for herring and young salmon. Feeding had been good and the seal had gained 30 pounds in the past two months to reach 185 pounds. As twilight approached in the long Alaskan day, a growing sense of uneasiness began to pervade her senses.

She rose to the surface frequently and raised her head above the water surface to peer up and down the rocky shoreline. Her male companion swam with confidence among the protective rocks near shore. A lonely gull called as it flew by, and the breeze blew a gentle ripple on the water. Perhaps one more herring before retiring to the safety of the crevices and shelves of the rocks on the shore only 200 yards away.

Tinga, submerged, silent and invisible from above, as always when hunting, banked around sunken rocks at the island's edge. Her sonar focused to scan the waters in the cove and near the shoreline beyond. The silent, powerful strokes of her flukes propelled her lithe, smooth body through the water almost effortlessly. She was anxious to make a kill.

With microsecond sonar pulses she determined instantly that a seal was present in the cove. The sonar response had been received through sensitive nerves in the lower jaw and passed through large nerve bundles to her specialized brain where it was correctly interpreted. She knew its underwater location in 40 feet of water just above a jagged, rocky bottom. To conceal the approach for the moment, she sent no further signals.

Tinga did not swim toward the seal: instead, she rocketed forward on an underwater interception course which would cut the animal off from shore access. If the seal could get up into the rocks it was safe, but she knew from experience that intended prey would often panic if a hunting killer whale blocked access to the rocky shore. Then it might foolishly try to outswim the hunters through an escape attempt into the Sound.

The seal broke off chasing a young salmon on the bottom when she thought she heard several clicks and paused with rising alarm. She quickly rose to the surface to peer in all directions like a nervous periscope. To her horror the seal heard the whuff of exhausted air and saw, 100 yards to the south, the dorsal fins of four of the creatures it feared most: the intelligent, swift, and large predators who chased, killed and ate her kind. Instinct told her there was a chance of reaching the shore, now less than 50 yards away. In panic she immediately dove and began swimming at top speed for the nearest rocks, not knowing that Tinga was already accelerating on a subsurface interception course. Kee and the other three front line whales were fully aware of the situation and ready for pursuit should the seal swim away from shore.

Closing swiftly and silently from the seal's left, Tinga suddenly began an intense send/receive sonar sequence. Silence was cast aside. In order to make the catch, she must now know the quarry's precise depth, shape, speed and direction of travel. Visual contact was not yet possible. She quickly determined, with the other whales watching on their own sonar, that the seal was making a run for the shore; she was on a good course to intercept. Streaking through the water, the silver-gray, bullet-shaped seal body suddenly came into her view, swimming from right to left toward the rocky shore.

Tinga opened her mouth to grab it in the middle, but the seal had heard the sonar and now saw her and, at the last instant, turned an underwater somersault back away from the shore. Her rushing jaws closed on water only. This seal knew better than to take a course away from shore; land was its only hope. It quickly turned another somersault as Tinga's 22 foot body zipped by, and it again swam rapidly for shore. Tinga banked sharply to the right, maintaining a high speed. Sonar told her the seal was again swimming for shore, and she accelerated after it. In less than a minute the seal reached shore just ahead of Tinga, but the only place it could get into quickly and away from the water was a narrow rock crevice sloping up from a ledge at the water's surface. It jumped to the ledge and began clawing to get up into the crevice, but with ease Tinga slowed her rush with her large front flippers and she and the water rose onto the ledge. Deftly her teeth closed on the rear flippers of the struggling seal and she plucked it from the crevice as a hungry otter might grab a panicky rainbow trout. As the large wave of water she had carried shoreward began to recede, Tinga slid backward with the flopping seal held firmly in her mouth. Although Tinga was not visible to the others waiting offshore, they knew, through sonar scanning, that she had made a catch the instant she slid back into the water. Visual sighting was unnecessary.

A chase and catch were something to be enjoyed, and, 50 feet offshore, Tinga released the injured seal, its back broken. The 4 lead whales now began to play with the captured seal as 4 coyotes would play with a captured prairie dog. The seal's injuries were not so serious that it would immediately die, but it could not escape. Tinga, blowing excitedly at the surface every 30 seconds, again picked up the seal and carried it around the cove with it's rear quarter in her mouth and the head projecting forward. The seal still was capable of biting, although it was in shock. Kee then signalled she wanted to play, so Tinga released the seal at the surface where Kee immediately grabbed it and shook it gently under water. The juveniles also wanted to play, but Zirgo, the male, waiting 75 feet offshore with Zinda, was very hungry and signaled to the playing females that he wished to eat. The females immediately began moving away and left the seal at the surface looking helplessly toward shore with large, dark eyes. Female killer whales, because of their smaller size and greater agility, usually caught more prey than males and they often fed the males.

With light strokes of his flukes the male Zirgo moved forward and, taking the front half of the seal in his mouth, sank below the surface. He bit down and the matching teeth in his upper and lower jaws came together to shear meat, bones and skin. He shook his head to neatly severe the body in two parts. First the portion in his mouth was swallowed and he then grabbed the remainder of the seal, crushed many of the bones with 4 inch long teeth, and swallowed. There was nothing left. The familiar taste of blood from a warmblooded animal was good. The 185 pound seal would satisfy his hunger for a day.

A dozen sea gulls had begun circling overhead in anticipation of some scraps from the killing, and as the waters calmed and the whales began to depart, they dropped to the water's surface to squabble over bits of meat and skin.

The start of the hunt had been successful and the pack, reforming into two silent, linear groups, continued its northward prowl along the east edge of the island. Because of the chase and the kill they were more excited and their speed increased. Zirgo, now satisfied, dropped back to the rear group of "observers" to be replaced in the front group by Kray, the large 17,000 pound bull killer whale. Kray was 29 feet in length with a dorsal fin which projected a full 7 feet above his back. Kray was hungry now for red meat; Tinga, Kee and Zinda, the prominent females, were well aware of it. Another kill must be made.

◆◆◆

Brooke had now waded out to her narrow waist in the cold water with the small bottle of detergent, her slender tanned body quivering in the cold water. She began splashing handsfull of water on her arms and breasts and squeezed some of the liquid into one hand and began to lather her body. The small plastic bottle floated on the gentle waves. Sea gulls called in the distance; the bald eagle shifted on the high branch and watched intently. Jim, now naked, muscular and tan, still hesitated on the dark sandy beach at the water's edge. An ankle-deep test wade into the chilling water renewed his doubts about bathing here. But Brooke persisted, "Come on in, it's really not that bad once you get used to it," as she lathered her arms. Brooke didn't appear to be shivering so Jim finally agreed, "All right, but let me build the fire up first so it will be going strong when we get out." He tossed some of the small branches and pine cones he had picked up earlier on the fire, and, in so doing, turned his back on Brooke and the cold Alaskan water.

Tinga and the other whales, excited and in their hunting formation, detected splashing at the surface 200 yards away even before they came around the small rocky point on the island. They also picked up sound vibrations, indicating communications, which they had heard before when passing fishing boats with the two-legged creatures on board. In anticipation of possible action, the whales surfaced in unison to blow before they rounded the corner so their approach would be unseen at the surface. As Tinga, in the lead, rounded the rocks at 6 knots 150 yards from the beach, she was 12 feet below the surface. She sent out a brief sonar pulse. She identified a creature in the water close to the beach. This was no seal or sea lion, and it stood on two legs and was splashing at the surface.

Closer study was needed. She sent out more sonar and received confirmation: the legs were thin with a bone structure running up the center of this warm blooded animal. It had no thick, undesirable body hair as did the sea otter. The other whales following now also rounded the rocky corner well below the water's surface and received their individual sonar definitions of the creature in the water. They were at once excited and curious by the sonar returns.

Tinga wanted visual confirmation. Still hidden below the surface, her stroking flukes propelled her swiftly toward the beach and the animal in the water. About 50 feet away she continued her forward speed but angled to her right and, with her body tilted so as not to expose her dorsal fin, rose very near the surface for observation with her left eye. The observation revealed the animal was very light-colored and was continuing the active splashing at the surface. It seemed to be looking the other way and Tinga felt undetected.

Brooke felt an unexpected wave of cold water rise suddenly to her breasts. She gasped. "Wonder what caused that?" she shouted to Jim as the wave washed ashore.

"Don't know," he replied as he again approached the beach, satisfied that the fire was now crackling and leaping higher. Brooke began to feel a deep-seated primeval uneasiness and hurried now to rinse off the last of the suds from her shoulders and breasts. Then she started toward shore.

Tinga's carnivorous tendencies and aggressiveness began to rule her actions as she swung around in 15 feet of water offshore to position her streamlined body toward the animal in the water. She had no fear, the only question was how edible the animal would be. Sonar told her the animal was starting toward shore and possible escape. She made the decision to capture this prey; a later decision would be whether or not to eat it. The rest of the pack was stopped silently underwater offshore, observing the scene through their hearing and sonar scanning. With several quick strokes of her flukes she accelerated toward the animal.

Brooke heard a sound like a knife cutting through water behind her and turned slightly to see what it was. The "knife" was a curved 2 foot high dorsal fin and below it a large, sleek black torpedo-like shape rushing at her 10 feet away in the shallow water. She screamed in terror.

At the last instant, Tinga tilted to her right at the surface to allow an easy bite of the animal at the top of the legs. As Brooke screamed she saw the creature roll on its side and open a large pink mouth rimmed with sharp ivory teeth. The white eye patch and white chin field identified the creature as a killer whale, which she had seen in seaquariums. Her screams intensified and echoed through the cove as the jaws closed on her upper thighs and waist. Three inch long teeth punctured Brooke's abdominal cavity and lower back muscles even though Tinga exerted little pressure. Teeth on the left side of Tinga's jaws penetrated Brooke's thighs just below the buttocks. Blood gushed into the water. Jim, too, had seen the torpedo-shaped whale approach at the last instant and he yelled "No! No!", but the words were in vain as he saw the killer whale roll and grab Brooke. Brooke's horrified screams caused his brain to focus on getting her out of the water quickly. A rush of water flooded up onto the beach and almost reached the fire.

With the animal in her mouth as a dog might carry a rag doll, Tinga returned to an upright position and began sliding back toward deeper water, carried by the seaward return of the wave of water she had caused in rushing the shore. The creature was softer than any she had taken before, and she kept her jaws gently closed so as not to cut it apart or kill it immediately. The other whales waiting offshore observed that a catch had been made. Kee, near the bottom in 40 feet of water 75 feet offshore, edged forward anxiously.

Jim instinctively ran and dove into the churning water to try to get hold of Brooke to pull her back to shore. He saw Brooke's head and one arm at the surface for an instant in the red foam. He grabbed the arm by the wrist and found himself pulled with astonishing power as the killer whale continued turning toward deeper water. As the whale dove, Jim could not breathe and was forced to release Brooke's arm. His blurring mind told him he *must* get hold of her as the only hope to save her. He *must* get hold of her! He swam with quick strokes away from the beach, hoping the whale would surface with Brooke one more time. He wished for the knife in his pack onshore.

Kee, waiting anxiously offshore, continued sonar scanning the shoreline action. After receiving clear signals of Tinga's catch at the beach, she was anxious for an opportunity to examine the catch closely and to determine what it was. But now she detected another animal in the water. This one was splashing at the surface and was moving away from shore as if in pursuit of Tinga and her catch. Catching this second animal was crucial and Kee quickly accelerated and struck the animal much as a hungry trout strikes a fluttering mayfly at the surface.

Jim felt momentary intense pain as the ivory teeth sank into his neck and chest. More blood gushed into the water as the teeth punctured his lungs and almost severed his head. The other whales observed that Kee, too, had made a catch. Hunting was good here. All 7 of the remaining lead group of whales now became excited, and, moving forward, surfaced to blow and take in air every 30 to 60 seconds. The two juveniles and the bull Kray crowded in closer to examine the catches and to determine if the catch could be eaten. Tinga, underwater, turnedv Brooke in her mouth so the feet were in her gullet and the head facing forward, just as she had done with the seal. She then rose to the surface. Brooke was not yet dead, and she gasped and coughed. Her bronze braided hair had come undone and was waving in the red-tinged water. Tinga released her, and Brooke, her legs useless, attempted to stay at the surface with her arms. One of the juvenile whales grasped Brooke by the waist and swam joyfully in a circle at the surface with her, as if taunting the others.

But Tinga sensed something was wrong here; these creatures were not a good food source. There was little fat and there were strange and objectionable chemicals in the water wherever the blood or the bodies had been. She signaled to the juvenile swimming with Brooke's body to drop it and the same signal went to Kee, who promptly dropped Jim's body. The two bodies sank to the bottom 40 feet below where crabs would soon move in to the feast.

The whale pack was confused. Two kills had been made and yet Tinga wanted the prey to be dropped. They milled about the area and quickly picked up the scent of the chemicals Tinga had found to be so awful. This sort of creature was not good to eat even when it did not have the body covering which they had seen so often on the two-legged creatures.

Tinga rose vertically to project her head above the surface to see if there were any more of the creatures on shore, but there were none. A flickering light was there and a blue-green object in which the creatures must have travelled on the water. But now the hunt would continue. Tinga again began swimming north along the shore, followed by the others.

Two dozen gulls had begun circling the carnage, waiting for an opportunity to feed on the food scraps they could see in the water. As the whales departed and the surface calmed, the feathered white opportunists screamed, wheeled and darted at the water surface to pick up a few pieces of flesh and skin. The bald eagle had watched the attack with great interest, anticipating scraps to eat afterward. Its acute vision now revealed a morsel near the surface and it quickly launched into a rapid glide from the tree perch to circle only once before descending rapidly, talons extended, to pick up a 2 foot length of intestine before the gulls could get it. Rising on beating wings, the eagle carried the morsel back to the tree and away from the noisy gulls. There would be no need to seek additional food tonight. Within a few minutes the crimson hue of the water faded and the normal quiet returned to the cove. A narrow column of smoke curled upward from the slowly dying fire. A southwest breeze rippled across the tent and rattled the aspen leaves

Orcas Described

It was a warm, sunny California afternoon as 40 year old Dr. Reed Remington drove his small sports car through the crowded parking lot and parked in a spot designated *"Reserved"* adjacent to the administration building of the Hydrosphere Seaquarium. He smiled shyly at a blonde in a bikini top and jeans, whose movements seemed suspended in the act of entering another low-riding sports car. Her companion, seated behind the steering wheel, snapped "Christ, Karen; get in!" Karen glared over her shoulder toward the driver and then looked back at Remington with a flashing smile that had nothing to do with shyness. The little sports coupe raced out of the lot. "Good looking woman," Reed thought.

It appeared to be another good day for business. The lot covered almost 7 acres, and he estimated 600 automobiles in the lot, which meant about 1,800 paying customers inside. He smiled. Although he owned no part of the business, he received research grants, direct financial support and use of many of the Hydrosphere facilities. Continued good business meant continued support. A marine biologist, Reed was generally recognized as one of the best. He combined an outstanding educational background, including a Ph. D. from Humboldt State University, with an excellent field study background of marine mammals worldwide. His reputation as an expert on marine mammals was built on a solid foundation of combining the best of the educational world with an uncanny knack for understanding how and why marine mammals behaved the way they did in the real world. Although Remington's views were often controversial in the academic arena, even his worst critics grudgingly admitted that he had made very significant contributions to man's understanding of marine mammals. Remington's personal popularity had led to a good retainer with Hydrosphere and a teaching position at nearby California Marine College.

As he approached the gate to the Hydrosphere research complex adjacent to the security building he waved to the guard and entered the glass door marked ADMINISTRATION ONLY. "Hi Barbara" he greeted as he strode past the desk marked RECEPTION. Barbara, a shapely honey blonde in blue on blue, smiled and waved without interrupting the message she was taking from a caller. She was hoping he would come back later to talk or perhaps go to lunch.

Reed went down the hall to a door labelled JILL SISSON - PUBLIC RELATIONS. The door was closed and he knocked lightly and listened. Placing one hand over the phone so the person on the other end was not interrupted, Jill called "come on in." Reed opened the door and peeked in. Jill waved him into the small but neatly arranged office. She signaled with an index finger that the call probably would not last much longer. Reed had been to this office many times before because Jill was his main contact with Hydrosphere management. The two of them had a natural creative compatibility, and together had been responsible for the development of many concepts and proposals for Hydrosphere which had proved to be enormously successful for Hydrosphere as well as for themselves. Yet, there had been a recent tendency toward belt-tightening by management which had cut short several research programs.

As usual, Remington took time to notice Jill's neat compactness and good organization. Here was a woman who never wasted a motion or a word. She was attractive the way fresh air and clean skies are attractive. Jill had started her career twelve years earlier as a secondary school teacher but became interested in journalism and had returned to Pallisades State University to get a master's degree. After five years reporting and writing for a small town newspaper she applied for an assistant PR position with hydrosphere. She had progressed swiftly to her present spot in the organization, and her work was a key factor in the good public relations enjoyed by Hydrosphere. Today Reed and Jill were going to watch the killer whale show, which was the top attraction at Hydrosphere. The management of Hydrosphere was thinking of installing another larger tank for the killer whales and they had requested the advice of Reed early in the planning stage. Jill ended the phone call by promising to call the person the following day. Then she stood and grasped Remington's hand. "Reed, it's good to see you again. We just about have time to get over to the arena for the 10:30 killer whale show so we should go right over. We'll have a visiting television crew there from the local PBS station recording some footage for a special on marine life studies in the San Diego area. They'll probably have some questions for us, so be ready." She smiled because Reed never had a problem with spontaneous questions.

"Great", Reed responded, and noticed again how attractive Jill was in the pale green blouse and skirt, which made her blue-green eyes even more attractive. Jill's only marriage had ended three years previously in divorce, and she had no children. She went out occasionally, but, for her, Mr. Right had not come along.

Remington's wife had been killed in an automobile accident the previous year and he had been hard-pressed to find adequate time for his three boys, eleven, fourteen, and sixteen years old, and he hired a nanny to help out. The paternal grandparents were good about helping with the kids. Someday he thought he might remarry, but virtually all of the women he dated who appeared to have possibilities for being a good wife were turned off when they learned he had three boys. Those interested in children usually wanted their own.

Jill picked up her camera and an auxiliary telephoto lens in a case as they were leaving her office. "Don't tell me you are going to take more killer whale photos," Reed said, laughingly. "Hydrosphere must have a 500 gallon tank full by now."

Jill responded as they walked down the hall, "We never know when that unusual situation may arise for a great shot. Remember, the best way to get a fantastic photo is to take lots of them. Besides, we're putting a new flyer together for special advertising in the Midwestern US, and the whales have learned a few new tricks since our last promotion was assembled."

"Sounds good," Remington said as they exited the administration building into the hot California sun and turned toward the park complex itself.

Leaving the administration building area, they could see the various components of the largest marine and amusement park in southern California. The park occupied 40 acres adjoining a bay just north of San Diego, and had proven to be an ideal location both for access by the public and for obtaining the fresh sea water needed for the many tanks and other displays present in the Hydrosphere facility. In addition, Hydrosphere's founders had a continuing strong interest in marine biological research and had established, as part of the facility, buildings, tanks, offices and laboratories for research which had achieved worldwide recognition. As Jill and Reed wound their way through the facilities and through the crowd, they discussed the concept for the new killer whale tank. "What do you think, Reed, of planning the new tank capacity at 6,000,000 gallons, more than twice as large as the one we use now for the killer whale shows?" she asked, and then continued. "It would be located in space at the south margin of the complex and would take a quarter of an acre from the parking lot. The current killer whale tank would be used for smaller whale and dolphin shows."

"Sounds great," Reed responded. "As we've been trying to tell management for the past two years, with a larger tank we may to be able to have successful births of killer whales in captivity as we did at the Florida facility."

"But we can't give them a guarantee," she replied. "One of their major complaints is the cost for refrigeration equipment and for continuously cooling that much water."

"That's understandable."

They were now approaching the arena containing the killer whale tanks where the show would soon begin. A crowd of about 2,000 persons was excitedly entering the mini-stadium in front of the big tank. The tank had been cleverly constructed with thick, clear glass walls 5 feet high at the top of the water level facing the audience, thus allowing the audience to see the bottom of the tank 30 feet down, as well as the killer whales in the tank even when they were below the water surface. In addition, it allowed the killer whales to see the people walking by or in the stands.

As they entered the stadium, Reed noted with interest that the two females of the three killer whales in the tank were indeed watching the crowd through the glass panels. The whales, swimming slowly very close to the glass, seemed to be extremely interested in observing the types of creatures on the other side. Both adults and children crowded to the glass for a closer look, and Reed silently wondered who was learning the most from this interspecies study. The third killer whale in the tank was a large male with a dorsal fin bent over to the left so much it rested on his back. The male was stationary in the tank watching the two trainers, smartly dressed in black and white wet suits with blue trim, on the stage at the opposite side of the tank from the crowd. The trainers were busy arranging containers of fish which were used to reward the whales as the show progressed.

Jill and Reed found seats near the center of the seating area. They knew better than to sit close to the glass panels near the edge of the tank. Because of the noise of the crowd and their own intense interest in the killer whale show, they postponed further talk until later. It was 10:30 and the show was about to begin. Stirring music began to boom over the loudspeakers and the excitement of the crowd intensified.

One of the trainers waved a hand signal to the male and it promptly exited the large tank and swam into one of the adjacent smaller holding tanks. A hinged, barred gate was swung into place and latched, thus isolating the male from the main tank and the two females. The other trainer waved to one of the females in the large tank and it immediately exited to the other adjacent smaller holding tank. Again a gate was swung into place and latched. Reed smiled at the quickness of the whale's response, and observed that the two whales were now motionless, watching and listening at the gates of their respective tanks as if to have a ringside position to see and hear the show. The lead trainer, John McCall, now stepped forward on the stage and announced that the show, with the killer whale Charu, was about to begin. He announced to the crowd that the star performer Charu was a female 21 feet in length and weighing 7,200 pounds, and that she had originally come from Iceland. He also cautioned members of the audience seated in the first few rows in the center that they might get wet and that now was the time to move unless getting wet did not bother them. Some of the children, eager for more fun, moved into the standing area near the glass panels.

With that the trainer rotated his right arm once in a circular motion and the orca, after watching intently from a position in front of the stage, swiftly swam from the stage to the 30 foot bottom of the pool and then accelerated to emerge and perform a beautiful arching leap 15 feet above the water's surface. She re-entered the water very gracefully, and Reed noted that her momentum carried her to the bottom of the pool in about one second. Such observations were extremely interesting to Reed because the killer whale shape had evolved over millions of years to become one of the most efficient configurations in the ocean. The United States Navy had carried out considerable research on shapes for submarine design and many of the characteristics of the killer whale could be seen in the newest nuclear subs.

As the crowd cheered, Charu swam to the stage where McCall was standing and slid her sleek black and white body from the water onto the shelf provided for the purpose. There she arched her back so her flukes were well off the concrete and opened her mouth as if to imitate a laughing expression. McCall placed two handsful of fish and squid into her mouth and Charu easily slid off the shelf and back into the water. Jill was busy with her camera and telephoto lens, and Reed continued watching the show. For the next ten minutes McCall put Charu through a series of spectacular performances, including jumping high over the head of McCall while he was in the water, swimming around the pool with McCall riding both on the dorsal and ventral surfaces of the whale, and pushing McCall high in the air from her snout as she leaped into the air with him. When Mary, a female trainer, entered the pool, other feats were performed including swimming on her back and "clapping" her flippers, waving her flukes to the crowd as she did a headstand in the pool, and carrying Mary around on her back. After each spectacular act the whale expected, and was rewarded with, fish and squid.

McCall now moved to a platform at the side of the tank near the audience and asked for a young volunteer. When he saw a boy of about 5 years old sitting in the front row, he asked him to come to the platform. McCall asked if he would like to feed and hug the whale, and announced to the crowd that the whale the boy was about to feed is the same type of whale which at one time had a reputation as a ferocious killer. Upon signal, Charu came over and raised her head above the water's surface at the platform. McCall then gave the boy a squid to place in Charu's mouth as she opened it. Charu swallowed the squid and rose even further from the water on command and the small boy put his arms around her snout. With another signal the whale remained still and this time the boy kissed the whale's black snout.

Cameras were snapping amid oo's and ah's from the crowd. Over the loudspeaker McCall asked "Now, does that look like a vicious killer?" The audience, in unison, said "nooooo." McCall next went over to the gate enclosing the other female whale and opened it. He announced to the crowd that "Icey", another female from Iceland, was now coming into the pool. The two whales began swimming rapidly around the pool in close coordination, but it was clear they were watching McCall for a signal. When he made a circular motion with his arm they dove to the bottom of the tank in unison and emerged to sail through the air and land on their side with a tremendous splash directly in front of the center section of the audience. Several hundred gallons of water splashed from the pool into the crowd. The children laughed and squealed with delight, but some of the adults with dripping cameras cursed and looked about forlornly. McCall shouted into the microphone: "We warned you that some of you might get wet!" The two whales together then made two more spectacular, perfectly synchronized jumps and McCall announced that the show was over for now, but that another show would be held at 2:30 in the afternoon. The crowd applauded loudly and then began to file out of the arena.

Reed watched as McCall went over to open the gate to the adjoining pool so the male killer whale would have access to the large tank. Charu had followed him over to the gate. As soon as he opened the gate she closed it and then backed off. He opened it again and she closed it again. Then she remained motionless as if watching him for the next move. McCall sensed that a game was underway, so he left the gate closed and backed away with his arms spread as if to say "OK, so YOU want to control the gate, then go ahead." Charu watched him for half a minute. Then, as if satisfied that SHE was in control, she opened the gate and swam into and around the pool with the bull. Then both whales swam through the open gate into the large tank. Reed was so absorbed in watching the episode that he had not noticed that Jill was standing there waiting for him.

"Come on," she said, "the TV crew is going to talk to McCall in a few minutes and we should get over there to monitor the session." As they walked past the whale's tank, Reed noticed that Charu was swimming beside him in the tank looking at them through the glass panels. He wondered if she recognized him and silently vowed again to take the time to attempt some new approaches to communications with orcas. The whales appeared to have their own communication methods, but man had thus far failed to figure them out. Jill touched up her lipstick and combed her hair lightly. Best to be prepared when a TV crew was around.

They found the television crew before McCall had changed into a dry suit for the session. One of the cameramen, Dave Perkins, recognized Jill and waved to her. "How did you like the show?" she asked.

"It's always good," answered Dave. "I will never cease to be amazed at the intelligence and cooperative behavior of these whales."

"*Mostly* cooperative," remarked Reed.

Mark Hedderly, the person who would interview McCall, overheard the remark. He knew Reed Remington's reputation for controversy. This could be interesting, he thought, and approached them. "Hi, Reed and Jill, how are you?"

Jill, always ready to project a positive image for Hydrosphere, answered brightly. "Great, and yourself?"

"Everything is fine. I believe we got good coverage of the show, and we're ready to talk to McCall. But since we're all set up and ready to go, would you mind if we have a brief question and answer session right now. Something usable may come out of it, but remember, we cannot let you review any segment before we air it." Jill looked at Reed, who shrugged his shoulders as if to say *Why not?"*

Mark didn't waste any time. "OK, guys, get ready to roll on an interview with Jill and Reed. Jill, could you and Reed please step over here." They moved in front of the cameras, positioned so a large HYDROSPHERE sign was visible in the background. The director indicated the go ahead with a wave of his arms.

Mark began. "We are here at the beautiful Hydrosphere facility just north of San Diego where we are speaking with Jill Sisson, the public relations director of Hydrosphere, and Dr. Reed Remington, marine biologist and instructor at Pallisades Institute of Oceanography. Jill and Reed, good to see you here today."

Together they smiled and replied. "Thank you, good to be here."

Mark addressed Jill first. "We understand Hydrosphere is keeping the two female killer whales and the male together in the hope that conception may occur and a killer whale birth may occur at some time in the future, is that correct?"

Jill responded "Yes, we have good evidence from a healthy birth at our facility in Florida that killer whales can be born and survive in captivity and it would certainly be nice to have that happen here."

"Very good, we wish you success." Mark then turned to Reed. "Dr. Remington, you have studied marine mammals in many areas of the world, and you have done a great deal of work with killer whales in Alaska and in the Antarctic. We have just filmed a great show here at the Hydrosphere facility, and the whales seemed to perform perfectly. How do you explain the docile behavior of these animals in the marine parks and yet they will catch and devour almost anything that swims in the ocean?"

Reed responded. "Killer whales are a very social animal among themselves, and, as we have seen, among man when fed by man in captivity. The whales, in my opinion, are sufficiently predisposed to getting along socially that they can, and will under certain conditions, substitute man for their own kind. In this captive environment they look upon man as a socially acceptable creature when there is no competition for food."

Mark continued with another question. "Are you suggesting that food is one of the primary factors in the docile behavior of killer whales in marine parks?"

Reed looked at the camera. "No, I am saying that it is more than just ONE of the factors. It is THE most important factor. You see, not many scientists have recognized that killer whales in the wild feed each other. In particular, the females often feed the males and the juveniles. Such feeding is a social affair among the whales. It increases bonds and induces harmony among the group. When man feeds a captive orca, the bond which would have existed among members of a killer whale pack is transferred to man as a provider. So long as they are fed by man they are no more likely to injure man than they would be likely to injure one of their own kind in the wild."

"But do they ever attack each other in the wild?"

"Yes, there have been instances of killer whale deaths caused by other killer whales."

John McCall, handsome in pale blue tightfitting nylon coveralls, now approached the trio from the side and out of view of the cameras. "That's fascinating, Dr. Remington", said Mark. "I see that John McCall, Hydrosphere's chief trainer has now joined us. John, congratulations on a thrilling show today and thank you for joining us."

"My pleasure, Mark," John replied as he shook hands with the announcer. Cameras were rolling.

"John, you have worked with killer whales at this facility for a number of years and know the animals on a day to day basis better than perhaps any other person. The whales seem so docile and well behaved, do you ever have any trouble with them?"

John pondered the question for a few moments. "No, we do not have any trouble as such with them, but it is important to understand that a good part of this results from our recognition of the whale's individuality and peculiarities. Each whale is different, just as people have individual personalities, and we must work within the framework of that individuality."

"Could you give our audience an example of how you work with each whale as an individual?"

John continued. "It is difficult to tell if any one of the whales is going to be psychologically, or you might say emotionally, prepared to do the show.

We cannot tell until the whale is in the tank and we give it the first few commands. If there is any hesitation or balking whatsoever, that whale is immediately moved to an adjacent tank and a different whale is brought in. We have learned that once the tendency for stubbornness appears, that whale should not be expected to perform."

"Is there any punishment for a whale which will not perform," Mark asked.

"Absolutely not," John responded. "We never punish whales under any circumstances. We operate on a reward system only. Furthermore, we have found that a whale which is hesitant for the 10:30 show may be emotionally perfect for the 2:30 show. We don't know why. That's just one of the peculiarities of the orcas."

"We noticed that you did not use the male whale in the show this morning. Is that related to the incident last year when the male jumped upon a trainer riding a female and seriously injured him, including a broken pelvis?"

McCall was under orders not to discuss the incident, which had cost Hydrosphere $1.3 million to settle out of court. But he managed an answer: "To some extent. The male is not as easy to control as the females, and unpredictable jealousy may get involved."

"So has the male been ruled out of future shows?"

"No. let's just say we always exercise caution in our program planning."

"Have there been any other accidents or injuries related to the whales in recent years?" the interviewer persisted.

McCall was now getting very uneasy. "Let me answer that, if I may," Jill interjected, smiling. "As you know, we did have one instance of Maru, one of our trainee whales, charging another whale in the tank and colliding with the wall with such force that she shattered the bone in her lower jaw. We had to put her to sleep."

"Was that another incidence of jealousy?" Mark asked, looking at either Jill or McCall for an answer.

"We don't know for sure," Jill responded, "but we now have our trainers, such as John here, watching carefully for any signs of hostility among the whales."

"Are there any happenings you could relate to our audience concerning working with the whales when they were not in a good mood?"

She evaded the question. "Let's just say we try to work with the whales when they are in a good mood."

Jill did not bring up a serious incident several years earlier which had led, for a time, to restrictions on trainers getting into the water with the whales. Hydrosphere had planned to make a commercial with a model in a bikini riding one of the whales, Charu, around the pool. For some reason the whale did not want to perform and the staff failed to recognize important clues when the animal balked at some of the first commands. In their haste to complete the commercial they proceeded to place the model on the whale. Halfway across the tank the whale bucked like a bronco and threw the model into the cold water. Then Charu turned around, picked up the terrified girl by the legs and brought her back to the stage. Not too much damage done, but the skin was punctured in five places on the model's legs with corrective surgery required. Settlement of the resulting lawsuit cost Hydrosphere $850,000 plus $40,000 medical costs. The Hydrosphere staff had felt fortunate at the moderate cost of the settlement.

Sensing an opportunity, Mark turned to McCall. "These descriptions suggest, then, that even killer whales in captivity could be dangerous to man. What about yourself, are you ever concerned about entering the tank with animals which could swallow you whole."

John smiled nervously. "No, not really. We know enough about each whale that I have great confidence none of them would harm the trainers so long as we recognize their moods and treat them accordingly."

"We have time for just one last question, John, and I'm sure you have been asked this many times. How would you feel about getting into the water with killer whales in the wild?"

McCall hesitated for a moment. Reed Remington stepped toward Mark and the microphone. "I can think of few circumstances under which Mark or any other intelligent person would enter the water with wild killer whales. In the first place, you might be invading their space. It is my belief that many animals, including killer whales, have territories they consider their own. If you enter their territory they may take offense and drive you off or remove you somehow even if they had no intention of eating you. Whatever their reason might be, it is not going to be good for your health. Second, you might become involved unknowingly in a situation where the whales were either very hungry or excited from just having made a kill which satisfied only part of the pack. Such a setting is also unlikely to be good for your health."

"'Pack' is a term you seem to use for the orcas while most other scientists refer to the groups as 'pods'. What is the difference?"

"When you have observed orcas hunting cooperatively in the wild, they are very much like a cooperative wolf pack," Reed responded. "Both kill living creatures and eat them. They also share food. It has never made sense to me to refer to their groups as 'pods' such as a pea pod. These are hunting packs and that is the best term."

The director signaled to Mark that they were out of time and the cameras focused on him. "That's about it folks for today from your roving reporter at the Hydrosphere in San Diego. Thank you John McCall, Jill Sisson and Dr. Reed Remington for joining us today. The comments were very enlightening and we look forward to more excitement here at the killer whale tanks at Hydrosphere. This is Mark Hedderly saying goodbye for now."

The cameras turned away to pan the surroundings at Hydrosphere, including the tank where Charu and the other two whales seemed to be curiously watching the camera crew. After saying goodbye to Mark and asking him to come back soon, Jill and Reed discussed the new large tank proposal as they walked back toward the administration building. Besides providing increased arena size, it was important to commence healthy live births in the facility because of the illogical public outcry about captures of new killer whales from the wild. As Reed drove home, he thought about ways the capture of additional whales could be made to make sense to the public. There must be a way.

———————— ◆◆ ————————

At the request of the local nature club, Dr. Reed Remington had agreed to deliver a 'layman's lecture' on the killer whale. A lecture hall had been arranged for at the campus of Pallisades State University. Dressed in a light blue blazer, ivory cotton pants and an ivory silk shirt, open at the collar, he arrived at the science lecture hall a few minutes before the scheduled 7:00 pm program. Dr. Rogers, the previous lecturer on marine mammals, had recently retired and this was the first general public lecture on killer whales for Reed. He thought it would go well, but he realized his views were divergent from those of some of the other Biology Department staff members. He knew a few of the existing staff members would be in the audience, ready to take him to task if they believed he was too far afield from "accepted beliefs."

Reed had come to be regarded by the faculty as a maverick, and even the university president, although he liked Reed, was concerned that some of the controversial viewpoints might antagonize a few of the wealthy contributors who provided substantial funding to the school. The Mountain Club, representing thousands of Californians, would be sure to have several representatives at the lecture.

Reed was pleased to see a crowd of about 200 persons gathered in the tiered room. A graduate student assigned to assist him, Cindy Simmons, an attractive brunette majoring in marine biology, was already there but it was doubtful Reed would need help with the computerized presentation. His laptop computer was in black leather briefcase. Cindy had been angling to go on an extended biology field trip with Reed since her arrival at the school seven months previously, but she knew there were several other female grad students, as well as undergrads, who wanted to spend time with him, whether in the field or not. Once in a while he *did* take a female student on a trip, and the rumors were that Remington was a masterful teacher of personal relationships in addition to marine biology.

Reed smiled at Cindy. He had been thinking she would be a good student to take on a field trip one day. Although at 23 she was a little young, such forays were mostly overlooked by the liberal school administration these days. If anything, there might be some jealousy.

"Here's the computer, Cindy. Once it is up and running the right program there should be no problems. I appreciate your coming in to help". He touched her briefly on her bare, tan shoulder.

Reed glanced around the lecture hall again. The crowd was enthusiastic, as they usually were when the topic was killer whales. He knew that most, if not all of them, had been to the killer whale show at the Hydrosphere facility and had developed a feeling of kinship with the black and white performers. Anxious to begin the lecture, he looked at the clock on the wall. At precisely 7:00 pm, even though a few persons were still straggling into the hall, he began. "Ladies and Gentlemen, thank you for coming this evening to hear this presentation on the killer whale. I feel honored to have the pleasure of addressing you. Some of you may have heard one of the presentations by Dr. Rogers, my predecessor, concerning killer whales. If so, you may find that this presentation will differ in certain aspects."

Two Biology Department faculty members in the audience nudged each other. Just as they suspected, Reed was likely to present some of his crazy ideas. They listened.

"For those of you with a technical orientation, killer whales are part of the family Delphinidae, genus Orcinus, and species orca. The great naturalist Linnaeus named the species in 1758, but, perhaps a fact not so well known, Pliny the Elder much earlier in history gave this mammal the name 'killer of whales' because it was known to kill other whales."

He glanced at Cindy near the computer, and she smiled in readiness. "But let's turn to some aspects of the killer whale with which most of you are familiar. The killer whale is the largest of the dolphins. Let's look at the first slide." He clicked the remote.

A slide came onto the screen with two killer whales jumping high out of the water in unison at the large Hydrosphere tank. Their 20 foot long bodies were at least 15 feet in the air. "It is interesting that these, the largest and most cunning predators in the oceans, have come to be regarded as 'puppy dogs' in the seaquariums because of their apparent docile nature, apparent affection for man, and because they are quite responsive to training. Prior to the evolution of modern man, and not counting dinosaurs, Orcinus orca was the top predator in the oceans and thus the top predator on Earth".

The next slide appeared showing a small boy 'kissing' one of the trained killer whales at the edge of the Hydrosphere whale tank. Another slide then appeared showing a trainer riding on the back of one of the killer whales. Reed continued, "The killer whale is a very social animal in the wild, and the social structure of the 'pods', as some biologists call them, is quite complex and not well understood. Underwater vocalizations of killer whales, both of the broadcast type and sonar, strongly suggest that members of specific killer whale pods are always in acoustical communication with each other".

A slide came onto the screen showing the black dorsal fins of a pod of at least twelve killer whales, all swimming closely together. Someone in the audience muttered "Looks like sharks."

"Most of you have seen the show at Hydrosphere involving killer whales, and I am sure many of you have looked at these sleek and beautiful black and white creatures and have wondered how they ever came to have the name 'killer whale'. Let me tell you that the name is appropriate. This mammal has evolved over millions of years to emerge at the very top of the oceanic predator chain, and it will eat literally anything that is in, or gets in, the water".

A slide is shown of a closeup of a killer whale's head at the edge of the big tank at Hydrosphere, followed by another slide showing a closeup of the whale's mouth and teeth with the trainer putting some squid in the mouth.

"This slide showing the whale's mouth is quite important. It illustrates both the size of the whale's mouth and the character of the teeth. The mouth is large enough, as you can see, to accept a piece of food perhaps 24 inches in diameter, and the specimen shown here is only a moderate sized female of perhaps 18 feet in length. Some males reach 31 feet in length and thus could probably take food one-third larger in diameter, or perhaps 36 inches in diameter. This is very important to remember as we continue."

"In this slide please note the teeth. They are conical in form, about the size of a large man's thumb, and they are sharp. The lower teeth curve back slightly toward the throat while the upper teeth are set with a slightly forward orientation. This match provides an efficient cutting action for the killer whale. Even though this creature is a warm blooded mammal, contrary to what we might expect there are no canine incisor teeth such as we see in, say, the large cats of Africa, or in the wolf, or even in the dog and cat you have at home."

Reed hesitated for a moment and looked at the audience carefully as another slide of killer whale teeth was shown, this one taken just a few inches from the teeth. It was important that they grasp the significance of the teeth and he noted with satisfaction they were studying intently the teeth shown in the slide. "The teeth of the killer whale are highly developed for the purpose of catching, killing, and preparing for consumption, anything from a duck swimming on the surface to the largest creature that ever lived on the face of the Earth, the blue whale. Please note in this closeup slide that the teeth are positioned to interlock when the jaws close, similar to pinking shears. And note the grooves in the teeth caused by the close meshing with teeth on the opposite side of the jaws."

He continued, "There are usually 24 teeth on the top and 24 on the bottom. Unlike the shark, if a killer whale tooth is lost it is not replaced."

The next slide came on and the audience stared in silence. It showed a male killer whale surging through the surf near a beach with a full grown, but apparently dead, sea lion in its mouth. "A killer whale in the wild will eat up to 500 pounds of food a day. That is one sea lion of the size you see here in the mouth of this bull *per day*."

"You will also observe that this particular sea lion is too large for the killer whale to swallow whole, so it must be cut up into smaller pieces.

The whale is believed to do the cutting (butchering, if you will) mostly underwater, where it bites and shakes the sea lion to produce pieces of the carcass which are small enough to swallow. Based on field observations of submersal time with a catch, the butchering seems to take place rather quickly, particularly if more than one whale is present. Thus we may assume the dental structure which has evolved in the killer whale is indeed an efficient one for its purposes."

The next slide came on, showing a pack of killer whales attacking a blue whale approximately 60 feet in length. "Killer whales are the top predator in the ocean, they are afraid of no other creature, not larger whales, not sharks, and not man unless man is trying to kill it such as with a rifle. This slide shows a pack in the process of attacking, and eating part of, a large blue whale. In this observed case, the attack went on for 5 hours, with the orcas biting large chunks of flesh from the dorsal (upper) part of the blue, leaving gaping, bleeding holes. The pack finally let up, probably full, and swam off. The blue no doubt died later."

"Documented items included in the killer whale's menu are seals, sea lions, fish of all types (even the speedy tuna), walrus, other whales, porpoise, crabs, octopus, squid, turtles, land dwelling deer (probably caught swimming from one island to another), and even water birds such as ducks."

The next slide came on, showing one of the trainers at Hydrosphere with his head in the mouth of a killer whale. The trainer, in the usual photogenic black and white wet suit, was smiling broadly for the camera. Reed paused for a moment to look at the audience. He had led them to the point where they were asking themselves how such an efficient killer in the open seas could be so docile, and even apparently friendly, when in captivity? Most of the audience, Reed suspected, had already posed this question to themselves when watching the killer whale performances at the Hydrosphere facility because the trainers there often had the whales come up and 'kiss' one of the children or attractive female patrons. The trainer might then ask the patrons over the public address system "now does that whale seem like a killer or a lover?" The answer was always "lover."

Reed went on. "Why is it that an animal that can and will eat almost anything that moves in the oceans behave so well in captivity? Is this contradictory behavior? Does it make sense?"

"There will be those who disagree, but it is my belief that the answer lies in the basic social structure of the killer whale pack. These animals are very intelligent and they learned long ago that a group working together is much more efficient at capturing food. They are gregarious animals and enjoy the company of other whales, both for friendly physical interactions and for acoustical communications involving the exchange of information, often over distances of several miles. Whales had the equivalent of the wireless telephone long before man ever thought of it."

Another slide was shown on the screen, this time of a group of killer whales blowing at the surface in a beautiful bay beneath some snow-capped peaks. "Killer whales remain together in groups, often the same group, for their entire lives. They are quite diligent about taking care of each other, particularly if one of them is in distress. They also feed each other, not just in times of trouble, but as a matter of group cooperation."

The faculty members from the biology department again exchanged glances, this time more worried. Was Reed about to expound on one of his speculative and unfounded theories?

Remington continued. "The practice of these animals feeding each other is crucial to understanding the true nature of the killer whale. I have personally observed that certain of the whales are better hunters, or perhaps more agile hunters, than others in a particular group. These whales, usually the mature cows (the females), will catch prey and turn it over to the juveniles and even to the bulls. Some biologists are, in my opinion, incorrect when they state that the bulls control the killer whale groups. The bulls are valuable for breeding, protection and certain matters such as helping kill large prey (other whales, for example), but the females are more agile and make more kills and more of the day-to-day group decisions than do the males. Observations I have made of killer whale groups strongly suggest they are matriarchies."

Low muttering came from the Biology Department faculty members. Just as they suspected, Remington was going off on one of his tangents contrary to most available published data concerning killer whales. The *males* led the groups, not the females, they whispered, and shook their heads.

As if he overheard the remarks, Remington continued. "Some researchers have suggested that the males lead the killer whale pack, or *pods* as some prefer to call them, but my research strongly indicates otherwise. Some observers have been misled by the leading role the males play when the killer whale pack is under seige from whalers, but that is the male defensive role and not the day-to-day functioning of the pack. You'll notice, by the way, that I refer to a killer whale *pack*, and not to a *pod*. The term pod simply is not appropriate for the orca. I suggest that the name pod is alright for gray, blue, fin, sperm and all the other whales, but it is not appropriate for the killer whale, which hunts and kills more like a wolf pack."

At this remark one of the faculty members took out a pad of paper and a pen and began to make notes. It was bad enough that Remington would introduce some of his crazy ideas to this audience, but it was even worse that he would challenge even the established nomenclature for whales. Good grief, was nothing safe from his rebellious thinking?

Another slide came onto the screen, this one showing one of the killer whales at Hydrosphere swimming upside down with one of the trainers riding on its white, upturned belly. Remington did not hesitate as he went on: "Let's return now to the question of why these intelligent ocean predators become so easy to manage in captivity. Again, this is my own theory, but I believe the killer whale has evolved to be cooperative, and *beholden*, if you will, to *any* creature that provides it with food, space to exist, consideration and agreeable physical contact. The animal also enjoys learning and play, but such requirements are secondary to those just mentioned.

He continued: "The killer whale is born and raised to be cooperative and nonaggressive with those who care for it and take care of it, and that is why you see them cooperating so well in the various aquariums. Please do not, however, confuse these characteristics with the scientifically unfounded notion that killer whales possess a need or desire to communicate with man, or that they have demonstrated special consideration of man".

The faculty members were hoping that there was no one present from Hydrosphere. One of the reasons the killer whale show was such a big drawing card was because many of the paying customers believed in some sort of special interspecies communication between man and killer whale.

Reed went on. "Under the right circumstances, man is able to act as a substitute in interactions which normally would take place between one whale and the other whales. By feeding and caring for a captive whale, the man earns the whale's respect. Under such circumstances the man is *generally* safe from attack or harm by the whale, just as members of a whale clan are *generally* safe from attack by each other."

On the screen a slide appeared showing one of the trainers at Hydrosphere using a long handled brush to groom a killer whale, with the whale seeming to smile in enjoyment. One of the faculty members could contain herself no longer, and she rose to her feet: "Are you saying that the actions of Homo sapiens just happen to fit into that area of activities to which the killer whale was adapted both by inheritance and training by other orcas?"

"Thank you, Miss Harris" responded Reed, enjoying the spontaneous confrontation of his ideas. "That is correct". He loved controversy because he firmly believed that disagreements led to a closer examination, and thus a better understanding, of natural phenomena.

But Reed had more points to make, and he went on. "There are those foolish enough to think that because captured killer whales are generally docile, killer whales in the wild must be similarly docile. Nothing could be further from the truth. Killer whales in the wild remain the top predators in the ocean just as they were long before man evolved to the present position of serious studies of the whales. They can, and *will* if hungry, eat anything that is in the water. And if it is not in the water and they want to eat it, they will attempt to knock it into the water so they can get at it.

"Now I know one of the questions many of you would like to ask is: would a killer whale attack a human being? Let me answer that right now." He paused briefly. "Despite the lack of documentation of attacks against man by killer whales, it is my belief that these predators, when hungry, can, and will, attack, kill and eat man almost as quickly as it would any other creature which enters its marine domain. Because the killer whale has a high degree of intelligence, it is able to recognize another creature possessing intelligence, such as man, and therefore is likely to hesitate to attack man. Much of this hesitancy may result from the fact that man is an unfamiliar item on the menu.

"But it is my personal belief that the orcas do not care to ingest a large amount of what they recognize as indigestible material, the clothing man wears."

A member of the audience could contain himself no longer: "Are you saying that killer whales in the wild will attack and kill man? I'm no marine biologist, but I know there are no well documented instances of killer whale attacks on a human being. In fact, I'm a scuba diver and there have been situations where killer whales swam around scuba divers without touching them. How do you explain that kind of interaction?"

Remington was delighted at the question: "You're only partly right. There is one reasonably well documented instance of a killer whale attack on a surfer, that was near Monterey, California in 1972... but, regardless, let's assume there are no documented instances of killer whale attacks on Homo sapiens. Where does that leave us? Are we going to be so foolish that we will assume that killer whales will not attack man?

"Let's try to look at the question logically. In a situation where the whales are hungry and man is present, there is no doubt in my mind that the killer whale will kill and eat man. It is a fact that the stomachs of killer whales taken in Antarctica have contained the remains of other killer whales. This is cannibalism by any definition. In this audience is there doubt in anyone's mind that, if man had been present, the whales would have eaten man before they would have eaten their own kind?

"Speaking of cannibalism, of course, even modern man can, and will, eat his own kind rather than die from starvation. Students at the University of Colorado in Boulder annually celebrate Alferd (not Alfred) Packer Day. Alf became snowbound in the Colorado Mountains with some other persons in the late 1800's and ended up eating most of them to stay alive. The joke in Colorado is that there were not many Democrats in the county and Alf, a Republican, ate most of them".

This brought a welcome laugh from the audience, but they continued to listen intently. They were eager to hear more of this portrayal of the killer whale as an actual killer rather than the friendly animal to which they had been attuned. Remington again focused on the question, "But *will* killer whales attack, kill and eat man? *Of course* they will, given the proper set of circumstances. And the circumstances need not be very farfetched. In my opinion, again, it is just a matter of time until we have well documented evidence of a killer whale attack on man. It is likely to occur where the whale preys on marine mammals, as opposed to fish, and it probably will occur at a time of the year when other food is scarce. In other words, when food becomes scarce, the killer whale will take any food available on what is a sort of preference list. Man is no doubt well down on the menu, particularly when fully clothed, but I'm sure he is, nevertheless, on the menu. We can assume man would be taken as food before other killer whales would be taken. It further would seem safe to assume that cannibalism is not one of those activities which the killer whale enjoys.

"That concludes my discussion. I'm sure there are many questions you have concerning Orcinus orca, so let's spend a few minutes on those questions, and then those of you who are interested may accompany me to the museum next door where we will have a firsthand look at a killer whale skeleton. Cindy, would you please turn the computer off?"

Reed looked questioningly at the audience. "Who has the first question?"

He could have guessed what one of the teenagers in the front row was going to ask. Sure enough, a hand went up and Reed nodded to the girl to go ahead with the question.

"Was the surfer eaten by the killer whale?"

Reed smiled. "The surfer was bitten by an animal which most investigators believe was a killer whale. The whale, if indeed it was one, could easily have killed the surfer, but it didn't. We don't know if that incident was a case of mistaken identity where the whale thought the surfer to be a seal, or what it was. There are no other reliable reports of killer whales attacking people that I know of, although some Pacific Coast natives have passed down stories of killer whales taking out revenge on people who harassed them."

Reed looked around the audience. "Other questions?" Another hand went up from a gray haired gentleman in the center area. "Go ahead, please," urged Reed.

"I understand that killer whales hunt as a group more often than they hunt as individuals. Could you tell us something about their hunting techniques?"

"Yes, I'd be glad to. As mentioned earlier, there are strong social bonds in a killer whale pack. Their frequent comparison to wolves is appropriate because both maintain complex social relationships, hunt their prey in a cooperative, coordinated manner, and are the top predators in their respective domains. One of the techniques which seems to be preferred by killer whales is the surrounding of a group of prey, such as a school of fish, by the pack. The pack then circles the prey as individual whales enter the central area to feed while those circling see that few escape. Some observers believe the whales use ultrasound to shock or stun the fish, thus making them easier to catch, but that is hypothetical at this time."

He continued. "Another technique, observed mostly in Patagonia, involves killer whales catching sea lion pups on a beach. I'm sure many of you have seen these spectacular catches on TV. The older whales have been observed teaching the young on how to best capture the pups. After the catch, the whales often play with the still-alive pups the way a cat might play with a mouse. There are numerous other techniques, and

I'd be glad to go over them with any of you when we have more time."

Again he looked around the audience. "Another question?" A hand went up, and Reed nodded.

A young lady near the front had a question. "What constitutes the primary food of killer whales?"

"Thank you, that's a good question," Reed replied. "The food utilized by Orcinus Orca depends mostly on the availability of various types of prey. In Iceland, for example, when the herring are in large schools, the whales feed almost entirely on herring because they are readily available. In Alaska during the salmon runs, evidence indicates strongly that the whales feed heavily on salmon. In Patagonia they feed mostly on sea lion pups when the pups are just a few weeks old. In Antarctica they will feed mostly on penguins at certain times of the year.

"This does not mean, however, that they will not feed on other prey during the time one species may be the source of most of their food. Indeed, my field observations suggest that the whales will make a special effort to occasionally mix their diet. In Alaska we have observed that whales feeding on salmon, when we know they are not hungry, will, every week or so, make a special effort to hunt, catch and eat harbor seals, harbor porpoise and other `choice' warm blooded prey. Sort of like a fisherman getting tired of eating fish so he goes to the field to hunt ducks and rabbits both for the fun of it and to provide variety in his diet."

Again Reed scanned the audience. "We have time for a couple of more questions." One of the boys in the front row raised his hand, and Reed smiled at him and nodded. "Go ahead."

The boy stood up to ask his question. "What would happen if a killer whale and a great white shark got in a fight?"

Reed laughed. Many who had read novels about large sharks or had seen movies about them had also seen the killer whales perform. It was natural for youngsters to wonder about a fight. "In the first place it it is highly unlikely that a *single* killer whale would encounter a shark because the whales are animals which travel together in groups. But what if a large killer whale did encounter a large great white and a dispute arose over food. Comparing size and weight, the whale would be about 31 feet long and weigh about 18,000 pounds. The great white would be about 21 feet long and weigh, say, 6,500 pounds. Thus the whale is 30% longer and weighs almost three times as much as the shark. But," he smiled at the boys, "let's make our imaginary confrontation more fair from a size standpoint. Let's say we have an average size female killer whale, which would be almost the same size as the large shark."

Reed looked directly at the boys, who were watching and listening in wide-eyed anticipation. "Now do you suppose there would be great slashing of teeth and pieces of flesh torn from each other in a frenzied attack?"

The four boys, in unison, nodded an enthusiastic yes.

Reed continued. "If you think that, you are mistaken. I would give the shark about one minute to live. But there would be no biting. The whale is much too intelligent to risk the possibility of injury from getting near the shark's dangerous teeth. The killer whale is also the fastest swimmer in the seas, while the great white shark is relatively slow. If the whale wanted to dispose of the shark rather quickly, I am quite sure it would attack the shark from below, but not with its teeth.

"While the shark was wondering where the killer whale went, the whale would probably dive down to a position below the shark for rapid acceleration in order to ram into the shark's vulnerable belly area. It would probably ram the shark at 15 to 20 miles per hour, and if you want to visualize how much force is involved there, try ramming your 6,000 pound automobile at 20 miles per hour into a slowly moving 6,000 pound automobile. Tremendous forces are involved, particularly when you consider that the force is concentrated in an area of about one square foot at the whale's snout. Many of the shark's vital internal organs would no doubt rupture with the first ram from the whale. The great white would likely die without ever knowing what really happened.

"But, if another ram was necessary, the whale could deliver it in a matter of seconds, even in total darkness through the use of sonar. It is even possible that the whale, after the first ram, could circle in the poorly-lit water and, from a safe distance, assess the internal damage to the shark much as skilled medical doctors today use ultrasonic scanning to examine the internal organs of patients." Reed anticipated another question from the boys.

"However, would the killer whale suffer from the encounter? That is unlikely. Remember, these whales have been observed breaking through ice several inches thick to get at seals and penguins on ice floes in the Antarctic, and they have been known to sink boats by ramming them if angry or harassed. Just west of San Francisco a killer whale was photographed holding a great white upside down and swimming with it until the shark drowned. That whale, and others in the pack, ate much of the shark. Then all the sharks left the area."

The two boys were obviously tickled with the answer to the question; they thought killer whales were really cool. More hands were going up and many in the audience were turning to their neighbors to discuss the things they had just heard. Reed, glancing at his watch, was pleased to see the intense interest in the discussion. However, time was running short.

"OK, everyone. Thank you for your attention. I promised we'd go to the museum next door to look at a killer whale skeleton, and if you have more questions I'll try to answer them there. To get to the museum, exit through the east door and go down the hall to the first entry on the left. Thank you again."

Reed smiled at Cindy once more as he stepped down from the podium with the briefcase to retrieve his slides. Cindy had them ready, and smiled at him. "That was great, Dr. Remington, but some of the other faculty members may not be happy, as usual, with certain of your ideas."

Reed shrugged his shoulders. "That's all right. I've developed a rather thick hide. Are you coming to the museum?"

"You bet," Cindy answered, smiling and looking Reed directly in the eyes.

On the way down the hall toward the skeleton in the museum, several people approached to tell him their own theories about the whales or to ask questions. There were so many that Reed could not handle them. When he arrived at the skeleton a hubbub was going on. A glance through the large room revealed that the faculty members who had attended the lecture were not present. It did not matter. Reed raised his arms for silence and then spoke with a raised voice. "May I please have your attention? Your attention, please." The noise died down.

"Thank you very much. We have here the skeleton of a killer whale. This specimen was a female about 22 feet long which was found dead and washed up on the beach near San Francisco. The cause of death was a full grown, 200 pound harbor seal which the killer whale had tried to swallow whole. The seal got stuck in its throat and the whale perished.

"What I would like you to pay particular attention to is the head and the teeth." He pointed to the teeth. "Note that the teeth are about as large as a big man's thumb and that they are conical and curved. Although the jaw of this skeleton is open, you can see how the 24 teeth on the top mesh precisely with the 24 teeth on the bottom. So well do they mesh that, as you see here, the teeth in the lower and upper jaws have striations or grooves on them where teeth from the opposite jaw have repeatedly meshed together in biting and cutting. "Although you cannot see it on this skeleton, the tips of the teeth fit into depressions in the gum on the opposite jaw, thus creating an excellent biting mechanism. "Remember, unlike the shark, which is constantly generating new teeth and replacing teeth, the killer whale does not replace teeth. Once the teeth are worn down or lost, the killer whale's life is finished unless it can somehow manage to catch salmon, herring or other prey which does not need to be chopped up. An older whale might be assisted by others."

The crowd was listening intently as Reed went on. "Another feature you should observe is that the killer whale has no teeth in front, either on the top or the bottom, for a width of about 6 inches. This allows the whale, should it choose to do so, to hold prey without seriously injuring it. Whales have been observed carrying seals and sea lions about with the rear part of the animal's body in the whale's mouth and the front part and head projecting forward. This is believed to be a sort of play before eating, much as a cat will often play with a mouse before eating it. The whales also sometimes flip their wounded prey with their tails, sending it sailing through the air."

"But scientists really do not yet know why the whales do not have front teeth. In many ways it seems illogical that a predator such as this would not have teeth there. The other predators with which we are all familiar such as the cats, wolves, bears and so forth, all have front teeth. If any of you have theories of your own, I'd like to hear them.

"And one last thing, this whale had a slight case of osteoporosis, as you'll see if you look carefully at some of the bone structure, especially here on the rear part of the spine."

Reed, with Cindy nearby, began backing away from the skeleton. Several of the people in the crowd were following him offering comments and asking questions, but they kept steadily moving toward the entrance as Reed parried the various ideas and queries. Finally they reached the door and Reed turned to the group with one last comment as they left the building, "Thank you very much, but I have another important meeting I must get to right away. See you next time!"

He grabbed Cindy's arm and strode quickly out of the building. Then they ran toward the parking lot. Safely into the darkness, they both began laughing, both at the relief to get away and because they were with each other. Cindy spoke first. "That was a great evening. You sure threw the faculty some bones to chew."

Reed smiled. "I'll be hearing more about this later. But, say, where are you going from here?"

"I don't have any plans, but it would be nice to relax."

"You live near here don't you," Reed asked. He already knew she had an apartment not far away and that she lived alone. "The nanny is watching the boys so I don't have to go straight home. Tell you what. Why don't you hop in with me and we'll stop by a liquor store for champagne and then have a little celebration at your place. That's a good way to relax. Later, I'll drop you off here to pick up your car."

Cindy was thinking ahead. "I have a better idea. Let's take both cars now. I'll follow you to the liquor store and wait. Then you can follow me to my place and I won't have to come back later."

Reed looked at her closely, and she again looked him in the eyes unhesitatingly. They both realized communication was good. No question about intent.

After Reed left her apartment at 2 am, Cindy lay in bed quietly thinking about this maverick marine biologist. He was the best lover she had ever had. So kind and considerate. Although she had only seen Reed's three boys one time, she realized that the oldest one, on the basis of age, could be her brother. She wondered what it might be like to get more serious with Reed, perhaps move in with him, begin motherly duties in a real home. Reed had advised her that he had a vasectomy so there was no chance of additional children; that lack of choice was disturbing. As she drifted off to sleep the best course of action with Reed seemed to be to try for a close but unpossessive relationship.

CHAPTER THREE

Halibut

T ed Barnes was the Chief of Police and head of the three man police force in Whittier, a small fishing village and shipping terminal perched at the edge of a finger of water projecting west from the main body of Prince William Sound. Barnes had reached the conclusion that the two kayakers from Nevada, Brooke Adams and Jim Tubbs, had been overcome by hypothermia and had drowned. It appeared the couple may have gone swimming, swam out too far from shore and had been overcome by the numbing cold of the waters. There seemed to be no other logical explanation. The tent, boat, clothing, vodka bottle and other items had been found in the small cove on the east side of Slate Island, but no other sign of the couple had been found. There was no indication of foul play. With dozens of people lost each year in Alaska as a result of boating accidents, two more didn't really make much difference. Besides, these two were `Cheechakos' who probably were ill prepared to deal with several days boating in the Sound.

When the charter boat *Ace of Spades* had arrived to pick up Brooke and Jim at the designated location on Knight Island just a few miles from Slate Island, no one was there, even though the Ace was three hours early for the prearranged arrival time. After waiting six hours into the afternoon, Perry Butler, the captain and owner, had radioed the Harbor Master in Whittier to tell them his passengers were "no shows." "Glad I got the full payment in advance" Butler remarked. After a brief conversation, they agreed that the best thing to do was for the Ace of Spades to motor south in the direction from which the couple would have been returning in their kayak. Because of the virtually continuous daylight, the search was carried on almost all night.

By 7 o'clock the next morning Butler radioed the harbor master that he must return to Whittier because of other commitments. Two days later an aerial search had confirmed the location of the tent, boat and other belongings of Jim and Brooke.

Captain Barnes called Ascuaga's Nugget Inn in Reno, the only known contact, to advise them that Jim and his escort were missing and that a search was underway. The Nugget manager provided the names and phone numbers of the next of kin, and Barnes called them with the news. He handled the usual questions of what was known about the disappearance, what was being done, that the relatives probably couldn't help. Jim's father and Brooke's brother called back to say they would come to Whittier as soon as possible to help with the search. Barnes had anticipated this reaction and said he would help them find a charter boat so they could go to the exact site and examine it for themselves. Jim's father requested that a charter be arranged starting two days hence in order for them to have time to travel to Anchorage and on to Whittier.

After hanging up from the call, Barnes telephoned Perry Butler at his charter office near the harbor to tell him that a lucrative charter was probably coming up as a result of the disappearance. "The relatives of the missing couple are coming in day after tomorrow and may need your boat for a couple of weeks," he advised. "Should be a moneymaking deal for you."

Barnes, originally from Montana, had been in the state nearly 20 years and had come to recognize the fact that Alaskans were always quick to take financial advantage of someone else's tragedy. The oil spill by the giant tanker *Exxon Valdez* in Prince William Sound in 1989 had been dubbed the "Alaska Full Employment Act," and the name of Joseph Hazelwood, the captain of the Valdez, showed up on bumper stickers in Anchorage as a nominee for the next governor because he had done so much to provide employment and a financial bonanza for thousands of Alaskans. The payments of a billion dollars by Exxon resulted in a classic Alaska feeding frenzy as the piranha-minded Alaskans flocked to file their claims or otherwise try to get on Exxon's payment list or payroll.

In the 1970's, Barnes recalled, Shell Oil had been financially raped by residents of Homer, Alaska when a Shell contracted offshore oil rig was towed into Kachemak Bay near Homer and crossed over a few crab pots. As soon as the word got out that Shell was accepting damage claims, greedy and ruthless Alaskans for miles around filed claims of fishing equipment damage against Shell to get on the band wagon. The fact that they were lying did not bother their conscience so long as they get paid and, at the same time, could enjoy some oil company bashing. Shell did not argue and paid virtually all claims as submitted, thus adding fuel to another feeding frenzy. The term 'opportunist,' Barnes acknowledged, was particularly fitting for many Alaskans, including Governor Ben Springfield. Springfield had gotten in on the cash payments by buying part interest in a fishing boat in Seattle within a week after the oil spill and contracting it out to Exxon for "cleanup," which was, in effect, standby.

The relatives of Tubbs and Adams arrived two days later and Barnes met them at the train. After going over maps and reviewing all that was known, which he admitted wasn't much, he took them directly to the *Ace of Spades* to meet Butler, who was waiting in smug anticipation. As undertakers often take advantage of bereaved relatives when a loved one dies, Butler was ready for the occasion. He explained that he was the logical one to hire for the job because he was the last one to see the couple and he "knew the area" better than anyone else. He was sure they would understand that he would have to charge a premium rate, however, because he had cancelled some other work so he and his boat would be available for this search. Further, he was ready to go with a fully stocked and fueled boat and could stay out two weeks if necessary. When he pointed out they might have to wait several days for another boat, the worried relatives agreed without argument. Butler and Barnes smiled knowingly at each other. Barnes would get a case of whiskey for this one.

The next day, eight days after the official disappearance, Barnes advised the state trooper office in Anchorage that he believed the official search should be abandoned by all parties, including the Coast Guard. He concluded there was essentially no chance of finding the couple alive. Exposure for even a few days without food or shelter in this northern climate, although it was June, would cause even a skilled outdoorsman to succumb.

The commercial salmon fishing season had been in full swing in the Sound, and most of the fishermen had been advised of the missing persons. No clues as to their whereabouts, other than the camp site, had been found. Barnes also wrote in the memo that the usual expected relatives had arrived and that he had helped them hire a search vessel.

Mike Mackenzie was alone on Prince William Sound when he heard the reports of the missing couple via the marine radio. He was on his 28 foot, diesel powered boat near the entrance to his favorite cove on the east side of Knight Island. He could understand why people would seek adventure, but his years of experience had taught him that venturing in a kayak onto big water like the Sound, where hurricane force winds could spring up in 30 minutes, was asking for trouble. Another two people would probably be added to the continuously growing Alaska Trooper list of "missing and unaccounted for." His attention turned to selecting a safe anchorage in the protected cove for the evening.

Professionally, Mike was a geologist, but he had a strong interest in fishing and marine biology. Working out of his Anchorage office-at-home, he tried to spend sufficient time on mineral exploration and mining projects to make a living and yet provide enough money so he could also pursue his intense interests in studying aquatic organisms. Mike sometimes described himself as a naturalist, which seemed incongruous to some of the preservationists he met, particularly those employed by the State of Alaska Department of Conservation. Fortunately for Mike, several years previously he had staked fifty 20 acre mining claims in one of the old placer gold mining districts on the south slope of the Alaska Range about halfway between Anchorage and Fairbanks. The company he leased the claims to three years ago had commenced gold mining. The modest five percent royalty he had retained was providing him with adequate funds to spend more time in his favorite haunt, Prince William Sound. The frequent reports of substantial numbers of stolen gold nuggets from the operation bothered him, but there was little he could do to increase security at the mining operation.

Mike had been introduced to marine mammals in the Sound by Dr. Reed Remington when Reed was carrying out research there under a program sponsored by Hydrosphere Oceanarium of California. For parts of three summers Mike and his wife, Tracy, had acted as volunteer assistants to Reed, and the three found they shared an acute interest in nature. Their very different backgrounds seemed to blend with and enhance each other in what Tracy jokingly called `Prince William symbiosis.' Reed and Mike were high calibre scientists, and while Reed was a practicing marine biologist and a teacher, Mike, 46 years old, brought to the trio the benefit of years of observations of nature in action, including careful studies of the earth through exploration and mining on a broad range of projects in many differed climates. Tracy's forte was her excellent background and abilities in computers and electronics, but she was also very keen as a naturalist and went with Mike to the field at every opportunity.

All three had become extremely interested in killer whales after observing them discretely for several weeks during the three previous summers. Unfortunately, Hydrosphere management had decided to discontinue funding of the Alaska killer whale research because of strong opposition from well-meaning but, in their opinion, misdirected and disoriented animal rights groups.

Killer whales, because of their intelligence and social behavior, came to be regarded by Reed, Mike and Tracy as *Earth* inhabitants on a special elevated plane, with intriguing communication potential. Their interest in Orcinus orca extended beyond the normal passing studies they accorded other species such as sea otters, or even other whales such as the humpbacks or gray whales which were frequently seen in Prince William Sound in the summer months. It was not difficult for them to understand why certain 'psychic' individuals and certain spiritual groups, including some Alaskan and British Columbian natives, worshipped the killer whale or believed it to be at least the equivalent of man on this planet. Some of the psychics even contended that the killer whale represented an extra-terrestrial landing on earth which had progressed to the present state of a sophisticated marine life. Certain native groups, which had lived along the northeast Pacific rim for centuries, after crossing the Bering Land Bridge, regarded the killer whale as a sort of supernatural being with magical powers.

Reed, Mike and Tracy, however, while granting the whales considerable mental dexterity, believed the flesh and blood whales had evolved as a top predator mainly because of food availability. Their efforts were directed toward a better understanding of the whales through a close examination of their behavior and practical aspects of their complex social life. Much data remained to be gathered, however. Research funds were difficult to come by. Unfortunately, one of the important investigations, which would have resulted from the capture and study of ten killer whales collected at a rate of two per year from Alaskan waters by Hydrosphere, was thwarted by maniacal opposition from Blue War, a self-appointed but financially powerful whale protection society. Some of the Alaska natives had also jumped into the fray both for publicity and because they didn't want the white man doing anything else with "their" wildlife. Governor Ben Springfield had gleefully stepped onto the band wagon in opposition of the project for political motives, hoping he might win some preservationist votes, and the matter was still in court.

Mike, alone on the *Czarina* for the past five days, had securely anchored in the protected cove on the east side of Knight Island for the night and had slept soundly. Tracy had grudgingly missed this trip due to a commitment previously made to an Anchorage bank that was converting to a new, more efficient computer system.

The sound of gulls arguing from the rocks on shore awoke him in the comfortable cabin just before 6 am. He arose and looked with binoculars to see what the ruckus was all about. A bald eagle was fishing on the beach 75 yards away and the gulls were upset that they weren't getting any of the fish. The eagle's fishing technique consisted of waiting quietly on the gravel only a few feet from the water, watching intently, and then springing forward with talons extended to grab some sort of small fish which was just under the surface 15 feet offshore. A few wingbeats would then carry the eagle and its catch back to the beach to dine. Mike could not determine the type of fish being caught, but presumed they might be young salmon.

Before preparing breakfast, he decided to set his heavy duty rod for halibut. A catch would be fun and would make for some excellent eating.

The halibut rod, always rigged with hook and sinker and ready for bait, was kept in an overhead rack in the cabin. He took it down and went to the stern of the *Czarina* and opened an old, banged-up cooler and dug from the ice a plastic bag containing a dozen 10-inch herring. He took out one of the herring and cut it in half. After threading the point of the heavy 3-inch hook twice through the front half of the herring, he picked up the rod, swung the bait and sinker over the side, released the clicker and watched the rigging disappear into the green-gray water and then stop. By looking at the reel, he estimated the depth to be about 80 feet. He reeled it about 2 feet above the bottom. Satisfied that the bait was just off the bottom, he set the clicker on the reel and inserted the base of the rod securely into a holder bolted to the railing. He returned inside to have breakfast of coffee, bran cereal and fruit.

While eating, he turned the radio on to hear the news and the weather report. Other than some expected wind, the report was quite good. Sounded like the search was about to be called off for the couple lost at Slate Island. Two days earlier he had passed by Slate Island and had scanned the shore line with binoculars, but had seen nothing.

As he crunched on the dry cereal and milk, his thoughts turned to plans. Today he would cruise the area near The Needle, an isolated, jagged point of rock in Prince William Sound, to observe the abundant sea lions on the rocks and in the nearby waters. With abundant salmon now migrating through that part of the Sound, some interesting things might happen. One of the groups of killer whales might come by. He would like to see the interactions again.

Whenever Mike had his line in the water, his attention never strayed far from the rod even though his thoughts might run to other subjects. An occasional glance told him if anything was happening to the bait, turning slowly near the cold and dark bottom 80 feet below. He knew that if he had erred and the bait was on the bottom, a starfish wide as a dinner plate would probably engulf it.

Head bent over a steaming cup, he spotted a slight twitch of the line. As he watched, the end of the rod jerked down 3 inches and then again straightened. This was no starfish. Deftly he placed the coffee cup on the table, moved to the rod and carefully picked it up so as not to move the bait. Two sudden heavier jerks on the line told him a good-sized fish was trying to take the herring. Mike lowered the rod slightly, providing some slack so the fish could take the bait if it would. One more slight jerk and then the bait and sinker began to move, the fish was carrying the herring. He struck hard by rearing back on the rod suddenly to set the hook. In response, the stout rod suddenly bent in a sharp arc and he felt the power of the fish as the drag on the reel screamed in complaint. From experience he knew such strength reflected a big halibut. The fish powered its way away from shore for 50 yards toward deeper water before it slowed the initial run. Mike's wrists and forearms were strained as he sought to slow the heavy fish.

For the next thirty minutes he battled the fish. Although it made no more long runs, it had no desire to leave the security of the bottom and be forced to the surface. By the heavy power displayed, Mike guessed the fish would probably weigh at least 100 pounds. It must be one of the `hens', female halibut which can weigh more than 500 pounds.

Finally the fish began to tire and, by exerting great pressure on the rod, as much as he thought the line could stand, Mike was able to begin reeling the heavy halibut slowly toward the surface. He had not yet been able to see the fish even though visibility was a good 40 feet.

After several more minutes of straining and reeling, he peered over the side of the *Czarina* toward the bottom to see a mottled green shape which was at least 6 feet long, slowly, slowly spiraling upward toward the boat in the clear, greenish water. That fish would probably weigh at least 250 pounds, he told himself. Halibut, because of their flat shape, could exert tremendous downward pressure. The grotesque, weirdly-located two eyes on the upward side of the head were now visible, looking like Dr. Frankenstein had erred when operating on the head of these fish.

It was fun to hook and fight one like this, but now he had to decide what to do with it. A large halibut, he knew, was an extremely dangerous fish to handle, not because of its teeth or because it bites, but because of the tremendous power it displays when flailing with its body and tail when trying to escape its captors, but especially when brought aboard a vessel. Mike knew that each summer in Alaska some inexperienced fishermen make the mistake of hoisting a large live halibut into their boat. At best such a blunder can result in broken fishing rods and damaged surficial hardware on the boat. At worst it can mean broken legs and other physical damage for the fishermen and, in the case of smaller boats, large halibut have been known to pound the bottom out of a boat and sink it.

Mike knew this big fish would fight for another ten or fifteen minutes after it approached the surface and would make several powerful runs back to the bottom before he could get it near the boat. He could then shoot it with his .44 Magnum, harpoon it and tie it to the boat with a stout rope. But he realized he then would be faced with handling a 250 pound fish by himself. Not an impossible task, because the *Czarina* was equipped with an electric winch for retrieving long commercial fishing lines. But he had no place to store such a large amount of fish even after filleting.

He decided the best course of action would be to release the fish. This could be done by simply cutting the line, or he could attempt to remove the hook with pliers if it was not imbedded too deeply in the halibut's mouth. As he fought the powerful, mottled fish closer to the surface, he saw that the hook was imbedded only at the edge of its mouth, and he decided to try to take the hook out. Fortunately, the needle nose pliers that he needed were available in the small aft tool box he could reach while still holding the rod firmly.

After picking up the pliers and stuffing them into a rear pocket, he stepped out of the boat and onto the transom, a small wooden slatted platform just above the propeller at the stern of the boat. Now he could see how big this fish really was. He guessed it must be 7 feet long, 4 feet wide and would weigh perhaps 300 pounds. The size, mottled green color and flat shape reminded him of a large rug, except this rug was about 2 feet thick in the middle. Halibut are indeed strange looking fish, he was reminded. They begin life swimming upright as any other fish does, but later one eye migrates across the head to the other side and the fish then spends the rest of its life swimming on its side. The gills and mouth, however, remain in their original position so that the mouth opens and closes in a side to side motion. The upper side of the halibut, where both eyes are located, becomes a mottled green camouflage color, and the side down becomes an off-white. The evolution of this form has been quite efficient for the halibut, because it has the ability to conserve energy by lying on the bottom rather than having to swim constantly upright as many other fish must do.

As Mike looked down at the huge, slowly circling fish, now in 15 feet of water, he again looked at the bulbous, staring eyes on the upper side of the mottled green head. He was reminded that Reed Remington had once told him that a 300 pound halibut lying on the bottom will eat almost anything that comes by: crabs, fish, octopus, eel, herring, salmon and even diving sea birds if the halibut happens to be in shallow water.

The fish was now getting weary and Mike stood on the transom, the bent rod in his left hand. He got the pliers out of his pocket and set them on the stern. In order to be closer to the water he kneeled on one knee. As he reeled the halibut closer, it seemed to be staring at him with the two deep black, yellow rimmed but efficient eyes. No matter how many halibut he had seen, the eyes still seemed out of place on the upper side of the fish's head. With the rod in his left hand and the pliers in his right, Mike reached out carefully and slowly, hoping the fish would remain calm. There was the exposed hook. With the pliers, he grasped the shank of the hook and started to twist it for extraction, but the barb was imbedded in hard cartilage. The halibut, now slightly rested, felt the twist and, with rapid, powerful strokes of the 2 foot wide tail, exploded at the surface. Water flew 30 feet into the air. The reaction was so quick that Mike could not release the pliers and he was jerked off the transom into the cold water by the strong surge of the fish.

He was under water only momentarily, but he dropped the pliers as he used his right arm for swimming toward the boat. The rod was in his left hand but the drag was set so tightly he was having difficulty swimming as the halibut once again stripped line off the reel and headed for the bottom.

Treading water, Mike managed to reach down and unlock the drag, thus allowing the fish to strip off line easily.

He climbed back up on the transom of the *Czarina*, cold and wet, telling himself he should have cut the line. Once again the halibut had proven itself a dangerous fish. Shivering from the cold water, it took Mike another five minutes to reel the fish to the surface, not wishing to cut a long length of fishing line because a long line might get snagged on bottom debris and result in the death of the fish. This time, with the fish 10 feet below, he simply cut the line. The big halibut, feeling no restraint, slowly disappeared back into the depths as Mike watched. He was confident the hook, non-stainless steel, would deteriorate with time and would not interfere with the halibut's feeding.

He returned to the cabin to dry off and change clothes. Getting soaked was only a temporary inconvenience, but, in thinking it over, there was no question in his mind that he should have cut the line in the first place. Operating alone in Alaska allows little room for error in judgment.

With dry clothing on, he finished breakfast and started up the diesel engine to allow it to warm up. At the bow of the boat he brought in the anchor, made easy by the electric winch. Returning to the cabin, he slowly idled the *Czarina* to the east and out of the cove.

Once in the open waters of Prince William Sound, he used the binoculars to survey the surface on the east side of Knight Island. No sign of whales, nor did he see any for the next two hours. Approaching The Needle, even from a distance of half a mile he, could see the light and dark brown sea lions crowded on the rocks, with many more heads bobbing in the rough water around the rocks. Sea lion defecation caused a terrible smell downwind from the jagged rocks, and Mike maneuvered the *Czarina* around to the windward side. After making several passes nearby to observe and to take photographs, he decided to head westward toward Whittier. Time to catch the train back to Anchorage and work on two more mineral exploration ideas he had conceived. Four hours travel time would be required to get to Whittier, and he could watch for killer whales on the way.

An hour passed with the *Czarina* throbbing steadily along. As he was passing the southern end of Green Island, the two tone blue of a familiar vessel appeared, anchored in a cove. It looked like Jerry Gallagher's *North Star* from Seward. Jerry operated in the Sound for a few weeks each year in June for commercial fishing for herring, halibut and salmon. Mike got on the radio. "*North Star, North Star,* this is the C*zarina* calling. Come in, Jerry."

The response was quick. "Hi, Mike, I thought that might be you. Where have you been?"

"Oh, spending some time fishing and watching animals. How's your fishing going?"

Jerry replied. "We had been doing were doing pretty well during the halibut opening, which closed just this morning, and we're about to go to Whittier to sell our catch."

Jerry's voice changed to a concerned tone. "But we ran into a problem I've never seen before. Yesterday evening, at about 6 o'clock, we had just started to bring in a two mile long halibut skate with a couple of thousand baited hooks on it when we noticed a group of about twenty killer whales approaching. We just assumed they would go right on by as they have always done in the past. But this bunch turned from their course and swam toward our skate as if to look it over.

"We continued to bring in the line on the winch drum and we were catching some good halibut. We were busy with the fish and the whales disappeared. We thought they had gone on by when the winch suddenly started straining. We could then see our skate was rising toward the surface, and a bull killer whale surfaced to blow with one of our large, hooked halibut in its mouth."

Mike was wishing the conversation was not taking place over the radio which allowed any other nearby fishermen on the same frequency to hear it all. Jerry was an excellent fisherman with 30 years of experience, and his observations could be depended upon as true.

Jerry continued: "The halibut must have weighed 100 pounds, but that bull was holding it like a piece of candy. Then he started to swim away and was tearing up our equipment because our line was still attached to the halibut. We had no choice but to cut the line and lose the entire skate, fish and all. We guessed that the rest of the whales were below the surface having a picnic as they plucked the halibut from the line. The whales milled around in the area for thirty minutes and we couldn't do a damn thing about it. One of the boys wanted to start shooting the SOB's, but I wouldn't let him."

Mike responded: "I'm glad you prevented the shooting, but I'm very sorry to hear of trouble with the whales. I have never heard of them bothering halibut gear before. We know they like black cod because they stole some last summer from a couple of long line fishermen, but this is the first halibut theft that I know of."

Jerry continued. "If they make a habit of this, many more of the fishermen will start shooting the whales when they come near. In all my years of fishing, I have never seen whales steal fish off a line. Wonder what made them do it?"

Mike thought a minute and then radioed back. "Fish and Game last month published a report suggesting too many herring were being caught in some areas, including Prince William Sound. Perhaps this group of whales normally feeds on herring. If the herring are not available they might turn to other food such as your halibut. By the way, could you tell which pack this was?"

Jerry responded. "Yes, I've seen this bunch before. It has a couple of big bulls in it, and one of the bulls has a sort of wavy dorsal fin, 6 or 7 feet high, with a notch at the rear. He's the one who picked up the big halibut."

Aha, Mike thought, it must be the A-T Pack and the bull must be A-T- 4. They had photographed that bunch several times over the past three years and had counted eighteen whales in the pack last year. A couple of births would increase the count to the number Jerry observed.

Then on the radio: "We'll look at our records and see if we can tell which group it is." The less known about which whale group it might be at this time, the better, he thought. If one pack seems to be at fault the fishermen might be merciless in persecuting them.

"Well, they'd better not make a habit of stealing our fish. That escapade cost me about 1500 dollars in gear and another $4,000 or so in lost halibut. My crew gets a percentage of the catch and this means money out of their pockets."

"I'm sorry this happened, Jerry," said Mike. "Hopefully, it's an isolated incident."

Jerry radioed back. "I hope so too, Mike. Well, we're heading into Whittier to unload the halibut we did catch, we've got about 7,000 pounds on board. Hope the prices are halfway decent this time."

The *North Star*, both 350 horsepower gasoline engines at a low roar, began to pick up speed and swing out of the cove toward the west on a course for Whittier.

"OK, Jerry, I'm going that way too, but I chug along at a fraction of your speed. Maybe I'll see you there."

Jerry had one more thought. "Another thing, Mike, a couple of the whales, including the other big male, appeared to have bullet holes in their dorsal fins. Someone has been shooting at them."

"Yes, many of the killer whales in Prince William Sound have been shot at, and I'm sure many die when they're hit in the body. Some of the shooting is by crazies who will shoot at almost anything, but we don't need confrontations between the fishermen and the whales over fish."

"Right, over and out," said Jerry as the *North Star* picked up speed. Commercial fishermen had learned that high speed boats allowed them to travel very quickly from one area to another in order to be wherever the fish happened to be, or wherever the Alaska Department of Fish and Game (called Moose and Goose by the fishermen) declared an "opening." A speedy boat was worth the additional expense.

As Mike watched, the North Star began to plane and sped away into the distance at nearly 20 miles per hour. Mike smiled, the diesel powered was slow, but he could go a long way on 10 gallons of fuel, and, more importantly, the diesel engines were not irritating to the whales and other mammals he liked to watch. In his opinion, gasoline engines, particularly the whiny small outboards, were disturbing to whales. He theorized that some marine biologists in British Columbia, based on papers he had read, improperly interpreted the normal travel speed of killer whales because they were following the whales in a small boat with a whiny outboard. The whales had simply speeded up to get away from the noise.

The *Czarina* throbbed away at 1400 **RPM** toward Whittier. It was 4 pm, and he'd be there by 7. Tracy had told him she was planning to arrive in Whittier on the six o'clock train from Portage, but it would be too late tonight to shower, eat, get everything tidied up on the and catch the train to Anchorage. He and Tracy would spend a pleasant night together in the *Czarina* and leave tomorrow.

A driving rain began to fall and Mike pondered the killer whale's taking of the halibut. If this indicated a trend toward conflicts with the fishermen, it would be disastrous for the whales because there would be more shooting whenever the whales appeared near fishing boats. There was no way, he knew, to attempt patrolling the vast areas of Prince William Sound in an effort to head off conflicts between competing interests of whales and fishermen. A better way would be to change the herring openings and catches, if it could be determined that this was the problem, in order to provide more food for the whales.

Excessive commercial herring catches could also have repercussions in other parts of the food chain, such as on king and coho salmon. But again, it was likely no data was available. He also knew that in Alaska, political pressure from special interest groups such as commercial fishermen could easily outweigh any consideration of food sources for the killer whales, or any other marine mammal for that matter.

The thoughts occupied his mind a good part of the way to Whittier. With the radio on, he monitored broadcasts from Whittier, including occasional mention of the disappearance of the couple from Reno. Their boat and gear had been recovered from the small beach on Slate Island with no sign whatsoever of foul play. The Troopers and Whittier police were still requesting information from anyone boating in the area. In the back of his mind Mike wondered where the A-T Pack had been hunting in the past two weeks, other than at Jerry's halibut fishing location.

The rain stopped and the skies cleared when the *Czarina* was 30 minutes out of Whittier. If the Chugach Mountain Range did not stand so high west of Whittier, the beautiful, all nightlong Alaska sunset would be visible for hours. Even this far south, sunsets in late June could be long lasting and gorgeous as the sun angled across the northwest horizon. As Mike looked westward, the Chugach Mountains seemed to form a sort of rugged cradle for Whittier, resplendent with glaciers, ice or deep snow covering most of the areas more than 1,000 feet above sea level. The effect was a gorgeous but chilling blue and white foreground set against flaming orange clouds high in the stratosphere. Here and there massive, jagged rock outcrops showed at the mountain tops and on the steep mountainsides. Lush green willows grew in abundance near the mountain base but vegetation was sparse on the slopes because of few places available for growth.

Whittier had never fully recovered from the major earthquake of 1964, which had made a shambles of many of the buildings, the railroad and the harbor facilities. Even without the earthquake destruction, the town always seemed to have a grim appearance it somehow could not shake.

As Mike steered the toward her reserved slip, he smiled upon seeing Tracy there dancing a jig and waving to him. What a terrific sense of humor, he thought. It was wonderful to see her again, even though he had been gone just a few days. With the *Czarina* secured, Tracy came aboard with hugs and kisses for Mike.

Reed had called from California, she advised him, with a request that Mike call him as soon as he got into port. Mike described for her the theft of the halibut by killer whales, probably the A-T Pack, and the disappearance of the couple from Nevada. She had heard of the disappearance, but fish thefts in this season was a new and disturbing development.

Tracy offered to begin warming up some of her homemade chili which she had thoughtfully brought along from Anchorage. Mike looked at his watch and thought he might be able to reach Reed at home at this hour.

With towel and overnight kit in hand, he made his way along the planked floating dock and up the steep ramp to the two story harbor headquarters building, where three public pay telephones were available. In the past summers in Whittier, when it was not raining, great clouds of dust were churned up by the small amount of traffic milling around town. But the State of Alaska, with income of $3 billion per year from oil royalties for a population of about 500t,000 people, had finally appropriated funds for paving the streets in this, an important terminal for passenger and freight traffic. Years earlier, tens of millions in state money had gone to build and pave roads to real estate developments in the Anchorage area whose owners just happened to be cronies of state senators or representatives, or of the governor himself. Whittier did not have the proper clout in Juneau to get the job done earlier.

As he waited for a phone, three of the fishermen recognized him as one of the whale researchers and filled him in on the latest rumors among the fishermen about problems with the whales. Jerry wasn't the only one with problems, they informed him. Black cod (sablefish) fishermen were suffering sporadic raids on their fishing lines just as they had the previous year. Some of them were starting again to set off subsurface explosions in order to scare the whales away from their fishing gear. Yet many were concerned that the explosives would also have an adverse impact on their fishing success. Further, the Marine Mammal Protection Act specifically forbade harassment of whales.

Mike thanked them for the information and promised to do what he could to look into the problem and to try to find a solution. He cautioned them not to shoot at the whales because they were a protected mammal and injuries or death to the whales could bring in the "Feds" to regulate the fisheries more severely. In his own mind, however, Mike knew that if it came to losing fish and/or fishing gear or shooting whales, many of the fishermen would start shooting.

Cell phones will not work in Whittier because of the terrain. For Mike, the delay in getting a phone was exceptionally long because fishermen were taking the opportunity to call home to Ninilchik, Homer, Seattle and various other points of origin. After an almost intolerable wait of fifteen minutes, he got to a phone. Fortunately, Reed was home to receive the call.

"Hi Reed, this is Mike calling from Whittier. How are you?"

"Great, Mike. I wish I could be up there with you right now. Tell me what's happening."

Mike cupped his hand over his mouth and spoke almost in a whisper into the phone. "Reed, I'm at a public phone so I must speak quietly. Listen, I just returned from six days out in the Sound. Things are looking worse up here. What clearly appears to be the A-T pack has picked halibut from Jerry Gallagher's halibut skate. Sounds like one of the A-T bulls, probably T-4, picked up a big halibut that was on the line and took off with it. Jerry had to cut the skate line. Then the orcas milled around as if picking off other hooked halibut. If this continues, it will mean more trouble between the whales and the fishermen, perhaps even worse than last year."

"I remember well, last year was not pleasant," Reed sighed, "but I had hoped the problem would go away. The last thing we need now is more problems between the fishermen and the whales. What do the fishermen have to say?"

"Unfortunately," Mike replied, "it's not just the halibut. The word here in Whittier is that killer whales, and I'm not sure which pack, have again been taking black cod from long lines. We may have a trend developing here where the whales regard the hooked fish as a sort of readymade buffet. Further, the whales are quite particular about the types of fish they will pick off the lines. Gray cod are out, black cod are in."

Reed chuckled but then again became serious. "But this could turn the entire fishing community against the whales. How did Jerry react?"

"He at least kept the crew from shooting at the pack. But if this happens again there will probably be some dead whales. The economic loss of the fish and gear is significant for these people, and they know, even if Blue War doesn't, that there are plenty of killer whales in Alaska. So far as the fishermen are concerned, the 'disposal' of a few troublemaker whales will never be noticed in the populations of Prince William Sound."

"Mike, do you have any new ideas on why the whales might be doing this? As we have discussed before, fish stealing is not a normal type of activity for the orcas. Why would they take hooked fish when they must be aware of the danger from the fishermen. Why has this been taking place the past couple of years?"

"The only possible connection I could think of, Reed, is depleted herring stocks as reported by Fish and Game. This may somehow be having an impact on killer whale food directly, or on the food chain. But, so far as I know, there is no data available to give us a clue as to what the real herring impact may be. Further, some of the thefts are taking place when there are plenty of salmon in the Sound for the whales to feed on."

"I wonder if we are dealing with a maverick pack," Reed mused. "In any event, let's review all possible reasons why this may have happened. I don't need to recite this to you, Mike, but if only we had been allowed to carry out more research we would know more about the whales and their life styles. The kooks who believe they are protecting the whales by blocking research, including hizzoner the governor of Alaska, are in fact contributing to the demise of the animals."

They had discussed the previous year, and had agreed, that even certain Alaska native groups, through opposition to research on the creatures they claim to regard as a type of deity, could, through ignorance, cause the death of many of the whales because scientists had been unable to collect and study a small number. There had been fierce opposition to the collection of a few whales for research, yet practically nothing was done to prevent Alaska fishermen and trigger happy boaters from shooting the whales at will. Where were the Natives when the whales needed them. Indeed, some of the fishermen who were suspected strongly of shooting the whales were of partial Native descent.

"Let's continue to gather information and see if we can establish a pattern to, or reason for, this activity," Mike suggested. "If these are isolated incidents it may blow over. If it continues...we can expect real trouble for the whales."

"Sounds good, Mike. Please keep me posted. And I'm still planning to come to Anchorage a week from tomorrow unless something new pops up here to delay my departure. If you're available, let's plan to spend at least a couple of weeks on the Sound getting all the data we can during that period. Maybe you can get more information from Game and Fish and other sources in the meantime."

"I'll be available, Reed. This time the whales seem to be in real danger." He cupped his hand more closely over the phone and whispered,

"By the way, there's one other thing, probably not related, but two boaters from Nevada disappeared from Slate Island about a week ago without a trace. Their small boat, camp, food and clothing was found, but nothing else. Nothing. No sign of foul play."

Reed hesitated. "Mike, you're not suggesting killer whales had anything to do with that, are you?"

"I just have an ominous feeling about it. Remember how aggressive the A-T pack has become in killing and eating seals and harbor porpoises the last two years? I wouldn't want to be in the water when that group was on the prowl!"

"Yes, but, as you said, they theoretically should be well fed on salmon at this time of the year, thus making it unlikely they would attack a strange quarry such as man."

"I know, Reed, but I'm uneasy about it. The A-T pack was the one tearing up Jerry's halibut gear. One problem group could cause all kinds of crazy things to start happening. You know how irrational Alaska officials are, and many with NOAA and the U. S. Fish and Wildlife Service are not much better. The situation could get out of hand, to the detriment of the whales, guilty or not."

"Keep me posted, please, on what is happening up there. I will arrange things here to break away as soon as I can. Some first-hand investigation is definitely called for."

"OK. That's it for now, Reed. Give my best to the boys. I'll call you as soon as something new develops, and in the meantime we'll be looking forward to seeing you up here."

Mike checked for an open shower stall and, finding one, climbed the stairs to the harbor master's office and paid the $1.50 required for the number 3 shower. Returning to the shower area, the hot shower felt wonderful after the previous several days on the vessel.

Back on the *Czarina*, Tracy was waiting for him with a crisp green salad, steaming hot chili and a good bottle of 1980 Silver Oak Napa cabernet sauvignon opened for breathing. Soothing music drifted through the cabin as they dined. They postponed further talk about the whales and devoted all their energy and attention to each other. In the forward bunk they made passionate love and were then gently rocked to sleep by the slight motion of the vessel.

CHAPTER FOUR

Champ

Nels Larson and his wife, Lydia, had built their cabin in 1947, 12 miles southeast of Whittier on Chimney Creek where the boisterous stream emptied into Prince William Sound. Retired, the couple lived in Anchorage through the winter, but in mid-May each year they would return to the cabin to spend the summer salt water fishing for salmon and halibut. Their children, now grown and with families of their own, would come to visit two or three times during the summer, and almost always in September, when bear, both black and brown, and moose were hunted.

For many years Nels and Lydia, now in their late 60's, had travelled back and forth from Whittier to the cabin site in a 25 foot dory, which was also used for fishing because it had the capacity to accommodate the fishing nets and the salmon when they were lucky enough to "get into them" as Nels would say. But the dory, although seaworthy and rugged, was also very slow. The previous year their son had convinced them that they should get a smaller, faster boat to use in the run to and from Whittier. For ease of handling and light weight they had selected a 12 foot model of the small but tough, inflatable sport boats called Zodiac. With a 20 horsepower outboard, the Zodiac would travel at more than 15 miles per hour. This meant that time to travel to or from Whittier was reduced to less than one hour while the dory took more than two hours.

It was early June and one four day "opening" time period for king salmon, as set by the Alaska Department of Fish and Game, had come and gone. "Lydie," as he called her, and Nels had caught nearly 1,000 pounds of kings in their one set net strung from shore out for 200 feet, and had been able to sell them "in the round" (ungutted) to a fish buyer for $1,882. Not enough to live on, but not too bad as supplemental income for a retired couple. The amount just barely exceeded the dividends they received from the State of Alaska from earnings from the Permanent Fund, a multibillion dollar stash of funds the legislature had decided to put away as investments in the days of big oil money. As a result of the investment, Alaska was the only state to make an annual payment to every resident, just the opposite of the usual practice of state income taxation.

The openings for commercial salmon fishing were now temporarily over for a two week period. Lydia had canned four cases of the kings in her home pressure cooker, most of which she would give to the kids in Anchorage. She had her special recipe which included a generous amount of garlic and dill weed.

Lydia had reminded Nels each morning for the past three days, gently without nagging, that it was about time to go to Anchorage for supplies. Besides, it was grandson Tim's 6th birthday. Nels had been working on a leak in the roof of the cabin next to the rock chimney, but finally, on a Tuesday evening, he said he would be ready to go the following morning. If they left Chimney Creek by 8:30 am, he told Lydia, they could be in Whittier in time to catch the Alaska Railroad noon train. Forty five minutes later, after the ride through the mountain tunnels to Portage Landing, they would be at the old pickup they always left at the railway siding.

In anticipation of the trip, Lydia was up at 5:30 am, but, with the long Alaska summer days, the sun was already well up. She made the strong coffee both she and Nels liked so well, and cooked breakfast. Their black lab "Champ" sensed the excitement and eagerly trotted around in the small kitchen as Nels and Lydia ate breakfast. It was obvious Champ knew they were going to town.

Nels looked at the dog. Champ, you like to go to town more than Lydie does and I'll be danged if I know why. Must be those grandkids you like to wrestle with. Well, just calm down, we'll be ready before long."

Lydia put a scrambled egg and some bread scraps in Champ's bowl near the door, and he eagerly wolfed it down. Then he scratched at the door, anxious to travel.

They agreed to take only one case of canned salmon to town because of the limited space in the Zodiac, but Nels had caught three fair-sized halibut the day before, fifty, seventy, and seventy-five pounds. With his fileting knife, Nels had deftly fileted the halibut to produce two long slabs from each side of each fish. The three fish produced twelve slabs of prime fresh halibut weighing about 120 pounds. Fresh halibut had become the premier seafood of Alaskans, replacing the still popular salmon, and the kids were always glad to receive a fresh supply. The Nelsons could catch more halibut for their own use when they returned from Anchorage.

Nels placed the halibut slabs in a cardboard box in the Zodiac two slabs at a time, with layers of wet cloth between. He dumped in 20 pounds of icy snow from a drift in a ravine behind the cabin to keep the fish cold and fresh. As Lydia closed up the cabin, Nels returned to get the case of salmon. Clouds had been moving in overhead and a breeze had sprung up. As usual, they dressed warmly and carried along rain gear in a plastic bag. No need to take too much, they'd be returning in two days anyway. Their orange flotation jackets were usually all they needed to wear, even if some light showers fell during the one hour trip to Whittier. They loaded in their usual fashion from the small makeshift dock: Lydia in front facing backward away from the wind and rain with a raincoat thrown over her shoulders, Champ in the middle, and Nels at the stern operating the outboard engine.

Before casting off, Nels snapped a light rope to Champ's collar so Champ wouldn't jump out and run off due to the excitement of reaching Whittier. As they cast off and got underway to the northwest, Nels began thinking of the couple who had, according to the radio broadcasts they had heard, disappeared at Slate Island only 4 miles east of Chimney Creek. Few people could last more than fifteen or twenty minutes in this cold water. Even when a person wore a life preserver or jacket, would-be rescuers usually found a cold, dead body floating in the jacket. Without insulating protection, the water would drain all the heat from the body in less than 30 minutes and death through hypothermia would come as the body core temperature dropped to a 40 degree Fahrenheit or so equilibrium temperature with the sea water.

In thinking over everything he had heard about the Slate Island incident, Nels had to agree that the most likely cause for the disappearance of the Reno couple was unwise swimming and resulting hypothermia. No bodies could be expected to be found because, as he knew so well, any fish or animal remains on the bottom are soon attacked and devoured by crabs and other bottom-dwelling organisms.

As he proceeded northwest, he kept the Zodiac within a quarter of a mile of the shoreline. This made the trip a little longer, but strong winds could come up suddenly and he still did not completely trust this new fangled air-filled boat. He reasoned that if, for some reason, it sprang a leak, he could head for shore and try to beach it before going down.

They were about fifteen minutes out from Chimney Creek when Nels noticed Champ intently looking at something behind the speeding Zodiac. He turned to look and, to his surprise, saw the dorsal fins of three killer whales 100 feet behind the boat and keeping pace with it. He slowed the engine to half speed and watched as seven more dorsal fins, followed by nine more, emerged in perfect unison. Included in the group were two large bulls, one of which had a tall, wavy dorsal fin.

"Lydie, look at the killer whales," he shouted forward to Lydia, who had been riding with the raincoat over her head. Nels reduced their speed sharply and turned the Zodiac to the right so they could have a better perspective when the whales again surfaced to blow. They had no fear. They had seen the killer whales in the sound almost every year since they first arrived in the 1940's and they were always curious about the whale's habits. They had never seen them feeding except one time when Nels and his son had been netting salmon and two sea lions came in to feed on the salmon school. Three killer whales had shown up and apparently caught, killed and ate one juvenile lion, while the other lion was able to get completely out of the water on the beach to escape. "We're ahead of time, let's watch them for awhile," Nels said, as he reached down to shut off the still-idling outboard engine.

It was silent now, except for the wind on their garments and the waves lapping against the boat. The Zodiac rocked gently in the waves. Champ stood up now with his front paws on the edge of the small air-filled boat. He whined softly, looking intently in the direction of the waves where the whales had last submerged a football field distance away.

———— ◆◆◆ ————

Tinga and the others had been resting that morning. Hunting for king salmon had been only fair, and while some of the whales had caught several fish, most of them had caught only one or two. The whales had detected the noisy whine of the outboard engine as soon as it was started, even though the sound originated 4 miles to the southeast of the whales' location. The small craft had proceeded almost into their path, and they had all submerged for six minutes as the noisemaker passed by. Then all of the whales followed Tinga as she swung to the northwest to follow the vessel. The engine and propeller noise were annoying, but they could tolerate it. Tinga again was leading them into an interesting situation and they were curious.

They had followed only a short distance, rising to blow every four minutes, when the noise suddenly was reduced and the small craft slowed and swung to the right. Then the noise stopped and the craft bobbed at the surface. Subsurface silence by the whales was unneeded and Tinga and the others scanned the scene ahead with sonar and redetermined the craft's size, shape and texture. This one, unlike the hard-shelled others they encountered frequently in the Sound, was soft and weakly reflected their sonar emissions in an unusual way.

Her curiosity aroused, Tinga decided to move in closer for a visual examination of the object and any contents. She accelerated from the group, which now slowed, and rose to the surface for a passing look only 15 feet on the right side of the Zodiac.

She saw a very dark animal on the edge of the craft, not the kind with two legs, but one with a head resembling a seal. Perhaps it was a seal, trying to hide or stay out of reach on the floating object. She had grabbed or knocked seals and sea lions from floating logs and icebergs before when they had attempted to hide there.

Without slowing her pass she submerged to 30 feet and made a circle underwater to once again approach the boat from the right. This time she made a pass so close to the surface that her dorsal fin cut the surface even though she rolled to her right to get a better view almost at the surface. On this pass she could see the animal clearly; it was not a seal, but it was an animal which was interesting and perhaps edible. She also saw two other animals in the floating object, but these were enclosed in a brightly-colored covering and were of little interest. Again she submerged as her rapid pass carried her swiftly beyond the object.

———— ◆◆◆ ————

Nels was getting apprehensive. Even though he knew of no one who had been attacked by a killer whale, he felt very vulnerable in the small boat and he wished they were in the sturdier but slower dory. Champ had become nervous and was whining and quivering as he stood looking into the water. Lydia was getting scared; these whales were acting strangely.

Underwater and unseen by the Larsons, two members of the pack stopped 50 feet from the boat to survey the action, and the other 17 began a wide circle around the site. Tinga, aggressive but cautious, swung around to pass closely by for yet another look, this time on the left side of the craft where she had seen the seal-animal. This time she blew steamy breath as she came to the surface.

The Larsons heard a loud WHUUFFF as the whale expelled air, followed instantly by vacuumed SSSSS as the whale inhaled. The spray and vapour from the exhale went 12 feet in the air and drifted in the wind over the Zodiac, reminding Nels of how large these animals really are. They could smell the fishy breath of the whale in the exhaled mist. This female, at 22 feet in length, was nearly three times as long as the Zodiac and more than ten times heavier than the vessel and all the contents. When Champ heard the whale on the opposite side of the boat he jumped over to look. He growled softly as the sleek black and white body swiftly passed by, the water boiling from the power of her flukes.

Tinga's acute vision saw the animal come to the other side to look nervously at her, much as the seals looked nervously when the killer whales passed closely by.

"Wow, did you see that?" Nels exclaimed to Lydia. "I believe that cow killer whale was actually coming up to take a look at Champ!" He patted the dog. "Champ saw it, didn't you boy?"

Lydia was frightened but excited. "I wish we had brought a camera along, no one will believe we saw a killer whale that close".

Tinga circled again, 10 feet below the surface.

Experienced fisherman that he was, Nels could make out her black and white form in the pale milky water and knew she was coming back again. Now he was getting seriously worried. His pulse rate went up and the adrenaline started flowing. For the first time in this encounter he felt their lives were in danger. He didn't know where the rest of the pack was, but he was convinced this one orca was up to no good.

For Tinga, there was no question that there was a seal-animal on the craft. It would be an easy matter to dump it into the sea where she and the others, now waiting or circling, could survey it more closely or capture it. Without altering speed, Tinga came up vertically with her snout under the left center of the Zodiac, easily lifting the entire craft from the water and spilling it's contents into the icy waters.

Nels and Lydia had no time to react. They felt a sudden jar and the Zodiac rose from the water. In an instant they were thrown to the right into the frigid water, along with Champ, the case of canned salmon and the box of halibut slabs. Lydia screamed as they went over. "That damned killer whale!" sputtered Nels. He knew they were in no danger of immediate drowning because the float coats they were wearing would keep them afloat. The Zodiac was upside down. Champ was swimming between them, trying to find a place to get out of the water. The case of salmon sank immediately and was gone, the box of halibut had been turned over in the water and the white slabs of fish left the floating box and began separating and sinking.

"Hold onto the Zodiac, Lydie!" cried Nels, "I'll try to get it turned over, but move to the left side." Now concentrating on righting the boat, Nels was now oblivious to any activity of the killer whales. He maneuvered around to the back of the Zodiac, where the engine remained attached, and began pushing up on the right side to try to bring the craft to an upright position. Two heaves produced no results. Lydia worked her way along to the front of the boat where she could get hold of the rope which went around the outside of the Zodiac.

"Let's try now", she cried, and, as they both heaved, the Zodiac hesitated and then flipped over to an upright position.

Nels hoped they could now get into the craft. They had been in the water only a couple of minutes but their leg muscle temperature was dropping quickly. As Lydia hung onto the front of the boat, Nels pulled himself in over the transom next to the motor. Then, crawling stiffly, he moved to the left side to get Lydia's hand and pulled her in. For a moment they both lay shivering in the bottom of the Zodiac, water running from their clothing. Champ, a good swimmer, was paddling alongside the boat.

Tinga, after turning the boat over, had made a circle to survey the situation with sonar. She and the other three nearby whales, Kee, Zirgo and Zinda, sent and received detailed sonar signals that three animals were in the water, one of which was a seal animal. The two others were the animals with thick, inedible surface covering and of little interest. The sonar also revealed a number of pieces of meat of a familiar texture, and Kee and Zirgo, now 50 feet below the overturned boat, moved in closer to investigate. As they came within sight and smelling distance, all senses indicated these were pieces of a familiar bottom-fish food, but without bones. They swam downward with the sinking halibut, eating each delicate morsel as they went.

Two slabs of fish they saved, however, and carried them back to feed to the two juveniles, still circling with the other five whales.

The cold water did not bother Champ. He often went into the Sound swimming because he enjoyed the water. Getting dumped into the Sound, however, had come as an unpleasant surprise, and now he wanted to get back in the Zodiac with his masters. The rope, attached to Champ's collar, was still tied to the Zodiac. Nels, having caught his breath slightly, turned to the dog as he heard Champ splashing at the side of the Zodiac and trying to get in.

Tinga had not deviated from her strict attention to the animals which had been dumped into the water after she turned the craft over. With sonar she had observed with satisfaction that Kee and Zirgo had been feeding on fish which had been spilled from the boat. Circling, she knew that the two creatures with the thick covering had gotten into the boat, but the seal-animal was still in the water. From 50 feet under the boat she turned upward to focus her sonar on the animal in the water. The legs were not the same as a seal, and it was not as fat or as heavy, but it had no thick covering or dense hair and it was edible. She lightly accelerated toward the animal on the surface, her mouth beginning to open.

Nels, still lying exhausted in the bottom of the Zodiac, reached over and got hold of the rope tied to Champ's collar to begin pulling him aboard, but just as he started to pull on the dog the rope went slack and then was jerked out of his hand as Champ, locked in the jaws of a killer whale, was lifted upward above the water's surface. The killer whale, rising straight up, took virtually the entire dog's body in its jaws. The black lab squealed as if hit by an automobile as he was lifted 10 feet in the air by the force of Tinga's rush.

Nels and Lydia gasped as the whale disappeared straight back down into the water with Champ in its jaws. The light rope tied to the Zodiac was still attached to Champ's collar, and the Zodiac jerked sharply as the end of the rope was reached as the whale descended, then it went slack. Nels, in shock, reached over and picked up the rope, hoping that, somehow, Champ would still be there. He pulled the rope in hand over hand and then saw the collar, still tied to the rope, with shreds of Champ's black hair and flesh dangling from it. A crimson stain began spreading through the water near the boat. Lydia began sobbing at the sight. Nels lay back in the boat, very worried now and wondering if the whale would again come to turn the

Zodiac over. He knew if it did, it would likely mean death for he and Lydia. They might not be able to get out of the water again.

Upon making the catch of the seal-animal, Tinga signaled to the others and began swimming to the northeast toward the three whales which had been circling the action. She was followed closely by Kee, who had eaten the dog's head as it sank. Kray, the large bull, responded that he would like to eat, and broke away from the others to move toward Tinga, who was 50 feet below the surface.

Before Kray arrived, Tinga released the headless dog's body and she and Kee examined it carefully. This animal had a different smell than either the seal or the sea lion, and a different structure. As they sensed the approach of Kray through the dim gray water they moved away. Kray, using sonar, swam directly to the dog's body and pushed it once with his rounded snout and then took it in his mouth. There was no need to bite this carcass into pieces and he swallowed it whole. The pack then began reforming 200 yards away to start off on a northward resting course for the next several hours.

For a few moments Nels and Lydia lay shivering in the silent boat, looking at Champ's collar and rope on the floor. The wind continued to blow and waves lapped at the Zodiac, rocking in the cold breeze. Suddenly two whales surfaced to blow 200 feet north of the boat. Then three more surfaced to blow, followed by five more 300 feet away. They appeared to be going north.

Nels decided the whales were gone, and he knew that he and Lydia must get to safety and warmth as soon as possible. He suspected the outboard motor would not start until the carburetor was taken apart and dried out. The fuel tank, which had been strapped to one of the seats, was still in place. The two small oars were still attached to the inside of the Zodiac, and he gratefully took them now to begin rowing back toward Chimney Creek. Fortunately, the wind was in their favor and helped move them along. Nels began to warm slightly from using the oars, but Lydia was bunched up and shivering in the front of the Zodiac.

A dreadfully long hour later they arrived at their own dock, still finding it difficult to believe what they had been through. The absence of Champ was a grim reminder of the close encounter with death. They both hurried into the cabin to get out of the wet clothes and to get a fire going.

"I'm going to try to call Cyrus in Whittier on the radio," he told Lydia. Cyrus McDuffy was the Harbor Master and a long-time acquaintance of the Larsons. As soon as he had changed, Nels got on the radio: "Whittier, Whittier, this is Nels at Chimney Creek, do you read me?"

The response crackled back dimly on the small receiver: "This is Whittier AQ 428... Nels, this is Cyrus at the Harbor, what can we do for you?"

"I want to report an attack by killer whales. They knocked our Zodiac over and damned near drowned me and Lydie. And they killed Champ and probably ate him. Over."

"... Nels, did you say an attack by killer whales? What happened?"

"Yes, you'd better notify Ted Barnes. Those damned whales might have killed us if we hadn't gotten back in the Zodiac. They might kill someone if they aren't stopped. Over."

"Nels, we have never had any such thing reported here. But we're glad to hear that you and Lydia are OK. Is there any way we can help? We'll notify the police immediately."

"I believe Lydie and I are going to be OK when we warm up. Say one more thing, call our son in Anchorage and tell him we're not coming in today. Maybe tomorrow."

"All right, Nels, we'll call them right away. Sorry about Champ. Radio again if you need more help. Radio Whittier AQ 428 clear".

"Nels clear".

Captain Ted Barnes was drinking coffee in the Coffee Cup Cafe in Whittier and reading the *Anchorage Times* when the phone rang. Mary Todd, the owner/waitress and the woman Ted was currently sleeping with, called him to the phone.

"This is Captain Barnes."

"Ted, this is Cyrus over at the Port. Nels Larson at Chimney Creek just radioed and said that killer whales attacked his Zodiac. He and Lydia are all right, but the whales killed the dog and he believes they ate him."

Barnes turned his back to Mary Stuart, the Coffee Cup owner and Kate Davis, who operated a charter boat, and the other curious people in the cafe and lowered his voice. "Killer whales? They never attack people or boats. Is he sure it was whales? Maybe they just accidentally bumped into the Zodiac. Wouldn't take that much to turn one of those over ...Where did he say this took place?"

"Didn't ask him," Cyrus answered, "but I told him I'd give you a call. Get on your radio he's standing by on channel 16."

Ted, tossing a dollar out for the coffee, told Mary "Gotta go."

Mary and Kate, ears always open for gossip, had overhead enough key words to know something interesting was going on. "Keep me posted, and see you later," Mary called to Ted as he hurried out the door.

Ted somewhat regretted having Mary overhear his conversation, but many of the fishermen no doubt picked up Nels' radio conversation with the Harbor Master anyway. Ted immediately got into his pickup and drove to the small Trooper's office. On the way he was hoping that whales had not actually been involved in an attack. Except for an occasional drunk fisherman, things had been quiet and he wanted to keep them that way.

As soon the radio warmed up he began the broadcast. "This is AQ 326 Police in Whittier calling Nels Larson at Chimney Creek. Come in, Nels." He repeated the message twice.

Finally a weak reception came in. "This is Nels. Go ahead."

"Nels, this is Ted in Whittier. Cyrus just called me and said you reported a whale attack. What happened?"

The message crackled in over the radio. "Lydia, Champ and me took off for Whittier in the Zodiac this morning about 8:30. We were about a couple of miles out when a bunch of killer whales began following us. I cut the outboard so we could watch them. One of them, a female, came by real close to look at us a couple of times, must have come within 4 feet of the boat. Then the next thing we knew we were being thrown out of the Zodiac. Do you read OK?"

"Reading OK."

"Must have thrown us 10 feet in the air, and the Zodiac was turned upside down. We had our float coats on but that water is damned cold, we almost didn't get the boat turned back over, and then we had trouble getting in. When we did get in, I started to pull Champ in and the whale came up and took him. It was a terrible sight, Ted."

"Nels, is there anything I can do? Would you like for us to call a helicopter or float plane out of Cordova to come and pick you up? Do you have any medical problems?"

Again a weak crackling response over the radio. "No, we're OK, but I would appreciate it if you would be sure Cyrus telephoned my son in Anchorage to tell him what happened. We'll try to come to Whittier and go on into Anchorage tomorrow. Tell him also that we're going to be in the dory next trip and not in that damned inflatable toy."

Ted responded. "Will do, Nels. Call us if there is anything else we can help you with. I'll report this to headquarters and they'll probably notify Fish and Game so you may be hearing from someone later today."

"OK, Ted, Chimney Creek clear."

Ted signed off: "AQ 326 clear."

When Ted Barnes telephoned district Trooper headquarters in Anchorage, he reported a "possible" killer whale attack in Prince William Sound. The Troopers advised him to play it cool until Nels came in the next day. Then more details could be gathered and a full report filed. No one had been injured, he was reminded, and there definitely was no need to call Fish and Game because no game animals, fish or protected species had been harmed, only a dog. A written report could be sent to Fish and Game when it was available.

"Who else in Whittier," the Trooper supervisor asked, "knows about this?"

Ted replied that only Cyrus at the Port of Whittier and perhaps Mary and Kate at the cafe knew for sure, but it was likely some of the fishermen would have overheard the radio message. Kate was a particular worry. She had lost a husband a couple of years back under strange circumstances. One rumor in Whittier was that he had not been performing to her requirements so she bumped him off. She became sole owner of the near-new fishing boat that was in perfect condition. Kate, better known locally as "Love Buns," delighted in getting men to go out for a cruise and trying to seduce them, often with success.

"Well, Ted, just play it down for now until we get more data. If the newspapers get hold of it, just tell them we have only a reported incident that is being investigated and that we'll give them more details when we have them available."

Ted was accustomed to handling rumors. "Yes sir, will do," he said in closing, but he knew this one would not be easy to dispel. If fishermen did hear the message they would be talking among themselves by radio already. And when Nels and Lydia came in tomorrow they would be relating first-hand what happened. He decided to wait near the harbor the next day so he would be there to corner Nels and Lydia and talk to them in privacy before the matter got totally out of hand.

The best thing to do with Mary and Kate was to tell them that it was something the Troopers were looking into and as soon as more information was available he'd let them know. If he told them nothing, they'd start making a big deal of it. Then he had another idea: his geologist friend, Mike MacKenzie, had said he intended to study killer whales in Prince William Sound and Mike would no doubt like to know about these recent events. He left a message on Mike's recorder to give him a call soon for some information on whale activity.

From the deck of her boat, the *Vamp*, Kate could hear the rumble of the train arriving from Portage, which often meant the arrival of a number of young, good looking males at least a few of whom might want to hire Kate's Vamp for a cruise. She ran a brush through her bleached blonde hair and wished she had some way to cover up the gray that was beginning to show at her temples. All the tourist traffic was good for business. The Vamp had been chartered almost every day this week and Kate had gotten lucky herself a couple of times. Like Juanita the old whore who sold hot dogs from a pushcart on the wharf always said, "A man will take a swing at anything that's thrown at him whether it is fifteen or fifty." Love Buns could pitch one hell of a game when she was prowling the Sound, all alone with some young fool who was worried about the wrong *predators*.

———— ◆◆◆ ————

CHAPTER FIVE

Rocky Bay

Vancouver Island lies like a green, humpbacked caterpillar 50 miles west of the beautiful Canadian port city of Vancouver, British Columbia. It is a large island, about 250 miles long in a northwest southeast direction and 50 miles wide. It is the southwestern-most projection of Canada into the Pacific Ocean about 1,000 miles southeast of Prince William Sound, Alaska. Killer whales have been common in the waters near Vancouver Island for all of the area's recorded history, and for millions of years before that. The whales are particularly abundant near the mouths of certain rivers during the summer months when the schooling salmon are preparing to begin their ascent of the rivers to spawn.

Dr. Dan Short, resident psychologist at the Central Province Hospital in Calgary, Alberta, south-central Canada, had been invited to British Columbia to spearhead efforts aimed at determining why there was such a high rate of alcoholism among the West Coast natives, and to try to find a means of alleviating the problem. He was ready for a change, and the opportunity had seemed so attractive that he did not even deem it necessary to travel to the village of Rocky Bay to check out the situation. Instead, he accepted immediately with the enthusiastic support of his wife, Claudia, who, as a practicing nurse, was also offered a position at the tiny Rocky Bay medical facility.

Many of the staff members at the Central Hospital, and many in the Calgary community as well, believed Dr. Short's departure was good riddance. His recent psychological studies and teaching seemed to stray more and more frequently into the world of parapsychology, hypnotism and, during the past summer, attempts to communicate with occupants of UFOs after a farmer in the area had reported strange markings in his wheat field suggestive of flying saucers. Dr. Short was always ready to strike off in some unorthodox direction, regardless of how irrational it seemed to his professional associates. But he adamantly defended his excursions, saying that someone had to break some new ground and he enjoyed accusing "conservatives" in the profession of simply being in a rut.

Dan and Claudia had met fifteen years earlier when he was about to receive the PhD he held in psychology. She had already been practicing for two years as a licensed nurse. Now Dan was 40 years old, still muscular and trim due to his workouts, and an imposing 6.3" tall. The gray hair beginning to show at the temples added to his imposing stature. Claudia, trim at 105 pounds when they met and were married, had taken up smoking and allowed her weight to climb to what she called a "fluffy" 145 pounds. Neither of them had any idealistic illusions left, about their professions or about each other.

Over lunch they had discussed the move to Rocky Bay. "Christ, Claudia," Dan began as she followed lunch with her third cigarette in fifteen minutes. "You're a nurse, you ought to know those things are taking years off your life."

Claudia watched the cigarette smoke curl away from her fingers and through the screen of the open window above the table. "That's right, Danny, I am a nurse and I know that life is taking years off my life."

"That's not funny."

"You know what is funny, Danny? A man your age who still thinks he's a young jock. That's funny Danny."

"Nothing wrong with keeping yourself in shape. If you're referring to my physical fitness program..."

Claudia laughed. "I'm referring to your middle aged madness."

"Physical fitness programs," he continued, "could drop some of that extra weight you're carrying around, not to mention starting a cleanup of your lungs."

"You think all this running and pumping iron is good. Well, maybe Danny. But as far as I'm concerned it's just prolonging the inevitable." She took another sip of coffee. "Age is something we all have to face, even in this youth-obsessed culture. I have no desire to outlive my family or friends..."

"But do you want to die first?" Dan interrupted.

"... or to end up at the age of 99 in a wheel chair with a heart and lungs that won't die."

As they left the cafeteria Dan shook his head. Their marriage was not what it once was. Where was it going? Would Rocky Bay make any difference? Hell, maybe he should just leave her in Calgary, but they had already accepted the positions.

The village of Rocky Bay, with its 1100 inhabitants, half of whom were natives, clung grimly to a northeast bulge on the caterpillar of Vancouver Island. There were no roads in or out of Rocky Bay, all travel was by float plane, weather permitting, or by private boat. The sea never froze but it never got warm. The chief claim to fame for the village was that it was the geographic location where the nomenclature of Discovery Passage to the southeast changed to Johnstone Passage to the northwest. Not even the provincial ferry system stopped at Rocky Bay, and yet there was a strange quality to the location which must have been observed by native hunters centuries ago. In the 1940's, to commemorate the village and pay homage to spirits, the natives had erected three climate-battered totem poles which now stood forlornly near the fast moving stream which cut through the town. Ironically, the stream now separated an area set aside for native tract housing, built mostly by the government, from the area where most of the non-native residents lived. A foot bridge had been erected over the stream and an occasional drunk, both white and native, would fall off in high water and disappear, swept into the salt water downstream where crabs would make short work of their alcohol laced bodies.

The "white man's community" clustered around the elongate dock. Prominent buildings included a hardware store, a two story apartment building, a three level Victorian home converted into Rocky Bay's only hotel, and a general store adjoining a restaurant and bar. Two saloons, a clinic and two small churches rounded out the main public buildings.

Although lumbering had once been an important industry at Rocky Bay, another 20 years would have to pass before replanting efforts began to pay off with additional harvests. Other than a few sport and commercial fishermen in the summer months, the village was seldom visited. Unemployment was high and alcoholism was rampant.

Before arriving at Rocky Bay, Dan had reached the tentative conclusion that curtailing the alcohol problem might be a simple matter of focusing the natives' attention on something in which their ancestors had an interest. He imagined returning them to crafts such as wood carving and the manufacture of leather and bone curios to consign to outlets in Vancouver for sale to tourists. Perhaps there was some way to resurrect the now lost Kwakiutl art of carving totem poles. He had read that museums long ago had taken the best poles, and only a few shoddy remnants remained.

Claudia had her own theories about alcohol curtailment, and was a staunch opponent of governmental agencies sending money to the natives unless it was earned. Over and over she had seen native Canadians cash government checks followed by mindless drunkenness for days until the money ran out. She was advised by phone that Rocky Bay tavern owners made certain their places of business were the easiest locations for natives to cash checks, and some even offered a free drink as an incentive to anyone cashing a check at their establishment. After the first drink many natives were hooked and would spend blindly at the bar until the money was spent or someone took it from them.

Dan wondered if there were any local problems with cruelty to animals at Rocky Bay. Many native tribes were known to eat dogs before they became more "civilized", but, he reasoned, from a dog's standpoint, being killed quickly and eaten was better than starving to death at the end of a chain. He had been a prominent figure in the Calgary Humane Society, and had personally investigated a number of cases involving animal mistreatment. Dan considered himself a sort of champion of good treatment for animals. He verged on opposing even zoos and animal parks because they kept animals in enclosures. On more than one occasion he had remarked that, with the development of movies and television, it was no longer necessary for people to go to a zoo to see animals when they could see them even better on a screen in their filmed natural habitat. In coordination with one of the animal rights attorneys in Calgary, he had successfully sued the owner of two dogs for cruelty to animals, making him a sort of hero for those in central Canada who believed themselves to be the proponents of "proper" animal treatment.

But Dan and Claudia looked forward mostly to being near the ocean in moving to Rocky Bay. They liked the water, and it had been difficult spending six years in landlocked Calgary. The coast of British Columbia would provide, they hoped, opportunities for boating and fishing that they never had in Alberta.

After their arrival at Rocky Bay by float plane, Dan and Claudia settled into their small one bedroom bungalow. Almost immediately they set about assessing the depth of the alcoholism problem; it was much worse than they had expected. It soon became obvious that the monthly compensation sent to the natives by Ottawa and by the provincial government had effectively removed almost all incentive for the natives to develop any of their skills or to work for a living. Their entire, unique culture was in danger of being lost.

Dan decided upon a course of working first with those natives exhibiting some measure of hope for rehabilitation, particularly those in their 20's; rehabilitating the old timers would be difficult, if not impossible, and would take considerable time to accomplish. His first attempts to meet the local shaman, witch doctor or whatever the natives here called their native priest, were met with rebuffs.

Claudia was shocked mostly by the extreme loss of dignity of this once-proud people as they were brought in to the clinic drunk, sick, dirty and smelling of urine and vomit. "Drying out" these sad cases would obviously be one of her major tasks and she did not relish it. Hopefully Dan would come up with a solution to prevent the alcohol problem and she encouraged him in his work.

Within a month of the Short's arrival in May, Sid Lockridge, the rugged, 6.4" bachelor owner of the Rocky Bay hardware store, invited the Shorts to go on a fishing trip in his 24 foot boat the 'Princess' to try their hand at catching some of the chinook (king) salmon which were now schooling offshore of the Johnson River. They jumped at the chance. It would be their first opportunity to get out of the Rocky Bay village since their arrival, and they were anxious to learn more about life in the area. In addition, Sid had told them that there was a possibility of seeing killer whales near the river mouth.

Both Dan and Claudia were familiar with killer whales in captivity, because Dr. Short had participated for four weeks in an attempt at the Vancouver, B. C. aquarium where two killer whales were kept in a large tank. His initial objective had been to gather data concerning killer whale communications. The experience left him fascinated not only with the communications possibilities, but also with the intelligence and friendliness of a creature which had such a reputation as a dangerous carnivore. He had requested funding for additional studies, but budget cuts had eliminated any immediate possibility of more work. In addition, he suspected his request was denied in part because there were those who believed a psychologist with no marine biological training was not well suited to conduct the studies, no matter how much empathy he expressed for the animals.

As he maneuvered the Princess away from the small Rocky Bay harbor, Sid remarked that luck was with them so far because it had stopped raining and blue sky could be seen here and there between gray and white puffs of clouds, although the tops of mountains both to the east and west were obscured in heavy gray clouds.

As soon as they were out of the harbor area and well under way, Dan could restrain himself no longer. "What is known about killer whales in this area?" he asked, speaking above the noise of the inboard engine.

Sid prided himself on knowing quite a bit about the fisheries and marine life in the Queen Charlotte Strait region, having once been a commercial salmon fisherman himself. "Studies in the past few years have suggested that killer whale groups in this area can be divided into two general types: those which are more or less stable residents of the area, and those which can perhaps best be described as transient. Many more studies will have to be done, but at least that is the current thinking. There is a possibility today that we may see one of the vessels the government has assigned to gather killer whale data; the mouth of the Johnson River has been designated one of the primary study areas because a large amount of timber cutting has been proposed in the Johnson River drainage. Initially the concern centered around the impact upon the salmon, but now the whales are also being studied to determine what, if any, impact the logging would have on the whales."

"How will we recognize the study boats?" asked Short, ready to seize any new opportunity to learn more about studies of killer whales.

"There are only two of them at the most" said Sid, "and we can call them on the CB. They're usually anxious to talk because they like to get information on where anyone has seen killer whales. Here, take these binoculars and scan for the whales. We could come across some anytime now." Little more was said for the next 30 minutes as they motored north along the eastern side of Queen Charlotte Strait toward the Johnson River. Dan was busy scanning with the binoculars.

Above the roar of the inboard engine and the sound of spraying salt water, Short tried another question: "How do we go about spotting the whales? Aren't they difficult to see in the open ocean, especially in rough water?"

Sid laughed. "The water is really not very rough today. But if we are more than half a mile from the whales, you're not very likely to see them.

When resting, they will surface to blow about three times every six or seven minutes. Your best bet is to use the binoculars; watch for the black dorsal fins and plumes of mist in the air from their blows."

Dan could hardly resist asking more questions about the killer whales, but he decided to wait the hour it would take to get to the Johnson River because of the difficulty in conversing above the engine and wave noise. Standing up to compensate for the roll of the boat, he continued scanning the horizon with the binoculars. He saw sea birds, flotsam and an occasional seal or sea lion, but no killer whales. Claudia remained seated and showed little interest in anything except Sid. The more she watched his body and movements the more interested she became.

Rain squalls occasionally swept across the strait, and the 3 foot swells made for a bumpy trip. Commercial fishing boats were here and there but they were not fishing because there was no current "opening" for salmon. The seasons for commercial salmon fishing were closely regulated by the provincial government, and "openings", as in Alaska, sometimes were for only twelve to forty-eight hours duration as the biologists responsible attempted to reach a proper balance between salmon escapements up the various rivers and the harvest by commercial fishermen. Impact upon the salmon in salt water by sport fishermen, and by killer whales and other mammals, was considered negligible.

As they approached an area where many more boats were present, Sid reduced the boat's speed and asked for the binoculars. He scanned the area ahead closely, and pointed to the northeast where a prominent notch could be seen in the mountains along the east shore of the strait. "Over there, although you cannot see it from here, is the mouth of the Johnson River. From here for the next 3 miles is heavily fished for salmon by the commercial fishermen. It also is a good place to see killer whales because they come here to eat the salmon. On top of those two predators here we are fishing for the salmon. Seems like the fish are picked on by everyone." Sid smiled. "But catches have been good, thanks to the Fish and Game staff."

Sid slowed the Princess to an idle. "Let's go ahead and troll from here on for the next mile or two. Never can tell when you might cross a school of salmon." He handed one rod to Dan Short and another to Claudia. "I'll get you two started and then I'll rig up my own outfit," Sid remarked as he reached into the bucket containing partially thawed 8-inch herring. "Here, this is the way to hook them on."

He passed the point of the hook through the herring just behind the gills and then again 2/3 of the way back on the body. Claudia made a face at the sight of handling the frozen but slimy fish. Sid smiled at her.

"That should do it," he said as he handed the rod to Claudia. "Now, here's the way you let out line and set the drag. Don't let out more than about 20 yards of line and the way to tell that is by counting the rotations of the spool." In showing her how to hold the rod and let the line out from the reel he put his arms around her from behind. Claudia smiled at this attention. Sid pierced another herring for the second rod and hung the bait over the side of the boat so Dan could also let out line to begin trolling.

Sid stepped up and took the wheel of the slowly moving vessel again. He scanned the scene ahead as he instructed them. "Let out about 20 yards of line. No use getting too much out; those jet planers will take the herring down 30 or so feet below the surface."

He then picked up another rod, hooked on a herring and dropped it overboard, letting line off the reel at the same time. After letting out about 20 yards of line and setting the clicker, he placed the rod in a holder and returned to the wheel again. The wind was dying down, and it appeared that a pleasant day was ahead, whether or not they caught any salmon. Without being obvious he admired Claudia's plump but well-proportioned body.

Dan took the opportunity to ask more questions. "Have there ever been any reports of killer whale attacks on people?"

Sid smiled, as if he had expected the question. "There is one instance that has been told here in British Columbia. A number of years ago, so the story goes, there were two British Columbia loggers cutting timber on a hillside above an inlet. They were skidding the logs down the slope into the water where the logs later were gathered together and towed off to the mill. A group of killer whales was observed approaching, and one of the loggers timed the release of a log so that it slid down and hit one of the whales in the side, injuring it but not killing it."

Sid noted with satisfaction the intent interest shown by both Short and Claudia. He continued the story: "The whales went away, but that evening, as these two loggers were rowing back to camp, they saw the whales returning and closing fast on the boat. They tried to row to shore, but one of the whales came up under the boat and flipped it over. The logger who had earlier injured the whale disappeared, but the other man survived and lived to tell the tale."

"My God, is that true?" asked Short. For a minute the idling of the engine was the only sound to be heard.

Sid looked at him, "So far as we know, it is. There are people in Rocky Bay who claim to have spoken with the survivor. He will no longer go on the water in a small boat; claims they might get him next."

Sid scanned the horizon again and suddenly picked up the binoculars. He looked closely at a boat almost dead ahead. "That boat 500 yards ahead appears to be one of the

Government killer whale study boats. Let me see if I can raise them on the CB." He picked up the handset.

"This is the Princess out of Rocky Bay calling the Bruin Bay, can you read me?" Thirty seconds passed and then the reply came: "This is the Bruin Bay, go ahead Princess."

"Say, we're here for some salmon fishing today, but I've got a couple of people on board who are very interested in killer whales, are you fellows still involved in that study?"

"Affirmative, the current project will last most of the summer. We have been following one pod of eight whales in this general area for about 3 days. We lost them last night, but we are expecting them to show up here at any time now because the salmon schools are here."

Sid responded, "Well, good enough. We'd appreciate a call on the CB if you see them."

"We'll be glad to do that, but remember that under the law, you will not be allowed to approach the whales."

Sid laughed, "No problem. From what I've seen of the whales, they are usually the ones who do the approaching unless some nut has been shooting at them. Are there any other study boats in the area?"

"No other *official* boats, but there is one boat with people on board who are trying to establish communications with the whales. They're in a blue, modified fishing boat with the name *Lingo*. Don't know what success they're having, but we have heard some of the noise they make."

"We'll watch for them; call us if you see any whales," he concluded. "Princess clear." Sid, pleased that he might be able to show his guests some killer whales *and* catch some salmon, smiled; he had brought them to the right place. He waved to the crew of the drifting Bruin Bay as the Princess idled slowly by trailing three lines and maintaining a northerly course.

Dan, anxious to see wild killer whales, scanned the horizon frequently with the binoculars, but none were seen. He turned to Sid, "Do you believe the story about the whales and the logger?"

Sid responded, "The whales are highly intelligent, but it really is doubtful that they would return to seek vengeance on someone who had injured one of their group. It's also unlikely, if they did come back, that they would know which person it was who released the log. Still, maybe they're smarter than we have given them credit for."

"They are indeed intelligent animals," said Dan. "I did research on Namu and another whale in Vancouver for 4 weeks last year. With more time I believe communications could have been established with them."

Claudia suddenly let out a squeal as the rod she was holding jumped up and down with line screaming off the reel. Sid stepped over beside her. "You've got a king on and a good one. Keep your rod tip up and, when you can, reel in some line but don't try to bring it in too quickly. Dan, let's reel our lines in so they won't get tangled."

As they looked beyond the stern, a bright silver fish, 3 feet long, leaped several feet into the air shaking its body in an attempt to dislodge the hook. It then dove as Claudia laughed and struggled with the rod and reel. With the Princess now idling and out of gear, Sid helped her keep the rod tip up and offered advice on handling the fish. Ten minutes later the fish was brought aboard in the large landing net. It was a beautiful king salmon weighing, Sid estimated, nearly 40 pounds.

"Lovely fish," he smiled at the exhausted but happy Claudia. "Good job. It wouldn't take many fish like this to make a killer whale full and happy." He dropped the live fish into a water-filled hold beneath one of the seats in the stern. The hold was constructed cleverly with two holes in the bottom allowing fresh sea water to circulate through it, thus facilitating keeping any catch alive and fresh.

Midday was approaching and Claudia opened the basket of food she had prepared. Smoked sliced turkey, whole wheat bread, mustard and mayonnaise, tomatoes, lettuce, radishes, celery and a large insulated bottle of hot coffee. Not to forget the dessert, she had made a large carrot cake with plenty of frosting. They each made their own sandwiches while the fishing continued with the rods in rod holders. The boat idled slowly along, rolling gently on the waves.

Sid picked up the binoculars again. "There's a blue boat over there to the west similar to the one the Bruin Bay crew mentioned. Now if I can make out the name. It starts with an 'L', let's see... L i n g ...it must be the Lingo, and there, 300 yards on the other side of them I see a dorsal fin. That's a killer whale! They're going west following some killer whales!"

Short became excited. "Fantastic! Can we go over to see the whales?"

Sid smiled "Why not? Reel in the lines!"

They reeled in enthusiastically and Sid revved up the Princess to 1,500 rpm and steered toward the blue Lingo and the whales. "What about the Bruin Bay?" asked Short.

"They're about 3 miles back," Sid replied. "and, if we want to get close to the whales today, we'd better not call them. If they see you approaching or following the whales they will either chase you off or arrest you."

As the Princess approached the idle Lingo, Sid cut the power and strange sounds could be heard above the decreasing noise of the engine. Sid throttled the engine back further and then turned it off so the entire spectacle could be seen and heard.

It was obvious that the whales were involved in some type of chase and catch activity. Rather than moving as a group, they were churning about rapidly either in individual activities or in twos and threes. Some quick turns could be observed when the whales were at the surface. They seemed to be blowing excitedly and frequently.

"Looks as if the whales have found some salmon, and they're feeding," Sid remarked as he looked through the binoculars at the black dorsal fins and the backs of the whales at the surface here and there. "And look, there's a jumper!" Sid pointed to a spot 50 feet from the Princess where a 15 pound chinook salmon made two leaps from the water.

"Why do the salmon jump?" Claudia asked.

"No one really knows," Sid responded. "In this situation it may be because of the whales, but salmon getting ready to spawn and spawning do quite a bit of jumping. Some people say the females jump to loosen the eggs, but I don't believe it. Both males and females jump."

A female killer whale must have detected the nearby jumping chinook salmon on sonar because she rose to the surface to blow at the last location where the salmon had jumped and turned quickly as if in pursuit. Two minutes later the female whale's scythe-shaped black dorsal fin appeared again 100 feet away, but now she was swimming much slower. It was a safe assumption that a subsurface salmon catch had been made.

Sid, Dan and Claudia were thrilled to be in the midst of feeding whales.

There was an overcast, but the wind had died to a whisper and the sea was calm; almost ideal conditions for observation. The whales appeared to pay no attention to either the Princess or the Lingo. Their erratic and seemingly excited blows over an area of perhaps one quarter square mile could be distinctly heard.

But now the volume of music emanating from the Lingo began to increase. Two large speakers could be seen on the stern of the Lingo, and there were floats in the water on both sides of the craft. Five people were on deck watching the whales with binoculars and excitedly laughing and talking. One of the men on board the Lingo now waved to the Princess. It was obvious they either had concluded the Princess was not one of the research boats, or else they did not care and were not worried about arrest for being near the whales.

The London Symphony Orchestra, playing Beethoven's Fifth Symphony, came booming out from the speakers. Then the operator apparently realized the volume may be too high and turned it down. Dan was pleased with the selection, he was very fond of the Fifth and especially liked the London Symphony version.

The Princess had now drifted to within 200 feet of the Lingo, and five persons could be seen on board: two males with long hair and beards, apparently in their late twenty's or early thirty's, and three women of about the same age. One of the women had a very dark complexion and was the only one attired in a dress. The others wore blue jeans.

After Beethoven's Fifth had ended there was silence. The whales, still scattered, could clearly be heard blowing. At locations where they were at or near the surface "footprints," areas in the water that appeared to be boiling made by the action of their tail flukes.

Dan was enthralled. Looking at the equipment both on board and attached to floats near the Lingo, he guessed that one of the floats supported a hydrophone for listening to or recording whale sounds, and the other larger float probably supported an underwater speaker. What a great research project and what fascinating people. He wondered if he might be able to participate.

A new tape now commenced with a solid bass, rock and roll beat followed by an attractive, almost falsetto voice. It was Michael Jackson and his brothers coming on with "Billie Jean." Dan wondered about this selection for an experiment with the whales, but "Who am I," he thought, "to question these people with field experience?"

The whales continued their activity, which clearly seemed to be chasing salmon and feeding, and, so far as Dan could tell, paid no attention to the music from the Lingo. When the "Billie Jean" number had ended, all was silent again except for the irregular sounds of the whales blowing and a background of screeching and bickering gulls making circles over the area where the whales were feeding, hoping for a morsel of salmon. No words whatsoever had been exchanged between the persons on the Princess and those on the Lingo. It seemed as if they were in the whale's space, and it was to be revered as one on shore might revere and remain silent in an ancient cathedral.

"How wonderful," thought Dan. "We're in the holy domain of the killer whale. The early native hunters must have felt the same way. No wonder they came to worship the orcas."

Whistles, clicks, creaking door sounds and crow calls then pierced the relative silence. Someone aboard the Lingo had decided to play assorted recordings of killer whale sounds and they were apparently playing them both through the underwater speaker and through the array of speakers on the stern.

Dan recognized the sounds from his work with killer whales in Vancouver. "They're trying some recorded killer whale sounds," he whispered to Sid and Claudia.

"This is amazing," Claudia observed. The broadcast killer whale sounds were suddenly faded out by someone on the Lingo.

As they watched, a strange thing happened. Three of the whales, two females and a juvenile, surfaced together to blow and then swam just below the surface toward the Lingo. As they approached the boat, it appeared they intended to check out the source of the broadcast killer whale sounds because they seemed to be swimming toward the underwater speaker. Fifty feet from the speaker they submerged. Everyone, both on the Lingo and on the Princess, breathlessly watched. Two of the whales, one female and the juvenile, glided past the speaker on the side away from the Lingo and continued on out of sight. The other female had obviously slowed, and passed only a few feet below the speaker, swimming on her side as if to have a close examination of this object. After passing, a few slow strokes of her flukes carried her swiftly out of sight in the direction of the other two whales.

The five on the Lingo began clapping and cheering. Obviously they considered the approach and study of their underwater speaker by the whales to be a significant contact. Dan himself thought it was one of the most exciting things he had ever witnessed. There was now total silence as everyone watched to see what the whales might do next. Three minutes passed.

The whales, fourteen of them, rose in unison to blow 500 yards to the west and then sounded as they continued swimming westward. One minute passed, then two, then five. With the binoculars, Sid finally spotted the group as they surfaced to blow a quarter of a mile to the west and going away. Sid spoke first. "Feeding time is over. There they are way out to the west."

Dan could restrain himself no longer. "That was one of the most fantastic things I have ever seen. Imagine initiating communication with highly intelligent and friendly animals that are the top predator in the oceans! Absolutely fantastic! If the Lingo was recording the whale sounds they may even find that the female was attempting to initiate communication with the sound source!"

Sid thought the use of "initiating communication" was going too far. As he saw it, the whales simply came to investigate the sounds and that was nothing new. Killer whales had been recognized as curious animals throughout recorded history. "Sid, could you start up and pull over to the Lingo? I've just got to talk to them."

Sid looked at his watch. They weren't going to catch any salmon this way, but then the killer whales might not have left had the salmon been abundant at this location anyway. He nodded to Dan and went to the controls of the Princess to start the engine. This could be interesting.

Sid started the engine of the Princess and began idling over to the drifting Lingo. "Ahoy there, may we come along side?" Sid called to the Lingo when they were 20 boat lengths away. One of the bearded males, who had been busy with a tape recorder on the rear deck of the Lingo looked up. "Of course, and please come aboard."

Sid eased up, and ropes were tied between the two vessels with tough, flexible bumpers between. They noticed that boxes of electronic gear and wires cluttered the deck of the Lingo.

Dan, Claudia and Sid crossed over to the pale blue vessel and introductions were made. The `crew' on the Lingo consisted of a silent and stern looking man known only as "Jammer," who seemed to be in charge, and the man who invited them aboard, Craig Martin. The three young women were Susan Marks, Paula Chang and Rolanda Jefferson. Quite an ethnic variety, Dan thought. Jammer looked as if he was part native, Paula was definitely Chinese, Rolanda was black and Craig and Susan were probably of northern European ancestry.

Dan could hardly contain his enthusiasm. "We were watching the whales and heard the broadcasts to them! They seemed to be responding!"

Rolanda hurried to the tape recording unit and said enthusiastically "Hey, just listen to this, man! We got some great sound from the whales in the last 20 minutes." She started the tape near the end of "Billie Jean," immediately followed by the short segment of whale sounds they had transmitted into the water.

Everyone on the Lingo was silent as the just-recorded true whale sounds started. First a long, escalating click train was heard, followed by sharp pops.

"Sonar focusing on our hydrophone and speaker," Rolanda whispered.

A chorus of whistles, rusty hinge sounds and crow-like calls were next heard, along with more click trains, some obviously in the distance and some very close to the hydrophone. Then relative silence.

"This is when the three whales approached the equipment for a visual inspection," Rolanda whispered as they listened breathlessly.

A long minute went by with hardly any sound from the speakers other than the recorded slight slapping of gentle waves against the float for the hydrophone. Craig whispered that the human ear was deficient and that the whales were hearing much more than the human ears could hear.

Then, not far from the hydrophone, a loud, crisp whale call had been recorded: Kreeeeeeeaaaaaaaaa, with the tone initially sharp and then descending and fading. More silence.

"The queen of the group is calling them to leave," Jammer said softly, his eyes closed and head back as if in ESP contact with the animals.

About 30 seconds later, from the same whale, the identical call again, but this time further in the distance. More silence. Then the same call, barely discernible in the distance followed by more silence.

"She has commanded they depart," Jammer observed, eyes still closed, "and they have gone."

Rolanda stopped the tape and nodded agreement with Jammer. "That's it. They were gone."

Dan, Claudia and Sid spontaneously began to applaud and cheer, joined by the others except Jammer, who sat in silence staring at the water slowly nodding his head up and down.

"What a stunning recording!" Dan exclaimed. "That gives me renewed confidence that communications with the whales is possible! It's wonderful!"

Jammer looked up, scowling. "What do you mean, `renewed?' You probably don't know a damned thing about orcas!" He rose threateningly to his feet.

"Hey, hey, let's calm down here," Sid commanded, looking directly at Jammer. "No need to get riled up. Tell you what, I've got some beer aboard the Princess. What do you say we have one and get acquainted?

"Sounds good to me," Susan cast a hard look at Jammer, "Maybe some of us will learn some manners and how to welcome guests aboard."

"Great idea," Craig said, "we've been out here too long without any beer. By the time we buy the equipment and food for the field work there isn't anything left for beer."

Sid was already crossing back to the Princess. He lifted a full case of Canadian Grizzly lager from a jumbo cooler and handed it across to Dan Short, who was still pondering the surprise of Jammer's hostility.

Beers were opened and passed around. With relaxation about to begin, Craig and Paula hurried to bring in the hydrophone and underwater speaker and stow the gear. Claudia asked Susan where they all were from. "We're all from the Vancouver area, except for Rolanda, and she's from Bellingham, Washington north of Seattle. What about you?"

"Dan and I just moved to Rocky Bay from Calgary. Sid operates the hardware store in Rocky Bay."

Jammer had taken out a joint of marijuana, lit it, took a couple of deep drags and passed it to Susan. She sucked on it eagerly and then offered it to Dan Short, who was sitting next to her. Jammer watched Short closely.

Unhesitatingly, Dan took the smoldering joint and puffed deeply. He was no novice to pot and had used it on many occasions in Calgary to reach beyond his condescending view of the normal Homo sapiens mental capability. He had even brought some to Rocky Bay, which he and Claudia smoked most nights in the privacy of their bungalow. Their pot source was in Vancouver and, when he tasted the potency of Jammer's joint, wondered if they had the same source for the strong "Maui gold."

As the one joint was passed around, Jammer got out another and lit it. One just was not enough for this crowd. Even Sid, who had never tried pot, took a couple of drags.

After 20 minutes of beer, marijuana and casual conversation, the tension had faded. The conversation turned to the whales. The case of beer was emptying. "How long have you been carrying out these attempts at communication with killer whales?" Dan asked Susan, still wondering about Jammer's hostility.

Susan explained that just this season had they been able to raise enough money to start the field program of attempting communications. For the previous two years it had just been all talk and theory with no action. They all considered the Lingo a poor excuse for a boat, but it was the best they could purchase with the meager funds raised through the efforts of OCS, the Orca Communication Society, headquartered in Vancouver. All on board were members of the society and were serving as unpaid volunteers.

The organization was new, she explained, and had enjoyed little success with raising money. However, they hoped that with some good video tapes and photographs, sound recordings and stories from this first field excursion they might be able to obtain more financial support to expand communication efforts. If the environmentalist and 'save the whales' group "Blue War" could raise $20 million a year, they should be able to raise $20 thousand.

"And it wouldn't hurt," Paula looked at Jammer, "if some of us weren't buying drugs, either."

Jammer ignored the comment. Dan returned the conversation to the whales as he took another quaff from his beer bottle. "Well, you got some good recordings of the whales we were just watching. Did you also take photos?"

Rolanda, her dark skin looking gorgeous in the reflected light from the sea and observed closely by Dr. Short, pointed to a primitive looking camcorder on top of two boxes. "That's the best we can do right now. The quality isn't what it could be or should be."

Dan had much better equipment in Rocky Bay, but he did not mention it yet. Instead, he had another question about the whales. "Are you able to predict the type of reaction you'll get from the whales when you play a certain type of music or recorded whale sounds?"

Paula Chang, her dark eyes flashing against her olive skin and obviously excited by the interaction, answered. "We never know what their reaction will be. This afternoon was great, but one of the best reactions we've had was to some rock and roll yesterday. Three of the whales, could have been the same three as we saw today, swam around the boat for several minutes as they tuned in to the Beach Boys and Jerry Lee Lewis."

Jammer grunted and shook his head as if to disagree but said nothing. Craig, ignoring Jammer and sharing Paula's excitement, added "I thought they might start singing a trio into the hydrophone, it was that great!"

They all laughed. Sid brought another case of beer from the Princess as conversations continued.

After listening to the efforts and results, Claudia got their attention. "You know what you kids need? You need some professional help. Dan Short here, *Doctor* Dan Short, may just fill the bill." She proudly revealed to them that he was a practicing psychologist licensed and funded by both the Canadian government and the Province of British Columbia.

With attention riveted on him, Dan substantiated the revelation and added that he had experience with killer whales at the aquarium in Vancouver where he, too, had come to believe that communications with whales and dolphins was entirely possible. Feeling heady from the alcohol and marijuana, he further advised them that, in his professional opinion, there was no reason why the studies and communications could not be extended to other animals and even to UFO's.

Jammer just nodded slightly, but the revelation was to the rest of the Lingo crew what a sparkling gold discovery would be to prospectors working their claim in rugged mountains. They had searched long and hard in the Vancouver area for even sparse support and thus far had struck out completely with efforts to obtain serious Canadian professional consideration. Most scientists simply considered them kooks.

Rolanda looked Dan Short directly in the eye. "You can't imagine how difficult it is to find supporters for our cause, and the professionals are worse than the general populace."

Dan returned her look, "We can probably do something about that." He experienced a feeling of extraordinary warmth toward the beautiful black woman.

The pot and alcohol consumption continued with more ideas passed back and forth. Jammer had remained silent, but now he spoke. "The queen sent them. It is a good omen." For the first time Dan, Claudia and Sid saw him smile faintly.

"What queen? Sent who?" Paula asked.

"The queen of the whales sent these three to find us," Jammer observed matter-of-factly. "This was not luck or happenstance. The queen knew we needed help and sent them."

Susan knew better than the others that Jammer seemed extremely psychic at times. "He means," she interpreted, "that the leading female whale has somehow intervened or provided guidance to bring your group here to us. Think about it," her blue eyes flashed at Dan, "why did you come out here today?"

"Why, it was my idea," Sid stated.

"Yes, but why here and why today?" Susan persisted, now eager to defend and promote Jammer, her occasional lover.

"Well, it was just an idea for an outing," Sid shrugged.

"But didn't you think about killer whales and that you might see some out here today?" she continued.

"We were *hoping* we might see some…"

"But, don't you see? Jammer is saying there was a force acting to bring you here to us today. It is a good omen." Susan looked directly at Dr. Dan Short. "You have been brought to us by the whales because *together* we can raise money for whale communication!"

"He may be right!" Dan exclaimed. "Perhaps we were guided here!" This idea was so gripping that they could talk of nothing else for the next half hour. Perhaps the whales had exerted a form of ESP or other unknown power to somehow bring them together. It must be a form of encouragement from the whales, they concluded, to intensify their efforts. Perhaps the whales recognized that the Lingo group was getting on the right track to interspecies communication.

Flush with the excitement, Dan related to them what he was certain would be good news. He believed that he had sufficient contacts in Vancouver, even among sceptics such as marine biologists connected with the Aquarium, that he could raise money for their research efforts. "We don't have to call it `communications efforts,'" he advised, his speech becoming somewhat slurred. "We'll tell them its research into Orcinus orca populations and behavior and they'll probably give us government grants, maybe even a new boat!"

Craig, Susan, Paula, Rolanda and even Claudia cheered and raised their bottles of beer as a toast, while Jammer remained sullen.

"Listen, our timing might be good," Paula exclaimed, "We're about out of supplies and were planning to go back to Vancouver in the next couple of days anyway. Maybe we can leave later today! What do you say, Jammer?"

The bearded Jammer glanced from one member of the party to the next with a flat gaze, followed by a shrug of his shoulders which meant approval to those who knew him. Then he added, "About time we picked up more pot anyway."

More ideas were exchanged about how to raise money, with most of the conversation oriented toward getting Canadian government help. Susan thought perhaps some of the natives living along the coast could be recruited, to which Claudia replied that she and Dan were certainly getting acquainted with those at Rocky Bay. Dan mentioned that someone, meaning himself, might have to take their plea all the way to Ottawa. After all, there was no reason why the government shouldn't support their work. He could, and would, write a grant request which the stingiest bureaucrat would find difficult to decline once the environmental community got behind them.

Of the eight persons present, Sid alone was able to maintain a measure of objectivity. He simply smiled as one seemingly weird conclusion after another was reached by the celebrating group. After the first round of pot he had declined further smoking, but he made it a point to stay near Claudia.

"Maybe we can help other ways, right, Sid," Dan continued. "When hardware supplies are needed in this area I'll bet you'd be willing to give a nice discount to help them out, hey?"

Sid nodded affirmatively, but with little enthusiasm. It was tough enough making a go of it in Rocky Bay without offering discounts to various groups which happened to be in the area. The crew, except Jammer, expressed appreciation for the offer. As more cold, dark beer was taken from the second case and opened, Sid looked at his watch. "This has been fun," he looked at Dan, "but the Princess should be departing for Rocky Bay.

Dan's eyes lit up. "Jammer, if you're going to Vancouver anyway, why not go as far as Rocky Bay this evening? Claudia and I could ride along with you." Then, looking at the rest of the crew, he added what he thought would be the clinchers: "We could kick around more ideas on how to raise lots of money. And there are nice hot showers available which you're free to use."

Either offer would have been persuasive, together they were irresistible.

Jammer was listening. "Might work. You've got a deal," He nodded, knowing just when to move to keep his crew from rebelling.

The other four crew members shouted enthusiastically: "All right!" and began stowing remaining loose gear.

Dan had been ignoring Claudia, but now he turned to her. "You ready?"

"Danny, if you're going in the Lingo," she coaxed, "why don't I go with Sid in the Princess? I really need to get back to Rocky Bay, and I'd rather not spend that much more time on the water." Claudia knew it would take the slow Lingo at least twice as long to get to Rocky Bay as the Princess and she was anxious to be alone with Sid to see if that body felt as good as it looked.

Dan glanced at Rolanda and smiled at this good fortune. He replied, "Sounds good to me. What do you think, Sid?"

Sid also was smiling. "No problem, let's go." He set the one case of empty beer bottles across on the Princess, leaving the other partially empty case on the Lingo. He then helped Claudia across to the Princess and said goodbye. He appreciated the way her soft, round body yielded to his strength.

"Don't wait up for me," Dan called. "This is definitely not a speed boat." The ropes were untied and, as the two boats drifted apart, the powerful inboard of the Princess roared to life. The diesel in the hold of the Lingo started slowly, almost painfully. The Princess accelerated quickly and hurtled southward across the gently rolling sea with the spray flying.

Twenty minutes later Sid backed off on the throttle to reduce the noise and make it easier to talk. Claudia left her seat facing the stern to come up and stand beside him at the wheel. Her body touched his.

Sid turned to her. "Do you like white wine?"

"I love it," Claudia replied. "Wish we had some."

"We do," said Sid. "Here, take the wheel for a minute." She took the wheel and Sid went forward and down to the refrigerator in the Princess' mini kitchen, where he always kept a few bottles of white wine. He noticed there was also one bottle of Mumm's champagne. Save it for later, he thought. He had learned it was a mistake to follow champagne with a still wine; drink the still wine first. He took out a bottle of Washington state chardonnay, St. Michelle vineyards, pulled the cork and returned with two wine glasses to Claudia at the controls. He handed one half full glass to Claudia and raised his own for a toast. "Here's to new friends and freedom, and may we enjoy both."

Claudia looked at him and smiled. "I'll drink to that."

Half an hour later the low angle of the sun reminded Sid that their progress toward Rocky Bay had been good, perhaps too good. Claudia had both arms around his waist and was obviously interested in further bodily exploration. She was giggling and cooing like a baby as he rubbed her back and rounded bottom. The bottle of wine was almost gone. Sid's watch indicated it was nearly 6:30 pm, and he had a suggestion. "Look, it's almost dinner time and we still have a ways to go. What do you think about stopping in a nearby secluded cove to have dinner? We don't have anything fancy on board to eat, but I can come up with something palatable."

Claudia thought it was a fantastic idea, and twenty minutes later they motored into one of the most beautiful coves she had ever seen. It was accessible only through a narrow passage and then opened into an area about the size of four football fields. Sheer rock walls rose for several hundred feet on three sides.

As Sid dropped anchor, Claudia went to the deck on the rear of the Princess to gaze in awe at the glistening slabs of nearly vertical pink granite rising toward a blue sky with cotton puffs of clouds rushing by. A small waterfall cascaded down a sharp gash made green by moss and small bushes clinging to invisible anchors. There was no wind whatsoever.

"This is fabulous! How did you ever find it?"

Sid moved to the stern and put his warm arms around her from behind. "You just have to know the right places to look." He turned her around and their lips met lightly at first, followed by tongues intertwining as passion swelled like waves riding an incoming tide to the Alaskan shore. They walked forward together to the bunk near the bow, undressed each other and made love as though each was starved for affection.

An hour later they prepared a light dinner of canned soup and crackers washed down with the champagne. Without saying so they knew they would be seeing more of each other, but extreme caution would have to be exercised in Rocky Bay, where, like most small towns, gossip was a primary occupation.

They didn't arrive at Rocky Bay until just after 8:00 pm. Claudia assumed no one paid any attention to their quiet arrival but the few slips at the dock were in perfect view of the Crow Bar, the most popular saloon in town located in the Chinook Hotel. Lee Lockridge, Sid's brother and manager of the saloon, watched as Sid tied the Princess in her slip and then helped Claudia from the vessel. Two of the bar regulars, Charlie Coats and Doug Marshall, also had ringside seats at the bar with clear visibility through the large double-paned window.

Sid and Claudia casually walked along the dock and then separated to go their separate ways. Dan Short was nowhere to be seen. "Well I'll be damned," Charlie observed, chuckling. "You don't suppose they threw the Doc overboard to get rid of him, do you?" He winked at Lee.

"Ah hell, Sid's too smart for that," Doug smiled. "But they might have put him off on shore for a snipe hunt 10 miles out. That would give Sid time enough to get the job done."

Lee was also smiling at his older brother's boldness. "I don't know what he was doing with her out there, but I know damn well what I'd do. She looks like she'd be one hell of a roll in the hay." He figured he'd find out from Sid later what happened but he didn't want to pursue it any further with these two town gossips.

After the departure of the Princess, the mood aboard the Lingo was a happy one. The aged, smoking diesel engine in the bowels of the Lingo throbbed away and they set course for Rocky Bay. Several hours would be required for the trip back, and the effects of the alcohol and pot still prevailed. Dan, as best he could, looked more closely at the crew. All three of the women were in their mid-twenties, and they were all very attractive along with being well endowed. He could not help wondering how Jammer and Craig could find such gorgeous women to bring out on a small boat like the Lingo, particularly with the sinister Jammer lurking about like the Phantom of the Opera.

It was obvious that the beautiful oriental Paula and scruffy looking Craig were more than just fellow research enthusiasts, while Susan seemed fairly close to Jammer. As close as anyone might care to get. But Rolanda seemed to be pretty much on her own. Rolanda interested Short, interested him a great deal. He also wondered how they arranged sex life on the boat.

The interior of the Lingo was arranged so there was one bunk for two people in the forward compartment, along with two single bunks above the bunk for two. In the main cabin there was a small sofa on each side, both of which could be folded down into a small bed suitable for two. Thus the Lingo could sleep eight without too much crowding if there wasn't so much junk on board. The two bunk beds in the forward compartment were being used to store electronic gear.

Dan noticed a foot tall, hollow pyramid, probably made of sheet brass, hanging over the bunk for two; he figured it must be one of Jammer's talismans. Perhaps the unfettered promiscuity Short had initially suspected was not taking place after all, although he was sure Jammer was getting into Susan's pants. He knew careful observation would reveal a great deal about ongoing relationships.

Rolanda seemed quite shy and intelligent and tended to keep to herself. Experience had taught him that some women were extremely hard to get next to, but worth every minute of time and effort expended. He watched all three attractive women with admiring eyes as the discussions went on. If they look good now, he thought, they must look fabulous cleaned up and in nice clothes.

Craig noticed the gaze and confided to Short: "One of the benefits of whale watching," he said. "There are dozens of them in Vancouver who would do anything to come on a tour like this."

Turning his mind to other matters, Dan had many things he wanted to talk to the Lingo crew about. In the cabin, with Jammer at the helm, the conversation continued with one idea seeming to follow another. He wanted to continue convincing them that association with him was a good idea, and he informed them that he knew a number of wealthy people in Vancouver and was certain many of them could be persuaded to provide financial support. However, he pointed out, assistance could only be expected for the killer whale communication project if the program plans were professionally prepared and presented. He was certain he could assemble, with their help, a program which would be well-received and would get results.

As Dan was speaking, Craig brought out a package of cigarette papers and rolled four more marijuana joints. Dan accepted one, lit it and handed it to Rolanda standing near him. After taking two heavy drags she placed it in his lips.

Hidden away in Rocky Bay, Dan had some of the cocaine brought from Calgary and he wondered what Rolanda would do for him if she knew he had coke, and other drugs as well, available. He had experienced the use of marijuana, cocaine and other drugs, some experimental, in Calgary during late night parapsychology sessions. Drug use was common among those attempting extrasensory perception and Dan was always in the thick of it.

Paula laughingly suggested one way to raise money would be to stage a concert of some kind, and that they should consider hiring a popular band for a concert in Vancouver. Craig was thoughtful for a moment. He kept glancing toward the place where Jammer had descended below deck. "I think its a great idea," he finally said. "Maybe we could persuade one of the groups to perform at no fee to help the OCS, but you know Jammer."

The crew of the Lingo exchanged glances that told Short they all knew him too well. "What about Jammer?" Dan asked, annoyed at having the hopeful mood of the session disturbed by the specter in the hold below.

"Jammer's a loner," Rolanda cleared her throat. "He doesn't trust a lot of people. But one thing he'd better trust is us, projects like this don't go very far without money and money means backing. OCS needs backing."

Craig took a last drag off a dying roach. "I'll talk to Jammer and see what he thinks."

Dan Short was impatient. "Let me talk to him now," he said as he stood up.

"Thanks Dan, but I don't think so," Rolanda's voice was firm as she pushed him back down. "Give us a little time to work on him. OK?"

Dan nodded his agreement. Paula and Sally got busy in the tiny galley area and soon brought out paper plates with beans, cream style corn, canned sardines and crackers. They apologized for the food, but Dan complimented them they could hardly have picked a meal which went better with the beer.

Rolanda appreciated Dan's easy going nature. He was so much different from other snooty professionals she had known, such as college professors. Here was a doctor worth getting to know.

The crescent moon played tricks on the waves as the Lingo chugged toward the dock at Rocky Bay, Jammer back at the controls. With the commercial salmon season under way, there were only two places left for the Lingo to tie up at the dock.

"Wow!" Rolanda sighed. "This place is hidden in one lovely bay."

"Man. I didn't even know this was here." Craig said.

Dan, pleased that they liked the village, smiled at his new friends' appreciation of his new home. Dan and Craig tied the Lingo to the wooden dock and the engine was shut down. The night was clear and the lingering smell of an evening barbeque drifted on the hem of the breeze, mingling with the fragrance of evergreens. The deep throb of the town's diesel electric generator could be heard faintly in the distance. The faint sound of revelry was heard from the saloons as the fishermen spent some of their earnings.

"This place looks great," Paula smiled.

"Well, there are no gridlocks or air pollution here, that's for sure. But if we're going to get cleaned up and have a drink we'd better hustle. They usually roll up the boardwalks here by 10. And one detail," he added, "the

two showers are in one room so it's not co-ed. I suggest the ladies go first."
Rolanda, Dan thought, was probably the only one with much modesty.

Paula, towel and cosmetic bag in hand, bounded from the Lingo onto
the wooden dock suspended 4 feet above the water surface on creosoted
poles. "Which way to the showers?"

"Right this way," Dan waved the three ladies forward, his spirits high.
He lead his new friends across the dock and uphill to the public showers
adjacent to the small, vacant harbor master's office. A donation of $1.00 per
person was requested by a sign over a slotted wooden box and he tossed in a
ten dollar bill. "When you have finished, I'll meet you at the Crow Bar, the
saloon on the ground floor of the Victorian hotel over there."

"OK, Dan, see ya then," Rolanda called.

"Right, about fifteen minutes." Dan smiled at Rolanda and turned
to walk up the street toward the clinic. From the corner of his eye he saw
Jammer, leaning against the cabin of the Lingo and staring at him with no
expression.

Strange bird, Dan thought as he crunched up the gravel road and
rounded the small clinic toward the toy-looking bungalow he and Claudia
shared. For some unexplained reason his step quickened and he began to
whistle. He knew it had nothing to do with going `home' but, once again, he
could not quite fathom his own feelings.

As Claudia had pointed out to him in Calgary after one of his patients
had committed suicide, "Christ Danny, here you are a psychologist and
supposed to help other people with mental problems, but you can't handle
your own. Reminds me of the song that goes: `If he can't even run his own
life, I'll be damned if he'll run mine.'" The accurate criticism had cut his
feelings like a knife.

As he approached the bungalow, the prospect of seeing Claudia was
depressing. She had ceased to excite him some time ago and he suspected
that she felt the same. But this was different than anything he had ever
felt before, a kind of throbbing just below his diaphragm, a euphoria.
Something important had happened to him on the Lingo, something he had
been awaiting subconsciously for a long time.

"That you, Danny?" Claudia called from somewhere past the small,
darkened living room as he closed the door.

"Yeah."

"Have trouble finding your way home?"

"No, I was enjoying the visit with the Lingo crew. They're taking a shower. Did you have a good time Claudia?"

He found her in the bedroom, seated at her dressing table. She was brushing her hair and the front of her robe was open, letting the amber light from a small lamp on the table fall on the round, pink softness of her breast. Dan wondered when he had lost interest in her. She was still beautiful, overweight and a little gone to seed, but beautiful.

"Sure Dan. I always have a good time." Her reflection smiled at his in the mirror.

"Listen, a couple of those kids from the Lingo are sick and tired of staying on that boat. I thought we could offer them the clinic." Rather than a `couple' he was thinking of one.

"What about the hotel?"

"It's quite full of commercial fishermen and I wouldn't recommend it to anyone. Besides, I'd like to show them some hospitality. This group could be a key to establishing communications with another species. By God, if I could do that the accomplishment would shock the scientific world. I could name my price and position at any institution in the world!"

"But you don't need that group. Do it on your own."

"No, they'll be valuable to have on the program. And right now, frankly, I really believe it will be easier to raise money with them than without them."

"I must admit," Claudia observed, running a brush through her hair, "that Jammer seemed to have some sort of ESP with the whales. And what if the whales really did exert an influence to have us meet their group?"

Without saying so she rationalized that perhaps the whales influenced her evening of lovemaking with Sid. "Anyway, if they stay in the clinic they'd be out early, before I open."

"Come on Claudia. What do you say?"

"Sure Danny. Any friends of yours are friends of mine. Besides, it's your clinic too. Just make sure they're out before I open at 9 am...and that the place is clean."

"You bet." He turned to leave the room. Then as an after thought, "I'll be back later. We're going to talk over more ideas before they leave for Vancouver in the morning." He didn't tell her they were meeting in the saloon.

"Take your time, Danny." She didn't really care when he returned. Or maybe even if. Dan Short jogged around the clinic and down the gravel street 200 yards to the hotel, took the front stairs two at a time, and, feeling twenty years younger, entered the dim red glow of the Crow Bar, which always smelled slightly of urine. He let his eyes adjust to the change in light from the bright outer hall and glanced around. At the end of the bar sat the regulars Charlie and Doug, with Sid's brother, Lee, tending bar.

"Hi, Doc," Lee greeted him, joined by Charlie and Doug. "Looks like you brought some strangers to town. We haven't seen that Lingo around here before."

"I'll have a Grizzly, Lee." Then smiling, "Somebody's got to act as the Chamber of Commerce and bring some new life into this burg."

"By God, I'll drink to that," Charlie raised his beer bottle. "This town could use some life other than these bloody commercial fishermen."

Lee slid a frosty bottle across the bar. "Who are they Doc? Look like sort of a motley crew."

"Group out of Vancouver doing a little research on killer whales. They'll be over here in a bit."

Lee smiled that there would be a little extra business and some new people in the place. "You get'n settled in OK, Doc?"

"We are indeed, Lee. Thanks."

"Where's your pretty lady tonight?"

"She was tired." Dan saw Jammer sulking in with the rest of the crew following a discrete few paces behind. "Decided to stay home. Excuse me, Lee." Lee watched Dan's back receding across the room and turned to Doug and Charlie at the bar, winking. "I'll bet she's tired."

"You folks find everything you needed in the showers?" Dan asked, showing his friends to a table.

"Sure did, Dan." Craig stepped back as Rolanda elbowed him away from the chair next to Short. "Hey Lee, how about a round of cold brew over here."

"Sure thing, Doc." Lee smiled. Paula, still feeling the effects of the dope, giggled.

"I am so impressed by men with titles."

Jammer's cold eyes locked onto the woman's profile. He had very little tolerance for superficial chatter, particularly inane superficial chatter. Craig caught the look on Jammer's face and, taking Paula's hand, said, "Let's go see what's on the music box." Jammer waved the beer away before the Lee could set it in front of him. "I'll take a double Jack Daniel's."

The music from the juke box began and Craig and Paula stayed out on the floor to dance to the loud, slow, heavy bass number. Rolanda was stunning, Dan thought, as he looked at her seated next to him. She had put on a flaring pink dress which made her dark skin look absolutely radiant and Dan turned and leaned closer to enjoy the natural fragrance of her body. "How was the shower?"

"Fabulous. Thanks for the thoughtfulness," she replied, leaning closer to him.

"Want to dance?" he asked, coaxing.

"I'd love to," she replied, standing.

On the floor, her lithe body twisted in perfect rhythm to the beat. She moved in against his body so he could feel every contour of her solid breasts, narrow waist and sculpted hips.

Dan Short held her firmly and closed his eyes as they danced. He had never been near a woman like this and he knew he had found a treasure. The music ended and they returned to the table along with Craig and Paula, who were also enjoying the dancing.

Jammer tossed down the Jack Daniel's and said nothing, but kept his cool gaze leveled on Dan. Craig and Paula returned to the floor as a rock and roll tune boomed over the speakers. One round of drinks gone, another on the way, and it seemed to Dan that Rolanda's eyes were getting larger and darker as they talked and held hands.

Jammer's coarse voice shot between the lyrics which laced the chords of an old Bob Dylan ballad together. "What do you want from us, Short?"

Dan needed a minute to organize his thoughts to respond to this unexpected assault. Then he turned to look directly at Jammer. "I don't want anything, Jammer. We seem to have a mutual interest in the whales and that's about it."

"Yeah, well you straight academic types always want something. To slander, to ridicule anything you don't understand. Which is a hell of a lot more than you're willing to admit." The Bob Dylan number played on as Rolanda scooted her chair closer to Short to indicate her full support.

Dr. Dan Short, fifteen years older than Jammer, had no physical fear of Jammer. Indeed, Short was getting so fed up with Jammer's antagonistic attitude that he was thinking someone should give him a good old fashioned beating, sort of like spanking a spoiled brat who is used to always getting his or her way.

"I have no interest in ridiculing you, Jammer. The whales are of interest to all of us. If I can help, I will." Jammer stood up, never taking his eyes from Short's.

"To help. OK, time will tell won't it, Doctor?" Then to his company seated around the table. "I want to get under way early tomorrow. Booze as long as you like, but if you're not on board in the morning when we pull out, you're stuck with the doctor here." Susan accompanied Jammer as he stomped out of the Crow Bar.

"Good night, Jammer and Susan," Short called sarcastically as they left. Maybe the Lingo group needed a new leader to replace the weird Jammer, and perhaps he, Dr. Dan Short, was the one to get the job done.

Dan glanced at the three remaining with him at the table. "Not a very trusting fellow. As a matter of fact he's a real ass."

Craig cleared his throat and chose his words carefully. "Look, Dan, Jammer's been burned, we all have. We believe in what we're doing. The last guy who said he was interested in our work turned out to be a biologist from U.C.L.A. who was only interested in using us as an example of the lunatic fringe for a paper in some damned journal. The story was picked up by AP and it hit the papers. That cost us several good backers."

"Jammer is a strange man, Dan." Rolanda leaned a little closer to Short than she needed to in order to be heard. "But he believes in his work and so do we. Just give him some time, OK?"

"OK," Dan responded warmly to the black woman's request. "Now how about another round. Lee looks kinda busy, I'll go get 'em."

Rolanda stood up and put her hand on his shoulder. "Stay put. A man in your position shouldn't carry his own drinks."

Dan's hand was warm when she took the $100 bill from him. A current ran up her back and she shuddered delightfully as she moved toward the bar. Charlie and Doug grinned at her approach.

"What can I do for you, pretty?" Lee smiled.

"We need another round at the Doctor's table." Rolanda smiled back.

"Get them for you in just a second, honey."

"Fine. I think I'll visit the little girl's room. Get 'em ready." She handed him the bill.

"Will do." Lee replied as he plucked the bill from her fingers, a wide grin across his face.

When Rolanda finished touching up her makeup and hair she strolled back to the bar where Lee was now talking and laughing with the man, Sid, who had left with Dan's wife earlier that afternoon. The drinks and change were ready and on a serving tray. Another heavy rock number was playing.

"Hey, man," Sid smiled to his younger brother behind the bar, "Don't underestimate the ones over thirty. You think they got to be young to be hot?"

Lee handed his brother a shot of whiskey. "I never said that, Sid. I just said that young and dumb might be safer."

"Safe's one thing, quality is another. After this afternoon I could get used to quality."

Rolanda picked up her tray and returned to the table unnoticed by the visiting men at the bar. She was smiling, things weren't gonna be so difficult after all.

Dan and Rolanda returned to the dance floor once more for a slow number. In the dim light Rolanda was dancing with her head on Dan's shoulder, happy to be there.

"Must you sleep on the Lingo tonight?" he whispered in her ear.

"No one tells me where to sleep," she whispered back, stroking his ear with sensitive ebony fingers.

"I have a place where you can sleep…in privacy and away from the Lingo" Dan responded. "Look, let's talk to Craig and Paula about breakfast, then we'll get out of here."

At the table, Dan told the other couple that he had a place for Rolanda to sleep and suggested they all meet for breakfast at the hotel dining room at 8 am. He would buy.

"But what about Jammer?" Dan asked Rolanda. "When will the Lingo leave?"

"Don't worry about him. He won't want to leave without anyone. And Craig will talk him into having breakfast, won't you Craig?"

"We can probably get the job done. But Paula and I will be there regardless. If he pulls out, what the hell…we'll get to Vancouver some other way."

"Way to go," Dan encouraged the attitude. "C'mon Rolanda, let's get out of here."

Lee, Charlie and Doug smiled and nodded at their departure. The village was obviously more lively with Dr. Dan Short and nurse Claudia in town.

Dan led Rolanda, overnight kit in hand, to the locked glass door at the front of the clinic. The sky had clouded over and the humidity-laden breeze indicated rain not far behind.

As they entered the stark cleanliness of the place, Dan locked the door behind them but turned on only one light. For a fleeting moment Rolanda wondered if it was a mistake to come here with a man she hardly knew. Dan led her down the narrow, dark hall and unlocked the door to his office, again locking it behind them. In the dim light filtering through the window she could see that he had decorated his office with soft wood and leather tones, creating a relaxed and homey feeling. A large leather couch, firmly cushioned, was against one wall. She had seen sofas like this in movie scenes of psychologist's offices.

Dan spoke quietly. "You can sleep here in my office on the sofa. Should be quiet. Let me get some sheets and a blanket." He kissed her lightly and stepped into the hall.

Within a couple of minutes he returned to the office with folded sheets and two pillows. Placing them on the leather couch, he turned to Rolanda. This should be a good place for you to sleep tonight. I'll come by and wake you about 7 in the morning."

"But where are you sleeping?" she asked as she pulled him close for another kiss. "It's not right to leave me out here by myself." She began to unbutton Dan's shirt and he responded by unbuttoning her blouse. In a couple of minutes Rolanda pulled Dan on top of her on the couch and they made passionate love for twenty minutes all the while telling each other how wonderful they had met.

After getting dressed again, Dan let himself out and made his way around to the rear of the building. It suddenly occurred to him that a distance of only about 100 feet separated the clinic from the bungalow where Claudia was sleeping. As he entered the small house he made as little noise as possible. Rather than disturb his sleeping wife, he took off his shoes and lay down on the small sofa. He pulled a small comforter across his shoulders and immediately went to sleep.

The next morning, Dan was at the clinic at 7:00 to wake Rolanda and put the sheets in the laundry. She woke up quickly and they hugged each other and talked briefly before walking to the Chinook Hotel. None of the rest of the Lingo crew was there so they took a table and ordered coffee.

Craig and Paula soon straggled in, followed by Susan and Jammer. As they sat down at the table Craig complained of a headache from too much beer.

As breakfast was eaten, Dan advised them that he would do his best to assist with the fundraising and already had plans in the works to go to Vancouver himself. "When do you think you might go?" Paula asked, although she was certain Rolanda already knew.

"I would guess in a couple of days, if I can get the AA program lined out that quickly. When I do go, I'll fly over to save time."

As they finished a last cup of coffee Jammer looked directly at Dan Short. "How was your night, Stud?"

"Fine, had a good night's sleep. Why?"

"Not a thing, man. Just make sure what you're gett'n at doesn't interfere with the Lingo mission. We got to keep our eye on the prize, you know what I mean?"

Dan felt rage mingled with scorn as he looked at the bearded Jammer seated across the table. "The mission is clear to me, Jammer," he replied. "Clearer than some in this group could ever imagine. And one thing a leader must learn is to coordinate group efforts rather than divide them and cause dissension."

Dan tossed a five dollar bill on the table and picked up the check as he stood. Followed by Rolanda, he went to the cash register, paid the check and walked out.

As they walked toward the dock, Dan questioned the wisdom of keeping Jammer with the crew, especially as the unofficial captain.

"I know he's weird and obnoxious, Dan," Rolanda argued in Jammer's defence, "but there are a few points in his favor. He really *does* know vessels and the sea, I have witnessed that myself. And he claims to have some strange communication ability with the whales, which has yet to be proven, but who knows?"

They were now walking onto the dock. Rolanda continued her explanation. "By the way, did you know he is mostly Tlingit Indian and a few times has mentioned his power as a Shaman among his people in the coastal villages? If so, his contacts may be of value."

"We can give it a try," Dan acknowledged. "But what about Vancouver, you going to be there when I arrive?"

"I wouldn't miss it for anything," she smiled.

Within ten minutes the rest of the crew arrived and the Lingo departed for Vancouver. As Dan waved them off, his psychological training picked up on the buoyancy of their spirits, related, he was sure, to the greatly improved prospects for significant funding for the project. Even Jammer smiled and gave him a thumbs up sign as the vessel chugged eastward into the bay.

The next two days in Rocky Bay went by slowly for Dan. He had difficulty concentrating on the AA program and the handling of individual native alcoholics when thoughts of communications with killer whales ran through his head. He searched the Internet and read and reread what little information was available in Rocky Bay about killer whales. One fascinating story, discovered in an old paperback, concerned cooperative whale hunting in Australia between killer whales and human whalers beginning about the year 1830. Over a period of almost a hundred years a pack of twenty-five or thirty killer whales appeared at the whaling community of Twofold Bay every year just prior to the time gray whales were to appear in migrations northward from Antarctica. Several of the whales were given names, including one large male called Old Tom who was quite mischievous.

The whalers, operating with oar-powered dories, would watch the killer whales offshore carefully for signals conveyed by the whale's visible activities. Experienced observers learned to recognize the signals so well that they could tell immediately when the orcas had one of the much larger gray whales "held at bay." If the whalers did not come out quickly enough, one of the killers would come into the bay and slap its tail on the surface and take other action to get the attention of the whalers, sort of like a baying hound returning to alert the hunters when a coon was treed. When the signal was recognized, the whalers would rush out to row through the circling killer whales to harpoon and dispatch the hapless gray, all the time assisted by the orcas who would even try to close the gray's blowhole by getting astride it as it surfaced for air.

Once dead, the lifeless carcass of the gray was towed into the bay, eagerly followed by the killers, where it was tied to an anchor but left in the water. The orcas, over the next few hours, would proceed to tear off the lips and work the mouth of the gray open in order to get at the large tongue, an organ they obviously relished. The body of the whale was then left for the whalers.

Had this not gone on for so long, and had the cooperation been less successful, it could have been considered a chance occurrence. But year after year the highly successful whaling went on with the killer whales and the whalers hunting together and sharing in the kill. Only in the 1930's, when mechanized whaling replaced the old style hunts, did the cooperation end.

This true story fascinated Dan. Such cooperation between two intelligent, independent mammal species in mutually beneficial activities was extremely rare, and this one apparently was initiated by the whales themselves. What a monumental psychological study that would have made!

But why not initiate communications with killer whales again? Why not learn what sort of benefit *they* could gain from an activity of man and see if they would reciprocate.

He found other references which described the Tlingit native's ideas concerning why killer whales would not attack man. One story related was that the killer whale was created by a native from a wood carving and the carver ordered the whale to harm no people. But not, he noted, before the whale had already killed two natives.

CHAPTER SIX

The mini-pigs

T he early June morning in northern Colorado broke clear and blooming as Mary Pantera ran her battered, four-wheel drive pickup toward the two square miles of poor grazing land, helter-skelter small metal buildings, and experimental crop plots the Colorado Agricultural College called the Experimental Farm. Mary, a petite brunette in her late 30's, had grown as tough as any ranch foreman and held a firm determination to make her swine animal husbandry program a success.

Flat and dry except for irrigated areas, the land around the town of Greeley, with 14,000 foot Long's Peak looming in the western distance, was a very different stomping ground from her home. The small New Mexican community of Chimayo, the name rolling off the tongue like the smooth, nearly pure Castilian Spanish still spoken in the region, sits forlornly on the west bank of the snake-like Rio Grande 50 miles north of Las Cruces. Mary was born and raised there in the small, pale adobe house of her grandfather, Fernando, not far from the Jornada del Muerto, the valley of the journey of death.

It was nearly three years since she had been home, and her brother wrote that the old man was losing his sight. Still, her schedule didn't leave much time for Chimayo or going home to see Fernando. Her professional ambitions often caused the old man to shake his flowing mane of silver hair and stare questioningly at the pepper plants he had grown in his neat and narrow little garden for as long as anyone could remember. Caressing the slender, brilliant red chilies, he would mumble to himself and shrug, as if they alone could explain why his granddaughter wanted to raise pigs.

"Education! A woman needs a husband, not an education," Fernando informed her when she accepted the scholarship to Colorado State University in Fort Collins after working hard for top grades in high school and junior college in Las Cruces.

"Grandpa, the world has changed," Mary advised him. "Times have changed. Women are educated now, they have careers. Our intelligence is good for something besides raising kids."

But Fernando was unmoved. "Women have children. Men earn life, women give it. That is the way it has always been, there is no reason to change. And what about grandchildren for me?" Mary shook her head in silence. She loved her grandfather but he was not going to get away with putting her on a guilt trip over having no kids. She would make the decision of when or even if.

Then began the long and tedious journey toward the PhD in animal husbandry, which she finally earned. Mary rolled down her window and smiled out at the rain-soaked summer morning. Before the end of the season northern Colorado would become deadly hot, but for now, the early hours of the day were blissfully cool, particularly after a gentle storm laid the beige dust to rest. Homesick though she might be at times, Colorado had become a very comfortable place for Mary. Upon her arrival at CSU in Fort Collins, Pantera had her heart set on becoming a veterinarian. However, as her course work progressed she became increasingly interested in animal husbandry, the field in which she finally obtained her advanced degree. As part of post-graduate research she had conducted a research project in swine intelligence and found herself convinced, as other researchers had been before her, that the pig is the most intelligent of all domestic animals. Swine, she learned, are capable of figuring out problems for themselves, a step above the dogs and horses which man tends to overrate. Her PhD thesis included the statement, not agreed to by at least one faculty critic, that pigs seem to regard man as a fellow traveler on the planet.

The bottom line was that the kindred physiology of swine to man, along with the value of the pig as an important food source, gave her academic interest a pragmatic edge. As she studied her subject, Mary's fascination with swine as a group became even more focused by accounts in the literature of small swine, about 1/3 the size of an ordinary pig, which had been developed by selective breeding several hundred years ago in Europe, particularly Spain and Portugal. A number of these pigs had reportedly been transported across the Atlantic in the 16th century by the Spaniards when they colonized Central and South America. The smaller pigs required much less space, food and care than larger hogs. Some scholars reported strong evidence that Columbus had brought small swine to the Caribbean area in the 1400's and that many of the pigs now present throughout the area were descendants of those early arrivals. The Italian discoverer and those who followed him left the small porkers on islands where they were likely to stop on later trips, thus providing a ready replenishment of meat for hungry sailors. Pantera concluded she could pick up the ball where the early seafarers of Columbus' day left off and develop an outstanding small swine which would find wide acceptance as a food animal and for medical research.

In the very early stages of Mary's infatuation with the swine, she had taken a trip to the Dominican Republic and Haiti, but found no living person who could report with certain knowledge the origin of swine in those parts. In addition, she found that breeding with larger swine stocks had altered the original animal to a bigger hybrid of little interest for her program. She also learned the answer to a question which had puzzled her for quite some time, how was the locality name `Caribbean' pronounced? A wise old Indian appreciated her concern. "The name," he advised her solemnly, "came from my tribe the Carib Indians and the word Caribbean is pronounced just as the tribe name is pronounced. It is "CARE-i-bee-an," not "Ca-RIB-bee-an" as it is pronounced, unfortunately, by many newcomers. Without knowing it, these people are defiling our tribal name." Mary was familiar with many Spanish terms which had been distorted by non-attentive readers, with Texans among the worst offenders. She promised to do her part to encourage use the correct pronunciation, just as she did for her mother language.

Mary's continued research at the CSU veterinary library did yield some valuable additional information. Small swine, weighing less than 250 pounds, were reported to be quite common farther south, in certain parts of Central America. Guatemala, in particular, seemed to have a substantial population of the "mini-pigs", perhaps because the climate and the peasant's need for a small swine breed were well matched. She had read that Guatemalan farmers kept the pigs around the house and fed them scraps from the kitchen, but for other food the pigs must scrounge from the floor of the jungle. The mini-pigs were slaughtered for food or were sold on the market. Larger pigs would be too dangerous for such a close relationship with people, particularly if small children are present, which a large hog could injure or kill.

In Fort Collins as Mary's academic and scientific prowess developed, her knowledge and reputation expanded. Unlike the narrow cultural roles of her New Mexico home, where female acquaintances grieved as she advanced into her thirties unmarried, in Colorado she was a respected peer, a scholar, a fellow scientist. In this atmosphere Mary found the self-confidence to complete her doctorate requirements and set about finding a location where she could both teach and pursue her dream of developing a mini-pig experimental and breeding station in the United States. Although one of the large meat-packing companies in the U.S., along with the University of Missouri, had a Europe-originated mini-pig program underway, she believed a better breed could be developed from carefully-selected animals from stock being raised in Central America.

The 50 pound Vietnamese pot-bellied pig, which was becoming quite popular in the States as a "lovable" household pet, was too small and just wasn't hardy enough to tolerate variable outdoor climates. Colorado winters with 30 below zero temperatures, for example. And she didn't need a bunch of animal lovers getting emotionally upset with her planned profitable marketing of her small swine for the table and for research. There was really only one way to prove she was right; go to Central America, locate and select high quality swine and export them north. Within a couple of generations she believed a swine with very desirable characteristics could be ready for introduction to the hog breeders of America and for her own marketing efforts and research facilities. A big job for a small Mexican girl from the Chimayo.

She needed a sponsor. Much to Mary's surprise, her support came from an unexpected quarter, Dr. Chester Buckingham, the president of Colorado Agricultural College 75 miles east of CSU in Weld County. Buckingham was an eccentric man, known to many professionally and few personally. He was a pure academician with an intense conviction that conservation of the earth need not mean deprivation of earth's inhabitants. Mary's first encounter with Buckingham was much less auspicious than one might have expected, considering the outcome. She waited for over forty minutes in his austere, little anteroom with his secretary, Martha, who stared blankly about, shifting her weight in her rolling chair and sighing.

"Oh, he'll be right along, Dr. Panther. He won't be much longer. I'm sure I told him you were coming today at two."

"Pantera." Mary corrected gently.

"What?" Martha blinked.

"My name is Pantera."

"What an interesting name, Pantera Panther. Are you Indian?" Mary smiled and re-directed her attention to the five year old National Geographic on her lap. Another ten minutes passed and she was on the verge of excusing herself, believing either that Dr. Buckingham had simply forgotten that he had summoned her there a week before, or that Martha had never told him she was coming. The door suddenly flew open and a small man with great blue eyes under a red receding hair line stormed into the anteroom.

"Do you know where I've been for the last two hours, Martha?" he puffed.

"Why, yes doctor, don't you?"

The blue eyes stumbled over Martha's features wonderingly for a moment before the head that housed them shook violently from side to side. "Of course I know!" He stifled adding 'you idiot.' "I've spent the last two hours having breakfast, at the request of the president of our Alumni Association, with the wife of Senator Elect James Harrel and Mrs. Gordon Russell." The last name was drawn out through the teeth as the mouth twisted into an angry grin.

"How exciting." Martha squeaked.

"Not exciting, Martha," Buckingham nodded in an exaggerated fashion, "It was an exercise in observing the lunatic fringe."

Martha shrunk back in her rolling chair and ran a dry tongue over her thin, pale lips. "Oh, the Senator's wife is a lun..."

"No, not the wife, Mrs. Russell. She's eighty years old and nuttier than a Christmas fruit cake. Do you know what she offered to do?" Martha opened her mouth to speak, then snapped it shut as Dr. Buckingham placed his face very close to hers and tapped a bulging vein in his temple with a stubby index finger. "She offered to give the Agricultural College a five hundred thousand dollar grant on condition that we set aside a quarter of the space in our Botany Building and use 90% of the money for her pet organization to conduct experiments in floral communications." Buckingham's face was becoming alarmingly red, his collar seemed to pulsate with the blood flowing through his protruding artery. "That's right, they talk to flowers: roses, carnations, snap dragons. Christ ..."

Pantera felt the laughter slip out from between her compressed lips the way one might feel a half-supressed thought slip into place. Buckingham turned his glowing blue eyes on her and took two steps forward. "Who the hell are you?" He demanded.

"This is Dr. Panther, she talks to pigs." Martha gushed.

Buckingham's head swiveled toward his secretary with such ferocity that the woman fairly shouted, "Well, *you* invited her."

For a moment Dr. Chester Buckingham was completely immobilized before he looked back around at Mary and sighed, "Dr. Pantera, I am sorry, I very nearly forgot our meeting."

"Sounds like you've had your hands full, Doctor."

Buckingham nodded slowly. "Please come into my office. Martha, hold my calls."

"Yes sir," Martha relaxed in her rolling chair.

There wasn't much to Chester's office, a desk, a large series of book cases on the north wall, a window looking out over the chemistry building. He'd never been much for the pomp and circumstance that surrounded the office of College President, as a matter of fact, he rather enjoyed ignoring the position all together. "Sit down and make yourself comfortable, Mary."

"Thank you, Doctor."

Buckingham's eyes took on a jolly character. "Call me Chester. I hope you and I are going to be friends and co-workers."

"I have to admit, I am a little confused." Mary watched Buckingham settle his small, square frame in a wicker rocking chair.

"I am not unfamiliar with your work. Dr. Phyllis Herrmann over at CSU has spoken of you often and fondly."

Pantera smiled as she thought of her role model, academic advisor and mentor. "Dr. Herrmann has been a great source of support for me."

"She's a brilliant woman and a fine educator. Her career is like a bright crown and she considers you the jewel."

"I am flattered."

"Nonsense." Buckingham snapped. "Flattery has nothing to do with it. A gifted pupil is a pleasure to teach, and Phyllis says you're the most gifted she's seen. Now, let's get down to business. As I said I am not unfamiliar with your work. When David Rodman..."

"The Business Manager of the National Swine Association in Ames, Iowa?" Mary interrupted.

Buckingham smiled, he appreciated sharp memories. "The same. Anyway when David told me about a letter he had received from a young Ph.D. here in Colorado with a notion of starting a mini-pig experimental program and breeding station, he rang a bell. Took me a couple a days to remember that Phyllis described the same kind of project to me a year or so ago. She said it was your concept. I'm like Sherlock Holmes, Mary, I don't believe in coincidence. You're the one who wrote to Rodman?"

"Yes, I am."

"I'm impressed, so is David. We think your idea is first rate. I don't mind telling you that CAC has a selfish interest; we think it will be a money-maker as well as put us in a better light with the farming interests in the United States. But, back to the practical aspects: you're gonna need some place to set up shop. How about the Farm? We have those four empty buildings which were used for that angora sheep program."

Mary's mouth was a little dry when she answered. "The Farm would be perfect, but first I need top quality pigs."

"When you wrote to David you indicated that you wanted to bring the stock north from Central America."

"That's right. I wrote to the Swine Association for money to finance a trip to Guatemala."

"OK," Buckingham took a pad and pencil from his desk. "Give me an idea of what you think it will cost."

"Traveling, purchasing twenty or more pigs and returning them here to Greeley would run around $75,000. Then we'll need operating funds of about $300,000 for three years until the program is producing enough revenues to begin standing on its own two feet." To Mary's amazement, Buckingham didn't even blink.

"Yes, I saw that in your well-written proposal. You can teach some courses here and we'll use other personnel part time to help at the Farm. The buildings out there aren't the best, but they'll have to do for now." Buckingham scribbled a few notes on his pad and picked up his phone. "Martha, get me David Rodman in Ames, Iowa." He turned to Mary with a general plan map of the entire Experimental Farm layout with a group of segregated buildings which were available. Their plan was coming together.

A few minutes later the telephone on Chester's desk buzzed softly. "I'm fine, David, how are you? Good. Yes she's here." The great blue eyes concentrated on something out past the window, Buckingham rolled his pen on the arm of his chair and listened. "About $75,000 for the trip and acquisitions. Half will help, my friend. Thanks, David. Tell Ruth and the kids hello… You, too."

Buckingham replaced the receiver in the cradle and focused his attention squarely on Mary. She was afraid to speak, afraid the sound of her voice would end the dream and she'd awaken. "The NSA will put up $37,500 for now provided they receive recognition and full reports on the progress of the program." Buckingham was scribbling on his pad now, talking more to himself than to the dumb-founded Pantera. "We'll try to get more from them later when we can show them how well the program is going. I know they'll get some heat from the Iowa schools for this, but Dave thinks competition is good for them."

He glanced at Mary, who sat utterly amazed at how quickly this man was operating.

Buckingham continued, "There is 20 grand in unused funds left from last year's soil conservation program, and I can get another 10 to 15 thousand from the general fund in a month or two when we need it. Can you get started immediately, Mary?"

"Yes, sir." Pantera managed to whisper.

"Good. I'll order maintenance to begin setting up for you, including fixing up that office out there. It won't be luxury but we'll be ready for you and your porkers when you head back north from Central America. Be sure to get all the required permits, we don't want the Department of Agriculture on our case."

Mary stumbled through the next few days in a kind of daze. She had never imagined that she would find such support so quickly, particularly since the letter she wrote to David Rodman had gone unanswered for nearly two months. She began to steady her course by methodically gathering all possible information concerning making the proper contacts in Guatemala, a country riddled by political unrest. Her belief, shared by Buckingham, was that she would be safe enough if she selected villages to visit not in the areas where rebels were active.

When she contacted the State Department, they agreed with her assessment, but cautioned that she should be sure to keep the embassy in Guatemala City informed of her location and activities. A lot of good that'll do, she thought. Most of the staff members of United States embassies, based on her experience and research, were racially-discriminating, incompetent oafs who could not even speak the language of the country in which they were serving. The embassy crisis and hostage-taking in Iran in the 1980's, she believed, may have been caused in part by just such ignorance. The

State Department staff probably couldn't be relied upon to mitigate a crisis in a culture which they, through bigotry or simple stupidity, could not bring themselves to understand. The author of THE UGLY AMERICAN was correct in many respects. To avoid any future hassles over her livestock purchases and shipment, however, she assured them of her cooperation.

The U. S. Department of Agriculture listed specific steps which must be followed in order to bring foreign swine, especially from Central America, into the country. The steps included inoculations, quarantines and anti-fungus and anti-parasite chemical dips.

Within ten days after her conversation with Buckingham she was boarding a flight out of Denver with her boxes of vaccines and treatments, bound for Guatemala City via Mexico City.

A few days spent getting oriented to the beautiful capital brought Pantera face to face with an old enemy, a deep and formless resentment she thought she had left in the Chimayo years before. She watched the tension seethe and swell as the free and communist worlds strove to dominate the minds and bodies of the hungry and impoverished Guatemalan people. While the Catholic Church loomed on the periphery preaching against birth control, the illiterate population exploded toward starvation and further stripping of the country's resources. Enormous stone cathedrals rising hard and pale against the clear azure sky tormented their souls with visions of hell fire and eternal damnation while proclaiming unquestionable Divine power. Insulting, that was how she found the situation. Just as she once found the intimidation perpetrated by the Penitentes -- a group of Catholics who still practiced the bloody rite of crucifixion -- against the starving Mexican peasants in the countryside. Hunger and want weren't enough, humiliation and terror had to be added into the bargain. Politics and theology, Pantera often wondered, which of the two fooled the greatest number of people with the least basis in truth.

After what seemed like an eternity of wondering through the mindless maze of Guatemalan bureaucracy, Mary finally made contact with Ricardo Romero, the head of the Nations Bureau of Agriculture. Ricardo spent the better part of an hour staring at her bosom, as if he expected it to expand into something he had never seen, and making lewd suggestions about how he might amuse her if she failed to turn up a sufficient number of four legged animals, before he finally relinquished the information she required. Clearly, Ricardo pointed out, the best area to search for high quality swine would be near Plano Verde, 80 miles northeast of Guatemala City. Once the best pigs were selected, he further instructed, she could have them hauled an additional 100 miles northeast to the port village of Puerto Barrios. Banana shipments were made from this port to Houston, Texas, and, with luck, she could get the pigs transported on a banana boat.

She departed for Plano Verde immediately. It didn't take much talking to enlist the help of the local livestock buyer, Jose Quintana. For each pig purchased she promised to pay Quintana a commission of ten American dollars, an arrangement with which he was delighted.

In addition, Mary believed it imperative to get to know the people of the villages and to determine how they felt about the mini-pigs, what they liked and what they didn't. Because there were no accommodations for travelers in the town of Plano Verde or in the surrounding villages, and because Mary was fluent in Spanish and had expressed her desire to become acquainted with the people who knew the pigs best, Jose arranged for her to stay a few nights with one of the best respected farm families in the area, the Borregos. "They are very fine people, Doctor," Jose beamed. "And they raise some of the best swine in the region."

"That's very good, Jose. But I will need to look at a large number of pigs in order to pick 30 or 40 good ones."

"Don't worry, Doctor. You can trust me. I will find plenty of pigs for you to take back to Estados Unidos. After all, I am now an international trader, I will find pigs."

The Borregos lived at the end of a rutted, dirt road in a house which looked more like a tin-roofed shed for livestock than the home of a successful farm family. On the afternoon Jose dropped her off, the oppressive heat and humidity made Pantera long for the dry Colorado climate to which she had grown accustomed. She was sweating profusely when four children, three girls and a boy all less than nine years old, came running out to greet her. They were followed by a pregnant woman in a brightly flowered dress. A baby about a year old rode in the woman's arms and pulled at the bright orange button on the front of the dress.

"I am Señora Borrego," she extended a warm, work-hardened hand and smiled at Pantera.

"It is a pleasure and honor to have you in our home, Doctor."

"Thank you for extending your hospitality, Señora Borrego."

The woman took hold of one of her children and turned the whole group toward the house. "Please, my name is Delores."

"Mine is Mary."

As they proceeded toward the open front door of the dwelling, Mary took some candy from her back pack to offer to the children. As her hand came free of the bag with the wrapped, hard sugar drops she heard a familiar snorting and three full grown mini-pigs came bustling and shoving around the corner. Mary was astounded. It was as though the pigs had a sixth sense and knew food was near even though they could neither see nor smell it. Mostly gray, with little hair, the pigs were 3 to 3½ feet long. Mary estimated that the trio was less than four years old, fully mature and weighing about 165 pounds each. The pigs looked at her closely, sniffed and tested her scent in the hot breeze. They could also smell the candy and looked longingly as the children popped the sugar in their smiling mouths. When Mary and the Borrego family entered the shanty home, the trio of pigs was joined by two more, including a boar, all of which proceeded into the dirt-floored structure with an easy freedom. Delores reached for the broom to chase them out, but the pigs were already on their way. Again, it was as if the animals knew what she was thinking.

Delores put the baby in a chair and sat the broom aside. "Señor Borrego, my husband, is clearing some trees two kilometers away, but he will return at dusk in time for dinner. In the meantime would you please make yourself at home."

The children were delighted to have a visitor, especially one from a foreign country who could speak their language, and they were full of questions. Mary led the discussion around to los cochinos, the pigs, so that both the children and Señora Borrego would tell her about the mini-pigs. The children did most of the talking. The pigs were treated much the way Norte Americanos might treat a dog around the house, but with little or no affection. The pigs had the run of the place and were fed table scraps. For most of their food the pigs rooted around in the nearby jungle for grass, roots, leaves and anything else edible. "On more than one occasion," Delores finally interjected, "we have found the pigs killing, and then eating, both poisonous and nonpoisonous snakes which ventured into or near the cleared area." She was pleased about this for the safety of the children.

"Aren't the pigs bitten?" Mary asked.

Delores smiled, hoping for a higher price if Mary bought the animals. "Oh yes, but the venom does not bother them. They are cochinos buenos, good pigs."

A little more conversation and the children insisted upon moving outside and showing Mary around a bit. The pigs, still smelling the candy, Mary thought, followed them as they wandered through the clearing. When Mary asked where el tocador, the toilet, was, the children laughed as Delores pointed to a small, rickety shed sitting on four posts about 6 feet above the ground. A makeshift ladder led from the ground up to the doorless facility. At Chamayo, outdoor toilets were commonplace, but even a cracked or broken door provided a measure of privacy.

"Why," she asked, "is the toilet raised above the ground?"

"For many reasons," responded Delores. "No dark places for spiders or snakes to hide in, and on the ground the pigs always are bothering when you defecate. This way you are out of reach, and the view is also better." Mary looked at the shaky outhouse and the ground underneath. The pigs obviously had been there because the earth was trampled and barren of grass. Another thing caught her attention, there was no evidence of human feces below the one-hole seat. She wondered, but feared to ask, if the excrement constituted part of the pig's diet.

"Oh yes, Mary," Delores smiled. "Our smart pigs can tell if you are going to defecate or urinate before you go to the toilet!" An observation which brought more laughter from the children. Pantera couldn't help joining in the laughter at this ridiculous bit of folklore. Just another way to try to increase the price of the pigs, she thought. But she did need to urinate, and perhaps she could go somewhere else. There was the jungle, but she quickly ruled that out because of too many unknown dangers, especially poisonous snakes. There was the edge of clearing, or trees in the clearing, but the pigs were there. Perhaps the elevated outhouse was the best choice after all. She excused herself and started toward the ladder. Delores, sensing her need for privacy, started to the house with the children. Before ascending the ladder, Mary scanned the area for pigs. Those visible were near the jungle edge rooting and eating grass. They gave her only an occasional glance. She climbed up the ladder and looked down through the one hole. Nothing below except trampled dirt and pig tracks. She concentrated on the view across the clearing to steady her nerves and allow her to relieve herself. Delores was right, looking away from the outhouse was very pleasant. Unlike the pale brown of the Colorado plains, the dense jungle growth offered a canopy of brilliant shades of green splattered with patches of yellow, red and purple flowers. The singing of birds was wild and glorious. Brilliantly colored butterflies danced across the clearing and along the jungle edge. A large wasp buzzed by. If it weren't for the heat, Mary thought she could enjoy life near the jungle. Now relieved, she made her way down the ladder and back to the house. The pigs, she noted, were still busy with what seemed to be their primary activity of rooting and eating in the clearing, which kept it nearly free of excess grass and brush. She found herself wondering how the family kept the pigs from wandering off. And what about jaguars?

The Borrego family apparently had eight adult pigs along with three juveniles and one sow with six piglets. Tomorrow she would examine them closely with Jose, the animal dealer, and Raphael Borrego and try and make a deal. A little over two hours later, as she continued to talk to Delores and play with the children, Mary began to feel a tinge of the cramping and general discomfort which signals an onset of the bowel irritation generally known as Montezuma's revenge. She had carried her own canteen of drinking water, but somewhere on the trip she must have eaten or drank from an unclean plate or glass. She cursed herself for having eaten the ceviche at the hotel in Guatemala City the previous night. As the discomfort increased she excused herself and headed toward the outhouse. Mary scarcely had time to clear the front door before the four pigs nearest the entrance were running for the outhouse, to be joined almost immediately by the others. Pantera was incredulous. How did the pigs know whether she was going to urinate or defecate? She had felt the urge herself just a few minutes before.

Delores came to the door of the little house and laughed. "Ah, los cochinos, I told you they know what you are going to do in the toilet!" Then she turned and went back to the children. Mary continued across the clearing. All 12 of the larger pigs were grunting, snorting and jostling for the best positions under the hole and around the four posts. The six piglets stayed off to one side to avoid being trampled. The rickety frame shed creaked and swayed on the posts as Mary reluctantly climbed the ladder. When she got to the shed and looked down through the watermelon-sized hole cut in the rough lumber bench, the pigs were looking up and seemed to be smiling. Despite the increasing cramping in her abdomen, the sight of the smiling porkers was more than she could stand. Mary started back down the shaky ladder. Perhaps, she thought, if I leave, the pigs will leave. Maybe she could confuse them by walking toward the jungle. Climbing down the ladder, she hurried to the edge of the clearing beneath the heavy natural canopy which effectively blocked the sun. The brush seemed impenetrable except for tunnels where the pigs had gone through. In order to proceed, she would have to crawl on her hands and knees. Her imagination conjured up fat vipers coiled along the crawl space, fangs dripping with venom. She turned back toward the outhouse. The pigs were unmoved by the attempted deception and held their ground under the wooden structure on stilts. Accustomed as she was to working with pigs, she had never seen any like these. It seemed they knew she really had no choice but to come back. The jostling was over. Each pig had its position. They waited. The cramps in her abdomen were now close to unbearable. Again she considered the edge of the jungle, but, were she serious, the pigs would no doubt follow her and things could get rough, not to mention messy, if a pig struggle developed while she was defecating. She thought of the explorers at the ice caps with their huskies. When the explorers defecated, she had read, they did so all at one time with all the humans squatting and facing outward. Otherwise the huskies would fight to get at and eat the human feces.

Mary, now desperate, turned again and started toward the ladder leaning against the outhouse. The pigs, still tightly clustered under the hole, grunted in anticipation as she climbed the rickety ladder once more. At the top she again looked through the single hole at the diabolical smiling faces, but she could wait no longer and positioned herself over the crude hole. Squeals and grunts sounded through the clearing as the bacterial infection swept her bowels. Jostling of the pigs caused the outhouse to sway on the posts. Mary had never felt such humiliation in her life, and she hoped Delores and the children weren't watching the spectacle from the house. Mixed with her personal feelings of degradation and even disgust, however, was an intense scientific longing to learn more about these creatures that seemed capable of reading minds. There was also a deep concern about the health of these pigs. If human excrement, and possibly excrement from other sources, formed a significant part of their diet, the pigs no doubt had serious health problems, including parasites. Pantera was hoping that pork would not be one of the items for dinner in the Borrego home that night.

Her hope was in vain, roast pork was offered as the main course. Mary ate very little, excusing herself as not being hungry due to the stomach ailment. "The small pigs," Raphael Borrego explained after the meal was finished, "have been in Guatemala for centuries."

"So I understand." Mary nodded her agreement, still humbled by the afternoon's experience.

"Some think the pigs are, in..., I cannot remember the American word, but it means, they have always been here."

"Indigenous."

"Yes, that is it." Raphael smiled, glancing up at the clear starlit sky spread above the shadow of the jungle. "But I believe that the Spaniards brought them in the 1500's."

Pantera followed Raphael's gaze. "I agree with you."

Just after midnight the cramping in Mary's stomach began again. She took the flashlight from her pack and moved out of the house onto the narrow porch. Even before she switched the light on she heard the pigs deep in the jungle darkness grunting and snorting. They seemed to have awakened just as she did. As Pantera threaded her way back to the outhouse, the pigs preceded her. This time she preferred not to look at them and carefully avoided shining the light down the hole. But she wondered if the squealing and grunting of the pigs awakened those in the shanty as she again emptied her large intestine.

After that first day in the Borrego home, the symptoms of the bowel infection subsided very quickly. She attributed her resistance to and ability to fight off such things quickly to her Mexican American upbringing. She had been told since childhood that the hot food, dry heat and clean air of the Chimayo grew children stronger than any place else in the world. She believed it.

Mary thought a lot about the Chimayo over the next few days. Watching the Borrego children play and argue she thought of her own brothers and sisters, seven of them, all married now with children of their own. Like her host's children, she and her brothers and sisters had not enjoyed much luxury, but they had love and concern, food and warmth. In the final analysis, Pantera believed, that is what gave children strong minds and bodies to take into adulthood.

Within 10 days of her arrival at Plano Verde, Mary had selected the pigs she wanted to take north. She expected that despite her best examinations and those of the local "expert," who also claimed to be a veterinarian, some of the pigs would prove to be too diseased or to have other problems which would make them unacceptable to the U.S. Department of Agriculture or unacceptable for the breeding program. For this reason she bought 30 pigs with the intention of reselling, or giving away, about 5 pigs before departing for Puerto Barrios. Another 5 would be weeded out during the initial quarantine.

Upon arrival at the Port with two trucks transporting the pigs, she arranged to have temporary fencing set up at the edge of town away from other pigs or pig enclosures. Her pigs would have to be kept clean, watched carefully and would receive vaccinations during a two week holding period before shipment. Any pigs exhibiting illness or physical defects would be removed from the group immediately and sold. The vaccines, louse spray and powder and disinfectants she had brought along for the purpose were now put to use. Mary also spent a good deal of time hosing down, feeding, caring for and talking to her herd. She believed the extra care, as well as her nearly-continuous company, would be the best defense against porcine stress syndrome in the two stages of the trip first to Houston and then to Greeley.

At the end of two weeks, Mary had reduced the swine herd to 22 animals, and she felt good about the group. They were looking healthier on the predominantly corn feed she had been purchasing for them. She hired two local men to keep the pens clean and to provide clean, fresh water. She was sure, barring any unforeseeable problems, she was on her way with the mini-pig program. The shipment of the swine out of Central America by banana boat was a 10 day ordeal. The pigs seemed, in their uncanny way, to quickly adapt. In fact, they were fascinated by the water.

Back in the states, Colorado Agricultural College had notified the Department of Agriculture that the pigs were coming, and a quarantine area had been arranged for in Houston. The quarantine period in Houston was for two weeks during which the swine were examined by two veterinarians representing the Department of Agriculture. Pantera didn't dare tell them about the nature of part of the pig's diet on the Guatemalan farms. In addition to concern about hog cholera, there was the major concern of trichinosis. After another round of vaccinations, worming and disinfecting, approval for shipment to Greeley was finally given. First, however, Mary was required to sign an affidavit stating that none of the pigs would be used as food for humans for a period of two years and that if any evidence of diseases showed up in the pigs the affected animals would be immediately destroyed. Additional inspections in Greeley were also planned by the USDA. During the trip from Houston to Greeley, Mary rode with the driver in the covered stock truck. She insisted on traveling during the day and stopping at night to give the pigs a chance to rest and be fed. By the time Mary Pantera and the tired, traveling pigs arrived at the Experimental Farm, she had two separate objectives in mind: continued breeding of a quality mini- pig, and down-size breeding to develop a micro-pig even smaller than the mini.

The swine were unloaded into newly fenced areas with segregation by age and sex. A key factor in her breeding program was that the pigs must be separated and selected in order to commence her selective breeding program.

Five years had passed since the beginning of the mini pig program. Many of the problems Pantera anticipated never materialized. Others, not completely unexpected, had reared their heads with a vengeance. Perhaps the worst was the increasing opposition to any use of animals for medical and other research purposes.

As her truck rattled up to the cattle guard at the gate to the CAC Experimental Farm, she noticed with relief that there were no pickets yet today. The animal rights activists had been driving her crazy. A rumor that the mini and micropigs were being used for toxicity and other testing by governmental and private agencies had sent them roaring to the farm where they picketed, threatened to steal the pigs and to burn the buildings.

"Why in hell," Mary muttered as mud from a puddle splashed through the open pickup window and over the dented hood of her truck, "don't they picket the Greeley Packing Company, 3 miles away? Cattle, hogs and sheep are slaughtered by the thousands there every year."

Pantera waved to Rex Hammond, the guard for the swine research facility. He was having a cup of coffee just outside the door of his camp trailer which constituted the "guard station." Rex had retired from the Greeley Fire Department four years before, and after losing his wife to cancer, was glad to find the night watchman's job at the school.

Once in a while, Hammond's life at the farm got a little exciting when the bombing threats and picketing were underway. But, thus far, things had not gotten too far out of hand. In front of the metal Quonset hut which held the offices, Mary pulled into her usual parking place. Just inside the door of the attached porch she took off her jogging shoes and placed them in a rack. She slipped on a pair of knee-high, black rubber boots with the initials M.P. painted on them and stepped into the vat containing the greenish yellow bactericide solution. Everyone entering the compound had to change from street shoes to issued boots and step into the solution.

Mary would take no chances on diseases being introduced to her swine from the street. She also would allow no employee, including herself, to enter the facility if a viral or bacterial infection was suspected in or on the person. One of Mary's latest investigative efforts was the possibility that *Candida albicans*, a yeast, was causing some sinus problems with her pigs. Some had exhibited symptoms of a respiratory illness and yet no viruses or bacteria had been identified as the culprit. As if to reemphasize the similarity between pigs and man, she had discovered that a prescription drug, nystatin, specifically designed for curbing Homo sapiens problems with the pesky yeast, also took care of the problem with her swine.

Coyotes were common in this part of Weld County and they had learned well how to adapt to life in and near a city such as Greeley. Usually they stayed out of sight during the day and carried out hunting and other activities at night such as raiding dogs feeding bowls left outside or catching and killing domestic cats that had wandered away from their owners. Rex Hammond had warned Mary about seeing coyotes passing by the outside pig pens on several occasions and they were obviously interested in the small porkers that were in the pens. One October evening two of the coyotes, perhaps a mated pair, decided to raid one of the pens for the micropigs. The three pigs panicked and ran around the pen squealing. The larger of the two coyotes picked out the smaller pig and sank sharp teeth into the back of the pig's neck. The pig bucked and squealed but the second coyote grabbed it by a hind leg and flipped it onto its back. The larger coyote then went for the pig's throat and cut off the pig's breathing. The squealing stopped and the coyotes proceeded to rip into the pig's intestines, eating as fast as they could pull out the heart, liver and other parts. They could not carry the pig back over the fence so they had to eat what they could, and quickly, in the pen. After eating only several pounds of the meat they again bounded over the fence and ran into the prairie.

Rex found the remains of the pig the next morning and the tracks told him what had happened. He called Mary, who advised him they would have to find some way to protect the pigs. Perhaps one of the large Maremma sheep dogs that are used to protect sheep from wolves in Europe. It was a possible solution they could think about.

Overall, Mary's pigs were in excellent condition. And, except for the coyote attack, they were happy. Overall, she was happy. Once in the office, Pantera took out the coffee pot, filled it with water, put coffee in the basket and plugged in the electric cord. As she started down the hall Kim Storey came in, black boots still dripping from the solution. "Hi Mary. Wow, it's a gorgeous morning, isn't it?"

"Lovely," Mary responded, smiling. "Let's go see how the families are doing."

Kim loomed a statuesque 5' 6" next to Mary's 5' 1" frame. She was beautiful in the raw, clean manner of Nordic blondes. Pantera hired her four years earlier as her assistant. Storey had proven invaluable. With a degree in biology and a strong interest in animal development, Kim had learned to run the entire facility during Mary's occasional absences. Storey, as intelligent and enterprising as she was beautiful, came with some independent ideas on breeding selection which had produced some excellent litters of the desired size and disposition. "Wonder if the 26C sow has popped yet?" Kim wondered as they walked along the dirt-floored walkway leading from the tiny administration building toward the large barns and outside pens.

The metal barns, one cluster for the minipigs and one for the micropigs, were actually in better condition than the office because Mary preferred to put any available funds into improving the pig habitat rather improve the space for her and her small staff. In time she hoped to construct a new, but compact, office building. Sales for the pigs had been good and cash income was increasing. The stalls containing sows and piglets had a bed of wood chips and straw which was changed every few days. "The biggest part of this job is house cleaning," Kim often laughed.

The facilities and feed were kept as clean as possible while still allowing for the raising of a substantial number of swine. The National Swine Association was providing financial support in the amount of $50,000 per year to CAC for the swine program. A number of U.S. farmers had indicated an interest in the swine for, as it turned out, the same reasons the Spanish had developed them in the first place: ease of handling, lower feed consumption and an excellent meat product for human consumption. Mary's mini pigs had come to be known as superior minipigs. She bred them not just for small size, but also toward good muscling, substantial frame (for their size), wide-set legs and relatively little fat.

"Update our inventory list this morning, I'm expecting a call from Japan. They may want 10 micros shipped later this week." Pantera stood up and looked down at her assistant kneeling next to a sow that had just given birth. "We received another order from the Navy for 5 of the barrow mini's. Apparently, their program using pigs instead of humans for studies of certain mammalian responses to underwater conditions is working out very well. I'm gonna have to see that someday. They've developed scuba masks, suits and weight belts for the pigs so they can function under water just the way humans do."

"What exactly are they trying to prove?" Storey asked as they walked toward the outside pens which housed the barrow minipigs.

"You know the Navy, they'd keep the Pacific Ocean a secret if they could figure out a way to hide it. However, I did manage to find out that some of the tests involved experiments on various combinations of gasses which might be used with scuba equipment to prolong the dive times of Navy frogmen." Then she looked at Kim closely. "The new order no doubt means that some of the pigs have died. The Navy keeps a constant inventory."

The two women continued in silence toward the buildings housing the minipigs. Picketers had begun to assemble about 100 yards from the fence and gate at the entrance to the facility. Under waving signs several voices were raised simultaneously in an angry shout, "Killers!" when the two women were sighted. The antagonism was clearly distressing to Kim. She looked at Pantera with a wounded expression.

"Look, Kim. Much of this is the result of what I call the 'animation syndrome'" Mary advised her as they entered the office, trying to ignore the noise. "Today's children are constantly and repetitiously exposed, from the time they can watch a television set or read, to numerous cartoons, movies, television shows and stories depicting animals as having intelligence, organization, guilt, sympathy and a "soul" just as Homo sapiens has." She poured coffee for both of them. "Witness the Muppets, Bugs Bunny, Mickey Mouse, Mr. Ed the Talking Horse and a zillion other characters. Kids on the farm or in small towns have sufficient exposure to real life animals that they can watch these programs and pretty well maintain their mental equilibrium on what is fact and what is fiction. Kids in the city do not have a similar broad perspective."

They sat down and Mary continued her explanation. "Kim, think about it. When many city kids grow up, guess what, they become misdirected animal rights activists. I would bet right now that if an honest poll were taken of those goons on the other side of the fence you'd find that 95% of the picketers were raised as city folk or otherwise had no opportunity to discover the real world of animals. This is the animation syndrome generation, and it's probably going to get worse before it gets better. But don't let it get you down."

From the window they could see the demonstrators. Efforts to talk to these well-meaning but unrealistic people had been fruitless, even though some of them were meat-eaters themselves. Mary saw clearly the concern expressed on Kim's beautiful face. "You have some doubts about all this don't you, Kim?" she asked softly.

"No, not doubts about my own position," Kim nodded negatively. "I just wish there was some way I could educate these people to the realism of man using his fellow creatures to learn about them, himself and the biological world. Not to mention food and clothing."

Pantera once more ran her eyes over the milling crowd, now perhaps 50 people, just past the entrance. "All of this concern for the rights of animals doesn't stop some of those people from wearing leather belts, leather shoes, eating a Big Mac. Christ, look at the leather industry? Nothing gets my Castilian blood boiling like being called a killer by some babe with an alligator purse who just had bacon for breakfast!"

Kim smiled. "I guess if I hadn't been raised on a Weld County farm and taken a biology degree I might even be picketing someone myself. But we RAISE the critters, why don't they picket the USERS?"

"Don't worry, they will if they can find them. We're going to have to be very careful to keep our customer lists confidential." They arose and walked into the adjoining office where the computer and data files were kept. Time to get back to business.

It was doubtful, they knew, that any of the mini's or micro's raised and shipped from the Experimental Farm ever lived to an old age, the same as with the livestock industry. Hogs, sheep, cattle, chickens, few of them were reared to be enjoyed for their company. Man raised them by the millions for slaughter, consumption and use of body parts. In many areas of the world, dogs, cats and horses were still on the list of edible animals, but much of the so-called civilized world regarded eating these "pets" as unacceptable. Yet man himself had proven time and again that cannibalism will take place if there is no other food available.

In answer to Kim's question Mary had answered, "The pigs we raise would seem to fit somewhere in between the food animals and the nonfood animals." Then she added, "But no, they really are food animals which have the additional valuable characteristic of being useful for research. So much the better for our pigs, their contribution is greater than their brethren although both make the supreme sacrifice."

◆◆◆

In the meantime, out in the far north Pacific near the coast of Alaska, several species of salmon are starting their annual swim to their river of origin so they can migrate upstream to find spawning sites. Killer whale packs are acutely aware of this potential food source and they also gather near the mouths of the larger rivers, or in migration pathways, to catch and eat salmon. Prince William Sound, east and over the mountains from Anchorage, is one of their favorite hunting grounds during salmon spawning periods. However, they have learned that they have a competitor who uses boats and nets to catch the fish. The whales try to avoid getting close to any of the boats or nets because the fishermen sometimes try to kill them with bullets.

But the whales usually hunt for and find salmon in areas where there are few boats. There is another competitor in Prince William Sound that the whales will kill whenever the opportunity arises. This competitor is the salmon shark, which can grow to lengths of 10 feet and weight of 900 pounds. They have sharp dagger-like teeth and can catch and consume large amounts of fish, with salmon one of their favorites. They often hunt individually but also in small schools of 5 or 6 sharks.

When the A-T pack is hunting salmon for food and come across one or more salmon sharks, a couple of the fast females, including Tinga, will outswim the slow shark and grab it by one of its lateral fins and turn the shark upside down. Sharks cannot process water to recover oxygen when upside down and, after several minutes, die from drowning. When the shark is dead, the orca may eat some of it and will release it to let it sink to the sea floor where it will be consumed by crabs and other bottom dwellers. Even great white sharks are killed in this manner by killer whales. Just offshore southern California biologists have observed killer whales killing a great white by turning it upside down. They were fascinated to note that all the other great whites in their study area then fled, apparently because they feared the killer whales.

CHAPTER SEVEN

Plans

Mike and Tracy Mackenzie sat waiting in the small seaside town of Whittier, waiting for the Alaska Railroad train to arrive from Portage, 25 miles to the west via the tunnels between Whittier and Portage. No vehicle road existed due to mountainous terrain, tunnels would be required. From Portage paved highways extended to Seward and Homer to the south and to Anchorage and beyond to the north. Vehicles were transported via flat cars between Portage and Whittier. No town exists at Portage, simply a loading ramp for vehicles.

With their vehicle holding a place in line, Mike suggested they walk over to the Trooper Ted Barnes' office to see how many reports had been received from fishermen having fish stolen by whales and to get all the information available concerning the missing couple from Nevada. As they approached the squat two room building housing the Troopers' office, they noticed a green pickup parked next to Ted's 4 wheel drive pickup. They recognized it as one from the Biology Division of the Alaska Department of Fish and Game.

Ted Barnes greeted them as they entered the one room cabin called an office. "Hi Mike, Tracy! Headed for the big city again?"

"Hi Ted," Mike replied. "It's not that we want to leave but we made a promise to go out to the gold mining operation and see how they're doing so far this summer."

"Gold, eh, sometimes I wish I'd stayed out in the hills prospecting instead of taking this trooper job. Say, do you know George Maxwell here, a biologist with Moose and Goose? George, this is Mike and Tracy Mackenzie, self-made researchers, gold miners and what-not?"

Mike stepped forward and shook hands. "Hi, George, I believe we met one time at the Fish and Game offices a couple of years ago when we had a meeting about a placer gold mining operation. And this is my wife, Tracy."

"Hi George, I also met you at that meeting," Tracy nodded as she shook his hand.

George smiled at her. "To tell you the truth I hadn't remembered Mike, but no man in his right mind could forget someone as pretty as you are, Tracy. Nice to see you again."

They all chuckled. Ted Barnes loved to talk about gold. "Did I ever tell you my Grandfather did pretty well on the beaches at Nome in the early 1900's? That's where the money came from to buy the family farm near Anacortes, Washington."

Tracy smiled, "No, but Mike and I have been to Nome several times in the past couple of years and it is a really nice little town, one of the best in Alaska. But, did you know that money to build Madison Square Garden in New York came from gold mined at Nome, primarily from the Anvil Creek placers?"

Ted shook his head. "I'd better quit thinking about gold or I'll turn in my time right now and head for the hills. This damned trooper business is bad enough in normal times and now we've got the killer whales raising hell and stealing fish. Can't shoot 'em and can't arrest 'em, even when they're caught red handed, or should I say red toothed."

Mike nodded, "But isn't that a problem for the Department of Fish and Game or the U. S. Fish and Wild life Service?"

"Supposed to be," Ted noted, "but that's what George and I were just talking about. Jurisdictional problems always pop up. Fish and Game is responsible for the fish and the fishermen, but under the Marine Mammal Protection Act, the Fish and Wild life Service is responsible for managing and caring for the whales. Some of these fishermen seem hell bent on keeping the whales away from their lines, but if the Service catches them injuring a whale there will be hell to pay. Someone's probably going to jail before this is resolved. The problem for me is keeping people from each other's throats."

Tracy looked directly into George Maxwell's eyes, "Is anyone carrying out studies to determine which whales are causing the problem and why?"

Maxwell nodded. "We'd like to do more, but frankly we just don't have the budget or the manpower. With the decline in oil revenues to the state our budget has been cut not just to the bone but to the marrow, twice. We're about three years behind now on high priority biological studies and, frankly, studies of killer whales are way down on our list, particularly since we regard the problem as mainly in the lap of the Fish and Wildlife Service out of Seattle. They don't *want* us to study the killer whales because that is their responsibility, and they are not about to help us get any federal money."

Mike looked seriously at Maxwell. "Perhaps the Department doesn't know it, but this is the third year Tracy, Dr. Reed Remington, marine biologist with Hydrosphere in San Diego, and I have been carrying out independent observations and studies of killer whales in Prince William Sound. We are interested in them and enjoy it. We undoubtedly know more about these whales than all other parties combined."

Maxwell was interested. "How are you financing your studies, and what do you do with the information?"

"Hydrosphere has been providing most of Remington's funding because the research will contribute to a better understanding of killer whales in the wild. Tracy and I pay our own way, even though the cost is considerable" Mike continued. "As for the data, we are compiling records of behavior as well as identifying photographs of all the whales in the various packs which we plan to publish through Hydrosphere Research Institute in San Diego."

"With the new Desk Top publishing system we just got, we may be ready to publish this coming winter," added Tracy.

"In my humble opinion we need all the help we can get," nodded Maxwell. "Are you in good communication with the Fish and Wildlife Service?"

"Very little," Mike responded, "But we were able to get a permit from them to observe whales in Prince William Sound. This may be another no budget/no personnel situation."

"Look," said Maxwell, "There is a meeting scheduled in Anchorage tomorrow between Fish and Game and the Wildlife Service and I'm going to attend. I seriously doubt that they will resolve anything, but it's worth a try. Why don't you two also plan to attend? Some of the bureaucrats may try to keep you out but I'll tell them about your work with whales in the Sound.

Give me your phone number in Anchorage and I'll call you to confirm the time, place and your presence."

As Tracy gave him a calling card Mike turned to Barnes again. "Anything new on the couple from Nevada? I heard on the radio they were still missing."

"Nope, nothing new on them but hell, Mike, people disappear in Alaska all the time with no trace. I don't regard their disappearance as any big deal and we've spent enough time on that situation already." He looked more closely at the three intent listeners. "I'll tell you what is new, though. As I was just telling Maxwell here when you came in, a pod of killer whales harassed old Nels and Lydia Larson down by Chimney Creek a couple of days ago and knocked them out of their Zodiac. Nels told me on the radio that one of the whales then ate their black lab like a piece of candy. He and Lydia got back in the boat and made it back to their cabin, but it scared the hell out of them."

"Oh, oh," breathed Mike and Tracy together. "Who's investigating?" asked Mike.

Maxwell responded, "No one at the moment. The dog was obviously not a game animal and no humans were injured so we're simply writing up the report as an isolated incident of unknown cause. But this won't help the whale's reputation with the fishermen."

"That's for sure," Tracy observed as she looked at Mike. They both knew it was best to make no verbal speculations and to reveal no emotions about the whales at this time even though fears were forming in the recesses of their minds.

"Is Nels coming into town?" asked Mike. "If he is, we'd like to talk to him. We'd go out there right now but we've got to go to town."

"Nope," said Barnes, "he's not coming in for a few days. He was going to but thought Lydia should rest up.

He's also fixing up his old fishing dory for the trip; they won't becoming in that Zodiac anymore."

Tracy posed another question: "Did he give any kind of a description of the whales involved? Any identifying marks?"

"Yes, he said that of the 18 or so whales there were a couple of large males in the pack, and one of them was especially large with a real tall dorsal fin. Oh yes, and he said the fin on that whale was strange because it was wavy."

Maxwell watched Tracy and Mike closely to see if the description produced any tell-tale reaction, the way a poker player watches the facial expressions of the other players, but no reaction appeared. More noise from the direction of the railroad loading ramp caused Mike to step out and look in that direction. The line of about 25 vehicles was beginning to move forward for loading onto the flat cars.

"Well, they're starting to move so we'd better run, Tracy. Ted, thanks and keep us posted. George, call us tomorrow and we'll plan to come to the meeting."

He and Tracy jogged the 50 yards to the vehicle in time to move with the line up the ramp and along to about the 4th flat car. They remained in their Suburban.

Within a few minutes the train began moving slowly westward out of Portage. Tracy poured them each a cup of coffee from the stainless steel insulated jug. "Mike, you know as well as I do that the wavy dorsal fin on a big male makes it almost certain that it was T-4 with the rest of the A-T pack which harassed the Nelsons. Didn't you say Jerry Gallagher also described him as one of the whales taking halibut?"

"Yes, I'm afraid so. We may have a rogue pack developing here."

"I'm really worried about these new developments for the sake of the whales. We already know some get shot every year by trigger happy fishermen even when they're not directly bothering fishermen and fishing gear. If they're becoming aggressive we could have dozens of whales killed in one season." Mike did not reply immediately as they both pondered the changing killer whale situation in the Sound.

From the silence, each knew that the other was mentally turning over both their past three years' experience and the new information they had just received about the killer whales. Tracy was unusually intense in her thoughts. In the past she had been perhaps more deeply impressed than Mike or Reed by some of the almost vicious predation by some of the killer whales. In watching them kill seals and other sea mammals over the past three years, she had developed a strong respect and fear for the creatures, a fear which she had not revealed to Mike. Her acute perception and sort of ESP had always fascinated Mike, although he was a total non-believer in such phenomena.

Nevertheless, on occasions when she would mention to him that she had been thinking about an old friend, followed within hours by a call from that friend, Mike was puzzled. In the remote sub-conscious of her mind a belief was developing that the killer whales may have had something to do with the sudden and unexpected disappearance of the couple from Nevada.

"Mike, I've been thinking about the couple who disappeared. Black bears, and even a few brown, are common around the Sound. We know they'll enter camps, tear things up and even kill people under some circumstances. But the bears always leave some evidence, and without fail they get into the food. From all reports, there was no evidence of a bear attack at the boater's camp. And bears seldom stay on small islands for long anyway. Trooper Barnes' theory that the couple from Nevada had gone swimming, gotten out too far and had succumbed to hypothermia is not believable."

"And we have the overturning of the Larson's Zodiac, and the killing of their dog, Champ," Mike added. "The Larson's escaped unharmed, although it seemed clear the whales could have killed them, or, at the very least, tossed them around as we have seen the whales doing with some animals they did not intend to eat, such as sea otters. Added to the puzzle are the reports of the theft of halibut and cod from the fishermen's lines."

In the latter two cases, they agreed, the pack involved seemed to be the orcas which they had labeled the A-T pack two years ago when they, along with Reed Remington, had been observing and photographing the whales. Even then it had been apparent that the A-T pack was strongly prone to attacking and eating warm blooded mammals, much more so than the other groups of killer whales which they had observed or which had been described in the literature for the Alaska-British Columbia, Pacific Coastal region. Some of the killer whales in Patagonia, they had seen on TV, were very aggressive in catching and killing sea lion pups at certain times of the year. In Antarctica there were reports of orcas aggressively hunting penguins and seals, including the breaking of ice to knock the animals into the water where they could be caught and eaten.

However, aggression by killer whales such as that seen in the southern hemisphere was not known in Alaskan waters, but they could think of no reason why a pack of killer whales in Prince William Sound would not, under the right circumstances, or perhaps simply because of the disposition of some of the whales themselves, become aggressive and begin feeding on whatever food was available and which suited their fancy at a given moment.

They agreed that Man qualified as food on all counts, except perhaps for the indigestible clothing he wore. Tracy wondered aloud what would happen if the A-T pack was on one of their mammal hunting expeditions and came across some people in the water without clothing. That was an unpleasant thought. As experienced as she, Mike and Reed were with killer whales, there was still a deep seated fear which arose in them when they were on the water in the vicinity of a whale pack hunting mammals.

Meanwhile, in Prince William Sound the A-T pack had been feeding heavily on red salmon moving into the area to spawn. But they weren't the only orcas dining on fish. Another pack of 12 whales had swam into the Sound from their usual hunting ground out in the northern Pacific. These were the type of killer whales known as transients and they usually hunted larger prey such as certain species of whales, dolphins, porpoises and warm blooded animals such as seals and sea lions. But they had come into the Sound because they knew there was good feeding to be had on the salmon. The two separate packs detected each other's presence when they were still 3 miles apart. They communicated within their group in a similar but not identical way as the A-T pack. As the two packs merged there was curious examination carried out on both sides but no hostility. There was plenty of fish for all and no territory disputes. After an hour of milling around together the two packs split and each went a separate way, the A-T pack to rest and sleep and the transient pack would hunt salmon.

Tracy turned to Mike and, over the clickety-click of the steel wheels over the joints in the track, posed a question: "Do you suppose it is possible that the couple traveling in the small boat had taken off their clothes, to perhaps bathe, just as the A-T pack came by and decided these creatures could be an interesting meal? I would like to believe not, but if this were to prove true, or even if a rumor started about it, the whales could have hell to pay from those seeking vengeance, or those simply seeking an excuse to kill more whales than they do already."

Mike, the moment Tracy mentioned it, acknowledged the view point. "You may be right. Even if innocent, the whales could be judged guilty with no chance to be proven innocent. However, if there are some bad characters out there, we should do our best to identify them and somehow isolate them where they can do no harm."

"When we get to Anchorage why don't you call Reed and see if he can get up here sooner. We could find the A-T pack and commence observations to see if they really are acting strangely. The less time that passes, the better."

"I agree," Mike nodded. "But what about the computer setup at the bank? Are you far enough along that you can get away for a couple of weeks in the Sound?"

"I can pretty well wrap it up if I don't go to the mine with you. Why don't you go alone this time and I'll have everything ready so we can spend a couple of weeks on the water when you return?"

"Listen Sweetie, I just spent a week away from you and that was too long. Do you want me to turn into a sex maniac?"

Tracy laughed, "Just let the pressure build!" and kissed him on the cheek.

Both Tracy and Mike were naturalists and they always noticed various natural phenomena wherever they went. It was always disappointing for them to hear anyone say that they were bored at some particular locality and had nothing to do. A true naturalist can find something of interest even if the location in which one finds oneself is in the midst of the concrete and skyscrapers of New York City. A recent example was an interesting article concerning the insect and plant-life which exists in the joints between concrete sidewalk slabs in Manhattan.

As they drove off the train at the Portage siding, they noticed again the dead trees on the flat land west of the siding near the Portage River, which empties into Turnagain Arm, the easternmost extension of Cook Inlet. In the 1964 earthquake this area was dropped about 5 feet and the invasion of salt water, as well as a shift in the groundwater table, had caused the death of almost all the trees at low elevations. As they turned onto the paved highway leading from Portage to Anchorage, they went over their thoughts again and formulated plans. Tracy got out a pencil and pad and began making a list.

A third of the way to Anchorage the highway crossed Bird Point, which projected into Turnagain Arm from the north shore. The old timers, in about 1900, had found visible gold in a vein at the edge of the water on this point and had tried to mine it, but, during a storm, the dam they had built to keep out the water had collapsed and they had to give up. There was still gold there, more than one ounce per ton in some places, but, as in so many areas of Alaska, the land on which the veins occurred had been included in a huge land withdrawal.

As they drove along, they noted that the tide was out, exposing the mud, silt and sand filled flats of Turnagain Arm to the sunlight. Fluctuations of 30 feet from low to high tide had been recorded. During periods of extreme low and high tides, the incoming tide was sometimes headed by a wall of water 6 feet high; this was the "bore tide."

Tracy looked south across Turnagain Arm to the old gold mining town of Hope. "By the way, Mike, did you hear that last week another person died on the mud flats near Hope?"

"No, what happened?"

"A gold prospector and his wife were going to try some gold sluicing at low tide and were taking some equipment out on three wheelers. She took a different path than he did and her unit got stuck. When she got off to try to get un-stuck she also began sinking into the mud. By the time her husband got there she was over her knees. The tide was still going out so time seemed no worry, but he went into Hope for help anyway, just in case. Several men came out to help but, as usual, they couldn't get her out. They called the Anchorage Fire Department and by now the tide was coming in. Despite all their efforts they could not get her out and her husband watched helplessly as she drowned even though they tried to keep her breathing through a length of garden hose."

"That happens every couple of years. I wonder if they can't design a sort of parachute harness, with special strength between the legs, to be attached to a couple of Zodiacs. When the tide came in there would be tremendous lifting power. Might not work but that beats hell out of that type of drowning."

"Yes," she replied, "but when will people ever learn how dangerous Cook Inlet really is?"

Arriving at Anchorage near noon, they drove straight to their log cabin home in Stuckagain Heights. With Tracy's cooperation, Mike would try to get all the urgent tasks done so he could depart for the placer gold mine immediately after the meeting the next day. On the answering machine, among other messages, was a message from Reed asking Mike to call as soon as he got in. He picked up the phone and dialed Reed's number at the University. Fortunately, Reed was there.

Reed had been worrying. "Mike, I've been thinking about some of the things which have been happening up there in the Sound, and I have a gut feeling something has happened to change the whale's attitude to result in these strange actions. The taking of halibut from the long lines doesn't make sense if the whales are getting plenty of food."

"That isn't all, Reed. We now have a report of an orca attack on a Zodiac. Remember the Larson's who have a cabin on Chimney Creek? An orca turned their boat over and reportedly ate their dog. The Larson's weren't hurt but it scared them and they're very upset about the dog."

Reed was startled, "Oh no, do you know which pack it was?"

"The bull description sounds like T4 so it was probably the A-T pack again," replied Mike. "Not only that, and I hesitate to say this, but Tracy and I are wondering if the disappearance of the couple from Nevada may somehow be related."

Reed was stunned to silence for a moment. "Do you actually believe one of the orca packs in Prince William Sound may have had something to do with that missing couple?"

Mike responded. "No, not *believe*, just suspect at this point. However, it seems that the A-T pack has been involved in every reported screwy event, and you remember how aggressive they are with mammals."

"Yes, but *people* is something else."

"Reed, there is no reason, as we have discussed before, why whales would not kill and eat people under the right circumstances. If those two people were in the water without clothes when the A-T pack, or even one of the other packs, was hunting mammals, it is possible they were taken."

Reed stopped to ponder this carefully. It was one thing to be in southern California participating in the captive killer whale program and teaching a couple of marine mammal courses, but it was something else to be dealing with an aggressive and intelligent group of the beasts misbehaving in the wild. If they ever became accustomed to eating people, it would likely be necessary to kill them just as it had been found necessary in India to kill man-eating tigers.

He posed a question to Mike. "How many people know about this theory?"

"No one other than Tracy and me. She came up with it on the way over from Whittier." His hand went to Tracy's knee as she sat intently beside him. He smiled at her.

Relying on Mike's judgment, Reed asked: "What do you think we should do?"

"If we want to try to help the whales before this crazy Alaska bureaucracy and many of the other so-called whale savers get involved, you'd better plan to come up immediately. There's a meeting tomorrow here in Anchorage with Fish and Game and the Wildlife Service and we're going to try to attend. Then I've got to go out to the mine east of Denali for a day or two. Tracy is going to wind things up at the bank so she can get away.

Why don't you clear things up on your end and plan to be here three days from now. Call and leave a message with Tracy so we'll know when one of us should pick you up at the airport."

"OK, Mike, but one thing I must do and that is inform Hydrosphere management of what is going on, except for the speculation about the Colorado couple. They should be advised both so I can get leave and to ask for their support and financial help. They're reasonable people, and we may have to count on them for more help this summer."

"Good. Give us a call when your plans are firm. And bring that new hydrophone you were telling us about."

Reed's voice took on a regretful tone. "By the way, the orca paper I was going to give at the marine mammal conference in Vancouver next week has been cancelled."

Mike knew how much Reed had been looking forward to describing field observations of the killer whales in the wild to better educate those who professed significant knowledge about Orcinus orca, but who, in actuality, knew practically nothing about the lives of the predators. "What happened? Did they cancel the conference?"

"No," Reed explained, "they just cancelled my paper. Apparently Blue War, and others like them who want no new studies of killer whales and they probably believe my appearance could only undermine their effort. They say to hell with new knowledge and a better understanding of the whales in their own environment, and they will do whatever it takes to get their way, including unethical acts."

"But why," asked Mike, "did they accept your paper for the program several months ago, and why did they wait until practically the last minute to cancel it?"

"Apparently, after the paper was accepted, the radicals swayed enough people over to their side to veto my appearance, and they waited until the last minute so that there would be insufficient time for me to protest the act and still get back on the program."

Mike sighed. "It's bad enough that they oppose anyone studying the whales, but now they are even trying to head off valuable information about one of the very creatures they profess to want to protect! It reminds me of idiot societies like the Nazis burning books."

"Well," Reed resigned, "let's forge ahead and do what is right for science and the orcas in spite of the hurdles presented by this sort of stupidity. I'll get my schedule in order and be back in touch in the next day or so."

"OK, Reed, I'll look forward to seeing you. Take care."

With the afternoon ahead of them, the Mackenzies went about their work with a vengeance. Tracy left for the Alaska National Bank in her own car. She had time yet this afternoon to make some reviews of the computer program functions. Mike began assembling the gear he would need for the trip to the mine. The gear would be left on the garage floor until just before departure time. There were too many thieves in Alaska to trust leaving equipment in an unguarded vehicle, even for a short time in a residential area.

He set out the two large, wooden boxes of field equipment along with food and water. Included were a .44 Magnum pistol and ammunition and a short barrel (so-called sawed off) 12 gauge shotgun and 2 boxes of buckshot ammunition. If the miners had some gold ready for transportation from the mine to town, he had better be ready to haul it. Water jugs were filled them from the kitchen sink. He would cross many streams but the water was hazardous to drink, not because of chemicals but because of a parasite named Giardia lamblia or sometimes "beaver fever," which could cause diarrhea, cramps, vomiting and severe weight loss. When the parasite was ingested by a mammal it would attach to the intestines and commence reproducing billions of additional cysts which, in the case of beavers or muskrats, were excreted with their feces into the water. Mike and Tracy were glad they had their own well with excellent water. Mike believed, however, that their well would one day be contaminated by effluent from the many septic tanks which were being installed in Stuckagain Heights as new houses were built in the area without the benefit of sewer lines.

The next morning Mike and Tracy arrived in two separate vehicles at the Mulberry Road offices of the Alaska Department of Fish and Game 10 minutes before the meeting was to start at 10 o'clock. George Maxwell had called them to advise that their attendance was OK and that he and Cynthia Scott, marine mammal habitat biologist for south central Alaska, including Prince William Sound, would represent the ADF and G. Helen Walker, *Dr.* Helen Walker he stressed, indicating her title preference, would be there from Seattle representing the U. S. Fish & Wildlife Service (USFWS). Alaskans took pride in avoiding titles, it did not matter if a person had a PhD Of greater importance was the person's intelligence and value in accomplishing the task at hand. Over Styrofoam cups of weak coffee, Cynthia and George reviewed for the Mackenzies the king salmon harvest in Cook Inlet for the new season. Cynthia had been sport fishing on the Kenai River 100 miles south of Anchorage over the past weekend and had caught a 71 pound king salmon; not a huge fish by Kenai standards, but not bad.

In response to Tracy's question, Cynthia advised them that Dr. Helen Walker, the lead marine mammal biologist for the USFWS, just happened to be in Anchorage because she was visiting her sister in Eagle River. Otherwise one of the field people would be there. Martha had the reputation, she confided, as a person who did not care for field work and it was difficult to get her out of her Seattle office. Her knowledge about marine mammals was unknown, and she had never taken a position on some of the issues which had arisen over whales.

Dr. Helen Walker arrived 10 minutes late with excuses about poor taxi service from the Captain Cook Hotel. Tracy and Mike noticed she wore no wedding ring and guessed, subconsciously, that she would probably be very difficult to live with. She was a little overweight and wore a gray pin striped skirted business suit, hardly the outfit to wear at a meeting with the ADF&G where blue jeans, plaid shirts and jogging shoes were the usual attire.

After introductions, Maxwell explained that the reason for the Mackenzies attending the meeting was their experience with killer whales in Prince William Sound. Dr. Walker made no response to these remarks but looked suspiciously at the Alaska couple. It was apparent she did not trust anyone who was not a civil servant, and the fact that neither of them was a trained biologist only increased her suspicions.

Cynthia reviewed the past two month's events in Prince William Sound: the theft of fish from skates by the orcas and the Larson "incident" as it was now called. Maxwell added "Dr. Walker, our department frankly does not have the manpower or funding to commence monitoring the orca activities in Prince William Sound. We will have our usual number of enforcement people out there monitoring compliance with the salmon, herring and halibut openings, and our biologists will be busy on escapement studies and the million other tasks which must be done at this time of the year. The bottom line is that we cannot spare people to carry out surveillance of the orcas without some sort of financial assistance."

"Well, Mr. Maxwell, as you know, the Service is charged with the responsibility of overseeing the welfare of all marine mammals in all waters

of the United States. We do not expect or want the Alaska Department of
Fish and Game to get involved with our programs. As you know, our budgets
are also very tight again this year and, as always, our major concern lies with
the protection of the whales. In the cases you have just described, the whales
are perhaps 'misbehaving' but nothing I have heard indicates any real threat
to the lives or health of the whales. Frankly, this situation is going to be way
down on our list of priorities."

Mike could restrain himself no longer. "But Dr. Walker, I believe what
Cynthia and George are telling you is that the residents and fishermen in
Prince William Sound are not going to tolerate the orcas interfering with
their means of earning a livelihood, and they are not going to tolerate
orcas attacking some of their friends such as the Larsons. We're trying to
warn you that the net result of these actions by the whales could be severe
retaliation, and none of us wants that."

Tracy looked directly at Dr. Walker, "What we would like to do,
with the best wishes but no money from the Service, is to intensify and
continue our independent surveillance of the orcas in the Sound. We have
a tremendous amount of information already and we can build further on
our data base." She showed Dr. Walker, Cynthia and George several albums
of whale photos with particular emphasis on good shots of the saddle area
markings which were specific for each whale. The photos were arranged by
whale group.

Dr. Walker became more interested. Here was a proposal which might
bring some positive attention to her department and yet would not cut into
the budget. "What we might be able to do," Mike explained, "is to discover
which whale pod (he knew she would not like "pack") may be responsible for
the fish theft and the Larson incident. If we can do that we may be able to
seek a course of action to alleviate the problem, with the full participation of
the Service, of course."

"And Fish and Game," Tracy added, smiling at George and Cynthia.

"What personnel would participate in the studies?" asked Dr. Walker,
looking at Tracy. If she had to deal with non-biologists at least she could
deal with another woman.

"Mike and myself and Dr. Reed Remington of Hydrosphere Marine
Research Institute in San Diego. We believe a small number of investigators
at this time is the best approach both so the orcas will be less disturbed and
because the confidentiality of the work can be better protected."

"Speaking for the Alaska Department of Fish and Game," Cynthia interjected, "We welcome this proposal from the Mackenzies and Dr. Remington. It seems to be a very cost effective and sensible approach to gathering more information about the orcas. Further, the fishermen will be less likely to take aggressive action against the whales if they are aware someone is out there observing the whales 24 hours a day."

"You must be joking," replied Dr. Walker, accustomed to the relatively easy work schedule in the Seattle office. "Nobody watches whales 24 hours a day. You mean the researchers are in the area 24 hours a day."

"No, we mean watching the whales 24 hours a day. If you don't stay with them every minute you are going to lose them," said Tracy, a little impatient that this so called expert seemed to know so little about field procedures.

"All right, all right," Dr. Walker stated emphatically. "We'll go along with this for the time being, but we'll expect prompt and thorough reports on progress. And never mind our local representative, communicate directly with me."

Tracy and Mike believed they had accomplished their objective of securing cooperation of both the state and the federal organizations, absolute necessities if they were to carry their studies forward. As they walked across the parking lot, Tracy said "I'll call Reed from the bank and advise him of this favorable development, and he may have his schedule arranged by now."

"Good idea. I'm going to leave for the mine immediately but I'll call you from there so you'll know I arrived. I'll be back as soon as I can; try to get that computer program lined out so we can leave for Whittier in a couple of days."

◆◆◆

CHAPTER EIGHT

Placer Gold

Stopping at their garage, Mike quickly loaded the stacked gear into the Suburban, placing the .44 Magnum pistol, the shotgun and the ammunition in the front seat. As he drove north from Anchorage his mind turned to the gold business. Four years earlier he had read about and then confirmed the existence of significant amounts of gold along the east shore of Cook Inlet south of Anchorage on the Kenai Peninsula. Unknown to most residents of the Peninsula was the fact that some pretty good placer gold values could be panned from sand and gravel along the east shore of Cook Inlet near the villages of Ninilchik and Clam Gulch. At one time Mike thought there could be substantial gold deposits on the sea floor just offshore but, through a public relations firm, Governor Springfield had demanded an under-the-counter cash payment of $250,000 before he would approve the needed permits. Mike would not pay and the project died for lack of permits.

Another hour's driving and Mount Denali came into view, rising magnificently above the clouds at its base. Two more hours, several more tapes and snacks from the grocery sack and Mike was at Cantwell, a town of about 300 people located where he could fill the Suburban with fuel before heading east toward the mine on a gravel road.

Where the highway crossed Beaver Creek 4 miles east of Cantwell, an area had been cleared for the mining of gravel for use on the road. There were fewer mosquitoes there, and Mike was glad to get out of the truck for a stretch. A couple of individuals were sleeping there in thin bags near their vehicle. They should be cautious, he thought. Whenever Mike and Tracy stopped along a road to sleep, they always tried to park at a location away from the main road. He kept the .44 Magnum in its holster, under his head between the bag and the pad. The most dangerous animals in Alaska were not the bears, more dangerous by far was Homo sapiens and there were too many of them around.

After a two hour drive Mike could look east 8 or 10 miles across the broad Susitna River Valley, where the mining camp buildings were visible along with the piles of gravel near the mining operations. The mine was located on Valdez (pronounced Valdeez) Creek, which flowed into the Susitna River from the east. Placer gold had been discovered on this creek in 1903 by prospectors who had made their way inland on foot from the small Port of Valdez on Prince William Sound. A rush of prospectors and miners followed, and for the next 40 years placer gold was mined from streams and benches in the area.

The original prospectors had discovered that much of the gold mined in the early days on Valdez Creek was being derived from an older river channel, which they found exposed in the steep gravel banks 30 feet above the level of the current Valdez Creek. They followed this ancient channel underground via an adit 25 feet wide and 7 feet high, and became extremely wealthy by standards of the times. It was tough work to dig the gravel underground and move it laterally to the surface in primitive carts to be washed through a slice box. The box was a long wooden u-shaped structure about 30 feet long, 3 feet wide and 2 feet deep with wooden lathes across the bottom. Gold bearing gravels were dumped into the upper part of the slanted box and large volumes or water, usually from a diverted stream were run through the box. Lighter sand and gravel were washed away while the heavier gold particles settled to the bottom of the box near the lathes. It had been discovered a couple of hundred years earlier in other parts of the world that sheep skin, with the wool attached, was great for catching the small gold particles as they passed by, hence the term golden fleece.

It was reported that the early Valdez Creek miners recovered as much as 1,500 ounces of gold during one season, which was worth $30,000 in 1907. Big money in those days and the price of gold was only $20 per ounce.

The ancient stream course, named the Tammany Channel, was followed by the workings for about one mile underground before the property was sold to another company, which began a hydraulic mining operation using high pressure water from hoses to wash light minerals away from the heavy gold particles. This operation was closed in 1942 under presidential order due to World War II.

When Mike had first examined the area 7 years previously, he reached the conclusion that good potential existed for additional undiscovered placer gold deposits quite deep below the current stream channel. He hired a crew to stake 40 mining claims extending eastward up the Valdez Creek valley for 2½ miles. A couple of years later he had been able to interest a Canadian mining company in the potential for the discovery of additional high grade placer gold on the 40 claims he had staked, and a deal had been made.

The Canadians agreed to pay $100,000 in cash for an option to lease the claims, and, in addition, would spend not less than $450,000 over a three year period to explore the claims. Mike retained an in-kind royalty of 3% and the option to "back in" for a working interest of 10%. The in-kind royalty meant that he would receive 3% of the placer gold produced from the properties, in all size fractions, without any financial contributions on his part. Exercise of the working interest would require him to provide 10% of the funds for the exploration and mining within a certain time window if he wished to participate in that fashion. Any gold received from the royalty interest was taxable at its fair market value when he received it, but any gold he might receive from the working interest was not taxable until he sold the gold.

Fortunately, geological consultants representing the Canadian company did a good job of exploration and had found three ancient gold-bearing river channels which had not been discovered by the old timers due to their depth. Mining operations had gotten underway in the third season after the deal was made. Last year the mine had produced 40,000 ounces of raw placer gold, and the 3% royalty brought him 1,200 ounces worth more than $500,000 even at the current $450 gold price. Some of the nuggets were as big as golf balls. Numerous assays of the gold produced showed it had an actual gold content of 86% along with 14% silver, which is about average for central Alaska placer gold.

Part of this gold he had sold for the market price of $450/ounce of contained gold with minor payments for the silver content. Some of the nicely-shaped fractions had been sold for jewelry overlay at a premium for $475/ounce. It was funds from the sale of gold which allowed Mike and Tracy the luxury of participating in, and helping to carry on, the killer whale studies in Prince William Sound. Gold that was not sold was stashed in a safe set in the concrete floor of the cabin basement in Stuckagain Heights.

After discussing the matter with Tracy, he had decided to simply retain the royalty interest and did not exercise his right to hold, and pay for, a working interest.

As Mike approached the one lane bridge over the Susitna River, the piles of gravel at the mine and large shop on Valdez Creek came into sharper view 3 miles to the northeast. A small herd of 12 caribou trotted across the gravel road just ahead of his truck, causing him to slow down as he topped a hill. They're tame now, he thought, but this fall when the season opens they'll run when you get within a mile of them.

The weather was good and he hoped the operations at the mine were going well with no serious mechanical breakdowns which would delay production. he EPA (Environmental Protection Administration) had been threatening to shut the operation down because of muddy water discharges into the Susitna River. The river, which originated in active glaciers in the Alaska Range just 10 to 20 miles to the north, was already choked with sediment and glacial flour as evidenced by the strongly braided channel. Any sand or silt contribution the mine might make to this river would be small and completely undetectable compared to the vast amount of active material constantly moving down the river bed. As Shorty, one of the old timers in the area often pointed out, the moose didn't have to swim the Susitna, they walked across. No salmon existed for 50 miles downstream due to the existence of falls they could not ascend. Yet the EPA was insisting that any water used to wash the gold from the gravel at the mine must be returned to drinking water clarity before it could be discharged into the muddy Susitna. It was one of those environmental situations where clear water regulations made no sense.

Two bull moose, their juvenile but quickly growing antlers covered with a fuzzy brown velvet, were busy gorging themselves on roadside willow sprouts as Mike drove across the single lane bridge spanning the river. They paid no attention whatsoever to the noise of the vehicle. Big game animals, he knew, were very tolerant of the presence and activities of man so long as they were not harassed. The caribou on Alaska's North Slope were a good example, and, contrary to dire predictions of many well-meaning but ill-informed people, the herds were found to freely cross over and under the great oil pipeline. Further, the size of the herds had increased as a result of being in close proximity to the oil production facilities where they were not harassed. Mosquitoes remained a problem for the animals, but not man or man's structures so long as man did not disturb them. Experience had shown that caribou near the North Slope oil production facilities often stayed near the buildings and producing oil wells for protection from the elements as well as from their natural predators, the wolves.

A half mile after crossing the bridge, Mike turned north off the main gravel road onto the graded trail which led to the mining operations. It was necessary to ford Windy Creek, where recent rains had raised the water depth to 3 feet and it was running very swiftly. He steered the Suburban slightly upstream, knowing the vehicle would be washed downstream 50 or 60 feet before reaching the other side.

Approaching the mine, dubbed the Tammany Mining Company for the previously- mined channel, Mike could see plumes of black diesel smoke rising from the heavy equipment working in the open pit mine. It looked pretty much like any gravel operation in the lower 48, with the usual backhoes and shovels to dig the material and trucks to haul it to the wash plant. But there was one major difference, at this plant the gravel was not to be sold, it was to be tumbled and washed to free the heavy yellow metal which occurred scattered as grains, flat particles and nuggets in the gravel. One of the key pieces of equipment needed at this operation was a large, steel, tilted sluice box divided into 4 separate channels, the bottoms of which were covered with a carpet of green plastic turf of the type developed for use on football fields. The heavy gold particles, along with magnetite and some other heavy minerals, settled out into the turf as the gravel bearing waters rushed through the box.

During operations, water to an individual channel in the sluice box was shut off at least once per day and the green turf from that channel was removed and turned over in a large water trough. Agitation would shake the gold and other heavy minerals loose from the turf and it would fall to the bottom of the trough for later recovery. The resulting concentrate was washed into buckets which were taken to the well-secured "*gold room*" where a vibrating table separated the gold from the unwanted heavy minerals, such as magnetite. The gold was also screened and sized in the gold room, with the large nuggets set aside in plastic baby bottles because they would not break if dropped.

In the earliest days of placer gold mining in Europe and Asia, sheep's wool on the original pelts was used to catch the gold in wooden sluice boxes, hence the term "golden fleece." Because fine gold, with its sharp hooks and angularities, was difficult to remove from wool, after a time the pelt was burned and the ashes were panned. Mike suspected that wool remained a superior overall material as compared to artificial turf for recovery of fine gold. Or even indoor/outdoor carpeting with its tight, wiry mesh, he suspected, was superior to the plastic turf for fine gold but tough for recovery.

A small cemetery had been established in the early 1900's on a hillside overlooking the creek, and all subsequent miners and prospectors were careful not to disturb the area. The weather beaten remains of wooden headstones and remnants of some of the original small cabins were still to be seen here and there.

It was nearly 8:30 am as Mike drove up the hill toward the mine buildings, with the first stop always the guard stationed in a small mobile home overlooking the operations, especially the sluice box and the gold room. During mining operations guards were on duty 24 hours a day to keep thieves and well-meaning prospectors alike away from the mining and gold recovery facilities. The guards knew Mike as the claim owner and waved him by as he approached their strategically located observation post. He parked in front of a 10' X 40' mobile home which served as the company offices. Next to it was a long, single story building, made of eight mobile homes fastened together and with a common roof. This large composite unit served as the bunkhouse for the crew and, on the south end, the kitchen and dining room. About 100 feet from the mine office, and in full view of the mine manager's office, was the gold room, a 15' X 20' metal building to which all the concentrate recovered from the sluice box was taken for final separation of the gold. Only highly trusted employees and company officials were allowed into the gold room. An attractive, single one ounce nugget, which would easily fit into a pocket, could be worth more than $1,500 when made into a necklace.

As with diamonds in Africa, employees in trusted positions of gold handling were known to swallow nuggets, hoping to recover them in the next couple of days after defecating in private in the brush near camp. Such activities were closely monitored by the professional staff and the guards of Tammany Mining. African diamond mines, they knew, had found it necessary to retain employees for two days before releasing them from the fenced compound for time off because diamonds were being swallowed in the mine with the hope of recovering them later from defecation outside the compound. Still, there was no question that a dishonest employee at Tammany could get away with some gold in spite of the best monitoring. Just an ounce of gold dust per day was 20 or

so ounces per month, worth more than $8,000, not bad for clever on-the-job pickings. Mike was aware that rumors in Anchorage held that every time there was a good gold cleanup at the Tammany Mine, a bunch of nuggets showed up for sale in the city. Some of that gold rightfully belonged to himself and Tracy.

Mike entered the Tammany Mining Company offices, and was greeted by Ginger, the secretary, handling the morning shift. With warm weather and 24 hour daylight, mining was carried out round the clock. Ginger's husband was one of the dozer operators, and they enjoyed spending summers at the mine. The pay was good, and during the winter they were able to spend 4 months in Hawaii because of the generous $1,000 per month unemployment benefits paid to each of them by the State of Alaska. It was a deal that was hard to beat.

"Hi, Ginger," Mike smiled. "How's it going?"

"Hi, Mike," she replied. "That's a fresh pot of coffee over there. Tom has been expecting you, why don't you go on in. He's frustrated over trying to talk to Toronto, but don't let that bother you. By the way, Tracy called a couple of hours ago and would like for you to call her."

Mike knew Tracy wouldn't call unless something had come up. He decided to return her call immediately. "Is there a phone I can use?"

"Sure use the one in Bill's office. He's out at the mine this morning."

Mike entered the office door with the label Bill Morrison, Geologist. In Anchorage Tracy picked up the phone as soon as it rang. Her voice was urgent. "Reed called this morning and I filled him in on the meeting with Fish and Game and Helen Walker. He's flying into Anchorage tomorrow night. He's convinced we should move quickly before things get out of hand. He talked to Hydrosphere management and they will provide some financial support but it won't be a blank check."

"Good," Mike replied. "Unless some problem develops out here I may even make it back tonight. If not, will you be able to pick Reed up at the airport? Good, and please fill him in on the details of what has been happening in the Sound."

"Can do, sweetheart," Tracy responded. "I also have the orca photos ready for review, and I'll get supplies together on the assumption we'll be going to Whittier and to the Sound as soon as you return."

"Fantastic, way to go. What would I do without you?" Mike was more serious than joking.

"You'd probably get by, but not very well," she laughed, "Well, be careful out there and let me know when you'll return."

Mike's mind churned for a moment with thoughts of the whale situation at Prince William Sound. But he knew the best course of action was to take care of everything at the mine while he was here so no loose ends remained to interfere with the upcoming time needed at PWS.

He went across the hall to the office door labelled Tom Powers, Mine Superintendent. Tom, still on the phone, smiled when he entered and motioned him to sit down. As Mike did so, he thought how this mining camp, though relatively new, was one of the best he had been to: Airstrip, good communications, dependable electrical power from their own generator, satellite TV, good housing and dining in large trailers.

Tom smiled at him. "Mike, what I want you to do is to stop fooling around with those damned whales in Prince William Sound and find another mine like this one. I'll never understand what a talented explorationist like you is doing studying whales anyway. They're not going to lead you to an ore body unless you're going to try another offshore program." He laughed.

Mike smiled. "Hey, you guys don't know it, but I'm secretly training orcas to find oil and gas offshore. Our new company will be called Orca Oil. Interested in buying a few shares?"

"I'd forget the orcas if I were you. The TV news last night said some of the killer whales in Prince William Sound may becoming aggressive toward people. Any truth to that?"

"At this time we just don't have enough information. I'll be going back to the Sound in a few days to have a first-hand look, but right now we're only guessing at what's going on."

"Well, now that you're here let's talk about mining. We have some good news. The `A' channel has proven to be about twice as good as we thought it was from the drilling. We're no doubt in a rich pocket right now, and we've averaged almost 750 ounces of gold per 24 hours of operation for the last seven days. Sure hope this lasts for a while."

Mike was elated. "You and me both." The claims he had staked were proving to be one of the best placer gold mines in the past 50 years in the

State of Alaska. Some of the drill holes had encountered so much gold that the geologists on the drilling rig reported that the drill cuttings became loaded with placer gold flakes and grains when they hit the high grade part of the gold bearing channel. Still, there was always some question about the reserves present and the grade of the ore until mining had been completed. It was the same story at many mining operations: one doesn't really know what the ore grade and quantities of ore are until after the mining is complete.

"Sounds fantastic for the grade," Mike smiled. "Maybe you'll make that 80,000 ounce goal for this year! Now if the price of gold would go up beyond the current $450 per ounce we'll be lookin' good! Would you believe there are people talking about $1,000 gold?"

Tom shook his head like a bull, "We're gonna try like hell. Come on out to the gold room and I'll show you what we're getting." He pointed to a brushy hillside 50 yards to the north on the other side of a road used by some of the heavy equipment. "There's that cow moose and her twin calves. They've been hanging around here for several weeks. The cow recognizes that she's safe from wolves and bears as long as she stays near the mine and camp with her new calves. When things are quiet they sometimes wander right in around the buildings. Cute, aren't they?"

Mike paused to smile at the two light brown gangly calves playing in the brush around their mother as she slowly browsed her way along the hillside only 50 yards from where they were standing near the gold room.

Knowing Mike's interest in wildlife, Tom added: "A grizzly showed up 1/2 mile west of here near the airstrip two nights ago, and it killed the calf of that cow moose which usually hangs out down there. The cow must have gone after the grizzly because we found her almost dead with a big gash in her left flank. We had to shoot her and then called Fish and Game to report it. The grizzly had eaten most of the calf. We never did see the bear but everyone in camp is on the alert in case he comes around the mine or camp."

Mike nodded. "Grizzlies kill quite a few calf moose each year. Just part of the scheme of things."

As they approached the locked gold room door, Tom took a set of keys from his jacket pocket and pushed the button on the intercom.

"Mary, this is Tom. I'm coming in with Mike." Then he turned two heavy deadbolt locks with separate keys, swung the heavy door open and they entered. The door was relocked behind them.

Inside three people were busy processing the "cleanup", which consisted of the heavy minerals recovered from the sluice box in the last 24 hours. Perhaps 1/2 of the material being handled was the so called black sand consisting mostly of the mineral magnetite. Shaking tables, spiral wheels, simple hand panning and magnets were being used to separate the gold from all the other minerals in the black sand. It was obvious all three workers, two of them women, had their hands full in processing the material. In the rush of the season they were working solid 12 hour days but were making good money.

Mary, the tough, slim and affable gold room supervisor, smiled when she saw Mike and lifted off the floor a white plastic 6-gallon bucket which was about one third full of placer gold.

"Not bad, ay?" she shouted over the noise of the equipment.

Mike signaled an "O" with his right hand, indicating "great." He had helped Mary get the job when the operation had first started. She was rugged, dependable and completely honest; a good person to watch over the handling of large quantities of placer gold each season. Mary lived the year around in a small cabin one mile from the mine with her 14 sled dogs. She was a frequent winner of sled dog races in the winter and was considering running the 1100 mile Iditarod race from Anchorage to Nome. Mary had remarked that the previous multiple winner, Susan Butcher, needed a good female challenger.

Large nuggets, marble size or 1/2 inch or more in diameter, which showed up in the buckets of concentrate brought to the gold room, were handpicked and kept in a gold pan separated from the rest of the gold. Mike looked in the pan and saw that one unusually large flat nugget was in the pan. The only way it could have gotten through the screens would be for it to be turned on end. Mike had often remarked that the operation was probably losing some good-sized nuggets because the screens would not allow any particles larger than 1/2" to drop through for transfer to the sluice box. "Tom," he had argued, "we've got to put in a nugget trap. You know very well we're probably losing fist-size nuggets with the setup you have now."

Tom's response was always the same, "We don't *know* we're losing big nuggets and, besides, the objective of this operation is not to look for large gold nuggets but to process substantial volumes of gravel to recover the maximum amount of gold at the least possible cost. We don't want to screw up our gravel handling procedure for a few hypothetical nuggets." As a royalty interest owner Mike could only make suggestions, he could not force any changes.

The sight of the abundant raw gold in Mary's bucket caused both Mike and Tom to smile. It was easy to see why men over the centuries had risked their lives, and even killed, to gain possession of the precious metal.

As Tom relocked the gold room door behind them he turned to Mike. "Looks good, doesn't it? What you saw there was about 500 troy ounces representing 12 hours recovery from the sluice box. I believe the `A' channel, where we are presently mining, is quite a bit richer than the old Tammany channel. Hope the grade holds for the rest of the channel we're planning to mine this season."

"That would be great," answered Mike, as they started toward Tom's pickup. "But, as I recall, results from the next line of drill holes 200 feet upstream did not look all that good."

"True, but we find we're recovering 50% more in mining than we had estimated from the drilling results. There's more gold there than we thought there was. But we'll see in the next two months or so." He paused. "I'm assuming you'd like to see the wash plant or the mine."

"You bet! Let's see how they're doing today."

They climbed into Tom's pickup and drove the short distance to the plant where the gravel from the mine was dumped in a pile from trucks before being fed into the plant by a large front end loader. A wash plant to recover gold is really a sizing plant using trommels, vibrating screens and copious amounts of high pressure wash water. In the process, washed rock fragments larger than a certain size are rejected and only the smaller material size, containing most of the gold, is run through the sluice box. Mike was convinced large gold nuggets were being discarded from the wash plant with the larger gravel fraction, but how to prove it? He had to conclude the Tammany Mining Company processing equipment and procedures were not the best, but they were passable and he and Tracy were making money.

The concept of washing heavy minerals from gravel was simple, Mike thought, but it was amazing how many amateur and even professional miners failed to include the sizing/separation system on their operations.

Making their way along the muddy, noisy gangway leading from the banging, rattling wash plant to the sluice box, Mike posed a question. "Done anything yet to try to catch the flour gold?" In addition to large nugget loss, he believed the very fine gold was washing right through the sluice box without being allowed to settle out.

Tom shrugged as they reached the sluice box. "We still believe we are getting almost 100% recovery of the gold in the original gravel, and our tests of the 'heads' above the sluice box and the 'tails' below it confirm that."

Mike saw that all four channels of the steel sluice box, 20 feet in length, running 3/4 full of fast moving, sediment loaded water, were in use. There was no way, Mike remained convinced, for tiny or thin, flat gold particles to settle out of that turbid, fast-moving medium. Tests of other placer gold operations in Alaska by engineers with the University of Alaska at Fairbanks had demonstrated that many sluice boxes lose 25 to 50% of the small particle gold contained in gravels processed through the box. There was no reason to think the Tammany operation was any different.

"There's one thing you shouldn't forget, Tom," Mike advised his friend, "this operation recovered 40,000 raw ounces last year. If you're losing 25% of the gold contained in the original gravel, you missed 10,000 ounces of gold which went right on through this box last year alone. That's a lot of gold and value, even at $450 an ounce."

"But I've told you before, Mike, we don't have any fine gold in our deposits," Tom argued.

Mike shook his head. "Right, and it doesn't get cold at Valdez Creek in the wintertime and snowballs don't melt in Hell. There is no good geologic reason why these placer deposits are different from hundreds of others in Alaska. There *is* fine gold here."

"But the deposits *are* different," Tom countered. "These are probably some the higher grade deposits mined in Alaska the past 50 years. That alone tells you there's something different about them."

Mike was unswerved. Gold was being lost, 3% of which belonged to he and Tracy. The test results showing no fine gold in the gravel had to be erroneous, it only made common sense that flour gold was present. But he would not have the time this trip to debate the point. During the coming winter he planned to prepare drawings of a different, but proven, system using shaking tables called jigs which would capture the fine gold and hopefully increase the system recovery by 15 to 25%.

They climbed back into the mud-covered four-wheel drive truck and Tom drove the 1/4 mile of muddy, rutted road, heavily used by the ore trucks, into the mine itself. Gravel from the "A" paleochannel, unknown to the early miners because it was hidden 40 to more than 60 feet below the surface, was being loaded into dump trucks for hauling to the wash plant.

When geologist Bill Morrison saw them drive into the mine, swerving out of the way of the large trucks, he came over smiling and shook hands with Mike. "Hi, Mike, how ya doin?"

"Fine, fine, but how's the *mine* doing?"

"Well, besides good gold in the `A' channel, we found something interesting in the overburden this morning. Come on over and look in the back of my pickup."

Even before they reached the pickup, Mike could see what they had found. A huge tusk, almost 7 feet long, curved and stained a hauntingly beautiful light to dark brown from centuries of burial in the frozen peat, protruded from the bed of the pickup. It was a massive, fossil ivory tusk from a mastodon. Mike and Tom both placed their hands on the tusk in silence; it was a sort of direct communications link with the past, to be respected and honored.

All such findings were reported to the University of Alaska in Fairbanks, and this tusk, along with photographs and a description of its location, would be delivered to the university. Work in that particular spot in the mine would be discontinued until representatives of the university could come out the next day to examine the site for other remains. Morrison had checked the area out already, however, and had concluded the tusk was all they would find.

"That's a beauty of a tusk," Mike nodded. "I'm sure you've contacted Paul Nichols at the U of A."

"You bet, they'll be out tomorrow."

"Keep up the good work," Mike encouraged, pleased with another example of good cooperation between industry people and those in academia.

Mike loved field work involved with exploration and mining, and he would have greatly enjoyed staying at the mine to examine the site in conjunction with the palaeontologists and archaeologists, but concern for the killer whales was again returning to uppermost importance in his mind. He must return to Anchorage.

It was now nearly noon and the weather had taken a turn for the worse. Strong gusty winds began driving rain squalls in from the west with clouds skimming the ground surface. The temperature was dropping quickly. "Tom, wonder if they have an extra lunch at camp?" Mike asked. "A bite to eat would hit the spot right now."

"We always have plenty of food. Remember, we're running three shifts at the mine and that means three shifts in the kitchen. They'll have something for us. And here's another thing to consider: We have been mining in some good ground and we have about a week's gold production on hand. The safe contains about 3,000 troy ounces, worth a bundle even at today's gold prices. That's more than we like to keep on hand at the mine at one time. The plane was supposed to come in from Anchorage this evening with the two security guards to ferry the gold back to town, but this weather has rendered that flight impossible. They just can't come in with this low ceiling."

Tom stopped the truck at the mine office. "What do you say to you and me making the run to Anchorage in your rig with the gold this afternoon?" He paused, then added: "In a way it may be a good idea… anyone who might attempt a gold heist will be watching for a pattern. If we always send the gold out by small chartered plane, someone will figure out a way to intercept it somewhere along the way, or they'll try some other scheme and may kill someone in the effort."

Mike recognized the wisdom of the comments and responded without hesitation. "I'll be ready anytime you are!"

After a quick lunch Tom said: "I'll have Mary get the gold ready from the safe. Don't mention that the gold is being moved. I'll restrict outgoing phone calls from the camp. Radio telephone calls can be easily intercepted and there's no need to let the world know we're heading out. Your Suburban is not full of fuel, so drive it over to the pump at the maintenance shop and fill it up. Then I'll meet you at the gold room."

"Will do," Mike responded, leaving the room immediately, taking two snack bags from the kitchen with him. Mike had planned to call Tracy, but, under the circumstances, it would be best to make no calls. He wondered to himself how many people at the mine knew of their planned run to town with a substantial amount of raw placer gold. After a fuel stop he drove to the gold room, put the .44 Magnum and the shotgun on the front seat, backed to the door of the gold room and opened the tailgate.

A security guard with a name tag reading simply "Bummer," sawed-off shotgun in hand, stood in a small lean-to near the door to the gold room and out of the rain. He looked suspiciously at Mike but said nothing.

Tom was ready and the heavy door to the gold room swung open. Mary and one of her helpers carried the buckets of placer gold to the door, almost 3,000 troy ounces of it in five sealed 6-gallon metal containers with metal locking lids. Tom and Mike lifted the buckets into the Suburban. Mike noticed one was considerably lighter than the others and it was marked "Mackenzie."

"Tom," Bummer finally spoke, "I want to go on record right here and now opposing the transport of gold by someone who is not a guard, is not bonded and is not even an employee. Seems like damn foolishness." Bummer was a die-hard union man and seldom missed a chance to promote union help.

"Back off, Bummer, it's OK," Tom told him curtly as the last bucket was swung into the truck.

Mike closed and locked the tail gate. Tom got in toting a short 12 gauge shotgun and a .38 Special in a holster at his waist.

On the trip to Anchorage the two of them talked hunting, fishing, prospecting and even killer whale speculation and observations. Seven long hours later they arrived in Anchorage as the late afternoon sun, seemingly resting on Mount Susitna west of Anchorage, projected red and orange shafts through the dark gray clouds. Certain that no one was following them, they drove straight to the mining company offices to unload all the gold buckets but one. The other bucket, containing about 180 troy ounces, the royalty for two months, was the 3% cut for Mike and Tracy. Mike took the bucket to the cabin home in Stuckagain Heights.

Within two days a shipment of nearly 3,000 troy ounces, worth more than one million dollars, would be sent by commercial airlines from Tammany Mining Company in Anchorage to Seattle to Toronto. There it would be delivered to the Royal Canadian Mint for processing, purifying and making pure gold Canadian Maple Leaf coins, the purest gold coins on Earth.

◆◆◆

CHAPTER NINE

Reed arrives

T racy, having completed her work with the bank computers, had been busily assembling information on the PWS killer whale packs, particularly the A-T pack, as she awaited Mike's call or return. They always took time to look at and handle the gold that was theirs before putting it in the safe or selling it. Upon Mike's arrival they opened the container containing this new shipment. About 50 troy ounces of this gold was nugget size, some as large as a golf ball, which they put in their safe. Mike would telephone the receiving offices of Englehard Precious Metals in Anchorage the next morning to tell them he would like to make a gold delivery.

Tracy reminded him that he must call Carl Baker, operator of a charter air service at Lake Spenard in Anchorage. The quickest way to find killer whales in the Sound was from the air and Carl had assisted them the past two summers when they needed surveillance or searches carried out. With his float-equipped Cessna 182, Carl could search for more than two hours and cover hundreds of miles in the Sound, an impossibility from a boat on the surface. Using GPS locations Carl could radio the location of whales to them without any other party knowing what it was all about. They had decided to use the code name "sniper" for the whales.

Mike got Carl on the phone and made arrangements for a whale search to take place two days later. Carl agreed to set the time aside and fly over to the Sound when needed. Summers were good to Carl because of the steady chartering of his three planes at $350 per hour. The two pilots he had hired as assistants had worked out well and had been there for three years. Mike and Tracy had been good clients and he would help them out when he could.

The next morning at 9, Mike was at the gold receiving office and was given a receipt from the buyer for 253.46 troy ounces of placer gold. Final settlement would be mailed to them from California after deduction of processing and refining costs and a determination of the London gold fixing on the day of the delivery.

His next stop, with Anchorage traffic painfully heavy and slow due to construction, was the Arctic Bait Shop, which stocked salmon eggs for sport fishermen along with frozen herring and octopus for halibut fishing by both commercial and sport fishermen. He was surprised to find a fresh frozen 30 pound octopus from Prince Rupert, British Columbia, stamped "Food Quality" by Canadian food inspectors known to be very particular. Octopus was favored as a bait by the commercial fishermen because large halibut apparently considered it delicious and, just as important, it stayed on the hooks well. This octopus (tako in Japanese) would bring at least $40.00 per pound in Japan and here it was offered at $3.00 per pound for bait. "I'll take 10 pounds," Mike smiled at Dick Carroll who owned the bait shop. "I'm going to keep it frozen; if we don't catch any fish we'll eat the octopus!"

"Knowing you, you're not kidding, either!" Dick responded. "I really think someone made a mistake shipping this one to us for bait. It's good-looking stuff," as he deftly sliced 1/3 of the curled up tentacles away from the rest of the octopus. It was weighed and placed it in a large plastic bag surrounded by shredded ice in a box.

Mike returned again to Stuckagain Heights where he joined Tracy in assembling food and equipment for the approaching trip to Whittier and the Sound. They both made extensive use of lists of necessities for their excursions and Tracy had several master lists stored on computer disks for recall whenever a trip was being planned. Because of the lists, they seldom found themselves forgetting important items. Tracy had done the grocery and wine shopping the previous evening.

For this trip they concentrated on healthy food needed for a period of up to three weeks for three people. Fortunately, all three of them were very diet conscious so most of the food was low in cholesterol and animal fat and high in fiber. Beverages included two cases of good red wine, mostly cabernet sauvignon, and two cases of high quality dry white wine, mostly pinot grigio. A couple of bottles of Balvenie Double Wood Scotch were added along with two bottles of Crown Royal Black whisky.

Cameras and recording equipment were vital and must be capable of taking shots during rain, overcast or other dim light conditions. Tracy had packed their camcorder, along with a couple of new rechargeable batteries. Reed had advised them that he was bringing two of the new camcorders which were smaller, lighter, had better optics and overall made older units obsolete. On this trip they planned to use hydrophones which would imprint the subsurface sound track, and subsurface if they wished, on the same recording as images of the killer whales. Reed had advised them that he was bringing along a sensing device which would help them determine from which direction underwater sounds, such as killer whale calls, were originating. By 6:30 pm most of the supplies were in good order and stacked on the garage floor ready for morning loading.

At Anchorage International Airport, Reed was one of the first ones off the flight and hugged them both. He was glad to be back in Alaska and away from crowded southern California. Small talk was exchanged as they waited for the luggage. Tracy, looking over the shoulder of another waiting passenger who was reading the *Anchorage Times*, saw a page five small heading *"KILLER WHALE FOUND DEAD NEAR CORDOVA."* As Mike and Reed visited she immediately went to a newspaper dispenser, inserted two quarters and took out a paper. Turning quickly to the article, she read that the bloated body of a female adult killer whale had washed up on shore near Cordova on the east side of Prince William Sound. A biologist for the Alaska Department of Fish and Game, who happened to be in the area, was quoted as saying that a number of bullet holes in the dorsal fin and the body clearly suggested that the whale was the victim of someone shooting a high powered rifle or rifles at the animal. She took the paper over to Mike and Reed and, as they read the article, shook their heads.

"Maybe it's already started," she remarked as they finished reading. "I wonder how many more might have been killed which have not been found?"

"Remind me in the morning," Mike requested, "to call Cynthia Scott at Moose and Goose to get photographs of the saddle area of that whale. We can probably tell which one it is."

"Good idea," responded Reed, "but I hope this is not a sign of things to come."

The luggage came creaking out on the moving belt and Reed picked off the 6 bags and boxes he had checked as luggage when leaving San Diego. "I knew we did the right thing when we brought the truck," Mike smiled. "What did you bring, half of the lab?"

"Lots of goodies," was the only response he could get from Reed.

"No doubt about it now, we're going to have to pull the trailer to Whittier," Mike observed. "No way can we get all of your gear and ours into the Suburban."

With the cargo loaded in the Suburban, they drove into the city and stopped at one of their favorite restaurants, the "Tempura Kitchen," one of the many Japanese restaurants in Anchorage. This one had a small but well-designed sushi bar constructed to allow full view of two sushi chefs and their clever work. The trio found three seats together at the bar and ordered Kirin beer along with raw fish favorites such as maguro (tuna), tako (octopus) and succulent hamachi (yellow tail).

"We'll have plenty of tako on board the ," Mike remarked as the smiling sushi chef passed two more hamachi sushi across the counter. "Maybe we can talk Tracy into becoming our own sushi chef out there in the Sound."

"Trouble is," Reed mused, "there aren't that many fish in the Sound which are safe to eat raw. The halibut are loaded with those small white muscle worms and even the salmon should be frozen to kill parasites before raw consumption. Herring would best be cooked or at least pickled in vinegar and salt. The tako may be the best choice if it's a good one."

"Let's just cook our fish out there," Tracy concluded.

An hour later they were at Stuckagain Heights reviewing the accumulated killer whale data and photographs. Mike opened a bottle of 12 year old Armagnac, the lesser-known French competitor of Cognac, and poured snifters 1/8 full of the fragrant liquor, which Tracy heated briefly in the microwave oven.

Planning for the next few days and strategies on how best to study the orcas were discussed until just past midnight and then they turned in.

CHAPTER TEN

Finding The Pack

Arising early in the morning, Tracy prepared a hearty pan full of old fashioned oat meal with added wheat bran, cooked in just a few minutes so the flaky texture would not turn into sticky glue. By the time she served it, along with toast and coffee, both Mike and Reed were at the table eager to start the day's activities. Later, as Tracy washed the dishes and took care of last minute packing, both the Suburban and the attached trailer were loaded with the equipment and food. A tarp was tied securely over the trailer to keep the contents dry until they reached Whittier.

The one hour drive to Portage landing went by quickly and they were in good spirits as they drove, along with 17 or 18 other vehicles, onto the eastbound flat cars to Whittier. Once again they enjoyed coffee and doughnuts in the Suburban as they passed through the rugged terrain via the tunnels. Plans were discussed and a tentative schedule made. They would try to gather specific data on the A-T pack to determine if there was anything that would indicate why that particular group would act differently. How aggressive were the pack members? Why would they steal fish if other food was available?

"You know," Reed told them, sounding a bit like a college professor, "we've got a lot to learn about animal behavior. Remember Jane Goodall's work with chimpanzees? This was a species which many mammalogists thought was well understood, yet she found unexpected and erratic behavior with the discovery of murder and even cannibalism among those mammals, a species long believed to live together amiably."

In the total darkness of a tunnel he continued. "For 200 years we have known there are rogue elephants, rogue tigers, lions. Sometimes these animals began preying on man for no well understood reason. Sometimes the predation seems to be related to old age and poor teeth, which make the usual prey difficult to catch and kill, but, in other cases, man seems to be a preferred quarry and the animals actually acquire a taste for human flesh. "Not a very pleasant thought is it: killer whales, the largest, and undoubtedly the second-most intelligent predator on the face of the Earth, acquiring a taste for the flesh of man?"

Tracy responded first. "Let's hope that's not the case in Prince William Sound. We seem to have enough evidence to involve the A-T pack in several incidents... and they had acted very strangely in those cases, but obviously we need more data."

"Of course," Reed replied. "I'm just tossing out some thoughts for consideration. We have much to learn." Tracy poured more coffee just before the train entered another tunnel.

"Well, all this points out the urgency in finding the A-T pack," Mike stated in the diesel smoke-filled darkness. "We need to find that pack and follow it so questions can be answered: is the pack composed of approximately the same animals as when last observed? Does the group seem healthy and well fed? Is there any outward evidence of erratic behavior? What constitutes the major food source, and does the food source correspond to the food of other whale groups in the Sound? Does the group behave differently around vessels in which there are people?"

"I'm afraid it's an impossible task in the time available," Reed shook his head negatively.

"We'll have to do the best we can," Tracy observed.

Arriving in Whittier 15 minutes later, Tracy, Mike and Reed found that it was fairly crowded and in the usual state of turmoil when a halibut opening had just taken place and a salmon opening was imminent. The motor home driving off the train just ahead of the Suburban was driven by a make-up laden woman whom Tracy recognized as one of the hookers she had seen working Spenard Drive in Anchorage. Also in the vehicle were two others, similarly made up, who anxiously peered out to locate their first scores in Whittier. "Looks like someone's here to fish for the fishermen," Tracy observed. "I've seen that driver hustling in town."

"But they don't kick the girls out of Whittier," Mike added. "Ted Barnes told me they let the `girls' know that, so long as there were no complaints, the police won't harass them."

Mike double parked near the *Czarina* to allow handy unloading of the gear from the vehicle and trailer. With all their equipment and supplies in a pile near the ramp, he drove on and found a spot 100 yards away. He jogged back to the ramp and noticed as he approached that a man and woman were talking to Reed. The man had a shoulder pack video camera which was not being used. Mike recognized them as reporters for one of the Anchorage TV stations; the woman was Clara Sutter. Mike nodded hello as he jogged up to them.

"Look," Reed was saying, "we appreciate your assignment to gather information on killer whales in the Sound, but we're simply going on one of our regular trips to study many marine mammals, including the whales."

Clara persisted, "But aren't you here from California, Dr. Remington, specifically to investigate these killer whale incidents and to protect the whales?"

"No, Reed replied, "as a matter of fact I was planning to come up anyway. The timing was coincidental."

"Clara, to tell you the truth," Mike pointed a finger at her, "you probably know more about what's been happening out here than we do. Tell us the latest news."

Clara was somewhat flattered that information should be requested from her. "Well, the last couple of years there have been quite a few reports of whales taking fish from long lines, mostly black cod. But this year they're also taking halibut. We're down here to check out those stories and to look into a report that a killer whale ate a dog belonging to some people, Larsons, who live about 12 or 15 miles southeast of Whittier. Unfortunately, we haven't been able to locate the dog's owners. But a dead killer whale was just found over near Cordova."

"Well, you know as much as we do," Mike acknowledged. "We've heard the stories too, but that's about it. We'll let you know when and if we have anything to say later. Now if you'll excuse us, we must carry our gear and stow it." He started off with a box as Tracy came up the ramp for another armful.

"But we thought you were interested in protecting the whales," Clara stated, this time her statement directed at Tracy in an effort to raise a response. "Several fishermen have said they're not going to put up with fish stealing and general hell raising by the whales. There may be more whales shot if this keeps up."

"Clara," Tracy replied, "You know how rumors are in Alaska; we'd rather deal with facts. Sorry, now we need to get loaded." She turned to help Reed shoulder a box.

"If you get any stories, be sure to call me first," Clara called as Tracy started down the ramp toward the .

"You bet," Tracy responded, walking down the ramp with an ice chest. Under normal circumstances Tracy and Mike would have been calling on any of their fishermen friends who might be in port to find out if and where they had seen any killer whale groups, but such inquiries at this time would only arouse more questions and speculation.

Mike again ascended the ramp and entered the Harbor Master building to use McDuffy's phone. He called Carl Baker and reached him at his small cabin of an office near the Lake Spenard float plane dock in Anchorage. "Carl, I'm in Whittier and we do need your help out here on the Sound. Publicity is heating up and the sooner we find the A-T pack the better. Tomorrow sounds good for us if you could come over and help locate them? I'm sure you'll recognize the A-T pack by the large male with the tall wavy dorsal fin. There were 19 orcas in the group the last time we saw them but we're not sure how many are there now...but approximately 19. We'll be at Naked Island by 10 tomorrow morning so if you could get a start in mid-morning maybe we can locate that pack tomorrow."

Carl responded, "We're supposed to have a hellaceous wind storm and rain tonight in the Sound, but tomorrow is supposed to be better. If you don't hear from me in the morning, just assume I am coming."

It was almost 2 pm before everything was stowed on the *Czarina*. After refuelling, Mike steered the vessel out into the fjord-like Whittier Arm but watched for other boats which might be tailing them. Fortunately, none were spotted and the two Volvo diesels were revved up. The *Czarina* headed east toward the main body of Prince William Sound.

The afternoon surveillance revealed no killer whales, although they did see a humpback whale and calf, harbor seals, dolphins and perhaps two dozen sea otters. "Just as we expected," Reed noted after seeing another three otters bobbing on their backs on the surface, "the Exxon Valdez had only a temporary impact on otters in the Sound. There are already too damned many of them in parts of offshore Alaska and the few lost in the Sound in 1989 were a drop in the bucket. But to hear the complaints of preservationists, a major part of the otters in Alaska were lost."

Mike agreed. "To properly manage the population, a season should be opened for otter harvest in a few areas, particularly the Aleutians where some of the otters are reportedly starving because they've decimated the food supply. But much of the public generally doesn't understand the harvest of animals, especially a species as photogenic as sea otters."

Clouds were moving overhead and the southeast wind was increasing as they approached the east side of Perry Island. The wind and heavy gray, racing clouds promising rain made the evening seem unusually dark and threatening as Mike guided the *Czarina* into a protected cove. After Reed assisted with dropping the anchor, they lowered the dinghy into the water and Reed rowed ashore towing a stout line which he attached to the trunk of a sturdy spruce. The sea floor anchor held the bow of the vessel and the shore line held the stern. Mike had learned that a two way anchor system was a valuable safeguard in strong winds, even when in a cove.

In the cabin, Tracy was busy preparing a tossed salad along with corn on the cob and poached fresh sockeye (red) salmon prepared from one of the two ten pound fish she had managed to buy from one of the fishermen in the harbor. Later, over dinner, they enjoyed a bottle of sauvignon blanc and discussed their plan. With the dishes out of the way, Reed showed Tracy and Mike how to operate the new camcorders and the directional hydrophone. At about 9:30, the wind velocity was up to 70 or 80 miles per hour and they could look out beyond the mouth of the cove to the open waters of Prince William Sound and see large whitecaps beating their way to the northwest. Even in the cove they were getting 3 foot swells and the *Czarina* tugged at one anchor or the other with most of the strain against the line tied to the spruce.

"Good thing we've got her tied down," Mike commented to Reed as they stood in the cabin looking at the tormented gray and black sky. Then the rains came; pelting sheets of large drops which poured off the *Czarina* in small rivulets. The noise of rain on the water resembled the amplified sound of dozens of frying pans full of bacon on a hot stove. Visibility was reduced to 50 yards.

With the rain and wind continuing, they decided to retire to their bunks; Tracy and Mike in the forward bunk and Reed sleeping on one of the foldout sofas in the main cabin, which also served as a dining area. Several times during the night each of them awoke as the wind velocity increased and the *Czarina* rolled and pitched. Waves periodically could be heard crashing against the large rocks which lined the entrance to the cove.

The next morning they awoke just before 7 am to receding winds, calming seas and a partly cloudy sky. Mike was up first and began making peanut butter and bran pancakes accompanied by soft boiled eggs and plenty of strong Colombian coffee. Cooking was a one-person-at-a-time chore in the tiny galley and all three cooperated. They didn't take turns cooking, it was more of "whoever was the least busy and whoever felt like it." Someone other than the cook washed the dishes. Tracy was very adept at operating the boat, spotting whales, photography or whatever else a good hand would do, in addition to being the best cook of the three. But they tried to divide the cooking equally, with Mike and Reed claiming it was therapy for them.

After breakfast they continued east toward Naked Island, an area where they had seen the A-T pack on other occasions and where Carl Baker would know where to find them. The weather report from Cordova was good.

As they motored along in 4 foot seas, they again realized that, in the thousands of square miles which was the Sound, help was needed to locate a particular pack. Experience had shown that they could spend days, or even weeks, searching in vain. Their best hope was Carl in the plane, but even then good fortune would have to play a role because the entire pack of whales, when in a resting mode, would usually submerge for 5 to 6 minutes at a time. They would then surface to blow two or three times and then submerge again. An observer going by in a small plane at 170 mph could easily miss a submerged pack.

At 10 O'clock they were at the southeast edge of Naked Island proceeding north at 5 knots and watching intently for any sign of whales. Suddenly Tracy shouted "There's a spout at 2 o'clock!" As they approached, they could see it was an average size humpback whale 60 feet in length and she had a calf with her. But it was 11:40 and no word yet from Carl. They had seen a small plane a couple of times in the distance, but they had no idea if it was Carl. They knew he would call them in due time.

Then the radio crackled and Carl said "Have spotted two parties of Snipers. One party is at L5, 165. The other is at Q7, 225." He then repeated the message and asked if they read it.

"Have received. Any other details?" Mike asked, hoping he might tell them that one was the A-T pack.

"Sorry, no other identification possible."

Reed had written down the coordinates and Tracy now repeated them to "Eagle Eye" so there would be no mistake. Carl confirmed that the numbers were the same. A float-equipped Cessna 182 suddenly came into sight low over the water and buzzed past the *Czarina*. Carl laughed over the radio. "See, I knew where you were all the time!"

Tracy laughed in return and said "Thanks, Eagle Eye, we'll follow up."

"Good luck, CZ, have no further data and must return to base." The Cessna climbed to the west and disappeared.

From the code Mike and Carl had worked out, they knew Carl had spotted two killer whale packs and had relayed the coordinates of each pack. They unrolled the coded map and marked the locations identified by Carl. However, Carl had been unable to determine which pack, if either, was A-T. The nearest pack was just east of Knight Island and thus closest to their present location, probably an hour's run away. Mike turned the *Czarina* east and accelerated. If they were fortunate, they would arrive at the location before the whales moved off in an unknown direction. The second orca pack, a 45 minute run away from the nearest one, would likely be in some other location before the *Czarina* could get there. Hopefully the first pack would be the right one, but they knew it was a less than a 50/50 chance because of the ten or so packs in the Sound.

"I wish Carl had been able to at least count whales to give us a clue," Mike called to the others above the noise of the two engines. After another hour at the higher speed he told the other two, "We should be getting close to the first pack." He maintained the higher speed.

Tracy suddenly shouted "Look behind us!" And she pointed in that direction.There, seemingly playing in the wake of the boat, were two juvenile orcas. They appeared to be having fun rolling, jumping and once in a while slapping their tails on the surface. It was fascinating to the three observers because they had never seen such activity previously.

Mike said "We must be near a pack," and reduced the speed. The two juveniles quickly swam past the *Czarina* and disappeared.

Four long minutes later Tracy again was the first to see something. "That looks like a dorsal fin at 11 o'clock," she said. "Reed, do you see it?"

"Yes, I see it. It's a female, and there's another one just ahead of it. Mike, could you steer over that way?" Mike was already turning the *Czarina* in that direction, when he saw two more whales at 1 o'clock. "There's a good sized bull," he exclaimed. Suddenly, they seemed to be almost in the midst of a scattered pack of killer whales. Mike reduced the speed to 1 knot and all three of them donned their warm jackets and caps. Mike and Tracy took their cameras with telephoto lenses and Reed slipped on the carrying case and the battery pack with the video camera inside. They exited the cabin and climbed up into the brisk air on the "flying bridge."

Whales appeared at the surface here and there at erratic times and going in erratic directions. There seemed to be ten to fifteen whales, including at least two good-sized bulls. They also observed an occasional "jumper" salmon at the surface. From their experience they assumed that this pack had found a school of salmon and was feeding on them.

Mike's familiarity with the whales led him to remark first, "Sorry, but this does not appear to be the T pack. The bull T-4 is so distinctive that he can be recognized right away. The two bulls here are not nearly as large as he is."

"I'm afraid you're right" agreed Tracy.

"Let's at least get some photos for identification" sighed Reed. Although it was urgent to move to the next coordinates given them by Carl, they found themselves watching the activity for 20 minutes. Whenever a whale surfaced near the boat, both Tracy and Reed took photographs of the dorsal fin and the distinctively patterned, gray "saddle" area just behind the dorsal fin, which could establish a positive identity for this particular pack.

"Aha," Mike noted. "This is the A (Alaska) F pack. The female with the notch in her dorsal fin is F-11, and the one with the new calf is F-8. Tracy and I saw them earlier this summer."

Mike again took the wheel, revved up the diesels and steered southeast as Reed and Tracy reviewed the coordinates on the map to relocate the spot on the west side of Montague Island where Carl reported seeing the second killer whale group. It would take about 45 minutes to get there. The wind was increasing under gray skies and the seas were growing more turbulent. Spray was now blowing from the bow onto the windshield as the *Czarina* bucked into larger waves. Mike turned on the windshield wipers occasionally to help visibility, but the wind, rough water, and spray made locating the whales more difficult because the black dorsal fins were nearly obscure and the exhalation plume was impossible to see at a distance.

Mike, watching both the map and the coastline, called out above the diesel engine noise: "Looks like we're about at the site. Hopefully the whales haven't gone too far." He cut back the speed of the *Czarina* to about 3 knots and kept the vessel oriented directly into the wind, which had changed from southeast to southwest.

Reed and Tracy donned their warm clothes again and climbed up to the flying bridge while Mike stayed at the wheel in the cabin. The *Czarina* was pitching and rolling which made viewing with binoculars difficult. Thirty minutes went by as they searched the rough waters for any sign of the whales, but they saw nothing. It became clear that the whales had moved off, but in which direction?

Tracy climbed down the ladder and entered the cabin, followed by Reed. Even in warm clothing, the 50 degree air temperature and a 20 mph wind made it uncomfortable on the bridge. "What do you think?" Tracy asked Mike, knowing his experience with the whales might provide a good guess as to where they went.

"My best guess, and it is just a guess, is that they may have gone with the wind to the northeast around the northeast end of Montague Island where there will be calmer waters. We don't know what they might be doing at this time of day, but if they have already fed on salmon, as the F pack was doing, they may be ready to rest or sleep this afternoon. What do you think, Reed?"

"Gone with the wind! Sounds good to me," Reed responded. "Seriously, it makes sense that the calmer water would be more conducive to rest even though 95% of the time they're under water anyway. Why don't we try it?"

Mike swung the *Czarina* around 180 degrees and headed northeast. He kept the vessel about 1/2 mile offshore from Montague Island to allow a check of the various coves for whales as they went. Rain squalls now began passing over the area, blown by a wind which seemed to be erratic in its intensity. Tracy made some hot tea. It was now 4:30 pm and time to start thinking about dinner. "Who's our cook tonight?" she asked. "I'll cook," volunteered Reed. "I'm a little rusty from California living, so there are no promises. How do hamburgers sound?"

"Sounds good," Tracy and Mike replied in unison. "But it's not typical hamburger," Tracy added, "it's ground round steak. Use olive oil for frying!"

The *Czarina* rolled along through the waves with the wind astern. It would be 45 minutes or so before they rounded the northeastern projection of Montague Island. Mike tuned in to get the latest weather forecast from Cordova; cloudy, windy and scattered rain for the next two days, the usual forecast for Prince William Sound at this time of year. Tracy took over the controls and Mike and Reed began going over notes and recording the sighting of the F pack near Knight Island. At such times they often exchanged ideas or discussed theories about killer whale behavior.

"You know, it's fascinating," Mike commented, looking over the map, "that the different killer whale packs hunt the same general areas, cross paths and occasionally intermingle, yet they almost always maintain their own distinct group."

"Yep, even with deaths or births," Reed agreed, "a certain group with, say, 24 members could be expected to have approximately that same number for several years to come. But yet we know there is sufficient variation so the health of the packs doesn't suffer from the effects of inbreeding. We just don't know how the whales go about maintaining diversity in their sexual relations."

"Another area where more research is needed," Tracy observed, now at the wheel and maintaining the heading to a location north of the island as indicated on the map, all the while scanning the rough surface for any sign of the whales.

The phenomena of constant killer whale group size had been discussed in previous brainstorming sessions aboard the *Czarina*. The trio had observed occasional variations in whale group size, which they assumed resulted from animals leaving their primary group and joining another, but, for the most part, whales identified in a particular group one year would be there the next. It was this very characteristic, strong family bonding, which led Mike, Tracy and Reed to suspect that if a group for some reason began a certain type of successful behavior, whether it be stealing halibut from long lines or killing dogs, that individual group could be expected to repeat that behavior. Further, the intelligent young whales would learn quickly from the older ones.

As the *Czarina* rounded the rocks at the north end of Montague Island, all three of them watched in vain for any sign of whales. An hour later, at almost 6 pm, they decided to give up the search for the night and enter a small cove. They could also fish for halibut. Over dinner they discussed further strategy. The best thing to do now was probably to go back to the second site where Carl Baker had seen whales earlier in the day. Perhaps there was some good feed there, such as salmon, and the whales might return. If that didn't work they could go west to Knight Island, south around the end of the island, and then northward on the west side of the island toward Naked Island. Looking for a particular whale group in Prince William Sound was almost as difficult as looking for the proverbial needle in the haystack.

With dinner over, the wind had decreased to only a breeze and the rain squalls had subsided. Tracy slipped on her wool cap and down jacket, picked up a pair of binoculars and stepped through the sliding door to the stern of the *Czarina*. Even at 8 pm on a cloudy night it was easy to see the trees and snow-capped peaks surrounding the cove. There were bears on this island and she wondered how often they came down to the shore. She glassed the shore line, hoping to see one. With the 8 power binoculars her view swept along the shore to the cove entrance and from there northward toward the high peaks west of Valdez, Alaska, terminus of the TransAlaska pipeline. She had gazed northward for several minutes when something caught her attention in the open water; it looked like a black dorsal fin a half mile beyond the mouth of the cove, going east. She watched intently. There was another one, and another! No doubt about it, a killer whale pack was travelling east past the entrance to the cove.

She quickly slid open the cabin door. "Mike, Reed, a pack of killer whales is passing the cove entrance going east!" They all rushed to the stern with binoculars. Three more whales surfaced to blow as they passed beyond the entrance to the cove, including a large bull with a tall dorsal fin. From this distance they could not tell if it was the T pack bull.

They sprang to action. Mike started the *Czarina*, Reed went forward to hoist the anchor, and Tracy began stowing items still on the table from dinner. As soon as the anchor was in, Mike swung the *Czarina* around and headed north toward the cove entrance. All three of the researchers watched intently as the *Czarina* reached the mouth of the cove and Mike swung the wheel to turn her to the east. In the excitement all thoughts of sleep were forgotten.

There, directly ahead, they saw one dorsal fin as a whale came up to blow. Then four together rose from the depths, followed by 5 more just behind. Three more blew 100 yards to the north, followed immediately by six whales, including one infant. "Looks like 19 whales!" shouted Reed. "And the dorsal fin on the big male is wavy like the T pack bull! Let's hope we've hit the jackpot!"

The whales, moving eastward as a group at about 4 mph in their "resting" mode, came up again to blow and this time all three of them got a good look at the male. Tracy spoke first: "No doubt about it, that's T-4 all right! Did you see that notch in the wavy dorsal fin?"

Reed and Mike were both exuberant. "Good going, Tracy," smiled Reed, "they would have slipped right by us if you hadn't seen them when you did."

"It's gonna be a long night," remarked Mike. "We're going to have to keep them in sight or we'll be back to square one."

"Right," Reed agreed, "but we can take turns tonight as usual."

Mike reduced the speed of the *Czarina* to stay the length of two football fields, about 200 yards, behind the whales, which they expected to surface three times to blow in a two minute period and then submerge for 5 to 6 minutes as they slowly moved ahead. All cabin lights were kept dim to facilitate vision outside the vessel and the *Czarina*'s diesel engines would not disturb the whales so long as the vessel did not crowd them.

"I'll bet they recognize the sound of this old gal's engines," Mike observed, smiling. Tracy and Reed nodded agreement in silence.

The whales were followed discretely for 3 hours and the time was now approaching 10:30 pm. Yawns became more frequent. Tracy had a suggestion, "Last year we took 3 hour shifts following the whales and it seemed to work out pretty well. I'll be first watch tonight, 11 to 2. I'm not sleepy anyway."

"OK with me," Mike offered, "I'll take 2 to 5 am because the least amount of light is available then, but I think I can follow them anyway."

"Well, that leaves me for the 5 to 8 am shift," Reed noted. "But last year we agreed that if the pilot for any reason lost the whales for more than 12 minutes the other two would be immediately awakened to help search for them. Let's do the same thing this year."

"Deal," Mike responded. "If we hang back and don't disturb them, they'll maintain a fairly constant heading with no strong deviations. As we learned last year, their resting speed is also quite constant."

Mike and Reed retired to their bunks and were hummed to sleep by the deep throbbing of the diesel engines. Just before 2, Mike came out to take over the wheel from a sleepy Tracy. By 5, when Reed took over, the sun was breaking through here and there. Tracy was up again at 7 to make coffee and begin breakfast. Mike arose to the smell of breakfast cooking at about 7:30.

The night had passed without incident but the pack had turned north so the whales, with the *Czarina* following discretely behind, were approaching the center of Prince William Sound. The wind had died somewhat, but the skies were still overcast.

Over a steaming cup of coffee, Mike watched the dorsal fins 200 yards ahead as they surfaced and the orcas blew plumes of mist into the cool morning air. "I wonder," he mused, "why they changed course over night? Do you suppose their sonar might have picked up signals of migrating salmon?"

Tracy came up from the galley to look forward. "In a way that makes sense because we know that this time of year salmon moving into the Sound from the North Pacific are schooling and swimming north toward the spawning streams."

"Following this line of reasoning," Mike predicted, calling on his experience with the orcas, "we might expect them to begin feeding on salmon about midafternoon, feed until evening, and then begin a rest/sleep period. If their rest period took them through a part of the Sound where schools of salmon were migrating, the whales could detect the fish on sonar and almost casually follow them north for feeding the following day. Could be an efficient feeding cycle."

Reed was extremely intrigued with the forecast. "Mike, that scenario gives the orcas credit for fairly complex advance planning for feeding activities. Do you think such planning is instinctive, or are they actually thinking through this in segments such as prey movement, timing, and distance traveled during resting?"

Mike smiled. "It's probably some of both. If they know that salmon schools pass this way at this time of the year, which I'm sure they do, then it makes sense that, during their leisure, they would take courses which would take them near or across the migratory paths of the salmon. Then, when they detect a school swimming near or beneath them, they simply turn and follow it just as we are following the killer whales with the *Czarina*."

"Sometimes I think you should be the marine biologist and teacher, Mike, instead of me," Reed chuckled.

They couldn't be certain, but on two occasions when feeding on salmon was underway, it appeared that one of the females had caught a salmon followed by an approach to one of the males. "I'm not sure," Reed had observed, "but it appeared that one of the females fed salmon to the T-4 male."

"Give the ladies credit where credit is due," Tracy chirped, who had also seen the event. "Remember, last year we concluded it made sense that the more agile females are better hunters than the large, bulky males."

"Yes," Reed agreed, "and feeding of the males by the females would help maintain order within the group as well as strengthen the matriarchy. Yet the feeding, and the ready acceptance by the whales of being fed, is exactly the trait which makes the whales in captivity docile and communicative. This is the message I've tried to get across at Hydrosphere."

During, but more often after, feeding, some of the whales would "breach" or jump completely out of the water to fall back on their side into the water with a resounding splash. Having just watched the killer whales at Hydrosphere, Reed noted that he had never observed wild whales emerging from and re-entering the water in a high, streamlined porpoise style leap as the killer whales at Hydrosphere and other marine parks did in crowd pleasing antics. Tracy and Mike concurred, they had never seen such action either. Apparently these wild whales leaped to make a splash, perhaps an expression of joy and perhaps partly to impress their group members. Whatever the reason, a smooth entrance back into the water did not suit their purpose. Some observers had suggested that the whales breached to dislodge parasites from their skin, but this theory had never been substantiated and none of the trio believed it.

With the approach of evening, the whales assembled into a group, seemingly sated with salmon, and proceeded to travel slowly southwest in their resting mode. The *Czarina* patiently trailed about 200 yards behind. Again the pack was followed all night with no unusual happenings. Tracy and Reed made written records of each day's events and they began to feel a close relationship with the A-T pack. Perhaps it was more a matter of getting reacquainted because they had followed the group several times in previous years.

Tinga and her group were fully aware that the vessel was following them. They had even recognized the peculiar tone of the diesel engines and knew that this one had followed them and even stopped among them in previous seasons with no harm or harassment. They would have fled from the sound of certain other vessels which had harassed them or from which shots had been fired at them. This friendly craft did not interfere when the whales were catching salmon and even became silent at times of feeding. Tinga somehow felt more secure because this vessel was present. Experience had shown that when this one was near, the other floating objects with the two legged creatures stayed away and caused no trouble.

The third day dawned and passed with no unusual events. It seemed that each day a general pattern was followed and the travels of the T orca pack in Prince William Sound seemed more than ever to be closely related to the movement of salmon schools. To the humans following them, the routine seemed monotonous.

On two occasions the group had passed within 300 yards of another PWS killer whale pack, but the whales apparently paid little attention to each other. With the *Czarina*'s engines silent, Reed had put out one of the hydrophones to pick up any communications between the groups, but nothing unusual was heard. He reasoned that sound travels so well in water that the groups were probably in communication most of the time anyway, even when several miles apart, so a passing at a couple of hundred yards would not be an unusual event for two friendly packs; thus no unusual communications were necessary.

Reed, Mike and Tracy began to wonder if the A-T pack was indeed the one which had killed the dog. And why would a pack well fed on choice fresh salmon steal halibut or black cod? Or, Mike had speculated, if this was the rogue pack, perhaps research into the habits of the pack were useless at this time because they were sated on salmon and would not deviate from salmon feeding activity until the salmon runs ended in September.

The three of them were still taking three hour shifts at night so the whales could be followed at all times. A time or two they had almost lost the whale group due to fog, heavy rain and rough water, but they had managed to keep the necessary visual contact. The short sleeping intervals were not easy to adapt to, but they made up for the lack of a good night's sleep by taking naps during the day before the T pack started feeding.

The fourth day began as usual with the pack moving slowly in a resting mode, the *Czarina* idling along behind. The weather was warmer and the wind had died almost completely. It appeared that the sun was going to burn away what remained of a few puny clouds. The confined quarters of the *Czarina* were beginning to tell on all three of them although they made a daily practice of stretching, sit ups, push ups and other exercises. Tracy would sometimes climb up and down the stairs to the flying bridge to increase her heart rate. A hot shower would have been luxurious, but doing so would jeopardize the amount of fresh water in the tanks and the time they might be required to spend at sea was unknown. Better not to take a shower than to run out of fresh water for drinking and have to spend eight or ten hours in a run to Whittier and return to replenish the supply. They would also lose the whales again. They could refill from a stream, but that, too, would take them away from the whale watch too long, and there was always the hazard of the Giardia parasites in the water. The use of paper plates in the galley conserved water by eliminating dish washing.

By 2 o'clock in the afternoon, the pack had traveled to a location about one mile northeast of Storey Island and was proceeding northerly. Tracy was at the helm of the *Czarina*, and they expected that the whales would again begin feeding on salmon. It became obvious the pack was "waking up" because there were tail slaps on the water, breaches, and the whales began milling around rather than proceeding on course. "Something unusual is happening," Mike noted. "Tracy, please turn off the engines," he requested.

Reed watched for a moment. "You're right, Mike, let's get the hydrophones out and get ready to film. I don't know what they're up to, but we've got to be ready." Tracy turned off the engines and they scurried to get the equipment in place. Two hydrophones were deployed, one was set up to record on normal recording tape as well as on the video tape when desired. The other was hooked up to a recorder and to a speaker so the crew could hear all of the sounds, including those being recorded.

As soon as the hydrophones were in the water, they heard a chorus of whistles, clicks and chirps, with the sounds obviously from many of the whales in the pack. It seemed that some sort of conference was taking place, or possibly the whales were in disagreement about what to do next. A couple of the younger whales made high speed forays for several hundred yards away from and back to the group as if anxious to get going. One of them made a high speed loop around the *Czarina* at shallow depth. The turmoil went on for about 10 minutes. Then a clear, sharp and loud call came over the speaker "Creeaaaaaaaaa", high pitched at the beginning and trailing off to a lower tone at the end. It sent instant chills up the spine of all three of the human observers, as if their subconscious mind had recognized some unseen primeval terror. To their amazement, all other whale calls and noise ceased. It was as if an unquestioned leader, a queen, had issued an order. Then the call came again, "Creeeaaaaaaaa", tapering to a lower note this time. All the whales were now below the surface and out of sight. There was total silence on the hydrophones except the gentle lapping of waves against the surface floats 20 feet above the hydrophones. Reed, Mike and Tracy listened almost breathlessly. Two sharp short whistles were then heard, again followed by silence. Mike started his stop watch.

The whales had disappeared. There was no sound on the hydrophone and nothing to be seen at the surface. Gulls could be heard calling in the distance. Four minutes went by, then six.

They scanned the surface of the water almost desperately with binoculars to find the whales. Without a word being said they all wondered if the pack had been lost.

Suddenly Mike spotted black dorsal fins cutting the distant surface. He called excitedly, "There they are, 1/4 mile to the northwest, and it looks like they're really moving out! Bring in the hydrophones and let's get going!"

He almost jumped down from the flying bridge to start the *Czarina*'s engines and turn to the northwest in the direction of the fast disappearing whales. Reed raced to pull in one hydrophone cable while Tracy pulled in the other. Quickly they gathered the video equipment and brought it down from the flying bridge. If the orcas were moving at anywhere near their maximum speed of over 30 miles per hour, there was no way the *Czarina* could keep up with them. The *Czarina* could attain about 20 knots, 23 miles per hour, maximum, and that for only half an hour or so before beginning to overheat and use excess oil.

Mike revved up the engines and shook his head, "We'll keep up with them if we can. Hopefully they won't go all out because they'll lose us in 30 minutes or less."

There was no reason to believe the whales were deliberately trying to "ditch" them. Experience had taught them that when a pack of whales wanted to get away from a slow tracking vessel they were extremely difficult to follow. Some of the packs, which had become "gun-shy" from having been shot at or harassed by fishermen, were almost impossible to approach.

Reed was looking at the best available map of the area. "I think they're headed for the mouth of Eagle Bay, about 11 miles northwest. We should be there in less than an hour."

"*If* this old gal can cut the mustard," Mike sighed.

"Even if we get there *after* they do, we might be able to find them," Tracy offered encouragingly, putting her arm around the man she loved.

"We'll find them," Reed offered encouragingly. "But it's a good thing we didn't give up the surveillance after only a couple of days." Another puzzle was unfolding before them. Where were the orcas going in such a hurry? Had they detected a school of salmon to the northwest and were speeding to intercept it, or were they going to rendezvous with another pack?

The possibilities seemed endless, but they were exuberant that something excitingly different was happening.

———————— ◆◆◆ ————————

Tinga and her pack had fed on salmon for several days. Many in the group, especially some of the young adults, had agitated for a change of diet and the excitement of a hunt. Some of the older orcas, however, did not desire to leave the area where salmon catching had been so good and go off to uncertain feeding in a different area. Turmoil and dissent arose in the pack and they circled, dove and exchanged a large repertoire of sounds.

Tinga, as the leader, properly gauged the time necessary to get to a familiar hunting ground. Hunting in the evening was often best when other animals were filling their stomachs as was their habit. Even though no true darkness came to the hunting area, many animals, including the fat seals, were accustomed to feeding in the normal evening hours and they were not quite as wary as other times. Upon Tinga's clear call to follow her to the hunting area, all dissent vanished. The pack would follow her lead wherever she took them. Bonds within the group were extremely strong and there was practically nothing that would separate them, certainly not minor decisions such as where to feed.

All of the mature whales knew the subsurface topography of the Sound very well because they had an almost continual scan of the bottom by sonar and their large brains retained the information. Just as animals which live on land learn to remember and recognize terrain by vision, the whales knew their underwater terrain and where they had enjoyed good hunting previously. As with other hunting animals, including man, the orcas tended to return to areas where they had been successful in previous hunts. They also remembered how to use individual or group action to advantage in capturing prey and, as an important plus, the whales had the capability to learn and adapt new hunting techniques to increase success.

The younger whales in Tinga's pack were very anxious for the hunt to begin and, once Tinga indicated the direction of travel, they excitedly swam ahead of the main, concise group. An occasional sonar scan was the only survey any whale needed to provide adequate bottom information.

———————— ◆◆◆ ————————

Little more was said as the *Czarina's* engines roared away in the effort to keep up with the disappearing group of whales. Mike watched the temperature and oil pressure gauges closely. "Temperature's going up," he called to Tracy and Reed who were scanning the surface to determine the course of the orcas. A noticeable heat increase from the engines could be felt in the cabin.

Due to their extra physical exertion, the whales could be seen surfacing every three minutes or so to blow and thus were visible more often, but they gradually out distanced the vessel and within 20 minutes vanished in the distance to the northwest.

When the dorsal fins and plumes from the blows could be seen no more, Tracy turned from staring through the binoculars and spoke loudly so she could be heard above the engine noise. "I hope they don't turn, I can't see them anymore. We're probably 30 minutes behind them now."

Mike, at the controls, responded. "It's the best we can do without blowing the engines apart. She just wasn't built for racing."

Reed added "I've got a hunch we'll find them in the vicinity of the mouth of the bay. They're not running from us, they're making a beeline for something out there and they're wasting no time doing it. My guess is there's another whale pack out there and they're going over for a rendezvous. But I wouldn't bet a penny on it!"

They throbbed on toward the northwest with no whales in sight. Visible ahead were the blue and white ice capped mountains rising to 4,000 feet around Eaglek Bay, and soon they could see the three small islands that lay just to the south of the bay mouth. Forty five minutes later they were near Little Axel Lind Island, about 2 miles out from the mouth of the bay. A mile further on was Eaglek Island and then the two mile wide mouth of the bay; too wide to spot a killer whale pack on the opposite side.

"I'm going to play a hunch," Mike called. "They may be near the west side of the bay." Without reducing speed he steered the *Czarina*, engines pounding, toward the west.

"And I hope they've slowed down," he continued. "If we don't cut back soon those Volvos will be screaming for oil."

They had gone about a mile past Eaglek Island and were intensely glassing the western part of the bay 1/4 mile away when sharp-eyed Tracy shouted "There they are, near those large rocks." With relief Mike reduced the speed of the *Czarina* to 3 knots and they all looked with binoculars to the west. Sure enough, there were the dorsal fins of a group of orcas appearing here and there very near the rocks along shore. The group was now moving much more slowly to the north. "Let's hope it's the A-T pack," Mike muttered.

"There aren't any salmon over there in that shallow salt water," Reed remarked, as he watched closely through the binoculars. "Wonder what they're up to. This is their normal afternoon feeding time."

"Maybe they decided to have crab for dinner for a change," joked Tracy. "After all, you'd get tired of a diet of nothing but salmon, wouldn't you?"

Mike revved up the engines again to half throttle and continued on a west heading. "Let's go on in to make sure these are our A-T friends and see what they are up to. We've been around them so much the past few days they probably wouldn't know how to act if the *Czarina* wasn't nearby."

The distance to the shore closed until the *Czarina* was about 200 yards out and Mike turned northward to parallel the shore. The whales were ranging from 20 to 100 yards away from the rocky shore. Mike adjusted speed so the was just keeping pace with what was, as best he could determine, the lead whales.

Again, the trio quickly donned warm clothing, picked up the cameras and recording equipment and hurried up to the flying bridge. Visibility was great. The cove was quite protected and lighting was good. The sun in the west had a glorious, iridescent orange glow. The hydrophone could not be deployed, however, because of noise from the *Czarina*'s engines, which must be kept running in order to maintain a position near the moving whales.

With binoculars they watched the whales closely to determine the nature of the seashore activity. Reed glassed the shore line 200 yards ahead of the whales and spotted two harbor seals cowering just above water level on the ledge of a large rock 30 feet offshore. The seals were looking nervously in the direction of the approaching killer whales.

"We probably have the answer right there on that ledge," Reed observed. "You may have been right Tracy, the pack has decided to change their diet, but it's not crab. They're planning on red meat for dinner tonight, and those two harbor seals don't want to be on the menu. Phoca vitulina scared out of their wits. Get the cameras ready, we may be in for some action!"

Mike turned the engines of the *Czarina* off just as Tracy spotted some rapid movement. "Wait! Look near that big rock, something's happening!" She didn't want anyone to miss important visual sightings while they were getting the cameras ready. Attention diverted away from the action for even a few seconds could be the loss of a once in a lifetime sighting opportunity.

The dorsal fin of one of the females indicated a starting position 30 yards from a small but deep channel cut into the bedrock of the island. The female rushed to the west side of the channel while the dorsal fin of a big male appeared rushing toward the east side of the channel. The water swirled with turbulence and the tall dorsal fin stopped and then shook violently. A red stain spread in the water. As the whale turned, in it's mouth a harbor seal was flopping the way a salmon flops in the jaws of an Alaska brown bear. The male submerged and the seal was seen no more. The kill was over in less than 30 seconds.

All three of the observers, watching through binoculars from the *Czarina*, were stunned. They had just witnessed what was clearly a cooperative hunting strategy. The female had literally scared the seal from one side of the channel to the other and into the jaws of the big male. They continued to watch, spellbound.

The scythe-shaped dorsal fin of a female orca cut through the water toward the ledge where the two seals were cowering, with the whale turning just before reaching the ledge. A wave several feet high, generated by the whale's momentum, washed onto the ledge and tumbled one of the animals into the water. Knocked from its secure position, the seal appeared to turn as if to climb back to the ledge, but the whales had apparently anticipated the move. No sooner did the seal roll into the water than a second black dorsal fin appeared and the foaming water turned red. This time the seal was not eaten immediately, but was carried at the surface proudly by the female captor. She turned it in her mouth so the head with the bulging, sorrowful eyes looked forward. The dorsal fins of two of the younger members of the pack appeared next to the seal as if they were examining the animal. The female then released the seal, and T-12, the younger bull of the group, moved forward and the seal disappeared. The trio of observers could only assume that the seal had been eaten.

"What an ambush!" Reed exclaimed, still looking intently through the binoculars. "Did you see that?" speaking to either Tracy or Mike. "She knocked that seal off the ledge so it was easy pickings!" exclaimed Mike, still watching.

"Great cooperation!" Tracy responded.

"But let's be ready next time," Mike urged as he took a large lens from a protective case. "The T pack has commenced an evening of dining on red meat and we'd better be ready to record it." Tracy and Reed immediately moved to get the equipment ready. Mike restarted the *Czarina's* engines because the whales appeared to be moving on.

Upon approaching the shallow, rocky area of the familiar bay, the younger whales had dropped back to rely upon, and learn from, the older, more experienced and more efficient whales, particularly the females. Tinga the queen, took the lead ahead of the pack and close to shore where she could take advantage of any situation in which they might encounter seals, porpoises or other prey. Quick, intelligent and aggressive, she was currently the best hunter in the group. After they had entered the bay and approached the west shore, her sonar detected three seals in the water 300 yards away. Two of them were near a large, striated, offshore boulder where the pack had enjoyed success before and which she remembered clearly. The third seal was perhaps 50 yards from shore near the surface. She correctly guessed that the two near the boulder would climb out of the water; the one out further was a good possibility for a catch.

The other whales "read" and understood the scene completely. Three of the whales fell in 20 yards behind Tinga and 20 yards out from shore, five whales were 40 yards behind Tinga and 50 yards from shore, and the remaining eight whales were 100 yards behind Tinga and 100 yards from shore. Kray, the large bull, was anxious for food and occupied a position in the trio nearest Tinga.

The hunting formation was a common one for them and allowed some of the best hunters to be in the lead. All of the sub-adult and adult whales in each grouping maintained a straight front with no whale ahead of or behind the others. They also came up to blow in exact unison. Such military-like regimentation allowed each whale in each group to have a clear sonic and sonar "view" of everything ahead, while breathing at the surface in unison prevented erratic subsurface noise from interfering with the whale's sensitive hearing and sensing of prey.

As Tinga sonar-scanned the area ahead, the two seals near the boulder disappeared from her "screen;" they had climbed, she knew, out of the water onto a rock ledge. The third seal had sensed the approach of the whales and was streaking toward the boulder. Tinga's decision was to "chase" the seal toward shore with great commotion at the surface, hoping to panic the animal into making a mistake. Her flukes churned the water as she quickly accelerated to become a 25 knot black and white torpedo. Her black dorsal fin cut the water with a sizzling sound and she emitted wavering screeches she knew would terrify the seal.

Anticipating action, Kray edged forward anxiously, sensing correctly that Tinga was going to the opposite side of the rock. He approached the near side, eager to kill and eat. There was no chance for the seal to turn from its panic stricken rush to get away from Tinga, and, by the time it realized the black object ahead was not another rock, Kray's 3 inch long, ivory teeth, which matched top and bottom like pinking shears, closed on the head and shoulder of the seal like the slamming of an automobile door. Kray shook his head so the teeth would severe vital parts of the seal. As he backed out of the area behind the rock, the seal was in the throes of death, twisting and flopping. Once out of the enclosure he submerged and his sharp teeth began cutting the seal into pieces. The head was discarded and a young whale picked it up for investigation. He bit into the front quarters and one of the females came over to disembowel the animal, discarding the intestines. The bull savored the front section as he swallowed it, followed immediately by the rear part. Total seal parts consumed weighed about 190 pounds and Kray would be satisfied for the evening unless some extra tidbits or pieces were available from later killings.

The other two whales of the lead trio, Kee and Ming, both mature females, had spotted the two seals on the ledge. As the other whales waited and scanned the scene with sonar, Kee, with Ming following behind, rushed toward the ledge and created a wave which washed one of the seals off. Kee was there to grab the seal much as a brown trout takes a hapless minnow. The seal's back was broken and its gut and rib cage punctured but it was not immediately killed. The whales enjoyed playing with captured prey, and the young whales had much to learn. Two of the youngsters moved forward to examine the seal, and the seal was alternately released and then grabbed again. The youngsters were hoping it would try to escape so they get could get the real thrill of the hunt, but the seal could use only it's front flippers and it was in shock. Zirgo, the ranking male after Kray, came forward to seize the front half of the seal. Kee seized the rear half and the two powerful orcas easily tore the seal apart. The parts were shared with several other whales which had approached for a morsel.

Hunting was good. The pack was excited and pleased. Kray moved back to the rear group of eight whales, and his place was taken by Zinda, a nearly full grown female anxious to get in on the action of the chase and kill. Kray was pleasantly full and would keep a position as the outside whale in the rear alignment for the rest of the hunt. At this location he could fulfill an important major role as protector of the pack.

As the pack continued north along the rocky coast, the hunting formation was maintained with Tinga in the lead. The orcas knew the exact location of the vessel paralleling them offshore and, once again, there had been no interference. The orcas, traveling again as a group, had proceeded a quarter of a mile north when they detected some other sounds offshore ahead in addition to the low throbbing of the *Czarina's* idling diesels. The engine sound now was operating to the killer whale's advantage because it tended to conceal from the animals ahead vibrations emanating from the whales sonar.

Upon analyzing the incoming sounds further, the orcas detected possible prey near the surface nearly one mile ahead. The two prominent females, Tinga and Ming, elected to split the group into two parts and, with faint clicks and whistles so as not to disturb the possible prey, communicated the maneuver to each other. Tinga would continue along shore with groups of three and five whales behind, and Ming would lead the group of eight whales to investigate the offshore sounds. Ming, a huntress nearly as skillful as Tinga, often was a leader of part of the pack. The eight which accompanied her this time included two young ones ten months and four months of age. This was good; they would learn more about hunting.

The rocky shore line swung to the west and Tinga's group followed it, hunting for more seals or whatever edible animal they might happen upon. They traveled in almost complete silence in order to maintain the possibility of surprise.

Ming's group did not turn west but instead continued north toward deeper water in the bay. Now the received sounds were much more definitive. They recognized the noises as those from a group of Dall's porpoises, the speedy black and white animals which sometimes roamed Prince William Sound in groups of up to 100. This sounded like a pod of about 25 or 30 and they were busily and noisily feeding on a small school of herring which they had driven near the surface. It would not be easy to approach the porpoises closely because they, like the killer whale, had excellent sonar and hearing capabilities. But the porpoises could not out-swim the orcas and any chase in open water would be lost by the small animals.

The whales split into two groups of four, with one juvenile and its parent in each group. The excitement of the hunt mounted among the whales. One group, led by Sheena and her calf, would circle around the porpoises and approach from the northeast, while Tinga and her four whales would wait until the subgroup was in position before advancing. They would try to disrupt, panic and confuse the porpoises and thus allow some kills.

The porpoises now detected the larger whale's presence, but they were not sure of the larger mammal's intentions. During other encounters, at times when the whales were feeding on salmon, the porpoises sensed they were safe, much as zebras, wildebeests and antelope sensed they were safe from lions at times when the lions were not feeding. The smaller porpoises could turn quicker than the whales but then a cottontail rabbit could turn quicker than a fox; yet the rabbit stood no chance unless it found the protection of holes, rock or brush.

So it was with whales and the porpoises, only obstructions such as shallow water or rocks could save the porpoises once they were targeted. But there was no safety indication now, and the whale's intent was clearly threatening. The porpoises could not run toward the open water of the Sound because they detected several of their large cousins blocking their way. Running to the ocean would do no good, they knew, because determined orcas could outswim them.

The split group of whales confused the porpoises, causing them to mill and blow nervously in a disorganized pod near the surface. They were also confused by the presence, not far from the whales, of a vessel at the surface which made a typical low rumbling noise they had learned to associate with such objects.

To complete the vice-like positioning, Sheena's group now turned directly toward the porpoises, which they could not see visually but which were clear as crystal on sonar. Sheena gave a call to Ming on the opposite jaws of the vice and both groups accelerated toward the now panic-stricken porpoises, calling, clicking and whistling as they advanced. The porpoises were making their own highly excited noises which added to the underwater cacophony. Three of the porpoises began a series of leaps, arching above the surface of the water as if attempting to fly from the approaching massacre.

The porpoise group leader made a dash to escape between the two fast-approaching killer whale groups but Ming detected the maneuver and veered off to intercept. At 40 feet in the hazy water she made visual contact with the quarry fleeing to her right. Her teeth closed on the porpoise's tail and last 6 inches of it's body. The force of her rush and her sharp clenching teeth broke the backbone of the small animal and blood gushed into the water from the puncture wounds, but she did not kill it. This one would flee no more and she turned her attention to the other animals much as a man hunting rabbits will leave a mortally wounded rabbit to be picked up after he has made the most of killing more in the bunch.

Other orcas rocketed into the middle of the terrified porpoise pod and caught 5 more of their small black and white cousins. The animals caught were killed, cut apart and eaten almost immediately. One of those killed was a female whose orphaned calf swam near the surface making plaintive calls. Sheena easily caught the young porpoise and fed it in pieces to her own offspring.

Ming returned to the animal she had crippled and found it barely alive near the surface. She was joined by another female with a calf and together they killed it and then performed a quick and skilful job of gutting, skinning and beheading it. The adults fed on the muscles and bones while the calf was given the heart and liver.

Several of the surviving porpoises made the mistake of attempting escape toward the west shore of the bay where two of them were pursued and caught by whales in Tinga's group, who broke off from seal hunting to feast on the smaller black and white speedsters. Sea gulls wheeled and cried over the area, picking up scraps of meat, skin and intestine.

The toll was 9 porpoises killed and eaten but approximately 16 escaped. Among those caught were the weaker swimmers and those with slower, or perhaps less intelligent, reactions. The entire orca pack reformed en echelon behind Tinga to continue along the coast in pursuit of more game. Those whales which had eaten moved to the rear group while those yet to feed took positions in the front ranks.

———————— ◆◆◆ ————————

On board the *Czarina*, emotions were mixed. They were astounded at the group hunting tactics of the whales and the ferocity and swiftness of their attack. They also felt a certain amount of sadness for the loss of the Dall's porpoises, which so frequently rode the bow wake of the *Czarina*. But this was the way of Nature, some perished that others may live. As always, observations were carefully logged into the hard-bound book which had pages that were water-resistant. They all participated in the logging as they had the opportunity.

Reed, Mike and Tracy had observed the division of the killer whale pack and had elected to stay with the group near shore because it had just scored two seal kills and they suspected more would take place. But Tracy had seen the Dall's porpoises through the binoculars and Mike had turned off the *Czarina*'s engines so the directional hydrophone could be deployed. They had then turned the cameras to the porpoise location in time to film the carnage visible at the surface. As the turmoil started, the speaker on the *Czarina* came alive with piercing whistles, click trains and other calls. They assumed the more highly pitched sounds were from the porpoises.

"What a scene!" Mike exclaimed, the excited whuuffs of exhaling whales sounding in the background. "How many porpoises do you think they got, Reed?"

"I would say 8 or 9 anyway," Reed responded, "including one juvenile which was taken after the others. The female that caught it appeared to be feeding jointly with another female and a calf, which was probably her offspring. That was the most incredible scene I have observed in years of marine mammal research. What do you think, Tracy?"

"It was scary. The porpoises were slaughtered. It reminded me of several expert marksmen with shotguns jumping a flock of mallard ducks at close range. The ducks haven't much chance. It's not a question of will any ducks be killed but rather how many will survive. A larger group of orcas might have killed the entire pod of porpoises... Did you see the other part of the T pack catch those two porpoises to the west?"

"Yes, and I think we got some good recorded shots," Mike replied.

"The sound should be pretty good, too," Reed noted, "although confusing because of all the hubbub." They watched as the dorsal fins of *Orcinus orca* appeared here and there moving toward the lead female, where the formation appeared to reassemble. The pack continued its hunting journey northward along the rocky coast. Mike restarted the *Czarina*'s engines so they could continue following. "We've got to get an identification of that lead female, Mike and Tracy. Any idea on which one she is?" Reed asked.

"She's probably T-7," replied Mike. "We'll see if we can get close enough this evening to get a positive identification."

Tracy, along with Reed watching the orcas through binoculars, nodded agreement. "When we followed the T pack last year it was clear that T-7 was calling the shots. Remember, Mike?"

"Yes, but we had no idea then she was also what appears to be the top hunter of the group as well."

Tracy's number orientation began to surface and she took a pad and pencil from an inside jacket pocket. "Tell you what, I'll start a running tally of the apparent kills for tonight. Two harbor seals and what, eight or nine Dall's porpoises? Let's call it nine, anyway."

Reed responded, "Good idea. And while you're at it, write down some approximate body weights so we can get an idea of how much meat this pack consumes on their 'evening picnic.' Put down 185 pounds for an average seal, and 160 pounds for an average Dall's porpoise. What is their total for the evening?"

Tracy added the weights. "Two harbor seals at 185 pounds each is 370, and nine Dall's porpoises at about 160 pounds is 1,440 pounds for a total of just a little over 1,800 pounds. Not bad results for just over one hour's hunting."

"Those are very rough numbers," Reed noted, "because the Orcas' often disembowel, skin or decapitate their prey. But we can always use a discount factor later."

The A-T pack continued hunting, with the *Czarina* paralleling the group 200 yards offshore. On the flying bridge, Tracy and Reed scanned the whale activity carefully with binoculars while Mike, at the controls, carefully maintained their position relative to the whales.

"Efficiency is one reason why large predators prefer to hunt larger prey," Reed observed, half thinking out loud. "One kill may feed an entire pack, as in the example of hyenas killing a zebra. For an adult male killer whale, which can eat more than 200 pounds of food each day, catching and eating a 185 pound seal is much more efficient than pursuing and eating 25 or so pink salmon which would weigh about the same. Catching the pink salmon, as you both know, might require several hours, while good hunting for a seal might take a fraction of the time."

Mike agreed. "Right, but they are subject to the same prey restrictions as other predators. If they hunt one species too much it will become scarce and the success rate will drop, thereby causing them to switch to more abundant prey."

"That's not what we're seeing here, though," Tracy interjected. "These whales have more salmon in large, easy to catch schools in Prince William Sound right now than they could possibly eat. Yet this pack took off to hunt mammals which are much less abundant."

Reed looked at them both thoughtfully. "Perhaps it's a combination of factors. Let's develop a working hypothesis here. How does this sound? First, the whales break off from feeding on abundant salmon because they need a variable diet for nutrition's sake. I have not seen an analysis of whole seal versus whole salmon nutritional components, but there no doubt is a significant difference. The seals are warm blooded and feed on quite a variety of fish; their meat, organs and fat are significantly different from fish. Second, the whales are sure to know their hunting area and seasons well and there are certain times of the year when there is good hunting for mammals such as seals. It is more efficient to hunt larger prey at those particular times."

Both Mike and Tracy nodded that so far they agreed, but Tracy had a question. "OK, but how would you account for this pack attacking a dog on leash in a boat, or stealing fish from the long lines when other food is available? Worse yet, what about the couple from Reno who disappeared?"

Reed nodded. "That's the third part of the hypothesis. This pack may be more curious or relish excitement more than most. It may be led by a female or females which can, and will, look for opportunities to kill and eat, or, at the very least, harass unusual animals which get in or on the water."

The *Czarina* throbbed along, Mike and Tracy carefully considering Reed's words. With binoculars they continued to glass the killer whales whenever the hunters blew at the surface. Reed pursued the idea. "You know, when you really think about it, there is no reason why Orcinus orca should not kill and eat Homo sapiens. In addition to determining if this whale species does attack and eat people, we should take a close look at why it would not."

Mike had been nurturing an idea for months, and this was a good time to bounce it off Tracy and Reed. "If man were an easily available prey for a hungry, feeding, excited pack of killer whales, there is only one thing I can think of which would turn them away from killing and eating him." He waited for their expected question. "What's that?"

He looked at them both. "Their clothing."

CHAPTER ELEVEN

Hunters

R eed looked at him curiously, wondering if they had reached the same conclusion. "Clothing? What are your thoughts on the connection between clothing and predation?"

"I've been thinking about this for a long time," Mike replied. Let this be my contribution to the working hypothesis. The killer whales will not take prey which is heavily furred or heavily clothed if there is other prey to be taken. While I admit I have not had the opportunity to observe how the whales would regard Homo sapiens, clothed or unclothed, under open ocean conditions, I have repeatedly seen them pass up the heavily furred but easily available sea otter in favor of other more difficult to kill but less heavily furred prey such as seals or porpoises. This suggests that the preferred food is not heavily furred. Not that they can't skin something. We all know killer whales can, and sometimes will, skin or disembowel, or both, various prey species including dolphins and sea lions."

"This will sound weird," Reed mused, "but I have reached the same tentative conclusion and was prepared to present the concept as part of the paper I was supposed to give in Vancouver."

Tracy took her eyes away from the binoculars for a moment as she picked up the train of thought. "So you both theorize that animals with either thick clothing or fur COULD be killed and eaten, but only as a choice several rungs down from the top choices."

"Right," Mike nodded. "This could explain why the Larson's were not taken but their dog was. They were heavily clothed and may have had life jackets on, but the dog was a black lab with a coat not much thicker than that of the harbor seal. If their dog had been heavy-coated St. Bernard, or even a Chesapeake Bay retriever, it might still be alive. The whale's sonar would have no difficulty determining hair or fur thickness."

"So," Reed pursued the concept, "if the couple from Nevada got into the water naked ahead of a pack on a hunting foray such as A-T here, they could have been meat on the table, so to speak."

"Exactly," Mike noted. "But remember, this theory is not a panacea. The whales may not be hungry at a particular time or for some unknown reason may be disinclined to eat an animal in the water, whether it's a doe deer or a dancer from Reno. Let's tread cautiously until we gather more data and firm up this hypothesis."

"It's basically sound reasoning though, guys," smiled Tracy. "I think we're on our way to getting answers to some riddles." It was 6 pm, but the light was still excellent.

"There's something on the water surface at 10 o'clock about 100 yards offshore," Tracy pointed out. "It might be a log… no it's a sea otter, it just raised its head. Do you see it, Reed?"

"Yes, I do. Now let's see what the approaching whales do. I'm going to run the video camera just in case something happens." Because of the slight rolling of the vessel, Reed held the camera on his shoulder for stability. The whales approached and then passed the sea otter, apparently paying little or no attention to it.

Tinga and her group were pleased with the way the evening's hunt had gone thus far, but many of the whales had not yet eaten and more kills must be made or fish would again be eaten. They had detected three more seals, but the seals had gotten out of the water at a rough and rocky location where Tinga had learned on previous hunts that capture was almost impossible. Better to move on to easier prey. They continued prowling northward, having progressed 3 miles from the mouth on the west side of Eaglek Bay. Just ahead lay a narrow, steep-walled fjord. Total length of the glacier-made feature was about 1/2 mile. Juvenile salmon and herring, as well as other small fish, frequented the fjord and it was, accordingly, popular with seals and porpoises. Tinga liked this hunting spot; they had been successful here before.

The killer whale pack turned toward the fjord mouth and, upon reaching it, the three whales behind Tinga joined her and they entered the narrow mouth four abreast. The five whales immediately behind fanned out at the entrance but did not enter. The eight whales in the trailing group circled slowly in the bay 100 yards out in a holding pattern.

Mike, Tracy and Reed aboard the *Czarina* saw the whales change pattern and the lead group proceed toward the entrance to the fjord. It was obvious that their view of the entrance from the vessel would be essentially nil because of the terrain.

"I remember this fjord," Mike declared, "it's narrow and trends north and then west. Good place for seals but we're not going to see a damn thing from here. What do you two think of edging up to the mouth of the fjord and dropping anchor?"

"Good idea," Tracy quickly responded.

"This group is very intent on hunting and they're accustomed to us," Reed added. "I don't believe we'll bother them a bit if we're cautious. Let's idle in and shut down. The water is calm there and we can see what happens."

Mike idled the *Czarina* past the milling outside group and toward the five whales waiting near the mouth of the fjord. Gravel became visible on the bottom in 40 feet of water. The five whales near the mouth came up to blow every four minutes and the trio almost held their breath as the slowly idling vessel edged past them.

With the *Czarina* gingerly on the right heading, Mike turned the engines off. The tide was coming in, however, and Mike could see they would be carried into the fjord on the current if they weren't anchored somehow. The 70 pound anchor on the bow was attached by a chain and would make too much noise in handling and further disturb the serenity. Mike kept on board a 50 pound weight attached to a nylon rope and it would probably hold the *Czarina* in the tidal current. He climbed down from the flying bridge to the stern and got ready with the anchor. When the vessel had coasted quietly to a position at the mouth where they could see the lower part of the fjord, Mike lowered the weight quietly over the stern and secured the rope. Next he carefully lowered a hydrophone on each side of the vessel, suspended 15 feet below. Floats at the water's surface kept the phones at the desired depth. He checked the reception and climbed back up to the bridge.

Tracy and Reed had remained busy on the flying bridge getting equipment ready and watching for whale activities. They spoke in whispers and moved the cameras and tripods quietly. Their jogging shoes made no noise on the deck. It was imperative that any sound they might make interfere as little as possible with either the prey or the hunters.

The cries of sea gulls blended with the gentle rippling of waves against the hull and splashing on the rocky shore. Every few minutes the five whales in a line 50 feet behind them would surface to blow, but even this seemed to be quieter than normal.

The trio was almost breathless with excitement. A trap had been set by these clever hunters. Any prey in the fjord would either be caught by the four sweepers on the inside or they would be ambushed at the exit. The high level of intelligence and the complex hunting skills of this pack of Orcinus orca were becoming more apparent.

Reed whispered, "The last time I saw organization like this was on a pheasant hunting trip to Kansas. Some of us would walk through to chase the birds while others waited at the end of the field to pick off the ones we chased through."

Tracy did a slow 360 degree sweep of the quiet but tense scene with a camcorder, recording sound at the surface on one audio channel and sound from one of the hydrophones on another. Reed stood by with a second camcorder and Mike had a telephoto-equipped camera ready. Other than an occasional whuufff followed by the vacuum-like sound of air intake by the whales at the surface, the only sound from the waiting five orcas off the stern was an infrequent click.

———————— ◆◆◆ ————————

The whales waiting at the fjord mouth, each almost as long as the *Czarina* itself, heard clearly the turn and approach of the vessel which had been following them. They would not move from their positions unless it truly disrupted their hunt, and this vessel had not interfered during the past several days. The noise could complicate their hearing of prey, however, and it was good when the throbbing noise ceased. With clicks they sonar-scanned the curious rope and weight as it was lowered to the bottom by the creatures on the floating object. Now they waited quietly and eagerly to see if Tinga and her companions flushed any prey.

Tinga and the other three whales were swimming swiftly and quietly underwater at about 12 knots. Speed was part of the element of surprise.

They had found nothing in the lower part of the fjord and they surfaced to blow before rounding a corner to scan the upper part.

Rounding the corner they immediately detected four animals in the water 300 yards ahead and made a positive identification. Four harbor porpoises had been feeding on juvenile salmon and were now faced by the top predator in the oceans in a steep-walled trap.

The porpoises instantly detected the whale's sonar and turned to bounce their own signals off the incoming predators. To the whales this was the equivalent of turning a spotlight on the porpoise's exact location because they could use the porpoise sonar to their own advantage in determining the prey's location and direction of travel. The whale's speed increased to 25 knots as they closed the distance to the quarry, the focus of their direction made easier by the panic sounds emitted by the terrorized small gray animals.

As with the Dall's porpoise, the small size of the harbor porpoise made it more agile and maneuverable than the killer whales. The porpoises evaded the initial rush of the orcas and began an all-out run for the mouth of the fjord. Tinga and the other three whales quickly banked through U turns and the pursuit was on. Top speed of the harbor porpoise was about 20 knots and the whales began closing the distance on the fleeing prey.

The porpoises began leaping from the water (porpoising) in their panic to get away, but also, with peripheral vision, to check the proximity of the orcas. They knew the whales were closing in behind them even though their sonar was nearly useless for any object to their rear.

The whale's sonar and hearing were slightly impaired by underwater noise created by water cavitation at their flukes and by the rush of their sleek bodies through the water. Even at 30 knots, however, they had sonar fixed on the four mammals ahead of them and they could hear the splashes as the porpoises reentered the water after jumping. The whales did not jump but blew at the surface every minute or so. They overtook the porpoise group just after passing the inside corner of the fjord, and again the porpoises took evasive action. Two of them turned sharply left to again evade the pursuing whales, but this placed them into the outside corner of the water body with three of the killer whales in hot pursuit. Despite jumping and crowding against the rocks almost to the point of getting out of the water, the two gray mammals were quickly caught, cut in pieces by the black and white trio, and consumed.

When the porpoise pod split into two parts, Tinga turned sharply right to follow two of the animals, knowing her associates would easily catch the other two which had turned left. The two she now pursued had turned right and were continuing south along the rocky shore line. Tinga could have caught them if she wished, but they were moving in a good direction and she herded them as skilfully as a good Australian sheep dog herds a band of sheep. She rose to blow frequently and created subsurface whistles and calls to move the prey along.

The attention of the porpoises was focused entirely on moving away from the whale in a direction which might lead to safety. They were tiring slightly and their speed decreased as they attempted to hug even more closely to the rocky shore while exerting maximum effort.

————— ◆◆◆ —————

Aboard the *Czarina*, Tracy, Mike and Reed heard some distant squeaks, whistles, click trains and splashes transmitted to the speaker by the hydrophone.

"Something is happening around the corner," Mike whispered. "Get ready!" The video cameras were focused on the corner of the fjord and turned on.

Suddenly four leaping harbor porpoises appeared at the corner with the whales in close pursuit. The two video cameras were operating, with Mike taking telephoto 35 mm shots. From the surface evidence it appeared that two of the porpoises had turned back toward the inside corner while the other two turned south toward the *Czarina* at the fjord mouth.

It wasn't entirely clear, but commotion involving orcas and porpoises at the outside corner indicated that the two porpoises which had gone in that direction were taken. This was confirmed by the slowed movement and surfacing of the three pursuers as if they were feeding at that location.

Now their attention turned to the two approaching porpoises and the female killer whale behind them. It became clear that the whale could have overtaken the porpoises, but she didn't. Her vocalizations were heard clearly on the hydrophone.

"Look at that, it's T-7 and she's herding them!" Reed was astounded.

"Right toward the trap," breathed Tracy.

————— —————

The five whales waiting 30 yards beyond the *Czarina* had picked up the entire chase and two catches in the sensitive hearing receptors located along their lower jaw. From there the sounds were transmitted in great detail to the large ear and hence to the large brain. Although lateral visibility was only 80 feet, they knew that two porpoises were approaching along the west side of the fjord, herded by Tinga. When the animals were 100 yards away the five whales surfaced to blow simultaneously and then submerged so the approaching animals would have less chance of detecting them as they came closer.

Tinga knew that two porpoises had been caught already, and she knew five whales lay in ambush ahead. At lower speed she could easily track the fleeing animals and she had also detected the sonar reflection from the hull of the *Czarina* and the rope to the bottom. No matter, the important thing now was to pursue the prey to the trap. She began emitting loud whistles well within the hearing range of the prey to hasten them on their way. She wanted no chance the two animals would turn from their attempted flight to safety.

The two porpoises detected the hull of the vessel in the middle of the fjord mouth and veered from the west side directly under the possible protection of the boat, but, with the orca a scant 50 feet behind them, there was no chance to try any maneuvers. Just as the two gray speedsters passed under the vessel, the center whale of the five waiting orcas made its move toward the porpoises. It almost caught one only 30 feet behind the boat, but again the quickness of the porpoise turns prevented the catch. One porpoise turned west and one east. The one to the east leaped from the water and was quickly caught by Ziza, a subadult male, as it reentered the water. The food was shared.

The porpoise to the west was herded toward the sandy shore line by Saree, a mature female, with Tinga's pursuing assistance. Sheena and her 10 month old calf quickly joined the duo, and the four whales effectively had the porpoise trapped against the beach with nowhere to escape. Sheena and her calf then made mock rushes at the porpoise, causing it to react with rapid swimming in circles or by jumping. She was teaching hunting techniques to her calf with the cooperation of the other whales. After just a few minutes, Sheena rushed in and caught the hapless animal by the rear quarter, crushing it enough to reduce its swimming ability. Her calf then moved in close to the quarry to see, feel, smell and even bite it. Later, when it bled even more, the young one would taste blood in the sea water.

Sheena carried the porpoise in her mouth by the rear half, followed by her calf, as the other three whales also swam near the catch. Then the porpoise was killed and cut and torn into smaller pieces, including some pieces small enough for the calf to eat. The three orcas still in the fjord had not yet made their appearance.

———— ◆◆◆ ————

The crew on the *Czarina* had observed the entire episode of chase and kill, and they were confident they had most of the surface action on video tape. The two audio recorders were operating at all times and they hoped they had some good sound to go with the tapes. But the whale pack had not yet reformed. Mike, his camera still on his shoulder, exclaimed "Let's go to the bow. We might be able to tape those three returning past the *Czarina* to join the others!" He grabbed a battery pack and clambered down the stairs to the main deck and hurried past the cabin to the bow, which remained facing directly into the fjord. He was followed by Tracy and Reed.

The three whales, perfectly aligned side by side, surfaced simultaneously 100 yards away to blow, on a course directly for the *Czarina*. Even though Reed, Tracy and Mike were all well experienced with killer whales, a deep feeling of terror crept into each of their consciousness at the direct approach of three of the large predators fresh from killing and eating their biological cousins. Breath came short.

There was no wake at the surface, no bubbles, nothing to indicate that large, highly intelligent carnivores were approaching. Even though clouds had reduced the light somewhat, gray and white gravel on the bottom was still visible 40 feet below the vessel. Mike and Reed, standing at the bow began taping almost directly below their position.

Suddenly and silently the three large black and white torpedo shapes were there, moving smoothly and almost effortlessly in perfect alignment and spacing at a speed of 12 knots 20 feet below the surface. The whale in the center was swimming upside down in obvious enjoyment of the activity. They banked as tightly as the Navy Blue Angels as they passed under the *Czarina* to head directly for the rest of the pack waiting for them offshore in the bay. In a span of 9 seconds they had appeared and disappeared like powerful demons. No sign or sound whatsoever had appeared at the surface and there was no revealing sound from the hydrophones.

As they passed, the size of the animals once again was startling for even an experienced observer, particularly after seeing mostly dorsal fins and saddles at a distance for several days. These three, two females and one sub-adult male, were from 18 to 22 feet long and weighed 5,000 to 7,000 pounds each, more than the average automobile.

"That was scary," Tracy whispered, still looking toward the bottom where the orcas had so swiftly appeared and disappeared.

"No kidding," Mike agreed.

"Truly awesome," Reed noted as he turned the camcorder toward deeper water where the pack appeared to be reforming into a hunting formation. As they watched, the whales started north again...

"They're taking off again, we'd better get moving!" Mike declared as he climbed down the ladder. "Tracy, get the hydrophones! Reed, pull in the anchor! I'll start the engines." Cameras and camcorders were hastily placed on the sofas in the cabin as they hurried with the chores.

Mike started the engines and called through the open cabin door. "Looks like we're still hunting," as he steered the vessel to position it 100 yards behind the whales and 200 yards from shore. He did not want to press the orcas closely when their next move could not be anticipated. Tracy and Reed joined him in the cabin.

"What's the tally now, Tracy?" Reed asked.

"You mean after the last snack? OK, what did they get? Four harbor porpoises that time, right? Reed, what is an average weight for one of that species?" she asked.

"They're quite a bit smaller than most other porpoises. Let's say 100 pounds average," Reed replied.

"Four at 100 pounds is 400 and they ate about 1,625 pounds already for a total of just over 2,000 pounds. In the A-T pack we have 12 adults, 4 sub-adults and 3 calves. How much shall we figure they will eat?" Her question was directed at Reed.

"All of the data I have seen is for killer whales in captivity, and it's a reasonable assumption that animals in the wild have larger appetites. Let's say 150 pounds average for the adults and 100 pounds for the sub-adults. The amount the 2 calves would eat is insignificant."

Tracy was using her note pad. "Twelve adults at 150 pounds each is 1,800 pounds, and four subs at 100 pounds is 400 for a total of 2,200 pounds. The numbers just about balance out, and yet they still seem to be hunting. What's happening?"

Mike smiled. "One thing wrong with averaging numbers like that is that one whale, one of the bulls for example, might have eaten 250 pounds of meat and one of the others may have not have had any yet. Until the group as a whole is satisfied they are probably not going to abandon the hunt. Do you agree, Reed?"

"Makes sense. Leaving some hungry would cause dissension in the pack, which they probably try to avoid. And I get the distinct impression they enjoy the excitement of the hunt. And remember... they may be gutting, skinning and beheading some of the captured animals. That would reduce the overall weight and bulk."

Reed and Mike returned to the flying bridge with their recording equipment as Tracy prepared some hot tea and sandwiches. It was now approaching 8 pm and the light was not the best for additional taping. It looked like another long night ahead.

———— ◆◆◆ ————

Tinga and her pack reassembled into a much less organized group now that most of the whales had fed. She had eaten very little, however, and the three whales which swam beside her were also ready for more food. They moved ahead at 6 knots 50 yards offshore, alert to any indication of prey. Tinga occasionally scanned the bottom and the water ahead with sonar and, as they rose to the surface every few minutes to breathe, she also scanned the rocks visually for any sign of seals. The low throb of the diesel engine behind them interfered only slightly with their perception.

After traveling 1/2 mile further north, Tinga and the other whales heard a sound in the distance ahead. It was faint and difficult initially to pinpoint. Listening attentively, they heard the sound again. It was the sea lion sound, at least two of them near the surface to the northeast. The rest of the pack in the rear had heard it too. The course was changed to the northeast toward the sound source. All whales came to the surface to breath simultaneously at about three minute intervals. Silence was maintained; the quarry should not be needlessly warned of their approach.

Another 1/2 mile was traveled and the occasional sound from the sea lions came through more clearly. Two of them were catching salmon near the center of the bay 300 yards ahead. But now the sounds were changing, the animals must have heard the approach of the whales. Tinga sent out a click train to determine the exact location of the lions in the water. The other whales sent no signals because they were able to get all the information they needed from Tinga's send/receive sequence. Yes, there were two sea lions, one large one and one smaller one, a juvenile. They were now moving off to the east away from the course of the whales. Tinga changed to a north northeast course.

The sea lions, which often encountered killer whale groups in Prince William Sound, could not interpret the whale's intention at a distance. Normally the lions would simply move out of the path of the whales and no encounter would result. The lions knew all too well, however, that at times the whales could and did kill and eat their kin, with major predation taking place when sea lion pups were first entering the water near the haul-out beaches. At any time the whales showed unusual interest, however, the lions regarded such signs as ominous. Now their sensitive underwater hearing detected the whale sounds again, and the whales had changed course. The older lion, with the sub-adult following, now turned north again to stay out of the orca's path.

——————— ◆◆◆ ———————

Tracy climbed to the bridge with sandwiches and tea in a small cooler, which kept the sandwiches dry in case of rain, helped keep the tea hot and reduced spillage. Mike and Reed eagerly dug in. Munching on half a sandwich, Tracy picked up a pair of binoculars to see where the whales might be going in such a hurry. Her sight had proven to be particularly keen at sea and in the dimming light she now scanned carefully. Far ahead she saw momentary objects at the surface which then disappeared. "There's something out there at 12 O'clock but they dove before I could make them out."

Reed also scanned ahead. "I see what you mean," he called out over the sound of the engines. "There are two of them and they look like sea lions. If that's what they are, the whales should be careful. Sea lions are extremely strong and agile animals and their bite can be vicious. Certain instructors of marine mammal courses are known to use grizzly bear skulls and sea lion skulls in final exams because of the difficulty in distinguishing between the two. The long agile neck of the sea lion can turn quickly like a thick, brown snake to put the canine fangs in a position to cut, rip and tear."

"I know what you mean," Mike added. "But I have confidence in the orcas. Just as a black widow spider protects its body and limbs by using its silken web material to subdue prey before approaching for the fatal bite, so the killer whale will not expose itself unnecessarily to danger. It's a matter of prudence, not cowardice."

"I just saw the two sea lions surface," Tracy said, without taking her eyes away from the binoculars. "They're running away fast. And there are the whales right behind them!"

"You're right," Reed noted. "One is fully grown and the other is a young one. They're in a panic and the whales are on course for them."

All three of them were now watching with binoculars. The *Czarina* was making 14 knots in choppy seas 250 yards behind the swiftly moving whales. Suddenly the dorsal fin of a male killer whale appeared well ahead of the main pack, slashing across at right angles to the path of the chase. The smaller sea lion surfaced just short of the dorsal fin as if to avoid a collision with the whale and peered about as if confused.

"They've caught up with the lions and something's happening," Reed noted. "That was the smaller lion at the surface."

"Yes," Tracy agreed, "and the larger one just surfaced about 100 yards further out. It's getting out of there!"

"The whales may have separated the two," Mike nodded.

From the vantage point of the approaching *Czarina*, the trio could see the dorsal fins of seven or eight of the whales circling the location where the young sea lion was last sighted, while the main group of whales remained off to the south of the action. With the vessel now within 100 yards, Mike cut the throttle back to idle. Suddenly a whale surfaced only 20 yards away and he turned the engines off. The silent boat rolled slightly in the choppy seas. As the whales circled, the erratic whuufff of an exhale followed by the vacuum-like sssss of an inhale could be heard clearly by the *Czarina* crew.

Without another word Reed and Mike picked up their video cameras. Tracy raced down the stairs to toss out the hydrophones and turn on the recorder.

The young, healthy sea lion was frightened at being trapped within the group of whales and was determined to escape and rejoin its companion. But every time it tried to get away, its way was blocked by one of the killer whales and it had respect for the teeth of the larger animals. The whales were making squeals, whistles and clicks to disrupt the animal's orientation.

During a quick pass, one of the younger whales nipped at the lion's rear flippers causing the lion to lash out with its sharp teeth, but the whale was already gone. The lion remained at and near the surface, bewildered but ready to fight for its life if need be.

The largest bull in the pack, Kray, had been observing the action and now joined the circle of several whales holding the dangerous 350 pound lion at bay. He swam toward the center of the activity and the other whales moved aside. Kray passed under the lion at shallow depth, his dorsal fin almost touching the animal. As the curved black surface of his tail came under the lion his flukes exploded upward in a powerful stroke. The lion was hurtled 40 feet end over end into the air. Completely disoriented, it fell and hit the water with a hard splash. Ming, one of the adult females was there waiting and seized the entire neck of the beast in her mighty jaws just behind the head much as a lion might seize an antelope by the throat. There was no chance of a lion bite. Her teeth broke the lion's neck in two places and the defence was over.

Several whales, including Tinga, then moved in to cut and tear the body apart into pieces small enough to swallow. The skull and flippers were discarded, as were most of the skin and intestines except the heart and liver. In less than 5 minutes the feeding was over. They regrouped now and turned toward the south. There was no discontent this time. All were fed. It was time to rest and sleep again.

On board the *Czarina*, the cameras were all operating as the whales circled the lion and prevented its escape. Tracy smiled as her sense of humor sparkled, "Well, I've heard of the O. K. Corral, but this is the first time I've seen an orca corral." Mike and Reed both groaned in appreciation.

When the lion exploded from the water it was tossed so high it was almost out of the zoomed-in telephoto field. With his camcorder still running, Mike whispered "What a slap!"

They saw the lion turn end over end and hit the water with a hard splash. A black scythe of a dorsal fin immediately cut through the water at the impact site and the sea lion appeared no more.

"That's the end of the lion," Mike concluded, continuing to tape the scene. "That was some fantastic maneuver!"

"Amazing," Reed and Tracy agreed.

For several minutes there was churning and blowing at and just below the surface as the whales appeared to dissect and eat the hapless lion. On the speaker connected to the hydrophone a variety of whistles, clicks and chirps could be heard.

The whale troupe then reassembled and began moving south. Reed finally spoke. "Dinner may be over. Tracy, better add one 350 pound sea lion to the food list." She didn't have to look. "That's about 2,500 pounds."

Mike shook his head. "That was the most amazing disabling technique I have ever seen or heard of. Have you ever seen anything like this, Reed?"

"No, I haven't, but I've seen video tapes of killer whales fluking sea lion pups in Patagonia. This is the first instance in Alaska that I know of. It's a very clever way to avoid those teeth!"

"Perhaps we'd better pull in the hydrophones and get underway," Reed suggested. "We don't know for sure if the hunt is over." He placed a camcorder back in its case. Tracy climbed down the stairs, pulled in the hydrophones and climbed back to the flying bridge while Mike started the *Czarina* and turned south to follow the whales. Physical and mental fatigue was setting in after 4 days of continuously monitoring the whales followed by several hours of intense observations and photography. They hadn't even had a chance to finish the evening food Tracy had prepared. As the *Czarina* throbbed south at 6 knots, the ice chest was reopened and the sandwiches and tea eagerly taken out.

A chill breeze had sprung up and streaks of gray and white clouds hung below the pale blue of the evening sky. Munching on the sandwiches and dill pickles, they took the opportunity for welcome relaxation. Their focus of attention changed from the whales to the lovely surroundings. To the northwest, beautiful orange and pale purple colors played through the clouds beyond the deep blue and white mountain peaks and valleys on the west side of Eaglek Bay. To the east stretched the wide expanse of Prince William Sound, with the Port of Valdez tucked in the northeast corner.

After gazing at the lovely scene, Reed's thoughts returned to the whales. "What do you say we follow the T pack until tomorrow evening, or about another 24 hours. If they go back to the salmon catching routine, we've got all the material we need to indicate that this pack, beyond any doubt, willingly deviates from what could be called *normal* resident killer whale behavior to carry out devastating raids on warm blooded animals. Mike, Tracy, I think we've seen ample evidence that this pack is capable of the reported aggressive acts, including the disappearance of the Reno couple." He stopped for a moment, staring pensively south in the direction of the whales. "Can you imagine getting into the water in your birthday suit when this pack was nearby in a hunting mode?"

Tracy nodded, "It's scary enough when they approach the *Czarina*, let alone if you were in the water when they're near, clothes or no clothes. Did you two feel the same way I did at the fjord when those three whales, having just killed the porpoises, were coming toward us?"

"If you felt a deep-seated fear," replied Mike, "I certainly did. There is something about facing the largest and cleverest carnivore on earth on its own ground. The feeling is emphasized when the orcas are carrying out organized group killing and eating warm blooded animals such as yourself."

"I've studied and observed killer whales for years," said Reed. "But, yes, I felt a tinge of terror myself."

CHAPTER TWELVE

Theory

L ittle more was said as they finished the food and tea. The cold breeze was increasing and the recording equipment, binoculars, and ice chest were taken down to the main cabin. The heat felt good. Tracy took the wheel and watched with binoculars to be sure they were still behind the whales even though there was little doubt the orcas would follow a relatively straight course in their resting mode. She also checked the stop watch so she could time the rhythm and timing of the blowing of the pack.

"How about a little Armagnac?" Mike suggested, with the bottle already out of the box. He guessed at the amount and poured several shots into a glass container, covered it and placed it in the microwave oven. In 30 seconds the liquid would be at a very warm temperature, just about right to help remove the inner chill. The fragrance of the heated Armagnac drifted through the cabin as Mike removed the cover from the glass container. "That's going to hit the spot." Reed predicted. "Just what the doctor ordered to warm the innards."

Mike poured ample amounts in two brandy snifters and offered one to Tracy at the wheel. "Care for a snifter?"

"No thanks," Tracy replied. "You two go ahead and relax. I'll take the wheel for a while." She looked ahead with binoculars.

Clouds rolling overhead were becoming more dense and the late evening light continued to decline. Following the whales, which came to the surface only every 5 or 6 minutes, became more difficult because of the decreasing visibility, but Tracy knew that, in their resting mode, the general course the whales had established could be depended upon.

Mike sipped the hot Armagnac as he relaxed on one of the sofas. "You know, I've been thinking about the significance of our observations." He looked at Reed. "It seems to me we've gathered the type of data we wanted on the A-T pack, but we lack sufficient data on the other orcas to know if they, too, behave this aggressively from time to time."

"True," responded Reed, swirling the hot glass of amber liquid, "but we have had no reports of other packs attacking or molesting people, dogs, and fishing lines. We do not know what happened to the Reno couple, but it seems clear that the A-T pack is the one involved in the other cases. If any other whale groups were misbehaving we'd hear about it pretty quickly. Tracy, sit down and take five. I'll take over the watchman/captain duties."

Tracy yielded the captain's chair and Reed slid into it, glass still in hand. Mike poured another snifter 1/4 full of the Armagnac and handed it to Tracy, who swirled it and looked through the distilled liquid toward the sky in the west before taking a hefty taste.

"I agree," she observed, "that it is not enough to identify this particular pack as the one which has been causing some problems. We've got to go further and determine under what circumstances this specific pack of killer whales, or others, might attack people or other unusual prey such as dogs. I guess it boils down to this: under what circumstances can the whales be expected to consider Homo sapiens as edible."

"Right," agreed Mike, "We must come up with a solution that does not cause harm to, or even destruction of this pack, which, after all, is simply carrying out hunting for prey in its own territory. And, in addition, which allows continued use of Prince William Sound waters for fishing and recreation."

"The problem could go beyond Prince William Sound, Mike," added Reed from behind the wheel. "We don't know where the A-T pack, or any other in this area, spends the winters. What if they go to Hawaii, California, or even Mexico. We just don't know. And there is no reason to believe their feeding habits will change just because they change hunting ground."

"True," Mike agreed, "and their predation on other species is likely to increase if they do not have access to an abundant, high quality food such as salmon."

The *Czarina's* engines throbbed along as three foot swells caused a gently rolling action to the vessel. Reed started the large stop watch kept on the shelf just ahead of the wheel as the whales rose to blow 200 yards ahead.

Tracy savored the Armagnac and looked deep into the glass. "We seem to be trying to get the answer when we don't have all the necessary data. Perhaps, in addition to simply passively observing the whales, as we have been doing, we should also set up some situations where we can observe how the whales react to experimental conditions."

"Interesting idea," mused Reed, "but we'd have to do such experiments without harming the whales in any way, *and* without harming any other protected marine mammals such as sea otters or lions. In addition to Blue War, we would definitely have the animal rights groups going bonkers over this one."

"They'd go bonkers if they saw the animals killed by the orcas when they're on a hunting spree," replied Tracy.

"If we're going to set up some feeding situations there are some definite no no's," Reed observed. "One is that we can't use people, another is that we can't use protected animals, and the third is we can't use pets such as dogs. Yet, to make this approach fruitful, we must have something which will give us good data about attack or non-attack by marauding killer whales. And remember Mike, we also need something without thick fur, or at least without heavy clothing!" He chuckled.

Mike sat up. "You know, Colorado Agricultural College in Greeley has a program which might fit the bill. Tracy, remember that uranium exploration project we put together northwest of Greeley a few years ago? That interesting person at CAC, Mary something, was breeding a special small pig for use in medical experiments."

"I remember," Tracy recalled with enthusiasm, "the pigs were also used for testing drugs and for equipment testing because they have many internal organs similar to man. In fact, when we visited Mary, Mary Pantera, they had two types, one was the mini-pig, which weighed 140 to 200 pounds, and they had a micro-pig which weighed less than 100 pounds fully grown."

Mike's enthusiasm for the idea was growing. "And the mini-pigs weigh about the same as an adult Homo sapiens! They have no fur whatsoever, only slightly hairy skin but much less hair than a seal. Another plus could be the pig's fat layers; seals have fat layers. And don't forget, certain parts of pig hearts are used to actually replace parts of human hearts through surgery. "

Reed turned from the wheel, excited by the idea. "Guys, this might be perfect! It's a food animal, readily obtainable and they can be trained. The lack of thick hair should answer the question of clothing or hair turning the whales off."

"Another thing," Tracy pointed out, "is that the internal structure, bones and other organs, should appear to a whale's sonar very similar to the internal structure of a man. And we can probably assume that the pig is unfamiliar prey to the whales, unless they do winter somewhere where pigs get in the water."

Reed smiled. "I helped out with some research on sharks one time, and it was amazing what was found in the stomachs of some of the larger specimens. Besides fish, we found parts of horses, a whole bulldog with it's collar on, chickens and part of a pig. It's almost impossible to figure out where the various food came from. Researchers in the Antarctic have found parts of killer whales in the stomachs of other killer whales which evidences cannibalism. Truly, the pig idea seems like a good one."

"The big difference between the pig and a human, from the whales perspective, is that the human is much longer for it's weight," Mike observed. "The pig's weight is concentrated in the body and it has short stubby legs. The human has longer limbs, where more of the weight is distributed. A human would be easier to cut up or to swallow whole."

"Yes, but the seal also has a relatively stubby body compared to a man, and it has stubby flippers," replied Reed. "A 175 pound harbor seal may be less than 5 feet long."

"Sounds like some Homo sapiens I know," laughed Tracy, and they all chuckled.

Mike became serious again. "Look, the mini-pigs in the 125 to 175 pound range may the perfect way to get a number of answers. Once again, they have little hair, the size and shape is good, they're available by the hundreds at reasonable cost, they are intelligent and can be readily trained, and they can be handled easily. On top of that, they should look good on the whale's sonar, right down to the heart, lungs and bone structure."

"But let's look at our objective," cautioned Reed. "We want to determine several things, most important of which is proof that the killer whales will molest or kill and eat man. We cannot use a man for this, and the nearest thing to a man is a chimpanzee, obviously out of the question for many reasons. You can rule out pets such as the dog, and I can't think of any other farm animals which have the right shape. You may be right, Mike, the mini-pig may be the best answer."

"Let's carry this logic a little further, though," Tracy added. "If we do establish that the whales will attack and eat pigs, then what? Will this be adequate proof that they can and will attack Homo sapiens? Remember, there are millions of people out there who are totally convinced that killer whales not only will not *attack* man, but that the whales are a friend and co-inhabitor of this blue ball we're riding around on. How would you handle criticism that whales killing and eating pigs only proves that they do indeed have tastes similar to man, because man also likes pork?"

"In many scientific experiments, as you know," Reed responded, "it is impossible to determine in advance what will happen in the course of the experiments, or what the results will be. If the answers were all available in advance there would be no experimentation. In this case there are dozens of questions to be answered about the whales and how they think and react in certain situations. To my knowledge, no one has ever carried out experiments of this type on wild killer whales. At this point we do not understand their sonar, we do not understand their sound communications and many other aspects of their lives. To the detriment of the whales, much of the experimentation which could have been done on captive whales has been thwarted by Blue War and similar groups because scientists are prevented from collecting a few whales per year."

Mike sipped on the Armagnac. "Yes, but Tracy has a good point. There is no doubt that many animal protectionists, biologists and others will attack the significance of a program which uses pigs to help determine if killer whales will attack man."

"This won't be the first time the thickness of our hide has been tested," Reed smiled. "Let's make careful plans. This is going to take some selling to a number of different people, including some politicians."

Weariness now began to take a toll on the crew. The little sleep they had been able to sandwich in with their activities, along with the spell of the Armagnac, made the thought of sleep impossible to overcome.

Mike pointed toward a cove on the nearby island. "Let's pull in there and drop anchor and get some sleep."

"Great idea" both Tracy and Reed agreed.

Within thirty minutes they were anchored in a quiet cove and ready to call it a day. No more food, no more drink, just sleep.

The next morning Tracy was up and around first. After making coffee she cooked some eggs over easy and heated bacon, covered in paper towels, in the microwave to get rid of much of the grease.

In another three hours they were back in Whittier and tied the *Czarina* into its slip. Another hour was required to pack many of the items to the Suburban to haul to Anchorage.

On the drive to Anchorage they reviewed the pig idea further. It continued to seem a great concept.

C H A P T E R   T H I R T E E N

Kids and orcas

Anchored 100 feet off shore from a sandy beach on the heavily forested north side of the small cove, two 28 foot pleasure boats, tied together with bumpers between, bobbed like one red and one blue cork on the swells. Two families from Anchorage, the Saunders and Hallorans, had just arrived the previous evening and had failed to get even a nibble in trying to catch halibut in water 80 feet deep in the middle of the cove. Two or three times each summer they took a few days away from the bustle of the city to fish, explore and absorb the serenity of Prince William Sound.

The Saunders children: Larry, seventeen; Sarah, fifteen; and Tim, thirteen, enjoyed outings with the two Halloran girls: Lenore, sixteen, and Heidi, fourteen.

On board, a late breakfast was over and the four parents sat in the morning sun joking and drinking double bloody Marys. A tape player was loudly playing a selection of country western songs with Willy Nelson singing something about on the road again.

"By damn, Harry," Dave Halloran observed, "we should get out here more often. This country's too pretty to visit only a couple of times a summer."

Harry Saunders took a sip of the reddish liquid in his glass. "I'll agree with you there, Dave. The halibut haven't been biting in this cove, but we'll try to get the kids into some salmon later today."

"Say, Dad," Larry Saunders asked, "We're not fishing this morning. How about letting us row over to that stream that comes in on the west side of the cove? We might see some salmon or crabs over there and it would do us good to get off the boats for a while."

"Yeah!" the other four kids chimed in.

"Sounds good to me," Ruth Saunders encouraged, stepping away from the small galley on their boat where she had been washing dishes. "These kids drive us bonkers if the fishing is slow."

"Let them go for a couple of hours," Carol Halloran agreed. "I'll put together some sandwiches and cookies so they won't starve."

Both men nodded and assisted the enthusiastic children as they untied and dropped a small oar-powered dinghy from each boat into the water.

"Boy- oh-boy, maybe we'll see a bear!" Tim Saunders chattered excitedly.

"Don't say that or they won't let us go," Lenore Halloran cautioned so the adults wouldn't hear.

The sandwiches were soon ready and in a back pack, along with apples, cookies, and soft drinks in cans. The kids climbed into the two small craft, anxious to go. At the insistence of Mrs. Saunders, they donned orange life preserver vests. Lenore rowed one dinghy and Larry the other as they splashed away from the anchored vessels toward deeper water and the west side of the cove.

———————— ◆◆◆ ————————

As Tinga's orca pack approached the entrance to the cove, four whales, two sub-adults, including Tinga's three-year old daughter, and two adult females swam playfully in advance of the main group, exploring the sea floor and the water ahead for interesting fish or animals. None of the pack was really hungry, but they were curious and feeling playful and they knew seals and sea otters frequented this area. They hoped to find one and have some fun. The four ahead turned briefly into the cove and scanned the area with sonar. They heard noises from the anchored vessels on the north side while a scan of the south side detected a yard-long, furry animal at the surface 300 yards away. It was a sea otter, bobbing on its back on the waves while pounding an urchin on a rock on its chest. They also scanned the two stationary vessels and picked up sounds coming from them indicating objects were being placed in the water. Communication noises between two-legged creatures of the type they had encountered previously were also heard, and they detected two small vessels leaving the larger ones. These objects were of little interest. But the sea otter offered a chance for some fun. Advancing into the cove, the four rose in unison to blow, submerged to 30 feet and swam rapidly toward the floating animal.

The five children from the two pleasure boats had entered into a race to see who could row fastest the 200 yards to the west side of the cove. They had rowed about half the distance, well away from the music they didn't like, when fourteen-year-old Heidi pointed and exclaimed, "Look, there's something at the entrance to the cove!"

Larry and Lenore stopped rowing and all the children looked toward the entrance. The tips of four black dorsal fins were disappearing beneath the surface and rapidly coming toward them. Mist from the exhaled humid breath of the animals hung in the cool air. They watched in silence as the black dorsal fins of four whales appeared in unison and then disappeared below the surface.

The oldest of the group, Larry, seventeen and just out of high school, shouted excitedly. "Those are killer whales! They might be coming in here to eat a school of herring or salmon or something! This is great! Let's watch!"

Tim, the youngest one of the five, wasn't so sure. "Larry, why don't we go back to the boats? We don't know what they're doing and they're scary."

"Aw, c'mon Tim," his sister Sarah chided. "You even touched a killer whale in San Diego. This may be our chance to see wild ones up close."

"Well, let's ask Mom," Tim requested.

"Look! Look!" Lenore suddenly pointed from the other craft. "There's a sea otter over there on the surface. Maybe the whales will go near it!" Without waiting for a response she began rowing toward the spot where the otter was bobbing on the surface.

"Let's go," Larry responded enthusiastically as he turned the other dinghy and began rowing in the same direction.

No sooner had they started rowing than a black shape arched rapidly up from the depths, like a huge northern pike after a mallard duckling, to seize the otter in its teeth.

With two of the younger whales following, Tinga dove with the sea otter to 50 feet near the bottom where she released the otter and its buoyant fur began taking it toward the surface. But one of the young whales caught it and swam to the surface. The two then began having fun with the otter and resembled dogs playing with an old sock as the otter was carried one way and then the other. After a couple of minutes of play, the otter was released and it floated upward to the surface where it gasped for air. The orcas had not bitten it hard enough to break any bones or kill it, but the skin had been torn in a couple of places and the slight stain of blood trailed the otter to the surface. The animal was terrified.

Sarah, in the front of the Saunders' dinghy, saw the sea otter taken. "Look, they've taken the sea otter. The killer whales must be killing it!"

Larry and Lenore stopped rowing to look at the spot where the otter had disappeared, now only 30 yards away. There was nothing at the surface except the whale "footprints," unrecognized by the children, indicating powerful flukes at work beneath the surface.

"It's gone, maybe they did kill it," Larry sounded forlorn.

Suddenly the otter reappeared at the surface, fur twisted and apparently cut in several places. The animal was looking at them with sorrowful eyes and it appeared to be pleading for help to save it from being killed. As they watched, two black dorsal fins rose and knifed through the water directly toward the otter. The first whale to reach the otter grabbed it and, with a great swirl, both whales and the otter disappeared beneath the surface. Close behind, two larger, fast-moving whales appeared, blew and then disappeared.

"Let's help the otter!" shouted Lenore. "If it comes up again let's take it away from them before they kill it!"

"Otters bite!" warned Larry. "But we might be able to drive them away so they'll leave it alone!"

They rowed swiftly to the spot where the otter was last seen, and, as they arrived and looked down into the water, they could see the gravelly bottom not more than 50 feet below. But they could not see the whales or the otter.

Suddenly the otter bobbed to the surface 20 yards away. Its fur appeared even more severely mangled and, as it gasped for breath, it looked at them with forlorn eyes. It made no attempt to escape. It seemed afraid to try to swim.

Larry removed one of the dinghy paddles from its oarlock and began slapping the surface of the water. "Lenore," he shouted, "let's try to distract them away from the otter! Splash on the water!"

Lenore removed one of the paddles and began to slap the water surface. The children watched the hapless otter, wondering what would happen next. But Tim looked around in apprehension.

The whales had detected, through hearing and sonar, the approach of the two small craft from the stationary vessels. But in their fun with the otter and each other they paid little attention to them. Now, however, the two small craft with their noisy creatures on board were in their play area and were slapping the water as if wanting to join in the activity.

The two adult female whales, each weighing nearly 7,000 pounds and three times as long as the dinghies, decided to approach the craft for a closer look. They were completely unafraid of the slapping on the surface; it only made them more curious. Side by side, 10 feet below the surface, they approached the two dinghies on the shoreward side, away from the surface slapping and the otter location. At 8 knots they rolled on their side and rose to within 3 feet of the surface for a close look at the creatures in the boats. No part of either whale rose above the surface as they passed by and looked closely at the face of one occupant and the backs of the others. Then they continued down toward the bottom.

Tim, still quite frightened, was looking down in the water fearfully and not at the otter as the others were doing. Suddenly he saw two black and white bodies emerge from the gray depths. Their speed and size scared him. Each of the whales appeared huge.

"The whales! The whales!" shouted Tim, but as the others turned the whales were no longer to be seen.

"Where are they?" asked Larry.

"They just came up on this side to look at us real close. You'd better stop slapping the water."

The sea otter was still at the surface and the two younger killer whales surfaced 50 yards away to blow.

Larry looked around. "Well, I think it's working. They seem to be leaving the otter alone." He and Lenore slapped the water a few more times, but they were wondering where the two larger whales were.

"Let's leave the otter and go back to the boats," Tim urged. "We don't know what the whales might do." Fourteen year old Heidi agreed.

"If they show up again, I'll let them have one!" warned Larry as he slapped the water with vigor one more time. "They should leave the otter alone!"

They heard shouting and the Halloran's boat horn honking. Looking in that direction they could see their parents waving wildly for them to return to the larger vessels. Larry waved back as a signal that all was OK. Nothing to worry about while he was there.

Larry also noticed, however, that exhaust was rising from the Halloran's boat indicating the engine had been started, and Harry, his father, was hurrying to the bow of the Halloran boat to begin pulling the anchor.

The two females from Tinga's group, Kee and Targa, considered the contact with these organisms another training exercise for the young whales. These were creatures they had seen a number of times but not this close. They did not intend to kill and eat now, but valuable lessons could perhaps be learned by such close study. In addition, these creatures were making slapping sounds as if they wanted to play.

Tinga and the rest of the pack, still cruising outside the cove, had become curious and had made a wide circle. They now approached the cove entrance, listening with interest to the splashing and other sounds coming from the area where their four companions had been harassing the otter. Zirgo, the nearly mature male, accelerated ahead of the rest for closer observation and perhaps participation in the activities.

In the cove Kee and Targa signaled to each other and rose in unison directly under the two dinghies, raising them both 8 to 10 feet above the water surface. The occupants and the dinghy contents were spilled into the frigid water.

The children screamed as they felt the dinghies lift from the water, although at first they did not realize what was happening. The power of the whales made the upward thrust feel as if a large machine was moving them. But, dumped into the water they became panic-stricken because they realized they were completely at the mercy of the whales. All were good swimmers, the dinghies would not sink, and their life jackets would keep them afloat, but they did not know what the whales would do next. They struggled to get back into the one dinghy which remained upright, but there were too many trying to get in on one side and they flipped it over.

Dave Halloran and Harry Saunders had watched nervously through binoculars as the children approached the area where killer whales were active. After honking horns and yelling to the children to move away from the area got no results, they had decided to go after them. As the women hurriedly untied the two boats, Dave started the engine and Harry clambered to the bow of the boat to weigh the anchor. In the interest of speed they would leave one boat there and return for it later.

Carol Halloran was frightened as she watched the two dinghies through binoculars. Ruth Saunders suddenly shouted "Carol, what is that near the entrance to the cove?"

Carol swung her binoculars in that direction just as five more members of Tinga's clan blew at the surface. The largest dorsal fin that appeared was wavy and had a distinct notch at the rear edge.

"My God, there are more killer whales coming. Dave, hurry, HURRY!"

Dave Halloran swung the boat toward the south side of the cove. Just as they started toward the dinghies, they saw them lifted vertically from the water as if toys by two killer whales. They did not hear the children scream because of the noise of the engine, but both mothers wailed and began crying.

Kee and Targa circled quickly after dumping the dinghies, joined by the two sub-adults and Zirgo, the young male from the main group. All the whale's sonar scanned the awkward creatures thrashing about at the water's surface. The scan revealed that the animals had a thin covering over most of their body, but the chest area was covered by a rather thick material which absorbed some of the sonar and revealed that it was not edible.

The whales as a group swam past and just under the children struggling at the surface. These were some of the same creatures they had killed but declined to eat previously and there was no interest in that now. Only curiosity and learning.

Tyree, the precocious daughter of Tinga, turned from the group and quickly rose to the surface to seize the largest of the creatures in the middle and take it down for closer examination.

Larry had been trying to right one of the dinghies so the children could get in when he was grabbed and taken under. It happened so quickly he had no chance to even catch a breath. Sarah, next to him, saw the whale grab him and immediately disappear. She tried to grab his arm but he was gone too quickly.

Kee, holding the creature gently in her mouth, descended 10 feet below the surface. She was surprised at its buoyancy. The other whales approached and she released the creature, which immediately and quickly began rising to the surface as a result of its own buoyancy. Two of the whales followed it toward the surface and then turned back.

The whales could hear the disconcerting noise of the engine of the vessel approaching fast across the cove, and Tinga, still outside the cove, was signaling them to regroup at the entrance. In her wisdom she sensed danger in this situation and was calling her pack together to retreat from the cove. Regrouping underwater, the five orcas in the cove swam toward those waiting at the entrance.

The Halloran boat arrived at the swamped dinghies just as Larry's seemingly lifeless body bobbed to the surface. The children struggled toward the boat. Dave Halloran dove in, swam to Larry and began towing him back to the boat. The killer whales had apparently disappeared.

One by one they pulled the frightened, cold and crying children aboard. Larry was coughing and choking, but at least he was breathing.

"He'll be OK," his father reassured Ruth Saunders, still sobbing and terrified. An examination of Larry's skin and clothing, including his life preserver, revealed not a single mark or cut.

"If they'd wanted to kill him, they sure could have done it," Dave Halloran remarked, the effects of the bloody Marys beginning to override the adrenaline. "Why would they take him and release him with no harm done?"

"No harm other than almost drowning him!" Ruth Saunders almost screamed at him. "Another couple of minutes and he'd have been dead!"

"All right, all right," Dave Saunders urged. "Let's tie onto both dinghies and get back to the other boat so we can get the kids warmed up and into some dry clothes.

They knew that if the killer whale which had taken Larry down had wanted to kill him, it could have done so easily. No marks suggested to them that it may have intended no harm.

With the shivering children inside the cabin getting warm, Dave swung the boat around and he and Harry up-righted the two dinghies and retrieved the back pack. Tow ropes were tied onto the two small craft and they motored back to the anchored Saunders' boat.

Their trip was over. The children wanted to get off the water and go home, and both mothers were anxious to get away from the animals which had attacked their offspring. Harry and Dave had to agree it might be best to leave and let everyone's nerves calm down. They did not want the families to develop a dislike for the Sound because it would disrupt future trips. Besides, there was nothing wrong with a little publicity and they were sure to get plenty when they contacted the media, especially with some of the stories which had already been circulating about the killer whales.

Together the two boats started the four-hour return trip to Whittier.

It was raining in Whittier when the two pleasure boats arrived. The children had been dried and warmed after their ordeal at Knight Island, and they were feeling better although seventeen-year-old Larry Saunders remained very shaken. They regretted cutting their outing short and returning to Anchorage, but both families wanted to settle in and try to get back to normal after a close call with death.

Conversing on the radio on the way west from the Sound, they decided to advise only their friend and police chief Ted Barnes at Whittier. No effort would be made to reach the media with the story at this time; perhaps after a few days had passed.

Unable to use a cell phone at Whittier, Dave went to a pay phone and called Paul Grant, office manager at the parts store where he worked. He told Paul Paul he would be in for work the next day because they had returned early from the Sound holidays.

Thirty minutes later the families were in Ted Barnes's small office. They related to Barnes the story of what had happened. Barnes was very concerned about the possible loss of human life.

"Let's see now," Ted Barnes reviewed the notes he had taken during the meeting while listening quietly to the tale. He looked directly at Larry. "The whales took the otter down but the otter kept coming to the surface... alive. Then you kids started slapping the water to scare the whales away? But the whales came back, tipped your dinghies over and took Larry here under water, but released him unharmed and with no wounds, not even a scratch?" He glanced over the families for any reaction. "But it seems you want me to believe that was a whale attack? Hell, if those whales had attacked you kids they'd have made mince meat of you in no time." He looked across the table at the families. "Sounds to me like they were playing."

Barnes continued, "Now all of you have seen the killer whales in San Diego. Damned if those whales aren't playful and curious. Didn't you kids stop to think you might have been inviting the whales to play? And the otter; they must have been playing with it, too, or they would have killed it. Where was the otter the last time you saw it?"

"It was still floating on the surface," Lenore stated.

"Was it dead or alive?" Barnes asked.

Heidi spoke enthusiastically, "It was alive! I saw it still looking at us with those big eyes as we left."

"But they almost killed my son!" Ruth Saunders protested, her arm around Larry. She could see that Barnes was about to write off the incident as play.

"OK now," Barnes continued, "One more time. The whales dragged that otter around for about 5 minutes and didn't kill it. They tipped the dinghies over after the kids slapped the water to attract them, and then they took Larry here under but let him go without so much as a scratch. Sounds like play to me." He closed the book in which he had been taking notes.

"By gosh, maybe they're right, Larry," his father remarked, looking at his still shaken son. "You had good intentions to scare them away from the otter but maybe they *did* interpret the slapping as an invitation to play."

"Maybe we blew it," sixteen-year-old Lenore Halloran observed, shaking her head. "Maybe we could have been the first people to communicate and play with wild killer whales."

As they talked, all adults in the group, even Ruth and Carol, began to conclude that the children may have missed a real opportunity to befriend killer whales in the North Pacific. xEven the children, who earlier had been convinced that the whales were trying to kill them, began to agree that there WAS a good chance the whales were playing. After all, the whales didn't eat the otter, and perhaps the slapping of oars led the orcas to believe the humans wanted to play. The whale which grabbed Larry could have easily killed or drowned him, there was no doubt about that.

"Well, I'm going to file a report saying you folks had a killer whale encounter," Captain Barnes concluded, but, with political savvy, looked at the parents and added "if that's all right with you folks."

They all nodded that yes, that would be fine.

Barnes continued, "But we're going to have to be careful how we word it because it is illegal under federal law to approach or harass whales. The orcas were really minding their own business when the kids approached them. NOAA could impose fines or, worse, if radical outfits like Blue War get hold of this, they might file suit on behalf of the whales or some other fool thing." He looked directly at the adults. "Do you folks agree?" Barnes had been around long enough to know that agreement with these points now could reduce the possibility of arguments later, or complaints to old Governor Springfield himself, should the media get wind of the incident. They all nodded agreement once again.

"For these reasons," Barnes added thoughtfully, "I'd recommend you keep quiet about this to avoid possible legal problems for yourselves. If it's O K with you folks, I'll describe this as a killer whale encounter and not as a killer whale attack. But," he looked at the entire group, "with appropriate warnings to anyone to be extremely careful when near killer whales for any reason."

Ted Barnes concluded the meeting by thanking them for coming in with their report and added that he hoped the experience would not sour them on enjoying the Sound for recreation. The families left Ted Barnes office with a different attitude than when they had entered. The children were particularly intrigued by the idea that they might have come close to having interactions with the large predators.

With more than three hours remaining before the train was due to arrive from Portage and then return in the opposite direction, the families returned to their boats for sandwiches, coffee and hot chocolate. The conversation centered mostly on what had happened in the Sound. The kids did much more listening than talking, for a change.

"Earlier I could see nothing wrong with informing the media about this." Carol Halloran remarked as she bit into a turkey on rye. But Ted Barnes' point about law violations for harassing the whales has merit. We'd better keep quiet."

"Yes," Ruth agreed, "let's just keep this to ourselves."

"I wish now we'd taken some photos," Harry observed, sipping at a large cup of coffee to which he had added a good charge of George Dickel sour mash whiskey. "But that never gets done in an emergency."

"Speaking of emergencies, I'm not totally convinced the whales were just playing," Dave noted. "It's possible the whales left because they heard our boat approaching. If we hadn't shown up they might have drowned one of the kids even if they didn't bite 'em."

"But let's tell the kids to just say they saw some killer whales," Ruth urged.

"You can't ask the kids to lie, Ruth," Carol chided.

Conversation went on for another hour and they then carried their belongings to Dave's truck. The kids, who had decided to wander around Whittier, returned when they heard the train arrive, unsuccessful at finding anything interesting. Once the two vehicles were on the train, the kids ran forward to one of the two passenger cars for the ride to Portage; even though visibility was poor through the consistently dirty train windows, there was more room for them to move around.

◆◆◆

CHAPTER FOURTEEN

Interview

Reed Remington and Tracy and Mike Mackenzie had arrived in Anchorage ready to plan the next steps in their attempt to solve the killer whale problems in Prince William Sound and to protect the whales. At noon Tracy was at Carr's Supermarket with her shopping list when she picked up a copy of the *Times*. After loading the groceries into the rear seat and trunk of the car, she took a moment to open the paper and scan through it to see what was new in Anchorage and Alaska.

On page three there was a short story about Whittier and how most residents seemed to appreciate the work of Ted Barnes, who kept the Town pretty much crime-free. Acting on a hunch, she used her cell phone to call Mike in Stuckagain Heights where he and Reed were cleaning the hydrophones, tape players, and video units. Tracy told him about the Whittier article and added: "It would be a good idea to call Ted Barnes to stay in touch and find out if anything new has turned up in Prince William Sound."

"You're absolutely right, and thanks for calling, honey, I'll call Barnes this afternoon.

Hanging up the phone, Mike advised Reed of Tracy's hunch and then looked up Ted Barnes' office phone number.

Barnes answered almost immediately.

"Hi, Ted. This is Mike Mackenzie in Anchorage. How's it going down your way?"

"Pretty good, Mike. Quite a few tourists passing through but most of them get out of Whittier as fast as they can. Not much for them to do here unless they fish."

"Well, Tracy, Reed and I still plan to be studying the whale activity in the Sound this summer and I like to touch base with you once in a while because you're our main contact down there."

"Yes, and we'll be glad to help when and where we can." Barnes replied. "By the way, keep this between us, but I did get a report of some killer whale activity a couple of days ago."

"Can you tell me much about it?" Mike asked.

"I recorded it as some kids attracting whales but neither the kids nor the whales had any injuries." He proceeded to tell Mike the story of the sea otter and the whales along with the kids slapping the water and the whales tipping their small boats over. "And then one of the kids was taken under and very scared but unhurt. The parents saw it all."

"If it is OK with you, Ted, this could be very important for our whale studies and, if possible, we'd like to talk to the parents and possibly even the kids."

Barnes cautioned "We don't want to get a bunch of bad publicity out of this. It could be bad for the whales and it may also bring in the feds."

Mike wrote down the information Barnes told him about the Halloran and Saunders families in Anchorage. Mike said it would all be kept quiet and, after hanging up, looked up the names, addresses and phone numbers of the two families on his computer.

The Saunders line was busy, but he got through to the Halloran's. After explaining to Carol Halloran that he was a researcher who had been studying killer whales in Prince William Sound for several years, he explained that he, his wife and Dr. Reed Remington would like to meet with all of them in a few hours, at around six if that was OK. Mike wanted a late meeting to be sure all the family members were there.

"Well, that should be all right. The children are at the library but they'll be back by then. And I'll call Ruth Saunders."

At the library and whenever they spoke with friends, the kids could not resist telling about the exciting adventure with the killer whales. Many of those who heard the story wanted to go on the next trip and wondered when it might take place. Lenore usually could calm down some of the excitement by telling them there might not even be another trip.

"Good, we appreciate that. By the way, Mrs. Halloran, did you take any photographs so we might be able to identify the particular group you encountered?"

"God, no, we didn't take any photos! Who's going to think about cameras when you're trying to save your kids!"

"Do you really think the kids were in danger?" Mike asked

"Yes, we did, but after talking to Captain Barnes in Whittier we decided that maybe the whales were just trying to play with the kids. But at the time I was absolutely terrified that the whales were going to kill them. I know Ruth felt the same way."

"Well, perhaps we can go over that later this afternoon," Mike said. "But if there were no photos, did anyone get a good look at any of the whales so we might try to identify them?"

Carol thought for a minute. "It all happened so fast, and we were quite a ways away from them... but, wait a minute. Yes, I was looking with the binoculars when we saw more whales at the entrance to the cove. The only one that was distinctive was the one with the largest fin."

A mature male, Mike thought. "Please go on."

"Now that I think about it, the shape of the fin struck me as a little odd because it did not seem to be straight as fins I have seen on other whales. This one was, well, sort of wavy. And there was a piece missing, a notch, at the back of the fin. There was nothing distinctive about the other whales, so far as I can remember."

There was silence for a moment. Mike knew that it must have been the A-T pack again. He was thankful that these innocent families had gotten no more than a scare. "Thank you, Mrs. Halloran. You are very helpful. We'll plan to see you this evening at about six? ...Good, thanks again." He hung up and noted that Tracy had returned from the grocery store.

Mike was pensive as he went back to the garage where Reed was working on the hydrophone cables. He asked Tracy to come to the garage. When she and Reed were both there he explained what he had heard from Barnes concerning another whale incident. "I just a few minutes ago spoke with one of the parents. Her children were among those who encountered the whales. We'll see them tonight at 6 pm. No photos, but she got a good look with binoculars at a male with the group."

Reed looked up from the connection between the cable and the hydrophone. "Don't tell me it was T4."

"Not much doubt about it," Mike nodded. "Tall, wavy dorsal fin with a notch in the rear. Those families don't know how close they came to disaster."

Again, it appeared, the A-T pack had given a clear indication it was becoming a "rogue" group. They knew they must continue to gather all available information and somehow come up with a good plan to avoid harm to either people or to the whales.

That evening they arrived at the Halloran home just before six o'clock to find everyone waiting for them. The Saunders' had been there for almost an hour and the margaritas had been flowing freely.

After introductions, Dr. Remington, who found it convenient to use his title in such occasions, explained the nature of the killer whale research he and the Mackenzies had carried out in the Sound over the past few years. He explained that it was important to learn all they could about the animals because they would then be in a position to help the whales and perhaps avoid difficult situations like the one they had experienced. Tracy brought out some photographs and Carol Halloran was able to tentatively identify one of them, the large male with the wavy, notched dorsal fin.

Reed advised them that the male identified was with the AT group of whales, a "pod" with which they were familiar.

The children and adults then went on to explain the encounter in full detail to the three investigators, who obviously did not need any warning about the whales. Through questioning, it was established that there were four whales in the cove, two big ones and two smaller ones. The main group of whales, including the large male, had apparently stayed near the entrance.

"We appreciate the information," Mike assured them, "but it is important that we try to figure out which whales turned the dinghies over and which might have taken Larry here under."

"I have no idea," Larry said. "I didn't see the whales at all after we got to where the otter was."

"I saw two of them come up near the dinghie to look at us!" exclaimed Tim. "They looked very big to me!"

"Could you tell if they were adults?" Reed asked.

"No, but they were big, three times as long as our dinghies!" Tim almost shouted.

"We had a look at the two which turned the dinghies over," Dave Saunders offered. "There was one whale under each boat one and they came up at the same time. They were big; I'd say they were adult females. What do you think, Harry?"

"I agree, they were too large for youngsters." Carol and Ruth nodded agreement. But no one had seen the whale which took Larry down.

Appreciative of their apparent intense interest in the whales, Reed explained that it was possible the whales were playing with both the otter and the children. "But you are all fortunate no one was seriously injured," he advised them. "The whales are powerful and intelligent," he warned, "and even a whale at play can do serious damage. You would definitely be well advised to stay away from them."

With the time approaching 7 pm the trio thanked the families for their assistance and departed for Romano's Restaurant where they served a fair fettucine with white clam sauce. The owner had changed the recipe two years previously and it just wasn't as good as it used to be, but still pretty good.

As soon as the trio had left the house, Lenore spoke up. "Look, I've been doing some research in the library and these whales aren't as bad as they're making them out to be. We came as close as anyone in this hemisphere has come to communicating with wild killer whales. In Australia they even had killer whales which helped whalers catch other types of whales. Why shouldn't we follow up on our original contact?"

"I agree with Lenore," Larry spoke up, having been severely ridiculed by his friends for the poor TV coverage. "I think we should go back to the Sound and find those whales again, but this time we should really be ready to communicate. We weren't ready on that last trip."

His father had been listening. He poured another margarita for himself, Dave and the two women. "Christ, Larry, you're the last one I thought would want to go back and find that pack of whales again. You got nerve, boy!" He slapped his son on the back.

Dave Halloran did not have a son but he was proud of Lenore's aggressive attitude about going back on the Sound to look for the whales. "Heidi, what do you think about this idea of going back out there?"

Heidi, who had also been ribbed about the poor showing on TV, did not hesitate. "Let's get ready this time and go. Let's show that we can do things with the wild whales!"

"By God, that's good enough for me," her father proclaimed, his speech definitely slurred. "Let's get our plans made!"

◆◆◆

Research

Lenore Halloran had blossomed into a sweet sixteen both in disposition and appearance. She began to focus her excellent scholastic abilities on the study of killer whales and every opportunity was taken to search for data about the species *Orcinus orca*. She and her fourteen-year-old sister, Heidi, had become well known among their peers because of the notoriety from the national news coverage of the whales in the Sound. Information available at her school library, to which the school principal granted access even though it was summer vacation, was almost nil and she quickly exhausted the references in the Anchorage Municipal Library. In frustration she confronted the head librarian for the Municipality, Esther Beasley.

"Excuse me, Mrs. Beasley, but I'm trying to get some information about killer whales and I've checked the Internet but I thought the library might have information more specific for Alaska. Am I missing something here?

"Orcinus orca, aye? Well let's see what we have." Mrs. Beasley typed in some information on the computer terminal in front of her and frowned. "This whale is common in southern Alaska waters and yet we have little information on hand about Alaska whales. Sounds like a good research project. I'll do more digging."

"That will be appreciated!" exclaimed Lenore. "A very important family project is involved and we need all the information we can get right away!"

"Here's a thought: The Alaska Department of Fish and Game site. Wait a minute, even better, I'll call them. I know the receptionist over there and she might be able to steer us in the right direction. They might even have a whale specialist." She punched the numbers into the phone and waited for it to ring. "Hi, Josephine? This is Esther at the library. How are you? Say, I've got a young lady, Lenore Halloran, over here who is interested in Alaskan killer whales and we have almost nothing specifically about them. Is there one of the biologists over there she could get in touch with who might be a good contact about this type of whale?"

Although Lenore could not hear the response, Josephine was telling Esther that George Maxwell, one of the biologists, had been doing some special research into killer whales and she was sure Maxwell would be glad to help. In fact, Maxwell had just arrived at the office if Ms. Halloran wished to speak to him. Not wishing to waste time, Esther said "Good, put him on." She handed the phone to Lenore and advised her, "One of the biologists who might be able to help you is coming on the line. Tell him what you need."

George Maxwell came on the line. "Hello, may I help you?" in his best public relations voice.

"Yes, my name is Lenore Halloran, an 11th grade student, and I'm trying to do some research on killer whales in Alaska but I can't find many references. Mrs. Beasley here at the library suggested we call for help."

"Yes, as a matter of fact, I do have quite a bit of information on hand here at the office. If you can come over I'd be glad to show you what we have." Maxwell thought it must be the recent publicity stirring up some interest in the whales.

"Good. Could I come by today?" Lenore asked.

"Of course, I expect to be here all day."

Carol Halloran would not yet let Lenore drive the family car and she and Muffy, the white toy poodle, were waiting impatiently in the library parking lot. When Lenore came out and said she wanted to go to the Fish and Game office on Mulberry Road, Carol agreed but said she had shopping to do and was taking Muffy in for a shampoo and trim. She would drop Lenore off and pick her up a couple of hours later.

As Lenore walked into the spacious entry at Moose and Goose, as her father called this state division, she was impressed by the mounted heads of moose, caribou, Dall sheep, and mountain goats along with pelts of many Alaskan animals including wolves, wolverine, fox, mink, and polar bear. A full size mount of a huge brown bear stood almost 9 feet tall in the middle of the reception area. On the walls of the hallways were mounted Alaskan fish: several types of salmon, arctic char, grayling, shee fish and rainbow trout. They were interesting, but the practice of killing the fish and animals and then displaying their heads or pelts seemed somehow vicious and weird to Lenore.

The receptionist directed her down the hall to the biology division, where she found George Maxwell busy going over some papers on the desk of his crowded small office.

She knocked on the door and stepped in. "Hi, I'm Lenore Halloran," and she held out her hand.

George Maxwell, thirty years old and a bachelor, was surprised at the appearance of the young lady. She was wearing a plaid skirt and a pale green blouse with matching green sweater and white sneakers. Her light brown hair was held back with a pale green ribbon and she was obviously proud of her ample bosom. George immediately concluded that she was one of the most attractive young women he had ever seen. He guessed her age at about nineteen or twenty.

"Come on in and sit down," he said as he moved some papers from the only other chair in the room.

As Lenore sat down her subtle fragrance pleasantly swept over Maxwell and he inhaled deeply. This was going to be enjoyable.

Lenore declined the coffee with a smile and Maxwell moved his chair closer. "So you're interested in killer whales. Is this for a college term paper?"

"No," she laughed, "I'm not in college yet. This is a research project I am starting myself because my family and some friends want to try to contact some of the killer whales in Prince William Sound, again."

"Again?" asked Maxwell, surprised.

"Yes, we were on an outing in Prince William Sound a few days ago and encountered a group of killer whales. Although they scared us at first, we decided it was very exciting and we plan to go back. I decided the best idea was to do some reading and research before we go." She was a little embarrassed to be telling a professional biologist that a kid in high school wanted to read about whales.

Maxwell leaned closer. "Would you mind telling me about the whales you saw and what happened? Some people are afraid of the whales and some people like them."

She briefly described the encounter and then continued: "We think the whales may have been trying to contact us to play and next time we want to be better prepared. We've seen the killer whales at Hydrosphere in San Diego and they are very intelligent and sensitive animals. We think we may be able to show them we're friendly... just as they were friendly with us."

"Almost drowning one boy does not sound friendly to me," observed Maxwell, looking closely at this adventurous girl. "Do you realize that killer whales are the largest predator on earth and that they kill and eat warm blooded creatures? They can be extremely dangerous."

"Yes, but that's why I want to do some research of our own. They could hurt people...but they don't." She was beginning to feel that Maxwell was picking on her and trying to discourage her.

"Look," Maxwell said, sensing her feelings, "I am not trying to throw cold water on your ideas, but you must realize that wild animal behavior can be unpredictable. At least one of the pods in Prince William Sound has begun stealing fish from fishermen's lines, and, even worse, the boat of an old couple was turned over a short time ago by an orca and their dog was killed and probably eaten. These are large, fast, intelligent animals and must be respected at all times."

Lenore was feeling intimidated and she looked about uneasily. She was not going to let this conservative biologist change her plans.

"OK, OK," nodded Maxwell. "I have this stack of references I've assembled for you. I can't let you take them out of the building, but you can read them here." He picked up the 2 foot high stacks of papers and publications and started down the hall. "Come down here a couple of doors to the library and you can read them there. If you need any copies, we'll try to make them for you so long as you're not asking for the whole book." Again he smiled at her and admired her figure as they went down the hall to the small library crowded with papers and books but with no one else there. An open table with four chairs stood in the center of the room and Maxwell placed the stack of reference material there.

"Hope you're a speedy reader," he smiled. Use this tablet for making notes. I'll come back and see how you're doing in a little while."

"I appreciate your help," Lenore said as she looked into his eyes and touched his hand. Maxwell didn't know it but she was playfully repeating a scene from one of the high school dramas in which she had been the leading actress the past spring semester.

Flustered, he backed away a few steps. "Good, good, I'll be back shortly. Just come to my office if you have any questions."

Lenore was a fast reader but she knew she would not understand many of the technical terms in the books. She wanted mostly case histories or descriptions of whale activities, hopefully by authors who did not use long and unknown words. After glancing through the textbooks on marine mammals to see what readable coverage there was on killer whales, she set them aside as low priority. But included among the publications were a couple of National Geographics with some good killer whale photographs. One sequence showed a pod of killer whales attacking a great blue whale, the largest creature on earth.

In another volume were photographs of whales killing sea lion pups in Patagonia. Several slick paper promotional brochures had been added to the collection, probably, she assumed, by Fish and Game people who had visited some of the marine parks. The photographs showed the captive whales performing the exciting feats she had seen at the marine park in California. The photos brought back happy memories and she smiled. Some of the trainers were women and perhaps one day she would be a trainer. It would look great on her resume if she had already made contact with killer whales in the wild.

Several of the references stated specifically that Orcinus orca, the killer whale, had never been known to attack, kill or eat man. In one publication she found a very interesting description of "Old Tom" and his "mob" of killer whales. Whalers operating out of Twofold Bay, near the southeast tip of Australia, beginning about 1830, found that killer whales observed and learned about their whaling activities. The orcas began to arrive every year to assist with the harvesting of humpback, right and certain other whales which migrated through the area. The cooperation increased to the point where the "mob" would spot some whales approaching offshore and would swim into the bay and attract the whalers by tail lobbing, fin slapping and other actions. The whalers would then haul out their row boats, ropes and harpoons and follow the mob out to the vicinity of the approaching whales. At times, the report said, the killer whales would harass and hold the other whales until the whalers arrived to harpoon the quarry. "Old Tom," a large male in the group, would sometimes playfully grasp the rope between the harpooned whale and the whaling boat in his teeth and try to help with the landing of the whale.

The mob was allowed to feed on the dead harpooned whales, especially the lips and tongue, which they truly enjoyed. With the help of the orcas, the whalers with their primitive equipment sometimes harvested as many as a hundred whales in a season and the cooperative efforts went on for almost a hundred years, with the whales rendered to whale oil for sale. "Old Tom" finally died and washed up on the beach at Twofold Bay and his skeleton now rests in a museum. The cooperative efforts ended only when whaling ships with power harpoons replaced the old hunting methods.

To Lenore, this was additional proof that killer whales in the wild can and will work closely with man under the right circumstances. In Australia, the orcas were given a food reward from the carcass of the harpooned whale. Killer whales in captivity at the marine parks, as she had closely observed, were rewarded by food throughout the performances and were fed on a regular basis by the trainers. Perhaps that was the way to befriend the whales in Prince William Sound: feed them. But what? And how?

"How are you doing?" Maxwell asked as he walked into the library room. "Are any of these what you were looking for?" He leaned over the table to absorb the sweet fragrance of her body and light perfume.

"Oh yes, some of them are great. I couldn't understand much in the textbooks, but some of the other descriptions are very good and understandable. I particularly liked the one which described 'Old Tom' and the whalers in Australia."

"Yes, that is a true story, but most of that took place before the advent of photography so coverage isn't the best. The whalers weren't much for writing, either," he smiled. "Have you reviewed them all yet?"

"No, but my ride won't be here for about another hour. Would it be OK if I continue reading?" Again she looked into Maxwell's eyes.

"You can stay here all day if you want to." And all night, too, he was thinking, if he could be there with her. But he put that thought out of his mind.

Lenore read on for another hour. Startling to her were the statistics about whales being killed. The Japanese were continuing the slaughter of whales of all types in almost all oceans on earth, either by using their own vessels or through whale meat purchases from pirate hunters. Much of this was done under the guise of "research."

According to the latest information, even endangered species were being taken with no regard for possible extinction. The number of killer whales being taken worldwide was not known but several dozen were probably killed by the Japanese each year. One study reported that, in 1970,

Russian whalers had killed more than one thousand orcas in Antarctic waters, probably for mink feed, but fortunately they had since stopped whaling.

Lenore noticed on her watch that two hours were nearly up and she walked down the hall to Maxwell's office. "Thanks so much for letting me read those publications. I would like to read more but my ride will be here shortly." She did not want to mention that her mother was coming for her.

"Quite alright," said Maxwell, sorry to see her leave. He would liked to have spent more time with her but she was so young, regrettably. "Come back anytime for more reading, and don't hesitate to call with any questions. I'm no expert on orcas but I'll do my best."

"I appreciate that. And could I get a copy of these pages with the description of the whales in Australia. This is the only reference I found which describes wild killer whales cooperating with man in a project, even though the project was killing other whales."

"That's the only one I've found in my reading too. Let's take that article down the hall to the copy machine." Maxwell led her down the hall and put the first page face down in a beat-up machine. Then he turned to Lenore again, "By the way, there are some people who are going to be out in Prince William Sound carrying out research on killer whales: Mike and Tracy Mackenzie from Anchorage and Dr. Reed Remington from San Diego."

They might be able to give you more specific information." He put in another page.

"Oh yes," Lenore replied. "They were by to talk to our family a couple of days ago and they warned us about going near the whales, but when we go we'll be sure to stay out of any dangerous situations."

"Sounds as if you've decided to go," remarked Maxwell.

"Going to the Sound is nothing new for us," she said, above the noise of the copy machine. "Our family has been going there since I was about five years old when my Dad got his first boat. One question though, what do you suppose is the usual food for the killer whales in the Sound?"

"I imagine its salmon at this time of the year. They no doubt feed heavily on the various salmon species as they move through the area. Right now it would be kings, soon followed by pinks and reds." The copy machine continued humming and clicking as more pages were copied.

Thoughtfully she said: "I'm glad to hear that. That's what I would have expected." Her family knew where to get salmon in the Sound, both by fishing or by buying them from the commercial fishermen.

With the copies completed, they went back to the library. "Well, guess I'd better go. Bye for now. And thanks for the reading."

Maxwell waved as she bounced down the hall, "Come back soon." And he meant it.

Carol Halloran and Muffy were waiting for Lenore in the parking lot. Muffy, standing on the front seat, seemed to be quite smug with her shiny white coat and polished toe nails. Lenore related the exciting information about the findings to her mother on the way home. Carol still retained a deep seated hesitation about going back to the Sound to look for the whales, but her husband and the kids had developed so much enthusiasm she didn't want to spoil their fun. Besides, it kept the kids out of drugs and alcohol in Anchorage and Lenore might finally start thinking about a profession. 'Marine biologist' had a good ring to it.

"By the way," Carol turned to her beautiful daughter, "your father talked to Harry Saunders and they want to leave for Whittier in two days. It won't be easy to find any particular bunch of killer whales out there and they are willing to spend more time to help you kids out. Besides, they want to get out of Anchorage again."

"In two days?" Lenore asked. "That doesn't leave much time to get ready. We're going to need lots of supplies."

"Yes, and you'll have to help. I have a grocery list ready and we can go there tomorrow. We can take the same clothing we took last time. Your dad will take care of the fishing gear, and he is going to pick up a new video camera."

"That will be neat. We can tape the whales when we find them and feed them."

"Feed them? Who said anything about feeding them? I'm sure they get plenty to eat without our help."

"But don't you see, Mom, that's the way we'll let them know we're friendly. You saw how they fed them at the marine park in San Diego! You must feed the whales to make them friendly and so they will stay near you. Otherwise they will just swim off with no reason to stay around."

"But what do you feed them, filet mignon? I'm sure they get sick of eating fish and more fish."

"No, fish is probably the only thing we could interest them in. They would want fresh, familiar food. We could catch some salmon, or maybe some herring or halibut."

Carol again looked at her daughter. "I can see this is going to get rather complicated. You'd better take this up with your father."

They both thought about the forth-coming trip in silence the rest of the way home. Lenore was thinking how wonderful it would be if they could get their own video tape of the family making initial contact and feeding the whales. Perhaps they could get the whales to respond to hand signals. She was convinced there were many exciting possibilities.

Upon arrival at their residence she immediately told Heidi, her eager and curious sister, about the findings. She also called Larry Saunders to relay the story. Larry's enthusiasm had not fully returned after his terrifying experience with the whales, but he listened with interest to Lenore's report. The possibility of publicity appealed to him; he had not been very popular at school and this could make him look like a hero. Several of his friends had even told him that they would like to return with him to the Sound if they ever went back to contact the whales again. Such ideas, however, were promptly vetoed by the Saunders and Halloran parents. With five kids between them already, they believed boats of the size they had were maxed out.

Two days later, near the end of June, with their two cars heavily loaded with groceries, liquor, clothing, fishing tackle, video cameras, dog food for Muffy and a thousand other items, the families headed south from Anchorage toward Portage. In two hours they were on the train in their vehicles rocking and clacking toward Whittier.

They arrived in a drizzling rain, with the dust on any of Whittier's unpaved roads immediately turned to mud. Transferring the gear and food to the two boats went quickly with the kids running to get the job done.

Dave Halloran had noticed two fishing boats coming in to the Whittier landing, and he and Harry Saunders went over to ask about possible killer whale sightings, but the only sighting they could report was several days ago near Montague Island and it was hard telling where those whales might be now.

"Do you suppose we should talk to Cyrus or Ted Barnes before going out?" Dave asked as they walked along the dock.

"All they're going to do is try to discourage us. And they don't know any more than we do," Harry replied. "I'd say we just ought to head out."

After filling the vessel's fuel and water tanks they were underway.

As the two families motored east in 3 foot seas out of Whittier in their separate boats, a light drizzle continued to fall and the mountain peaks were obscured by low, gray clouds. The children were very enthusiastic and optimistic that they would be able to find the whales in a short time. The parents had previously agreed with them that, in the absence of good reason to search elsewhere, they would commence at the same cove where they had earlier encountered the whale group. The specific one identified for them by Reed Remington and the Mackenzies as the A-T pack.

Carol Halloran had done her best to sketch the dorsal fin of the large male to help with recognition of the group when they found it. She sketched a tall dorsal fin, somewhat wavy at the rear and with a notch in the middle of the trailing edge.

The children had convinced themselves that ANY killer whale group would be a candidate for contact. After all, the marine parks seemed to be able to take any healthy whale from the wild and feed it and train it in a short time. The animals were very intelligent and, they reasoned, it was simply a matter of contact with the right people in the right way to win the whales over. They had seen the hit movie E. T. several times and, were it not for the help of children in the movie, E. T. might have been killed by the adults hunting him. They reasoned that the killer whales might have a similar orientation; perhaps they needed contact with some understanding humans. The Halloran and Saunders kids were prepared to lead the way.

Larry Saunders had succeeded in purchasing some cassette tapes of whale sounds, including some of killer whales, and the flute his parents had tried to get him to play when he was ten had been dug out of the attic. He was driving his parents, Harry and Ruth, crazy playing the killer whale sounds on the portable tape player and then trying to imitate the sounds with the flute, even though the noise of the engine tended to drown out much of the squeaks and whistles. His sister Sarah and little brother Tim also tried their turn with the flute when they were not to-side watching for killer whales. Larry was proud that he could hit some of the same notes heard on the tapes. Even though the sounds weren't perfect, he was sure the whales would recognize the attempt at communications and respond. But they had found no hydrophones in Anchorage and the two fathers had promised to try to fabricate some sort of subsurface listening device from three old microphones they had been able to acquire.

By the time they reached Knight Island three hours later, no whales had been sighted and the downpour had increased while visibility had decreased. It was obvious they might as well put in to one of the sheltered coves and wait. Had they passed some whales in this weather they wouldn't have known it because of the poor visibility.

The kids didn't mind, though, this gave them a chance to try to catch some halibut for use in enticing the whales when they found them. Fortunately, the rear deck of both pleasure boats were covered thus making fishing possible without putting on full rain gear.

Once inside the protected cove, the water was much smoother and the wind, although reduced to 5 knots, swirled in from different directions rather than steadily from the southwest. After anchors of the two boats were dropped in opposite directions the `Saucy' and the `Primrose' were tied securely together side by side and stern to stern with several bumpers in between. At the west end of the cove half a mile away was a steep granite cliff that soared 600 feet above the water surface with large rocks at the base. A good area to avoid with their small boats.

The kids immediately rigged up their rods with half a herring each and dropped the baited hooks near the bottom. But, after forty-five minutes of no action from the fish, all of the children but Tim became bored and decided to reel in their hooks, still baited with chunks of herring. Heidi's bait had been resting on the bottom and was engulfed by a heavy starfish. Looking like a heavy, purple, wet mop head, it was reeled laboriously to the surface by the fourteen-year-old. It was thrown back after being cut from the hook. With the rain continuing to pour, all of the children except Tim, the youngest, went inside to warm up and find amusement. Games brought for the purpose were ignored in favor of tapes of action movies played on the Saunders' VCR/TV combination. The parents, aboard the Halloran boat to avoid the noise of the movies, had opened a bottle of dark rum shortly after anchoring and were enjoying their second round of hot buttered rum, strongly fortified with the liberal amounts of the sugar cane-derived liquor.

Twenty minutes later Tim's persistence paid off as he let out a yell heard by the adults but not the other children. Five minutes were required for Tim to fight the fish up to the stern of the boat, smiling adults standing out of the rain in the cabin. Finally, Harry Saunders set down his steaming brown beverage to proudly gaff and bring aboard a twenty-five pound halibut. "Nice going, son, I told those other kids they can't catch any fish if they're not out here, lines in the water, and paying attention."

Within a few minutes four white filets weighing a total of almost 10 pounds were sliced from the halibut and the bones, head, and guts intact were tossed overboard. The two mothers prepared a delicious meal with the main course the fresh, succulent fish prepared by lightly broiling the filets followed by baking them over a bed of red onions. A creamy, fresh mushroom sauce topped off the gastronomic delight. The adults enjoyed two bottles of sauvignon blanc with the fish while the children had apple juice. Muffy also liked halibut, but Muffy ate anything people ate, including vegetables, nuts, candy, fruit, anything.

The rain subsided and the water surface in the cove was quite calm. All five kids were now paying more attention to fishing and the halibut seemed to be more aggressive on the bottom. Suddenly the water surface began a strange oscillation and they looked shoreward where the trees were swaying as if pushed by an unseen force.

"Oh Oh!" Harry Saunders yelled so everyone could hear. "Looks like an earthquake."

From the steep-walled west end of the cove they heard a sound like rocks falling into the water. This was followed by huge splash as a large part of the cliff fell into the water.

"This could mean trouble!" Dave Halloran shouted. "Get ready for a big wave! Grab a life jacket!" He had read about a situation like this where a wave estimated at 100 feet high swamped anchored boats in Alaska's Latuya Bay thirty years ago following a large rock slide into the bay. Several people had drowned.

Then they saw the wave approaching. It happened so quickly they did not have time to locate the nearest life preserver. The wave appeared to be about 12 feet high.

'Hold onto something, here comes a wave!" Harry shouted. "This could get rough."

As the wave passed it quickly lifted both boats vertically about 12 feet. The chains to the anchor on one boat was broken and any item that was not secured was dumped onto the deck. Everyone on both boats hung on to any secure handhold. What had been relatively clear water in the cove suddenly turned cloudy. But no one on either boat was injured.

"Wow! We were lucky on that one, it could have been much larger. That earthquake shook a slab of rock loose. Good thing we were out a ways from that cliff!" Dave pointed out. "Is everyone OK? Harry, I'll help you rig up a rope for your smaller anchor."

The kids thought it had been exciting and were chatting about how they had all been very scared but all was now OK. The two wives wondered if they should move away from this cove; perhaps there could be another, larger rock slide.

"Nah, we're OK here." Harry assured them. "Anything that was shaken loose has already fallen. And the fishing might even be better now!"

The rain started again and the kids gave up on fishing for the day. They wanted to play some video games and then watch old movies such as Moby Dick. The remainder of the evening passed uneventfully with the rain continuing. After the end of "Raiders of the Lost Arc" the children were chased off to bed by their mothers at nearly 10 pm. Both Harry Saunders and Dave Halloran had gone to bed at about 9 pm after getting exceedingly sleepy from the five or six hot buttered rums they had each consumed.

◆◆◆

CHAPTER SIXTEEN

Hunting sea lions

O ut in Prince William Sound, the A-T pack had gotten tired of eating fish and decided to hunt mammals for a change. Tinga, as a transient orca anyway, was delighted to again hunt a warm blooded creature. One of the places where they had been successful previously was a jumbled bunch of rocks that rose only 20 feet above sea level. This was a hangout for quite a number of sea lions and there always seemed to be some young there who had not yet learned to fear the orcas. She started off in the direction of those rocks and signalled the others to follow. Within less than a half hour the pack was approaching the rocks and they split into three groups of five, six and eight orcas. By stealthily approaching the rocks from three directions they had a better chance of one of the sea lions making a mistake of either failing to get out of the water quickly or of panicking and swimming toward some orcas when they thought they were getting away from others.

The plan worked and Tingas group caught two young adult lions quickly. Orcas in one of the other groups had found calves on rocks where they could be picked off and they killed three. The third group had spotted a fairly large lion that appeared to be coming back to rest after a hunting foray in deeper waters. Two of the adult females approached the fast-swimming lion and it lashed out at them with sharp teeth, including fangs that were almost the same as those of a grizzly bear. The skull of an adult sea lion is almost identical to that of a grizzly. The orcas backed off, it was not worth risking severe injury to try to capture a sea lion, and they had learned that the flesh of the older lions had an undesirable taste anyway.

There were an abundance of young sea lions and soon all members of the pack had eaten their fill. Tinga signalled to them and the pack started swimming back toward Knight Island at a leisurely pace. Their course would take them past a beach that had a bottom consisting of small rounded pebbles instead of just sand and the pebbles extended offshore about 100 feet. This, for the orcas, was a wonderful spot for rubbing their bodies over the pebbles and the pack orbited around and around the beach so that each orca would have a chance to body rub their bottom and sides. Their dorsal fins prevented any back rubbing but they spent almost two hours at this beach, one of their favorite spots in the entire sound.

———— ◆◆◆ ————

Back at the *Saucy* and the *Primrose*, they searched for the next day and a half, with decreasing enthusiasm, for whales around the islands of southwest Prince William Sound. They saw sea otters, seals and once a black bear was spotted walking along an island shore. Near Montague Island they had come across a humpback whale and its calf, which they were able to recognize from a whale identification manual they had on board. A couple of times the kids were sent to shore to hike, fish and burn off excess energy. But the only time they thought they had found killer whales occurred late in the evening and, because no one had eaten dinner, even the children had easily reached the decision to put into a cove rather than try to follow the group.

The kids were becoming discouraged. They had caught a few halibut and were saving the filets, but each passing hour lent more support to the possibility that the search might be fruitless.

Harry Saunders had commitments in Anchorage and the two boats returned to Whittier with both vessels requiring refills of fuel and water. A phone call made by Harry revealed they did not need him for a few days.

While Ruth and Carol were picking up a few groceries at sky-high Whittier prices, Harry and Dave were making more phone calls and found they could stay a couple of more days. Larry and Lenore left the other three children at the dock and climbed the stairs to Cyrus McDuffy's office.

"Cyrus, you remember us, don't you?" Lenore asked the old man seated on the other side of the small desk. "We were in here a while back to talk about meeting up with the whales."

McDuffy's eyes brightened. "Why, of course I remember you. That little episode you had with those orcas really set things to spinning here in Whittier!"

"We're glad you haven't forgotten us," she smiled, "but we would like to ask your help." She looked directly into the blue eyes of the old man. "We would like to find the whales again and we haven't had any luck so far."

Cyrus hadn't had this much attention from a young attractive lady for forty years and he was enjoying every second of it. "I'll help any way I can," he smiled over the rim of his pipe and winked at the attractive blonde. "Those research people were in here just this morning. You know, that Remington fellow and the Mackenzies. They went out in the Sound on the *Czarina* and, they didn't tell me, but they're probably looking for the whales." If they could find the vessel, he advised them, they might find the whales as well. He described the as a 30 foot turquoise vessel that looked more like a version of a harbor tug than either a fishing or pleasure boat.

"Do you know where they went?" Lenore asked, sensing McDuffy's intense interest in her.

"Well, they did say something about Naked Island, but I believe they were going to look in a number of parts of the Sound. Probably won't do you any good to go to any one spot. Go out and search systematically. And if you find them, don't mention that I told you they were out there."

Lenore beamed at the idea, "Thanks, Cyrus, we appreciate the advice." Turning to Larry she nodded "C'mon, let's go."

Cyrus smiled at these kids. They reminded him of his own adventurous self in earlier years, and, shaking his head as they left, wondered to himself if he ever had a woman who looked as good as this Lenore.

Descending the stairs from the Harbor Master's office, Lenore smiled, "Hey, that was a nifty idea of Cyrus's. We know what the *Czarina* looks like, and we might even try to reach them on the radio."

Once again the two vessels motored eastward into Prince William Sound. This time there was much less enthusiasm, but they felt better when Lenore in one craft and Larry in the other told them about the plan to find the research vessel.

A close look around Naked Island revealed no sign of the *Czarina* and the two boats headed toward the north part of the Sound. They soon found that the Alaska Department of Fish and Game was having an "opening" for pink salmon in the Sound. Certain areas, such as the large inlet named Port Wells, which led to College Fjord further north, were crowded with odds and ends of small commercial fishing boats, some of which looked like escapees from a junk yard. White plastic floats supporting purse seines were common while floats for drift nets made lines, circles and arcs on the water surface as they waited in ambush for unwary salmon making their way toward spawning streams. The searchers decided to specifically avoid those areas. They assumed the whales, and the *Czarina*, would too and they headed south.

Cruising on the west side of Knight Island, they decided to put in at Drier Bay because there were several good places there for the kids to go ashore. As the two craft turned into the mile-wide entrance to the bay, thirteen-year-old Tim in the *Saucy* was busily scanning with the binoculars. "Whales!" he shouted. "I think I see whales!"

"Where, where?" asked Larry and fifteen-year-old Sarah at once. Larry, proudly at the helm, cut back on the speed of the boat. Harry and Ruth came forward from the rear of the cabin.

"Over there, near those rocks."

Larry took the binoculars and looked toward the rocks half a mile away. The boat was rolling in the 3 foot seas. Dave Halloran, trailing the *Saucy*, saw the reduced speed and also cut back, waiting for some word on the CB of what was going on.

At first Larry saw nothing in the area near the rocks, just the sun in sparkling flashes off the reflective sides of the waves. But then a black dorsal fin appeared and disappeared, and then another and another. No doubt about it, there was a group of whales over there. Larry wasn't sure they were orcas because he had read that certain other whales such as false killer whales, pilot whales and even dolphins are sometimes mistaken for killer whales. At this distance he couldn't be sure. He handed the binoculars to Sarah and picked the CB microphone off the overhead hanger.

"Dave, there are some dorsal fins at nine o'clock near those rocks but I can't tell if they are killer whales. Let's go over and see." He turned the *Saucy* toward the rocks and increased speed; the *Primrose* followed. Excitement was building.

When they had approached within 200 yards of the spot where the whales had been seen, they both reduced speed to an idle and Lenore suggested to her Dad that they stop the engines completely so as not to disturb the whales. Dave agreed and radioed the message to the *Saucy*.

"Will do," responded Larry cheerfully. "Let's just watch."

The two vessels, 30 yards apart, rolled from side to side in the 3 foot swells. The whales had not yet been seen at close distance, but a dorsal fin suddenly cut the water 100 yards ahead, followed closely by a much smaller fin.

"It's a female killer whale and her calf!" shouted Lenore excitedly as she watched through the binoculars. Dave relayed the message to the Saucy.

Dorsal fins of six other whales now appeared here and there, in the same general area, including one fairly tall, less-curved fin which Lenore guessed must be a small male.

After ten minutes of watching, Larry guessed that there were a total of eigth whales and therefore it must not be the same group they had encountered before. However, Lenore pointed out, perhaps the group had split up and this was only part.

Suddenly a 13 foot whale appeared just below the surface between the two boats. It came to the surface to blow and its black and white coloration and smooth skin were clearly visible.

"Look, look!" shouted Tim as he saw the whale coming to the surface. "There's one right here!" Everyone on the *Saucy* looked in time to see the whale come up, blow and submerge again. Aboard the *Primrose* they heard Tim's shout and the blow and looked in time to see the whale submerge.

"Quick, get the fish!" shouted Lenore as she ran to the box at the stern of the boat. Aboard the *Saucy*, Larry ran for his flute, Tim ran for the herring and Sarah ran for the halibut filets they had saved.

Additional whales surfaced in front of the two boats and disappeared after blowing. The kids were ecstatic and began throwing ten-inch herring and small slabs of halibut they had prepared for such an event.

The whale had turned underwater and again rose between the two crafts to blow, this time traveling in the direction of the other whales. Larry tried to play the flute but, in his excitement, couldn't get a decent note to come out. Lenore threw several herring and some halibut strips overboard and Tim managed to throw one of the herring 10 feet in front of the whale so the fish was sinking as the whale went by. But, so far as they could see, the orcas paid no attention to the offerings. Some of the fish could be seen sinking as far as 30 feet below the surface in the somewhat cloudy water.

"Did you see it looking at us?" asked Ruth, now as enthusiastic as the children.

"Yes, it *was* looking at us," agreed Harry. "Maybe it will come back again."

The kids continued to throw herring and halibut pieces into the water and Larry had finally been able to get a few notes out on the flute. He was trying to make some of the same sounds he had heard on the tapes. Dave

Halloran had gotten out the video camera and was busy trying to position himself for a shot of both the kids and the whale between the two boats in case it showed up again. Everyone was happy and excited.

A whale surfaced where the other whales had been seen 100 yards away.

"There he is!" shouted Heidi. "He's out there with the others."

The other seven whales surfaced in unison, oriented toward the mouth of the bay.Everyone was quiet as they watched intently for the whales to reappear. Larry continued blowing on the flute in an effort to call them. Two minutes later, after what seemed like hours to the waiting kids, Tim again saw the whales surface to blow 200 yards to the west.

"There they are!" He pointed in the direction of the whales.

All eight of the orcas surfaced in unison to blow and then again disappeared. "Looks like they're headed out of the bay," Dave remarked as he scanned for them with the binoculars. "If we're going to stay with them we'd better think about moving." He got Harry on the CB. "Harry, looks like they may be moving out of the bay, what say we start up to follow them?"

"Sounds right to me, let's go," he said as he hung up the microphone and turned the key to start the engine. He looked at the kids still straining to see the whales, "OK, kids, let's move out to follow them."

"All right!" Tim exclaimed, excited about the encounter.

The two vessels swung to the west and began accelerating.

"Better not crowd them," Harry cautioned Dave over the radio. "They might get the idea we're chasing them."

For five minutes they moved forward, everyone looking for the whales to resurface. Ten minutes passed, then fifteen as they re-entered the open water of the Sound. But no whales.

Dave's voice came over the CB: "Harry, where in hell did they go? Have you seen anything?"

"Not a thing," replied Harry. "They seem to have disappeared. They should have come up for air by now."

Unknown to those in the boats, these particular whales had been shot at by commercial fishermen twice in the previous week and they had no desire to be close to humans again.

Four hours of searching revealed no whales and the kids began hoping they might find another bunch instead of spending more time looking for this one. But by five o'clock in the evening, as they entered Drier Bay without seeing any more killer whales, their spirits were again sinking. The boats were anchored and lashed together for the night and the children took the two dinghies to the sand beach for some welcome physical activity in unconfined space.

The adults assembled on the Primrose to discuss the situation over scotch and soda. "I don't want to disappoint the kids," Harry observed, "but I've got to get back to town and go to work."

"Yes, and I'm getting tired of the close quarters," Ruth nodded."

"Amen," Carol agreed.

"I guess we're all getting discouraged," Dave agreed. "What we thought would be a fairly easy search has turned out to be tough. We've all got obligations in town. Maybe we should call it quits for a while."

"For a while?" Ruth smiled. "I'm not sure I ever want to come out here looking for whales again."

The three younger kids had taken some snacks along and were busy building a sand castle on a beach 50 yards away from the anchored boats, their bare feet cold on the 45-degree sand. Larry and Lenore had wandered off down the beach and were 100 yards away where some lichen-covered dark rocks were exposed in a cliff face above the gentle swells of bay waters.

A large black bear had caught the scent of the kids and their snacks and emerged at a slow walk from the dense foliage. It stood up on its rear paws for a better view. The parents saw the bear first and began yelling at the kids to get back in the Zodiacs and return to the offshore boats. Larry and Lenore began running back to the small craft that had been pulled up on the beach sand. They pushed the small craft back into the water, got in and began rowing away from shore. The bear casually walked to where they had been building the castle and ate the few snacks that had been left behind.

Once the kids were safely on board, Harry observed: "Well, seeing that bear was interesting, but let's give up for now on the whale search. Perhaps we can come back one more time this fall." There was no disagreement and even the kids thought it was a good idea once they were told that there would be consideration given for another try later.

About three hours were required to return to Whittier and another two to catch the train to Portage and drive to Anchorage.

CHAPTER SEVENTEEN

OCS – Orca Communication Society

C laudia had been up and gone for over an hour when Dan opened his eyes. There was a faint scent of burnt caffeine toying with his senses. He stumbled out of the bedroom and into the kitchen where the hot plate under the automatic coffee pot was turning the few remaining drops of brown liquid into a charred crust.

"Careless damn..." he didn't finish. Setting the glass pot aside and turning off the machine he headed toward his shower.

Even Claudia's nonsense, he suspected deliberate, couldn't ruffle him this bright morning. He had made his plans at the clinic the previous night before falling asleep and his mind now churned as he lathered in the hot shower. Jammer obviously disliked him, perhaps enough to attempt to block his entry into, and planned leadership of, the Orca Communication Society. Dan felt that, aside from raising money, there was only one good way to circumvent Jammer's personal feelings; he must be made to feel that Dan and Dan alone was the key to gaining legitimate scientific recognition for the Society's efforts. Whether Jammer himself would be given any credit was another question and Dan would like to get rid of the obnoxious character anyway, once things were going his way.

By the time Short finished the shower his thoughts were crystallizing on how to help obtain recognition for the Society. He would enlist the support of his friend Doctor Jacob Early, Chief Marine Biologist of the respected staff at the Vancouver Aquarium. Of course, Short himself, he figured, would ultimately enjoy the lion's share of the recognition, first as a duly accredited scientist, and second as the person responsible for bringing the Orca Communication Society to the attention of the academic world. Early and Short went back many years and many secrets, and Jake owed Dan more than one favor. Once Early was convinced of the work Jammer and his group were doing, Short figured he would be more than happy to support the effort.

Short shaved and dressed quickly, then placed a call to Early's office at the Aquarium. After convincing the secretary with a very throaty voice (a smoker, he thought) that he was indeed Jake's old drinking buddy from days gone by, Dan finally heard Early's voice on the other end of the line. "Christ Danny, where you been, boy? Hell, this place is not the same without ya."

"I miss you too, you old fool. I am up in Rocky Bay, doing some work with the Indians."

"I've been in Rocky Bay." Early announced. "About four years ago. Great hotel. How's Claudia?"

Dan hesitated then lied to his old friend. "She's fine. We're getting along great."

"Bull."

"Yeah. How's Ginger?"

"Filed for divorce. Says I work too much."

"Bull."

"Yeah. So what can I do ya for?"

"I am coming to Vancouver. Like to see you. It's important."

"OK." Early sighed, "When?"

"Thought I'd fly out tonight."

"Can't get away until tomorrow morning, Danny."

"Fine. What time?"

"How about, say eleven. I'll spring for lunch in that little joint we used to like in Gastown."

Dan was having a hard time containing his exuberance. With some effort he managed not to blurt the whole thing out over the phone. "OK, Jake. See you then."

Short made arrangements to take a float plane from Rocky Bay to the Bayside Hotel in Vancouver at 4 pm that afternoon. He had hoped to get two of the local natives on the AA program before leaving, but one of them was too drunk to comprehend what was going on. Around mid-afternoon he left the drunk in his cabin and stopped by the clinic to complete his progress report to the provincial headquarters in Vancouver. If they saw no progress he might be released or sent elsewhere and that's the last thing he needed right now. The position he now held gave him freedom of time as well as a comfortable income.

"So you're going to the big city, hey Danny?" Claudia smiled when he told her he was leaving. "How long you gonna be gone?"

He correctly interpreted her tone as indicating pleasure with his departure. "Is there anything you would like me to bring back from the city?"

Claudia smiled again. "No thanks. I have everything I need right here, Danny."

The bumpy, thirty minute flight on the float plane from Rocky Bay to a rough landing on choppy water just east of Stanley Park was more unsettling than usual. Between the motion sickness tablets Claudia had given him before take-off and the hypersensitivity to his own body functions, such as breathing and heart rate, which always preceded his anxiety attacks, Dan rode a precarious wave of mounting panic as the plane taxied over to the dock near the Bayside Hotel. As soon as he found himself again on the solid dock and then terra firma, he struck an unsteady but rapid course for the solitude of his hotel room and sleep.

The fitfulness of his rest and the content of his dreams, the most vivid of which saw Jammer setting Rolanda afloat in a casket of gold-tinted wood while he looked on helplessly, dying from poison administered by Claudia in the form of tablets. Even as he blamed the medication for the cold, sweaty disorientation with which he greeted the morning, the phone on his night table erupted. "Hello!" He managed, only partly aware of his location.

"Hey Danny, you alright boy?" Jake's voice was like a cold cloth on a fevered brow.

"Yeah sure, Jake. Still sleeping, bad flight."

"Too bad, old buddy. Listen, just called to ask you if it's OK to bring somebody along."

"Only if she's good looking."

"No, hell I haven't the time, money, or energy for any more good looking women. I'm talking about my assistant, name's McAllister. You'll like him, and he's heard enough about you that he would like to meet you. Any problem?"

"None that I can see." Dan answered, beginning to feel the effects of his dreams slide off his conscious mind. "Same time? Same place?"

"Right. Want us to come and pick you up?"

"No thanks, think I'll walk part way then take a cab."

"See you soon."

"Yeah."

Short stood under a cool shower trying to dispel his dream hang-over. There was that terrible feeling of knowing that he was going to die, left from the nightmare, which refused to follow the water down the drain. Feeling his hotel room closing in on him, he dressed quickly and began walking in the general direction of Gastown.

The walking felt good and he wondered why in the hell he hadn't picked out a woman who was into physical exercise. Claudia had always been a little flabby but lately she was becoming an absolute slob. He had never been able to make her comprehend how running, the straining of his muscles against the tension in his mind, kept him sane. Even walking, which he enjoyed only slightly less, was, to Claudia's way of thinking, a waste of time. He often wondered when it was that she became so fatalistic. Was a nursing career the cause or had she always been like that, a characteristic he just hadn't seen in the beginning because of being blinded by her beauty and intense sexuality?

But Claudia was soon pushed out of his mind as he maintained his east-bound course and covered the streets of Vancouver with his restless stride and hungry eye. This was THE city in Dan Short's mind, the quintessence of civilization. Heavily British in orientation and background, Vancouver nonetheless had assimilated people from all nations of the world in an amalgamation as timeless as the sea which had brought them here. As the mighty pulse of the city quickened his own, he began to feel the confidence he had felt with Rolanda in Rocky Bay and had somehow lost in the nightmare stupor which followed his terror during and after the flight. Once again jubilant in the knowledge that he had found something he had been seeking all his life, he jumped in a cab and soon found himself seated across the table from Jake and his young assistant in a place with many fond associations.

"Well Danny, you don't look too bad for an old man roughing it out in the middle of nowhere. How about a drink?"

"Thanks, Jake, " Dan gave the menu a once over. "It's a little early in the day for me."

"Since when?" Jake hooted.

"Since I began to be an old man roughing it out in the middle of nowhere." Short turned his attention to the man sitting quietly, if somewhat ill at ease, next to Jake. "Your boss has always had the manners of a goat. I'm Dan Short."

"Rolly McAllister. Pleasure to meet you, sir."

Jake Early looked about him impatiently. "Well, now that we have the social crap out of the way, what do you guys say we eat?"

The waitress, a redhead in a skirt that made Jake's mouth water with a different kind of hunger, appeared as if on cue and took their order. This particular Vancouver eatery was known for serving a great meal without a great delay, and the three men soon found themselves too busy with the crab and fresh shrimp on the table to indulge in much conversation. However, once the urgency of a sixteen-hour fast had been reduced as a psychological handicap, Short got to the point of his visit.

"Jake, I have discovered something wonderful off the north coast of Vancouver Island, something I want to share with you."

"A mermaid?" Jake swallowed a mouthful of California wine.

"No jackass, not a mermaid. A group of young men and women who are doing great work. Work that's important, maybe the most important work in the history of marine biology."

McAllister had lost interest in his lunch all together. He was staring at Dan with the keen interest a detective might show in the only clue in an unsolved murder.

"OK, Danny. Tell Uncle Jake what's got your pressure up."

Dan's eyes sparkled with the delight of a man who knows he has total control of a situation and will take his own sweet time about relinquishing any part of that control. "The Orca Communication Society."

"The Orca Communication Society?." Jake tilted his head to one side, like a playful puppy, and furrowing his brow looked at Short.

"That's right."

"What the hell is the Orca Communication Society?"

"Begging your pardon sir," McAllister ran his tongue over his thick, richly pigmented lips. "The Orca Communication Society is a group of individuals, amateurs of course, who believe it is possible to establish some form of meaningful communication with the great whales, particularly, the killer whale."

"The killer whale?" Early was holding his glass up and looking around for the waitress.

"Well, what's wrong with this idea? Next to man, these are the most intelligent creatures on the face of the Earth." Short looked intensely at Early..

"Meaningful communication with a killer whale." Early repeated. "Like what: conversations, perhaps dating and intermarriage?"

Dan Short sat back in his chair and sighed in disgust. "Jesus, Jake, will you be serious."

Jake Early looked across the table, his eyes squinted and his square jaw set hard. "Serious? About what? How serious can I get about another bunch of crack-pots who have confused research with metaphysics?"

"These people are not crack-pots Jake! They are students of another life form, just as you are."

"Just as I am? Look, old friend, I'm a marine biologist, not a mystic. My interest in the killer whale lies in what it is, not what I would like it to be."

"Jake," Dan began slowly, attempting to control his mounting anger. "Why would you deny these people and their work scientific validity? The ability of the great whales to communicate is documented."

"The ability of the great whales to communicate with their own species is documented, Dan." Jake signaled the waitress again and asked for the dessert menu. "There is no reason to believe they can or will communicate with ours."

McAllister reached for his water glass with a series of quick, jerking motions. "There have been individuals, Jake, who claim to have established a kind of personal bond with the orcas...and who believe..."

"Believe what?" Early's blunt features reddened as he stared at his assistant. "That the whale would like to be human. That's what this all boils down to, Rolly. Some humans believe that certain other forms of life on Earth would prefer to be human, or, at the very least, be admitted into our society on some level."

"OK, Jake," Short interrupted the exchange between Early and his assistant. "Let's agree that you disagree with the basic thesis of the Orca Communication Society. Fine. But you can't argue with the fact that any well-directed study of the species, at this point in our understanding, might yield something worthwhile. You also can't argue with the fact that any organized study needs funds. If the Aquarium could see its way clear to recognize that Society's work, at least financially, I am convinced that the return on the investment will be much greater than you or I could expect."

Early Smiled down at his strawberry cheesecake. "So this is a touch. I mean, you want me to extend Aquarium funds to your friends out in Rocky Bay.? What do you think I am running, Dan, a savings and loan? I spend half my time worrying about having enough funds to conduct the research the Aquarium was designed to conduct. Do you think research grants fall like manna from heaven? Christ, Doctor, you've been in academic medicine long enough to know better than that."

"The answer is no then?"

"The answer is that I can't, Danny. Frankly, even if I could, I am not sure that I would. There are so many important questions to be answered."

Short stood up and tossed twenty dollars down on the table. "Who decides what's important? You? You're some kind of mystic? Is there a possibility that you could be wrong, that you could be missing something? No possibility?"

"Dan… Danny." Short heard Early's voice following him out the door and into the street. Very disappointed and unhappy, he caught a cab at a nearby corner. All he could think of was what he was going to say to Rolanda about his failure to find funding.

Back in the hotel room at the Bayside, Short called room service and ordered a bottle of single malt Scotch, Balvenie Double Wood if they had it on hand. After covering the ice in the tumbler twice and savoring the pale amber liquid, he took out the notes he had made in Rocky Bay. He picked up the phone and dialed the number Rolanda had given him. The number was for a black family, the Robinson's, in Port Coquitlam, a community on the Fraser River about 25 miles east of Vancouver. Rolanda had told him she often stayed with these friends because they were great people and she avoided the expense of staying at hotels in the city.

The phone rang a few times and a child, nine or ten, he guessed, picked it up. "This is Dr. Short calling, I would like to speak to Rolanda, please."

"A doctor? Is Rolanda sick?"

"No, no, this has nothing to do with sickness. I'm a friend of hers and I'd like to speak to her."

"She ain't here. Momma told me she was going to be coming, but she ain't here now."

"When do you think she might arrive? Did she say when she was coming?"

"I don't know and my Mom's at the grocery."

"Fine, get a pencil and write this down." He had to repeat the phone number at the Bayside three times before the child had it right. "Now when your mom gets home tell her to give that number to Rolanda so she'll know where I am, OK?"

"Sure."

"Good, thanks for your help." Hanging up the phone, he poured himself another generous Balvenie. Scowling, he pondered the adverse reaction of Early and how he might go around him to get funding. Maybe there was a way to actually find funds somewhere in the myriad of Canadian government programs so they could be used for OCS work.

C H A P T E R   E I G H T E E N

Blind Justice

R olly McAllister seldom experienced peace of mind. There was always some aspect of insecurity eating away at him, some little doubt making him jump at every unexpected sound or new face he encountered. People could never understand how a young man who stood to inherit many millions of dollars would ever feel anything but confident, how the son of Edmond Stanley McAllister could ever be bothered by any form of self- doubt. But astute observers knew that Edmond Stanley, the bank president and chairman of the board who had inherited his wealth, instilled insecurity in people around him the way a syringe can inject an antibiotic into the blood stream. He was recognized as overbearing and uncompromising.

While no one opposed McAllister openly at the bank, the senior staff members did their best to keep Edmond Stanley away from the bank's business activities and, whenever possible, to keep the name of the bank disassociated from his name. The staff confided to each other that it was just a matter of time before the Vancouver Stock Exchange or perhaps Canadian tax authorities caught up with him and they wanted as little adverse fallout as possible for the bank.

When Rolly McAllister had lunch with his father, it made him feel the way he imagined Joan of Arc must have felt when asked to spend the evening with the Fathers of the French Inquisition. Rolly knew extreme feelings of hostility smoldered just below the surface of the old man's attempt to appear friendly to even his own son. When his mother was there, her presence was so overshadowed by Edmond Stanley that her plight could bring tears to the eyes of any empathetic person.

The boy had tried for years to find the formula, phrase, series of actions or good deeds that would give him the key to his father's approval. Rolly, as a healthy young man, tried to visualize what life might become after the eventual end of his father's life. But he had just about reached the end of his tolerance after failing to be worthy in Edmond Stanley's eyes. He knew, had always known, that love had nothing to do with the relationship between he and his father. Neither of them had any respect for the other.

As Rolly motored over Lion's Gate Bridge and along Burrard Inlet into West Vancouver, he really believed that this time he'd found a way to make Edmond Stanley genuinely proud of him. He hadn't exactly lied to Doctor Short the night before when he'd said, "Well sir, he is very proud of my work." Perhaps 'very' was an exaggeration, but not a lie. Edmond Stanley wasn't very anything, except controlling. What approval the sixty-year-old man had conditionally offered his son was always based on Rolly performing according to Edmond Stanley's standards. Doctor Short had been very cordial and encouraging when Rolly had asked him about joining the OCS. Short was not an officer of OCS but he knew Rolly would be an acceptable and welcome new member.

This time meeting with his father was going to be different, Rolly was certain of that. After all, Edmond Stanley was very fond of whales; one of the Icelandic companies in which he had owned a substantial interest had made a fortune slaughtering them and selling rendered oil in previous years. And Edmond Stanley attacked only worthy opponents.

"If whales could talk," Edmond Stanley had told him one time, "Think what we could learn about harvesting the seas. Boy, we'd make another fortune."

Well, his son was now going to help make that possible. His son, who was only too certain that Edmond Stanley would like nothing better than to be in on the ground floor, so to speak, of this particular investment.

The shade of the English style manor house was beginning to lay a moist, dark green shadow on the extensive lawn of the McAllister family estate when Rolly breezed up the winding drive. He rang the front bell. He always rang the front bell.

"After all, son," Edmond Stanley firmly held. "We can't have people just barging in and out, not even you."

A tall, well-dressed, Asian-looking butler opened the front door and let his long shadow mingle with the one on the front steps. "Morning, sir."

"Good morning, Philip." Rolly returned lightly. "Dad up and about?"

"Oh yes, sir. But, I am afraid you can't see him until straight up twelve. At luncheon, you know."

"What is he doing?"

"Making notes in his journals, sir. Today we are making notes in the blue and green journals. Let me see sir, that is people and moral impressions." Philip's swarthy brow was furrowed with the effort of memory. "Yes, I think that is right. He has left clear instructions that no one, not even Mrs. McAllister, can see him until straight up eleven. At luncheon, you know."

Rolly was reminded of Philip's consistent tendency to repeat specific parts of his conversation with the elder McAllister verbatim, giving his speech a kind of chanting, but slightly annoying, quality. "OK, Philip. Where is my mother?"

"In the morning room, sir."

Now that was another annoying habit of Philip's, Rolly thought as he followed the butler. Why did he insist upon referring to the small study with the built in bar as the morning room? Perhaps because Hope Douglas McAllister spent every morning there, but then she spent every afternoon and evening there as well.

"Morning, mother." Rolly said without much feeling. Her alcohol problem, of which he understood very little, had made him fearful of displaying, even to himself, the extent of his affection for her.

"Good morning, dear." Her speech was already becoming slurred and her gestures unsteady. "Is today the day you are to have lunch with us?"

"Yes, mother."

"How nice. I think that I really must rest ... ah ...before lunch ... ah ... however."

"Mother, it is eleven forty five. You know how father feels about all of us being prompt for family meals."

"Of course. He's right. But I can't imagine that my absence at lunch will be of much concern to your father, dear."

She attempted to rise and in so doing pulled the small, round table next to her chair sideways, spilling the content of her drinking glass across the lap of her satin dressing gown. Rolly crossed the room quickly, set the table upright and picked the glass up off the floor. "Alright mother, I think you probably should rest for a while. Let's have Philip get your maid. What is the new one's name?"

Hope Douglas McAllister shrugged loosely. "Can't remember."

Philip promptly answered Rolly's summons, was dispatched, and returned quickly followed by a large boned woman in her mid-fifties. Even though she wore none of the professional garb, except thick, white hose and white orthopaedic shoes, she had the brisk manner of a trained nurse, as indeed she was. It had been many years since Mrs. McAllister's care had been left in the hands of mere domestics. Besides, a nurse had a professional responsibility to keep what she saw in the McAllister home confidential; a maid couldn't be counted on for that.

For the past five years Mrs. Hope McAllister's condition had made it necessary for her to nearly stop making public appearances. Philip and his wife, who was the McAllister's cook, as well as Hope's "maid," were the only servants kept on permanent retainer. The other people needed to keep such a large household in order were brought in by order of Phillip as conditions dictated.

Rolly looked at his watch, it was twelve o'clock exactly. "Did you get her upstairs alright?" Rolly asked Philip when the butler returned to say that Edmond Stanley was ready to receive his son in the dining room.

"Yes, sir," was Philip's simple response.

"Well Rolly, how is everything in your life?" Edmond Stanley wondered from the far end of the long, linen-draped dining table without much interest in his voice.

"Oh, just fine, Dad. How was China?"

"Lovely. But I understand your mother was ill a good deal of the time I was gone. Speaking of your mother, where is she?"

"Ah ... upstairs Dad." Rolly swallowed. "She wasn't feeling very well."

"Nonsense!" came from the banker's mouth like lightning from the hand of God. "Philip! Go inform my wife that luncheon is served, and that I expect her downstairs immediately."

The butler exchanged a quick glance with Edmond Stanley's son and bowed himself through the door.

"How is your work coming along at the Aquarium?"

"Great, Dad. That is one of the things I want to talk to you about. I have a really great opportunity to get involved ..."

"That will keep for the time being, son." Edmond Stanley said flatly. There is something I want to discuss with you."

Rolly was startled into silence. He could count on one hand the number of things his father had ever deigned to discuss with him. "Of course, Dad. What is it?"

"Your mother's condition is getting steadily worse. I never had any doubt that it would get worse." The indifference in the older McAllister's tone seemed to emphasize his lack of faith in anything other than business. "I think it is time that we discussed the possibility of discretely allowing her to relocate."

"Relocate?"

"Yes. As you know when her mother died, let's see, twelve years ago was it?" Rolly nodded.

"Right, twelve years ago. Hope inherited the Douglas' villa on the Italian coast. I think that we should consider allowing her to make her home there. The climate would do her a world of good. I don't think she has ever cared for Vancouver."

The younger McAllister was stunned by an unfamiliar sensation welling up in his chest. "Does she want to go to Italy to live, Dad?"

"Oh, she doesn't know anything about this yet. Monday is her birthday you know. I thought we could surprise her."

"We?"

Edmond Stanley looked at his son and smiled woodenly. "Yes, you'll be coming for dinner."

"Ah ... well, Dad ... I mean ... maybe we should ....well you know ... think about ... ah ... this ..." A wave of resentment swept over Rolly, making his conversation more hesitant than usual.

"Nonsense, be good for her. It's settled then. We'll tell her Monday."

The resentment Rolly was experiencing was becoming very pronounced when Philip opened the door and more or less carried his semi-conscious mother into the room. With a pathetic attempt at dignity and leaning heavily on the butler, she took her seat and struggled to keep her limp frame in an upright position.

"Really, Hope, you know how I feel about people being late for meals." Edmond Stanley never looked up from the napkin he was neatly positioning in his lap. "Philip, serve the tomato aspic."

"Allergic to tomatoes." Hope muttered.

"Nonsense! Allergies are in the mind." The banker assured her. "Serve my wife, Philip."

The dislike for his father was becoming sharper and more focused.

Following the service of the aspic, he found it impossible to tear his eyes away from his mother, who was taking tentative mouthfuls of the soup and swallowing them with a terrified gulp.

"Rolly, answer me." Edmond Stanley demanded.

"I'm sorry, Dad. I didn't hear you."

"I asked you what 'really great opportunity' you had stumbled across while I was in China."

It was an effort for the younger McAllister to think past the feeling in his chest, but once he recalled meeting Doctor Short the burning began to subside. "I met a friend of Doctor Early's yesterday. His name is Doctor Daniel Short. He is very interested in an organization which is doing some studies up north."

"What organization? What studies?"

"Well," Rolly's enthusiasm began to take over now. "Studies with killer whales. They call themselves the Orca Communication Society. Dad, these people are really on to something. They believe that this species of whales has the potential for communication with humans."

"Indeed." Edmond Stanley said dryly. "What does Early think about this?"

"Doctor Early is very conservative. He feels that communication is a," choosing his words carefully, "premature issue."

"Probably right."

"I don't think he is."

Edmond Stanley laughed. "You don't *think* he is. Listen, Rolly, Early is the best man in his field, that's why I got you the job as his assistant."

Rolly's face reddened. "Doctor Early said that I got the job on my own merit, Dad."

"Well, of course he'd say that. Early is a very discrete man."

"Look, Dad, Early isn't the issue here, neither is the job. I have every intention of giving the job up if Doctor Early won't let me have the time to go along with the Society on their next expedition."

"You'll do no such thing, Rolly."

"Yes, I will, Dad." Rolly McAllister wasn't sure when the burning in his chest began to expel his fear. "You've said yourself that if we could talk to the whales we could learn …"

"Oh Rolly. A figure of speech, nothing more. The idea that people could or would want to talk to dumb beasts is poppycock."

"Dumb beasts? What do you know about it?" Edmond Stanley's son tossed his napkin on the table.

The banker turned on what Rolly called his board room stare. "I know that insolence is something I don't have to stand for from you. I am no longer interested in discussing this."

"I suppose it would be pointless to ask you for a little financial support to help fund the expedition."

"Pointless, yes. But not nearly as pointless as looking to me for support of any kind should you leave Doctor Early's employ."

Hope began to choke. Rolly turned toward her just in time to see her fall out of her chair, face first, vomiting profusely.

"Good Lord!" Edmond Stanley snapped. "Philip get her maid."

Rolly went to his mother who had pulled herself up on her hands and knees. He placed his arm around her shoulder and listened to her mutter the word allergy over and over again.

When the big-boned woman entered the room this time, she was several feet ahead of Philip and at a dead run. "Alright Mrs. McAllister, I'm here. We'll go upstairs."

"Tomatoes ... allergic ... tomatoes." Hope whispered.

The nurse looked at Mrs. McAllister's plate. "Who in hell gave her tomatoes?"

"Allergies are in the mind." Edmond Stanley said smoothly.

"Please don't ever take up medical practice, *sir*," the nurse sneered. "You could cause lots of trouble for lots of people."

Before E. S. McAllister could respond, the nurse had taken his wife in her big arms and was leading her from the room. Rolly followed the two women half way up the staircase.

"Sorry ... very sorry ... very sorry." Hope kept repeating.

"You're sorry." her maid commented bitterly. "Somebody should shoot that bastard, and you're sorry..."

Rolly turned around, walked past Philip, out into the foyer and out the front door as his father called "Rolly, Rolly..."

Meanwhile, at Vancouver's beautiful Bayside Hotel, a burst of steam filled her lungs as Rolanda pulled the shower curtain aside. "Not bad for a white boy," she commented as she looked down approvingly and nodded her head.

"How in the world did you get in here." Dan Short's voice was full of surprise as he looked up from rinsing his hair.

"Desk clerk. I told him I was your wife."

"My wife and I have been coming here for years, Rolanda." Short laughed, turning off the water and reaching for a towel.

"Well if anybody says anything, tell them I've got a great tan."

As Short emerged into the outer room in his terry cloth robe and slippers, he saw a large, brown leather bag near the foot of the bed. Rolanda apparently planned to spend some time. The situation held promise for some very good times. He started to speak, but Rolanda signaled him into silence. "OK, Andy," she said into the phone. "Soon as I can get the good Doctor dressed, we'll be up."

The two women in the luxury hotel suite still hadn't been able to find their tops and they seemed to be permanently stationed at the backgammon table. Sweets was once again bent over the coffee table and using a rolled-up one dollar bill to inhale the white powder up off a small mirror. In fact, Dan Short thought that nothing had changed in Boxcar Allan's suite since he left there the night before. Nothing except the solitary figure standing tall and proud on the balcony, looking toward beautiful Stanley Park and the small groups of people walking, jogging, and bicycling on the well-maintained paths.

"You look great, baby." Boxcar shouted, kissing Rolanda when she entered the room.

"Thank you. It sure is good to see you Boxcar. Hey, Sweets!"

"Hey, Rolanda." Sweets stumbled forward. "Want some toot, honey?"

"Sure do." Rolanda took her turn on the mirror, then moved unceremoniously out to join the man on the balcony.

"Scotch rocks, man?" Boxcar asked.

"Sure." Dan smiled, watching Rolanda kiss the man leaning over her. Dan assumed that must be the black band leader named Andy.

They remained outside for a few minutes chatting with one another before she took his hand and led him inside saying, "Come on, Andy, I want you to meet him."

Andy's round, sad eyes met Dan's and held them. He put his hand out slowly, shook the other man's quickly, and shoved it back in his pocket. When Andrew Webster, leader and lead singer of Blind Justice, spoke, the sound was a low, melodic rumble. "So you want me to put on a concert, for whales?"

"Well, not exactly." Short answered. "We would like you to help us raise money for the Orca Communication Society, Mr. Webster."

"You call me Andy, man."

"Alright, Andy."

"They talk to whales, Andy." Boxcar chirped. "Crazy, right?"

Andy's narrow face became bright with affection. "I don't know why, man. I talk to you. Some people might think that's crazy, too."

Boxcar threw his head back and laughed.

"Listen, Andy," Rolanda took hold of his arm. "I brought some tapes I would like you to hear."

Webster took hold of her hand and kissed it. "OK, Babe. Boxcar, put her tapes on."

Beethoven's genius in Symphony Number 5 boomed through the suite from the big speakers for perhaps thirty seconds, to fade out into total silence from which emerged the subtle sound of water moving and a series of clicks. The clicks in turn gave way to a long, piercing cry.

"Whale?" Boxcar was incredulous.

Short nodded.

Andy's solemn features were fused into a mask of concentration. Each eerie peal, each upscream and downscream, a kind of tonal spasm, seemed to touch a cord of meaning in the musical sound chamber behind this musician's eyes. Webster understood, as only a creative musical mind can understand, the barely-probed realm of possibilities yet to be explored in sound. The whales, with their vast repertoire of sounds as well as hearing, were eons ahead of man in this area and somehow this rock star sensed that.

The tape continued on to someone picking notes on a guitar, trying to imitate the notes and sequences of the whales. The sounds of the whales during the guitar sequence were of special interest to the black musician.

"No, no, no…" Webster noted, "whoever that dude is on the guitar has missed it. He's not in sync with the whales. Man, if I was there with my synthesizer…"

A few minutes later the tape ended. Webster walked back to the balcony in silence. No one said a word as they waited for his reaction.

"We'll do it. I like those whales," the singer announced.

"What? When?" Boxcar demanded.

"We'll give them the net proceeds from the concert we did last week."

"Andy …"

"I've made up my mind, man. You take care of the details, Boxcar. But there's one requirement…"

"Which is?"

"Blind Justice is going out with the whales. We've got to try this first hand. We need to be out there on the water. And it will be a nice change of pace for the band."

Boxcar Allan rubbed his big chin. "OK," he agreed as Andrew Webster went back out on the balcony to think about a concert for the whales and to watch another freighter sailing west into the Strait of Georgia.

Boxcar motioned Rolanda and Short over near the bar and lowered his voice. "You heard what the man said. We'll do it, but our accounting firm is going to raise hell if this isn't a charitable contribution, know what I mean? Why should Blind Justice pay taxes on money they're going to hand over to your group?"

"Don't worry" Rolanda said as she placed a hand on Boxcar's large shoulder. "We're going to take care of that tomorrow, aren't we, Dan?"

"Why, yes, absolutely," Dan sputtered, not sure of exactly what he was committing to.

As the three days before the concert seemed to evaporate, Dan Short found himself wondering occasionally what ever happened to Rolly McAllister. Rolly never phoned nor came by the hotel the night the Lingo docked. In all the excitement of having Rolanda with him, the love-making, the bicycle-for-two trips through Vancouver's gorgeous Stanley Park, getting an attorney to push for a tax-exempt status for the OCS and the tours of the city's best restaurants, Dan's head had been mostly in a whirl. But it was going well, even if Short himself had agreed to pay the $2,000 legal fee on behalf of the OCS to become tax-exempt. Rolanda had promised him a lifetime honorary membership in the group for his generosity, regardless of what the others might say.

"Is McAllister a wimp?" he had asked Rolanda. "One of those young scientists without the backbone to break out of the role his senior academicians, and perhaps his father, had defined for him?" But something bothered him about that. McAllister, for all his jerking and shaking, had left Short with a distinct impression of strength, perhaps dormant, but strength nonetheless. On the morning of the day the concert was scheduled, Dan decided to call the Aquarium.

"Rolly McAllister." The tone was abrupt, the voice somehow different from what Short remembered.

"McAllister, this is Dan Short."

After a moment's hesitation Rolly sighed and asked. "How can I help you, Doctor?"

"Well, I was just wondering if you'd had a chance to speak to your father yet."

"It is a little difficult to talk about it at this time. Perhaps, I could meet you somewhere this evening."

Yes, Short was convinced that something was definitely wrong with this boy. "Are you familiar with the rock group, Blind Justice?"

"I, I've heard of them. Why?"

"They're putting on a concert tonight, they have promised to give the net proceeds to the Society."

"Oh, I didn't know that."

"Yhea, we're having a little bash afterwards, about eleven or so in the group's suite at the Bayside, 1500. I want you to come as my guest."

Again McAllister hesitated, "OK. I'll be there."

"Good. See you then."

Rolanda was one of the most beautiful women Dan had ever seen. He watched her dressing for the concert, pulling silk stockings up over her long legs, wrapping her firm curves in a silver film more skin than dress, and he wondered if, after this, he would ever be able to touch Claudia again.

"How about a little nose candy for the road, babe?" she crooned in his ear. "OK."

Rolanda cut four smooth, wide, white lines on a little hand mirror, snorted two and handed the mirror and tightly rolled dollar bill to Dan. The cocaine burned into his nasal passageways, pooling in a bittersweet chemical sensation, it couldn't rightly be called a taste, at the back of his throat. His heart rate began to accelerate, a palpable euphoria battered at his diaphram creating a mental high.

His black Madonna was applying perfume to the area between her lovely breasts when he came up behind her and slipped his hand under her dress, letting it slide up her leg to her soft, silk panties. She turned and kissed him. Dan felt her whole body conform to his. He wanted to get closer, bare skin closer, but there wasn't time.

They took the elevator down to the ground floor and started through the cocktail lounge/dining area. Someone yelled to them: "Hey Short and Rolanda, where you off to?' It was a half-loaded Jammer at the bar looking as hostile as ever.

Rolanda spoke first. "We're off to a concert and don't have much time to talk, Jammer."

"No problem. But I wanted to find out if the rumors I hear are true or false."

"What rumors?" Dan asked him.

"Rumors that you are not going to use my boat, the Lingo, any more for your program. And that I am being pushed aside or maybe even kicked aside."

Dan looked him directly in the eyes. "No decision has been made on that yet Jammer, but we are looking into a larger boat with accommodations for more researchers. We appreciate your work but must do what is best for the program."

"Hell, you dumbos can't find your own ass using both hands, how can you expect to find killer whales out there in the open ocean."

Rolanda was becoming angry. "We'll do just fine, Jammer. We'll let you know if we need any of your help. Now we're off to the concert. Let's go, Dan." They walked past the front desk and a doorman signalled a cab to pick them up.

"Interesting to see Jammer again," Dan observed. "But the guy was always hostile toward me and we'll be better off without him."

Rolanda brought his hand up and kissed it. "I agree 100%, honey."

Short had not been to a rock concert in many years. He searched his memory, trying to remember exactly how long it had been. Oh yes, early and late 70's. Much younger then, he'd been part of the electricity, now he was a sensitive observer. The light cascading down on the stage seemed to be refracted off the group and their instruments, throwing random bands of color across the darkened music hall which was filled to capacity.

The audience was a mixed bag of teenagers in faded jeans and T-shirts bearing the name Blind Justice, and young adults in more opulent costumes designed to resemble, in age at least, the dress of their younger co-worshipers. They spent most of their time on their feet, shouting and singing the lyrics to the songs they seemed to know by heart. Wherever the light from the stage touched them, their intensity became doubled, even tripled, and some of the females began throwing articles of clothing, shirts, bras and panties, up to the men on the glowing platform above them.

After an intermission, Rolanda lead Dan into the smoke-filled area behind stage where the band was relaxing. They remained there throughout the duration of the second and third sets. Short was glad later that they hadn't stayed out front in the pushing, the shouting, and the screaming. He had discovered something fascinating: Andy Webster, the solemn, lonely figure on a balcony whom Short had met the night before, now seemed like a butterfly's cocoon that had released an iridescent creature whose total existence was somehow more music than man. There was nothing within the sound of his voice that wasn't somehow enhanced by the glow of his energy. By the time the last curtain call had been taken, Dan was so exhausted with the spectacle of Webster that he never saw the metamorphosis reverse itself; never saw the solemn, lonely figure return as if returning to the cocoon.

Rolly McAllister had spent the better part of his day wondering what in hell he was going to tell Doctor Short and the other members of the Society about his father's refusal to provide any funding. And Dr. Short had said the research vessel, the Lingo, was already in port, which meant the crew would probably be there too. A wonderful opportunity for him to make his debut in the group if only he could show that he could help them somehow.

He had been so sure, so very sure, that Edmond Stanley would want to help. But then he had been so sure of so many things, all of which seemed to have vanished like sea fog when he talked to his father over that lunch.

Riding up in the elevator of the Bayside Hotel, Rolly was driven by a need to be accepted by the people his father had ridiculed. But without the money, well, it didn't seem very likely. Stepping off the elevator he could not believe that the noise he was hearing could actually be coming from suite 1500, but, as he approached, it got louder. It sounded like a mini-convention. People were laughing and talking loudly, the stereo was booming and the heavy smell of marijuana hung in the hallway. Before he could knock on the door of the suite it was thrown open by a strange, small, black woman wearing nothing but a halter top and cutoff jeans; no shoes. The noise and smoke were intense. She looked right at him, but didn't seem to see him, and instead peered down the hallway toward the elevator.

"My name is Rolly McAllister." he said. "I am looking for Doctor Dan Short."

The woman ran her tongue over her teeth and seemed to be looking for something in the clutter of her mind. "Short ..." she whispered. "Short ... oh yhea, the guy with Rolanda who talks to whales ... right ... over in the corner." She shut the door in his face, and he knocked again. When she opened it a second time, Rolly walked in past her and made his way through the crowd, mostly black, toward the corner.

"Hello, Doctor Short. Some party," he almost shouted to be heard above the din.

Dan's pupils were dilated and he seemed a little disoriented when he turned to McAllister. "Well hi, Rolly. How are you? Did you catch the concert?"

"No, sir." McAllister stated, trying to brace himself. He intended to simply blurt out his failure and try to make the best he could of it. "About the money, sir ..."

"Wait a minute, pal, you haven't got a drink yet. Scotch wasn't it? Wait here a second." He pushed his way to the bar, poured half of glass of Scotch, no ice, and brought it back to the wide-eyed young man.

"Let's drink a toast to Rolly McAllister, newest member of the Orca Communication Society! Bottoms up, pal."

Rolly took a healthy swig and coughed.

"Dan!" The most beautiful black woman McAllister had ever seen pushed herself between he and Short. "Dan! Andy is planning to do a concert for the whales."

"Fine, babe." Dan answered, kissing her neck. "We need another concert."

"No Dan, you don't understand. He wants to go out, go out on the ocean, and perform a concert for the whales, for *them*, sing to them, play for them. Great, isn't it!"

Short looked down into Rolanda's beautiful, dark eyes. The meaning of what she was trying to tell him finally passed the cocaine barrier. "Yhea, that really is great, baby."

"We only got one problem, bro." Boxcar Allan had the strange woman who had met McAllister at the door tossed over one big shoulder. "What are we going to go out on? Man, we'd need the Royal Navy to haul this bunch, their instruments, their dope, their women..."

Suddenly Rolly McAllister felt the kind of joy that only comes from knowing how to get even. "Would a seventy 5-foot cabin cruiser do?"

"Yhea, Rolly," Short breathed. "That would do, that would *really* do!"

"Well, let me place the McAllister yacht at your disposal."

◆◆◆

CHAPTER NINETEEN

The Pharoah

Before Rolly McAllister left the Bayside Hotel he made a cell phone call from a remote corner of the lobby. The woman he spoke with was a woman he often called. Her name was Jules; no first name, no last name, no Ms, just Jules. Yes, she would arrange to have a friend of hers meet him in the bar of Gastown's Hotel Europe, and yes, she would arrange a room for later. Yes, indeed it could be done quickly, yes and thank you.

Rolly McAllister never touched a woman who wasn't in the business. After all, you couldn't hurt one of them, you couldn't soil a working girl. She'd already done it for you, she was pre-soiled, like the American jeans that are pre-shrunk.

He met Jules' friend half an hour after he decided to steal his father's yacht. She was French or Italian or something, he wasn't sure. They didn't talk very long, had a drink and went upstairs. As so often happened, Rolly couldn't get in the mood; despite the girl's best efforts, he couldn't get it up. After forty-five minutes of fruitless contortions he paid her and left. Climbing into his Jaguar, Rolly motored across the Lions Gate Bridge with the beginning of a plan in mind.

At the Bayshore he had given Short some lame excuse about why his father's crew would not be available. "Probably better anyway." Short had mumbled. "Lingo crew can sail the damn thing."

"Of course we can." Rolanda agreed. "We'll all meet in the morning at the yacht club."

"Oh no," Rolly interjected. "I think it's better if I pick you up at the yacht sales office on the northside of the hotel." Then as a nervous after thought, "Save the band having to haul all that expensive equipment around."

"Good idea." Rolanda nodded, patting Rolly on the shoulder.

Rolly responded nervously: "I am reasonably certain I can take the helm for that short a distance."

Rolanda smiled at him. "Why, haven't you ever handled your Dad's yacht, Mr. McAllister?"

"No, I never had the opportunity, but I'm sure I can do it."

"Well," she put a slender, brown finger between her beautiful lips. "Let's call Craig Martin. He was a sort of co-captain of the Lingo and he can handle it. Craig could meet you at the club, and the two of you can pick the rest of us up."

"Fine. Can you have Craig arrive about nine thirty tomorrow morning?" Rolly asked.

"Sure. I'll see him tonight. He'll be there," Rolanda assured him.

That solved one part of the problem. Now the big problem, and this is where his plan would come in, was how to get the yacht club authorities to allow him to take the yacht without confirmation by his father.

"Your father is in New York until Monday, sir." Philip informed him on the door step of the McAllister home.

"For Christ's sake, Philip, will you at least let me in before you inform me who I may or may not see?"

"Of course, sir." Philip responded.

"Where is my mother?"

"In the morning room, sir."

"Philip," Rolly ran his right hand through his hair. "That is not a morning room, it's a bar. That's why my mother stays in there, because it's a bar. And you know what Phil, old buddy, I don't blame her a damn bit."

Mrs. Hope McAllister was seated in almost the same position her son had found her in the last time he saw her. The only difference being that she was propped in front of a wide screen television dreamily watching Gloria Swanson stalk through her nightmare on Sunset Boulevard.

"Hello, mother." Rolly kissed her cheek.

She seemed surprised. He didn't blame her, it had been years since he kissed her.

"Rolly!" Hope timidly touched his cheek. "Mrs. Payne, could you turn the movie off?"

The big boned woman rose from the shadows and switched the VCR to pause. She then started to leave the room.

"Oh no, Mrs. Payne," Hope pleaded. "She can stay, can't she Rolly?"

"Of course, mother."

"You know, Gloria Swanson was very beautiful when she was young, Rolly?"

"I am sure she was, mother."

She took the glass from the side of her chair and brought it clumsily to her lips. "That movie is about a woman who finds herself getting old, and no one remembers her anymore. It's very sad."

Rolly looked at Mrs. Payne who looked back dispassionately. "Mother, I've come to ask a favor of you. I need to use Dad's yacht."

"Oh... well, my dear, I have nothing to say about ...about the yacht."

"Listen mother, I am going to the club in the morning to pick up the yacht. I am afraid that they will try to contact Dad in New York for permission before they let me have it. You know he won't give ... let me take the ... damn thing ... and well, I need ... I need that yacht, mother."

Mrs Hope McAllister was very confused now. She really wasn't certain what Rolly wanted her to do. Lord, what could she do, what had she ever been able to do? "Well, my darling ... I ... don't know ... I am not sure ... what I can ..."

"If, instead of calling New York," Rolly began carefully choosing his words. "They can call here, and you can tell them that it is alright. I am sure that they would accept that."

Confusion in his mother's face gave way to genuine terror. Hope McAllister tried to stand up and lost her balance. Rolly caught her as she pitched forward, Mrs. Payne was at his side instantly, helping him put the limp woman back in her chair.

"No Rolly," his mother cried. "... No ... please. I can't."

"Mrs. McAllister you settle down now, I am going to turn your movie back on." Mrs. Payne stepped back into the shadows near the VCR for a moment, then turned and glared hard at Rolly. "You, outside. I want to have a little talk with you."

Rolly McAllister did exactly as he was told. When she joined him in the hall, closing the door behind her, there was no malice in the nurse's manner, no anger in her demeanor, only a determination of purpose born of many years of taking firm action when someone she cared for was in great physical danger. "Do you have any idea how terrified she is of that son of a bitch?"

"I beg your pardon?" Rolly stuttered.

"Oh, cut the crap, kid! Your father, do you have any idea how frightened she is of him?"

"My father is ..."

"Your father is an a-hole. But that is not the point. The point is," Mrs. Payne had hold of Rolly's collar now, and was dragging him down the hall in the direction of the front door. "Your coming here, asking her to help you steal his yacht, is somewhere between cruel and moronic."

Rolly forced his left foot inside the door just as she was about to shut it in his face. "I need that yacht!!"

"You get your foot out of that door or you'll pull back a stump." Hesitating, she looked at him thoughtfully. "How bad?"

"What?"

"Are you deaf as well as stupid? I said, how bad do you need the yacht."

Something in the way Rolly was looking at her must have annoyed Mrs. Payne greatly. Suddenly she took hold of his collar and pulled him back into the foyer. She slammed the door, and after muttering something about Rolly being a great living argument for legalized abortion, demanded, "Do you want that boat bad enough to do something for me?"

"Like what?" Rolly McAllister's tone was sceptical.

"Like, give me the money to get your mother out of here?"

"Where ... how ...?"

"The where is a clinic in Seattle for alcoholics. The how, a check from you for enough to get the two of us down there so she can be admitted to dry out. I figure about five grand for now."

"But Dad would ..."

"Your Dad is not going to know anything about this, sonny. Now can you get that much money together all by yourself?"

"Yes. I can give you a check now." Rolly hesitated. "But how do I know that you'll do what you say, I mean the clinic and all that."

Mrs. Payne smiled sardonically. "There isn't much I could do to her that is worse than what's being done to her in this house, kid. One more thing. If he finds her, I want you to get your ass to the Seattle clinic and keep him from dragging her back."

"How am I supposed to do that?"

"Any way you can." Mrs. Payne sighed.

Rolly's throat was very dry when he asked, "What about the yacht?"

"You have the boys over at the club call here tomorrow. I'll say that I'm her secretary, that she can`t come to the phone, but that your father left his permission, no, ORDERS, for you to have the boat for as long as you like."

"What about Philip. I know Dad gave him instructions not to put calls through to her."

"Screw Philip, he knows better than to interfere with me." She looked at him sternly.

"I'll bet he does." Rolly whispered as he wrote out a check for $5,000, the amount she demanded.

"You and I will run him off one of these days. Just make sure the Yacht Club asks for Mrs. Payne and tell them that I screen all her calls."

He handed the check to her. "They probably won't call much before a quarter of ten."

"No problem."

"That Philip, your old man's mouth piece, goes out every day about two. Comes back with the stuff cook needs from the market. God forbid a delivery boy should see Edmond Stanley McAllister's wife drunk. I'll get her out then." Mrs. Payne held the door open for him.

"You must think a great deal of my mother."

"Hardly know her. Haven't ever seen her sober."

"Why are you doing this?"

Mrs. Payne ran her big hand over her chin. "If you have to ask kid, I don't know how to tell ya."

Admiring the beautiful Canadian morning, Jack Ormond was sipping coffee and watching the sunlight reflecting from the gently undulating water supporting the magnificent vessels moored in the Royal Vancouver Yacht Club. He'd been in the office since sunrise thinking about the yacht exhibition that was planned for the following Wednesday. Although why he spent so much time thinking about such an event was beyond him. But it was a good opportunity for owners who wanted to sell their boat and for boat sales people to show off their new models. The McAllister yacht was always popular with visitors.

"Morning," came a voice from over Ormond's shoulder.

Jack started, turned around and offered, almost involuntarily, "Good morning."

The man standing in front of him was in his late twenties, shabbily dressed, with shoulder length hair and features reminiscent of west coast

Indians. Ormond's first reaction was to send this person packing because he was obviously in the wrong place.

"I'm supposed to meet a man named McAllister here. A Rolly McAllister."

"Well ... ah, sir," Ormond found the stranger's habit of intense eye contact unnerving. "We are not expecting Mr. Rolly today."

"Is that right? Well I am. When he shows up I'll be over there." He nodded toward some seats near a large bay window looking out over the western harbor. "You tell him that I'm here. He's never met me but we'll soon get acquainted."

"And your name sir?"

"Just tell him Craig. He'll know who I am."

Ormond set his coffee cup down and put his hands in his pockets. He thought of calling the police but then decided to watch the situation further. What could this poorly-dressed individual possibly want with Mr. Rolly? Perhaps it was going to be an attempt at kidnapping. No, ridiculous, but someone could target Rolly as someone who could bring substantial money in a ransom demand. Not Rolly, Ormand you idiot. Edmond Stanley. Someone wanting to even a score with that bastard, and there must be alot of people who would like to, might consider, taking or killing his son. Oh yes, Jack Ormond knew he was on the right track. The deductive instincts he had nurtured, in the isolation of his little apartment, in the company of novels by Ross MacDonald, Raymond Chandler and Mickey Spillane, told him that he was definitely on the right track. Now the question was, how to handle the situation. The whole thing was up to him at this point. Again, his mind wrestled with the alternate possibilities of calling the police or simply trying to throw the rascal out the door when Rolly McAllister walked into the yacht club office.

Jack Ormond glanced at the stranger near the bay window who had apparently not seen the young man enter, then stepped across the room and threw his arms around McAllister. He turned Rolly back in the direction of the door and whispered, "You have to get out of here Mr. Rolly ... no time to explain ... must go before ..."

"Ormand! What in hell!" McAllister shouted trying to shake himself free. The stranger turned his attention on the two men struggling near the door. Ormand spoke louder than he needed to, and began rolling his eyes in the direction of the bay window. "I am sorry sir, there is no one here who can give you any information about the yachts that are for sale by the owner.

If you'll come back …"

"Ormand," Rolly took two steps back away from the man. "What are you talking about and what's wrong with your eyes?"

"If you'll just come back tomorrow, sir," Jack Ormond continued. "Someone will be here to help you and discuss the vessels that might be available this season."

"Look Jack, I don't know what you've been drinking, but I'm Rolly McAllister, remember me?"

"Oh I am sorry sir. We aren't expecting Mr. Rolly today. I told the other gentleman that. The one over there by the window. So why don't the two of you come back …"

Jack Ormand swallowed the end of his sentence in astonishment as Rolly strolled over to the stranger and shook his hand. The two men chatted for a moment before rejoining the Yacht Club custodian.

"This lunatic," Rolly indicated Ormand. "Reads too many mystery novels, Captain Martin. He probably thought you were going to kidnap me and sell me to some terrorists, or God knows what. Right Jack?"

"I am sorry, Mr. Rolly." Ormond stuttered. "I didn't realize that you had arranged to meet the Captain here."

Craig Martin surveyed Jack's hand with indifference and then shook it with a strong grip.

Rolly McAllister cleared his throat. "I've come to pick up the *Pharaoh*, Jack. Dad said he had no objections to my taking it out for a while, and Captain Martin here is coming along so that I won't need Dad's crew."

Ormond looked from Martin to McAllister uncomfortably.

"This is very unusual, Mr. Rolly. Your father has never allowed anyone else to take the *Pharaoh* out, and with the boat show coming up in a few days, well, I just don't know."

"I understand, Jack," said McAllister with a calm he did not feel. "Dad knew you would be skeptical so he left his permission with my mother. Feel free to call her. By the way, ask for Mrs. Payne, her secretary. She screens all mother's calls."

Jack Ormond nodded and disappeared into a small, glass enclosed office directly behind him. Rolly's chest wall quivered as he watched the Harbor Master speak, then wait, then speak again.

By the time Ormond finished and came back out of the office, Rolly was so agitated that he snapped, "Well, did you get what you needed?"

"Certainly, Mr. Rolly. I would feel a little better if I could speak to your father directly. However Mrs. Payne told me, your mother could not come to the phone it seems, that Mr. McAllister is in upstate New York fishing, and can't be reached. However, he left instructions with your mother that you were to be allowed to take the yacht out. Shall we expect you back for the show on Wednesday?"

"Certainly. You don't think Dad would miss that, do you?" Rolly felt Craig give him a sharp look.

"Of course not, Mr. Rolly. I'll make sure that she's fueled and ready to weigh anchor."

"Back by Wednesday, huh?" Craig inquired after Ormond was out of ear shot. "Short said you guys talked about staying out at least a week."

McAllister's breath caught in his throat, then he relaxed. Lying was getting easier. "Dad's bringing a new yacht in for the show. He doesn't want the club to know. That's why he needs the Pharaoh taken out. They'll have to let him enter the new yacht if we aren't back."

Craig's look was doubtful, but he said nothing.

There were few things in life that could thrill Craig Martin and a fabulous yacht with large twin diesel engines was one of them. After the shock of finding himself temporarily in command of the 70 foot beauty, Craig took a few minutes to look around. The yacht had the capacity to sleep at least twelve in five separate cabins, a formal dining room, well-stocked mahogany bar and upper deck with a hot tub, a fully-equipped and well stocked galley, fishing equipment, and a 14 foot aluminium runabout suspended above the stern. Every item was first class; no corners had been cut when the *Pharoah* was built and furnished.

Craig stepped to the controls and, starting the big twin diesels, ordered Rolly to cast off. He handled the vessel with the ease of a man long accustomed to living on the open sea. As Jack Ormond stood on the dock open-mouthed and incredulous, Craig gracefully and effortlessly ran her out of the Yacht Club dock and across the bay to the dock at the east side of the Bayside Hotel. The musicians were in the hotel at the ground floor arboretum bar but Boxcar was keeping an eye out for the yacht. The instruments and electronic equipment belonging to Andy Webster and Blind Justice had been placed carefully in the shade next to the hotel. Boxcar was standing vigilant guard over them.

By the time Boxcar and the crew from the Lingo had loaded and stored the musical and scientific equipment in one of the staterooms located on the *Pharaoh's* lower deck, Rolanda, Short, and Webster had joined Craig Martin on the bridge.

"What's our E.T.A. in the San Juan Islands?" Short asked casually.

"'Bout two hours." Craig replied.

"Great, man," sighed Webster. "I need some sleep."

"Hell, sleep when you're dead." Rolly McAllister almost shouted as he came up from the bar with a large magnum of champagne he had just opened. "It's time to party."

"If I don't get some sleep soon, I will be dead, bro. I been party'n for two days now." Webster even sounded tired.

"Hey, Andy." Boxcar shouted from the door.

"Yo man." Webster replied.

"Everything's loaded. Me and Sweets are go'n back to the Bayside. See you in about a week, right?"

"No." Webster objected. "We can't stay out no week, got that concert tour deal in L.A. We'll be back in a couple of days. You stay here. We'll all go back to the hotel together."

Boxcar Allan had not been very comfortable with the idea of dragging one of popular music's most valuable, in terms of bookings, rock groups out into the middle of bum-dink nowhere to sing to a bunch of fish that, as far as he could tell, didn't have ears. Now in the face of Webster's sober and cocaine free attitude, enthusiasm waning, Boxcar was downright nervous. "OK, Andy. Whatever you say, man."

"Andy, I thought we agreed that we would stay out at least a week." Rolanda's eyes had lost their alluring softness.

"Yeah, sorry baby." Andy yawned. "I just think the group needs to be get'n back to Vancouver by Tuesday, Wednesday at the latest."

Rolly McAllister dropped a half-empty glass of wine as he tried to fill it to the brim. Craig glanced at him out of the corner of his eye and then turned to Andy. "What do you say we bring you all in first thing Wednesday morning?"

"Sounds good, skipper." Andy agreed.

"Wednesday it is, man." added Boxcar as Rolly poured another glass of wine.

Dan Short sat with his black Madonna in the warm swirling water of the yacht's Jacuzzi hot tub. His mind was drifting on a white powder cloud in a gentle swell of Scotch. Rolanda's nude body was completely submerged, her eyes were closed, and her head rested on the cool, tawny marble lip of the tub. Dan was fascinated by the action of her breathing, the rhythmic rise and fall of her breasts just above and below the waterline. He put his hand out and lovingly caressed one dark mound as it broke the water's surface. She shuttered, sliding over closer to him, her lips slipping under his to be kissed. His hand moved down the fragile ladder of her rib cage, over her firm belly and into the pliant velvet between her thighs. Rolanda's breathing was now deep and guttural. She was positioning her body and his so that she might mount without pushing him down into the water when a heavy knock on the door broke the silence just before Boxcar burst into the room.

"Jesus, sorry Rolanda, Doctor Short, but Captain Martin wants everybody up on deck." Boxcar stopped to take a breath. "We've spotted a pack of killers and we're in pursuit."

"Where's Andy?" Rolanda asked, trying to regain some composure.

"One of the group went to get him. Everybody else is helping set up instruments and equipment near the pool."

Craig brought the *Pharaoh* into the heart of where he could see orca activity. There was some game afoot, he thought. The young whales were accelerating, diving, changing direction and sounding for no apparent reason other than their own amusement. The immense, glistening black and white torpedoes seemed totally indifferent to the presence of the yacht.

"Susan!" Craig shouted.

"Yhea skipper." She ran to the bridge.

"Is our recording equipment in place?"

"Sure is."

Craig's rigid face had taken on a strange kind of animation. "Before Webster and his bunch get started, let's record some tapes of the whales themselves. They're having a hell of a good time, and we might get an idea of how to entice them into playing with us."

He slowed the diesel engines to idle and then turned them off completely so the recorders could pick up sounds from the whales. Craig felt much more comfortable with these great predators than he ever could with people. Human beings were petty, stupid, and irrelevant in his estimation. But Orca was a superior species, a profoundly intelligent and meaningful life form. The sound of their clicks and cries tugged at a deeply primal and fundamental part of Craig's being. Like the ancient shamans he had met with the Tlingit tribe, he seemed to instinctively understand Orca's meaning, Orca's divinity.

The sounds of the killer whale's voices were now amplified over the ship's speaker system. To Craig some of the sounds were like projectiles, shattering the fragile surface of human's imperfect verbal communications. Craig believed that he was the only one on board who could hear certain of the sounds or appreciate the messages being sent via the sounds. He believed that some people tried to bring the brilliant Orca down to their intellectual level.

While the whales were still nearby, the Blind Justice band had set up their instruments and microphones. Speakers were lowered into the water and the band began playing. First a couple of slow and easy numbers and then silence to listen for the whale response, if any. The whales continued communicating with each other just as they did before the music was played. A couple of the younger whales did circle the yacht a couple of times for some unknown reason.

Andy wondered if they might like some old time rock n roll and they tried that with no obvious results. But Boxcar had an idea: "Hey, Rolanda has done some great singing in the past. Maybe she'll sing now for the whales."

"Good idea," Andy replied. "Hey Rolanda, how about singing something and we'll see what happens?"

"Well, OK," she responded, "but it will be something sweet and not rock and roll. How about 'What'll I Do' the song made famous a few years ago as sung by Linda Ronstadt. All I need it a little guitar and piano background, no drums."

Andy turned to his band. "Hear that? Rolanda wants some nice background so she can sing sweetly to the whales. Guitar and keyboard only." The band nodded yes.

Rolanda, with Dan smiling next to her, took the microphone and began singing softly: "What'll I do when you are far away and I am blue, what'll I do?" Her sweet voice was transmitted to the underwater speakers.

Within a minute of the start of Rolanda's singing, the noise from the whales fell off sharply. It was assumed the orcas were listening. Three of the whales approached the yacht and seemed to stop near the speakers.

Andy whispered to the band: "They're listening."

Dan Short was dumfounded. Perhaps they had stumbled upon a way to start communications with the whales. Rolly, sitting in a deck chair, was smiling, he could report this to the Orca Society. When the song ended everyone on deck applauded politely. Rolanda signalled to them: one more. She began singing "Crazy." A few low whistles and clicks from the whales were heard, but again they seemed to be listening. Once again, when the song ended the on-deck audience applauded politely. Dan hugged Rolanda and said "Wonderful." Together they walked to the bar to get a celebratory drink.

Someone shouted "Try Reggae" and the band launched into a catchy Bob Marley number, which prompted a reaction by the whales but not what they had hoped for. By the end of the piece, almost all orca communications stopped and the pack seemed to gather together and depart, heading west into more open water. Andy signalled the band to be quiet and then turned to Captain Craig, "The orcas may have decided to beat it. What should we do now? You have orca experience."

"It would take quite a while to even find another pack," Craig replied. "We were fortunate to find this one and we found out what kind of music they like, Rolanda's singing, and what they don't like. They don't seem to like reggae; when the band started playing that they took off in a hurry."

"Well, the whales should visit Jamaica. But what do we do now, man?" Andy Webster wanted to know. "Me and the band needs some rest before we hit the road again and this boat ain't a good resting place."

"We know we've got to get back to Vancouver in a day or two," Craig responded. "Why don't we head back now? We'll arrive at the hotel after 10 pm but the instruments and equipment can stay on the boat overnight. Rolly probably doesn't care as long as the yacht is back in place when his old man returns in a couple of days".

"Yeah, yeah" Rolly mumbled when told of the revised plan. "Gives me a chance to get this boat back before my old man returns. If it ain't there, he'll come look'n. He'll come, ya know, ta handle things himself, the way only he and Superman can handle things."

Craig watched Rolly stumble down the stairs and around the corner. He was thinking about the whales now, about the whales and how future communications efforts might be designed via the music approach.

◆◆◆

CHAPTER TWENTY

Shipping plan

R eed, Mike and Tracy were pleased to arrive in Whittier after several days aboard the *Czarina* following the whales. But their spirits were also elevated because of the newly-hatched plan for determining which of the whales might be a rogue or rogues and to determine their reaction to a food animal which was not a part of their normal diet.

As soon as the *Czarina* was tied in place at the harbor facilities they quickly made their way to the waiting Suburban carrying duffle bags and overnight cases. Fortunately, the train to Portage was just beginning to load and if they hurried they would be able to get aboard. With the Suburban crawling forward in the loading line, Tracy trotted over to the small grocery store and picked up two bottles of apple juice; $5 each for what would sell for less than $3 in Anchorage. Tracy and Mike gave each other knowing glances when they saw Reed dash to a public telephone to call the Anchorage office of Japan Air Lines to speak to his female friend.

When Reed returned to the railroad, he found Mike and Tracy parked on the 10th flat car from the ramp. After crunching through the gravel in which the railroad ties were bedded, he climbed aboard via the short steel ladder on the end of the car.

With a jerk, the train began to move westward toward Portage and they settled into their seats in the vehicle to continue contemplation of the events and thoughts of the past few days.

"You know, the pig idea has a lot of merit," Reed observed, as he sipped some of the apple juice from a Styrofoam cup. "But we can expect that holy hell will be raised when the word gets out about what we're doing. And note that I didn't say *if* gets out, I said *when*." He looked at Mike and Tracy in the front seats.

"Listen," Tracy pointed out, "I was in San Francisco last fall and there were pickets in front of Macy's and several of the other large stores downtown. I stopped to ask them why they were picketing and they informed me that they were animal rights activists picketing against the sale of fur coats. They said it was cruelty to animals. I asked them if they also picketed the slaughter houses where they killed thousands more animals, and larger ones at that, but they chose to ignore the question. It seems they oppose killing of fur-bearing animals but not the food animals. I thought they might be wearing some leather shoes or leather belts, but they had already thought of that and where wearing only synthetics and natural fibers."

"And they also spray paint on fur coats people are wearing to discourage the purchase of furs," Mike added. "The Times had a story a couple of weeks ago about some woman caught in Aspen, Colorado sticking wet chewing gum in fur coats in some of the stores down there. If I owned one of those stores and caught her doing that I'd be tempted to punch her lights out."

"Sure, and she'd sue you," Tracy stated.

Reed nodded, "A couple of weeks ago activists fire bombed a couple of department stores in London because they were selling fur coats. These people are crazy. They don't seem to realize that by far more animals are brought into the world because man utilizes them than would ever live without man's programs."

"Yes, and don't forget the attacks on research facilities that use animals both in the U.S. and overseas," said Mike. "The new facilities are being built like wartime bunkers to preclude attacks by the nuts."

The flat car their Suburban was on was approaching the first tunnel just west of Whittier. Tracy poured more apple juice before they were enveloped in complete darkness. "It seems like a good idea to keep the work as confidential as possible, but a certain number of people are going to have to know about the project or we won't get anything done," she noted.

"You're right there," said Mike. "One of the hurdles we must cross is working with Fish and Game and, more importantly, NOAA because they're responsible for marine mammals. If they don't go for our program we may not get to first base."

"We got along well with Dr. Walker when we met her in Anchorage," Tracy looked at Reed, "But do you think she'd go along with our plans?"

"I have met her," Reed said, "and from what I could see she may go along with the concept if she can; a) avoid committing NOAA funds, b) avoid embarrassing situations, and c) have a chance to bring a little glory to her division. Without her cooperation it's going to be tough. And I'm sure she will want to monitor the program somehow."

Mike thought a moment then noted, "Perhaps the best approach would be to get her approval for our work and then see if she'll assign monitoring to the NOAA biologist, Herb Bracken. We've talked to Herb on several occasions and he seems like the type who can take some heat if he likes a project. He's a retired Navy commander with Vietnam experience."

"What's his biology background?" queried Reed. The train clickety-clacked out of the tunnel so they could once again see each other.

"Strangely enough, "Mike replied, "he's about sixty or so and has a PhD in parasitology; don't ask me how he landed this job. I can only presume they wanted someone who could address parasite infestation in Alaska marine mammals, but I'm not sure.

Tracy added, "He must be short on field experience if he retired from the Navy."

"Well," said Mike, "I can tell you this much, he's a tough old coot and very independent, perhaps because he receives retirement pay from the Navy. I've heard him tell some of the Fish and Game people to go to hell, including Fred Pennyworth, the Commissioner. If we could get him on our side in the program it would really help."

Tracy smiled with an intuitive thought. "Why don't we just lay it on the line with Dr. Walker. When she hears how controversial this may get she'll probably be glad to pass it off to Herb. If things get hot later on, she can blame Pennyworth or even run Herb off as the whipping boy."

Reed also smiled. "That's a great idea, Tracy. Knowing how the bureaucracies work, she just may go for it."

"Good. Reed, maybe you could call Dr. Walker in Seattle when we get to Anchorage," Mike suggested. "I have a distinct feeling a call from a Ph.D marine biologist would go over better than a call from Tracy or me even though we seemed to hit it off at our meeting in Anchorage. If we can get her general approval I'll call Herb and set up a meeting, but we're going to have to proceed carefully because if Walker gets the idea we're trying to railroad her, so to speak, she may balk."

"I'll be glad to call," Reed responded. "You know, I think we're really on the right track with this approach."

"Speaking of tracks, here comes another tunnel," Tracy noted and poured another round of apple juice. "But we've got to figure out how much all of this is going to cost. Mike, you and I have prepared many an estimate for costs of your mineral exploration projects. This one won't be much different, and it actually should be simpler." She took out a tablet and pen she always kept in the console between the front seats of the Suburban just as they entered the tunnel and total darkness enveloped them. "Well, I can't write until we have some light," and she switched on an overhead light.

Reed led off. "We all know from experience up here that the big items are going to be labor costs and the costs for whatever vessels we need. The pigs and shipping the pigs are going to be a hefty item; they may have to come by air. Do either of you know if the contact of yours in Colorado has pigs on hand? And if so, do you think she'll give us some kind of a break on the price?"

"I never did price the pigs in Greeley, but, as a special breed, I imagine they sell for a premium above normal pigs." Mike replied. "Tracy, how about you calling Mary in Greeley when we get to town and find out what she has available and what kind of deal we might get. If we get everything going on this concept, we're going to need the pigs pretty quickly to take advantage of the summer weather."

"Yes, and we know the A-T pack is somewhere in the Sound," added Reed, "a very important factor."

The train emerged from the tunnel; Tracy continued making a list. "We've got to start somewhere, how about the vessels? How many, what kind, and what's the cost?"

"The fewer, the better," Mike stated. "The *Czarina* should, as usual, be the lead research vessel. For tax purposes it's our second home anyway, and the price to the project is good: nothing!"

Reed smiled. "For the second vessel we need something larger with deck space and winch capability."

Mike thought a moment. "Say, I'll tell you where we might be able to get not just a boat, but a damned good skipper as well, Remember Mario Petrovic over in Cordova, the guy who was so great at coming up with equipment ideas? He's about sixty-seven now and decided to sell his seining permit. He's also trying to sell his boat the '*Karen Marie*,' but hadn't sold it the last I heard. The boat is a 48 foot pocket seiner with a power block and boom and plenty of deck space for the containers holding the pigs. Could be ideal, not too big."

"I remember him, he's the one who invented that power block pulley," said Reed. "And when we saw him last year in Cordova he said he'd like to go out with us sometime to watch the whales. If he hasn't sold the boat he would be ideal if he'd do it; he knows Prince William Sound like the back of his hand."

"I'll try to call him as soon as we get to town," Mike volunteered. "Hopefully he'll be available and may not charge more than fuel and groceries."

"Ok, two vessels," noted Tracy as the train lurched around a corner where a small waterfall fell 500 feet down the precipitous slope of the narrow canyon through which they were passing. "But what shall we put down for fuel and grocery costs? Shall we say $300 per day or $9,000 for one month for the *Karen Marie*, Mario, fuel and groceries? Might not be that much, but better to err on the high side."

"That sounds pretty good," said Mike, "and you'd better put down $150 per day for a crewman/cook to help Mario. We might find a volunteer, but don't count on it."

"Ok, one month at $450 per day is $13,500. Good thing we have the *Czarina* with a crew that works for nothing," Tracy smiled. "The *Czarina* will run $100 per day just for food and fuel alone."

"The next item will be the pigs and shipping," observed Mike. "My guess is the air freight per pig will be much more than the purchase price. And how many pigs will we need? I'd say we'd better get about twenty. What do you think, Reed?"

"Just as a guess, if we use four or five on each trip out that would give us only four trips. And better to order too many than not enough. Besides," Reed winked at Tracy, "if we close out the project with five or six pigs left over they'll look damned good in your freezer. I remember that pork roast you cooked for us last year, Tracy. That was fabulous!"

Tracy mused, "If we ended up eating some it would be the most expensive pork in Alaska, but then it probably would not cost any more per pound than some of the Dall sheep or moose Mike brings in. By the time you figure all the costs, wild game probably runs $30 per pound not including the time it takes Mike to actually do the hunting and meat handling.

"But it's the sport," Mike smiled. They had been over this many times

before. The train was approaching Portage where they could drive off and
then cruise into Anchorage as they discussed planning. About thirty minutes
were required to get all the vehicles off the flat cars.

"Speaking of pork," Reed asked, "what are the chances of getting some
pigs right here in Alaska so we can avoid the shipping charges?"

"Practically no chance," Mike replied. "You might find a few pigs up
around Palmer, but they're kept mostly as a hobby; it costs too much for feed
up here. Besides, they'd most likely be the full sized variety."

"Back to the question," reminded Tracy as the train slowed. "How
much for the pigs and how much to ship them?"

Cars and trucks began driving off the flat cars in Portage and Mike drove
the Suburban off and onto the highway heading north toward Anchorage.
The conversation about pigs continued.

"To have some numbers to work with, let's say the pigs weigh an average
of 150 lbs each and we can get them for 75 cents per pound on the hoof."
Mike offered. "That would round off at $112 per pig average, times 20 is
$2,250. Add in costs to ship them to Denver, get them loaded aboard an
aircraft and shipped to Anchorage and you're talking big money. Oh! And
one other thing, we've got to ship them IN something."

"I've been thinking about that," said Reed. "We've found at Hydrosphere
that the fiberglass dog kennels made for shipping dogs by air work very well
for small seals, sea otters and other animals. They have no sharp edges and
they have a good sized, secure heavy wire door. If we got those large units
they might do fine."

"Wait a minute, wait a minute!! Mike suddenly exclaimed. "Why are
we talking about all these high shipping costs? We might be able to find
someone in Colorado who has a truck and who would drive the pigs to the
west coast, specifically Portland. SeaLand has cargo vessels that leave that
port almost every day headed for Anchorage. The trip takes about two days.
If we find the right deal on a truck we could just buy it and ship it with the
pigs. We're going to need a way to haul the pigs from Anchorage anyway."

Tracy liked Mike's idea. "Good thinking! When I call Mary in Greeley,
I'll ask her if they might have a used truck we could buy from them. It might
be possible to truck the pigs directly from Greeley to Portland and ship the
truck with the pigs inside to Anchorage. Someone would have to be there
with the pigs to make sure they were fed and watered, but that approach
would avoid the transfer hassle."

"And we might be able to ship feed with the pigs," Reed added.

"But, remember the time factor," reminded Tracy. "If you lose a few pigs because of more stress due to the travel, the cost advantage of surface transport could soon dissipate."

"Please ask Mary about the risks when you call her," Mike suggested. "I was thinking that if we could buy a decent truck from Mary or from someone else in Greeley, we could use it to transport the pigs to Alaska then sell the truck to someone up here. After all, this is a one way trip for the pigs."

As they neared Anchorage it became apparent that they needed one key person who could act as a jack-of-all-trades to not only take care of miscellaneous purchases but could also build the pens, coordinate supplies, feed the pigs and whatever else needed to be done.

Mike had the answer. Five years earlier he had met Don Schwartz through Don's wife who worked at one of the banks in Anchorage. Don had shown up, recently arrived in Alaska, for work on a grubby project involving assembling some gold separation equipment for testing of gravels. Don, a logger from Oregon, had shown up for work in clean, close-fitting blue jeans, western shirt, polished cowboy boots and a cream-colored cowboy hat. Mike had immediate questions about the work ability of this person, but Don soon proved that he liked hard work and would go twenty hours a day, seven days a week if that was what it took to get the job done.

Don had the reputation of a bar fighter in the logging towns of Oregon where he was raised. Not that he went looking for fights, he just couldn't resist the fun and excitement of a fight after drinking a case or so of beer. But he seldom held a grudge. If he had a fight one night and saw the opponent the next morning, he would buy breakfast for him and laugh over a few jokes. Don almost never lost a fight but he had numerous scars and healed broken bones from logging accidents. He was about 6 feet tall and 210 pounds of solid muscle on a stout frame. Don was honest and dependable, could operate any kind of equipment and was a fair mechanic. Despite the bar fighting reputation, he got along well with people and, to top it off, he was an excellent cook and enjoyed cooking. At the moment Mike had assigned Don to one of his gold exploration projects but that work could be postponed until September.

"We're going to need all kinds of work done on this project," Mike advised them, "We need sort of a handyman/roustabout/expediter and Don Schwartz will fill the bill. He's over in Nome working on our Anvil

Creek Gold Project, but I can call and have him back over here in a couple of days."

"Great idea," Reed agreed; he had seen for himself what a worker Don was. "Don can handle the supplies and tend the area where we keep the pigs. Speaking of areas, where are we going to keep the pigs, and how are we going to protect the confidentiality of the project?"

"That's something I've been thinking about," replied Tracy. "The Department of Fish and Game took over that place at Herring Bay on Knight Island that was a salmon cannery and then was converted to a hunting and fishing lodge by that group from Fresno. When they were caught illegally taking fish and wildlife the state seized it under provisions of state law. It is reported to be in good shape and Game and Fish would like to have someone out there to protect it because there is no one out there right now. Remember Mike, we stopped in there and looked at it last year? Why don't you see if they'll let us use it?"

"Good idea, Tracy," Mike smiled. "That place has about two acres of grassy sloping hillside behind it and a good spring for water. Fish and game also fixed up the dock so we can get a couple of vessels in there. What do you think Reed?"

"I remember that place," Reed noted. "That's where we saw a couple of float planes at the dock and some fancy fishing boats. The state probably got those too. And isn't that the place that has a good generator and fuel tanks."

"That's the place," Tracy agreed. "And we might be able to spread the word that the pigs are there for a state research project. We could say the state is studying the effect of climate on pigs or some such."

"That's great!" laughed Mike. "We could say the state is trying to figure out what to do with all the barley the state spent tens of millions of dollars on getting farmers to produce up around Delta Junction, which is too high-priced to compete on the world market. The governor himself might like that rumour."

Reed smiled. "I like the innovations you two come up with. It sounds good, but what about getting the pigs to the island from Anchorage. Shouldn't we try to avoid the Whittier rumour mill?"

"You can avoid it for a while," Tracy pointed out, "but sooner or later stories will get out and you may expect some of the more nosy characters to stop in at the camp to see what's going on. We may be able to function for a few weeks before they find out what we're doing. One thing I might suggest is to take the pigs though the Port of Seward rather than Whittier. The drive from Anchorage to Seward is longer by about an hour than the trip to Whittier but the railroad would be avoided. The trip by boat from Seward to Knight Island is a few hours longer than going thorough Whittier, but rumors could be delayed by going that way."

Traffic density was picking up as the Suburban entered the southern outskirts of Anchorage.

"Well, we've got our work cut out for us," Mike stated as they drove into Anchorage. "Let's go straight to the house and get on the phone."

"Mike, if you don't mind," Reed said, "I know I'm welcome at your place, but could you drop me off at the Voyager Hotel? I can get on the phone there and I'll also be right downtown for any meetings which might pop up."

"Yes," Tracy smiled, "and of course staying at the hotel has nothing to do with the fact that you're within a few blocks of the office where Mariko works, does it?" They all chuckled.

"Well, that might have a *little* to do with it," Reed responded. "We must consider all aspects when looking at efficiency of operations."

Mariko Suzuki was a beautiful thirty-one-year-old former stewardess who now worked for the Anchorage office of Japan Air Lines. Reed had met her two years ago when planning a trip to Japan and they had dated on a regular basis whenever Reed was in Alaska or she was in southern California. Mike and Tracy thought Reed was actually quite serious about Mariko, much more so than the other women he had dated in Alaska.

"Leave your duffle bag with us and I'll throw your clothes in the washer," Tracy smiled. "You don't have any place at the hotel to wash clothes."

"But I don't want to put you to the trouble, Tracy." He knew she wouldn't budge. "OK, you do the clothes and I'll buy dinner while we're in town."

"Deal."

They pulled up at the Voyager, across from the Captain Cook Hotel, and dropped Reed off with only his suitcase. His electronic gear was left in the Suburban to be stored in the Mackenzies garage.

As soon as Reed reached his room, he began calling the people on his list. His first call went to Dr. Walker with NOAA in Seattle. She was on the phone when he called and Reed asked the secretary to give her a note stating that he was on the phone with an important call, and, yes, he would wait, thank you. Within less than two minutes he heard an icy voice: "This is Dr. Walker speaking."

Reed reintroduced himself as Dr. Reed Remington and confirmed Dr. Walker's understanding from the meeting in Anchorage with Mike and Tracy. He went on to update her on the situation with the whales, fully acknowledging that the mammals were under the jurisdiction of NOAA. But he pointed out that finding the problem whales was the best approach and everything he and his associates might do would help protect the whales. The fishermen might start shooting more of them if the whales really appeared to be trouble makers. At the end he stressed the need for immediate cooperation and suggested that one person at the NOAA office in Anchorage be appointed as liaison for the project, with that person responsible for keeping her office informed. He specifically did not ask for any money and he did not mention any names of personnel in Anchorage. But he added that if their project was successful, and he believed it would be, the success would reflect well on her division.

Upon hearing the explanation she said tersely, "What's your number up there? I'll call you back later today."

He gave her the number of the hotel and said that if he happened to be out or on the phone to leave a discrete message.

Reed's next call was to Mariko at the JAL office. He had called her from California to advise that he was coming and had left another message from Whittier. She was now delighted to hear that he was in Anchorage. They agreed to meet in the Crow's Nest bar of the Captain Cook Hotel for a glass of wine at 7 in the evening and then go to the small but elegant Marx Brothers's restaurant for dinner. Sometimes, Reed thought as he hung up the phone, the loneliness of being a widower was somewhat offset by the excitement of meeting a lovely lady for a wonderful evening. But not totally offset.

Mike and Tracy had reached home and Mike began unloading some of their gear. Tracy immediately got on a computer and searched for the Colorado Agricultural College Animal Research Center. As soon as she had the number she dialed. A voice answered, "Research Center, Kim speaking."

"This is Tracy Mackenzie in Anchorage, Alaska calling. Could I please speak to Mary Pantera?"

"Alaska? Hey, how's your weather up there?"

"It's wonderful at this time of year. Lows in the 50's and highs in the 70's. Nearly twenty four hours of daylight too."

"Sounds great," Kim said, "I've always wanted to go to Alaska, but haven't made it yet. Just a minute, Mary's in the next building and it will take me a bit to get her."

"Fine, I'll hold on," replied Tracy, willing to hold until Mary got on the line whatever the time. Shortly she heard someone pick up the phone.

"This is Mary Pantera, may I help you?"

"Hi, Mary, this is Tracy Mackenzie in Anchorage. You may not remember Mike and I, but we became acquainted with you when we lived in Greeley several years ago when Mike was working on a uranium project."

"Of course I remember you. It isn't very often people who are not animal researchers or farmers get interested in a program like mine. And that Mexican party you had at your place with the Mariachis was fabulous. How are you and what are you doing?"

The mention of the party reminded Tracy that she and Mike had thrown some great parties in the past but had gotten away from parties now that they were in Alaska. She was pleased to hear that Mary remembered the party. "We're doing great, Mary. But we have an important project up here and we need some information about your miniature swine program. First of all, do you have some of the swine available, and if so, how many?"

"Well, as you may recall, we have both mini-pigs and micro-pigs here. We're pretty well stocked right now because the Cystic Fibrosis Research Center in Cleveland just cancelled an order for pigs for research because they were picketed by some animal rights group. What size did you need, Tracy, and what were you going to use them for?" Mary fully supported use of the pigs for important research, or even for food, but she was not going to send her pigs to a program she considered distasteful.

"Mike and I, along with a marine biologist from Hydrosphere in San Diego, are researching killer whales in Prince William Sound. The whales, I should say one particular pack of the whales, have been causing problems by attacking small boats, stealing fish, and even killing and eating a dog. Two people have disappeared and we suspect the whales may be involved, but please keep that confidential, it's just a theory of course. But we believe we can determine much more about the whale's tendency to kill and eat other mammals, perhaps even mammals strange to them, if we can carry out some observations of their reactions and predation in a controlled situation."

"Killer whales?" Mary asked. "If I remember correctly they're the largest predators on earth. But how do the pigs fit in?

"We want to set up an experiment so some of the pigs are presented to the one pack we think is causing the trouble. We'd like to do it at a time when that pack is hunting mammals such as seals or porpoises, which are a normal part of their diet. We can see how the whales react to the strange possible food source. We suspect there are a couple of the orcas that are more aggressive and perhaps we can determine which ones may be causing problems. A couple of transient orcas may have gotten in with the more docile fish eaters. If we can identify them we may be able to remove them to an aquarium for study and later release."

But Mary had more questions. "Why did you pick pigs to work with, what do they have to do with whether or not the whales will attack people?"

"They're the best food animal we could think of that has many of the same characteristics as seals and certain other marine mammals and also has similarities to people."

"We see people every day who appear to be close relatives of swine," Mary replied jokingly. "But, yes there are significant physical similarities."

Tracy laughed, "Yes, other than shape, we were thinking of more internal organs such as the lungs, heart and circulatory system. The fat layers should resemble that of the seal. Perhaps just as important is the concept that pigs are completely foreign to Prince William Sound and do not constitute what can be called 'normal' food."

"Are you going to put the pigs live into the water, and do you expect the whales to attack and kill the pigs?"

"We don't have the answers to all the questions right now, but we do plan to actually put live pigs in the water when the whales are present. We believe it is extremely urgent to commence the study and we're seeking the support of state and federal agencies. Can we count on you for some pigs if this all comes together? We are hoping we could get twenty that would average about 150 pounds each, with none more than about 200 pounds."

"What are you going to do with the pigs not used in the project?"

"Truthfully," Tracy responded, "any remaining, and we doubt there will be many, are likely to be sold in Alaska for whatever use a buyer might have for them. But they will be well fed and taken care of throughout the program; I personally will assure you of that. We cannot carry out the experiments, of course, without some risk to the pigs exposed to the whales."

"Well," said Mary thoughtfully, "as I said, an order for twenty-four pigs was just cancelled by the Cystic Fibrosis Research Lab so we do have some available, and they're the size you want because that is our most popular size, about the weight of an average sized person."

"I'm sorry to hear about the cancellation, many of those activists would rather have a child suffer a terrible disease than to have a food animal used in an experiment," Tracy noted. "Makes you wonder what some of those idiots might do in a situation where we are trying to save the lives of noble creatures like orcas by using food animals such as pigs." She sighed. "But there is little use for a rational analysis of their activities because those people are not rational."

"Amen," said Mary. "We have had pickets here at our facility but they won't picket the slaughterhouse down the road where they kill thousands of pigs, cattle, horses and sheep."

"Well I'm pleased that you do have some pigs which we might use, but how much are they going to cost?"

"Who's funding this program?'

"Thus far, my husband Mike and I are personally committed to at least part of it. Hydrosphere will provide some funds, and we're hoping we might get a contribution from Fish and Game and perhaps from NOAA, but right now we don't even know if they will go along with the program, much less give us any money."

"OK," Mary Responded, "I'll tell you what. We'll let you have the twenty pigs for two dollars a pound, and we'll throw in a week's feed to get them to Alaska."

"Oh, oh," Tracy hesitated. "That's about twice as much as we thought we'd have to pay. And I have no idea what the feed is worth."

"That's only a couple of hundred dollars worth of feed, but that is a good deal for the pigs. We normally sell them for $3.50 to $4.00 per pound but we're overstocked right now. That's about the best we can do. On the positive side, we could be ready to ship in a couple of days. How are you thinking of shipping them?"

Tracy sighed. "We had thought of shipping them by air but it is such a hassle and is too expensive. So we concluded we might try to find a truck to buy for the shipping. The truck could also be used in Alaska. We were thinking of dog kennels to put the pigs in."

"Strong dog kennels are a good idea so long as you don't try to put more than one pig in each kennel.

Tracy then asked "You wouldn't happen to have an old truck at your facility we could buy to ship the pigs in would you? We were thinking of taking the pigs to Tacoma, Washington by truck, about a three-day trip and then two days by boat to Anchorage, so say a week total. Would the pigs survive a trip like that?"

"With good food, water and clean cages the pigs should do fine because there won't be any really cold temperatures on the trip. An enclosed truck would provide shelter even if they were on the top deck on a ship. But the truck?" She paused in thought. "Let's see, we do have an old Ford one and on-half ton truck here with about 120,000 miles on it we were planning to get rid of. We'd expect to get about $9,000 for it, but we'll let you have it for $7,500. It's pretty good sized with an enclosed bed which could hold the pig containers and some feed and straw as well. How does that sound?"

Mary hesitated before speaking again. "Thinking this project over, I believe you should take a person experienced with pigs along to Alaska. From what I've heard so far, no one in your group knows much about pigs and how to take care of them, much less train them. And you'll need someone to drive the truck anyway. My right hand person here, Kim Storey, would probably be willing to go and this could be a good opportunity for her. She deserves it and has several week's accrued vacation. You will pay all of her travel, lodging and related expenses, of course. Pass that on to your partners and see what they have to say."

"I certainly will," Tracy agreed, "and we'll try to get back to you within a day or so, as soon as we can get some word from NOAA. By the way, tell me something about Kim."

"She's about twenty-nine, is very bright and has a degree in animal husbandry from our school here. She's single and teaches aerobic exercise at the local health club every night. She has six years experience with the pigs and is very good at working with them. Oh yes, she's about 5'6" tall and a gorgeous blond."

"Sounds like someone the back woodsmen in Alaska might go crazy over," laughed Tracy. "Thanks, Mary, I'll call you soon."

She smiled as she hung up. If Kim came to Alaska, she thought, a good joke could be played on Reed and Mike by telling them in advance to expect a tough, overweight old blister.

Mike was pleased to hear the good news about pig availability. Tracy threw some clothes in the washer and booted their computer so she could begin plotting cost effectiveness of getting the pigs to Alaska. She would also do some critical path planning so they could coordinate getting everything done on schedule. There was little time for error.

Now it was Mike's turn at the phone, and he first called Reed at the Voyager to get the latest on NOAA. Reed advised him the wheels were turning but no answer yet. He next called Fred Pennyworth in Juneau, the commissioner of the Alaska Department of Fish and Game. Fred, an economist by training, had shown an amazing ability to survive from one governor to another in the appointed post and he was currently serving under his fourth Alaskan governor, Ben Springfield. If anything, Fred was an expert at working within the Alaska governmental system and, while keeping a low profile, he knew the legislators. Fred had even cleverly avoided the controversy over the Exxon Valdez oil spill by laying the assignment at the feet of the director of the Department of Environmental Conservation.

Fred's secretary tried to pass the call off to one of the other staff members in the office, but Mike insisted on talking to Fred himself, stating that it was extremely important. Fred finally came on the line and Mike brought him up to date on the killer whale situation. Then he informed him of the general plan and the need for confidentiality.

"Listen," Fred acknowledged, "here in Juneau we've been plenty concerned about the clashes between the fisherman and the whales. And I was afraid it was going to get a lot worse."

Mike asked Fred to assign one person in Anchorage to monitor the project from Anchorage. That person could provide information to Fred. He also asked for funding assistance if Fish and Game had any funds they could spare, to which Fred responded he would see but doubted it. After all, he correctly pointed out, as marine mammals, the whales were the responsibility of NOAA and not the state. He promised to take the matter up with his top staff assistant in Juneau and then get back with Mike soon, probably the next day.

Mike hung up and told Tracy that he couldn't ask for much more at this stage. He thought Fred's reaction on the phone was reasonably favorable.

A call to SeaLand revealed an estimated cost of $2,500 to ship the loaded truck from Tacoma, Washington to Anchorage, plus $300 for the person accompanying the truck. Tracy estimated it would take three days to drive from Greeley to Tacoma with costs of about $250 per day for fuel, food, and lodging, assuming Kim could drive the truck. Mike suggested she figure a resale value of the truck at $6,000 although they might do a little better if the truck was in good shape. Tracy ran the numbers on the computer and concluded that shipping by boat was a good way to go and selling the truck later in Alaska made sense. She recommended to Mike that they try it.

The phone rang. It was Reed and he was elated. Herb Bracken had called him to say that Dr. Walker had given him instructions to investigate the project and, if it made sense, to cooperate in the effort to identify the particular killer whales causing the problems. Welfare of the whales was given top priority, which coincided with the existing plans. A meeting was scheduled with Herb the next morning at 9.

Mike related to Reed the findings and recommendations for purchasing and moving the pigs from Colorado, including the truck purchase. He also relayed the comments from Fish and Game and hoped they were going to cooperate. Tracy had reviewed the budget numbers and they looked favorable.

Two hours later the phone rang. It was Fred Pennyworth with the message that he was assigning Area Biologist Cynthia Scott to monitor the project, but that she was busy on a salmon program and would probably need some help from George Maxwell. Knowing Cynthia, Mike advised him he thought the choice was a good one. He also told Fred that they could plan to meet at the offices of Fletcher Marshall, who was their Anchorage attorney for mineral deals. "That's a great location," nodded Tracy. "For the kind of money we pay Fletcher we could have paid for that meeting room and half of the building by now."

After calls to Reed, Herb Bracken and Cynthia, the meeting was set. Cynthia advised that she was bringing George Maxwell but, she promised, the project idea would go no further in the Fish and Game offices. She was very interested in the program and was pleased she had attended the earlier meeting with Mike and Tracy so she wasn't in the dark when Fred called her.

Reed was feeling great at 5 pm as he jogged along the new coastal trail leading from downtown Anchorage past the International Airport northwest runway and out to Point Woronzof. The light breeze blowing in from the west was brisk. As he approached the Point he observed the huge concrete standpipe looking like a giant tombstone. The structure indicated the location where the Municipality of Anchorage's large sewage discharge pipe ran 150 yards out into Knik Arm. Millions of gallons of chlorinated sewage were discharged daily into the arm and, to Reed's knowledge, no one had ever done any studies to determine the effects on organisms in the area, including salmon and beluga whales which were present four months of the year. No one knew what the sewage might do to razor clams which were harvested at many locations throughout Cook Inlet. Interesting, he thought, how the various environmental groups with offices in Anchorage were determined to shut down the placer gold miners who had been working in and near Alaska streams for more than a hundred years with no serious lasting effects on the streams, and yet they turned their backs on a more serious problem in their own back yard. Fighting the miners was popular and they could raise money from folks back east for it; fighting the city over sewage discharge wouldn't win many points. Besides, they themselves used toilets which drained into the sewer and there were more advantageous battles to fight. Similar to the "greenies" weird position on oil exploration; heat your house with natural gas and drive your automobiles using gasoline, but fight like hell when some company wants to drill another oil well.

He arrived back at the hotel winded and sweating but refreshed and hurriedly showered and dressed. As usual, Mariko was on time at the Crow's Nest bar, dressed in a beautiful red silk Chinese Mandarin style dress with gold embroidery. The colors set off her golden brown skin perfectly. Her knee length black hair was pulled back and clipped with a gold and red beret. She was beautiful. Reed considered himself very fortunate to be with this lady.

After two glasses of Kendall Jackson chardonnay, they walked the three blocks to the Marx Bros. Restaurant, a converted relatively small house. Dinner was very good and very intimate and seemed to pass quickly, but none too quickly for Reed, who was anxious to have Mariko accompany him to his hotel room. She had a plan of her own, however, and told him he should come to her apartment to look at some new Alaskan paintings she had acquired.

When they arrived, she kept the lights dim, turned on some gentle music and poured Napoleon Cognac into two snifters. She took off his jacket, hung it in the closet and guided him to the sofa. Then she went into the bedroom and, a few minutes later, came out wearing a gorgeous blue silk robe and, so far as Reed could determine, nothing else. She smiled, kneeled before him, took off his shoes and gently massaged his feet. He reached out and ran his fingers through her long hair and along the sides of her beautiful face. She raised up to massage his legs and then bent over to him to kiss his lips, her black hair enclosing them both like a veil. Her warm, soft tongue, fragrant from cognac, then entered his mouth. He pulled her onto the sofa beside him and pushed the robe aside. Within a few minutes they were in the bedroom enjoying each other's bodies.

The following morning Mike and Tracy arrived early for the nine o'clock meeting carrying two boxes of freshly-baked doughnuts picked up on the way in. One they would put in the coffee room for the legal office staff and the other was placed in the conference room. The view westward from the conference room across Cook Inlet to the northeast end of the Aleutian mountain chain was striking. The mountains were mostly white, reflecting the ever-present snow, with scattered bluish-green in the lower elevations reflecting denser tree growth. Four mallard ducks flew past the seventh story windows, so close the brilliant green of the drake's head could be seen clearly.

With everyone present shortly after 9 and the usual talk about the nice weather, Reed began with an outline of the observations of killer whales in Prince William Sound over the past three years and a summary of the events of the past few weeks: fish being taken from fishing skates, the tipping of the Larson's Zodiac and Champ's death, the incident with the Saunders and Holloran kids. Tracy displayed some of the photographs taken of the whales, with particular emphasis on the A-T pack hunting mammals, and then added the theory that the couple from Nevada had disappeared under circumstances which might possibly be related to whale activity.

Reed then told them about the necessity of determining when and under what circumstances the whales would attack a mammal which was not part of their normal food. In addition, the identity of the aggressive "pod" should be determined if at all possible. He admitted that it would be impractical to conduct a study of every group in the Sound, but with the tentative identification of the A-T pack by a couple of observers, as well as their own observations, the trio believed they were on the right track. He also explained the crucial timing before any more incidents occurred and so they could take advantage of the good summer weather.

Herb Bracken, with a head of hair that looked like it had been scalped from a grizzly bear, listened with interest to the descriptions. He personally had not worked much with whales, but he was an avid reader and was pretty well up on the literature. "Now that you've told us about the conflicts, how do you propose to go about gathering predation information on wild killer whales?" Herb asked Reed.

"That is a question we grappled with and it was not easy to come up with a satisfactory answer," replied Reed. "We concluded that we need to set up a situation so we can observe how the whales will react, and this means the use of some type of live animal. Marine mammals are out because they're protected and they're also part of the whale's diet. We need something foreign. Dogs can't be used for obvious reasons. We finally concluded that we need to use a food animal which has many of the same characteristics as a seal, or perhaps the same as a man."

"Why hell!" Herb exploded. "I can give you the answer to that one right now. Pigs are the answer, boy. In my Navy research days we used pigs all the time for testing. They are wonderful test animals. The Navy used pigs for the successful testing of animal respiration under water and to develop some new devices and breathing compounds for human activities underwater. We also studied how to save victims in a container, and with that optimum gasses, such as in submarines on the ocean floor. From my own studies of parasitology and cures for parasite infestation, pigs were almost ideal once we got past the mice, rat and rabbit stage."

"Wait a minute, wait a minute," Cynthia half shouted. "Before we get carried away, let's look at this again. The objective is to study killer whale predation to protect the whales, and now we're thinking about bringing in pigs to see if the whales will eat them? If this gets out we'll be the laughing stock of the biological community. I can see it now in the Journal of Mammalogy: 'Killer Whales Enjoy Pork Dinner', or how about 'Sausage on Hoof Fattens Orcas!'"

George Maxwell nodded. "Not only that, but animal rights sympathizers are going to riot when they hear about this one."

"Yes, yes," Mike agreed. "There are those who are not going to like it, but they've got to realize that we're trying to save the killer whales from being wounded or killed by antagonistic people including fishermen. The question is: are we justified in possibly sacrificing some pigs to save a substantial number of whales?"

"And remember," Tracy pointed out. "Except for Muslims, pigs are a human food item."

"By God, I like it!" Herb snorted. "Those damned animals worshippers can go to hell. They don't know what's going on up here anyway and if we decide it's the way to go, that's what we'll do. We have the Marine Mammal Protection Act passed by Congress and signed into law but we sure as hell don't have a pig protection act. The choice is clear to me."

"But maybe there is some other way," Cynthia said softly, somewhat of an animal rights person herself. "Perhaps there is something else we could do to that would accomplish the same end."

"We're all ears," Reed stated.

"What about using an artificial body, perhaps made of pig parts in the shape of a man," suggested Cynthia. "Maybe that would accomplish the same thing."

"Let me get this straight," Herb looked at her incredulously. "You're suggesting we kill a couple of pigs and sew the parts together to look like a man to avoid the possibility that the orcas may kill a couple of live pigs.?"

"Well, uh, I'm just thinking," Cynthia replied, somewhat embarrassed.

"That idea won't work anyway," Reed pointed out. "The whale's sonar and hearing is so good there is no doubt in my mind they can analyze muscle and bone structure, breathing, heart rate, the works, and are not going to be misled by something that looks like something. Think of an orcas brain as a giant sound processor exquisitely tuned to process data from its own sonar. The whale can operate as well at night as it can in the daylight. One killer whale was found tangled in a submarine cable at a depth of 3,000 feet; it must have been hunting food down there and needless to say, it's damned dark at that depth."

Tracy tried to help Cynthia out. "We have honestly tried to think of alternatives, but the pig is almost ideal in configuration, fat distribution, and vital organ characteristics, and it is a food animal. In addition, they are pretty good swimmers."

"I can't think of anything better," Maxwell observed, "but pigs get too big unless you try to stay with young ones."

"We thought of that, too." Mike responded. "Tracy and I are acquainted with a miniature swine research program in Colorado and we have already contacted them concerning pig availability. We can order twenty pigs today which, fully grown, will weigh between 150 and 180 pounds, none over 200. They will average 160 pounds, or about the same as an average Homo sapiens and are very easy to handle."

"Say, if you have any trouble getting pigs," Herb said, "I can call some of my friends who are still with the Navy research program and see if they have any extras, although they usually don't because of long term studies. Many of their pigs are also specially trained. Have you ever seen a pig swim near the bottom in 50 feet of water with scuba gear on? Damned if they're not pretty good at it," he chuckled.

"Time is short, Cynthia," Reed pointed out. "If you have a viable alternative we would be pleased to hear it. If not, then we would like your vote of approval for the project so we can get down to the brass tacks."

"Where do you plan to keep the pigs, if that is what you end up using?" Maxwell asked.

"Thanks for bringing that up, George," Mike answered. "We need a place to keep the animals on shore, and we would like to get the approval of Fish and Game to use the idle facilities at Herring Bay on Knight Island. From what we have seen of the site it would be almost perfect, although we'll have to put up some fences to keep the pigs in. What do you say, Cynthia, will we be able to use it?"

"Let's get past the question of whether pigs will be used at all before we talk about where to keep them," Cynthia said pensively. "But, frankly, I can't think of anything better to use than swine. So we'll go with your program, with one stipulation. This is YOUR idea, Remington. If all hell breaks loose, the Alaska Department of Fish and Game is there only as observers, if at all. If you try to drag us into adverse publicity we'll deny that we had anything to do with it. That's the bad part. The good part is that internally we appreciate what you're doing and later on may make some equipment and perhaps some money available. George will be the liaison between myself and your operation, the hunting lodge on Herring Bay. I'll check into it to be sure it isn't in someone else's plans already and, if not, I see no reason why you can't use it."

"Is Fred going to tell the governor?" Tracy asked.

"I don't know and don't even want to ask," Cynthia responded. "The less some of the politicians know, the better. They typically will take any situation and try to turn it to a political advantage no matter what the consequences."

"What you might call opportunists," nodded Herb, in full agreement with her statement.

Cynthia looked at the trio, "Count us in for now."

"All right! That's great, Cynthia!" Reed practically shouted.

"And Herb, can we count on NOAA for support?"

"We don't want to get our tit in the wringer either," Herb observed. "But it appears to me your approach is the best one which can be taken under the circumstances. We'll participate as side line observers and, if I can get away to go to the Sound, will participate as active observers."

"Any funding available?" Mike asked Herb earnestly.

"No promises, but we may have a little money left over from a walrus study in the Bering Sea. I'll look into it and let you know. Remember, however, that any funding which might come from us will be for Orcinus orca research in Prince William Sound and of a general nature only."

"Then we can count on you?" Reed asked again.

"Yes, but don't let anything happen to the whales or there'll be hell to pay, by everyone." He looked at them all.

"Great!" Reed, Tracy and Mike clamoured.

But Reed had a second thought. "Herb, we would like to get the permission of NOAA to radio tag one or two of the whales in the A-T pack so we'll be able to locate and follow them more easily. We would provide the tags and radios at no cost to the service. Do you think Dr. Walker would go along?"

"You're asking for a tough one there, Remington. If you're just observing the orcas with hands off is one thing. You start talking about nailing them with a dart or tag and questions will be raised about infection and interference with the whale's natural movements and reactions. I can ask, but my forecast is you're not going to get approval. It's doubtful she would even approve NOAA personnel taggin' the whales, let alone some yay-hoos with, as she sees it, questionable qualifications."

"Well, please see what you can do." Mike urged. "In the meantime we'll get moving immediately. With the personal money Tracy and I are going to provide, along with Hydrosphere, we have funding for our preliminary budget to get started. We hope your agencies will be able to help us later."

"One more thing before we split up," Tracy said as she held up her hand as a stop signal. "We probably need a code name for the project so we can refer to it among ourselves and perhaps in needed reports, without arousing suspicions. I would suggest the code name "Project Barley" because that ties in rather well with our plan to find more uses for the excessively-priced Alaska barley, including pig feed."

"Good idea," Reed nodded. "What do the rest of you think?"

"Sounds good to me," Herb stated, and everyone nodded.

"And in line with that," Tracy turned to Mike, "it would be a good idea to buy a few hundred pounds of Alaskan barley even though we'll pay more than we would pay elsewhere."

"I don't know much about pigs," Mike responded, "but I'm sure they would like some straw. Let's get about a hundred bales of barley straw while we're at it."

"If that's all you need us for, I've got to be going," Herb noted as he stood up. "Paperwork waiting."

"I think we've got most of the bases covered," Reed observed. "Thank you all for coming in. We'll run a good program."

"We'll be in touch," promised Tracy as the group left the meeting room to return to their offices. Tracy, Mike and Reed stayed behind to do some planning.

"Give me the bad news first, Tracy," Reed said. "How much money are we looking at to get started?"

"Right now I'd say we'd better plan on about $30,000 rather quickly. More than $15,000 may be required to get the pigs up here, but we plan to sell the truck later to recover part of that."

Mike had a suggestion. "Reed, perhaps the best way to make funds available for various purposes will be to open a bank account and deposit funds as they're needed. I suggest that we Mackenzies and Hydrosphere each put in $15,000 to get started. That $30,000 will carry us into the first phase. I'll pay Don's wages and expenses from my own account and can be reimbursed later."

"I'm sure Hydrosphere will go for that," replied Reed. "In fact, they have said they would advance $50,000 for the initial part of the program if we got Fish and Game and NOAA to go along. I'm going to request the entire amount immediately. And one other thing, Tracy and Mike, I greatly appreciate you putting your own money into this. You know I'd do the same if I could afford it, but a teacher in the United States makes a pauper's wage and a biologist not much more."

"That's OK, Reed, right now we can afford it," Mike assured him, "but there have been times in the past when we would have been glad to have the pigs to eat ourselves."

Reed returned to the Voyager Hotel and Tracy and Mike returned to their home in Stuckagain Heights to continue planning for the coming program. Tracy made lists for both herself and Mike.

Don Schwartz was called in Nome and told to return to Anchorage as soon as possible. He advised Mike that he could wind things up quickly and be in Anchorage the next day, rarin' to go. He liked exciting new projects.

◆◆◆

CHAPTER TWENTY ONE

Knight Island.

Mario Petrovic was called in Cordova and Mike learned he had not yet sold the *"Karen Marie"* and he'd be glad to participate in the killer whale program for just fuel for the boat and grub for himself and whoever else might be aboard his vessel. He would need a couple of deck hands and he had two good ones already working for him. And these deck hands could also cook, so much the better. He would bill Mike's group for the actual cost of the deck hands plus 10% to cover accounting expenses.

Tracy called Mary Pantera in Greeley to see if a little better deal could be made for the pigs and truck, but Mary couldn't go any lower because the school could become unhappy if she loses money on the pig program. Tracy gave Mary the go-ahead and promised to wire $14,000 the next day for the pigs and the truck; the details of other funds due, if any, would be handled later. Mary had talked to Kim, who would be delighted to take the pigs to Alaska.

Kim was there and Mary put her on the phone. Yes, she was fully capable of driving the truck to Tacoma for shipping and would see that the pigs arrived in good condition. She would take along ninety days supply of vitamin supplements for the pigs, including vitamin E which would help relieve stress. Kim also advised Tracy that they should figure on about 5 pounds of food per day for each pig, along with a suggestion not to skimp on the feed. She would have enough feed on the truck to get the pigs to Alaska, but they should have good feed available for the pigs once they arrive.

At Reed's suggestion, Tracy called the manufacturer of the dog kennels and got the name of the distributor in Denver. She then called the distributor and ordered twenty large kennels to be delivered with no transportation cost to CAC in Greeley. The money would be wired the next day by Tracy.

Tracy called SeaLand for the shipping schedule to Anchorage and told them a truck with live animals would be arriving from Colorado and to be sure to get it aboard. She also called Kim in Greeley and gave her the shipping information and the phone number for SeaLand so Kim could make specific timing arrangements with the shipper. She also arranged to wire $3,500 to SeaLand for shipping the truck with the pigs, Kim, and containers of pig feed. The amount was more than enough but a refund would be issued for the overage.

Mike called a wholesale grain distributor in Tacoma and ordered 6,000 pounds of high protein bagged feed for the pigs at a price of $40 per 100 pounds. It would be delivered to SeaLand in Tacoma and loaded in two shipping containers provided by SeaLand. It would arrive in Anchorage in a few days.

While Tracy went shopping for groceries and wine, Mike and Reed made up a list of equipment and supplies needed for the camp. From George Maxwell they obtained a description of what was already at the camp. It sounded almost ideal. In the transition from a cannery to a hunting camp to a Fish and Game outpost, considerable money had been spent in upgrading and refurbishing. There were ten sleeping rooms, a kitchen and dining room complete with pots and dishes, a small diesel generator for electrical power, a substantial oil-fired water heater and a septic tank and leach field to accommodate sewage disposal. The spring fed gravity water system was working well the last anyone knew.

When asked how Fish and Game happened to gain possession of such a place, Maxwell responded that the hunting camp had, over a period of several years, turned into a poaching and illegal hunting camp. Moose, Dall sheep, caribou, bear, and even bald eagles had been illegally killed by hunters operating out of the camp in float planes and boats. An undercover operation by Fish and Game personnel had resulted in a sting. Under Alaska law, the equipment used in carrying out an illegal fishing or hunting activity can be seized and becomes the property of the state. In this case the state got two power boats, two float-equipped aircraft and the hunting camp itself. The department was using the planes and the boats for other projects but Maxwell said that one boat and one plane might be available for use on this project if needed.

Maxwell advised them that the only thing they needed to take to the camp was groceries; even the fuel tanks were nearly full. He added that Fish and Game was actually pleased that someone trustworthy would be staying at the camp because there was concern about security. There were keys needed to enter the buildings, and Maxwell promised to drop them by the Voyager Hotel later.

The next day, Don arrived on Alaska Air Lines from Nome and Mike filled him in on the concept of a research camp at Herring Bay, Knight Island. Don was to handle transport of the pigs from Anchorage to the camp and was to be general camp manager and operator.

With a cash advance from Mike and a list from Tracy, Don immediately began acquiring the fencing and other items needed to prepare the camp area for the pigs. At Tracy's suggestion, he called Kim and found that one large general enclosure for the pigs would do for now, perhaps 20' x 100', depending on the terrain. Kim said that if smaller separate enclosures were needed later they could be erected so long as he had the materials. Saplings should be nailed or wired to the bottom wire of the heavy wire fencing to discourage the pigs from digging under the fence. She said a gently sloping hillside would be best for good drainage, and, if he could manage to make some sort of wallow, the pigs would be forever grateful.

Don also called Mario in Cordova and arranged for Mario to cross the Sound to Whittier the next day so the supplies could be loaded aboard the "Karen Marie" for transport to Herring Bay after a stop in Seward. The Karen Marie had deck space, a crane and winch on each side, a kitchen, sleeping quarters for eight (but could crowd twelve), and plenty of fresh water storage. The deck was also configured for easy hosing down. At the stern was a 14 foot Boston Whaler and a 10 foot Zodiac were nestled over the main cabin.

Don also told Mario that from Whittier he was to sail down to Seward to pick up additional cargo. Don was feeling great as he headed his 3/4 ton Ford four-wheel drive pickup, toward the south edge of Anchorage. He was dressed in his usual blue jeans, western shirt, cowboy boots and western hat. Didn't make any difference that he was a lumberman from Oregon and had only been wearing western togs just to be different, but it caught on and he found himself wearing them most of the time. He also had taken a liking to country and western music and Don now had an old tape in the player with Dolly Parton singing a love ballad.

The pickup was heavily loaded with tools, rolls of wire, 5-gallon cans of gasoline and other paraphernalia Don thought he would need at Herring Bay. Also included were tools needed such as a power post hold digger and chain saw. Miscellaneous shovels, picks, hammers and the like were loaned to the project by Mike. Four boxes of groceries were crowded with him in front on the truck seat. He had found room in the bed for three cases of beer.

He was a little thirsty and pulled off at the last liquor store at the edge of Anchorage to pick up a couple of cans of Alaskan Amber beer in the jumbo cans. Arriving at Portage half an hour before the train arrived, he whiled away the time by listening to CDs. Two people, a man and a woman in their late twenties, apparently also waiting for the train, had been back and forth along the tracks pacing up and down the track and again, walked beside the truck. Don figured they were from "outside" because of the way they looked and talked; they were probably 'greenies' and it might be fun to talk to them. As they approached his truck he rolled down the window. "Pardon me," he said, using his best French accent, " But do you have any Gray Poupon?" He smiled broadly, a can of beer in his right hand.

For a moment they thought the man in the truck was serious and they started to say, "No, we don't..." but Don's laugh made them suddenly realize they had heard that line before. "Oh, you," the female smiled. "We don't have mustard of any kind."

"No harm in askin'," Don smiled again, noticing how pale their complexion was. "Goin' to catch the ferry?"

"No, we're going to stay in Whittier for a while," the male answered. "We're trying to find out more about what's happening over there with the whales." Then he added proudly, "we're with Blue War."

"Oh yeah," Don smiled. "I spend some time over in Nome and I'm familiar with some of Blue War's activities on the Russian coast trying to get the Russians to stop feeding whale meat to mink."

"That's our group!" he said proudly. Then he moved closer to the pickup where Don was sitting. "Say, you don't happen to know anything about the killer whales in Prince William Sound, do you? We'd like to learn all we can about what's happening here."

"About all I know," Don replied, "is what I see on television or read in the papers. I guess they've had a couple of incidents out there. One I read about involved some kids, but I guess no one was injured.

The woman now stepped forward. "We were told in Anchorage that the whales killed someone's dog and that they have been taking certain fish from the fishermen's net lines."

"Yes, I believe that was in the paper too. But what are you going to do about it?" Don thought he'd see what response he might get from them.

The man responded. "We don't know yet, but we intend to see that the whales are not harmed."

Don knew that the fishermen were very proud and protective of their livelihood and could, and did, shoot the whales when their fishing activities were disrupted. "How are you going to keep the fishermen from shooting the whales if they're stealing fish from the lines?"

"We don't know that either. We're hoping we can come up with some way to keep the whales away from the fish that are on a line."

Don noticed the train was pulling in and would soon be discharging Anchorage-bound traffic.

"Where are you staying at in Whittier?" Don asked them, knowing that Mike would be interested to know where they were located.

"We don't know yet. We're going to ask around when we get there, but we have sleeping bags if we can't find a place. Do you have any suggestions?"

"You might try the Whittier Inn. It's not much but it'll keep the rain off your head." Don looked at them seriously, "Watch out for drunk fishermen, especially if they think you're anti-fishing. I'd tread lightly if I were you."

The traffic from Whittier was now driving off the flat cars.

"Are you a fisherman?" the woman asked, looking at the rolls of wire and boxes of gear in the pickup.

"Naw, I'm in mining and lumber, two industries not in favor with your group," Don replied with a smile.

"We're not anti-industry, we just want to protect the environment and, in this case, marine mammals." The man replied.

"Looks like we're going to be loading right away," Don noted. "Wish you lots of success with your project."

"Thanks," they both responded as they walked away. Don noticed that their backpacks had some patches from places they must have visited: Vancouver, the Caribbean, Mexico. Probably some rich kids who think staying in a hotel is roughing it, he thought. They have time to watch out for whales because they don't have to work for a living.

After driving onto the train, Don considered going forward to the passenger car to talk to those two again but decided against it and rode in the pickup to Whittier.

Upon arrival he drove to the Whittier docks near where the cruise ships came in and found the *Karen Marie* tied up 12 feet below the level of the pickup on the dock.

"You must be Mario," Don shouted down to the grizzled person who came out of the cabin to look at him.

"That's me, and you must be Don."

"Yep, here and ready to transfer this gear."

"Good. We're right where this boom and winch will work so we'll load into that basket and then swing the basket over and lower it to the deck. I've got two helpers here and one of them will come up there."

Don expected two men but instead two husky-looking young women, both wearing blue jeans and knee high rubber boots, came out of the cabin.

"The blond is Sally and the brunette is Evelyn," he advised Don, watching for Don's reaction, but Don just smiled.

The blond quickly climbed up the ladder and shook Don's hand with a grip that was surprisingly powerful and yet she wasn't showing off. "Hi Don, I'm Sally. Let's get moving."

As quickly as they loaded the 4 foot wide basket, Sally operated the winch and lowered it to the deck of the vessel where Evelyn and Mario unloaded it and secured it on the *Karen Marie*. The basket was then returned. Don noticed that Sally had no difficulty handling her half of heavy objects unloaded from the truck, and she was very quick. The last items to go down were the groceries and beer.

"If I'd known you girls were going to be along I'd have picked up a couple more cases of beer," he told her.

"Relax, Don, we already have four cases on board," she smiled. This was Don's kind of woman and he figured there would be some fun ahead.

With the truck unloaded, Don parked it at a remote spot in the parking area and returned to climb down the ladder to the *Karen Marie*. First Mario and then Evelyn shook his hand. He noticed strong, solid handshakes from both of them. Yep, this was going to be fun.

"Cast off, girls," Mario commanded as he started the engines. The girls quickly cast off the lines and the *Karen Marie* swung gracefully into the Whittier arm called, for some obscure reason, Passage Canal. They entered the cabin to escape the cool breeze and Don got a better look at the two helpers and to look around the boat, which appeared to have accommodations for eight to ten people in separate quarters. The galley was neat and clean. It also had plenty of room on board for the pig kennels.

"Don, if you're wondering about these two deck hands," Mario offered, "they worked for me last year when I was commercial fishing and they proved to be damned good hands. When I found out that they were in town again and didn't have a job yet, I was tickled to take them on again. Only trouble is," he winked at them, "they treat me like a father and I want them to treat me like Rudolph Valentino! Getting old is hell." The girls laughed at this and Evelyn gave him a hug. Don's eyes sparkled.

A round of beers was opened. Don's suspicions that this could be one helluva project were being confirmed. Three hours, a case and a half of beer and a couple hundred of Don's jokes later, they could see the northwest part of Knight Island looming above the horizon. The trip from Seward had been such fun that they were not eager to reach their destination.

As they entered Herring Bay, a humpback whale surfaced to blow ahead of them. "Thar she blows, man the skiffs!" Mario jokingly sang out.

Soon they could see the camp nestled in a small cove on the east side of the bay. The setting was even prettier than Don had heard. The lush, green-bearded mountains rose majestically to nearly 2,000 feet behind the buildings and made them appear like toys. Rock outcrops, abundantly covered with moss and lichens, lent a variety to the landscape. Don noted an area of perhaps 5 acres just up-slope from the camp, an area Mike had told him was probably used for horse pasture by the hunting camp. A fair-sized stream tumbled down a sharp cut in the side of the mountain, slowed as it passed the margin of the hillside pasture and then emptied into the salt water. Too small, Don thought, to host any salmon.

As they approached the dock, Don began to appreciate the amount of work and expense that had gone into this place, which in no way resembled the canneries he had seen. The roofs of the several buildings had been recently covered with green asphalt roofing interspersed with fiberglass panels to admit light into the buildings. The buildings themselves were of solid log construction and had been allowed to weather without paint so they blended well with the terrain, except for an attractive blue trim around the windows. One section of the longest building had many windows facing the bay and he guessed that was the dining area.

Mario skilfully steered the *Karen Marie* up to the dock and the girls made her fast. The unloading went quickly and soon the supplies were stacked on the dock. Don was wishing he had thought to bring a cart of some kind to move the gear across the dock to the buildings. Mario saw his dilemma and brought from the hold a cart he had found very handy for such purposes. The girls and Don moved the fencing and related gear to one compartment in a building near the pasture which had been used as a barn. They noted the smell of horse manure.

After Don unlocked the door to the main building, groceries and beer were taken into a room which looked like a pantry near the kitchen/dining area. Sally was the first one in and was pleasantly surprised by the layout. The interior was nicely panelled in light birch and there was a large rock fireplace at one end.

"Hey, this is all right," she smiled. "This place must have been one first class hunting lodge."

There were ten sleeping rooms with two single beds in each and the quarters were reasonably clean. Two of the sleeping rooms had been converted to storage. Don figured that as soon as the pen was in, he would do some cleanup. He liked this place and wanted it to look as good as possible when Mike, Tracy and Reed arrived.

Don found a note telling how to turn the water on, which was just a matter of closing a couple of valves and opening a couple of others. The water system was a simple gravity flow through a PVC pipe from a spring 200 yards up on the mountainside. Another note told how to start the generator and how to operate the water heaters. All very thoughtful, but Don wanted to look around before getting into the nitty-gritty of the camp operation.

After surveying all the buildings with the girls and Mario, who had now come ashore, Don walked out toward the pasture and the stream flowing by. Grass was thick and lush in the pasture and it looked like a great place for the pigs. There was a marshy area which Don immediately thought would make a good pig wallow and he walked over to take a look at it. He stopped suddenly as he looked at the marsh. There in the soft, brown, mushy peat were the fresh clear tracks of a large bear. The four inch claws showed distinctly at the front of each large paw print; it was a big grizzly. The bear had travelled from south to north and Don guessed it had been grazing on the lush grass. Bears did not worry him, but a hungry grizzly wouldn't be good for the health of the pigs. He'd have to take that into consideration in laying out the pen.

Dinner time was approaching and Evelyn and Mario went back to the galley of the *Karen Marie* to prepare dinner. Mario had suggested that Don eat on board with them tonight and he said he'd be delighted.

In the meantime, Sally helped Don begin with all of the turn on, turn off, set up, start and light up all of the different components of the camp. By the time they were called to the *Karen Marie* for dinner at 8:15 they had gotten most of the systems functioning. The water was on and the water heaters were working. The generator was checked out and started.

Over a dinner of pork chops, apple sauce, cream style corn, rice, and whole wheat and oatmeal bread made by Mario, Don learned that the *Karen Marie* was for sale and that Mario had sold his limited entry seining permit the previous fall. At sixty-seven, he was ready to slow down and relax a little. He had made good money over the years and his investments were yielding substantial dividends. He also received royalty payments from the Seattle equipment company manufacturing the fishing tackle block he had invented. Even at his age, much of the earnings went for taxes. Smiling at the girls, he said they had each made about $40,000 in five months the previous two years because of generous fish catch bonuses he paid them.

"Sorry, girls," he had told them, "but I can't do that this year." They assured him it was OK. At least they had a job and they sincerely wanted to make him happy.

Mario's right, Don thought after hearing the story, they do treat him like a father.

Mario also advised Don that Mike had agreed to pay him only for his actual costs of fuel, groceries and deck hands. "That's a helluva deal for Mike," Don commented. "You could be getting quite a price for renting this hummer out for seining."

"Yes, but look at the fun we can have out here. I don't know much about what they plan to do, but Mike said it involves some studies of killer whales and may last a couple of weeks. Mike likes the *Karen Marie* for the work because of her deck space and boom and it certainly has worked out well on hauling the pigs from Seward. What are they really planning to do, Don?"

"I don't know much more than you do. They're supposed to send some pigs out here and I've got to set up some pens starting tomorrow. The best thing we could do is avoid speculation and wait until they come out to tell us what they have in mind. Whatever the project, it looks like it will be fun."

"Say, you're going to need some help to get things going here," Mario observed. "The girls will come ashore in the morning and help out. Mike's paying them so let's keep them busy," he smiled.

"I'll appreciate the help," Don replied. "I'm going to start cutting posts in the morning. Sally, maybe you could help me out on the hill and Evelyn could start cleaning up the camp. Those cabinets ought to be cleaned out before we start putting any groceries away and the floors should be cleaned. We want to set things up so everyone will be happy."

"My contribution will be to provide some fresh halibut or salmon," Mario smiled. "Cutting trees and cleaning camp are not my idea of fun or excitement. Sounds to me like a good day to go fishing."

Sally, Evelyn, and Mario decided to call it a day and stayed on the vessel for the night. Don returned to the lodge and selected the room nearest the kitchen and rolled out his sleeping bag. He placed his .44 Magnum and its holster on the stand near the end of the bed.

The next morning Don was up before six and stepped outside the lodge. The rush of the stream down the mountain created a sound which seemed to bounce gently off the low-hanging clouds blanketing the mountain peaks. The lush green vegetation of the pasture and the surrounding trees seemed to release a refreshing fragrance. Within two minutes the first mosquitoes arrived to risk death in order to feed on the hot blood coursing through his arteries and veins. He wondered if they could hear his blood the way he could hear the stream cascading down the mountain.

Looking toward the calm water of the bay, Don noticed that someone was stirring on the Karen Marie. It was Mario, who waved him over for some fresh, strong coffee. Evelyn arose and cooked ham and eggs. The morning was gorgeous with no wind and a bright sun climbing into the sky from the northeast. The *Karen Marie* rocked gently at its mooring to the dock.

After breakfast the two women, along with Don, dispersed for the work on shore. Mario started up the diesel engines and moved out into the bay to fish.

Don, carrying a chain saw and accompanied by Sally with a double bladed axe, crossed the pasture to the forest beyond. He commenced cutting down pine trees about 4 inches in diameter with the chain saw. "Too damned thick anyway," he told Sally. "These saplings will never get very big," as another small tree was cut into a 7 foot length. They continued cutting until twenty posts had been cut, not enough for the planned 12 foot post spacing for the enclosure, but they'd cut more later. And they'd probably need some extras. After a quick lunch they went about cutting more posts and, near the end of the day, had sixty stacked up. Sally trimmed off the branches with the axe. Some trees the size of a man's arm were then cut down and were cut into 12 foot lengths for use at the base of the fencing. By the time they were through cutting and carrying the posts to the pasture area, it was 6 pm, and Don was extremely impressed with the physical strength and endurance of Sally. She could work as well as any male her size he had ever met.

Mario returned from fishing and reported that he had caught only a couple of small halibut and had put them back. But now he knew where to fish and would get some keepers tomorrow.

Evelyn had prepared some Salisbury steaks, canned peas and carrots, fried potatoes, and onions and a loaf of fresh bread. Beer and iced tea were the drinks. Everyone pitched in on washing dishes and further cleaning in the kitchen and dining rooms. It had been a long day and all retired early.

After a light breakfast in the newly cleaned dining area, Evelyn went back to her chores. Don pointed out to Sally that now the tough work would start. "The power post hole digger," he said, made to be operated by two people "is like trying to hold a mad Brahma bull by the horns, especially in rocky ground."

Don laid out the shape of the pen by pacing and tied a piece of colored plastic ribbon to the grass wherever a post should be placed. Because of the bear evidence, he placed the 30 x100 foot enclosure closer to the buildings that he otherwise would have. The lower end of the enclosure took in 20 feet of the bog and he knew posts there would have to be held in place with rocks. He put a slight jog in the northern edge of the enclosure just into the stream so the pigs would have good access to water. He allowed for two gates, one nearest the buildings and another near the stream.

The post hole digging went well except for two rocky areas. Evelyn stopped cleaning long enough to come out and help with the noisy digger. Between the three of them they got all the holes dug and the posts in place by 6 pm. It was a tough day of work and not entirely free of blisters. The hot showers in the lodge were wonderful.

Mario had gone out again and caught two halibut of 20 and 40 pounds and had also caught 4 pounds of shrimp in a shrimp trap. He proceeded to prepare dinner and, by the time showers were over, he had the shrimp hors d'oeuvres ready and a couple of the halibut filets ready to cook. Perfectly seasoned, he fried them lightly in premium olive oil. He also had baked five medium-sized potatoes and opened a large can of lima beans. His preparations included two bottles of Washington state chardonnay. The girls and Don complimented him on a gourmet dinner.

The following day Don and the girls put up the fencing including the bottom poles to help keep the pigs from digging under the fence. By three o'clock the pen was looking good.

"Looks like we're ready for the porkers," Don said. Mario had observed the last part of the project and remarked that it looked very good.

Back inside the lodge they found Evelyn still cleaning, but the place looked so much better. "As with any house cleaning" she said, "it will be a continuous job."

Once again, Mario did the cooking for the evening on the *Karen Marie*. This time he prepared a tossed salad with his own dressing, beef roast with mashed potatoes, gravy, peas, and green beans. For dessert he had made a chocolate cake. Don commented that Mario should consider opening a restaurant, to which Mario responded that in thirty-five years of work aboard a boat you must learn how to cook or suffer your own incompetence.

There was some talk about going back to Whittier and to Anchorage but Don said he really did not need to go and, anyway, if there was something that was needed they could ask Mike, Tracy, and Reed to bring it when they came out. The idea for going back to Whittier was scrubbed.

Sally continued to sleep in the vessel and Don began to wonder if she would ever sleep in the lodge. She had told him on several occasions that she had a boyfriend in California she really cared for, but it made no sense to Don for her to be celibate when spending much of the year in Alaska, boyfriend or no. But he and Sally were working hard and having fun together. Don figured with time and understanding she would warm up.

CHAPTER TWENTY TWO

Kennelsto Herring Bay

With the telephoned order from Tracy in hand, Mary Pantera immediately went into action. It was now critical that she take a serious look at the old Ford truck which was going to be sent one-tenths of the way around the Earth. Fortunately, this truck had been used for hauling livestock on many occasions and it had a large plywood-covered bed.

Although it did not have the typical slotted "stock rack" type of construction, it did have adequate ventilation ports which could be opened front, sides, and top so any animals inside would have plenty of fresh air. The tires were OK she noted, but, after starting the engine, decided to send it into town for servicing and a tune up. There was no doubt in her mind that the Alaska purchasers would not object to paying for the additional expense.

Mary then called Kim to her office to discuss the transportation and which pigs should be sent. "What are they going to use the pigs for?" Kim wanted to know.

"It's a research project," Mary replied, "I don't have all the details and it will probably be best if the people in Alaska fill you in. But I understand it involves some research on marine mammals."

"What type of pigs do they want?"

"Average 150 pounds and none over 200. As always, let's send good, healthy stock, but no sows with litters and no very young pigs." She turned to the idling computer on the credenza behind her desk. She brought up a complete listing of all pigs on hand. Another command and a listing all pigs on hand which had the desired characteristics appeared. With another command the printer printed two hard copies of the three page list. She handed one to Kim and together they went over the information which included vital statistics for each pig.

They check-marked four older sows (two already pregnant), six gilts (younger females), nine barrows (castrated males) and one boar. "Are they planning to start raising pigs up there?" Kim asked. "But I assume not or they would have paid more attention to sex rather than weight in their order."

"Well, I considered sending no boars at all," Mary noted, "but there's always the possibility that Tracy and the Alaska group will decide to raise more pigs in the coming years."

Several of the sows selected were Kim's favorites, including one she had named Daisy because of the pink flower shaped spots on her gray back. Another she called Minnie because Minnie's dark rounded ears reminded her of mouse ears. Mary suggested, and Kim agreed, that Kim should keep records of the trip and how the pigs responded so they would know in the future how the "kennel shipping" technique worked out. They might want to use it again sometime.

They carefully reviewed the rations the pigs would need in preparation for the trip and in travel. They both agreed that with plenty of fresh straw or hay daily in the kennels, along with good water and food, the pigs would get along well on the one week trip. As a matter of fact, the pigs would, they thought, be better off in their individual kennels than competing for space and milling around in a stock truck with the typical slatted wood sides.

Two days later a delivery truck from Denver arrived with twenty large fiberglass kennels. Both Kim and Mary were pleased that such high quality kennels had been ordered.

The units were even made so as to allow easy stacking, but three high was probably going to be too much weight without some support. Jeb Raymer, the handyman around the facility, was called over to look at the truck and the kennels. Together they concluded that it would be best to construct some racks in the truck to support the containers. Jeb thought he had enough scrap lumber on hand to do the job and he recommended that the supports be bolted into place for strength rather than nailed.

He also suggested they install the kennels in the racks and load the pigs in them later, another advantage, he observed, to having small pigs. A second rack would be built opposite the pigs in order to have a place to place feed and straw without having it underfoot. He got right to work.

Kim began winding up her personal affairs for the several week stay in

Alaska. She was very excited about going, but it seemed strange to be packing warm clothes for a trip in mid-summer. Her boyfriend-of-convenience was not happy that she was leaving for such a long period, but Kim welcomed the opportunity to get away from sleepy Greeley. The thought occurred to her that she might never return.

Among the rations planned for the pigs was plenty of high-protein feed containing abundant soy bean meal. They also included a two week supply of vitamin and mineral supplements, including vitamin E which was effective in reducing the possibility of porcine stress syndrome, caused by mental stress on swine.

Kim was highly interested in nutrition and physical condition of humans and she found it extremely interesting that the nutritional requirements of pigs and people was almost identical. A highly nutritious, low fat diet wellsuited for people was also good for the swine. If, for some reason, she needed additional vitamin and minerals while on the trip with the pigs, it would be a simple matter to stop at a drug or discount store and purchase additional amounts.

Mary received another call from Tracy in Anchorage. There was a vessel leaving in four days from Tacoma and they were hopeful Kim could arrive there in time to get aboard. To confirm matters, the phone number of the shipper, SeaLand, was given to Kim so she could be in touch with the Tacoma offices directly.

Kim immediately called and talked to Ruth Swanson, expediter for SeaLand. Ruth was surprised to learn that Kim was a woman; she had been expecting a male truck driver. She advised Kim that they normally did not take any passengers because the airlines and cruise ships opposed it. Their insurance agent didn't like it either. In this case, however, where live animals were involved, they would make an exception. Ruth warned her not to expect any special treatment and that she would have to eat with the crew. They could, however, give her a small cabin with a bunk so she wouldn't be in general quarters.

Kim knew that to reach Tacoma on time she would have to depart the following day, but all preparations seemed to be in order. Jeb completed installing the kennels in racks in the truck and had built a sturdy rack on the other side where he now was loading the selected feed and straw. Four heavy duty, 5-gallon plastic water containers were loaded in the event water was scarce on any part of the trip. A dish for food and water for each kennel was set aboard, and each kennel was filled with a good bedding of straw. Looked very cozy, Kim thought, the pigs should do nicely in here. It was hot in the truck, sitting there in the broiling Colorado sun, but at 60 miles or so per hour on the road, ventilation would be good.

Kim hurried back to her own apartment to finish packing and say last minute phone goodbyes to her friends. The next morning she rose early and a friend dropped her off at the swine research office west of town. She was wearing faded blue jeans, a denim shirt and some well-brokenin western boots. Her blond hair was tied back in a ponytail.

The previous day they had segregated all the pigs to be shipped into a separate pen except for the boar, which was kept in its own pen. Each pig had an individual ear tag with an identifying code number.

At 7 am the pigs were herded to a final holding area near a ramp leading to the truck. Then, three at a time, they were driven up the ramp into the truck where Jeb, with the help of one of the school's football players, physically picked up the pigs and placed them in the upper kennels one by one. The smallest pigs went in the top kennels, the heaviest in the bottom. The identifying number for each pig was written on the kennel with a permanent marker. Pigs tend to become possessive, Kim knew, and she would try to return each pig in its own kennel once they were taken out.

"Wolfy," the boar was the last animal to load. As expected, he was also the most difficult. He had been named for his ugly appearance, with a head Kim thought most closely resembled the beast in the movie "An American Werewolf in London." If makers of Halloween masks or horror films ever needed a model, she knew right where they could find one. It was the male hormones which made the difference; castrated males, the barrows, did not have the ugly features and grotesque tusks.

In helping with the loading, Kim remarked that if any of the upper level pigs had to be removed from its kennel on the trip, she definitely was going to have to find some help. Even Daisy weighed in at 125 pounds.

With all the pigs, water, feed, vitamin supplements and straw aboard, Kim threw her luggage in the front seat along with a briefcase containing the pig data. Armed with a road map on which she had plotted her course, she said her goodbyes.

The truck seemed rather heavily loaded as she pulled away from the buildings and down the lane to the county gravel road. The only two animal rights picketers on site that morning stood up from the shade of a tree to wave their signs as she drove by.

Those people she thought, probably belong to the Society for the Prevention of Cruelty to Animals. She wondered what they'd think if they knew some of her pigs were on their way to be used in marine mammal research. She waved gaily to them.

Her travel took her from Greeley through Wyoming and then into Idaho. With stops for fuel, for feeding and watering the pigs and cleaning out their kennels, she still managed to make it to the Oregon border by the end of the second day. She called Mary back in Fort Collins to tell her where she was and Mary called Tracy in Alaska.

Heading into Washington State she asked herself "Why not give the old Ford truck a name? She had spent lots of time in the old crate, and why not become familiar? After thinking over several names she arrived at Freddie. That's it, Freddie Ford.

"Hi, Freddie! My name's Kim!" she introduced herself loudly and patted Freddie on the instrument panel. "I'll introduce you to our passengers at the next stop." With a name for the truck, the cab somehow seemed more comfortable and homey.

Temperatures cooled noticeably and were welcomed as the highway descended the west flank of the Cascade Range. She was surprised at the rapid change to humid, cloudy weather as Freddie rambled down the highway toward Seattle and Interstate 5 which would take her south to Tacoma.

The directions were simple enough to depart the Interstate and drive directly to the SeaLand parking lot where lines of vehicles were being driven by a crew of drivers onto a waiting ship, the Kodiak Queen. Kim parked Freddie near a mobile home-turned-office and stepped down out of the truck. The pigs grunted in anticipation of more attention from her. The air was very humid and smelled of the ocean, a smell she hadn't savored since a trip to San Francisco two years previously. She took a deep breath and then walked into the office. A red-haired woman in her mid-fifties greeted her.

"I'll bet you're Kim, the young lady with the truck load of pigs," she smiled.

"And you're Ruth, right?" Kim responded.

"Yep, glad to see you on time, but we don't have any time to waste. The Queen sails in three hours and there's still lots to do. For one thing, take these papers and drive over to the scales on the other side of the lot where they'll weigh your truck and take more exact measurements. Then come back and we'll proceed."

"OK," Kim replied. "Will it be necessary for me to drive the truck on board, or will someone else do it?"

"No, don't worry, the crew will drive it on. Because it has animals in it we 'll try to put it on one of the lower decks so it will be out of the weather in case it turns nasty."

"I'd appreciate that," Kim nodded as she pushed open the door.

As she drove up to the scales a motor home was driven off. A small man with a cigar in the side of his mouth came out and waved her forward. He stood there motioning as she drove Freddie onto the weighing platform and climbed out. The cigar smoker motioned her out and into the small adjoining building.

"This must be the load of pigs I heard about," he said, as he adjusted the beams on the scales. "Who'd want to send live pigs to Alaska? Costs too much to feed them up there; better to ship ham and pork out of Washington." He looked at her curiously.

"I understand they're going to be used for some sort of research, but I'm not sure yet," Kim replied, trying to be polite to this opinionated person.

"I was in Alaska once, to Katmai National Park." Wouldn't dare take any pigs in there. Too many bears." He wrote down the truck weight on the form. "Let's go out and get the dimensions." Kim helped him with the measuring tape and he wrote down the dimensions of the truck, including the height. "Need the dimensions so we know where it will fit on the Queen," he said. "How many pigs you got in there?"

"Twenty," Kim replied, "but they're not large pigs."

He handed a piece of paper to her. "Take this back to Ruth. She 'll tell you what to do next."

Ruth studied the weight and size data for a moment and then showed Kim on a diagram of the lot where to park so the vehicle would be in proper position for loading.

"You'd better stay with the truck so you won't be separated from it when they take it aboard. After the truck is parked and blocked in, go to the bridge and meet the captain, Carl Kasilof. He's from Alaska, somewhere down on the Kenai Peninsula, and supposed to be part Indian and part Russian. Carl knows you're coming and will show you to your quarters."

"One question," Kim asked. "Is there plenty of fresh water on board the ship?" She was thinking of the pigs.

"There's enough water on that ship to last from Tacoma to Hong Kong and back again with the crew taking five showers a day," Ruth smiled. "I can't imagine you and the pigs using more than that."

"I just wanted to be sure, that's all," Kim replied.

With Freddie parked in his designated spot, Kim opened the rear doors to tend to the pigs. She always talked to them in a gentle voice and they responded with quiet grunts and oinks. She proceeded with changing the straw and found a dumpster in which to deposit the waste. The pigs were doing well but seemed excited. Kim concluded that it was probably the smell of the ocean which excited them, or they were detecting and responding to her own excitement, or both. There was a pounding on the side of the truck and a voice said "Let's go!"

She quickly closed the doors and found a man of twenty-five standing near the driver's side door. Kim crowded in the front seat between the driver and her luggage, much to the amusement of the driver.

"Quarters are a little crowded," he said, "but I'm not complaining." He looked at Kim appreciatively.

"Fortunately, this will be a short trip," she responded.

It was nearly 5 pm when the truck was driven across a ramp and through an entryway in the side of the ship. It was quite dark in the hold and Kim immediately began thinking of ways she could get some additional light to the pigs during the daylight hours. She would also need light for the cleaning and feeding. The truck was pulled in with the front against the hull, thus allowing access to the rear of the truck. With the rear doors open, the pigs would have plenty of fresh air.

The crew member told her how to reach the bridge and she walked in that direction as the truck was being blocked into place. Trucks, automobiles, boats on trailers and miscellaneous vehicles were loaded on the lower deck.

After climbing the stairs to the main deck, she found huge stacks of cargo containers, with some container stacks four high reaching 40 feet above the deck of the ship.

Walking past the stacked containers, she could not help wondering if there was a chance the Kodiak Queen might capsize; the top deck appeared to have enough bulk on it to flip the vessel over once it had left the dock. She had read a number of accounts of fishing boats capsizing in Alaska waters, but, under the circumstances, she could only assume that the experienced crew knew what they were doing. She climbed the stairs to the bridge and entered.

A tall, slender, dark-haired, ruddy complexioned man about 45 years old was looking out toward the activity on the deck. He turned to look at her as she entered. His dark eyes, set below shaggy black eyebrows, seemed to scowl. In a way, he reminded her of Abraham Lincoln.

"Hi, I'm Kim Storey," she said, walking forward with her hand extended. "You must be Captain Kasilof."

The captain showed no emotion and little interest as he grudgingly extended a hand.

"Have a seat," he commanded. "I'll have someone show you to your quarters as soon as we're loaded. Is your truck on?"

"Yes," Kim replied, "it is."

"I'm not crazy about hauling a truck-load of pigs. It will be up to you to see that the area is kept clean. You are responsible for your own safety on board. You will eat when the crew eats; if you miss a meal, don't complain." He looked at her disdainfully. "Don't complain about anything." He watched with binoculars as the crane swung another container on board and it was chained in place.

Kim sat on a hard bench. There seemed little use in talking to this hostile character.

The door to her left opened and a short, somber-looking man came in. He smiled as soon as he saw her.

The captain spoke again. "Cal, show her to her cabin and the mess. Tell the crew that anyone found fooling around with her is finished."

Cal said nothing but motioned to her to follow him. She was glad to get up and follow. The captain continued to scan the scene on deck, but Kim said "Thank you" as she exited, hoping he'd learn some manners.

Once out of the control room and the door was closed, the man smiled and offered a hand. "Hi, I'm Cal Sisneros, the first mate. Welcome aboard."

Kim was pleased that someone seemed friendly. "I'm Kim Storey. Nice to meet you."

"Follow me and I'll show you to your cabin. And don't mind Captain Kasilof, his bark is worse than his bite."

"His bark gets tiresome in a hurry," Kim replied. Cal showed Kim the location of her cabin. It was small but was clean and perfectly adequate. The mess was nearby and there was a port hole which could be opened for ventilation. The vessel was preparing to cast off and Cal excused himself to handle some of his duties. She looked around the cabin and mess areas while she waited for him.

She felt the vessel shudder and heard the engines rev up and assumed they were underway. A look out the port hole confirmed it; the dock facilities of Tacoma were sliding by.

Within ten minutes Cal returned and accompanied Kim back to the truck to get her luggage and to see what could be done about additional light in the area. Cal promptly rigged up an extension cord and three trouble lights which lit up the interior of the truck brightly whenever Kim plugged in the cord to the nearby outlet.

"Plenty of electrical power on the Queen," Cal advised.

In the next two days Kim found that the food was actually quite good. The sea air was wonderful and the pigs were doing fine. Kim had brought along a tape player and some tapes and she experimented with the pigs by playing various types of music. They seemed to like Strauss waltzes best, but she suspected much of the reaction was a result of her being there with them. Refuse from cleaning the kennels, an almost ideally biodegradable material, was simply tossed overboard.

The crew of the Kodiak Queen became interested in the pigs and there were frequent visits to the truck. Kim answered dozens of questions and she was beginning to think the truck was a petting zoo. Little "goodies," such as cookies and apples, began showing up in the pig's food dishes after crew meals. In response to Kim's question, the cook confirmed that interest in eating pork, bacon and ham had not changed since the pigs came aboard. The crew wanted to take some of the pigs out of their kennels to wander around the deck but Kim would have none of that idea. Too risky; a pig overboard was a pig lost.

Even Captain Kasilof came by to look at the pigs. He said it was to check the cleanliness of the area, but Kim noticed a smile on his face at the happy grunting and apparent smiling of the pigs from their kennels.

The pigs themselves quickly caught onto the idea that they were a prime attraction and Kim observed that they seemed to do their best to make faces and noises which would please the viewers. To record the unexpected interactions, Kim took many flash photos and made copious notes. This could constitute subject matter for a PhD thesis on animal behavior, she thought, with the reactions of Homo sapiens just as interesting as the pigs.

Two and one-half days out from Tacoma they were approaching the Alaska coast. In anticipation of the arrival, Kim repacked her bags and took them down to Old Freddie. Because much of the straw and feed had now been used from the storage space near the pigs, she was able to stash all of her bags there. She also looked in on the pigs, changed their straw and gave them food and water.

Cal invited Kim to the bridge to see maps of the terrain appearing to the north and to see the planned course of the Kodiak Queen into Cook Inlet and past Fire Island to Anchorage. Cal showed her why the timing of the entry of the Kodiak Queen into Cook Inlet was so critical. Due to the latitude and Inlet configuration, the slanted, Y-shaped body of water, extending northward toward Anchorage from the Gulf of Alaska, was host to some of the greatest tidal fluctuations on Earth. At Anchorage, twice-daily maximum and minimum tides frequently differed by as much as 24 feet. The tides in Cook Inlet were so strong, Cal pointed out, that a vessel trying to go in against an outgoing tide could actually be trying to go forward at 8 knots but be carried backwards by a tidal current moving at 10 knots. On the other hand, a vessel going in with an ingoing tide could travel not at 8 knots but at 18 knots, thus saving a tremendous amount of time and fuel.

With this explanation Kim was not surprised when the Kodiak Queen seemed to be making little headway when first entering Cook Inlet, but then seemed to fairly fly the distance from Seldovia on the east side of the inlet to Fire Island just a mile west of the Anchorage International Airport.

With the ship sailing north-northeast into the Inlet, she saw the majestic blue and white Aleutian Range on the west side of the Inlet. She saw the steaming vent of the volcano Augustine just west of Kachemak Bay. Augustine had erupted within the past four years and no one knew when the next eruption might occur. The position of the volcano in Cook Inlet, Cal explained, was positioned in such a way that any violent sub-surface eruption would almost certainly unleash a tsunami (often incorrectly called a tidal wave) that could easily devastate those parts of the town of Homer which lay within 100 feet of sea level. A tsunami warning center had been established, but an energy wave released from Augustine would require only about fifteen minutes to reach Homer, not enough time for an evacuation.

Another volcano, Redoubt, had been erupting over the past twelve months, often covering Anchorage and the entire length of the Kenai Peninsula with fine gray rock powder. Kim could see a plume of steam rising to at least 20,000 feet over the peak. Cal told her no one knew when the next eruption might take place.

Kim noticed that the closer they got to Anchorage the muddier the water became. By the time the Kodiak Queen was near Fire Island the water looked like liquid mud and the tidal flats not yet covered by the incoming tide appeared to be a dark gray mud. She assumed the mud was from the action of the volcano but Cal advised her that it was always like this, volcano or no. A large amount of suspended particles, including glacial flour, were carried into the Inlet by the various rivers, he said, and tidal activity kept the mud constantly stirred up.

As the vessel approached the Anchorage docks, Kim went to Freddie so she'd be there when the truck was driven off. She looked forward to meeting the Alaskans but she also wanted to get the pigs out of their kennels as soon as possible. They had been in their containers for more than one week now and she was becoming apprehensive that problems might develop.

At the Herring Bay camp a float plane belonging to the Alaska Fish and Game Department had stopped at Knight Island because the pilot wanted to see how everything was going. Everyone at the camp was pleased to find that the plane was headed back to Anchorage and that three passengers were OK to take along. Don and the two girls all had things to take care of in Anchorage and they were happy to find a quick way back to the city. Mario said he had some things to take care of in Whittier so he would take the *Karen Marie* to Whittier by himself and would meet Evelyn and Sally there.

After landing on the small lake near the middle of Anchorage, the three of them walked to Don's pickup, parked nearby. There was lots of shopping to be done and they all pitched in at a large grocery and liquor store to get the items on their list. About four hours were required.

In the pickup were Don's four-wheeler all-terrain vehicle, trailer for the four-wheeler and other supplies for loading aboard the *Karen Marie*. From there it was planned that the *Karen Marie* would motor south to the Port of Seward to await the arrival of the truck and animals from Colorado. Evelyn and Sally dropped Don off at the Port of Anchorage where he was to meet the driver of the truck with the pigs. They then headed for Portage and then to Whittier with Don's loaded pickup.

Meanwhile, the *Kodiak Queen* was nearing the Port of Anchorage at the northeast end of Cook Inlet. Captain Kasilof steered her through the extremely muddy water to the dock. Some maneuvering had to be done around a dredge working under contract to the Corps of Engineers to remove silt, sand and mud from the Port docking area. The strong tidal currents were continually moving sediment about in the entire water column in this part of the Inlet and the Corps had never figured out how to avoid dredging and yet keep the water in the dock area deep enough for ships the size of the *Queen* to dock.

Don Schwartz looked at his watch; it was 6:30 pm and the *Queen* was only twenty minutes late. He poured himself another cup of coffee in the dockside offices of SeaLand where he had been visiting with the secretary/expediter. On the intercom they could hear the radio conversations between the *Kodiak Queen* and the Port Authority. Everything seemed to be on track.

As the *Queen* was being secured to the dock, Don walked over to the large parking lot where disembarked vehicles were left pending their pickup or receipt by owners. Don waited near the small security office. After a dozen vehicles had been driven off, an old Ford one and one-half ton truck rumbled out of the bowels of the vessel. There was some sort of cargo on top beneath a bright blue tarp and the plywood-covered bed had what appeared to be hinged ventilation doors on the sides. A rather tough-looking character was driving, with a blond woman sitting in the passenger side of the truck cab.

Don was convinced this was the pig delivery truck and he walked over to the vehicle as the driver was getting out. He could hear the pigs now and could detect an unfamiliar, acrid odor. The driver was telling the blonde woman: "You'll have to sign the receipt papers at the security office before you can take the truck off the lot. Then she's all yours."

"OK, thanks," she replied as she climbed down out of the cab. Her shapely figure and beautiful face immediately impressed Don. He stepped forward smiling, "Hi, I'm Don Schwartz. Welcome to Alaska!" He offered his hand.

"Hi, Don. Thanks. I'm Kim Storey, as you might have guessed."

"Any problems on the trip?" Don asked as he placed his bag on the hood of the truck so he wouldn't forget it.

"No, really, it was a good trip overall. The captain of the *Kodiak Queen* wasn't my favorite person, but that's not important."

"You may have heard that I work for Mike and Tracy Mackenzie. Mike is a geologist and Tracy is a computer programmer. The other person involved in the program, as you probably know, is Dr. Reed Remington, a marine biologist from Hydrosphere near San Diego. They make quite a trio."

"I'm very anxious to find out more about what they're doing and why they need some pigs," Kim looked at him earnestly, "but I'd better get this paper work taken care of first."

They started walking toward the small office. "How are the pigs doing?" asked Don.

"So far, so good. But they've been in their kennels for about a week now and I don't want to waste any time getting them to wherever we're going."

"If your truck is running well it will take about four hours to reach Seward where we'll put the pigs on a boat. It's going to be late, but we have twenty-four hours of daylight up here as you probably noticed. By traveling during the night we should be able to reach the island by tomorrow morning. Can the pigs hold out for that?"

"I think so, and I'm anxious for you to fill me in later on some of the details of where we're going."

They entered the office where an unshaven, lean man in scruffy clothes was shuffling papers at a desk behind a counter. A cigarette hung from the corner of his mouth. He ignored them and went on moving papers and making a note here and there with a pencil.

After waiting a few minutes Don posed a question: "Say, do you suppose we could get some service here? We 'd like to get on the road with a truck that was just unloaded from the *Queen*."

"Cool it, Buster. When I get to it, I'll get to it." The clerk cast a scornful glance at them.

The language and attitude toward Don was like waving a red cape before an angry Spanish bull. He considered going after the clerk immediately but hesitated because he didn't want to embarrass Kim. "Now, go sit down until I call you," the clerk sneered.

Don vaulted over the counter, grabbed the clerk by the collar with a powerful right arm and drug him halfway across the desk.

"You little bastard," Don said, his face only a few inches from the gasping face of the clerk, hanging upside down in Don's powerful grip. "You are going to pay attention to our papers right now, because if you don't, I'm going to mop this floor with your head. And you damned well better be courteous!" Don released his grip and stood glaring as the clerk struggled back off the desk.

"OK, OK," the clerk said as he came around the desk toward the counter, eyeing Don suspiciously. Don stayed on the clerk's side of the counter in case additional discipline was needed.

"Now process those papers so we can get out of this place," Don ordered.

Kim was watching with amazement. Was this typical of Alaska? Was

Don always this tough? In just a couple of minutes the papers were ready and Don crossed back over the counter. He had one more comment for the clerk. "If I ever come back in here again, I'll expect a different attitude." The clerk just stared with nothing to say.

Outside, Don growled to Kim as they walked back to the truck. "That bum was lucky I didn't work him over. Sorry about that welcome to Alaska, but I don't put up with that kind of insolence."

Kim could see he hadn't calmed down yet, but she had the feeling Don was a good and fair person. The clerk was insulting, she was just surprised at Don's hair trigger reaction.

"That's alright. He was aggravating and it is important that we get going," she commented, and then asked, "Are you going to ride with me or do you have your own vehicle?"

"I'll ride with you," Don replied, "My truck was taken to Whittier already," although he knew she didn't know yet where Whittier was located. He would fill her in later.

At the truck Kim opened the driver's door. "Old Freddie here isn't the best truck in the world but it got us here. Don, why don't you drive since you know your way around."

"All right with me," Don replied. Kim climbed in and Don tossed his bag in the middle of the cab and started the truck.

"This old hummer reminds me of a truck I had in the logging business in Oregon. Fords were the best highway trucks on the job and this one has less than 100,000 miles on it," he observed as they drove out of the fenced lot. The clerk was watching out of a small office window but Don ignored him.

"You are now seeing the great Port of Anchorage," he told Kim as they drove along railroad tracks and past a hodge-podge of fuel storage tanks, containers for containerized cargo, tractor trailers and miscellaneous equipment. "And ahead lies the great downtown part of Anchorage."

Kim notices that the tallest building was about fourteen stories.

"Because we're going straight to Seward I'm not going to give you the grand tour. Perhaps when you come through here later on I can show you around," Don offered.

"I would like to look around," Kim replied, "but today is not the day."

Don drove Old Freddie through the moderate evening traffic and noticed that the fuel gauge indicated the need for fuel. "Looks like we need some petrol," he noted, using the Australian version of the word.

"Yes, I'm sorry, but they prefer nearly empty fuel tanks for vehicles being transported on the *Kodiak Queen*. Must be related to the fire hazard."

Don filled the tank and checked the oil at a quick-stop station while Kim looked in on the pigs. Within ten minutes they again were heading south out of town on the four lane 'New Seward' Highway. Kim was impressed by the fact that, except for the mountains just east of town, Anchorage seemed just about like any other western U. S. town. Don said the population at one time had been about 500,000 but it had declined to about 400,000 with the demise of the domestic oil industry.

As they travelled down the decline from town past Potter Point Bird Refuge, Don pointed out the Chugach Mountains to their left and Turnagain Arm of Cook Inlet to their right. The mountains were more spectacular than anything Kim had seen in Colorado. The tide was now fully in and the water lapped at the rocks protecting the highway, which had narrowed to two lanes.

"Don," she asked, "tell me more about what the pigs are to be used for. I have heard only that the project involves marine mammals."

"I don't know much more than you do," Don replied. "As we discussed on the phone, they've had me set up a pen for the pigs over at Herring Bay on Knight Island, that's in Prince William Sound east of here. They have two boats they plan to use for observations. Mike, Tracy, and Reed have been studying these whales now for three or four years but they've never done anything like this before."

"Well, they're spending quite a bit of money on getting the pigs up here so it must be pretty important. Tell me about this island camp you mentioned."

Don described the camp history and location, including the fact that the setting was gorgeous. "If you were going to a camp like this as a tourist or sportsman," Don pointed out, "you'd be paying $3,000 to $4,000 per week to stay there. I think you're going to have a good time and the pigs probably will too." Don did not mention the bear tracks he had seen at the camp. Time enough for that later.

Nearly two hours down the road they wound their way up the road to Turnagain Pass south of Turnagain Arm and Kim suggested they make a pit stop as well as to take a look at the pigs to see how they were doing. Don obliged and pulled over in the large roadside rest area not far from two large outdoor toilets, men's and women's, built several years earlier. No restaurants or gas stations, only toilets.

Kim immediately went to the rear of the truck and opened the doors, while Don went to the men's toilet. Although it was now nearly 9:00 pm, it seemed to her as if it was only 4:30 in the afternoon. She was in the process of giving each of the pigs two of the molasses cakes when Don returned. He took over the task, fascinated by the little porkers.

Back in Old Freddie again, they drove the wellengineered highway toward Seward through spectacular scenery of steep, snow-covered peaks, rushing mountain streams and U-shaped glaciated valleys. On several occasions Don pointed out moose browsing in willows near the road and Dall sheep grazing or resting high on the mountain slopes.

"But where are the large trees?" she asked. "We have seen only small trees and willows."

"We're just about too far north for large trees," Don observed. "In a few protected spots there are some trees 24 inches or so in diameter, but most of the trees this far north are quite small. The large trees are in southeast Alaska along the coast. North of here, up around Fairbanks, there are few trees more than 5 or 6 inches in diameter."

"Another misconception," Kim laughed, "when many of us think of Alaska we always tend to think of large trees because we have seen pictures of large trees in Alaska. Those of us from down south don't realize how big this state really is, or the diversity, until we see it for ourselves."

After nearly another hour and a half of driving through equally spectacular scenery, they began seeing a few cabins and houses near the road. "We're only about 8 miles out of Seward now," Don pointed out. "We'll be there in a few minutes. Do you want to stop and get something to eat?"

"I'm fine, unless you'd like to stop for something. Frankly, my main concern now is getting the pigs to the island and out of their kennels. But what about you?"

"Don't worry about me and eating," Don replied. "I can always get something to eat aboard the *Karen Marie*. But I'll tell you what, let's stop at a liquor store and I'll get a couple of cases of beer. There's a new beer out of Juneau called Alaska Amber that won a national tasting contest and I'd like to try some. There's a liquor store right by the road so it won't take much time."

"It's OK with me," Kim replied. "Say, if they have an inexpensive beer I think I'll buy a couple of cases for the pigs. It might sound crazy but they really enjoy beer. When we take them out of the truck they're going to expect to be released from the kennels, but we can't do that yet. I think a couple of beers would do them good."

"Those are pigs after my own heart," smiled Don.

Jokingly Kim asked "You haven't had any valves replaced have you, Don?" smiling at the pun.

Don laughed, "Nope, not yet."

More houses began appearing and then Blying Sound, a northward extension of the Gulf of Alaska, came into view. Seward was in a location which reminded Kim of some of the photos she had seen of Norwegian ports at the head of fjords. The steep walls of the mountains rose directly from a choppy blue sea while snow capped the high peaks.

Don stopped the truck near a small building with the name Seward Liquors on a Pepsi Cola sign above the door. On the window, a hand written poster indicated that Old Milwaukee beer was on sale. Stepping out of the truck, Kim felt the refreshing but cool ocean breeze and she pulled on a jacket.

Inside the store, Don found out that they did have Alaskan Amber, although it was a little more expensive than most domestic beers. He said he'd take two cases anyway. Kim had found the Old Milwaukee and asked Don if it was any good and Don remarked that, so far as he was concerned, it was far better than the so-called "king of beers" and only two-thirds the price. Kim ordered two cases un-chilled, which surprised the clerk. "Our friends prefer it warm," she told Don. The clerk, overhearing the remark, said "I've got some friends like that too. They can't drink it fast enough if the beer is cold so they drink it warm. I guess that's the way they like it in England."

Don added several sticks of buffalo jerky to the order and the clerk rang up the purchases. Kim offered to pay but Don said he was under orders to pay for all supplies. With each of them carrying two cases of twenty-four cans, they returned to the truck. "Does Mike know you're spending money buying beer for pigs?" Kim asked, smiling.

Don opened the rear doors of the truck. "He knows I usually use pretty good judgment. And besides, if there was ever a question he knows I'd pay it from my own pocket."

Starting the truck again, Don offered Kim a piece of the jerky and, chewing on a tough, leathery stick himself, drove a winding street toward the water. He wasn't sure exactly where the *Karen Marie* might be docked but he thought it would be near the Port of Seward facilities. They drove along looking at the myriad of sport and commercial boats tied up in the harbor. Finally he spotted it near one long section of dock. There was a ramp nearby where the truck could be backed up and the pigs unloaded.

Don stopped Old Freddie near the dock within 100 feet of the *Karen Marie* and they stepped down from the truck. As they looked down upon the deck of the vessel, they noted two stacks of some type of material under waterproof tarps on the deck.

"That must be the feed and straw we sent down," Don advised Kim. "There are 2 tons of feed there and a hundred bales of straw. My four-wheeler and trailer are on board but we won't use them here."

"That's wonderful," Kim replied.

"Hey, down there! Anybody aboard?" Don called.

Mario came out of the cabin. "Hi, Don. We been waiting for you. Come on in and have some coffee, we're just watching a video tape."

"Thanks, but we're kind of anxious to get our load of pigs moved. Mario, this is Kim Storey from Colorado. She's had these pigs in kennels for more than a week and would like to get them to the camp."

"Hi, Kim. Nice to meet you. Hell, let's get going. I'll roust out the girls and we'll get right with it. What do we need?"

"Bring your tool box," Don replied. "The pigs are in individual kennels in racks in the truck and we may have to take the racks apart. It won't take long once we get started. And bring that dolly of yours so we can wheel the kennels over to the *Karen Marie* for loading."

Don got in the truck and backed it to a nearby elevated ramp, which almost reached the level of the truck box. As soon as he stopped, Kim opened the rear doors and began setting out the beer and her luggage. Don removed the few remaining bales of straw.

Sally and Evelyn were approaching from the *Karen Marie* with a tool box and the dolly, and Don turned to introduce them to Kim. They shook hands and Kim was very impressed with the strength of these two; Alaskans clearly seemed to be more physical that Coloradoans. They in turn were impressed that she had individually brought a load of 20 pigs all the way from Colorado to Alaska and they had many questions but they'd wait until later. Mario walked up, shook Kim's hand and surveyed the situation with his analytical mind.

"Did you load those upper kennels with the pigs in them?" he asked Kim.

"No, we installed the kennels and then put the pigs in," she replied. "And I suspect that we'll have to do the same thing to get them out."

"Do they bite?" Mario asked, looking in several of the kennels.

"These pigs won't bite but be careful with the male we call Wolfy. He has tusks that could do some damage."

"It'll be kind of messy even at that," Mario noted. "But with one of us on each corner I think we can handle the pig, kennel and all. The heavier pigs are in the lower kennels and we can just wheel them out of here, but right now we need to unbolt the retainers. "Eve and Sally, take the cart and wheel all the straw and feed down to the boom. The rest of us will start on the bolts."

With everyone pitching in, they soon had the top layer of kennelled pigs ready to move. With Mario, Don, Evelyn, and Sally on the four corners of each kennel they found they could easily set them on the dolly and wheel them to the dock. Using the winch and boom, they swung each kennel over the vessel, lowered each to the deck of the *Karen Marie* and secured them with nylon trusses. Within two hours the job was done, but it was now 11 pm. When Kim looked at her watch she was again amazed at the continuing daylight, but she was getting very tired now. In Colorado it was long past her usual bed time and her biological clock had not adjusted.

"Where are we going to park Freddie?" She asked Don.

"There's nothing much here to steal," Don replied, "I'll just park it over there at the end of the lot well out of the way. We'll be coming back to get it one of these days."

While Don parked the truck, Kim went aboard the vessel to observe the final lashing down of the kennels and to tie the cover over them with each door accessible. Mario knew what he was doing and he gave the girls excellent instructions as they hurried to finish the job. With everyone aboard, Mario started the engines, the girls cast off the lines and they pulled smoothly away from the dock.

Here we go, thought Kim, another step taken in this once in a lifetime experience. She removed the pig's water dishes from a box, began pouring in beer from the cans replacing the dishes in the kennels. Sally saw what she was doing and began popping cans for her, two cans for each pig. The pigs loved the beer and showed their pleasure by grunting loudly. She followed that with two molasses cakes each.

"They'll be OK now until we get to the island," Kim smiled. Entering the cabin they found the others enjoying a bottle of the Juneau-made, orange-tan Alaskan Amber. Only those who liked a heavy-bodied beer appreciated it, but that included everyone on board.

The passing scenery was gorgeous in the dim light near midnight. A rose and sliver tint was cast from the sun, which was just beyond the horizon to the north.

Evelyn reheated some delicious lamb stew they had saved for Don and Kim and served it along with some of Mario's homemade bread with butter and a sprinkling of garlic powder. They both ate heartily and washed the food down with beer. After eating, everyone but Mario and Don tried to get some sleep. Kim collapsed on a sofa in the cabin and went to sleep immediately. Don and Mario exchanged stories about Alaska. Don drank several more beers but Mario said he was going to stop at two; he had a vessel to navigate. Finally, at 2 am, the rhythmic pulsing of the diesel engines lulled his senses and Don fell asleep in one of the chairs in the cabin.

At 5:15 am the *Karen Marie* idled toward the dock at Herring Bay. Kim continued to sleep on one of the sofas in the cabin and Don was snoring lightly in the reclining chair where Mario usually sat to watch the video tapes. The smell of freshly perking coffee filled the cabin from the pot Mario had started further out in Herring Bay. He always tried to purchase fresh-ground Colombian coffee, a combination of French roast and medium roast, which he kept in sealed containers in the freezer to retain freshness. He enjoyed coffee and didn't like to settle for less than the best. Evelyn and Sally had anticipated a short night and slept fully dressed on their bunks. Evelyn awakened at the change of tone of the diesel engines and the great smell of the freshly-brewed coffee. She got up and shook Sally.

"Wake up, we must be at Herring Bay." She went to the control panel where Mario was carefully maneuvering the vessel toward the dock.

"Good morning!" he said to her cheerfully. "I was beginning to think I might have to dock this old gal myself."

"All you have to do is holler," Evelyn replied, as she slipped on a jacket. The weather was overcast but it was not raining. A moderate breeze was blowing from the southwest.

"The weather is cooperating," Mario observed. "I don't believe we'll have any rain for a couple of hours." His judgment was based on experience gained in hundreds of days of dealing with south central Alaska weather.

Sally came out to the bow and Evelyn at the stern. As Mario

maneuvered the vessel in against the dock they jumped across and tied down the mooring ropes. Don began to stir after hearing the voices and changed pitch of the engines. He looked up through bloodshot eyes. "Seemed like a short night," he told Mario, "but that coffee sure smells good."

"Help yourself," Mario smiled. "Pour one for me, too."

Evelyn and Sally returned to the cabin and each poured a cup of the dark, fragrant brew. Kim was still sound asleep. "Tell you what," Mario said, looking out at the dock and the camp. "Let's let Kim sleep and we'll start unloading the feed and the straw. As soon as she wakes up we'll start on the pigs. Don, go ahead and get that Honda four-wheeler and trailer of yours and we'll start the Herring Bay shuttle service. Let's have breakfast after the job is done."

They all nodded agreement over their coffee. "Why'd you feed me all that beer last night?" Don jokingly asked Mario.

"Must be your German heritage," Mario responded. "Damned if I can see how some people can put away so much beer. I had a German deck hand one time, name of Hans Schmidt. That guy could drink twelve bottles of beer before dinner and another half dozen bottles with dinner. Wasn't that big either. I don't know where he put it."

"I've been known to drink my share," Don smiled, as he sipped the last of his coffee. In his logging days he had often consumed more than a case of beer himself in one evening.

"We'd better get with it," Evelyn said as she slid the door of the cabin open and went out on deck followed by Don and Sally. They uncovered the feed and straw and began setting the bales in one stack on the dock and the feed in another. The fifty-pound feed bags and sixty-pound bales were no problem for either of them.

Don's four-wheeler and trailer were picked up with the winch and boom and set on the dock. Don started the machine and began shuttling between the dock and the barn building. Evelyn and Mario helped load the various items on the trailer and Sally helped Don unload at the barn.

When they had most of the feed and straw unloaded from the vessel Kim emerged from the cabin stretching and rubbing her eyes. "Good morning!" Mario greeted her. "Welcome to Herring Bay!"

"Good morning," she replied as she looked toward the camp and the beautiful forested slopes leading to the mountain peaks, some of which were obscured by clouds. The camp buildings blended pleasantly with the background and she saw the green area which must be the pasture near a stream with fresh-looking posts. That must be the pen, she thought. She could faintly hear the pigs grunting under their cover, and she immediately went to remove the cover and check on them. The pigs appeared to be fine, but restless. As always, they seemed to sense when something was going to happen and conveyed their feelings with body language and sounds.

Don was about to make another shuttle run with five bags of grain on the trailer and motioned for Kim to hop on behind him on the four-wheeler, which she did, smiling. The engine of the Honda revved up and they rolled across the boards on the dock, 100 feet toward the camp. A good gravel path sloped upward from the end of the dock toward the camp buildings and then split into smaller paths. The path to the barn had not been gravelled and a number of small but muddy potholes had developed, which were now filled with water.

Don seemed to delight in hitting the potholes at a good speed so water flew in all directions, including up. Kim found herself wiping muddy water from her face, a sight which made Don chuckle devilishly.

"I'll get you later!" she laughed.

The barn where Don and Sally had been stacking the straw and feed was about 25 x 50 feet with two large doors and a small pole corral. "Someone had horses here," she said. "I thought the climate in Alaska was too tough for horses."

"In most parts it is," Don replied, "unless you keep them inside and spend a fortune for feed. The people who were using this place as a hunting camp apparently had plenty of money. Come on out and I'll show you the pen."

They walked out past some willows and the beautiful green pasture spread out before her. She could smell the fresh earth and sap from the newly installed fence. A couple of the biggest mosquitoes she had ever seen circled near her head.

Kim was astounded at the size of the insects. "Wow, are these mosquitoes?" she asked as she swished them away from her face and then swatted one on her jacket sleeve. Don had forgotten that Kim had not yet encountered the pesky blood suckers.

"You're now being welcomed by the Alaska state bird," Don smiled. "Just be thankful there are not many of them around because of the well-drained ground. The few of them that are here probably come from that wet area over there I thought might be a good hog wallow. By the time the pigs get that churned up there won't be much left in the way of mosquito home sites."

"The fenced area looks great, Don," Kim remarked, "with one exception. We should erect a separate enclosure for Wolfy, the boar. He gets a little too aggressive with the other pigs and we don't want to start any breeding yet."

"OK," Don replied. "That won't take long because we have plenty of fencing and I cut some extra posts. Where do you want him?"

"Let's put him over there by the creek where he can have some of the wallow as well. Pigs love to wallow and it wouldn't be right to let the other pigs wallow and not him. We can also place the edge of his pen just over the edge of the creek so he can have plenty of water."

"All right, now let's get this feed off the trailer and go back for another load."

"Just set it off," Sally smiled, her brow covered with perspiration. "You go back for another load, Don. I'll stay here and carry it into the barn and stack it." She picked up a fifty-pound feed bag and carried it into the barn with ease. Kim also picked one up, not as easily, but without undue strain.

Don was impressed. It wasn't very often he ran into women who could and would handle their end of heavy manual labor, and there were three of them on this project already. He hummed a tune as he drove the Honda and trailer though the mud holes and out on the dock for another load. He loved adventure and Herring Bay was looking good.

In another half hour they had unloaded and transported all of the feed and straw and it was time for the pigs. Kim stayed at the pen and while Don, Mario, Sally and Evelyn loaded the kennels two at a time on the trailer. Don then hauled the kennels across the dock and to the enclosure where he and Kim slid it off onto the ground. While Kim coaxed each pig out of the kennel Don went back for more. Soon all twenty kennels were there, and nineteen pigs were frolicking in and exploring what seemed to them an immense area with thick lush grass such as they had never seen before.

Sally, Evelyn and Mario walked in from the dock to take a look at the pigs and to see how they liked their new home. They couldn't help smiling and laughing at the antics of the pigs as they pranced, dashed, and rolled around. Daisy had just explored the stream when she pranced to her left. It seemed that a look of disbelief came over her face when her hoofs stuck in wet, slushy mud. She stuck her snout in it, she jumped in it, and at last rolled in it, grunting and squealing in delight. The other pigs soon had mud-spattered bodies and were sounding very happy. Mario and the rest of the group laughed when they saw the other pigs running to join Daisy in a glorious wallow in the mud, large enough so that all nineteen of them could get in at once.

"By gosh," Mario remarked, laughing, "that looks like so much fun maybe I'll get in there!"

Wolfy was hitting the sides of his kennel with his tusks and making loud grunting noises. He was anxious to get out.

"OK, OK, We'll get to you as soon as we get your pen ready," Kim said, partly to the pig and partly to Don. She opened the door to Wolfy's kennel, fed him two of the molasses cakes from her pocket and closed the door.

"That is the ugliest pig I have ever seen," Sally exclaimed as she looked into the kennel.

"I'd hate to meet that pig in a dark alley," agreed Evelyn. "Why is he so ugly compared to the other pigs?" She asked Kim.

"It's the hormones. Believe it or not, twelve of the other pigs in the group are also males, but they are called barrows and were castrated at an early age," Kim replied.

"You mean I could have been even better looking?" Don joked. They laughed.

"I don't know about the rest of you," Mario told them, "But I'm about ready for breakfast and then a little shut-eye. Eve, let's get on back to the *Karen Marie* and prepare some vittles. If you two are going to set up another pen, go ahead and Sally will help you. We'll call you when breakfast is ready."

Don and Sally immediately got out the post hole digger and dug more holes. Kim went about feeding the pigs and moving their nineteen kennels into the pen with them. She wasn't sure the pigs would return to their individual kennels, but she wanted the kennels there to serve as shelters should the weather turn nasty. To help keep rain out she put small rocks under the rear of each kennel to tilt the entrance downward.

The horn on the *Karen Marie* sounded and echoed twice through the Bay and off the mountains.

"Sounds like grubs on," Don observed, as he set down a post he was carrying to Sally for setting. "C'mon Kim, let's get some breakfast. The pigs have had theirs, now it's our turn."

They enjoyed a breakfast of whole wheat hot cakes, eggs and sausage washed down with more of the good coffee. They were happy that one major part of their mission was over; they had successfully gotten the pigs to the island in good condition. After the hearty breakfast Mario said he was going to get some sleep while Sally and Evelyn said they'd do the dishes and then help with the fencing. Don and Kim went back to the pens to finish Wolfy's 10 x 20 foot section. They did not put a gate between the two pens and instead put a gate in Wolfy's pen facing the barn, the same as the large pen. At Kim's suggestion they doubled the wire between the two pens and doubled the poles at the bottom. When Sally and Evelyn arrived from the Karen Marie a hefty pole was added at the top of the fence between posts to discourage Wolfy from climbing over to get back in with the sows and gilts.

Now it was time to get Wolfy into his own pen. With the help of Don, Sally and Evelyn, Wolfy's kennel was skidded over near the gate to the new pen. She opened the door to the kennel and Wolfy looked out hesitatingly. At Kim's coaxing he suddenly bolted out into the pen. He was obviously happy to be out of the kennel and, after checking out the perimeter of the enclosure, rolled on the ground. Then he rolled and rooted in the mud wallow that was near the creek.

Everyone was weary from the work and the lack of sleep the previous night. Don suggested they all get some rest for at least a couple of hours and he offered to help Kim move her gear from the boat to one of the lodge rooms. Before they left the pen area, however, Don felt there was something he should tell Kim."

"Kim, there is one thing I wanted to mention to you. We're going to have to keep our eyes open around the pigs in case we have a furry visitor. There was a fresh set of tracks here the other day before we set up the fencing."

"Furry? Oh, you mean a black bear," Kim responded.

"A black bear might be just as bad, but this was one of the big boys, a grizzly."

Kim was concerned. "What can we do?" She asked Don.

"The best thing is to know when the bear is around so we can run him off," Don answered. "Can we depend on your pigs to make a lot of noise if a bear shows up?"

"I don't know, they've never been around a bear before, or any other carnivore for that matter. I think they would make noise, but I'm not sure."

"Well," Sally advised, "I've seen what remains of a 1500 pound moose after a grizzly attack and its pretty grim. A 150 pound pig would probably be just a snack."

"The pigs are strange fare for a bear," Don observed. "I may be wrong, but I believe if a bear comes around this area it will first do some reconnaissance to check out these strange critters. If we keep our eyes open we should be able to see tracks and droppings before it makes a serious move. But we'll have to be on our toes. Now let's get some rest." After getting the luggage from the Karen Marie, Don showed Kim into the lodge and she picked out a room, not near his. They both collapsed for some needed sleep.

CHAPTER TWENTY THREE

Training

M ike, Tracy, and Reed had completed their shopping in Anchorage and have arrived in Whittier where they excitedly transferred their supplies to the *Czarina*. They had been in touch with Don at Herring Bay and knew that all had gone well in getting the pigs from Anchorage to the camp.

After they were under way, Tracy said above the muffled roar of the engines, "I haven't told you what I heard about the person who is bringing the pigs from Colorado." Then she waited for a response.

Reed and Mike looked at each other. "OK, so you want us to guess, or what?" Reed asked.

"She's a biologist."

"Not another Helen Walker, please", Mike pleaded.

"Would you believe a face that would stop a clock?' she asked, smiling. No response. "Or would you believe someone who could make a female walrus look beautiful?"

"Show a little mercy," Reed pleaded. "That does not sound like someone it would be fun to work with. However, if she's a good biologist…"

Tracy smiled to herself. She had heard that the gal from Colorado was a blonde beauty.

As they continued to motor out toward Knight Island they discussed what the best approach might be to locate the A-T pack and what to do after they found it. In early afternoon they arrived at Herring Bay and were delighted to see that Don, always dependable, had set up pens for the pigs.

Tracy was looking through binoculars. "Looks like hog heaven where Don put the pigs. It appears there may even be a wallow there."

The *Czarina* idled up to the dock and Reed tied her firmly to the dock next to the *Karen Marie*. Mario emerged to welcome them. He had met Mike and Tracy previously but Dr. Remington was a new face. "Just call me Reed." He shook Mario's hand.

Don had seen them approaching and was already driving his four-wheeler with the trailer out on the dock. He stopped next to the *Czarina*. He was followed out by deck hands Evelyn and Sally and then Kim, a beautiful young woman with long blonde hair.

Mike looked at Reed, who could hardly take his eyes off the blonde, and said "What was that remark about stopping a clock?"

After introductions, all hands turned to unloading the groceries, equipment and various other items bound for the lodge and loading them in the trailer. Kim and Evelyn went to the lodge to unload as Don arrived with a full trailer. Several trips were required.

"We're not going to run out of food." Tracy observed after she saw how much had already been brought to the site on the *Karen Marie*. The two refrigerators were operating very well and were keeping perishable food cold.

"Come on out and I'll introduce you to the pigs." Kim urged. Mike, Tracy, and Reed followed her to what was being called the "pig pasture." They were surprised at how friendly the pigs were as they ran to meet the visitors. Kim showed them Daisy and Petunia, two of her favorites, along with Minnie and Patsy. She had names for them all. Over in the corner was a separate pen for the only ugly pig, the male Wolfy. They reached over the fence and scratched the pigs behind the ears, which the pigs really appreciated.

Back in the lodge, Evelyn and Sally made sandwiches with roast beef that had been brought out in a cooler and chips and dip were put on the table. Beer, coffee, and tea were offered. The food was very welcome.

Kim's curiosity was now bubbling over once she found out what Dr. Remington's specialty was, but she directed a question at Mike, who was sort of the group leader. "No one has told me yet why the pigs have been transported to a remote island in Alaska. I have heard it has something to do with research on marine mammals but pigs are not known as water-loving creatures."

This caused some chuckles and everyone at the table looked at Mike, including Mario who had come in from the *Karen Marie* to have a sandwich.

"Well, Kim", Mike explained, "We're trying to find out if killer whales might attack and eat Homo sapiens, you know, a man or woman in the water. There is one pack of whales here in Prince William Sound that has been doing some strange things and we'd like to find out if people might be on their menu."

"OK." Kim responded, "But what does that have to do with pigs?"

"Pigs are the nearest animal we could think of that might have sonar reflective characteristics similar to those which a human might have in the water. That's why we went for a certain weight of the pigs. And they are a food animal." Mike pointed out.

Kim wanted more information. "So you're going to have the pigs in the water with the whales and you want the whales to attack the pigs?"

"Not necessarily," Remington noted. "We want to see how the whales will react to a creature in the water that may have a similar sonar response as a man would. The pigs seem ideal, they don't have much hair, they have layers of fat just as seals do, and some people do. The internal organs are similar and the bone structure is similar. So we believe it is important to observe the whale's reaction when these critters are put in the water."

Kim wanted more information and was getting apprehensive. "Do you think they might kill and eat the pigs? Some of them are my darlings such as Daisy, Minnie, and Petunia for sure."

Mike responded this time. "We are not going to deliberately make an effort to have the whales take the pigs, but we must see what their reaction might be to this strange creature they have never encountered before. There is one specific group that we believe may be responsible for aggressive acts. We call it the A-T pack. A for Alaska and T for the designation we gave this pack a couple of years ago. There seems to be one particular female that is exceptionally aggressive and she is the pack leader. We intend to locate that pack and be prepared to carry out our experiment."

Kim still seemed to have some questions but she said nothing more as she thought about what might happen to her friends, the pigs.

As they got up to leave the table Tracy told them "Mike, Reed, and I are going out to search for the A-T pack this afternoon. We'll be in touch by radio, if we happen to find them we'll let you know, but we may have to get some spotting help from the air. We may be out there a day or two."

With Don Schwartz in charge of overseeing the camp, Reed, Mike, and Tracy spent the rest of that day and half of the next day on the scouring familiar areas in Prince William Sound for killer whale packs. They were hoping to find the A-T pack, but they carried out several hours of observations of any *Orcinus orca* group they happened to find. A salmon opening was scheduled for the Sound by the Department of Fish and Game and, when this happened, the northern and northeastern parts of the Sound would be crowded with commercial seining boats. Experience had shown that areas with so many boats in the water were generally avoided by the whales, a practice with which the salmon seiners were in complete agreement. A good way to have a net torn up, experience had shown, was to have a killer whale wander into it or get entangled while chasing salmon.

Although several groups had been followed, including the A-P and the A-R packs, the A-T pack was proving to be elusive. Nevertheless, information the trio gathered about the other groups helped them to continue developing behavior profiles of orcas in the Sound and how each particular group tended to behave. All of the groups followed were feeding primarily on salmon, which were near the peak of their abundance in the Sound. Both pink and red salmon were bunching together and moving toward the spawning streams and rivers. Some king salmon were still present and the silvers were beginning to school.

At the jagged rock promontory called the Needle, between Knight and Montague Islands, they observed glossy brown sea lions, stinking from their own excrement, lying on the rocks, their bellies bloated with fresh salmon. Scattered seals lay asleep on sand beaches and on low rounded rocks in the coves. It was a time of plenty for all of the marine mammals which fed on salmon. Sea otters bobbed here and there among the waves although they did not feed on finfish most likely because they were too slow to catch them.

Aboard the *Czarina*, Reed, Mike, and Tracy noticed and recorded the fact that the smaller marine mammals, which often comprised part of the diet of the killer whales, were much more relaxed around the whales when the whales were feeding on salmon. Indeed, at times the smaller animals were even brazen. Following the A-R pack one evening not far from the Needle, they observed the killer whale group joined by four or five sea lions as they fed on a school of salmon moving through the Sound. The sea lions sometimes apparently dove ahead of one of the whales to catch salmon being casually pursued by the orca. It appeared to be a matter of a super-abundance of food diminishing the need for attack of one species on another. Reed theorized the whales might even use such encounters as an opportunity for a learning experience about the sea lions, how they moved, how they reacted, how they communicated. Valuable information for times when the sea lions would become the prey.

Tracy remarked that the situation, with the `sometimes prey' paying little attention to a `sometimes predator,' reminded her of grazing animals in Africa paying little attention to a band of lions when they knew the lions were not hunting. Or perhaps, she added, the situation was closer to a setting where the lions had already killed and were feeding on a carcass; the remaining prey animals sensed they could graze in peace for the time being.

Part of their information concerning the location of killer whale packs came from monitoring radio conversations between passing fishing boats. Occasionally they would ask the skipper of a passing boat if any killer whales had been seen, but the only leads were two unidentified groups or two groups they could see were not the A-T. No new reports of whales stealing fish were heard on the radio.

"The next time we come out on another search we definitely should use an aircraft spotter," Mike lamented.

"Wonder how they're doing at Herring Bay?" Tracy asked as the *Czarina* idled along behind the A-R pack, traveling in the general direction of the Needle.

"The people and the pigs should be well settled-in by now," Mike replied.

Reed nodded, "You know, we've been out here for a day and a half, what do you say we follow this group to the Needle and see what happens there. Then let's go back to Herring Bay. We'll be only two hours away. What do you think, Mike?"

"I think it sounds great. Wonder if Don has gotten the showers working, I sure could use one."

"Knowing Don," Tracy observed, "I'll bet he has everything up and running unless some unusual problem showed up."

The whales they were following, in a sleeping mode, approached and then passed The Needle without so much as even a minor change of course. They appeared to pay no attention to the sea lions in the water around the rocks.

"Well, had enough?" Mike asked twenty minutes later as The Needle grew smaller behind the stern. The whales continued monotonously forward.

"Let's go to the lodge!" Tracy almost shouted, "I'm ready to step onto terra firma and take a shower."

Mike turned the toward the northwest and increased the throttle. The sound of the engines seemed to lift everyone's spirits. They looked forward to seeing the camp again; hopefully all would be in order so the project could proceed.

Two hours later, proceeding south into Herring Bay, they could see the buildings of the camp and the Karen Marie at the dock. It was a welcome sight.

It is Sunday at the Camp on Herring Bay and Don has gotten all operations in good running condition. He has been particularly pleased with the pantry, kitchen and propane cook stove at the camp. He can hardly wait for the *Czarina* to return so he can do some cooking for the trio Tracy, Mike, and Reed.

Kim had settled in at the camp and, in spite of the frequently rainy and cold weather, loved the Alaska setting. The pigs had quickly made themselves at home and were enjoying the new clean pen, the lush grass, now mostly eaten and trampled, and the mud wallow. Kim was pleased with their condition and she was eager to discuss further the plans for using the pigs to study whales. She had additional concerns about research the Mackenzies and Dr. Remington had in mind for the pigs. It didn't quite make sense that pigs were going to be used to find out if the whales might kill and eat a man or woman.

She had asked Don to cut down an "old snag of a tree" as Don called a twisted dead tree not far from the camp. He used the four-wheeler to drag it into the pen. Because of the shape, which allowed the pigs to go under part of the twisted wood, it immediately became, as Kim thought it would, a scratching station for the pigs.

"Pigs love to scratch," she told Don, "and there's no reason not to give them something to scratch on. If you ever have occasion to want a pig to lie down, just start scratching its belly. Works almost every time."

"I can't imagine why I'd want to have a pig lie down," Don laughed, "but I'll keep that in mind."

The lush growths of brush and timber on the mountainsides were fascinating to Kim because she had always lived in the arid Rocky Mountain region, but she took care not to wander far from the camp because of her unfamiliarity with bears. She did not want to encounter one in an unpleasant situation even though Don had told her she should not allow bears to interfere with whatever she wished to do in the woods. "Just keep your eyes open and make plenty of noise so you don't surprise them," he said. Over coffee one morning the conversation turned to bears. Mario, Evelyn and Sally had also stayed to chat.

"Don't surprise a grizz, whatever you do," Don cautioned a wide-eyed and attentive Kim as he sipped on his coffee. "Surprise one and you don't know what they're going to do. You're forcing them into a quick decision and that quick decision may be one of aggression. Let them know you're coming. They have good hearing, so you want to talk, whistle, wear bells, whatever. Most of the time they will get out of your way and you will not even know they've been there."

"That seems strange," Kim observed. "When I'm in a wooded area I usually like to be quiet so I can be more in tune with nature. You know... listen to the birds and trees, watch for strange insects, watch for animals."

"That's fine for "Outside" but it is not a good policy up here in bear country," Don stated. He loved bear stories and he also liked to have her attention.

"I'll tell you one thing," Don said as he looked directly at Kim, "I'll take one of our Alaska brown bears anytime over the grizzlies I've read about in Wyoming or the grizzlies that were once so abundant in California. They were and are tough hombres. The Alaska browns are bigger, but the abundant salmon they feed on apparently makes them quite a bit more docile than a grizzly toughing it out on whatever they can find in the lower forty-eight."

"But what's the difference between a brown bear and a grizzly?" she asked. "Don't they both live in Alaska?"

"Yes, they do. So far as I know they are the same and can interbreed. The browns are much larger than the type called a grizzly just because of the richness of the feed."

"What kind of bear made the tracks you saw near the pig pen?" she asked. "You mentioned the term `grizz'."

"I suspect that here on the island there are probably some salmon spawning streams and, if so, we really should call it a brown bear. Judging from the tracks I'd say this customer would stand at least 8 feet tall when standing upright and would probably weigh more than 1200 pounds." Don looked around the room. "The ceiling of this room is about 8 feet high."

It was only 7 am but the pigs had been fed and breakfast was over. Don continued with bear stories. The previous summer, he told her, he had spent a week at Mike Cusack's King Salmon Lodge near the village of King

Salmon just inland from Bristol Bay in southwest Alaska. "Dr. Mike" was a well-known dermatologist in Anchorage who operated the lodge as much for a hobby as for profit. On each day of the week when Don was there they had flown out in small planes equipped with either floats or balloon tires, to a different fishing area. There were bears everywhere, with particular concentrations in and near Katmai National Park.

"At one place we buzzed the beach at low tide before landing at the mouth of a river full of incoming red salmon. There were five brown bears on the beach, with one large honey colored male obviously in control of a choice spot on the river. As we landed, all the bears scattered except the big male, who just stood his ground, staring threateningly, as the noisy plane taxied along the wet surface and up onto the sandy upper beach where it could not be reached by the incoming tide."

Kim and the others listened intently as Don continued.

"As we got out of the plane the bear crossed the river to the other side and climbed up a small hill into some brush where he stood looking at us over his shoulder. There were four of us there to do some fishing and we got our gear out of the plane along with a hefty lunch in a good-sized metal cooler. The pilot carried the lunch and a shotgun as we started upstream to a nearby salmon-filled deep spot on the river. The bear had disappeared, but I had some concern that the bear might decide to get into the plane while we were gone. If he did, it would not be difficult for him to trash the plane so it wouldn't fly and we'd be stuck for a while." He got up and poured more coffee for all.

"We walked upstream along the brush-lined river, making noise all the way. We all figured the bear would stay where he had been fishing and, after going a couple of hundred yards we stopped to see what we could catch. The pilot set the cooler containing the lunch down on the bank and we all started catching red salmon, which were so thick in the river it was difficult to avoid snagging them. We released every fish we caught because a bear has a great nose and can smell a fish, and probably a pig, a mile away."

He continued the story with Kim and the others listening attentively. "It would not be wise to get in a fight with a bear over a salmon; in fact, if you have a fish on the line and a bear shows up you'd best cut your line to get rid of the fish. If you bring the fish in, the bear will watch you and then come to take it away from you. Your arm or neck might get in his way." It was very quiet in the lodge.

"Well, first thing you know we're about 10 yards upstream from the cooler with the lunch but on the same side of the river. I happened to look back as I'm fighting a big red and there's that big honey-colored bear standing upright over the cooler looking at us. He had `taken possession' of the cooler and it was obvious that the best thing for us to do was back away from him upstream. We broke off our fish and backed away cautiously until we put about 30 yards between us and him. The pilot had the shotgun ready just in case the bear decided to charge. Instead, that bear ambled toward us about 10 yards and then sat down on his rear looking at us. The way he sat reminded me of the way a dog sits looking at you when you're eating dinner.

"This bear felt he was completely in charge of the situation. It was clear he came toward us to determine our intentions. If there was going to be a fight over the food, he wanted to fight on ground away from the grub. We concluded he sat down to watch us carefully and there is no doubt in my mind that, if we'd gone back toward him and the food, he would've threatened us, and if we forced the issue he would either mock charge or all-out attack."

"We decided to wade across the river both to slow any charge he might make and to assure him we did not want to fight over the food. When he saw us wade cross he relaxed and went back to the cooler and popped it open as easily as you'd open a can of soda to feast on sandwiches, pie, candy bars and whatever else the gourmet lodge cook had put in there for us. We went on upstream and continued fishing but it was a hungry afternoon for us although we would have cooked some salmon over an open fire had we really been starving. When we went downstream later, the bear had disappeared but we would not approach the chest because he could have been in the brush still guarding the find. But then we saw him back near the plane and we cleaned up the plastic, aluminum foil and other trash to take with us."

"So the bear wasn't really interested in you as food?" Kim asked.

"That's right. They'd much rather eat an easy meal; they're great opportunists. Give one of them a chance like a lunch and they'll take it. It is extremely dangerous for hunters to leave a moose or other carcass in bear country for even a short time. If a bear takes possession, you'd have to kill the bear to get the moose away from it. Hunters have been known to return to their downed moose carcass after going for help in butchering it, not realizing that a bear is concealed nearby and in possession. The bear would likely attack the hunters who, in the bear's judgment, are trying to take away its food."

"That makes sense from the bear's standpoint," Kim noted. "If it has protected and defended its food all its life it cannot be expected to change simply because a man, rather than some other animal, is trying to take food it believes to be its own. Seems to me the hunters should be smarter than to get into a spot like that."

"Hey," Don replied, "don't give the average big game hunter much credit for brains. If an IQ test was required to get a hunting license many of them would not qualify. Yet when they tangle with a bear through some act of stupidity they make the front page of one of the sporting magazines with an article about how brave or smart the hunter was."

"Well, what about the bears here, what can we expect?" Kim asked.

"Bears are curious and a strange smell like a pig will probably bring 'em in. I'd say the one thing you can depend on is that at least one bear will come by here, maybe the same one." He thought for a moment, "What it might do around the pigs is anyone's guess, but it could kill a pig the way you and I swat a mosquito."

Don could have gone on with more bear stories but he noticed that Mario had walked out to the *Karen Marie*.

"There's Mario, I'll go see what he has in mind today. I expect the *Czarina* to come in anytime now." Don walked toward the kitchen, which was clean and in good operating condition.

"While you see what his plans are, I'll go out and check on the pigs," Kim smiled. "They have been doing well. It definitely was a good idea to leave the kennels in the pen so they could use them for shelter."

"Well, taking care of the pigs is one of the most important jobs out here." Don smiled.

Mario saw Don coming across the dock and poured an extra cup of coffee. "What's doin', Don?" the older man asked. "Say, when do you think the *Czarina* will show up?"

"I was wondering the same thing. Could be sometime today, but you never know, they might arrive at night. I've been out with them when they've followed those whales twenty-four hours a day, day after day. Unbelievable dedication."

"We've got a little time today, why don't we drop the Boston Whaler in the water this morning and the girls will take you and Kim down south about a mile and a half to that little stream that has some salmon in it? You'd probably have some fun and fresh salmon would go pretty good for dinner. You might get some dollie varden as well."

"What about you, why don't you go, too?" Don asked.

"Aw, hell, Don, I'd rather stay here and take it easy. I'll keep an eye on the pigs; might learn something. I've got a couple of spinning rods here you can take, and a few lures. That's all you'll need if the reds are in."

"I think I know the place you mean; the creek mouth is sort of hidden among some big boulders."

"That's it, you can't miss it. And Sally knows where it is. Not many people go ashore there because they think the creek is smaller than it actually is. Say, the wind is starting to pick up," Mario observed, looking up at the partly overcast sky with strings of gray clouds racing toward the northeast. "I'd say if you are going you'd better go pretty quick so you can get back in a couple of hours."

"I'm ready!" Don volunteered.

Mario called the girls and told them of the plan to look for salmon in the stream at the big rocks. They had gone ashore there exploring two years ago and Sally remembered exactly where it was. Enthusiastically, the Boston Whaler was swung over the side with the boom and lowered into the water. Don went to get Kim and his .44 Magnum while Mario got the fishing equipment and a cooler to put in the skiff. Sally and Evelyn put together sandwiches along with some apples and a thermos of hot coffee. As soon as Don and Kim arrived, all four of them got into the skiff wearing warm float coats supplied by Mario rather than bulky life jackets. Don and Sally wore hip waders while Kim and Ev wore knee high rubber boots.

"Be sure to keep an eye on the pigs," Kim reminded Mario. "They've been fed this morning, but I noticed Daisy has been rooting near one particular spot in the fence and I wouldn't want any of them to get out."

"Don't worry, I'll watch them," Mario assured her. "Go have some fun."

"We're off!" Sally exclaimed as she revved up the fifty horsepower Yamaha outboard and swung the craft away from the Karen Marie's blue and white hull.

As they skimmed, bounced and rolled along the water, Don, Sally, or Evelyn would point out some of the wildlife to Kim. A sea otter here, a harbor seal there and they shouted the identification of each to her above the noise of the engine, the water and the wind. Kim had not previously seen these animals in the wild and she was fascinated.

Within ten minutes they had nearly covered the distance to the large rounded rocks, some of them as large as a house. Suddenly a 2 foot long, silver, attractive fish arched out of the water ahead of the skiff.

"A jumper!" Sally exclaimed. "That was a nice red."

She slowed the skiff to reduce the noise and to watch for more possible jumpers. Another fish jumped to their left and another swirled at the surface.

"Looks like we've got some schooling reds here," Evelyn smiled. "Fishing in the creek might be good if they've moved into the fresh water."

"And if they haven't we can probably catch some out here," Don observed, nodding his head.

"Why are they jumping?" Kim asked. "Are they feeding?"

"They're not feeding, but no one we've talked to really knows," Evelyn answered. "They jump both in the salt water and in fresh water when they're on a spawning run. Some people think it is to loosen the eggs in the females, but males also jump." Smiling she added, "We always like to think they're jumping for joy."

"Yes, but we've also seen them jumping when sea lions and killer whales were nearby and I can't imagine them jumping for joy then," Sally observed as she turned the Whaler in toward shore, cutting the speed so she could see and avoid any rocks just below the surface. A sandy beach soon appeared between two of the large boulders and she expertly beached the skiff there, raising the engine at the last moment to prevent damage to the prop.

"Here we are," she said. "The tide is still coming in so the skiff will be OK." Evelyn tied the bow rope to a stout 6-inch tree 40 feet higher up the beach. They got out of the boat and gathered the fishing equipment.

"Might as well take the cooler," Don noted. "If you three can fish as well as you do everything else we're sure to bring back some salmon." They smiled at the compliment. "But one thing I suggest is that we stay pretty close together in case we run into Mr. Bruin."

As they walked the hundred yards across sand and gravel and among more boulders toward the mouth of the stream, Don walked in the lead and every few steps would say "Hey bear, hey bear" in a loud voice. He's practicing what he preaches, Kim thought as she brought up the rear and remembered Don's words: "Don't surprise a grizz."

Don suddenly stopped, looking down at a patch of sand near the water's edge. "There's somebody fishing here besides us," he observed, as the other three came forward to see what he had found. There in the sand were the unmistakable tracks of bears, one large one and two small ones.

"Female brown and two cubs," Don noted. "They've been here just this morning."

"How can you tell they're brown bears and not black?" Kim asked.

"Look," Don pointed to the larger set. "See those claw marks extending 3 inches ahead of the pads? That's a brown or grizzly. A black bear's claws are not exposed when they're walking... and the print is smaller for a black."

"What should we do?" Kim asked, looking a little nervous.

"Aw, I think it'll be OK," Don replied. "We'll just stay in and near the stream where we can see around us and where any bears can also see us." He started forward again with the others following. "Hey bear....hey bear," his chant began again.

As soon as they reached the mouth of the stream, light gray shapes of fish lying in the two pools immediately became visible. Sally pointed out to Kim that the larger fish were red (sockeye) salmon and the smaller ones were pinks and the pinks were not very good eating.

"You gals try to catch some fish," Don suggested, "I'm going to look around a little." They all knew that Don was sufficiently concerned about the bears that he wanted to maintain vigilance and they were glad without saying so.

"A word of caution," Don added, "if you happen to have a fish on and a bear shows up, break the fish off immediately or cut your line. Also, any fish we catch will be killed and kept under water on this short length of twine I brought. Keeps the scent down."

Kim, Sally, and Evelyn positioned themselves at three places along the side of the hole where they could cast their chrome plated spoons. The wobbling lures had orange plastic egg-like bubbles attached on one side.

In just a couple of casts Evelyn shouted "got one," and the sides of a bright, silvery salmon flashed as the fish leaped into the air in an attempt to escape the hook.

"Nice fish!" Sally called. "About 10 pounds."

In the next hour the three fishermen caught nine premium red salmon, all fresh in from salt water with sea lice still attached to several. Kim landed two of the reds, the largest fish she had ever caught. She had thoughtfully brought her camera and they took turns taking photos of the fish and the fishermen.

Don cleaned the fish and put them in the cooler because he planned to leave right away. Egg clusters from the females were placed in small plastic bags. The cooler was almost full and weighed nearly 50 pounds. The flesh of the salmon was very firm and a bright reddish-orange. Don explained that Alaskans called this species of salmon "reds" because of the flesh color, although the canning industry called them "sockeye."

"No wonder I've never seen "red" salmon on the grocery shelves," Kim remarked. It looked fabulous. She had never eaten really fresh salmon before and she knew this was going to be delicious.

A misting rain started falling and the temperature went down as the wind velocity increased.

"Shall we head back?" Don asked Sally, the skipper of the skiff.

"We've got a nice mess of fish. No use getting drenched. What do you think, Ev?"

"I'm ready," Evelyn replied, reeling in the monofilament line and attaching the hooks on the lure to the rod handle.

Sally reached for the handle on one end of the cooler to help Don carry it, but Don hoisted it to his left shoulder. "Easier to carry this way," Don noted as he started downstream on the cobbles and rocks. Sally, Evelyn and Kim followed. "Heaay bear...here bear," Don began again as he walked.

A few minutes later they were nearing the salt water and could hear the waves rolling in among the rocks above the increasing noise of the wind. They would be facing into the wind on the way back to the skiff. Sally, walking behind Don suddenly grabbed his right arm.

"Don, there's a bear up there in the brush to your left.

Don set the ice chest down so he could see better. No one other than Sally had spotted the bear yet. "Where is it?" he asked looking in the direction Sally was pointing.

"Over there in the brush near the edge of the trees; about 40 yards away," Sally continued pointing.

Neither Kim nor Evelyn had seen it either, but they now crowded near Sally to determine what she had seen. Then the tops of the brush moved and they saw the shaggy brown hair with humped shoulders.

"It's a brown bear, all right," Don noted, his voice now a whisper. "It hasn't seen us yet and it can't smell us because we're crosswind. Let's just wait a minute to see what it's going to do."

The noise of the waves through the rocks and the sound of the wind through the brush seemed to increase as they stood silently watching the bear, a light rain falling.

Suddenly the bear stood up on its rear paws and began nervously sniffing the air; it also looked in their direction. The bear appeared to be nearly 8 feet tall and dark brown with a yellowish patch on the chest. The clearly visible 4 inch-long claws which tipped its front paws looked like mottled sabers.

"Wow! It's huge," whispered Sally.

"He may have picked up our scent," Don whispered. Kim noticed that he reached down with his right hand and unsnapped the retainer strap on the .44 Magnum holster.

The bear raised its nose and continued to sniff the air, again looking in their direction.

"If he comes this way, don't move unless I tell you," he warned his companions in a low voice and took the .44 out of its holster.

Kim noticed her breathing was shallow and her heart was pounding in her ears.

Suddenly the bear dropped to all fours and tore through the brush toward them with unbelievable speed. Kim was ready to run but Sally grabbed her arm and held it firmly. Don quickly raised the .44 and held it with both hands ready to shoot. The bear covered 25 yards toward them in a matter of a few seconds and emerged from the brush at the edge of the beach under a full charge heading straight for them. Fifteen yards away it slowed and stopped. Then it stood up again, snarling and growling menacingly but lowly.

At this distance the bear looked absolutely huge and the four fishermen stood transfixed, fearful of the confrontation with the bear but with no way to get out of it. Don kept the .44 Magnum aimed squarely at the bear's chest. Although a head or neck shot would be more lethal, he knew it was stupid to try sharpshooting in a situation like this. Better to hit the bear and slow it down for more shots than to miss altogether when trying for a head or neck shot.

But the bear had seen enough. Snorting, it dropped back to all fours and loped back into the brush in the direction from which it came.

Don breathed a sigh of relief and put the .44 back into the holster. "He won't bother us anymore." He looked at his companions. Sally and Evelyn were nearly as composed and under control as he was. Kim was pale and very shaken.

Sally was thrilled by the experience. "You know, you won't find one person in 100,000 in Alaska who has been charged by a bear and lived to tell about it. That was the experience of a lifetime! I loved it!"

"Did you see the size of that bruin?" Evelyn asked. "I'll bet he would go 1400 pounds and at least 8 feet tall! Those claws were 4 or 5 inches long!"

Kim stood transfixed. She couldn't believe that all of them had just stared death in the face and yet her companions were thrilled about the size of the bear! "Don, just tell me one thing," she looked at him and the pistol at his side. "Could you have stopped the bear with that pistol if he had attacked?"

"Hell, no!" Don answered. "I would have gotten off a shot or two before he hit us, but there is no way that would have stopped him. Might have even made him mad so he'd really tear hell out of things. Once a bear gets into a group of people you can't shoot anyway because you'll end up shooting the wrong animals. Sort of like the cops shooting in the middle of a fight with several persons involved; a participant or even bystander may be hit."

"Yes," Kim gasped, "but why did it charge us?"

"That was a false charge," Sally corrected her. "That bear was crosswind from us so he could not smell us. Their eyesight is poor and when he looked, he probably wasn't sure what we were but he didn't give a damn and wanted this 'whatever' out of his fishing area. He might have thought we were other bears, but, regardless of specifics, intended to run us off. When we turned out to be something unexpected, he reconsidered and backed off."

Don was very impressed by Sally's steely nerves and explanation. That was almost exactly the way he saw things.

"Well, one bear crisis over. Hopefully, that's it for today," Don chuckled as he picked up the cooler again and started for the skiff 150 yards down the beach. He would pay more attention this time. He was also hoping they did not run into the female with cubs whose tracks they had seen earlier.

The rain began to fall in earnest now, and they were glad to arrive at the *Karen Marie*. Mario had seen them returning in the distance and had put on a fresh pot of coffee. They handed the cooler full of fresh salmon up to him.

"Say, you did all right," Mario remarked as he hefted the weight. "Must have been a lot of reds up there."

"Lots of nice reds and one helluva big bear!" Evelyn said. "A brownie made a false charge on us."

"No kidding? Was he after the fish?"

"He didn't know what we were and wanted to run us off, but when he got a closer look he just ambled off."

"Yes, it looked like he just wanted us intruders out of his area," Evelyn continued. "But he backed off as soon as he had a close look and saw we weren't other bears."

"Close, I'd say REAL close," Kim remarked, smiling now that it was all over.

They tied the skiff alongside the *Karen Marie* and climbed aboard. For the next hour they relived the bear encounter in the warm cabin of the *Karen Marie*, each telling his or her version of the incident.

"I'll tell you one thing Mario," Sally nodded, "the next time I go fishing in bear country I'm taking that sawed-off 12 gauge automatic of yours and some slug ammo. That .44 of Don's is not going to stop a bear of that size."

Finally the bear talk began to fade from the conversation and Mario looked out at the rain pouring down on the vessel. "This cold rain might not be too good for the pigs," he said looking now at Kim. "Should we be doing anything else to provide shelter for them?"

Kim pondered the question before responding. "Well, I would like to put up some simple lean-to shelters for them. Pigs are very sociable animals and they haven't taken kindly to getting back in their individual kennels. I noticed there's some old plywood behind the barn and maybe we could put up a shelter this afternoon so they'll have a place to get out of heavy rain." She thought for a moment. "But you know, what really worries me are the bears. How are we going to keep the bears away. A bear like the one we just saw could kill all the pigs in a few minutes; that would be terrible."

"There are several things we could do" Don pointed out. "And I have one idea that will cause any bear to run 20 miles away before stopping."

"What is it?" asked Sally.

Don smiled. "I won't tell you now but I'll show you later on."

"I know the pigs will appreciate it," Kim acknowledged.

Within fifteen minutes all five of them were pitching in to pull the beat-up, mostly 4 x 8 foot plywood sheets from the barn and begin to erect temporary lean-to shelters for the pigs by leaning the plywood against the old tree they had dragged in. The pigs themselves tried to stay out from underfoot but enjoyed the activity in their pen. They were quick to realize how nice the shelter was going to be, especially when Evelyn and Kim brought fresh straw from the barn and scattered it under the newly erected shelters.

There were more bear tracks and Kim said the tracks seemed to show up every evening as if the bear was checking things out.

That evening Don invited the *Karen Marie* crew ashore for a fresh salmon dinner, which they happily accepted. He and Kim took four of the red salmon from the cooler, now loaded with ice, and walked down the dock to the lodge and into the kitchen.

Don broiled the salmon after injecting them with his own special sauce of fresh garlic, chicken bouillon, butter, soy sauce, and white wine. The salmon were some of the best the entire crew had ever tasted.

The next day they endured a light drizzle as they completed building the lean-to's by nailing the plywood to the old tree lying in the pen. By afternoon their attention had turned again to the bear problem because more tracks had been found near the pen.

"OK, Don, time for your bear idea" Sally smiled at him. "Let's hear it!"

"I'll get it ready and then I'll show you," Don smiled as he disappeared into the barn.

Mario looked out into the bay and saw a vessel approaching. "Say, I don't have my glasses on, but that looks like the *Czarina*. Can you see, Ev?"

"Yep, I think that's it. Hey guys, looks like the *Czarina* coming in!" Evelyn called to the others.

"All right, good timing," Sally noted. "It would be nice seeing Mike, Tracy, and Reed again. And who knows, maybe more adventure."

But the trio did not have any good reports on finding the A-T pack. They had seen a killer whale pack or two and lots of other sea life, but not the important pack.

Mario had made a batch of chili using ground moose meat and a side sauce using a habanero pepper for those who liked it hot. He and Don were the only two who could eat the hot stuff.

With dinner over and they were still enjoying their red wine, Sally was on Don's case again. "OK, Don, what about this answer to the bear problem?"

"All right," Don replied as he walked to the refrigerator and took out 4 strips of uncooked bacon and showed them to the small group.

"I get it," Sally remarked. "That bacon smells so good to the bears that they leave the pigs alone." There were chuckles from the group.

Don took a medium-sized can from his pocket and began wrapping the bacon around it. He then wrapped twine several times around the can to keep the bacon in place. Then he showed them the label on the can: *Starter Fluid.*

"What's the point?" asked Evelyn. "The only engines we have to start here are on the boats and your four-wheeler."

"It seems that large bear has been coming every evening. I'll have a surprise for him this evening." Don walked out to the trail that the bear had been using. He simply laid the can down in the middle of the trail and then walked back to the lodge where the others were watching and chatting about ways to get rid of a bear without killing it.

Suddenly Kim exclaimed "There he comes on that same trail!"

They all looked and there was a large slightly cinnamon-colored brown bear, his head swinging back and forth as if he was sampling smells from air currents. He stopped about 50 feet from where the can had been placed and stood up. This was a huge bear and he was using his nose as a direction-finder. He dropped back to all fours and again began walking on the trail. This time he went directly to the can location and came up with it is his mouth. Swoosh, a misty spray enveloped the bear's head, neck and chest.

He turned around and ran at full speed back down the path but ran into a tree and seemed to be knocked out for several seconds. But then he was up again and running. He disappeared into the trees.

"Wow" Kim said. "Great way to get rid of a bear! Did it hurt him?"

"Naw," Don replied, "But that bear won't come around here for quite a while. And he won't be able to smell or taste anything for the next day or two. That's ether in that can, under pressure."

"I've got to remember that," said Mike. "I often run into problem bears in my field work."

"Great technique" Reed noted.

After coffee and cake they walked over the foot bridge, built by the previous occupants of the lodge, to look at the pigs, the enclosure and the kennels. The pigs heard them coming and were waiting near the fence for goodies or for some attention such as a scratch behind the ear.

"These pigs are perfect," Reed commented. "Just the right size for what we need."

Kim responded, "We're worried that a furry brown visitor may show up at any time, perhaps at night."

"There were bear tracks here when I arrived," Don explained, "and we saw a big brownie this morning just a mile and a half away when we were fishing for salmon. They can be expected to come in here to see what's going on. We're still figuring out what to do for protection for the pigs."

"The last thing we need is bear trouble," said Mike. "Don, we appreciate it when you're aiming to discourage bears from coming around, short of shooting them, that is."

As they walked back to the lodge, Kim spoke to Reed: "Needless to say, I'm extremely curious to know more of the details of your plans. Thus far no one has told me how this testing of the whale's interest and abilities is going to be accomplished. And I am concerned about the safety of the pigs."

"Of course, we'll be glad to fill you in," Reed looked at her sincerely. "And your help is definitely going to be needed."

Don showed them around the lodge and suggested they pick out rooms. Reed picked one next to Kim's while Mike and Tracy selected one of the rooms at the far end. Then they returned to the *Czarina* to get their belongings.

Back in the lodge, they had another round of coffee and tea at one of the lodge's rough-hewn dining tables. Reed proceeded to describe activities of whales in the Sound based on observations they had made over the past three seasons, and how Orcinus orca, the killer whales, had recently been involved in turning a Zodiac over, eating a dog, stealing fish from set lines, turning over two small boats, and taking a boy under water. He described why, for the good of the whales, it was crucial that they identify the particular rogue pack, or perhaps particularly vicious whales within a pack.

"What's a `rogue'?" Don asked.

"It's a term which usually refers to an individual animal that functions alone and is fierce and wild," Reed answered. You may have heard the term `rogue elephant' meaning an elephant that tears the hell out of things, sometimes just to cause trouble. There are rogue tigers which kill livestock and sometimes people. It just seems like a good term for the particular pack, the A-T pack, which we believe is causing much of the trouble here in the Sound. OK?" Don nodded yes.

"Now, what we plan to do," Reed continued to the attentive group, "is to locate the A-T pack and follow them, day and night, until they go on what we believe will be one of their mammal-killing sprees. We will need both vessels there: the *Czarina* with equipment and for observations, and the *Karen Marie* with the pigs and also for observations." It was obvious from the questioning looks on their faces that more explanation would be needed.

"The reason for the pigs," Mike explained, "is so we can observe the whale's behavior in a structured setting. We need to know how they will react to a strange, but what we believe could be an attractive, food source."

Tracy saw the concerned look on Kim's face and spoke to her. "Kim, we don't know how the whales are going to react to the pigs. When we considered this study we tried to arrive at a test animal which was a food animal for people and yet would have some characteristics similar to a person. The pigs came out on top for many of the same reasons they're used for certain laboratory tests, and even the valves from pig hearts are implanted in human hearts."

"We're fully aware of the uncertain future of many of the pigs we raise," Kim responded, her blue eyes somber, "but what good will it do to risk having some pigs killed, a pig sacrifice, for whales?"

Reed looked at her closely. "We suspect that, in addition to the incidents mentioned to you earlier, the orcas may be involved in the disappearance of two people from Nevada who were camping on Slate Island. The island is too small for bears and all their camping gear and food was found intact. We suspect they may have been in the water at a time when the A-T pack came by hunting mammals, but there is no proof. However, if we demonstrate that a killer whale pack can and will take non-standard, non-human food animals in the water in the presence of Homo sapiens, then we can reasonably conclude that they would take people as well, no matter what the so called authorities say about orcas never killing people."

"Right," Mike added, "and if they will kill people, they will undoubtedly eat them as well. If we can confirm, as we suspect, that the A-T pack is really the one causing problems, with perhaps individual responsible whales within the pack, we can take steps to capture and remove those individuals."

"Hell," Mario remarked, "even if you do identify the whales, they'll never let you capture and take any from the Sound. I remember the big fight that arose over Hydrosphere trying to take only two whales a year for research and training. The fishermen kill more than that. I've personally seen them shooting killer whales."

"We can only hope," Reed continued, "that once identification is made we can get enough support to take action. Any politician or bureaucrat who refuses to let us capture and remove rogue killer whales is going to be in the hot seat when the whales kill somebody. The same goes for Blue War and the other preservationist groups."

"But I thought Blue War has done a great deal of good," Kim said.

"Their literature indicates they combat commercial whaling around the world."

"Yes," Tracy nodded, "and we agree with what they have done in several of their 'save the whales' programs. But they have gone too far in successfully fighting to prohibit the limited capture and study of whales when such captures not only do not adversely impact the wild populations, they actually benefit them through research. You're right, Mario, at the present time it is likely that fishermen annually kill more orcas than Hydrosphere may need for their study and training program."

"I can tell you from my work at Hydrosphere," Reed added, "having killer whales at the park to educate people and, yes, to perform for them, has tremendously advanced the cause of not just killer whales but for whales of all kinds. Yet, there are many in Blue War who want to shut down the killer whale facilities at the park and simply release all the whales. We have learned a tremendous amount about the whales, their physiology, diet, and other factors, by having them there to observe and work with. Just recently, in Florida, we had a successful birth of a killer whale. The first time that has been done in captivity and the first time it has been observed and filmed anywhere."

"Yes, but there are lots of people out there," Mario interrupted, "who believe Hydrosphere wants to capture them and display them strictly to make money at the park. Some of the protestors were in Cordova a couple of years ago to wage war against whale studies and tagging, even in the wild."

"Marine parks such as Hydrosphere are there to make money, no question about that," Reed answered, "but at the same time, we're using part of the money to gather a tremendous amount of data about the whales: their physiology, nutritional needs, reproduction, parasites, adaptation to stress, and mental acuity to name just a few. More importantly, the whales we proposed to capture, one every other year for ten years, would have no detrimental effect on the wild population. Perhaps we can figure out a way to get the fishermen to stop killing whales and then we'd be ahead on the count."

Reed paused a moment. "One other thing we are seriously looking at is the possibility of having an exchange program: orcas captured in the wild could be kept in captivity and studied for three or four years and then returned to the place where they were captured. That way we could study the whales and observe them for education and pleasure, and yet return them to the wild."

"I've never had an opportunity to study marine mammals," Kim stated, "but that approach certainly seems reasonable to me."

"Tracy and I aren't marine biologists either, and we know they don't have all the answers," Mike added, "but we believe we're on the right track. Time is important and we need to move ahead promptly. What we want to do, Kim, is to train the pigs to swim from a boat offshore toward the shore when called, perhaps from a distance of 100 yards, the length of a football field. Can we do that?"

Kim quickly responded, "Pigs are very intelligent animals and they're good natural swimmers. I don't believe we'll have any trouble at all once they become accustomed to the cold water."

"How should we start?" Tracy asked.

Kim thought for a moment before answering. "Let's start by food training. Don, let's extend the fencing across the creek and we'll start having them cross to get fed. Let's also deepen it so the pigs will have to swim and not just wade across. The training should go pretty fast, my pigs have high IQs," she smiled and looked thoughtfully out toward the bay. "After the creek we can start taking them a short distance out from shore and let them swim in for food."

"Good, I suggest we get started immediately," Mike said. "Don, how about starting on the fence this afternoon?"

"I'm ready," Don replied as he took his coffee cup into the kitchen.

"One last thing," Tracy added, "the nature of this project should be kept strictly confidential. We don't need any of the animal rights people coming around here doing something crazy. If we need a project code name it could be `Project Barley' because we're using some Alaska barley in the pigs' feed."

Sally and Evelyn went to start on moving the pen, followed by Kim. Don was in the kitchen and selected eight nice potatoes from the pantry, washed them, coated them with corn oil margarine and garlic salt, and placed them in a pan in a 250 degree oven. He then went out to work with Sally and Ev. Don was finding Sally very attractive.

Reed, Mike and Tracy, accompanied by Mario, returned to the *Czarina* to bring some of the electronic gear, notes, and maps into the lodge. They reviewed the maps with Mario to get any advice he may be able to offer with regard to finding and approaching the whales. A general plan was laid out, including using a plane to spot whales again. The photographs of the A-T pack and several others were shown to Mario. They also gave him prints of photos of the saddle areas of ten of the whales in the A-T pack to aid in his identification. He was sure he would not have any trouble recognizing the large bull with the wavy, notched dorsal fin.

"But, you know what?" Tracy added as they went over the photos. "Wouldn't it be better if one of us was on the *Karen Marie* both for whale identification and to better coordinate our efforts? Reed, perhaps you should go with Mario, Kim, and the pigs; one of Mario's deck hands could go with us on the *Czarina*."

Reed pondered the suggestion a moment. "You're right, Tracy. That would be better. We can have audio and video equipment on board both vessels that way and I can help Kim with the pigs," a chore he was looking forward to.

"That Sally is one helluva hand with a boat," Mario stated. "She can go with you on the *Czarina* and Evelyn can stay on the *Karen Marie*."

"Sounds like a good plan," Mike agreed. "Don can stay here and watch over the camp and the pigs, although I'm sure he'd rather go than stay."

"Speaking of pigs, how many are you planning to take at once?" Mario asked.

"I would say about eight and in their kennels," Reed answered. Wouldn't you, Mike and Tracy?" They nodded.

For the remainder of the afternoon, everyone pitched in to extend the fence and deepen the creek by taking gravel cobbles and boulders out of a hole and piling them just below the hole to make a sort of dam. The dam also provided a place to cross the creek wearing only knee-high boots. The pigs were curious and seemed to watch the activity with interest.

At about 4 pm, Kim returned to the lodge to work on the diary and notes she was so careful to maintain. Part of good biological practice, she had learned, was maintaining good records. It would also be a key factor in learning more about how the pigs might react to strange environments.

By the time they quit for the day, at just after 6 pm the desired scene was taking place. Don had moved rocks, some of them weighing nearly a hundred pounds, out of the hole and onto the porous dam. The hole, where the pigs would have to swim across, had been deepened nearly to the tops of Don's hip boots.

"Looks good," Don commented as he surveyed the work. "With no feed for the pigs tonight, Kim should be able to start training with the first feed tomorrow."

Back at the lodge, Don was the first one to get in the shower because he was anxious to start another salmon dinner even though they just had one the previous night. "When they're fresh," he laughed, "you eat 'em." He had decided to cook five of the reds and had them laid out.

In order to save fresh water on the *Karen Marie*, both of the deck hands and Mario showered in the lodge. Sally, freshly showered, came out to help him in the kitchen. "First thing you can do is open some beer," Don smiled. She obliged for both of them. Don was busy chopping two whole fresh elephant garlic bulbs, which he then put in a stainless steel pan with some water, chicken bouillon cubes, white wine, butter, soy sauce, fresh lemon juice and fresh ground pepper and turned it on to boil. There was about two quarts of solution.

"My gosh, you don't like garlic, do you?" Sally exclaimed as the fragrance erupted through the kitchen.

"Oh, I've been known to use a little now and then," Don chuckled as he popped another can of beer. With the fresh fish laid out on the table he cut off the heads and tails and set them aside. "Kim should boil these and include them with the pig feed," he told Sally. "The natives consider the heads a delicacy when they're boiled a couple of hours to make a broth."

"Yes, I've tried it," she replied. "Sounds gross, but it's delicious." She rinsed some brown rice and put it in the electric rice cooker Don always carried with him. She then chopped up a salad.

The others came into the kitchen to observe the proceedings and to have a drink of their choice. Reed, before going to shower, had set out a bottle of his favorite light, single malt scotch whiskey, Balvenie Double Wood.

"This is just like the parties I have at home," Don remarked with a laugh. "Everybody always crowds into the kitchen to be where the action is, but that's just the way we like it."

He filtered the garlic/wine solution through a strainer to remove the large particles and pieces and then took out a very large hypodermic syringe which would hold almost one half pint of liquid. Much to everyone's delight, he filled the syringe with the flair of a good heart surgeon and commenced injecting each of the fresh salmon with the solution. "No use basting them from the outside when you can do it from the inside!" Don smiled as he took another quaff of the Alaskan Amber beer. He laid the fish on two large buttered baking sheets, covered the fish with aluminum foil and placed them in the oven. He would later add small amounts of water or wine from time to time, baste them and turn the fish.

Reed, now freshly showered, was pleased to have an opportunity to visit with Kim. When each of them had sampled some of the Balvenie Scotch on the rocks, she invited him to go out to take a look at the pigs. Reed regarded this as an invitation to solitude, but Kim, in addition to getting to know this professor of marine biology better, was simply curious to know if the pigs would venture across the creek to check out the other side.

"Hey", Don half shouted. "If you're going out by the pigs I've got some freshly-baked potatoes here you can take and give them a treat." He had cut the cooled potatoes into pieces and placed them in a plastic bag, which he handed to Reed.

There was a thick patch of fresh green grass over there which Kim thought would look especially good to the pigs particularly when they smelled the potatoes. Putting on jackets and taking their scotch and the potatoes, they walked up the path to the pen. It was a beautiful, but typically cool evening. Rays from the sun lit up the mountain slope to the east in a brilliant green and the sound of the creek tumbling down the rocky slope could be heard clearly.

The pigs heard them coming and crowded to the fence, hopeful of getting fed. "They're hungry, but they haven't crossed yet," Kim noted. "These are dry land pigs and they don't know what to think of the `deep' water," she smiled. "But they'll learn."

They crossed on the foot bridge to the side away from the pigs and their kennels so the pond they had created was between them and the pigs, who were watching them closely. Kim took out a couple of pieces of potato and waved them so the pigs could see them clearly and she called to Daisy, Petunia, and Minnie by name. She tossed a couple of pieces of potatoe into the grass near the water.

That was all it took for Daisy to decide to swim and she jumped in and swam easily across the pond, but the other pigs balked. They paced back and forth on the shore but would not enter the water. Daisy enjoyed the potato pieces and Kim tossed the rest over to the pigs that had refused to swim. "It will take more training for all of them except Daisy,."

"Well. At least you have one swimmer here." Reed nodded to Kim, who was smiling broadly. "What do you think, more training tomorrow?"

"Absolutely" Kim responded.

Watching the happy pigs, Kim and Reed briefly described each other's backgrounds. Kim was surprised to learn that he had three sons in California. The handsome Reed didn't appear that old. She had been engaged once, she told him, but it didn't work out. Her fiancé had been very egotistical and they finally split. Now she maintained only casual relationships. Just then Sally called from the lodge: "Come and get it!" and they walked back to the lodge feeling very comfortable with each other.

Don and Sally had laid out a sumptuous spread of baked salmon, homemade bread Mario had baked on the *Karen Marie*, cream style corn and a finely-chopped and seasoned green salad prepared by Sally. Vouvray wine from France went perfectly with the meal. After dinner Don put some logs on the fireplace and, before the crackling blaze, they enjoyed some of the Armagnac Mike had brought in from the *Czarina*.

Don was up early as usual the next morning, a Monday, and had breakfast of coffee, orange juice, whole wheat pancakes, crisp bacon and basted eggs ready by 6:30. Kim was also up early to check on the pigs, which were squealing and grunting by now to let her know they were hungry again. The crew came in from the Karen Marie and ate breakfast in the lodge.

Over breakfast, Reed expressed an idea: "Kim, I was thinking about the training. What do you think about blowing a whistle every time you have food for the pigs. They will quickly associate the whistle with the food and soon they'll come whenever you blow the whistle. Should work much better than simply calling, don't you think?"

"A Pavlovian cause and effect...Good idea, but bad timing" Kim responded. "I don't have a whistle... unless I just pucker."

"We can probably take care of that," Mario acknowledged. "A couple of the life preservers on the *Karen Marie* have police-type whistles on them. We'll just borrow one."

"Good," Kim responded, "let's try it."

After breakfast Kim put on her knee high pair of rubber boots, put a handful of leftover pancakes liberally splashed with syrup in a plastic bag and, after stopping at the barn for a 5-gallon bucket of feed, went to the pen accompanied by Mike, Tracy, Reed and Mario. Evelyn had picked up the whistle and brought it out to them.

All the pigs, including Daisy, had returned to their kennels at night so they were on the opposite side of the creek and pond from the crew. Kim kneeled with the feed and pancakes and called to them. She also blew on the whistle so they would begin associating the whistle with food. Daisy and Minnie got into the water up to their shoulders but, for some reason they would not swim the short distance, not even Daisy as she had done the previous night.

Don and Sally arrived after finishing the dishes. "Why don't you just throw them in?" Don asked.

"We're training them, Don, not forcing them," Kim responded. She sat down on the grass to think it over and Reed sat down beside her. "You know," she told Reed, "The pigs need motivation as Daisy had last night, but they just don't know what to do. They want to come across, but the water seems a challenge for them this morning."

"Perhaps we need more food to attract them. Last night Daisy went for the potatoes." Reed observed. "What about trying some varieties of food they really like?"

"No, that would take more time and besides, they can do it." She hesitated, "I guess I'm going to have to show them."

"You mean you're going to swim across?" Reed asked, smiling.

"No, no, I'll just try to lead them across," and she got up and moved toward the stream.

"Don't you want some hip waders? That water's ice cold?" Reed warned.

"No, I'll just wade," and she started across the stream toward the waiting and watching pigs, immediately going over her knee-high boots. As she waded out on the other side, the pigs crowded around her, eager for feed. She tore off small pieces of pancake and fed them to the pigs, especially Daisy who she thought might be the first one to cross. Backing into the icy water once more, she continued waving a pancake to the pigs. As Kim emerged from the other side, Daisy plunged into the water and quickly swam across. As she arrived and went after the small ration of food, Kim blew on the whistle and rubbed her back. Soon all eighteen of the other pigs had crossed and received the rest of the pancakes or, when that was gone, some of the grain and molasses cakes.

Kim then waded back to the other side carrying feed and blew the whistle again. Daisy and the other pigs, ready for more food, quickly followed again. Don led the laughter at the comical sight of the pigs eagerly swimming back and forth across the creek.

"By gosh, you're right," Reed observed, smiling, "they do learn fast."

"They know how to cross now so I won't have to wade anymore," she said, shivering from her wet pants and cold water-filled boots. "But I'll tell you what, if someone has to show them how to swim in that cold salt water offshore YOU do it, count me out!" she laughed and her eyes sparkled.

"I've got my dry suit in the *Czarina* and, if that's what it takes, I promise to swim," Reed smiled. "Now c'mon, let's go get some warm dry clothes on you. As fast as those pigs learn you'll soon have them swimming across Herring Bay."

"Go ahead and change," Don urged, "we'll take care of feeding the pigs."

Mike and Tracy, as well as Reed, were pleased with the progress made with the pigs and they told Kim they were truly glad she had come along.

Back at the lodge Sally had built a nice fire in the fireplace and the coffee pot was on. Don and Sally had cleaned up the dishes and Sally was busily putting three loaves of Don's combo rye and whole wheat bread in the oven. Kim hurried to her room to change.

"Sally, everyone is making this place so comfortable we're not going to want to leave," Tracy complained.

"Nothing wrong with getting spoiled," she responded.

"Say, there's another boat approaching out there," Sally called out. Tracy looked with the binoculars, but they did not recognize the name of the boat *Columbo*.

"We don't know who it is, so mum's the word," Mike reminded them. "Mario, let's walk down to the dock and see who the visitors are."

Mike and Mario arrived at the dock about the same time the boat came alongside the Karen Marie. Herb Bracken of NOAA came out on the deck smiling and threw a line to Mike.

"Hi, Mike. George and I thought we'd better come out and see how you're doing." George Maxwell, Alaska Fish and Game biologist and department head, was piloting the boat. There was no one else aboard.

"Pretty nice boat, gentlemen," Mike observed. "I presume this is another one confiscated by Fish and Game?"

"You presume correctly," Herb responded as the *Columbo* was tied alongside the *Karen Marie* with bumpers between. Mike introduced Herb and George to Mario and they walked up to look at the pigs where Kim, Reed and Tracy joined them. Kim was introduced.

"Good looking bunch of pigs," Herb observed. "About the same size as many we used in the Navy. Have you tried them in the water yet?" he asked Kim.

"Yes, they took their first swim last night and this morning, except Wolfy the boar. We're not going to take him swimming." Kim wondered silently from the remark about the Navy if any of the pigs from Greeley had been used in the programs to which Herb referred.

"Just as well to leave him in the pen," Herb advised. The boars have only one thing on their mind and it's not swimming. Good idea to have him in a separate enclosure but he'll soon dig his way through if you don't keep that fence in good shape." He looked in Wolfy's pen, "Ugly, isn't he?"

"We know we're going to have to watch for bears," Mike noted. "And we need to come up with a non-lethal way to run them off."

"Good thinking," George nodded and then cautioned, "Good idea not to shoot any bears just because they come around the pigs. As you know, one quick way to start trouble with the Department of Fish and Game would be unnecessary bear killing. And *any* bear killing will be considered illegal on this project unless one of them decided to have a *Homo sapiens* for dinner."

In the lodge over coffee, Herb told them things were moving along rather well from their perspective in Anchorage, but Dr. Walker wanted a report on what was going on in the Sound. "One positive development," he said, "is that NOAA will allocate some money from the Bering Sea walrus project to an 'unspecified' marine mammal study in southern Alaska. But", he added, "the funds will be available to you as reimbursement for specific items for which billings are sent through the purchasing department."

"Such as what?" Mike asked.

"Such as actual costs for fuel, boat charter, aircraft support, even groceries so long as they are properly billed."

"That's great, Herb," Reed acknowledged and then turned to George Maxwell. "How are things at Fish and Game?"

"Not bad, not bad, at least we haven't heard too much static yet. Commissioner Pennyworth asked Cynthia for a report and she passed it on to me. I'm glad to get out here personally anyway so I could bring out something that will help communications. I dug up a good confiscated radio transmitter/receiver for this project. Cell phones don't work well out here in the Sound. "

"Better than the one on the *Karen Marie*?" Mario asked.

"Not necessarily better," George answered. "But at least the camp should be able to talk to boats in the Sound, and should reach Valdez, Cordova, and perhaps Whittier with this unit. You'll also be able to talk to

Fish and Game planes and boats in the area if you use the frequencies I'll give you. I suggest you top off one of the tall trees and put the antennae up as high as you can get it; we brought plenty of cable. With this unit Cordova marine radio should be able to patch you through to our Anchorage office; easier to stay in touch."

"Yes, but that has its pluses and minuses," Mike cautioned. "We don't want to be wasting our time on a bunch of unwanted calls from the state or from the feds."

"Hell, just don't answer if you don't want to talk to them!" Herb almost shouted. "Can't get any easier than that."

"Good idea, Herb," Tracy acknowledged. "And we'll all have to be extremely cautious about what is said on the radio."

"Nevertheless, we're glad to have the radio, guys," Reed added, "but we don't know when we'll have it in operation unless one of you two is an expert and can stay here and hook it up for us."

"We study critters, not electronics," Herb smiled. "You're on your own there. But the paper work goes on and I've got to get back to town."

"OK, we appreciate the help, guys," Reed nodded, "We'll be out on the Sound as soon as we've found our pack and the pigs are trained. We don't know when that will be, but we've got to have a date to shoot at. Mike, Tracy, Kim, what do you think about being out on the water in four days? If we plan for that now, George or Herb can arrange with Carl Baker to fly out here in his Cessna so we can plot our strategy for finding the A-T pack."

"The sooner we get started, the better. Kim will do her best, I'm sure, to get the pigs ready," Mike responded.

"OK, we'll tell Carl," George said. "That will be next Saturday, right? And what time do you want him in here."

"Let's say Saturday at 10 am. We'll either go up with him in the plane or have him spot for us and then go out."

"If Carl can't come, we'll send someone else," George added. "We may have one or more of the Fish and Game planes in the area and we'll ask them to stop in if he can't make it. They don't need to know exactly what you're doing, just tell them you're doing some whale research."

"That'll be OK if Carl isn't available," Reed responded, "but he's been an excellent spotter for us in the past and we'd sure like to have him back. I don't need to remind you, Herb, that radio-tagging the A-T pack would have made this task very much easier."

"Nope, you don't have to remind me, but Helen sure didn't go for it. One of the reasons she wanted me out here today was to make sure you weren't `harassing' the whales. By the way, if I can get away in a week or so I'd like to come out and visit the operation. I know you won't know where you're going to be, but keep your radio on and we'll try to find you from the air."

"Remember the project name," cautioned Mike. "There will probably be a hundred or more commercial boats in the northern part of the Sound."

"Will do," George responded.

"And tell Carl to bring out about two weeks groceries for eight people from Bush Camp Shippers," Don added. "They'll know what to send and we have a charge account there."

Back at the boat, George and Herb passed across the radio unit, the antennae, a substantial roll of cable and a set of installation instructions to Mike and the others on the dock. George started the boat, Herb cast off and they departed for Whittier.

As they left, Reed looked at their departing vessel and shook his head. "You know, I like those two but they still operate under the `government employee syndrome.' They can't stand working more than about seven hours a day, with half of that coffee time. I'll bet fifty dollars they have the timing worked out so they can get back to Whittier, catch the train to Portage and drive to Anchorage by 5 pm

Working for the government often destroys individual initiative."

"Fortunately, they're not all like that," added Mike. "Many of the game wardens in the field work twelve hours a day, seven days a week and get paid damned little for it. I have some friends who are game wardens in Wyoming and the amount of time they put in throughout the year is unbelievable. Probably more than most entrepreneurs."

They walked back to the lodge where they piled the radio equipment on one of the unused tables.

"Good luck in getting this thing hooked up," he told Don. "Supposed to have a much wider range than the radios in the boats."

For lunch, Don and Sally prepared grilled salmon patties from the leftover salmon, along with soup and some of the homemade bread. Throughout the day Kim continued training the pigs to respond to calls for food back and forth across the creek. She was pleased to see now that the pigs crossed even when she was not calling them to offer them a reward. It appeared they considered it fun and exciting to plunge into the icy water and rapidly swim the 20 feet across to the other side. By evening she was satisfied they could start the salt water training the next day. But thus far she hadn't figured out exactly how they should go about it. Perhaps, she thought, a raft would be the best way; put a kenneled pig on a raft and pull the raft offshore.

Kim was looking forward to talking to Reed again; this matter of the pigs being used to test the whale's reaction was troubling, but she attributed a good part of that reaction to the fact that she was so fond of the pigs. If she were an uninvolved bystander, she reasoned, a loss of a food animal would not be troublesome. In the present situation she and her companions were eating parts of this species of animal for breakfast almost every day.

Brushing away mosquitoes, she looked around the camp for lumber scraps from which to build a raft. In the rear of the barn she found one 4' x 4' piece of exterior plywood and she pulled it out and took it to the barn. "Don," she asked, "do you suppose you could cut some logs to put under this so we can use it as a raft to float the kennels one at a time for the pig training?"

"Sure," Don replied, "but let me go out in the morning to find some dry logs for the best flotation. Green logs are really heavy and they won't float as high."

Kim was still turning the raft idea over in her mind when 6 pm rolled around and it was time to shower for the day. At the lodge everyone was busy. Don had taken over the radio assembly problem and had the pieces spread out on one of the lodge tables. Mario, Sally and Evelyn looked like they were having fun in the kitchen, and Reed and Mike were working on what appeared to be a video camera on one end of a table while a hydrophone was on the other. Tracy was typing away on a laptop computer. "This place looks like an electronics shop," she remarked as she walked over near Reed. "It's after 6, isn't it toddy time?"

"I'm ready," Reed responded as he got up from the bench.

Don was also ready. "Remind me to stop working on this thing after a couple of beers or I'll have it so screwed up we'll never get it together." He chuckled as he walked to the refrigerator in the kitchen.

"Scotch sounds good to me," Reed laughed. "How about you, Kim?"

"Sounds great, but I'll go shower and be right back."

"I'm going to pass," Mike responded, "I've got to get the autofocus working better on this video camera before we go out again."

"Pass me too," Tracy called, "my typing goes to hell when I'm drinking."

Before dinner, Kim and Reed went for a walk past the dock and along the beach, sipping Balvenie Scotch on the rocks. They enjoyed each other's company, with light-hearted joking and now and then a touch.

Reed suddenly pointed down to the sand. "Oh oh, we've had a visitor on this beach and it was a grizzly, look at the size of those tracks and long claws." These were fresh tracks and he scanned around them to see if the bear might still be near but saw nothing.

Kim wanted no bear contact. "Well, we'd better get back to the lodge, dinner is probably ready."

Over a dinner of beef roast, baked potatoes and gravy, green peas, cole slaw and chocolate cake the entire group was enjoying each other's company and they were becoming friends.

After dinner, Kim outlined her plan for the next step of training the pigs. If a raft were built sufficient to float at least 200 pounds, they could pull the raft toward the L-shaped dock with a kenneled pig on board. Once away from shore the door could be pulled open with a cord and the pig called to shore with the whistle for a food reward. By taking the pigs further offshore in steps, the animals would gradually become accustomed to swimming substantial distances to shore to be fed. They could also experiment with having the pigs swim to a boat offshore if they had a small floating platform so the pig could get out of the water for some food.

"Good idea, Kim," Mike volunteered. "But one question, What if you pull the raft out and the pig does not want to get out of the kennel?

"I think they'll exit the kennels with some food inducement. You noticed how they learned to cross the pond with just a little motivation?"

"Yes, after you taught them how to swim," Reed laughed, rubbing Kim's shoulder.

"Well, I hope they get used to the cold water," Don chuckled. "I'd tackle that brown bear anytime rather than jump in and freeze my buns."

—————— ◆◆◆ ——————

CHAPTER TWENTY FOUR

Contact attempt

O nce again Harry and Ruth Saunders, with the help of Dave and Carol Halloran, coordinated plans to take the children back to Prince William Sound. Larry Saunders, 17, had finally gotten a job bagging groceries and decided not to go on another whale hunting trip because he was trying to save some money for the coming freshman year at the University of Alaska - Anchorage. The other Saunders kids, Sarah and Tim, each wanted to take a friend but the parents argued that three kids on the `Saucy' were enough. This time Sarah would take a friend; next time Tim could take one.

Sarah's best friend was Kelly Masters, also 15 years old. Both attended Service High School in Anchorage and lived in the same part of the city. Kelly had been agitating to go with the Saunders back to the Sound ever since the earlier publicity about the encounter with the killer whales and she was thrilled when Sarah asked her to go. Kelly, 5' 3" tall and 165 pounds, was a plump girl by any standard; even as a baby she had been heavy. Her mother, also substantially overweight, had spoken many times about how she was determined to get Kelly to "get trim," but it never happened. "Seems to run in the family," Ruth Saunders remarked. "Too bad, because Kelly could be a pretty girl if she would lose about 50 pounds."

"Yes, and she eats twice as much as a normal kid," Harry added. "Better take some extra grub if she's going."

Kelly's parents made her promise not to do anything foolish if they did happen to see any whales. "Stay in the larger boats," her couch potato father had belched after his fifth can of beer. "Don't go near the whales in anything small. Too easy to get knocked into the water, and you aren't the world's best swimmer, kid." Kelly promised to take no chances.

When Lenore and Heidi Halloran found out that Sarah was taking a friend they immediately began pestering their parents to also take a friend. To settle the matter, Carol Halloran finally said they could only take one and she would toss a coin to see who it would be. The child not winning this time could take a friend next time. Heidi won the toss and she invited 14 year old Dena Lambert, a very excited fellow student.

"Gee," Tim Saunders complained when he heard the news that every other youngster on the trip was going to be a girl, "that doesn't seem fair. I won't have anyone but a bunch of dumb girls to play with. At least the Halloran's have a dog on their boat; we don't even have that."

"You know, he's right," Dave told Ruth Saunders. "When I was a boy it wasn't much fun to go camping or on a field trip if you didn't have another boy to play with. I think we ought to let him take a friend even if we're a little crowded. This trip will be for only a few days."

Ruth relented and Tim happily called Robin Fletcher across the street. As soon as they had permission from Robin's parents, Tim and Robin began making plans for the killer whale trip. Tim told him about the plans to feed the whales when they found them and how they might be able to establish the first real contact with wild killer whales. It was almost hopeless for the children to try to sleep that night because of the excitement. They were determined to make contact with the whales and show once and for all that it could be done.

The next morning the two families and guests left Anchorage in two automobiles loaded with seven kids, Muffy, groceries and plenty of liquor. They arrived at Portage in time to drive the two vehicles bumper to bumper onto the morning train to Whittier, which arrived and departed half an hour late, as usual. Carol Halloran had made up a jug of margaritas and generous cups were enjoyed by all of the adults before the train left Portage. Once the train was underway, Harry Saunders made the dangerous wobbling trip from his vehicle to the Halloran truck to get margarita refills as the train rocked down the rails from one tunnel to the next. As he was returning, the train entered a completely dark tunnel and Carol did not know if he had fallen off until the train emerged into daylight. Harry was still there, one hand hanging onto the grill of the truck and the other waving one cup of margaritas, the other having been consumed in the tunnel. "My God, get back in here Harry," she shouted out of the window, "you're going to fall off and get killed." Harry managed to stagger back to the truck and, handing the cup with the remaining margarita through the window to Carol, climbed in.

At Whittier the children scampered to unload all of the supplies from the autos and reload them aboard the Saucy and the Primrose. "I'm going over to Cyrus McDuffy's office," Dave told them when the load was mostly aboard the two vessels. "I want to find out if anything new had been reported about the killer whales."

"Naw," Cyrus told him, "we're all so busy here with the commercial fishermen and regular tourists that we haven't paid much attention to the whales for some time. I haven't heard a thing about any excitement with the whales, either. Just the usual sighting now and then."

"What about those people who were doing some studies of the whales?" Dave asked. "What was their name, Mackenzie?"

"Oh yeah, that's Mike and Tracy. I understand they're back out in the Sound again. One of the fishermen said they have set up some kind of an operation at that old hunting camp on Herring Bay on the northwest end of Knight Island. They must still be looking for the whales but damned if I know if they've found any."

"Herring Bay, eh?" Dave noted. "We've been by that old camp. Isn't that the one the state took over after they caught that bunch poaching?"

"That's the one. Supposed to be pretty nice."

Dave started for the door. "Thanks, Cyrus, we'll be out in the Sound for a few days."

"Goin' fishin' or whale huntin'?" Cyrus called after him, remembering the publicity from the earlier whale encounter. Dave smiled but did not answer.

After refuelling at the harbor fuel station and refilling the water tanks, the two boats were at last ready to go. As they motored eastward through Wells Passage, Harry contacted the *Primrose* on the radio and suggested they go first to the north end of Montague Island in southern Prince William Sound because the north end of the Sound would still have too many fishing boats and the whales would likely avoid that area. The maps showed an anchorage called Stockdale Harbor near the north end of the island and they decided to stop there.

Sarah and Tim took turns piloting the *Saucy* and Lenore took over the *Primrose* as they rolled through 3 to 4 foot seas on the way to the anchorage.

Carol made more margaritas and the kids maneuvered the boats close enough to allow passing a plastic screw top container over to the Saunder's boat. Harry, laughing and staggering, almost fell in as he reached over to grasp the jug.

When they reached the anchorage in late afternoon, the kids, fortunately experienced, took the boats in to a safe spot for the night. The two boats were anchored side by side and lashed together with bumpers between. The parents all decided to have cocktails aboard the *Primrose* and asked the children to show their independence by preparing dinner from the food they had set out. The kids did a thorough, if not delectable, job of getting the dinner ready. By the time it was over the parents went to bed saying they were "sleepy."

The kids watched some ocean adventure movies on the CD player after dinner. After the movies the group of seven children talked about killer whales. Lenore, looked up to as the oldest and the wisest of the group, told them about her research into killer whales and that there was no evidence they had ever attacked a human. She also described the assistance orcas gave to whalers in Australia and how "Old Tom," the male killer whale, was a favorite of the whalers for several decades.

"But killer whales are much larger than a great white shark," Lenore cautioned, "and we shouldn't take any chances if we find the whales. And remember," she continued, "the whales may seem rough and dangerous, but in their own way they may actually be trying to demonstrate their interest. Let's do our best to try to communicate with them; we may be able to understand better than adults what the whales are trying to tell us."

They chatted excitedly until the parents ordered them to bed at 10:30 pm. There was ample light at their anchorage to have played a baseball game.

The next morning, a Friday, the parents arose late complaining of headaches, but nothing a bloody Mary wouldn't take care of. After a bloody Mary each, Carol and Ruth managed to prepare breakfast while Harry and Dave discussed where they should go for the day's search for the whales.

"By God, we've looked plenty in the interior islands and coves," Harry stated over his second bloody Mary. "And we didn't find them. I say we ought to go into a different environment, like the side of the island facing the North Pacific."

"Sounds good to me," Dave replied. "I'm damned tired of looking for 'em, and if we don't find 'em this time it's all over for the Hallorans this summer."

After a late breakfast and two rounds of margaritas were over, the two vessels pulled anchor. They headed on a northerly course, turned east for forty-five minutes and then southeast past the northeast end of Montague Island. The geologic "fabric" and glaciation of this island had created complex indentations which closely resembled a giant `E'. Turner Bay and Zaikof Bay formed the two indentations in the E, and Zaikof Point the bottom of the E. As the two vessels cascaded their way around Zaikof Point in four foot seas, the character of the waves changed. Where previously they were encountering relatively low swells, they now found the two small pleasure boats were bucking large rollers and breakers arriving from the huge stretch of the open Pacific. Two of the children became seasick in the 7 to 8 foot waves and it soon became obvious that the pleasure boats were no match for this type of water. "Christ, Harry," Dave called on the radio, "We can't hack this kind of water with our small boats. We'd better get the hell out of here."

"Amen," Harry responded. "But how are your margaritas holding up?"

"Fine, fine," came the response, "we're not going to run dry."

As they traveled northward, once more passing Zaikof Point, Tim spotted the dorsal fins of what looked like a group of about a dozen killer whales swimming south between the boats and the shore. He alerted the others. The whales were headed toward the rough water on the open Pacific side of the island. As they watched the whales through binoculars from the bobbing, rolling boats, the animals seemed to have an aggressive, fast-moving manner. Even their blowing at the surface seemed ominous. The large male's dorsal fin was very straight, tall and sharp.

"Gee, those whales look scary," Lenore remarked. "I'll bet those are some of the transient killer whales I read about which feed mostly on mammals rather than fish."

"They look different all right," Dave, her father, agreed. "Definitely don't look like the type you'd want to try to make friends with."

Aboard the *Saucy* excitement was running high. "Do you think we can try the hydrophones on them?" an inexperienced Robin asked Tim, who was watching the rise and submergence of the black dorsal fins as the orcas passed in the swells to the southwest.

"No. it wouldn't work, Robin, you need pretty calm water before you put out a hydrophone, and we wouldn't dare turn off the engine in these rough seas."

The boats continued northward for forty-five minutes and then turned northwest past the E shaped end of Montague Island. The severity of the waves became progressively subdued as they left the proximity of the open North Pacific.

"Harry, what do you say we find a sheltered place to anchor?" Dave called to the Saucy on the CB radio. "This rough water gets tiresome in a hurry."

"How about the Bay of Isles on the east side of Knight Island?" Harry replied. "There are lots of rocks on the south side of the bay, but once you get inside there's no rough water. There are usually some seals there, too. Good a place as any to run into the whales."

An hour later they were approaching the entrance to the Bay of Isles. Lenore, watching through binoculars, thought for a moment she had seen a black dorsal fin 300 yards south of the entrance, but the fin had disappeared and she saw nothing else as confirmation. The two boats entered the bay carefully on the north side to avoid the rocks both at and just below the surface, and the water became much smoother once inside. Even the sun seemed to shine brighter. The children on the two decks scanned eagerly for various types of wildlife. They saw several harbor seals on and near the rocks as they entered the bay, and they were thrilled to see a group of four small gray mammals they recognized as porpoises, but they weren't sure what kind.

Dave got out his camcorders and began recording the passing scenery, the kids, the dog, and each other's boats. He tried to get the porpoises with the zoom telephoto lens on his camcorder unit, but the creatures were visible near the surface only momentarily when they rose to blow.

Lenore, always a good student, referred to her *Handbook of Whales and Dolphins* and found that the best matching descriptions were described under the suborder Odontoceti. She did not know the meaning of the Latin terms and was not even sure how to pronounce them. How the names were selected didn't make sense either because mammals which seemed to be closely related had totally different names. She was puzzled why the people conferring the names didn't have better organization. But, using the photographs in the book she found the family Phocoenidae, the true porpoises. The photograph of the harbor porpoise seemed to best fit the animals they had just seen, and its Latin name was Phocoena phocoena.

The scientist who named that one must have ran out of a choice of names, she thought. The harbor porpoise was described as a small (4 feet long, 100 pounds), chunky, rather shy and secretive mammal which did not ride the bow wave of boats the way other porpoises did, but tended to remain aloof and in small groups. It was considered, according to the reference, a likely prey for both great white sharks and killer whales.

"Look at this photograph in my handbook," Lenore told Heidi and Dena. "Those were probably harbor porpoises we just passed back there between the rocks. They're not very big but are common in Alaska waters. But listen," she spoke up so everyone on board could hear her, "Killer whales sometimes feed on porpoises like the ones we just passed!" She relayed the same information via the CB radio to the *Saucy* where Sarah, Tim, Kelly and Robin heard her message. Lenore was proud that she had a possible identification, especially the fact that the small sea-bound mammals were sometimes prey of killer whales.

"Maybe we'll see some killer whales in this bay!" Robin exclaimed, much more excited about seeing the whales than Tim, who nodded agreement. With the possibility of seeing whales again, Tim was reminded of the previous experience with orcas and, subconsciously was afraid to get close to them again. If his older brother Larry was there he would feel better, he thought.

The two boats proceeded carefully on into the bay and, within ten minutes, dropped anchor in water only 40 feet deep and 100 yards from shore. Once past the rocky south shore they found that the bay opened into a delightful cove 300 yards across with precipitous cliffs on two sides and a steep but timbered mountain side on the north. A gravel beach with splotches of sand graced the base of the slope. The location was well protected from the wind and waves of the Sound and only gentle swells occasionally rolled across the serene surface.

The water was relatively clear in the bay and, with the aid of polarizing sun glasses, they could see rounded cobbles on the bottom reasonably well. Anchors were dropped and once again the two boats were tied side by side with bumpers between.

"Little shallow for halibut," Dave noted, "but I'll drop a line over anyway just in case."

Ruth Saunders saw an opportunity to get the four kids on board the Saucy out of the crowded quarters on the boat and onto shore. "Carol," she said, "It's almost 1:30 and the kids haven't had lunch yet. Why don't you and I make a picnic lunch so they can go in to shore and have some fun on the beach?"

"Good idea, Ruth. Lenore, get the kids organized to go ashore... and please take Muffy," Carol Halloran said, "she's going to go crazy on this boat and that beach is a good place to let her run."

"OK, Mom. Hey, good idea guys. Let's take the dinghies and go to shore for a picnic! And it's so sunny we'd better take our shorts or swim suits!"

The idea was greeted with enthusiasm by all the kids, who were tired of being crowded into the small space on the pleasure boats. They scurried to get into their bags for their shorts and light tops. While the adult males on the boats were busy with setting halibut baits and mixing more margaritas, Ruth and Carol hurriedly assembled sandwiches, fruit, cookies and soda and placed the lunch in two knapsacks. By the time the lunches were ready, the kids had placed the dinghies in the water and set in them the lunches, a battery-powered tape player to provide music, life preserver vests to serve as cushions to sit on and a couple of fishing rods and frozen herring bait in case they decided to fish. With the calm water and a short distance to shore, no one suggested they wear the preservers.

Lenore, Heidi, and Dena got in the Halloran dinghy, the *Ace*, along with the knapsacks, plastic bag with extra clothing and the tape player, also bagged to keep it from getting wet. Carol handed pure white Muffy to Lenore while Heidi took the oars. Sarah, Kelly, Tim, and Robin got in the other small craft, the *Spice*, along with the fishing rods and a half dozen foot long frozen herring in a plastic bag. The craft sank low in the water, especially on the end where Kelly was sitting, but, with no waves, all seemed well. Sarah took the oars of the second dinghy.

As they rowed toward the beach they got into a mock race with Heidi trying to show she could beat Sarah at rowing even though Sarah was two years older. But Sarah won amid the cheering of her four passengers. On the beach the kids were thrilled at the feel once again of solid ground beneath their running shoes. The clouds had dissipated, allowing the July Alaska sun to display some of its power. The temperature climbed to 80 degrees on the beach, an extremely warm day for an area bordering the icy waters of Prince William Sound.

High up on the beach they found some logs which had been stripped clean of any bark and tossed up by some past storm. There they ate the late lunch with the sun shining warmly. Kelly complained that it was too hot. But it was good to be there on shore with lots of room and they didn't even turn on the tape player. During lunch, Lenore told them another killer whale story. She had read of bull killer whales sinking boats larger than either the Saucy or the Primrose when angered. One such verified incident took place in Washington state when a research group had netted a female killer whale and the male came to her rescue and sank the boat by ramming it. Unfortunately, both the female and male were killed by rifle fire before the boat sank. The children loved the killer whale stories.

With lunch over, convenient bushes were found and clothes were changed. Halters and shorts for the girls and swimming suits for the boys. The roly-poly bulges of Kelly Masters were emphasized by the skimpy attire and she had obviously gained weight since she last wore the purple shorts and halter.

Lenore had brought along a Frisbee and she, Tim, and Robin began tossing and catching the flying disc. Muffy was learning quickly how to chase and catch the plastic disc on the fly and the kids laughed and cheered every time she was successful. The other four children went for a walk along the beach looking for interesting shells and floats lost from fishing nets. They particularly prized the green glass floats used in the past by Oriental fishermen before a switch was made to plastic.

Offshore, the Saunders and Halloran adults were enjoying the afternoon sun and another batch of margaritas while they played bridge on the deck of the Saucy. Between hands Dave took a few minutes to pan the scene with his camcorder. "That'll be nice to look at next winter," he remarked.

With an uncomfortable number of fishing boats in the northern part of Prince William Sound, Tinga's group had been cruising the southern islands area, feasting here and there on salmon schools they encountered as the salmon swam northward toward their spawning streams. Feeding had been good and the whales were having no problem getting all the salmon they could eat each day. But now they hadn't fed for almost twenty-four hours and hunger pangs were beginning.

As they cruised slowly half a mile offshore from the Bay of Isles, waking up from the afternoon nap, Ming had been cruising ahead of the others and happened upon a foolish seal several hundred yards from shore. Catching it just ahead of the rear flippers, she cracked its spine, thus disabling it. The seal became an instructional aid for the young whales, which soon had it bleeding profusely from open cuts and wounds as they dashed and tore at it. As the seal slowly died, two of the adult females showed the younger ones how to cut and tear the animal into sizes more easily swallowed.

Catching and eating the seal sparked the interest of the young whales in hunting more mammals and they made their desires known to the others through signals and actions. Tinga's natural inclination to catch, kill, and eat mammals became aroused. The pack began circling, with communication whistles and calls echoing through the island waters. Several of the whales breached and struck the water surface with a resounding splash, while Kray slapped the water surface with his large, downward-curved flukes. Other marine mammals heard the calls, much as prey animals in a jungle might hear the roar of lions without knowing which of them would be the lion's next victims.

Any whale preferring to catch more salmon or some other fish, rather than hunt mammals as the pack now seemed to want to do, could go off in another direction because it could easily find and rejoin the group later. But none declined; they were all eager for the excitement of the hunt again and looked forward to the chase and the taste of flesh of a warm blooded animal.

Tinga called to them and they formed the hunting formation with she, their leader, near shore. They were always in familiar territory in the Sound and the entrance to a bay, where they had caught both seals and porpoises before, was recognized. The entrance had a large number of rocks and small islands on one side. Now seriously hunting, they swam northward and then turned to the west into the passageway to the bay.

"I'm tired of losing," Harry told them as he threw down his cards. Hell, let's just drink margaritas and enjoy the weather. In the small galley he poured a can of Foster's lager beer into the blender, followed by a can of frozen limeade concentrate, a dash of triple sec and half the limeade can of Sauza Gold tequila. The blended mixture was poured over crushed ice.

As he was mixing the drinks, Ruth put some Mariachi music on the tape player of the Saucy and turned the volume up. Even the kids 100 yards away on shore could hear the trumpets, guitars and singing.

"And I thought kids were the only ones who played loud music," on shore Lenore complained to the others. "We're enjoying the sunshine and quiet for a change and listen to that noise."

The normally cold sand had warmed to the point where they also took off their shoes to experience going barefoot, a rarity in Alaska. Muffy was running herself ragged chasing the flying blue disc.

Harry Saunders, setting down the half-full glass of the freshly-made margarita, decided to reel in the line on the halibut rod hanging over the end of the Saucy to check the bait. As he did so, he noticed a swift, 4 foot long, gray shape swim under the boat near the bottom, followed by three more.

"Say Ruth, Dave, Carol, it looks like those small porpoises we saw in the water on the way in here may have followed us. They just swam under the boat. Ruth, turn that damned tape player down and I'll tell the kids. Maybe they'd like to come out and try to feed the little buggers some herring."

One of the porpoises surfaced to breathe 20 yards away; it seemed to do so very quietly and secretively and immediately submerged again. Even with the tape player off, they could barely hear the blow. As soon as the halibut lines were reeled in, Dave and Carol Halloran stepped across to the *Primrose* to get their video camcorder and still camera.

Harry called toward shore "Hey kids! Those four porpoises, or whatever we saw on the way in here, are near the boats! Come out and try to feed some of that herring to them."

"Hurry up while they're still here," Carol called. "But get your clothes on and wear life preservers."

"ALL RIGHT!" the kids said almost in unison as they dashed to get their clothes and shoes back on. Lenore, as the oldest, reminded them that they were also to wear the orange life preservers. She placed Muffy in the small boat that she would paddle and, with all aboard, Lenore and the others paddled both small craft toward the boats anchored offshore.

"We'll stop off and get the hydrophone and more herring," Lenore called to the others as she rowed toward the anchored boats. "Go on out and see if you can feed them some of the herring you have in the bag. The book said they eat herring and that might keep them around for a while."

Sarah began rowing strongly to get out past the two anchored boats as soon as possible. "Get the herring ready," she told Kelly and Robin, who were not fishermen and really didn't relish the thought of picking up the dead, smelly, slimy silver fish. They simply opened the plastic bag as their contribution to the effort.

Lenore reached the two anchored craft and picked up the hydrophone and more herring. The two dinghies were rowed out further from the anchored boats. All the kids but the two rowing were anxiously looking into the water for the porpoises but they could see nothing yet. "Where are they?" Sarah asked.

"They were circling under the boats about 20 feet down but then they headed out further into the bay." Dave Halloran called. "They seem to be acting nervous the way they were darting around. Wonder if they'd drink a margarita, might settle their nerves." He and Harry laughed. But the next time the porpoises surfaced to breathe all four were further out toward the mouth of the bay.

"Where are they now?" Sarah called back to the boats. "Should we throw in some herring?" The four porpoises rose in unison to blow but now 40 yards away and appeared to be heading toward the more open water of Prince William Sound.

"There they are!" shouted Heidi excitedly. "But it looks like they're leaving. Row a little further out and we may be able to get them to return!"

Sarah again began rowing and Heidi took one herring from the bag and threw it toward the spot where the porpoises had been seen earlier. Muffy, in the other dinghy, stood with her feet on one of the small seats and began to whine.

"They don't seem to be under the boats now," Ruth called. "But maybe they'll come back for the herring. Tim, throw out another one and we'll see if they'll return."

The tossed herring splashed into the water. A stillness fell over the cove as all the adults and the children strained to both watch the sinking herring and to see if the porpoises might return.

◆◆◆

At the mouth of the bay, Tinga's group split into two parts: eight whales, including Tinga, entered the mouth of the bay. The eleven others circled among the large rocks and small islands just outside the bay mouth. They were fully aware of several seals taking refuge on ledges and in shallow areas among the rocks. Occasionally a whale would do a spyrise so its head was above the water surface to visually locate a seal and to determine if the seals were vulnerable to being scared into deeper water or plucked off a ledge.

Upon entering the bay mouth, Tinga and her group's sonar had detected the four harbor porpoises and their location in the bay. Knowing the shape of the bay, they realized there would probably be no escape from the enclosure for the small mammals unless they swam into extremely shallow water among the rocks, something the porpoises hardly ever did.

Tinga's group of eight split into two parts, she and three other whales swam below the surface, making almost no sound, along the rocky and island-studded south side of the channel leading into the bay. The other four whales lagged behind Tinga's group and stayed on the right side of the 200 foot wide channel to preclude any escape through that avenue. As usual when hunting, the whales kept sonar to a minimum. The water was clear enough to see the bottom and any obstructions ahead and the element of surprise could result in a kill.

A seal raced into the rocks ahead of them before they could launch a pursuit, although they hesitated at the location long enough for Tinga to rise above the surface to look the situation over. The seal surfaced and peered nervously from the shoreward side of two large boulders. The seal was safe; Tinga knew it and the seal knew it. As the pack moved on, they detected people sounds and splashing in the bay ahead, around a slight turn in the channel leading to the head of the bay. They could not determine the location of the porpoises yet, but they knew the small mammals lay ahead. In unison the whales surfaced to blow as they rounded the bend.

In an unusual action, the leader of the four porpoises had decided this enclosed cove was not a safe place to get away from the black and white hunters and they began a run in shallow water on the west side of the cove, trying to get back out to the rocky shore or further out in the Sound.

The explosive "whuff!" as the whales blew, quickly followed by "ssss" as they inhaled, echoed throughout the still cove as four killer whale dorsal fins disappeared below the surface on the west side of the bay. As Tinga and the other three whales rounded the bend in the channel, they had a clear sonar view of the entire bay. The picture 150 yards ahead was taken in immediately by echolocation even though visibility was no more than 70 feet. There were two vessels and two smaller ones a short distance away. Swimming away from the vessels and toward the whales were four porpoises at high speed. Near the vessels some small dead fish were drifting down from the surface for reasons none of the whales could understand.

The whales now clearly detected the four porpoises making a run for safety on their side of the cove. Four of the whales would cut off the porpoise's path in the shallow water on the west and the other four on the east would guard against the porpoises turning back or heading further out into the deeper water of the cove. A trap was thus set. The porpoises realized there were killers ahead but they thought their safest path was in the shallow water closer to shore and they swam at full speed.

The eight whales rose in unison to the surface to breathe before the action of catching the porpoises started. Their acute senses detected their four companion whales approaching from the other side of the channel. At times like this the brains of the whales became large sound and sonar processors, able to process and discern signals from their own sonar and from that of the other whales, producing a three dimensional acoustic view of all the action. Submerged, they surged ahead, anxious for the chase and the kill.

The porpoises, terrified at the approach of the whales, split into two pairs. One pair panicked toward the west side of the channel and crossed the path of the whales on that side. After just a couple of jumps and some quick turns, one of the porpoises was captured by one of the whales which bit the rear third of its body to sever crucial swimming muscles. Thus crippled it was released near the surface to swim feebly for a short time before being taken again. The second porpoise was killed immediately when its head was caught between dagger-like teeth. Tinga and her three companions caught the other two mammals and likewise crippled them by severing tail flexing muscles. They took them to the larger group of whales waiting further out in the Sound where they were eaten.

———— ◆●◆ ————

Carol had been watching with binoculars and had seen the commotion further out in the bay. "Hey, it looks like killer whales may have gotten the porpoises! If you kids want to try to interact with them, why don't you try to entice them to come in here near the boats?" Although she had a deep-seated fear of the huge predators, she wanted the kids to have a chance to try their possible interaction with the whales.

"Helluva deal!," Dave half shouted. "We been looking for the damned whales for a couple of weeks and now they're coming to us! Let's make the most of it. Get your cameras ready." He then turned to the children, "OK, kids, this could be what you've been waiting for, try to get those whales to come in here where we're anchored!"

Lenore asked, "Where are they?"

Carol responded "They're up there to the north near the entrance to this cove."

Lenore said: "Looks to me that we're in a good spot." They were about 30 yards from the two larger boats. "Let's make some commotion!" Lenore urged them and she and Sarah began slapping the surface of the water with their small oars.

Carol was still watching with binoculars and she saw eight dorsal fins as the whales surfaced to breathe. They were headed toward the dinghies and boats. She shouted to the kids: "They're headed this way! Get some herring ready to throw out?"

"We're ready!" yelled Tim. Muffy was nervously whining.

"Quiet!!" Lenore told the other kids and they all stopped talking to listen and watch.

Tings and the other seven whales, after making their porpoise kill, turned their attention to the area near the boats and what might be happening there. They had heard the slapping at the surface, something they had heard before when near these particular boats. Ming, a whale that was sort of a joker in the pack, began swimming toward the boats and the others followed. This might be fun, Ming was thinking.

Sitting quietly in their small craft, the kids waited almost breathlessly to see what the whales, which had disappeared, might do next. Muffy continued whining. Suddenly, eight swiftly moving whales, which now looked enormous, surfaced 50 yards away to exhale and breathe in unison. Upon hearing the whales and then seeing the black dorsal fins of the large carnivores approaching straight for them, the bravado displayed previously by the children suddenly disappeared and they felt extremely vulnerable as the large predators neared. "I'm scared," Kelly moaned. "Me too," echoed Robin. "Let's go back to the boats."

"No! This is the chance we've been waiting for!" Sarah screeched at them. "Stop whining and let's try to communicate!" Then she shouted to Lenore: "Quick, the whales are coming, put out the hydrophone."

"The phone is ready!" Lenore replied. "Throw out some herring!!."

Tim remembered the terror of the previous encounter with the whales and told Lenore: "I want to go back to the boat. I'm scared." He was ignored as the other kids focused their attention on attracting the whales.

"Tim, throw out more herring," Harry called from the boat. "Maybe the whales'll start feeding on them."

The kids threw out two herring as two of the killer whales passed under the anchored boats like large black torpedoes at such a high speed that the bulge of the water at the surface rocked both dinghies. Six more whales then passed under the two small craft; two of them were swimming upside down as if having fun.

The whales disappeared but the kids and their parents knew they were coming back. It was frightening that these large predators could disappear so easily and quickly. The kids again started slapping the surface with their paddles and tossed out two more herring. Muffy had started barking excitedly.

All eight whales turned around leaving only footprints at the surface and started once more toward the two small craft and the two larger ones at reduced speed. Ming was now in the lead and she rose near the small craft with the white, noisy creature. She rose in a spyrise so her eyes were above the water level, thus giving her a view of what was on or above the surface. She saw the kids, their paddles and the small animal that was making the noise. She again submerged. The other whales were now slowly cruising 30 feet below the surface and watching Ming. They paid no attention to dead fish occasionally drifting down from near the small craft.

"I got it, I got that spyrise!" Dave Halloran crowed, looking at his recorder. "Let's see what they're going to do next."

"I think I got it too!" Ruth Saunders echoed from the deck of the Saucy. "What about you, honey?"

Harry Saunders was busy with a 35 mm with a telephoto lens. "I think so."

The parents were thrilled when the female killer whale rose near the dinghies and continued to tape and photograph the exciting events. Over the speaker on the hydrophone/recorder they could hear whale whistles, clicks, pops and sounds like squeaking door hinges.

"Wait'll Anchorage TV sees this!" Dave Halloran chortled. "Throw more herring!" he called to the children in the *Ace*, "And slap the water, maybe they like that."

One of the young male orcas swam up and gently seized the paddle Sarah had been using to slap the water. It swam off with the paddle just below the surface. "Hey, one of them got my paddle!" she yelled. All the kids watched in fear thinking a whale might come after them next. But the whale turned around, released the paddle in the water beside Sarah and then submerged. "But now it brought it back!" she yelled.

"Maybe they like the paddles!" Lenore smiled. She resumed slapping the surface.

Ming wanted to have some fun today. She rose vertically under the small craft with the white animal, raised it 8 feet above the surface and gave it a flip. All three kids and equipment, including the small white animal, were thrown into the frigid water.

The parents, still filming, saw the raft raised from the water and tossed as easily as a seal would throw a ball from its whiskered nose. Sarah screamed as she saw the craft and its occupants fly through the air. Two camcorders on the boats took in the action, but, with the realization of what had happened, pandemonium broke loose among the Halloran and Saunders adults.

"My God, they might get the kids!" Ruth Saunders shouted. "Do something, Harry."

As the three children in the water coughed and cried for help, the kids in the other small craft tried to help them but they could not pull them aboard. Lenore, Heidi and Dena fortunately had their life preservers on and did not sink below the surface, but they would have to get out of this cold water quickly. Lenore, holding onto the side of the *Ace*, saw the best opportunity. "Let's turn this over and try to get in!" she shouted to Heidi and Dena, who were both gasping for breath.

With the craft flipped, Tinga and her companions rapidly surveyed the situation with the creatures struggling on the water surface. They scanned them with echolocation to evaluate size, bone, fat, outer covering, construction. Tempestuous Tyree had focused on the one animal what was much like those eaten before, the white one. But this one was small and seemed like a waste of effort to kill and eat.

Ming, still looking for fun, spotted the small white animal swimming at the surface. She swam directly under it so her tail flukes were just below the animal and, with a quick flip, threw the animal end over end 30 feet in the air. The dog landed with a splash, looked around dizzily and then swam toward the kids in the water.

The whales were circling, watching and listening. They had no interest in trying to make a meal of these creatures and their indigestible padding.

Harry was confused, uncertainty and alcohol clouding his brain. "Should I swim?" he asked and then answered himself. "No, no, you fool, get the gun!" He staggered into the cabin, camera hanging from his neck, and grabbed the .270 Winchester he kept on a wall bracket near the wheel. His mind cleared a little and he decided he couldn't shoot near the kids but he could shoot into the water. Just as he brought the rifle to his shoulder Ruth pushed the barrel into the air. "No, Harry, you can't shoot into the water, you might hit one of the kids!"

Dave Halloran had untied the *Primrose* and the *Saucy* and he started the engine of the Primrose. Carol pulled the anchor and they headed toward the children struggling in the water. "Dave, hurry, HURRY!" Carol pleaded. "Get them out of the water!"

Lenore had succeeded in turning the dinghy over and she pulled herself in. Then she helped Dena and Heidi get in. They were all shivering, but felt safer in the small craft. In the confusion, no one gave a thought to look for the whales and what they might be doing.

Dave Halloran stopped the *Primrose* between the two dinghies and pulled the kids aboard. The kids who had been dumped in the water were shivering and still frightened. Muffy was caught with a long-handled fishing net and brought aboard.

With these creatures rejected as food, all eight of the whales decided to depart. Their collective intuitions warned them that there was something ominous developing about this situation, particularly with the larger craft now located near the remaining animals in the water.

"Well Christ then, I'll shoot in the air!" Harry Saunders exclaimed as he pushed Ruth away. He began shooting the bolt action rifle toward the cliffs. Kaboom, kaboom, four shots echoed through the rock-enclosed bay, the empty brass shell cases fell to the deck of the boat.

The sensitive hearing of Tinga and the others detected the sharp sound and knew that this was the creature at the surface sending dangerous, high speed objects which could injure or kill animals of their kind. They could feel the concussion from the sound even though the projectiles did not enter the water. Tinga had seen the dorsal fins of whales perforated, and some whales which died, after being struck by objects propelled by the noise.

It was clearly time to depart. Tinga signaled the others to move out; they had more hunting to do. Her plaintive, piercing call could be heard clearly over the speaker on board the Primrose. The eight whales moved away from the scene quickly and back toward the Sound where the others waited for them.

With the two dinghies in tow, the *Primrose* motored back over to the

Saucy and the two boats tied together again. The wet kids are taken to get dry clothes from their wardrobes.

"That was one helluva close call," Dave said. "Those orcas could have killed one or more of the kids. We'd better not try this again."

Sarah voiced her opinion, "They could have killed someone but they didn't. We have proven again that they won't kill people and maybe they'll communicate when we know how."

"Yeah," Tim added. "It was scary out there but they tipped only one dinghy and that may have happened because Muffy was in that one."

The chatter about the whale encounter went on for another hour and the three kids were now in dry clothing.

"OK, OK," Ruth Saunders told them. "Let's take a break and have drinks and dinner. You kids will feel better and we can hear more of your side of the story."

They all gathered on the deck of the *Primrose* and exchanged views of what happened.

Carol had them laughing when she told them about Muffy flying so high end over end but yet came away with no visible injuries. Muffy was chewing on a Milkbone.

"We found the whales all right," Dave told the group on the deck of the *Primrose.*

"And we had a close call. Those orcas could have killed the kids in a few minutes time. The people were right who told us to stay away from the whales."

"But we didn't find them, they found us!" Tim pointed out. "And we don't even know if that was the group we were looking for."

"In Whittier," Harry said, "Cyrus told us those people looking for the whales are at a camp on Herring Bay just the other side of the island. Why don't we head for that location tomorrow? We can tell them what happened."

"The whales could have killed everyone in the water," Robin pointed out. "But they didn't."

"True," Dave Halloran replied, feeling the effects of the tequila, "but firing that .270 may have convinced them we weren't going to be pushovers."

Ruth summed it up: "It was a good encounter but those orcas are so big and fast they could kill someone in a matter of seconds. Instead of us trying to communicate with them, perhaps we should leave it to the professionals."

"Damn good idea," Dave Halloran replied. "This is twice now the kids have come close to being a snack for the orcas. Let's get back to Anchorage tomorrow but we'll stop to see the whale hunters at Herring Bay."

There was more conversation over dinner, but none of the kids wanted to get close to the orcas any more, at least the way they were approached this time in small dinghies.

———— ◆◆◆ ————

After the encounter with the boats in the bay, Tinga and her seven accompanying whales swam the entire mile length of the entrance in silence. They were not afraid, they wanted to be secretive of their whereabouts, much as they did when unwanted boats were pursuing them. They rejoined most of their comrades outside the mouth of the bay and turned northward to swim once more as a united pack. From 2 miles away they picked up sounds of the other six whales indicating a large school of sockeye salmon had been found passing through the area. The whales were gorging on them. It was not easy to pass up wonderful eating such as prime salmon because there were times in the winter when food was quite scarce. In addition, all of the females with calves were teaching their offspring some of the skills of catching salmon, a swift and elusive fish. Although the youngsters were incapable of sonar amplification shock until they were three or four years old, the adults showed them how to focus the sonar beam on a fleeing salmon to stun it enough to catch it.

Tinga and the others, returning from the mammal hunt, joined in the food orgy until they could eat no more. Tinga herself ate twenty of the ten pound red salmon in addition to the 25 pounds of porpoise eaten earlier. The pack would hunt mammals again another time.

CHAPTER TWENTY FIVE

Close look

A t the Herring Bay camp, planning and preparations had been carefully laid out for commencement of the search for the A-T pack the following day. It was planned that during the time Mike and Tracy were in the plane with Carl Baker searching the area for the whales, Sally, Kim, Evelyn, Don and Mario would be loading supplies aboard the two vessels and making preparations to load some of the pigs in kennels aboard the *Karen Marie*. Reed assisted Kim in picking out which pigs would take the trip first.

They all hoped that by about noon the next day Carl, Mike and Tracy would call in or would return after having found the sought-after pack. The two vessels would then move out to establish contact with and follow the pack. Food, water and other supplies, including straw and feed for the pigs, had already been placed aboard the *Karen Marie*. Recording and videotaping gear was also in place on both vessels. The weather that day had been fantastic, one of the warmest Mario could remember, allowing the loading to progress without a hitch.

At about 6:00 pm, the group had celebrated getting the chores completed by enjoying cocktails in the dining area of the lodge. By 7 Sally and Evelyn had dinner ready, terriyaki pork and chicken over noodles. A bright green salad and fresh asparagus topped off the main course, with freshly made apple pie for dessert.

"I can't believe it's almost eight o'clock at night," Kim remarked after dinner as she looked out on Herring Bay. "Looks more like 4 in the afternoon. Say, aren't there a couple of small boats coming our way?"

Mario looked through the binoculars. "Nobody I know, but they're coming pretty fast," he said. "Any of you heard of the *Primrose* or the *Saucy?*"

"Say, those are the names of the boats of those people from Anchorage," Tracy remembered, turning to Mike. "You remember, the people who had the encounter with the A-T pack."

"Yeah, I remember 'em," Mike replied. "Wonder what they're doing out here again."

Reed nodded. "Let's hope they're just fishing this time."

Don got up from the table. "You folks go ahead and enjoy your drinks. Maybe they're just going to anchor in the bay for the night, but if they come to the dock I'll find out what they're up to."

As Don walked down to the dock where the *Karen Marie* and *Czarina* were tied end to end, the two vessels came closer and it became apparent they were not just going to anchor in the bay; they were coming to the dock.

"Mind if we tie up?" Harry Saunders called to Don.

"No, bring her on over," Don responded. "We'll tie her alongside." The *Saucy* came alongside the *Karen Marie* and was tied securely with bumpers between. The *Primrose* was tied alongside the *Saucy.*

Harry and Dave stepped onto the dock and introduced themselves to Don. "Are those people here who are looking for killer whales?" Harry asked Don.

"Well, sometimes they look for them. Why?"

"Big trouble. We found them, or they found us. It was another close call with the whales. They flipped one of our dinghies and dumped the kids and dog. By the way, I'm Dave Halloran and this is Harry Saunders."

"Nice to meet you, I'm Don Schwartz. Did the whales harm the kids? Did you see it?"

"Hell yes! We were right there. We thought the kids might be killed," "Harry answered.

Don looked at the two men and asked "But were the kids harmed?"

"Not that we have been able to determine thus far, but it scared the hell out of all of us," Harry replied.

. "C'mon up to the lodge, they'll want to hear about this immediately. Does anyone else want to come?" Don asked, looking toward the two boats.

"Our wives are fixing dinner for the kids," Harry replied.

"Did you take any photos?" Don asked as they started along the dock toward the lodge.

"Yes, we did!" Harry nodded. "And I hope we have some good ones."

As they approached the lodge, both Dave and Harry noticed the pens containing pigs but, with their attention directed at meeting the whale researchers said nothing about them. As they entered the lodge, Reed, Mike and Tracy instantly recognized the two men. Introductions were made to the others.

"You look like you need a drink," Tracy observed. Can we get a beer for you, or something stronger?"

"Got any tequila?" Harry answered. "Straight up."

"Make that two," Dave echoed and Evelyn poured two generous portions from the assortment of bottles in the cabinet. "Guess we should have listened to you," Dave addressed Mike and Reed, looking sincere and edgy. "You told us to stay away from the whales and we were damned foolish enough to actually go looking for them again because the kids wanted to try to contact them." He took a shot of the clear Mexican liquid.

"Do you mean killer whales?" Reed asked.

"Yes, killer whales," Dave nodded. "We'd been out a couple of times looking for the same group so the kids could try to contact them again but we couldn't find them, no luck. Then this afternoon we anchored in the Bay of Isles on the other side of Knight Island and the whales seemed to find us."

"What happened," Harry blurted, "is the killer whales dumped one of our dinghies that had three kids and a dog in it and then nosed one of the kids and flipped the dog in the air."

"But did the whales actually harm anyone?" Mike asked.

"Not so far as we've been able to tell," Dave replied

"Like I told Don here, we watched the whole thing and couldn't do anything but fetch the kids and dog out of the water after the whales left." Harry took another drink.

"Could you give us the entire story?" Reed asked, leaning forward intently. "Try to start at the beginning. Start at this morning."

"We been looking for those damned whales a couple of times since the kids got the idea they could communicate with them. This was going to be our last trip because we hadn't been able to find them. This morning we looked near Montague Island for a while and then, after noon, decided to go to the Bay of Isles because there is a nice beach there for the kids." Harry took another drink and continued. "Four porpoises showed up where we were anchored at the head of the bay just off the beach. They acted as if they were, well, sort of hiding under the boats. Is that what you'd call it, Dave?" Dave just nodded yes.

"What kind of porpoises were they?" Reed asked, leaning forward in anticipation.

"I wasn't sure, but Lenore, Dave's daughter, looked them up in her book and said they were harbor porpoises."

"Aha," Reed commented. "Please go on."

Dave had now recovered his composure sufficiently to speak. "Four of the kids were in our dinghy on the water trying to feed herring to the porpoises when killer whales showed up. I'm not sure how many there were, but probably seven or eight. It appeared they caught the porpoises near the bay entrance and may have eaten them. We could not see the details."

Evelyn started to refill the glasses but Tracy nodded a subtle no, indicating too much alcohol was being consumed too fast. Evelyn understood and backed off.

"The kids were slapping the water with oars to attract the whale's attention; trying to communicate..." Dave continued. The stupidity of the dangerous situation for the children appeared to wash over him.

"And they were throwing herring to 'em," Harry interrupted.

"To the whales or the porpoises?" Reed asked.

"Whatever," Harry replied, obviously feeling the tequila. "And one of the orcas took a paddle from Sarah, my daughter, swam off with it and then returned it to her. Damned strange."

Tracy, Mike and Reed exchanged glances. These people had really been asking for trouble.

"One of the whales came up under one of the dinghies," Dave explained, "and threw the thing over. Three kids and a dog dumped in the water just like that." He snapped his fingers. "And we were concerned they were going to attack the kids."

Harry continued. "The kids were trying to upright the dinghie and Muffy, Dave's dog was swimming around in circles. One of the orcas got under her and flipped her end over end about 40 feet in the air, but the dog seems to be OK. I started shooting my .270 into a cliff or we don't know what else the whales might have done."

"This was a close call," Mike shook his head, looking at the floor. "But look at the positive side, it appears none of the kids was injured and even the dog came out OK."

Reed continued the quest for information. "Could you tell if it was the same group as before? Did you take any photos?"

"Hell yes, we got photos," Dave answered, "and a video tape too. But no, we couldn't tell if it was the same group."

"Probably was though, they're vicious," Harry added.

"May we see the tapes?" Tracy asked, but didn't wait for an answer. "Evelyn, Mario has a tape player on the *Karen Marie*, could we look at them there?"

"You bet," Evelyn replied, knowing Mario would agree as soon as he got off the radio.

"Let's go," Mike urged, rising from the table. "We might be able to determine which pack this was. If it was A-T we'll have a good start on finding them tomorrow."

Everyone left the lodge, including Sally and Evelyn, who decided to finish washing the dishes later. They all wanted to see the tape. Dave's camcorder was brought aboard the *Karen Marie* and the tape was taken out. Neither Dave nor Harry had seen the tape yet and had no idea what Dave might have gotten or missed. All nine of them crowded into the cabin of the *Karen Marie* to watch.

After rewinding Dave's tape on Mario's unit, they began playing it. The quality of the tape made by the new unit was good, including the sound. Dave was anxious to see once more what happened and he fast forwarded through some early footage of the Primrose, the kids, the dog mostly in cloudy weather. As he reached the part where they were entering the channel into the Bay of Isles Dave commented, "There it is. There's the channel." The tape was now run at normal speed.

Mike and Tracy recognized the terrain around the entrance. They had anchored there a number of times themselves because it was such a delightful spot, especially in bad weather. The camcorder zoomed in on something and two small gray dorsal fins emerged from the water and then submerged followed by two more. The excited chattering of the children could be heard on the audio above the engine noise.

"Those are the porpoises," Dave remarked.

"Phoecoena phoecoena," Reed noted. "No doubt about it. Your daughter was right, those are harbor porpoises."

The next brief scene on the tape was the scan of the boats anchored in the bay and the kids on the beach followed by the three kids in the *Ace* rowing out to the *Primrose* to get the hydrophone and the four kids and the dog in the *Saucy* rowing out to try to feed the porpoises. The excitement of the scene was obvious as the children tossed herring into the bay waters. Muffy was barking nervously. Dave had tried to tape the porpoises swimming under and around the boat but only gray shadows could be seen.

The porpoises disappeared from view and the camera operator could not find them near the boats. There was a filming gap and the next scene was a distant view out toward the entrance to the bay. The dorsal fins of killer whales came into view and there was a commotion and turbulence where they were sighted.

"We think that's probably when they caught the porpoises," Harry noted.

The view shifted to the kids wearing life preservers in the two dinghies rowing out further into the bay. The parents encouraged them to throw some herring out to see if the whales could be attracted and they slapped the surface of the water with their paddles. The view shifted to show dorsal fins of four whales headed directly for the small boats.

"That was getting really scary," Lenore said quietly.

"The video went on to show the whales circling and then swung back to the *Saucy*. One of the girls, Sarah, Dave noted, was lightly slapping the surface of the water, but it was obvious the girls were apprehensive. No more herring were tossed. Muffy was barking more nervously. Dave had panned the scene trying to locate the whales, but he had focussed directly on the dinghy when a female killer whale, glistening black and white in the late afternoon sun, emerged vertically and, it seemed, majestically, near the small craft. The orca clearly seemed to be examining the occupants of the small boat.

Then a whale came up under the dinghy, dumping the kids and the dog out and into the water. The three kids were trying to turn the dinghy over and Muffy was swimming around in circles. One of the orcas could be seen taking the end of Sarah's paddle and jerking it from her hands, but it quickly released the paddle so she could pick it up again.

A whale cruised under the dog and used its tail to send Muffy flying up in the air. "Wow!!" Mike observed. "That's the way orcas play with sea lion pups in Patagonia. We've seen that on TV."

"Yes" Tracy chuckled. "And you can bet the other whales nearby were laughing!" That brought smiles to the faces of everyone watching.

The filming ended there as the parents tried to help the kids.

Reed told them they had done a good job filming but he asked if they would please show the spyhopping whale again so the saddle area could be seen.

When the dorsal fin and saddle area of that whale was shown again Mike said the marking could be compared with photos they had of killer whale individuals. "The saddle marking on that female is quite clear and I don't believe that is T-7, the leader of the A-T pack. But this could still be that pack."

"Remember T-6 was a sun loving orca," Stacy reminded Mike and Reed:

"That may be T-6," observed Mike. "What do you think, Reed?"

"I can't be sure. This is a partially exposed right side, but the scars we know T-4 has are on the left side."

The recording ended and Dave said "That's where I decided to take the *Primrose* to go after the kids to get them out of the water," Dave explained.

"Did you see where the whales went?" Mike asked.

"No," Harry replied. "It looked like when the whales got together they disappeared. We never saw them again. Not even when we looked further out toward the open water."

"Look, it's 9 at night and we're all tired," Tracy observed, "You said the kids were going to eat but what about the adults? Why don't you come over to the lodge and we'll fix something for you all to eat."

"Yes, and leave your boats tied up right where they are for tonight," Mike added. "Get some food and a good night's sleep and you'll feel better tomorrow."

"We appreciate the offer of food," Dave remarked. "The kids have eaten but it has been a while since we ate anything. And we sure as hell don't feel like trying to get our boats to Whittier tonight, do we Harry?" Harry nodded agreement.

"Good, let's go to the lodge," Mike concluded. "Mind if we keep this tape so we can review it some more?"

"No, not at all. I would like to get it back in the morning, though."

"We'll have it to you in the morning," Mike assured him.

Don and Sally carried Mario's tape player and viewer into the lodge where they replayed the section of the attack on the porpoises and the tossing of the dinghy.

Harry and Ruth Saunders and Dave and Carol Halloran ate a hearty meal of leftovers, including dessert. Later, over Armagnac, a request was made of the guests not to discuss this incident with the news media. More publicity at this time would not do the program any good. "But we've got to tell the Troopers something about the whales!" Dave protested,

"No, you really don't," Tracy advised the group. "There was no one injured in this encounter and there were no laws broken, the whales came to you. Getting some word out now could result in more attacks on the whales by fishermen. So please keep it quiet for now so we can carry on our studies. And that goes for the kids too. Ask them to keep it quiet for now and next fall they can tell the whole school about it! Is that a deal?" The parents nodded yes.

"Well, we're tired," Dave sighed. "It's been a long day. Let's go back to the boats for the night." They returned to the *Primrose* and the *Saucy*.

With the visitors gone, the researchers felt they could talk more freely. "There's no doubt the whales could have killed those kids had they wanted to," Reed observed. "Why didn't they? This seems to be more proof that the whales will not attack people."

"Remember," Tracy pointed out, "Harry said he started firing his rifle. Maybe the noise was enough to convince the whales to leave. Most whales in the Sound have been shot at before and may be gun-shy."

"Good thought," Mike added. "The whale activity seemed to be mostly before the shooting started. But did you notice one other factor which fits our earlier theory?"

Reed and Tracy looked a little puzzled. Then Tracy's eyes lit up. "I know, and you're right, they were wearing life preservers and were fully clothed."

"Good observation," Reed responded, "but there was one other important factor. The dog. We know they have killed dogs before so why not this time?"

Mike responded. "This was a small dog and white. Perhaps the orcas didn't think it was worth the effort or it had little fat, or both."

Kim, who had been listening quietly, now spoke. "If you want my thoughts as an inexperienced observer, these orcas are extremely dangerous to have around people in small boats. The whales were presented with an excellent opportunity to kill someone and they didn't, this time. But if the whales are sufficiently aggressive to turn a boat over you shouldn't need any additional evidence. And what if someone in the boat can't swim or doesn't have a preserver on?" She looked directly at Reed.

Reed nodded an acknowledgement of Kim's logic. "You're right to a certain extent, Kim, but more important in this encounter is that these whales did not kill or even injure anyone. But are there packs or individuals within a pack that will take man as prey? There are lots of unanswered questions and our research with the pigs hopefully will help provide some answers."

"We're back, Kim," Tracy advised solemnly, "to specifically identifying which pack may contain rogue whales and to carrying out reaction testing without using man for the tests. This is the need, the type of reasoning, which brought us to the conclusion that we should use pigs in a controlled situation."

"If they'll kill a dog, such as that black lab, they'll probably kill a pig," Kim responded, beginning to feel protective of the pigs. "And this dog today didn't fare so well either!"

"We have a report whales tipped over a boat earlier this summer and killed and ate a black lab," Mike responded, "but, in this encounter they apparently had killed some porpoises but even that did not excite the whales to go beyond that with humans in the water.".

"Right," Reed added. "Now we need good, solid evidence concerning the reaction of the whales in a natural setting with an animal which is not one of their standard prey. And we need to study them when they take off on one of their mammal hunts, not when they're feeding on fish. That brings us back to the pigs unless we can find a human volunteer or two."

"I'm damned sure not getting in with them," Don noted. "They're too big and fast in the water for me."

"And smart," Mario added, smiling wryly.

The discussions continued on for another half hour on the planning for the next day. The best course of action appeared to be the one they had decided earlier to follow. The day's encounter in the Bay of Isles lent support to the concept that it was the A-T pack causing most, if not all, of the killer whale problems in the Sound.

At Herring Bay the next morning, Don was up at 5:30 am, anxious to get on with the many chores involved with getting the vessels sent off. The usual southwest wind was blowing across the bay and it was overcast, but at least it wasn't raining. As he drank the first cup of coffee and looked out toward the moored vessels, the radio crackled with a call relayed through Cordova from Anchorage. Don answered the call. It was George Maxwell with ADF&G wanting to know how everything was going out there on the Bay.

"Hold on, George." Don responded. "He's not up yet but I'll get him." He walked down the hall and pounded on the door to Mike and Tracy's room. "Radio call from Maxwell, Mike." Mumbling could be heard and the door burst open as Mike came out in his blue terrycloth robe.

"I figured action might be picking up today" he told Don, "and they're getting started early." He picked up the microphone. "Mackenzie here."

"Mike, just thought I'd call to see if all is going well out there. Yours is an important study."

"We're doing OK," Mike replied as Don handed him a cup of coffee. We had a little bear problem but that seems under control now."

"Remember, if you need any help just call and I can fly over if the weather is decent."

Mike looked at Don standing nearby and Don, who was listening, shook his head no. "Nope, we seem to be in good shape. Thanks anyway." He had a second thought: "But hey, would you please call Carl Baker and tell him we'd like him to fly out here tomorrow so we can start a search?'

"No problem, I'll do it this morning. But, keep us posted on events. By the way, as word gets out about what your group is trying to do we're going to get more and more inquiries, but we're just telling them we don't know much. Good luck!"

Although the details could not be revealed on the radio, Mike knew that Cynthia Scott of ADF&G was handling most of the calls and she was very good at it. Frank Costello, the state trooper stationed in Cordova and a certified search and rescue diver, would be available if any state help was needed.

Meanwhile, Dr. Dan Short, Rolanda, and Rolly had landed at Anchorage International Airport and, after checking into the Captain Cook Hotel, a search on the Internet led them to call the Harbor Master at Whittier. Their call was answered by Cyrus McDuffy, who sounded as if he might have a hangover. Dan asked him what the situation was with regard to chartering a boat to go out to Prince William Sound for a week to ten days.

"Well, the only one I know of that isn't chartered already is the Vamp owned by a woman named Kate Davis. It's a good sturdy boat. How many are going?

"There are just three of us, all from Canada. Me, my name is Dr. Dan Short, and my girlfriend Rolanda and Rolly, a bright young man who is studying to become a marine biologist."

"What kind of doctor are ya? Another of these environmental kooks?" Cyrus asked.

"No, no, I'm a psychiatrist and interested in some studies of marine life."

"I'll tell ya what," Cyrus advised "Where are you and I'll have Buns, uh, Kate Davis, call you if I can find her."

"We're at the Captain Cook, room 1232. We greatly appreciate your help."

"I'll see what I can do." Cyrus smiled as he hung up the phone. He thought to himself:wait 'til Buns hears about this possible charter including a young guy from Canada. She might even offer to take them for almost nothing. He picked up the phone and called the Coffee Cup. Yep, Buns was there and she got on the phone.

Cyrus was still smiling to himself. "Buns, this is Cyrus. I had a call from some folks from Canada. They just arrived at the Captain Cook and are looking for a charter to go out in the Sound for a week or so to study some kind of marine life. Are you interested?'

"How many of them are there?"

"Just three. A doctor who is a psychiatrist, his girlfriend and a young man who is a student. Marine biology or some such."

"Why, hell yes I'm interested. These damn one day deals I've been doing are the pits. What's the name and where can I reach them?"

"They're at the Captain Cook and his name is Dan Short. Room 1232. Give him a call."

Now Kate was smiling. This could be one helluva good deal. A couple of weeks ago she had made a list of needed items for just such a charter. Lots of hard liquor and wine along with some food.

She called the hotel, room 1232 and Dan answered.

"Dr. Short, this is Kate Davis down at Whittier. I understand you are looking for a charter for a week or so on the Sound. I have a boat that will handle it but it's gonna cost ya."

"Yes, we are definitely interested,." Dan told her. "Can you handle three people? And what is the cost?"

"My boat will sleep six or seven people so three is easy. And I'll give you a good deal: $2,000 per day and you pay for the fuel. $10,000 up front. You also provide the food and drinks, do your own cooking and wash your own dishes. How does that sound?"

"Hold on a second, Kate." Dan held his hand over the phone and asked Rolly and Rolanda what they thought of the proposed deal. "Sounds good." they both nodded.

Dan spoke to Kate again. "OK, sounds good here but we'll have to rent a car and get supplies together. Can you tell us what to bring?"

"You damn right I can tell you what to bring. I'll send a list by fax to the hotel and you can pick it up there. When do you want to leave?"

"We need information from a person who is probably out there already, guy named Mike Mackenzie. He's the one we must contact."

"Well, hell, I know Mike and his wife Tracy. Damned nice people. I may be able to reach them by radio. Do you want me to try calling Mike?"

"Yes, would you please call and tell him the three folks from Canada are here and need to know when to head for the Sound and how long we might be out there?"

"OK, Dan, I'll do that and call you back."

Kate walked over to McDuffy's office and asked him if she could use the radio to make a call. Cyrus nodded yes and motioned for Kate to walk over to the radio.

Out at the Herring Bay camp the radio buzzed again. This time it was Kate Davis in Whittier. "Mike, this is Kate in Whittier, how's everything going out there?"

"All is OK for now," Mike answered. "How are you doing?"

"I just spoke with a doctor from Canada who said he is supposed to meet you out in the Sound somewhere but he doesn't know exactly when or where. He wants to charter my boat to get out there. Three people and they're at the Captain Cook."

"Oh yes, I remember a guy named Dan Long, no no, it was Dan Short. Yes, I knew he was coming to Alaska. What are his plans?" Mike asked.

"Sounds like he's leaving that up to you, so you say when and where" Kate responded.

"OK, how about three days from now you bring them out to our camp at Herring Bay. Used to be a hunting and fishing lodge but we're using it for now. We may not be at the camp but you can reach us by radio out there. You remember my boat is the *Czarina*. I know you'll advise them to bring plenty of supplies because we won't have any for them."

"Fine, I'll pass this on. Dr. Short and his friends can start shopping. I'll look forward to seeing you and Tracy out there, Mike."

Kate hung up the radio and noticed that Cyrus had been in the next room but was obviously listening. "Well, Cyrus, looks like this old gal is going to be back in action again. Getting a nice charter lined up. If I bring a document over could you fax it to the Captain Cook in Anchorage?"

"Absolutely, bring it on over and I'll send it," he told Buns.

The fax document was delivered to room 1232 and Dan and Rolanda looked it over. "Good thing we don't have much luggage" Rolanda shook her head. "If we did we'd have to get a truck to take this food and booze down to Whittier."

In their rented car the three of them went shopping at local grocery and liquor stores. All were paid for with the cash from the concert in Vancouver. The next day they headed for Portage and the train to take them to Whittier.

The radio at Herring Bay buzzed again. This time it was Dr. Dan Short from Canada. "Hey, remember me? From the Orca communication society?" he asked Mike, who was wishing they hadn't shown up but maybe, just maybe, there would be a use for them. And Dan had said they were bringing funding.

"Yes, I remember you, where are you?"

"Rolanda, Rolly, and I are in Whittier and I'm at the Harbor Master's office. That's how I was able to call you. We've made arrangements for a charter boat to take us out there. The one we have found is operated by a person named "Buns". Know anything about her or her boat?"

"She knows her way around, that's a fact. Her boat should be OK for a few days to a week, but be sure there are plenty of supplies and water on board. And remember, you will have to stay on the boat. When are you planning to show up?" Mike asked.

"We were planning to leave tomorrow," Dan replied. "Buns said it would take three or four hours to get to Herring Bay. Buns has a radio in her boat and we could call you if anything happens to delay our travel. Once out there we may be able to help you find some whales. I brought some hydrophones and recording equipment."

"OK, head this way tomorrow. We don't have a schedule yet but there is one particular orca pack we will be looking for. You may be able to help. Radio when you are getting close to Herring Bay, we have a camp here and a dock. Buns will know, she's been here previously."

"Will do, see you soon. Over and out." As Dan left the office, he noted that Buns had really taken a liking to Rolly and, out near her boat, was laughing and joking with him. Other than some Alaska natives, Dan noticed that Rolanda seemed to be the only dark-skinned person in town.

Back at the Herring Bay lodge, with everyone arising from sleep, Kim looked out toward the dock and saw the kids stirring on the decks of the two

R. V. BAILEY

pleasure crafts. She thought the curious youngsters might like to see the pigs.

Kim waved to them "Come on over here." Kim hoped someday to have kids of her own and was always delighted to be around children.

The kids were fascinated by the live pigs, which none of them had ever seen before. And the pigs seemed happy to have some visitors. The kids were shocked at the appearance of Wolfy and saw that he had been trying to dig his way out of his pen.

Kim smiled, "Hey, you guys, how would you like to feed the pigs this morning?" She showed the how to scoop up the feed and put it in their troughs. The kids were delighted and excitedly used 1-gallon cans to scoop feed from the bags and carry it to the hungry porkers. They asked numerous questions about the pigs, including which were males and females and which parts were used for bacon and ham. Kim did her best to answer, but she gave no clear answer to the question about what they were going to do with the pigs. "These are special pigs for a special purpose," she replied. "And another thing, these pigs are being fed partly on Alaska barley and we see that they are doing just fine. But here at this location we must be watching for bears to make sure the bears don't decide to sample some pork chops."

With the pigs fed, Kim invited them to the lodge where Sally and Evelyn were busy preparing breakfast and they joined the others in a meal of pancakes, eggs and ham. By 7:30 there was more activity on the *Saucy* and the *Primrose*.

"Looks like Dave and Harry are up," Don noted. "C'mon kids, let's walk out there." As they went, he talked with them about gold prospecting in the historic Nome area on the Seward Peninsula. He told them about the largest gold nugget ever found in Alaska that was recovered when placer mining on Anvil Creek. The original gold prospectors at Nome recovered several fortunes in gold and it was reported that some of that money was used to build Madison Square Garden in New York City.

Harry, Dave and their wives came out on deck looking somewhat bedraggled. Don invited them to go on over to the lodge for some breakfast, an offer which they gladly accepted.

Over more coffee at the lodge the tapes were reviewed again by Reed, Mike, and Tracy and Mike then handed the tape to Harry. "One other thing we should talk about before you leave," Mike advised them. "The media is going to keep snooping to see what they can find out about our activities. This could go on for a few days, or maybe for a couple of weeks.

We know we can't ask you to just say nothing, but could you please try to avoid saying anything that will cause people to become overly antagonistic toward either the whales or toward our research efforts? We'll be doing our best to investigate the whales and more publicity and possible interference is something we don't need."

"We won't disclose anything and we have already talked to the kids so we'll try to keep it quiet," Dave said.

With that the folks from Anchorage pointed out that it was time for them to leave and return to Whittier. Obligations were piling up in Anchorage. They thanked everyone at the camp for their hospitality and returned to their two boats. The kids had no problem with thoughts of leaving Prince William Sound.

"Well," Reed said after the guests had left, "we haven't been able to positively identify the A-T pack, but it probably was them. We'd better stick with our original plan and find that pack. And once we do find them we'd better stay with them constantly, we can't afford to lose them again during the period of our study."

They heard a small plane circling overhead. Don came into the lodge and told them it looked like the Fish and Game pontoon-equipped plane they'd seen previously.

The plane landed on the rippled water and taxied up to the dock where Don secured it. George Maxwell and Herb Bracken got out and Don walked them to the lodge. Evelyn poured coffee for them and Reed, Mike and Tracy told them about the Halloran and Saunders experience with the whales.

Reed explained their plans. "Right," Mike added. "But George, if we decide we need more help can you get a Game and Fish boat out here with a couple of good people to help us? When we find the pack we'd like to follow them 24/7."

"We'll have to see if we can find a boat with a galley and adequate sleeping quarters because they'll likely be out a while." Maxwell thought a moment. "Frankly, I'd like to participate in this one, Mike. You, Tracy, and Reed are really breaking some new ground, and Kim should be counted in because she is an important player."

"And I might be your second hand on this expedition," Herb commented as he took another bite of a cinnamon roll, "But, speaking of new ground, how is the training going with the pigs?" He turned to look at Kim, gorgeous in a turquoise shirt with matching bow holding back a blonde ponytail.

Kim's blue eyes sparkled. "They're doing fine. We've got them trained to swim from an offshore raft 150 yards or so to shore. They're good swimmers."

"You damned right they are," Herb smiled. "Let me tell you sometime about the pigs we had in the Navy. They'd wear scuba gear and dive in 30 feet of water."

"I'll look forward to that," Kim smiled, making Herb wish he was thirty years younger.

"Getting back to the matter of the A-T pack, Herb," Reed noted, "would you talk to Dr. Walker in Seattle again and see if she will approve radio tagging at least one of the whales in the group? A tag would assure that we weren't going to lose them again, at least for the short term."

"And if T-7 is one of the culprits and we tag her," Mike urged, "we could also get a better idea of the role she plays in the predation."

"I'd like to be able to give you better news," Herb told them shaking his head. "But there isn't much chance because Blue War and the United Wildlife Federation have tuned in to what they think may be a good PR opportunity in `defending the whales' and have already been issuing warnings that they would tolerate no harassment or damage to the mammals."

"Ask her anyway," Reed urged, "it would really help our tracking."

"OK, I'll try to talk her into it, but remember, she dances to the tune out of D. C." Sally poured more coffee.

"Speaking of D. C.," Maxwell pointed out, "we'd better pay some attention to how any publicity is going to be handled for this excursion."

"No publicity is best but poorly directed publicity we don't need either," Mike warned.

"Our entire plan could be fouled up if too many boats show up when we're looking for whales. Let's keep the spectators out of here."

Reed asked: "Do you suppose the Gov would consider closing the Sound to all small boats, say under 25 feet, which do not have a permit? Permits could be issued automatically to anyone holding a commercial fishing permit so the fishermen won't miss out on a season opening, and fishing guides could also operate."

"Trouble with that whole idea," Tracy inserted, "is that when you give the damned government more authority to do anything, they almost always screw it up. For now we're better off to just quietly keep doing our work and move the project forward."

"Sounds pretty good," Herb observed. "But the Gov probably doesn't have the authority to close the Sound. The Coast Guard and NOAA will have to go along with it, but the same logic should work with them. They're political animals, too."

"OK, so do we agree to try to keep things quiet for now?" Mike asked. "Carl Baker is due to fly in here any minute and we're going out to look for the A-T pack. Once we find them we must stay with them...and get the pig experiments underway."

"Low profile and try to keep the feds from interfering," Reed nodded.

"OK, we'll head back to Anchorage." Maxwell and Bracken started toward the dock. "Let us know if there is anything else we can do." They climbed into the state-owned plane and it taxied away from the dock and took off.

Mike, Stacy, and Reed laid out a map and began figuring out where they should start looking for the A-T pack and where there were some areas that they knew the whales liked. Evelyn and Sally were busy making lunches when another small plane was heard circling over the lodge. Again, it was a high-winged Cessna float plane, the best for observations.

"That must be Carl," Tracy said. "Let's get out gear together and head out to the dock. Perhaps we'll be lucky today."

Everyone was bustling about to get ready. Don moved luggage containing personal items and equipment from the lodge to the two waiting boats in preparation for several days on the Sound. He carried out a series of baggage runs with the four-wheeler and trailer from the lodge across the dock to the vessels.

Anxious to start the search, Mike and Tracy took binoculars and cameras and stepped onto the pontoons of Carl's waiting Cessna. Mike climbed into one of the rear seats and Tracy sat to Carl's right. The plane idled away from the dock and, with a roar and spray of water, took off. Carl circled the camp once and then turned north at an altitude of only 500 feet.

It was a late 10:30 in the morning when Don and the rest of the crew started hauling the pigs in kennels to the Karen Marie. Eight pigs, including Daisy and Minnie, had been selected by Kim on the basis of training and weight. Four barrows were chosen, which were heavier than the other pigs at nearly 190 pounds each, and four sows. Feed and straw had been loaded the previous day.

CHAPTER TWENTY SIX

Aircraft

"Where do you want to look first?" Carl asked Tracy above the noise of the engine and prop.

"We talked it over this morning and we'd like to fly around the north end of Knight Island and then east to Smith Island. From there let's go southwest to Manning Rocks and the mouth of the Bay of Isles," she halfshouted into Carl's right ear above the droning engine. "Then maybe east to Seal Island." Carl nodded and turned his attention back to the plane and watching for whales.

The high wing structure of the Cessna made the aircraft almost ideal for spotting. Banking away from Herring Bay, they looked down upon a rugged, wavepounded shoreline of mottled brown rock fringing the lush green and blue green of the steeplysloping hills of the island.

Spotting the whales could be extremely trying. If the whales were in a sleeping mode, and thus staying under water most of the time, they would be very difficult to spot, especially if they were in an area where the water contained abundant glacial flour. Fortunately, no glaciers were near the north end of Knight Island so the water was relatively clear. Although the southwest wind was kicking up, there were only small white caps on the Sound thus allowing reasonably good visibility.

Several times they observed seals, beached and sitting among the rocks or lying near the water's edge, but seals were so common it was not an observation worth mentioning to each other. Several sea otters were observed bobbing on the waves and, here and there, the white head of a bald eagle stood out against the more somber background of the rocks and forest. Nothing worth photographing although their cameras, as usual, were ready.

As they turned east around the north end of Knight Island, Tracy turned to Mike but speaking so both he and Carl could hear. "There's a humpback and a calf," she pointed down to her right.

Carl heard her and saw the direction of her point, He banked the plane around sharply to the right so they all could have a better look.

"It's a humpy all right," Mike agreed. "Look at the size of those flippers, they're as long as the calf!"

"And look at those teeth marks on her flukes!" Tracy exclaimed as the whale's tail emerged from the water. "She ran into some orcas somewhere!" Both cameras were now snapping. The whale was sounding, probably in response to the sound of the aircraft. She and the calf disappeared from the surface.

"Want to go around again?" Carl half shouted.

"No, they might be down for a while. Let's go on," Tracy responded. Then she turned again to Mike. "That was this spring's calf. Those teeth marks and pieces torn from the mother's flukes must be from a previous killer whale attack or she wouldn't still have that calf with her; the orcas would have killed it. Get any photos, Mike?"

He nodded yes and smiled.

Carl turned the plane east again toward Smith Island, 6 miles away. They were over the waters of Prince William Sound now and much less to see. They concentrated on looking for the black shapes under water, the dorsal fins or the mist jetted into the air when the whales blew at the surface.

Smith Island itself was not much more than a northeast trending rock promontory a quarter mile wide and 3 miles long projecting little more than 100 feet above the water surface. Nowdead shellfish growth lines suggested mean sea level marks on the perimeter of the island which had been raised 30 feet in the 1964 Alaska earthquake. Mike observed that some of the rocks now visible at the surface would have been well below the surface when killer whales were hunting seals here in 1963. Some changes in nature are not gradual, he thought; they're learning that in California.

Carl flew along the long northwest side of the island and around the northeast end and southwest along the other long dimension. Again they saw seals and a couple of sea lions, but no other whales. Three commercial salmon boats passed by, heading toward the north end of the Sound. He continued the southwest tack toward the mouth of the Bay of Isles 10 miles away.

"Whoa, whoa," Mike suddenly exclaimed and grabbed Carl's shoulder. "Over there at nine o'clock, about a quarter of a mile away, going north. That's a pack of orcas."

"All right!" Carl exclaimed, happy that they'd found some whales so quickly. Now if it would just be the right bunch. He banked the plane to the left and began to gain altitude. Carl had learned from previous experiences that, although spotting the whales from a low altitude could provide more details, the whales were best observed from not less than 1,500 feet and never buzzed.

As they climbed, the whales again came into Mike's view on the left side of the plane. "There they are, and there's a big male! It looks like T4's dorsal fin! It's wavy and there's the notch in the trailing edge! It's them, it's the T pack!" He could hardly believe their good fortune at finding them.

Carl made wide circles at 1,500 feet. Photos were taken, but there was no doubt in anyone's mind that they had found the group they were seeking. A confirmation count revealed nineteen whales.

"Must be good food here," Mike shouted. "This pack has been hanging around here now for a couple of days at least."

"Let's hope they stay a while longer," Tracy commented as she took one more photo with the telephoto lensequipped camera.

"They're in no hurry, just slowly cruising north," Mike observed. "If they stay on this course we should be able to intercept them between Smith and Naked Islands this afternoon."

"Back to Herring Bay, Carl," Tracy smiled. "We know where they are now!" Carl turned the plane southwest directly toward the Herring Bay camp. With a little dodging, their 1,500 foot altitude would be adequate to clear most peaks on the island.

Reed, Mario, Evelyn, Don, and Sally had gotten plans together for moving eight of the pigs into kennels and then to the boat when the time came to move them. It was all going smoothly. Reed and Kim were getting better acquainted. Others staying in the lodge had noticed, on more than one late night, Reed stepping over to Kim's room.

When those at the camp heard the plane approaching there was surprise. "Don't tell me they're back already," Mario exclaimed. "I thought they'd be flying until they were low on fuel."

"We'll soon find out," Evelyn responded. All those at the camp waited on the dock for any news.

At nearly 11:30 the Cessna's floats touched the water near the dock and glided across the water's surface before sinking slightly as the plane's speed decreased. Carl revved the engine and guided the plane toward the dock. The plane taxied to the end of the structure and Carl cut the engine as Don tied the plane to the dock. Tracy, Mike, and then Carl climbed out.

"We found 'em,"Tracy smiled to everyone. "And they're not far away, but we'd better hustle back out there."

"It was fantastic to find them so quickly!" Reed exclaimed. "Now we can start some solid planning!"

Mike said "We'll leave right away in the *Czarina*. Mario, you can some out when ready with the pigs. We'll be in touch by radio so you'll know where we are. The *Czarina* is already loaded with most supplies and water so we'll get out of here quickly." Then he turned to Don, "Is everything loaded?"

"Everything on the list and then some," Don replied, smiling. "As far as I know you're ready to go."

"We can have eight pigs ready and loaded in a couple of hours!" Reed added, smiling at Kim and looking forward to spending more time with her.

"We'll get them loaded in short order" she replied, and then smiled at Reed. "But there are no promises on swimming performance."

"Let's go then," Mike urged Sally and Tracy. "The whales aren't going to wait for us." They all started hustling. Sally moved her personal items from the *Karen Marie* to the *Czarina*.

Mike turned to Don. "Stay in touch by radio, Don, but not too often."

"You call me," Don smiled.

Mike started the *Czarina*'s diesel engines and Sally cast off the ropes and jumped aboard. Propeller turning, the vessel moved out. Tracy and Sally smiled waved to those on the dock.

Don hooked the trailer to the four-wheeler and headed for the pen. The pigs knew something was going on and were running around excitedly. Reed, Kim, Mario and Evelyn arrived at the pen with the plan to get the individual pigs into their respective kennels. Then they would skid each kennel to the trailer parked just outside the gate and lift the kennel into the trailer. Don and Evelyn did most of the lifting. The trailer would hold four kennels. As soon as four were loaded Don drove via the dock to the *Karen Marie* and the kennels containing the pigs were placed on the dock. Mario, with Evelyn's help, would swing a boom over from the boat and pick up each kennel, pick up each kennel and position it over the deck to be lowered. They strapped the last kennel in place and tied down the waterproof cover over the tops of the kennels. In two hours they had the eight kennels on board and ready to go. Straw and feed were also loaded.

Don pulled the trailer back to the lodge and Kim and Reed put their suitcases in the trailer along with the boxes of food they had prepared in anticipation of this search in the *Karen Marie*. Evelyn's and Mario's personal items had remained on the boat.

Carl, the Cessna pilot, who had been waiting to see if any more air support was needed, now returned to the dock.

"Say, Carl," Don asked, "got any starter fluid on board?"

"Might have a couple of cans. Why?"

Don grinned, "You never know when a quick start might come in handy on an island like this. How about loaning me whatever you've got."

"Why, hell yes, but what are you going to use it on, that Honda four-wheeler?"

"Let's say I may use it on a large critter that needs a quick start," Don smiled.

Carl handed over two yellow cans from a bag in the Cessna storage compartment. "Put this on our bill," Don said, "and thanks."

Kim, Evelyn, and Mario boarded the *Karen Marie* just ahead of Reed. Don cast off her ropes, which Evelyn quickly stowed. Mario started the diesel engines and the *Karen Marie* left the dock on a northerly course out of Herring Bay. Don waved to them but the person he was really going to miss was Sally, who was on the other boat.

Carl patted Don on the shoulder. "Well, they're off and running so it's time for me to head back to Anchorage."

Don nodded "OK, and thanks for finding those whales so quickly. That really speeds up the program here."

Don untied the Cessna. The red and white plane taxied away and was soon airborne.

That plane climbs quickly with no load, Don thought as he watched the plane disappear. He looked around and it suddenly seemed very quiet except for the low throb of the generator behind the lodge. But there was plenty to do. He'd be busy as always. Hell, maybe another bear would even show up for a little excitement. He started up the Honda and drove back to the barn.

CHAPTER TWENTY SEVEN

A-T found

The *Czarina* was in the lead as the two boats churned northward. The *Karen Marie*, the larger, more powerful and faster vessel would soon be in the lead and she would flatten out some of the waves for the following *Czarina*. The wave size gradually increased as they emerged from Herring Bay into Knight Island Passage.

Maps of the area were laid out in both vessels. Tracy was acting navigator in the *Czarina* and Reed in the *Karen Marie*. Tracy knew where they had seen the whales and their direction of travel so they would try to intercept them. It had been agreed that radio calls would be held to a minimum; too many boats out there with ears.

Mario picked up the radio microphone. "Looks like it'll take us about two hours to get to that location Tracy marked on the map," he radioed to Mike without disclosing where "location" was.

"The sooner the better," Mike responded. "You stay in the lead but not too fast. This old gal will get there eventually but I don't want to burn up an engine in the process."

"OK, now let's see what we can find." Mario left the powerful engines on the *Karen Marie* at a moderate speed.

Kim left the cabin to see how the pigs were faring. Even in good weather, the spray from the *Karen Marie's* bow and the wind made a warm jacket necessary. Reed slipped on a jacket and joined her.

"How are they doing?" he shouted above the noise of the engines and the splash of waves against the hull. Footing was also a little tricky due to a slight rolling of the vessel.

"They probably don't like the noise but otherwise they seem to be OK," she shouted back and then gave each pig a molasses and grain cake.

Together they returned to the warm, relatively quiet cabin.

"Are they all right?" Mario asked Kim.

"Seem to be fine," she nodded, taking off the jacket.

Reed again picked up the binoculars to scan the waters ahead.

"Kim, has anyone explained to you about float coats and survival suits?" Evelyn asked as she entered the cabin.

"No, not yet."

Evelyn proceeded to show her the float coats Mario always provided for use of the crew while on the Karen Marie. They were orange with a heavy nylon shell and lining. An interior layer in the sleeves and body was made of a dense foam material half an inch thick. A heavy zipper and hood were included along with Velcro sleeve fasteners. Evelyn explained that the jackets were very warm but, more importantly, if you fell overboard the jacket would act as a life preserver as well as help retain body heat. She then took down one of the large orange suits Kim had noticed hanging conveniently at the rear of the cabin. The suit was obviously made to cover the entire body including feet and head except the face. It was made of a dense, spongy material about half an inch thick, which felt like that in the float coat.

"This," she told Kim, "is a survival suit. Without it you wouldn't last twenty minutes in the water." The zipper was already open and Evelyn held the suit open. "Here, step in."

"With my shoes on?" Kim asked.

"Everything." Evelyn answered. "If you ever have to put one of these babies on, you probably won't have time to take anything else on or off. These suits are made to keep you afloat and retain your body heat for several hours in this frigid water. People have been known to survive more than twenty-four hours in these, but the longer survival times are probably related to body fat. Fat people survive longer."

"I wouldn't last long, then," Kim remarked. "And neither would you," noting Evelyn's muscular and attractive body.

Kim stepped into the suit. It felt like it was made for someone 6' 4" tall and 250 pounds. Evelyn started zipping it up and pulled the face opening down to where Kim could see.

"Never mind that, it is too large," she advised, "better to have a suit too large that you can get into quickly, jacket, shoes and all than to have one so small that you can't get into it in a hurry."

"But when would this be used?" Kim asked looking out from the face opening and feeling like a spaceman about to step out onto the moon.

"In emergencies. Like if the *Karen Marie* were to start sinking, get into a suit, quick."

"But what could make her sink?" Kim asked, finding it hard to believe that a boat like this, with an experienced captain like Mario, could get into trouble. She unzipped the suit to step out.

"In Alaska, expect the unexpected, if that makes any sense," Evelyn replied, brushing her dark hair back. "We might hit one of the large, partially submerged logs which are common in the Sound. Or, following the whales, we're probably going to be in some shallow water with lots of rocks just below the surface. Mario's good, but he doesn't have Xray vision."

"Thanks for warning us," Kim acknowledged. Reed nodded yes.

"Any trouble is highly unlikely," Evelyn added, "but Mario always reminds us of the Boy Scout motto, `Be Prepared'. That's why he's still here to tell about it while many of the other boats and crews, especially those who tried king crabbing in the Aleutians, sleep with the fishes." That's a mafia expression, Kim thought, and wondered about Evelyn's background.

They returned to viewing the passing terrain and to look at the marine life. Kim was thrilled to see sea otters, seals and, best of all, the speedy black and white Dall's porpoise which obviously had great fun riding the bow wake of the *Karen Marie* as it plowed through the waters of Knight Island Passage.

An hour and a half later they approached the south end of Naked Island. Kim could see why the island had such a name; it was almost barren of vegetation except for a few patches of trees and brush here and there among the rocks. Reed had calculated that the whales, when observed from the air, were traveling at about 2 knots (3 mph) and, unless they had deviated course significantly should be in the vicinity.

Mario reduced the speed of the *Karen Marie* and all four of them donned float coats and exited the cabin to climb the ladder to the flying bridge. On the bridge Mario removed the covers from the controls. Viewing was much better from this elevation above the water, although the rolling of the vessel was amplified.

Twenty minutes later they were still traveling east with no whales sighted.

"What's happening, Mario?" Mike's voice was recognized on the radio. "See anything interesting?"

Reed climbed back down the ladder and entered the cabin.

"Nothing yet, Mike," he responded to the *Czarina*. "We're continuing east and Mario believes it is a good idea if you go north along the west side, if you know what I mean."

"Sounds good, we're about in a position now to turn north. Keep us informed."

"Roger," Reed replied.

Kim had never seen a killer whale before and was somewhat unsure about what to look for except black dorsal fins. But she was interested in seeing whatever type of marine life they came across. With everyone else scanning forward, Kim had climbed down from the bridge and was near the stern of the vessel leaning against the blue covers on the kennels. The pigs grunted recognition that she was near. She gazed out at the blue water and the churning wake of the vessel.

A black scytheshaped object rose from the water 200 yards behind the *Karen Marie*, traveling in the same direction as the boat. Then four more, six more, eight more. Then they all submerged.

She ran to the ladder. "Reed, Reed, I think the whales are behind us," she called. All eyes turned toward the stern, waiting in anticipation. Six black dorsal fins rose in unison and six misty blows climbed into the clear air. Two more aligned groups followed, including one large bull.

"It's them!" Reed shouted. "That bull is T4!"

Mario cut the engines to an idle and then turned them off. They rolled on the waves in silence. The whales were coming toward them and would pass within 30 yards on their present course.

"Good spotting," Reed congratulated Kim as he hurried down the ladder to call the *Czarina*.

Kim stood watching for the whales to reappear as Reed called Mike. "This is the *KM*. Mike, we have the subjects at close range. Invite you to join us."

"Will do," Mike responded, keeping his excitement under control.

As they watched, the first six whales came to the surface in a line within 100 yards of the *Karen Marie* to blow, continuing their same course. Thirteen whales followed them. Kim was amazed at their apparent organization. Reed called her to the bridge for even better visibility, where he had his camera ready with a telephoto lens.

"That bull with the tall wavy dorsal fin is the quickest clue to the AT pack," he pointed out to her. "Watch, you'll see that it also has a notch in the trailing edge."

The whales again came to the surface to blow, this time only 30 yards away and their nearest point of approach. The whuff as they expelled air reminded Kim of steam escaping from a locomotive. Reed snapped off several photos as the various whales broke the surface.

"They're probably in a sleeping mode," Reed commented after they had submerged again. "If so, they may be down for six or seven minutes this time." He took a stop watch from his pocket and pushed the stem to start it.

"How can you tell they're sleeping?" Kim asked, thinking that they looked quite active to her.

"We don't really know for sure," he replied, "but after you've followed them as much as we have, you develop a certain sense for what they're doing."

"How do you know they'll be down for so many minutes?"

"Experience again." He turned to Mario. "Let's wait about five minutes before starting the engines, then we can follow them a couple of hundred yards back so they won't be disturbed."

"Will do," Mario answered, intrigued with the idea of learning more about the type of whale he had seen so often before while fishing. He looked with binoculars past the stern and saw another boat approaching in the distance. "Must be the *Czarina*," he nodded and started the engines.

They continued surveying the scene. Reed looked at the stop watch. Six minutes. The first four whales rose 200 yards ahead of them to blow. Kim smiled at him and nodded.

"Reed, take over will you?" Mario asked. "Eve and I are going down to put a lunch together."

Within ten minutes the *Czarina* had caught up with them. Mike brought her up on the starboard side (right side they told Kim) but stayed 40 yards out.

An hour later they were still idling along on an easterly course behind the whales, still in a sleeping mode. They were now almost in the southbound traffic lane, as shown on their maps, for supertankers transporting oil from the Valdez terminal; the southern end of the TransAlaska Pipeline. Through binoculars Mario saw one of the huge vessels coming south. Due to the curvature of the earth, the only part visible initially was the superstructure of the ship, looking like part of a city on the horizon with mountains rising in the background. He pointed it out to the others and, as they watched, idling along, the structure seemed to rise from the ocean surface as the great ship approached.

"We don't want to be in the path of that baby," Mario observed. "It takes her a couple of miles to get stopped."

Several minutes later it was apparent the whales had begun turning northwest toward the north end of Naked Island.

"Maybe they heard you," Reed laughed as the two boats turned to follow the pack.

As they moved slowly northwestward, the huge tanker, as long as four football fields, passed half a mile away going south. Even at that distance the wake reaching them several minutes after the tanker had passed rocked both boats.

By about 6 pm the two vessels were following the A-T pack at a slow pace. A few red and pink salmon jumpers were sighted. An obvious increase in the activity of the whales began to take place. They split into subgroups and there were several breaches along with fluke slaps on the water. The engines of both vessels were turned off. Mike put his hydrophone in the water and connected it to speakers and a recorder on the *Czarina*. Reed deployed one on the *Karen Marie*. There was abundant chatter between the orcas.

"Too bad we don't know what they're saying," Reed told the listeners on both boats.

One of the juveniles came back to circle and look closely at the crew on the *Czarina*.

"I'll bet she recognized us," Tracy told Mike and Sally.

"That might have been T8. Maybe she came to the *Czarina* because she knew the sound of the engines."

The whales apparently had encountered one or more schools of northwardmigrating salmon and had begun to feed on them. Video cameras were ready but most of the action occurred below the surface. One of the questions Reed, Mike, and Tracy wished to answer was whether the orcas were using bursts of sonar to stun the salmon. Such a question would be difficult to answer because killer whales, perhaps more than most predators, appeared to enjoy the chase as much as the kill so long as they were not desperately hungry. An orca enjoying the chase of a ten pound red salmon was not likely to zap the fish, particularly if it was teaching good hunting tactics to a juvenile.

On one occasion a female with a juvenile came very near the *Czarina* after a jumper salmon had sailed through the air near the boat, and there seemed little question that they were after that particular salmon. Speakers were attached to each hydrophone, as well as a recorder, and those on board the two quietly rolling boats could hear the contentedsounding clicktrains, buzzes, popclicks and rusty gate sounds of the whales. The recorders were picking up a much wider range of sounds than the human ear could detect and the tapes would be analyzed later in the Hydrosphere labs as they tried to sort out which calls and sounds the orcas made when feeding on salmon. Hydrosphere technicians had rigged up a directional device for the hydrophone Reed had deployed, but it was of little value with the group of whales circling and feeding in all directions around the two boats.

Aboard the *Czarina*, Kim blew the whistle as she fed and watered the pigs every couple of hours and made sure they had their vitamin supplements every day. She had become impressed when reading about the layers of fat all of the mammals living in these icy waters seemed to develop, and the pigs would probably do best if they, too, had more than the usual insulating layer. "I'm trying to add weight to the pigs, should be able to tolerate the cold water better," she told Reed, Mario, and Evelyn when she returned to the flying bridge. They were watching the orcas occasionally flash or twist at the surface while chasing their silvery prey.

"They're not the only ones putting on weight," Reed replied. "I'll bet these whales add 25% to their body weight during the salmon runs in June and July. This is the time of plenty." They watched the salmon for a few more minutes and listened to the whale calls coming in on the hydrophone.

A call came over the radio for Mike. It was Kate Davis saying the Short trio had arrived in Whittier with their supplies, which had been loaded onto the Vamp and they were ready to head out. "Now, where am I supposed to take them?" she demanded to know.

"Take them to Herring Bay where we have a camp. There is a dock and they can go ashore for a bit and meet Don Schwartz, our man of all trades who is there. Then call us and we'll give you directions."

"OK, Sweety, we'll be out of Whittier in about one hour."

Back at the *Karen Marie*, "You know," Reed observed, scanning through binoculars at the surface of the water, "these orcas in this one feeding will probably consume 3,500 pounds of salmon. If you figure an average of about 8 pounds each for the mix of reds and pinks, that's about 440 fish in this one feeding session."

"Yeah," Mario added, "from the fisherman's standpoint that salmon is worth about $8,000 in one day or $240,000 for one month...no wonder the Japanese kill whales and dolphins as competitors."

"The Japanese are killing whales of many kinds under the guise of scientific research," Reed noted. "They can't seem to break a bad habit, even under international pressure."

The whales began splitting into what appeared to be two separate groups. One group of nine, which included the large bull Kray and what appeared to be T-7, seemed to want to remain in this area. But the other ten whales headed northwest and soon disappeared.

"This is not unusual." Mike pointed out. "We have noted a pack splitting up and then regrouping several days later. We can follow only one so we hope it is the aggressive part of the pack that we will follow. The large bull has remained here and perhaps the females that cause problems may be here too."

"Yes, particularly T-7", Stacy agreed. "Let's stay with this one."

"And staying with them means we must follow them" Mike noted. "How about the *Czarina* crew taking the first shift and the *KM* can follow?"

By 7 pm the sea was calm. The remaining whales formed a close group and started west. The *Czarina* followed the pack at a distance of 50 yards and the Karen Marie 50 yards behind the *Czarina*. Evelyn had already started dinner in the *KM* and Sally was busy in the *Czarina*. The whales were not as active now and it appeared they might have eaten their fill.

"Reed, why don't you have Mario take the *KM* and go into one of the safe anchorages tonight," Mike called on the radio. "We'll follow the subjects and let you know by radio tomorrow where we are. They've filled up this evening, not much activity expected."

"OK," Reed called back, "or we could take the first shift tonight."

"We'll do the first duty and you can take it next. At least we know we've got decent weather tonight," he smiled at Tracy. "Oh oh, they're moving now and looks like T-7 is leading."

The main course for both boats was ham and lima beans, cooked with fresh garlic. It had been started by Evelyn earlier in the day at the lodge and it was a simple matter to reheat a pot half full of the steaming mixture. Green salad, homemade bread and chocolate chip cookies rounded out the meal.

On board the *KM* Evelyn asked as she passed the beans around: "How about a bottle of good Malbec?"

"Great idea" Reed responded. "We need some sleep tonight because we won't get much tomorrow night."

The two vessels separated and Mike steered the *Czarina* behind the slow-moving whales. No time to delay, he and Tracy would take turns eating while the other steered to follow the whales, which started on a leisurely northerly course.

The radio buzzed. Mike answered and found Dan Short on the other end. They had left Whittier as planned and were approaching Herring Bay. "Right where you are is the best spot for tonight," Mike advised him. "We have found some characters and are aiming to get better acquainted. We'll call you tomorrow morning with more info. Over and out." He hoped Dan would understand. Mike then told Stacy and Sally who it was and what the call was about. "Perhaps the Canadians will be useful," he mentioned to Tracy.

Kate Davis steered the *Vamp* toward the dock at the Herring Bay camp. There was one guy there who waved to them to pull up to the dock.

"That must be Don Schwartz," Kate observed. "He's the handy man at this camp."

Don tied the *Vamp* to the dock and helped each of them out of the boat. First Dan Short, dressed in obviously new outdoor clothing. Then Rolanda, the beautiful black woman, wearing turquoise tights and a matching jacket. Don had recent experience with the only black woman in Nome and nodded appreciation at meeting Rolanda. Next was Rolly McAllister who appeared to Don to be in his late twenties and in good physical condition. Then Kate jumped to the dock and gave Don a big hug and laughed with a sort of raw, wild sound. Don noticed that for a woman in her, he guessed, mid to late forties, she had a firm, full body which had been conditioned by years of self-preservation. And she had a way of moving that suggested she knew how to enjoy that body and didn't give a damn who knew it.

"My name is Kate," she said. "But some of my male friends call me Love Buns or just Buns for short."

"Welcome to the camp," Don smiled. "Let's walk over to the lodge and I'll show you around." Don was proud of the facilities and had grown rather fond of the pigs. Dan, Rolanda, Rolly, and Buns had no idea why the pigs were there and asked Don many questions. Don's consistent answer was "You'll have to talk to the scientists, I'm just the camp tender."

In the lodge they enjoyed a good Canadian whisky, Crown Royal. Don went out and fed the pigs. Buns smiled at Don, "We've got a ton of fresh groceries out there on the *Vamp*, Don. Why don't you come out to eat with us tonight?"

"Pretty good idea, Buns, but I've got a better one. Just bring some groceries in here and I'll cook dinner, we'll have some drinks and chat."

Dan and Rolly volunteered to get some of the grocery items and bring them in to the lodge. Don looked them over and said "Ground beef, OK? How about hamburgers tonight with a nice salad?"

Rolanda helped Don in the kitchen and chopped up the salad. Dan, Rolly, and Buns got better acquainted while sipping the Crown Royal. It was obvious Buns was aiming to get closely acquainted with Rolly and she began filled in some details about the cabins on the *Vamp*. As an ex-fishing boat it did not have deluxe accommodations and most of the cabins had bunk beds, a small table and a chair. Dan remarked that he and Rolanda would have no problem with that because they could both get in the lower bunk at first and then Dan would get into the upper bunk. Buns told Rolly, both now feeling the alcohol, that she had better plans for him, he could sleep with her in the double bed in her captain's cabin. Rolly, who hadn't been with a woman for weeks, looked at Buns's attractive body and just said "We'll see."

Dinner went by quickly with Don telling his usual jokes and everyone laughing. By ten o'clock the dishes had been washed and they all called it a day. Dan promised to cook breakfast the next morning and he, Rolanda, Buns, and Rolly walked back out to the *Vamp*.

Buns got Rolly by the arm and practically dragged him into her cabin and shut the door. She threw her arms around him and began kissing him on the face and neck. Rolly began to warm up, particularly when Buns ran her hand down to his crotch and began rubbing. "Listen," Rolly whispered in her ear, "I've had a problem with getting it up, you know, some kind of disfunction they call it. I may be a failure."

"Nonsense," Buns told him. "Here, sit on the bed while I get a potion I've made." She went to the cabinet at the foot of the bed and brought out a bottle that looked like some kind of soda. "I figured out a way to get some of the male enhancement drugs to work faster, I grind them up and dissolve one in cola and that's what this is. Here, drink up!"

"Well, what the hell," Rolly mumbled. "This stuff requires a prescription, where did you get it?" He took a sip and it tasted OK so he emptied the bottle.

"Some of my contacts have a pharmacy in Anchorage and they send them to me once in a while. They want to be sure the tablets are on hand when they come down to Whittier. Now, let me show you a few things." She unbuttoned Rolly's shirt, took it off and then pushed him back on the bed. Next were the shoes and then the pants and underwear. "See, my potion is working already" she smiled as she rubbed Rolly's naked body. After removing her own clothing she climbed on top of Rolly, who was now smiling and ready. Buns showed him some body movements he had never seen before and soon had him gasping for breath as she twisted and bounced. After several minutes they were both exhausted and collapsed on the bed.

"See, this is going to be a good trip," Buns told him as she kissed him.

"Looks like it will be one helluva trip. Now I know why they call you Love Buns," Rolly responded and then fell asleep.

Meanwhile, out in Prince William Sound aboard the *Karen Marie* they had settled in to enjoy dinner before moving to one of the coves for a sheltered anchorage.

"There's a pretty good anchorage in a bay on the south side of McPherson Passage on Naked Island," Mario suggested as he savored another mouthful of beans. "Only a couple of miles away. What do you think about going there?"

"You're the skipper," Reed answered, "but the closer the better, I guess. We don't know where we'll rendezvous tomorrow."

A half-hour later they had dropped anchor in the bay. Not as protected as some, but adequate unless a northeast wind came up. Kim continued to be amazed as one gorgeous view after another was revealed in Prince William Sound. Even this anchorage, with only sparse vegetation on a relatively low island had its own beautiful charm.

Kim had raked the soiled straw out of the pig kennels and replaced it. The used straw was swept overboard as completely biodegradable material. "Makes more plankton," Reed had said.

The pigs were fed and watered. They weren't very happy about being in the kennels again after the freedom they had enjoyed in the pen at Herring Bay and they let Kim know it with unhappy grunts and squeals. But they had plenty to eat. There was a small portion of the ham and beans left over and Evelyn suggested Kim give it to the pigs. They relished the change of diet, particularly the ham.

"Wonder if they realize they're eating one of their brothers?" Mario asked, watching the pigs slurp up the food from their heavy plastic dishes.

"I'd like to think my pigs are different, but the truth is they would probably even eat raw pork. Hogs commonly kill and eat piglets if they get a chance, so a little ham with beans won't give them a guilty conscience. Besides, they like the garlic."

Mario and Ev started washing the dishes while Reed and Kim got a large cushion and float coats and went up on the bridge. Reed brought binoculars and two small glasses of Glenfiddich Scotch. Kim was still fascinated by the mountains, trees and the ocean itself.

"Why is marine life so abundant in these colder waters?" she asked Reed. "And many of the fish and animals seem so large". They both sipped the Scotch.

"Well, that's a complex question, Kim, and nobody seems to have the entire answer but it seems that many fish and their prey grow larger and more robust in cold waters and there tends to be more of them because there is more food. However, lots of fish in the tropics also. But let's not talk technicalities, I'd like to tell you how beautiful you are, even in that orange float coat."

"Thanks, it's not easy to look good out here on the briney," Kim smiled.

"This project will not last more than a few more weeks and I'd love to have you come to Southern California to see my work and school there. And I know my boys would love to meet you and get acquainted."

They chatted on about possible future plans for another half hour before deciding to call it a day. When they entered the cabin, Evelyn and Mario were watching a video tape of `On Golden Pond.' Reed and Kim excused themselves and said it had been a long day. Both Mario and Evelyn nodded their understanding. The *Karen Marie* was large enough that there was a captain's stateroom with one double bed, along with three crew bunk rooms with two bunk beds in each. When loading their gear Kim and Reed had selected one of the empty bunk rooms for their gear. There was no way two people could comfortably sleep in one of the bunks, but they were perfectly adequate for making love followed by sleeping in separate bunks.

Kim and Reed did not ask about the sleeping arrangements between Ev and Mario. It was none of their business, but they were curious about the lovemaking abilities of a man in his midsixties.

Aboard the *Czarina* the engines were idling along. Tracy had taken the first turn at the wheel and was moving slowly along to the northwest behind the pack of nine killer whales. Sally washed the few dishes while Mike looked over the maps to again see where they had been during the day and where they might be going. Fortunately, in a resting mode the whales did not go into shallow or rockstrewn water.

One of the females, they could not tell which, began rolling and cavorting at the surface, with two males rolling with her. Through the binoculars Tracy could see, even 200 yards away in the Alaska twilight, the erect penises of the two males as they rolled.

"Looks like a little lovemaking going on out there," Tracy told Mike and Sally. "The two males with that cow are hot to trot."

Sally picked up a pair of binoculars to watch while Mike got out the video camera and put on a float coat and wool hat.

"I'll go up and see if I can get some footage of this," he said. "We don't have much coverage of sexual activity. If you can get a little closer without disturbing them it would help." He smiled at Tracy.

"I'll do what I can," she said, looking ahead with binoculars.

On the flying bridge Mike sat down and rested the camcorder on his upright knee for stability. Looking through the unit he zoomed in on the location where there had been turbulence in the water, but did not turn the unit on. No whales. Tracy kept the boat idling toward the location where the whales were last seen.

Suddenly on the port side Mike heard a loud "Whuff" followed by two more. He swung the camcorder and turned it on at the same time. Three whales were so close he had to back off from the zoom lens magnification and he missed recording what he had seen: two males with erections, both attempting to penetrate the female they were rolling with. Tracy cut the engine and they drifted in silence. Mike kept the unit running this time and, as the three whales again surfaced to blow within 100 feet of the *Czarina*, he filmed the whales including the large male. That was T4 he thought, after having a good look at the dorsal fin, but he wasn't sure of the identity of the other male or the female. Again the whales rolled and T4 and the female were now stomach to stomach. Although he couldn't see for sure, the male might have achieved penetration.

"Did you get that?" Tracy called out from the foot of the ladder. "Copulation close at hand!"

"I'm pretty sure I got it," he called back with the camcorder still running and picking up everything they said.

The whales continued cavorting in the area for another thirty minutes and on one occasion Tracy thought she saw the second male penetrating the female. The three orcas then speeded up to catch the other whales in the distance and Tracy, piloting the *Czarina*, followed. Mike came down from the bridge where it was getting colder with the decreasing sunlight and the more swiftly moving air.

"Looks like two different males may have bred that female," Tracy said. "Interesting. Wonder if that reduces stress and competition within the group."

"Looked like a regular `menage a trois' to me, or whatever they call it in France," Sally laughed, and they smiled with her.

"We have never seen the males compete for a female," Mike added. "But it makes you wonder how they prevent inbreeding. That was definitely T4 there, and the other one appeared to be T12, but was that one of their sisters they were breeding, or their mother? There must be some diversity of breeding stock or the orca tightlyknit groups are going to get into inbreeding trouble."

"How are you ever going to find out?" Sally asked.

Tracy answered from the wheel where she was carefully trailing the orcas. "We need more studies. More funding and better studies."

Sally had another question. "Are you two biologists?"

"No," Tracy smiled, "Mike is a geologist and I'm a computer programmer. We're out here because we like the whales and want to help them if we can."

"In college in Minnesota I joined Blue War one time. They were trying to get everyone behind the effort to stop the studying of whales and leave them alone," Sally said.

"That's the `head in the sand' attitude," Tracy answered. "How do those people expect to learn anything about these creatures? Here we are trying to live on the water planet with these gorgeous, powerful mammals and those fools want concerned, knowledgeable scientists to stay away from them."

"There is little doubt that Blue War would not agree with what we're doing," Mike added, "but we know these whales and we know the fishermen. If we don't find out damned quick which of the whales is causing trouble, and hopefully why, and come up with a solution, there could many orcas killed in this Sound."

"There is no way the `greenies' sitting in Washington D. C., or London, or wherever," Tracy added, "are going to understand the situation here in the Sound. We're here to help the whales in the best way we can, and we hope our plan will work."

"But we don't need to get on a soap box for you, Sally," Mike nodded.

"You'll see how we care for the orcas and intend to protect them."

The conversation turned to planning for the nightlong surveillance of the whales. Sally was sufficiently experienced in handling boats that she would have no trouble at all with the *Czarina*. They decided to take three hour turns at the wheel. Tracy offered to take the nine to twelve shift and Mike said he would take the midnight to three 'ordeal' as he smilingly called it. Sally was game for any shift but said the three to six would be OK with her. Mike advised Sally that the rule was that if any one of them lost the whales for fifteen minutes they were to immediately wake the others.

Sally agreed and went to brush her teeth and get in the bunk. Tracy and Mike sat together on high stools at the wheel of the *Czarina* following the whales. There was little chance of losing them unless a storm came up or the whales decided they did not want to be followed and gave the *Czarina* crew the 'slip.' Mike put on one of the tapes they'd had on the Czarina for years, Frank Sinatra singing Strangers in the Night and other classics. But he kept the volume low so Sally wouldn't be disturbed.

At about 10 pm Mike laid down on the sofa just toward the stern from the wheel and went to sleep. Stacy was at the wheel until midnight and then woke Mike. Sally was awakened at 3 am to take over. The night passed uneventfully. Tracy came out of her bunk at 6:00 am rubbing her eyes. Mike was still asleep on the sofa and had not even bothered to get undressed and into his bunk the previous night.

"Mike just toughed it out, huh?" she said to Sally.

"He probably thought it wasn't worth it for a few hours, and maybe he thought I'd need help."

"Whales still there?" Tracy asked confidently as she looked past the bow of the
Czarina.

"Right there, 200 yards ahead," Sally pointed. "But they're going south now instead of northwest. About the time we got to where I could see a number of commercial fishing boats up north this morning the whales turned south. I think they're smart to stay away from those fishermen; most of them are good people but there are derelicts and I can say that from first-hand experience."

The whales, visible every few minutes, were moving at a leisurely pace toward the northwest end of Knight Island in the vicinity of Herring Bay.

"Wouldn't that be something if they turned into Herring Bay," Tracy laughed. "We could stop in and have coffee with Don and still keep the whales in sight. Oh, and remember, Mike planned to meet the people from Canada who were stopping in Herring Bay. Speaking of coffee, how about some?" She went down to the small galley to draw water and put a coffee percolator on the propane stove.

The radio buzzed. It was Buns at Herring Bay. "We're ready to head out this morning, where are you?"

Mike replied: "You're at Herring Bay so just head north out into the Sound and you'll see us a couple of miles out. We're following at a slow pace so you'll catch up in no time. We'll watch for you and call again."

"OK" Kate replied. "We're departing now." Those on the Vamp waved to Don as they pulled away.

The smell of coffee filled the cabin of the *Czarina* as Mike began to scan with binoculars. The steady, pulsing throb of the engines and the gentle roll of the boat were sensations he appreciated. The *Czarina* was still following the A-T pack.

"Everything OK?" he asked Sally, who was in the captain's chair steering.

"No problems," Sally responded. "The orcas are 200 yards ahead, and we're going south now."

Tracy poured coffee for all three of them and set one cup near the wheel for Sally and one on the small table for Mike. He took a sip and then staggered to his feet to look out. He saw island terrain at about ten o'clock in the distance but wasn't sure which island.

"Where are we?" he asked Sally.

"Believe it or not, that's Knight Island in the distance. We're about an hour from the entrance to Herring Bay."

"That's a twist. The *Karen Marie* could have stayed at camp and joined us this morning" Mike chuckled.

Tracy was in the galley. "I'll go ahead and prepare breakfast, Mike. Maybe you should call Don and tell him where we're located."

Mike reached Don immediately on the radio and Don chuckled when he heard the location of the *Czarina* following the whales. He told Mike about the *Vamp* just departing and should be in sight soon. He also suggested Mike call Mario or Reed and pass on the location.

"By the way," Don said, "yesterday George from Moose and Goose called and said three of them are coming out later today. He'll call when they get in the area to find out your location. Anything you want me to tell him?"

"Three?" Mike questioned.

"Didn't ask him for details," Don replied, followed by a moment of silence. "Can you see the *Vamp* yet? 'Ol Buns should be showing up any minute."

Tracy had been watching with binoculars and she exclaimed "There's a boat approaching and it may be the *Vamp*."

"If it's the *Vamp*, Buns probably has her radio on." Mike noted. "Hey Buns, can you read me."

"I sure as hell can!" buns replied immediately. "I'm glad I found you bastards before you got out any further. I've got Dan and Rolanda with me and a really sweet guy named Rolly."

"OK, fall in about 50 yards behind the *Karen Marie* and follow. We're on an interesting trail.

Reed called Mike on the *Czarina*. "How's it going?" he asked Mike.

"There was a split of parties" Mike told him, "and we hope we have picked the right one. We're now back near camp and don't know what is next. But there now seems to be some sort of change underway. Best idea: stay where you are and we'll follow the party. Buns and her group just joined us."

Reed hung up the radio and the spoke to Kim, Evelyn, and Mario: "The *Czarina* has been following what they believe is the core of the A-T pack after the pack split. They are now back near Herring Bay and Mike suggests we stay put until they see something important is happening. They'll call us then and we can join them. The *Vamp* just joined them."

Aboard the *Karen Marie* breakfast was over. Kim had fed and watered the pigs, blowing the whistle as usual. The pigs continued to register unhappiness with the confinement by squealing, grunting and rattling their kennels. Kim remarked that they had gotten spoiled by the conditions in the pen at camp.

On the *Czarina* it was noted that the whales had apparently awakened and were now turning to the northeast and picking up speed. Mike radioed the *KM* again. "Change of course and speed. Now heading NE and will be approaching your area in one hour." Mario acknowledged the call.

Mike radioed the *KM* and the *Vamp* again: "We're getting near the north end of Montague Island and this is likely a good time for the *KM* to start over to intersect our trajectory." Mario acknowledged the message and checked one of his maps. He and Reed also looked at the

GPS and wrote down their location and where they should be going.

The radio crackled, it was Dan Short on the *Vamp* with Buns, Rolanda, and Rolly calling for Mike or Tracy. "We believe we see the *Czarina* up ahead and I was hoping we could get more details about your planning. Is that possible?"

"Yes", Mike told him. "We're going slow now so come alongside and I'll fill you in."

Within five minutes the *Vamp* was alongside the *Czarina* and there were introductions followed by Mike and Tracy telling them of the plan to use the pigs as substitutes for people to see what the whales would do with a strange animal."

Both Rolly and Dan thought this was a fantastic idea. Rolanda wasn't so sure and Buns thought it was hilarious. "You're gonna feed those whales fresh pork? They'll be so damned spoiled they won't want to eat fish anymore." And she laughed as she pointed to Mike and Tracy.

Dan wanted to know if there was a chance he might try to communicate with the whales and Rolly expressed enthusiasm for the possible opportunity.

"Won't be much chance to try it on this expedition but you can record and observe all you want. Just don't interfere with what we are trying to accomplish." A small plane passed overhead.

Meanwhile, on the *Karen Marie*, Reed helped stow the anchors and Mario steered north out of the bay and then turned southeast. The two vessels remained in direct radio contact and within an hour Mario had the *Czarina* and the *Vamp* in sight. "Hey, there you are!" he radioed to the Mike and Buns. "We'll swing in behind you two."

"So far, so good," Mike responded. "Might be a good idea to hang back there one hundred yards or so. Less noise."

"Will do."

CHAPTER TWENTY EIGHT

𝓕𝑜𝓁𝓁𝑜𝓌

The whales picked up speed easily, much easier than the *Czarina*, which was having trouble staying not far behind the cruising black and white hunters. Occasionally an orca would jump clear of the water and land with a big splash.

Once again the radio crackled. This time it was George Maxwell. "We're on our way, about two hours out of Whittier. You don't have to tell us where you are, one of our planes is in the area and they have already spotted you for us. We'll be there in about thirty minutes."

"Terrific," Mike replied.

The *Czarina* was now 200 yards, the length of two football fields, behind the northeast bound whales, moving more quickly along the west coast of Knight Island. The *Karen Marie* and the *Vamp* were half that distance behind the . The whales were fully aware that the three vessels, including one they recognized, were behind them.

The pigs continued grunting and squealing protests about the confinement. Kim remarked that they could see all the deck space and couldn't understand why they weren't allowed out.

Within five minutes of the time the *Karen Marie* joining the *CZ*, Mike radioed to Mario and Buns that something was up. The whales had stopped and were milling around. "All engines stop," he called to Mario and Buns. Then to Tracy: "Phones might be a good idea," referring to hydrophones.

Welcome silence overtook the *Czarina*. After hours of listening to the engines, quiet was a sudden adjustment to reality. Hydrophones were quickly deployed and camcorders made ready. Considerable chatter could be heard among the whales.

"Wonder if they're getting ready to go hunting?" Tracy asked, almost in a whisper.

The whales started northeast again as a group, and picking up speed. Mike was looking ahead with binoculars to see if there was anything visible. "There's something out there!" he told Tracy and Sally. "Looks like three heads of some animals." As they got a little closer he became excited. There are three deer, they must be swimming from island to island and they are out here in the path of the whales! This could be interesting." He radioed the news to the other boats but did not use the term deer, he just used "swimmers."

The whales had detected the deer before Mike ever saw them. It would be easy to cut off their access to shore and this was not their first encounter with this type of animal. To be cautious they circled around the deer and examined them visually and with sonar. None of the deer had antlers. Three of the whales swam near the surface, exhaling, and the deer panicked and began swimming in circles. The *Karen Marie* and the *Vamp* pulled up and stopped next to the *Czarina* and they all watched.

Tinga signaled to other whales that this was good food and, at moderate speed, she seized the lead deer by the neck and dove with it. Other whales grabbed the other two. In the subsurface the whales began tearing them apart and feeding. The bony lower legs were severed and dropped to the bottom. The heads were also severed and discarded. Crimson blood clouded the water.

"Swimmers taken and likely eaten!" Mike shouted over to the other boats. "Perhaps they're going to start feeding on mammals today!"

"If they are, we want to be there!" Reed shouted back. Dan and Rolly cheered.

Four of the whales suddenly surfaced to blow within 100 feet of the *Czarina*, two females and two older juveniles, for no apparent reason. They surfaced and disappeared so quickly there was no opportunity for identification.

Tracy spotted them again, they were slowly moving under the *Karen Marie*. She called to Reed and told him what she saw and added: "I wonder if they are down there listening to our cargo?"

Tinga and three of the other whales had sensed something different about this boat. They all had a noisy device with dangerous blades on one end but this one seemed to be carrying something that made strange sounds and that could be some kind of animals. The whale's sensitive hearing picked up the sounds and aroused the whale's curiosity. Tinga slowed her travel, with the entire group responding, and they circled to listen. As she did so, the noise from the vessels stopped and the whales could hear more clearly other sounds from the boats. They heard sounds of the two-legged creatures communicating between themselves but they also could hear the strange sounds but now louder and more frequent from the larger vessel.

Tinga signaled the others to wait as she, her three-year-old calf, Tyree, and two other females went back to determine more closely the source of this sound. They surfaced to blow near the familiar, smaller vessel, knowing there was no danger, and continued under the surface to the other. Sonar indicated wires hanging down from both boats, something with which they were again familiar.

All four of them circled slowly under the hull of the larger vessel, listening intently. The sounds were coming from one end of the boat and somehow stirred ancient instincts in the whales. The sounds indicated there were several of the creatures present.

The front third of Tinga's body rose from the water as she came above the surface in a spyrise to look on the deck of the craft. She could not see the sound sources because of a cover. She went to the other side and rose again, but still she could not see the source.

Curiosity not satisfied, the four whales swam past the smaller, friendly vessel. As they passed, Tinga led the group to the surface and looked at the familiar forms on the deck. To her these were interesting creatures who did them no harm. She had no urge, or need, to communicate. The whales lived here. This was their home. They could live in peace with these creatures and the creatures should live at peace with the whales.

Tinga and the other three rejoined the orca pack and they started off in their northeast direction again.

The whales kept up a moderate pace, rising for air every four minutes. As evening fell they came across a large school of salmon and spent an hour and a half at one location catching and eating salmon until all had eaten their fill. It was a time of plenty.

While the whales were catching and eating salmon and all three boats were in one place, they were pulled together within talking distance; no snoopy radio on. Everyone was introduced, with Kim even introducing the noisy pigs. Reed explained the goal of the "expedition" as he was now calling it. The three from Canada were fascinated, particularly Dr. Dan Short who wanted to try communication experiments, and Rolly, who thought this might be his chance to be a hero to the Orca Communication Society. The hydrophones were picking up whale chatter.

Tracy spotted four whales that had split away from the main group and were headed for the idle boats. 'Looks like we've got four visitors coming!" she called to the others.

All of them crowded the rails looking into the water; it seemed only seconds before the whales were visible, passing under the vessel. The hull and surroundings were being scanned by sonar. The pigs squealed and grunted.

Kim was looking down into the water as four black torpedo shapes silently but rapidly passed by in perfect alignment. She was awestruck by both the organization of these intelligent creatures and their huge size. Reed whispered to her that the whales were probably listening to the pigs.

Just then one of the females, an unusually large female, passed on the right side of the *KM* and exhaled with a loud Whuff!!

"That was T7," he told Kim. "She's a large female, and did you see those three tooth scars across the saddle field on the left side?" Kim was astounded by the size and speed of the whale.

"Yes, I saw it," she said. "But, you know, this is the first time I have ever felt that I was the one being studied by an animal rather than vice versa."

"T7 clearly appears to be the leader of this clan and we suspect she's also highly intelligent and aggressive. Almost as if she's a different type of whale."

The female killer whale now passed on the opposite side of the *Karen Marie* as cameras and recorders caught the action. "She couldn't see on one side so she tried the other," Mario observed. "She wants to see what's makin' all that noise."

Click trains, crow calls, whistles and pops continued to be received by the hydrophone, but with greatly reduced intensity. The four whales surfaced to blow, but appeared to be moving out after joining the other whales.

"The visit may be over," Reed commented.

"Those are some animals," Evelyn said as she shook her head. "One of these days man might figure out how to communicate with them."

"Hell, Ev, what makes you think they'd want to talk to man?" Mario responded. "They been doin' fine here for millions of years before we showed up, and they communicate fine among themselves. They'd probably be happy if man would disappear from the scene, which, perhaps unfortunately, doesn't seem about to happen."

On board the *Vamp* with Buns, Dan and Rolly were ecstatic at getting close to the pack of whales that is being studied. Dan is trying to think of new ways to try to communicate with them. Rolanda wonders if they should try music.

Kim was thinking it all over. "Can you imagine being out in a small boat with those whales coming to take a close look at you?" she asked. "Or worse, to have them dump you into the water the way they seem to have done with some kids."

"They are the kings and queens of the waters," Reed said. "The top predators in the oceans. In their own environment, which covers most of the globe, there is nothing on earth which can hold a candle to them."

"Looks like we're moving again," Mike shouted to them as he started up the *Czarina*. "Looked like you were being inspected, and the cargo too."

On the radio once more Mario voiced his opinion: "That must have been the inspection committee, but all the noisemaking cargo was covered." Everyone knew he was referring to the pigs and that the whales had come to determine the source of the noise.

With the engines on three vessels started the procession was whales, *Czarina*, *KM* and then Buns and her passengers. The whales turned south along the west coast of Knight Island. Aboard the *Czarina* Sally went to her bunk to catch up on sleep. Mike and Tracy would take turns napping throughout the day.

Aboard the *Karen Marie*, the unhappiness of the pigs was disturbing Kim. The skies were overcast, but it was not raining and the wind was only moderate. "Reed," she said, "do you suppose we could take these kennels and turn them all facing toward the stern and the wake behind the boat? I think if the pigs can see more open space and the water they're not going to complain so much."

"I don't know why not," he replied, "but let's get Evelyn to help. Hey Ev," he called into the cabin where she was standing by Mario, "would you help us move these kennels?"

There was sufficient width to the stern of the *Karen Marie* to place the kennels side by side with the wire doors facing toward the slowly churning wake of the vessel but there was still plenty of room for Kim to move along the stern side of the containers to check on her passengers, feed them and clean the kennels. The side rails would prevent any lateral movement. They lashed the kennels in place with stout rope to prevent any movement.

The maneuver seemed to work. The pigs, seeing the vast expanse of water, seemed to conclude that they were better off in the kennels where, even though crowded, they were well fed and had fresh straw to lay on. The squealing and grunting stopped as they lay quietly.

It was nearly 2 pm when they heard a familiar voice on the radio. "Herring Bay, Herring Bay, this is the Goose, do you read me?" They recognized George Maxwell's voice. .

"Goose, this is Mike, where are you?"

"Northwest of the Bay about 8 miles, looking to meet up with you very shortly."

Mike knew George would rather wait on shore than to spend a lot of time searching for the whales in the Sound. "Slow movement here but we're latched on, heading south. We'll watch for you." Mike guessed they were probably going about 10 to 15 miles per hour and getting very close.

"Sounds good," George called back.

It was a little after 3 when George called again. The whales, with the three vessels trailing, had passed the southwest end of Knight Island and were traveling southeast through Knight Passage at a leisurely pace.

In another half hour they could see a vessel approaching from the stern, back about 2 miles. In fifteen minutes the "Goose," actually named the *Glacier Bay*, had passed Buns' boat and was alongside the *KM*. The *G Bay* was a 40 foot diesel powered "bow picker" fishing boat, so named because the fishing nets were brought in over the bow rather than the stern. Along with George was Herb Bracken and a female they recognized as Cynthia Scott, ADF&G biologist they had met in Anchorage. One of the game wardens for Alaska Fish and Game, Greg Wallace, was piloting the *Glacier Bay*.

The *KM* and the other three vessels came closer together at low speed allowing information exchanges to take place without resorting to the radio. Evelyn took over control of the *Karen Marie* and Mario stepped back to the stern.

Reed told George, Herb and Cynthia, over the sound of the engines and the water churning from the propellers, that the whales had fed on salmon the previous evening and that the *Czarina* had followed the pack all night. All seemed to be going well, the next move was up to the whales.

"Have you heard the weather forecast?" Herb called across between the rolling vessels.

"No," Reed replied. "What's up?"

"They're calling for a helluva blow starting sometime late tonight, probably lots of rain too."

Reed shook his head, "That's all we need when we're following this pack. We could easily lose them in a storm."

"Ha!" Mario scoffed. "If we get a blow like I've seen out here you'll be damn glad to find some shelter, let alone trying to follow some whales."

"I guess we'll just follow as long as we can," Reed offered. "If it gets too bad we'll have to quit." He went inside and called Mike on the radio to advise him of the weather forecast.

"Guess we'd better tune in to the weather forecast," Mike responded and tuned in to the weather report.

"Hey Reed" Herb Bracken practically shouted over the engine and wave noise, "I got approval from Dr. Walker to put a tag on one of the whales we're watching. Here, I'll hand over the tagging rod with tags attached. There's more than one tag here but we have approval for only one. You have the animals on board and you'll have a better chance to tag than I would."

"Fantastic, Herb," Reed replied. "We'll try to tag T-7 the first chance we get."

By 5 pm the orca pack, followed by the boats *Czarina*, *Karen Marie*, *Vamp* and *Glacier Bay*, had traveled southeast and east and was now approaching the Needle. The pointed, rugged rocks jutting from the lower bowels of the Sound always seemed ominous, but even more so when a storm was imminent. As they passed the rocks, sea lions barked, growled and roared. The whales did not even slow their pace as they passed the rocks, apparently paying little attention to the sea lions. There were plenty of the animals both on the rocks and in the water, their dark brown heads bobbing here and there in the swells crashing against the rocks. Several large bulls had taken commanding positions on the choice rocks and fought off any other lions that tried to approach.

As the four boats passed just downwind from the rocks the pungent, acidic stench from sea lion defecation was almost overpowering. Tracy radioed back to the following vessels, "Get ready to hold your noses!"

"I'd hate to smell that if it wasn't washed with distilled water every couple of days," Tracy commented to Mike and Sally referring to the abundant rainfall in the Sound. Then she turned to Mike. "Do you suppose ignoring the lions means they won't hunt mammals tonight?"

"Let's hope not," he replied. "If we don't see some action this evening we may lose them in the storm. Some of these storms can develop winds of over 100 miles per hour, not a pleasant time on the water."

Sally had prepared a snack of sandwiches and tea. They had learned long ago that, when following whales, regular meal times cannot be scheduled. Better to snack through the day and not be extremely hungry if the whales should commence activity and meals are missed.

At 5:30 in the afternoon, 2 miles north of the Needle it appeared resting and sleeping time may be over. The whales departed from the rhythmic slow travel in one direction and became active. There was rolling and splashing interplay between the whales and a general milling around along with a couple of jumps.

Mike called back to the other vessels. "Something happening, we're shut down. You might hold back and we'll put a phone in," referring to the hydrophone. Reed deployed his equipment and Dan on the *Vamp* did the same.

Over the hydrophone whale conversation came in loud and clear. Whistles, crowcalls, squeaks, clicktrains and rusty hinge noises strained the range of the listening devices. The recorder was running. "I'll bet Reed, Dan, and Rolly are enjoying this," Tracy smiled.

"You bet, and recording it too," Mike responded, watching the whales through binoculars. After fifteen minutes of the milling, including tail lobbing and jumping by several of the members. The clear call they had heard before came in again over the speaker.

"Kreeeaaaaah." Complete silence for thirty seconds. "Kreeeaaaahh." It was a bloodcurdling sound no matter how many times one might have heard it. After another minute or so of silence a few chirps and whistles were heard. The whales all disappeared from the surface.

"I recommend we bring in the hydrophone and get ready to move, honey," Tracy advised Mike. "Every time we've heard that call they are getting ready to move, and fast." Even before he could answer, she had turned the unit off and was bringing in and coiling the cord.

Mike knew Tracy had a good sense for the whales and their movements.

He started the *Czarina's* engines and began moving forward. He called the others. "Looks like we're going to be moving and it may be fast." All four boats in a line continued in the direction the whales were last seen.

"Keep your eyes open," he urged Sally and Tracy. "If they're swimming fast they may come up so far away we'll have trouble seeing them when they blow."

Both Mike and Tracy had lost the whales on other occasions when the whales took off rapidly in an unknown direction and were not seen again for several days.

Five minutes passed. Mike wasn't even sure in which direction to steer. He could only assume the orcas would continue in the same direction they were traveling earlier.

"There they are!" Tracy shouted, looking through binoculars. "They're at about ten o'clock and going northwest fast."

Even before looking, Mike revved up the *Czarina's* engines and surged forward turning northwest from the previous north heading. He picked up the microphone. "*KM*, subjects on northwest tack. Suggest following pronto like the hare. We may be more like turtle. Dig? Three will hang back."

"Dig," Mario chuckled a response and accelerated the powerful engines of the *Karen Marie*. He would soon overtake the *Czarina* and pass her. Mario also had better visibility because he was higher above the water surface. With binoculars he, too, now saw the distant blows and dorsal fins of the departing whales. The *Vamp* and the *Glacier Bay* stayed behind the *Czarina*.

——————— ◆◆◆ ———————

CHAPTER TWENTY NINE

Kennels over water

By running the *Karen Marie* at nearly 20 knots, Mario was able to keep the whale dorsal fins in view, but the whales forged ahead for only about thirty minutes and then veered toward the rocky area at the southwest end of Green Island. This island, a 7 x 2 mile, treecovered mass of schist and slate, is situated almost midway between Knight Island to the west and Montague Island, the largest in Prince William Sound, to the east. All of the large islands had a strong northeast elongation, reflecting large breaks in the earth's crust.

On the northwest side of Green Island was a rockstrewn bay known locally as Gibbon Anchorage, named after one of the early salmon seiners who frequented the area. The bay was open to the southwest and to the northeast, not a secure place to anchor in bad weather coming from those directions.

"We're slowing down here," Mario radioed back to the three vessels behind. "Looks like there's some interest in the nearshore area." He didn't disclose many details because other ears might be listening.

As they slowed, Kim checked on the pigs. They were all right, but in the high speed run they had taken a little more spray than they liked. Kim wished now she had returned the kennels to their original position, but, in the back of her mind, she wasn't sure how many would live through the evening anyway should the killer whales commence mammal hunting.

The weather report was ominous, but the high winds were not scheduled to arrive in the Sound until near midnight. Mario began thinking about safe harbors; he knew the Gibbon Anchorage was not it. The storm, moving in from the North Pacific, had hit Kodiak Island, 400 miles to the southwest, with wind velocities of 110 miles per hour. Hurricane strength, but they were not referred to as hurricanes or typhoons in Alaska, just strong winds.

Mike, Tracy and Sally, approaching in the *Czarina* with the *Vamp* and the *Glacier Bay* following closely behind, also had heard the weather forecast. Although an overcast still prevailed, the moderate surface winds gave no indication of the approaching storm. Tracy had stepped out of the cabin to look at the sky. High clouds were racing by at several times the speed of the surface winds. She reentered the cabin thinking that this was another typical Alaska experience. Things seem to be going well and making sense and then the unexpected strikes, usually with devastating results and, often enough, loss of human life.

"The weather sounds really grim," Mike observed. "If we don't make some observations this evening we may lose the pack for a week."

Reed's voice came over the radio, "Some definite interest in pinnipeds," he said abruptly, knowing those in the other two boats would recognize the nomenclature for seals and walruses.

The three trailing boats now approached the position of the *Karen Marie*, where Reed and the rest of the crew were intently watching the whales to see what action the orcas might be planning for the evening. The three boats idled forward so the whales, now apparently searching near some large, partially submerged rocks, could be kept in sight.

Radios were used as little as possible to avoid the possibility of fishing or pleasure boaters discovering what they were doing. Mike brought the *Czarina* in close to the *Karen Marie*, and turned the controls over to Sally, who seized every opportunity to handle the boat because she wanted to have her own fishing outfit one day. The engines of all four boats were turned off and hydrophones deployed.

"What do you think they're up to?" Mike asked Tracy as they leaned over the railing.

"Right now they seem to be checking out this rocky area for some reason. Maybe they're taking some sort of census of the mammal population," Tracy said, only half joking.

"High winds are supposed to reach here about midnight," Mike noted. "Hope we can make some observations this evening. Look, if the whales do start hunting, why don't we take the *Czarina* and the *Karen Marie* and loop out ahead of the pack. The other two boats can follow the whales and tell us when they're coming. And Tracy, tell Mario to watch out for rocks if we go into that bay called Gibbon Anchorage. We were in there one time before and there are quite a few rocks just under the surface. Right now we'll hang in here closest to the whales because of our shallow draft; the other three boats can follow out further from shore."

"Will do," Tracy replied, and went into the cabin to advise Mario.

Mike got on the radio and advised the other three boats of the plan in brief terms, including a warning about the rocks. The *Czarina* edged ahead of the other vessels and swung in closer to the shore for observations of the whales. They idled ahead to within 100 yards of the whales, a distance they knew from experience would not interfere with the whale's activities, mostly because the whales were familiar with the vessel. Tracy was prepared to sit on the bow, as she had done many times before when following whales, to scan the slightly murky waters ahead for subsurface rocks.

"All stop," Mike radioed, indicating he had stopped the engines to observe the whales. "Let's get up on the flying bridge," he told Sally. Tracy already had the hydrophone in the water and was climbing the ladder to the bridge. Mike grabbed his camcorder and followed.

The whales were circling at the mouth of a small, sharp bay which appeared to have been cut by a giant knife into the side of the island. The bay was no more than 200 yards from mouth to head and 50 yards wide with steep sides and practically no beaches. Tracy had been watching intently with the binoculars to see why the whales were there, knowing that when the whales were hunting they usually did not spend time idly.

"That's it, that's it!" she cried. "They're after what looks like a small group of Dall's porpoises that are in the bay."

Mike zoomed in on the bay with the camcorder and Sally focused binoculars on the surface. In a few seconds they saw what appeared to be tiny blows from small mammals swimming rapidly just below the surface.

"Too bad we don't have better light," Mike complained.

"I see them, but they look awfully small," Sally remarked.

"They can weigh up to 500 pounds, but the average is probably more like 300," Tracy responded. "The only reason they look so small is because the orcas are so comparatively large. T4 in the pack is about thirty times the size of one of the Dalls."

"We've seen Dall's porpoises many times riding the bow of the *Karen Marie* when we're going fishing," Sally said. "They seem like they're fast swimmers. They even make a sort of rooster tail at the surface when they're really swimming fast."

"They are fast," Tracy smiled, still looking through the binoculars. "But have you ever seen one of the female orcas at high speed. They're awesome!"

"Something is happening," Mike reported. "See those three or four orcas going into the bay? The rest of them seem to be staying outside." He picked up the microphone. "Something happening," he radioed to the three vessels waiting 50 yards further out.

"We see it," Mario radioed back.

Suddenly in two places the surface of the water in the bay was churned to a froth as the whales appeared to commence chasing the porpoises.

"Wonder why they don't beach themselves," Tracy half whispered. "If they just got out of the water..."

One of the porpoises jumped 3 feet above the water surface, apparently to escape an orca. It was headed for the bay entrance, but five orcas were waiting there, frequently rising to blow and obviously excited with the hunt under way. There was more churning at the surface and they could only guess at the action invisible below the surface. One of the porpoises appeared to escape the orca `net' and made a run for open water to the west, pursued by a female orca and a juvenile perhaps two years old. It was a high speed chase with the female orca actually passing the porpoise to turn it back toward the following juvenile.

"She's herding it!" Tracy exclaimed.

Together the two orcas then seemed to drive the porpoise back toward the rest of the pack. As they approached the group, the female came to the surface with the flukes of the porpoise in her mouth; the animal was struggling to get free. The female then released it at the surface and the juvenile made a fast run to grab the rear of the hapless porpoise by one of its flippers and dove with it.

"This is a training session," Tracy said excitedly. "I think she caught the porpoise, crippled it and then turned it over to the juvenile for practice."

The activity between the whales seemed to go on for several minutes, with a couple of juveniles swimming among the adults. When the porpoises had all disappeared, apparently killed and eaten, the whales regrouped to continue searching to the northeast along the steep and rocky coast. Tinga and her pack sensed the approach of windy weather. Beneath the surface the weather was almost always consistent, but a strong wind with breaking whitecaps at the surface made quite a bit of noise. It could also change the migration patterns of the salmon and cause the seals and other mammals to remain closer to shore than they otherwise might. It would be good to feed well on red meat before the storm arrives. They decided to enjoy a hunt before the storm, fully aware of the four vessels following them at a distance.

It mattered not if the vessels followed so long as they did not interfere with the hunting.

This particular evening, the orcas found themselves near a location they had hunted many times before with success for various types of warmblooded animals. After the slow pace of the day they enjoyed the rapid, exhilarating swim toward the hunting area.

Upon entering the area with its many large rocks, including some protruding above the surface, the entire pack immediately sensed five porpoises swimming together near the mouth of a small bay. If they could drive the porpoises into the bay they would have an excellent chance of catching them either in the bay or when they tried to escape through the waiting group.

Tinga, her calf and two juveniles eager for excitement, swam rapidly ahead of the pack, calling and broadcasting click trains. The porpoises took the most readily available route away from the orcas, into the cove. Intelligent creatures themselves, they realized it was possible the orcas might pass by and pursue other prey such as seals.

With the mammals in the bay and the rest of the group waiting at the mouth, Tinga and the others had nothing to lose by moving directly into the bay for pursuit and, if they caught any, killing and eating. It was all over very quickly. The first four porpoises were caught, killed, and dissected quickly. The fifth one was pursued by Bree, a mature female with a two year old calf, and driven back toward the pack. She had crippled the animal so her youngster could learn more about it. Bree and two other females and their offspring cut the animal into desirable and undesirable parts. The heart and liver were choice and were fed to the youngest juveniles. The rest of the intestines were discarded, along with the head and skin as one piece. The meatbearing bone structure was torn apart by the adults and swallowed. The whales regrouped to move on with the hunt.

◆◆◆

Tracy was still looking toward the spot in the water where the last porpoise had been caught as Mike started the *Czarina's* engines.

"Mike, wait a minute," she said. "There's something there in the water. Let's see what it is before we leave."

"OK, but let's make it quick. The whales are moving again."

Tracy climbed down the ladder and got out the large sport fish landing net which had a handle extendable to 10 feet. Sally pulled in the hydrophone cable. At the bow Tracy directed Mike with hand signals until she reached down with the net and brought up the black and white neatly skinned head and cape of a Dall's porpoise.

"Look at this," Tracy called as she lifted the stillbleeding cape from the net. "They skinned that porpoise as neatly as a hunter getting a skin ready for the taxidermist."

Mike held it up for Reed and the others to see at a distance and then advised them on the radio that he would save it in an unused cooler so they might all see the cutting agility the orcas possessed. "Good going!" Reed radioed back. "That's great for later study. But we'd better get going if we're going to keep up the watch." Mario revved up the engines of the *Karen Marie*. The *Czarina* with Sally at the helm was already moving out. The *Glacier Bay* and the *Vamp* remained in the rear.

Tracy and Mike looked at the detailed maps published by NOAA. About 2 miles ahead, between the main body of the Green Island and a small offshore mass of rocks, a channel perhaps 300 yards wide was shown. It appeared the whales would pass through the channel if they continued their present hunting course.

"What do you think, Tracy?" Mike asked.

"Looks like a good bet to me, and we should be able to get there and be ready when they arrive," she responded.

"Call the others," Mike urged as he proceeded to the wheel. "Ask the *Glacier Bay* and Buns to stay with the group in case they decide to go off in another direction. With the *KM* we'll loop around the whales to get in front of them so we can try the pig experiment." He revved up the *Czarina*.

The two vessels swung away from the shore and traveled about 2 miles. The objective was to loop around the whales without disturbing their hunt and be wellpositioned, and ready, ahead of them should their mammal hunt continue. Mike and Tracy could only guess at how far ahead they should be positioned. Two fishing boats passed by in the distance, apparently paying little attention to the four boats.

Thirty minutes later two anchors were dropped for the *Karen Marie*, one at the bow and one at the stern to keep the vessel from swinging in the tidal currents on just one anchor line. "Water's about 40 feet deep," Evelyn told Mario.

The tide was coming in and the two boats had been positioned 100 yards offshore with the bows facing southwest into the incoming tide. According to their prearranged plan, Mike brought the bow of the *Czarina* in about 100 feet northeast (down tide) from the stern of the *KM*; easy talking distance with the engines silent. Sally dropped the *Czarina's* anchor using the power winch. The wind had died almost completely, lending an eerie silence to the scene except for the noise of the pigs. Heavy clouds continued to race high overhead and it seemed unreal that there was no wind and no rain at the surface.

The plan was to send Kim ashore in the skiff from the *Karen Marie* and have her call the pigs with the whistle at the right time; everyone else would be busy on board. Mario and Evelyn hurriedly swung the small craft over the side with the boom and gently lowered it into the water. Evelyn stepped in, positioned and connected the 5-gallon fuel tank which Mario handed to her. Kim seemed ready to go in her orange float coat, wool cap and knee high rubber boots. The whistle hung around her neck along with binoculars.

Reed looked into her worried eyes. "Are you going to be OK?" he asked, his hands on her shoulders.

"I'll be all right. It's just a little scary ...and... I love those pigs." Tears welled in her eyes and she wiped them away.

"I'm sorry," Reed whispered sincerely. "Be careful, Kim." He kissed her lightly on the lips. Her response was extremely cool and distant. "I'd go in with you if I could, but I've got to run the camcorder and hydrophone recorder. Mario and Ev may need some help, too." He suddenly realized that such a statement might sound to Kim like he was staying on board to execute some of her friends. Maybe this whole idea was crazy, he thought. Maybe they should stop now and avoid devastating someone's feelings.

Mario and Ev held the skiff as Kim climbed in. "Better hustle," Mario encouraged Kim, who started the Suzuki outboard engine on the skiff. "Those orcas can move plenty fast when they want to."

They cast off the rope and Kim shifted the engine into forward, pushed the accelerator and headed for shore. In just a few minutes she approached the sand beach at the shore, turned off the engine and stepped out to wade onto the sand with the bow line and small anchor.

On board both vessels preparations were made hurriedly. Three hydrophones were dropped overboard and turned on. Cameras and camcorders were made ready.

Mike picked up the microphone. "George, this is Mike. How's progress?"

"Two `pinnies' for dinner," George responded, meaning pinnipeds. "Progress again under way. Status OK."

"104," Mike replied and replaced the microphone. Outside the cabin he called across to the others. "Did you hear that report from the Bay? The pack must have caught two seals and are now on their way again."

"We'd better get a sample ready," Reed replied.

Reed helped Evelyn and Mario run two quarter of an inch steel cable loops under the nearest kennel. "You know, if I'd thought about it I'd have built a platform to place under the kennels so that when we lower the kennels the pigs would have something to step out onto," Mario observed. "Ev, get that long handled gaff, if the pigs won't get out of the kennel, lift the back of the kennel with the gaff and dump them out."

"Good idea, Mario," Reed agreed. "We can't have them balking now."

At the winch controls Mario lifted the kennel nearest to the water and Reed and Evelyn pushed it toward the side of the vessel. Once over water they turned the door, still closed and latched, facing shoreward so the pig could see the gravel beach where Kim was waiting near the skiff.

With preparations now ready tension began to build. Dark clouds continued to race by 2,000 feet overhead and a light rain began falling. Other than an occasional call from a sea gull on shore or passing by, the only sound was from the hydrophone speakers picking up the gentle lapping of waves against the hulls of the boats. The pigs were mostly quiet now, wondering what was happening. Occasionally one of them would grunt or squeal lightly in the kennels. The pig in the suspended kennel was panting heavily.

They waited. The top predator on earth waiting to observe the top natural predator of the oceans. Both highly intelligent; one trying to learn more about the other to save many of its brethren from possible death.

Five minutes passed. Seven minutes.

After the porpoise kill, Tinga and her pack had reformed into their hunting pattern. Tinga was in the lead and very near shore, closely accompanied now by her three-year-old rambunctious calf, Tyree. Close behind and out further from shore were three whales and behind them, further out, were the others in the group, also aligned. This was skilled cooperation. Within the first ten minutes of moving further northeast along the coast they had caught and killed an adult and a yearling harbor seal. The seals had been happened upon in an area where they could not reach the shore or get into rocks quickly enough. Tinga was proud that it was Tyree who had caught the younger seal almost singlehandedly. The pack reformed and continued the hunt, quite excited and anxious to find more prey.

"There's a seal," Tracy whispered to Mike and Sally as they waited uneasily in the flying bridge of the *Czarina*. "At ten o'clock."

The head of a harbor seal protruded above the surface of the water 50 yards away from the vessel. It seemed to look around nervously and then disappear from sight. In less than a minute it appeared again closer to the shore and not far from where Kim was waiting. After just a few seconds it disappeared again. The pig in the kennel grunted and shuffled. The seal reappeared very near an outcrop of rock which sloped at a gentle angle into the water. To their surprise the seal hauled out of the water and scrambled onto the sloping rock ledge. It lay there looking about apprehensively.

"Now that's something odd," Mike observed quietly. "Normally, with people nearby in boats there's no way you'd get that seal out of the water. The seal may sense that the orcas are coming."

They watched anxiously with binoculars toward the southwest. A corner of rounded glacial boulders existed about 400 yards away, around which the whales would likely come as they approached. From their vantage point on the flying bridge of the *Czarina*, they could see across the point and about 200 yards beyond to where the coastline curved east again. In the distance they could see the *Glacier Bay* and the *Vamp* coming their way at a pace which indicated the whales were on the prowl again. Tension was thick in the nowstirring and cooling air. Darkening clouds continued to race 2,000 feet overhead.

"Here they come," Tracy whispered as the black dorsal fin of a female cut through the reflective gray surface of the water 150 yards away. A strong jet of hot breath and mist was ejected into the air and the fin immediately disappeared.

"She's moving really fast," Mike noted somewhat breathlessly.

Four more black dorsal fins, perfectly aligned, rose near the same spot, but slightly further from shore.

Reed called the approaching two boats. "Greg, take the *Glacier Bay* over to about 100 feet from the *Czarina* and same distance out from shore. Buns, take the *Vamp* about 100 feet from the *Glacier Bay*. We want to be in a line for best visibility. Kim is on shore ready to call."

Both boats speeded to their positions, turned off the engines and dropped anchor. Hydrophones and recording equipment was made ready.

"The other whales have rounded the corner!" Mike called over from the *Czarina*.

One of the whales had spotted the seal on the rocks and another had spotted Kim on shore. The whales slowed their progress to investigate.

Mike gave a thumbsup signal to Reed, who had also seen the whales approaching. At Reed's whispered request, Evelyn opened the doors of the kennels and wired them open. The pigs stayed far back from the door. Mario released the brake on the winch to lower the kennels quietly near the surface of the water. Three foot swells caused the suspended kennels to rise and fall. Evelyn stood by with the gaff to tilt the cages if the pigs didn't come out voluntarily.

Kim, watching silently from her rock perch on shore, saw the kennels being lowered and knew the whales must be approaching. She could not tell which of the kennels had been picked up first. She was ready with the whistle.

Mike and Tracy had watched the whales so many times before they could just about tell how long it might take the lead female to reach the vicinity of the anchored boats. But in the calm evening water they saw clear evidence of the whale's power. Even though the lead whale was well below the surface, with binoculars they could see, 100 yards away, the boil marks or 'foot prints' made at the surface by the powerful up-thrusts of the lead female's flukes as she came around the corner. Depending on how deep she was and how fast she was moving, they knew the prints were probably at least 10 yards behind her. She was really moving fast.

The hydrophones had been silent, but now a few extremely sharp pops and clicks were heard. Then silence again. They knew she was echo-scanning ahead while trying to remain undetected. Despite their experience, all of the participants in the experiment began to feel an uncontrollable primeval terror, the kind of terror which paralyzes your muscles and voice during the worst nightmares. The terror was rooted in the fact that a group of the largest, swiftest and most intelligent predators on earth, other than man, was approaching with the possibility of killing and eating warmblooded animals.

Unknown to the orcas, an unusual experimental offering at this site was in kennels ready to be discharged into the orca's domain.

"There!" Tracy pointed down into the water only 20 feet from the boat. They looked quickly to see the sleek black and white form of a killer whale shooting by rapidly 15 feet beneath the surface. Her body was rolled at 20 degrees and she obviously was looking up at them. The length of the whale was almost the length of the *Czarina*.

"She's here faster than we thought," Mike exclaimed and stood to point downward so those on the *Karen Marie* would know the first whale had arrived. Then he gave the dump signal to Mario and Evelyn; the first pigs should be put in the water. Although their timing to have the first pigs swimming for shore just before the first orca arrived was not perfect, there were more whales coming.

"The plan to put in two pigs at a time as suggested by Kim is a good one," Reed stated. "And we'd better hustle because the whales are closing in."

Reed signaled to Kim to call the pigs. She began alternately blowing the whistle and calling to the pigs. The bottom of the first kennel was rising and falling near the surface of the water with the kennel bottom occasionally flooded with salt water. But the pig would not come out. With the lead whale already past the two anchored boats and more whales approaching, time was absolutely critical.

"Dump the cage, Ev," Reed called impatiently.

With the gaff Evelyn hooked the bottom rear of the kennel and lifted. The reluctant pig began squealing loudly as it tried to stay in the kennel, but Evelyn jerked on the gaff. The pig slid, still squealing, rear end first through the open kennel door and splashed into the frigid water. Mario and Evelyn quickly latched onto the next kennel, opened the door and swung it out over the water.

The first pig was swimming, noses held high, in a circle next to the boat. The second pig would not exit either so Evelyn again used the gaff to raise the rear of the kennel and dump the pig out. There were now two pigs swimming in circles next to the boat intending to get back aboard.

Kim was watching the kennel through binoculars and saw the familiar markings of the two pigs as they were dumped out of the kennels and into the water. "Oh, Oh. There's Petunia and Rosy" she thought to herself. She continued blowing the whistle and calling to the pigs, which continued swimming near the side of the boat.

"Ev," Reed called. "Take that gaff and push the pigs away from the boat. Maybe they'll start swimming for shore!"

Using the opposite end of the gaff, Evelyn pushed each pig away from the boat, dunking each of them briefly under water. She called to Reed and Mario, "They're trying to get back in the boat." And she pushed them away again. Suddenly it seemed Rosy had enough and she started swimming toward Kim on the shore.

The whale's echo-scanning revealed these creatures at the surface to be strange and unknown. Its body form was not the same as the seal but it had a generally familiar bone structure. The creature had little hair and good layers of fat, which showed up clearly on sonar. It was not a water animal because it swam at the surface with short stubby legs. Deer they had killed when caught swimming between islands had long legs and were slow but had almost no fat. This creature does not dive, she knew, but she could not scan its head because the head was out of water. The nature of its teeth were unknown and caution was justified. Just as the black widow spider seldom attempts to paralyze a victim before wrapping it in silk, the killer whales had no intention of risking physical harm by tackling an unknown animal before close study.

The whales had been watching the action via sonar and by an occasional spyrise for visual confirmation. They were somewhat hesitant to approach these strange creatures in the water when they were next to the boat. But when one of them started swimming for shore it was like open season for investigations. Tinga was in the lead as she and three other whales swam directly behind Rosy for a close-up look and more sonar evaluation of this beast's configuration. Rosy, now terrified, swam as hard as she could toward shore. The other whales in the pack got a good scan of Rosy as she swam.

Petunia had continued swimming near the boat and hoping she could get back in but Evelyn kept pushing her away. Now she, too, began swimming for shore where Kim was calling and blowing the whistle. "Rosy, come on, Rosy. Swim, swim! Petunia, swim!"

The whales were scanning all the activity and were getting more excited. This was a new experience and they loved it. New animals in the water, possibly food animals.

Rosy was now only about 20 yards from shore with her four legs pumping away and her snout held high. Tinga made one more close pass and then decided to pursue this one no more. She had noted that a new one had entered the water near the boat and was now swimming toward shore. It was time to do some closer examination of these critters. She passed under the second swimming pig and then turned and accelerated. She hit the pig with her open mouth just behind the front shoulder and bit down, not enough to kill the creature but enough to cripple it. She dove with it as the other whales watched the action via sonar or visually. Upon Tinga's signal one of the whales joined her and they began tearing the pig apart and eating it. Blood clouded the water. They signaled to the other whales that this was good food.

Rosy could finally feel sand under her hoofs and she trotted up to where Kim was standing. "Rosy, good girl, good girl," Kim said to the pig. When she looked out to see what happened to Petunia there was no pig in sight, only the occasional dorsal fins of whales and their heavy breaths as they exhaled and inhaled.

On board the *Czarina*, the *Glacier Bay* and the *Vamp* there were exclamations of what a wonderful concept this had been. Video and audio equipment had been rolling and some good shots had been taken by everyone who tried. Buns was the only one not excited. Dan and Rolly were both complaining that they wanted to do something besides watch, they wanted to try to communicate.

"But there is more to come" Reed pointed out. "There will be more pigs."

On board the *Karen Marie*, Mario and Evelyn were getting two more pigs ready to go.

Mike gave them the thumbs up sign and Reed acknowledged it. "OK, Mario and Ev, let's get two more ready to go. We're getting some good action here."

Mario and Ev were getting better at releasing the swine. They could now pick up two at once, open the doors and then swing them out over the water. The remaining six pigs had heard the squealing of the first two and wanted nothing to do with the water, but, as before, Evelyn used the gaff to dump them out of their kennels.

As the next two were dumped out squealing, Kim was again watching from shore with binoculars. "Oh my God, it's Daisy!" she whispered to herself. She began alternately blowing the whistle more intensely and calling. "Come on, Daisy! Swim, Daisy! Hurry! Hurry!"

Daisy was confused. She and Porky knew Kim's location but she sensed something definitely different here from the training. Her first reaction was to try to return aboard the vessel and, looking up at Evelyn for help, she swam back and forth near the *Karen Marie*, trying to find a way to get back aboard.

On shore, tears were running down Kim's frantic face. She would blow the whistle and then call to Daisy and Porky, pleading with the pigs to swim to her and get out of the water.

Reed looked down at Evelyn and the pigs from the flying bridge of the *Karen Marie*. "Give them another push away from the boat, Ev!" he called.

Evelyn reversed ends of the gaff and pushed the swimming pigs away from the boat with the blunt end. But again Daisy and Porky swam back toward the boat.

Some intense click trains now were detected by the hydrophones, the pack of whales was scanning the scene near the two boats with intense bursts of sonar.

Evelyn was getting frustrated. "Swim to shore, you little bastards, if you value your hides!" She again pushed the swimming pigs away from the boat with the force of the push taking the pigs under water.

This time Daisy seemed to recognize that she was not going to be allowed back on the deck and she turned toward shore, her short legs pumping away and her snout held high. As she swam away from the vessel the intensity of sounds from the speakers attached to the hydrophones increased sharply. Intense click trains, sharp clicks, and both high and low frequency sounds were heard. Porky remained swimming in circles near the boat.

"They're scanning her with sonar," Reed stated. "And it looks like the lead female is coming back," he said as he pointed in the direction of the first whale's travel.

Mario and Evelyn looked across the stern of the *Karen Marie* and saw the dorsal fin of the lead female orca. She was rapidly returning to the vicinity of the vessels from the northeast. Four other whales passed under the anchored boats.

"You're right, that first female is coming back," Mario agreed.

"I think we're going to get more action," Reed commented to Mario and Evelyn while looking through the viewfinder of the camcorder.

Daisy continued doing her best in swimming toward Kim on shore. She had gone about 30 yards, a third of the way to shore, amid a barrage of echoscanning from the orcas. The whales were obviously carrying out intense surveys and studies of this new creature in the water. The hydrophones were picking up apparent excited conversation between the whales.

On board all four boats surface action was being recorded on video and audio tape and through the use of still cameras. Fortunately, light was adequate even though the racing cloud cover persisted.

One of the female whales arced upward from the depths just in front of the swimming pig. Its flukes noisily swept across the surface toward the pig, pushing a wave and creating a whirlpool. Daisy splashed and was spun around in the whirlpool eddy, but then she reoriented and continued to swim toward Kim, who was calling tearfully and blowing the whistle from shore.

Tinga continued to cruise near the vessels and scanned both the creature swimming toward shore and the one near the boat. This was good food and she intended for the rest of the pack to try eating some. The animal continued swimming toward shore. Something had to be done. Tinga rose directly in front of the animal and pushed a wave of water toward it with her flukes. The whales noted the almost helpless reaction of the animal as it was swirled in the water, but its head remained out of water and out of reach of the sonar. It continued swimming toward shore.

Kray, the large male, who had been with the group further offshore, swam near the bottom into the circling group of whales. He concluded that this creature may be food but chances were not to be taken that the creature might bite in a counterattack. Best to be safe. Kray rose just under the surface with his powerful flukes beneath the paddling pig and whapped it upward end over end 25 feet into the air.

Upon hitting the water the creature, almost unconscious, submerged for a few seconds. Now the whales could scan the entire animal. This one had a strange head with a long face; its teeth were nothing. Its neck was extremely short and could not possibly turn the head for biting as could the dangerous sea lion. The whale's excitement increased.

The creature was disoriented but not seriously injured; it coughed as it rose to the surface and swam in a small circle for a half a minute. Then it once again started for the *Karen Marie* and another attempt to board.

Tinga was getting more excited. She made another pass close to the *Czarina* and Porky. Reed leaned out and speared the top of her dorsal fin with a fluorescent tag. Minor pain for the whale.

Tinga was now satisfied that this swimming creature would be good food. With a few strokes of her flukes she accelerated toward the animal and, with a passing rush, bit into the animal's body where the rear legs met the torso and submerged with it. She bit hard enough to cripple the creature, but not hard enough to severe body parts.

Two other females approached and the creature, in the throes of drowning, was carefully examined beneath the surface. This creature was again to be studied and tested for eating; no need or desire to play with it at the surface. The pig was disemboweled and the internal organs examined. The heart and liver were tasted and eaten. The skin was rather tough but was digestible. The creature had an excellent layer of fat and the meat was good. Small pieces of the animal were picked up by other adults as they were allowed to sink. The head was severed from the rest of the body and ears, flesh and the snout were chewed from the bony skull. The skull was crushed and brains were extracted.

The high fat content of this animal pleased the whales. It also had a good taste. If they could find more like this, it would be good. Perhaps there were more.

They could hear communication sounds of the twolegged creatures through the hulls of the four vessels and recognized them as nonthreatening. They also heard more sounds of the strange creatures, which they now began to associate with those they had just killed and eaten. Three of the whales circled the two vessels at shallow depth to see what would happen next while the remaining pack remained 100 yards further offshore.

Aboard the four anchored boats, the entire episode had been recorded on video tape and with still camera shots. Daisy had been lofted so high and suddenly into the air that zoom lens settings on the camcorders had narrowly missed catching the maximum height. Just after Daisy hit the water and submerged, intense sonar scan sounds were heard over the hydrophones.

"They're scanning her," Reed said to Mario.

They saw that just after Daisy struggled to the surface, one of the female orcas appeared swiftly, seized the hapless animal and submerged. Although the hydrophones picked up a wide variety of sounds from the whales and there was obvious commotion going on under water, Daisy did not emerge and a crimson trail spread through the water where the whale had taken the pig. The only logical assumption was that Daisy had been killed and eaten.

On shore Kim was sobbing softly. Daisy was gone. Although the eventual loss of the pigs had been expected, the personal bond she had formed with the animals, especially Daisy, was strong.

"I'm certain that female was T7 that Reed tagged," Tracy called from the *Czarina*, speaking to the crews on all vessels. "And the male was probably T4."

Reed looked at Kim through the binoculars and shook his head regretfully. "Yes, and the pig was Daisy," he said sorrowfully from the deck of the *Karen Marie*.

"I think I got a good photo of T7's dorsal fin and saddle area," Tracy proudly declared. "Including Reed's tag."

"I was looking through the camcorder and didn't see," Mike noted. "But it should be on the tape on a replay."

"What do you think?" Reed called over to the *Czarina*, wondering if Mike and Tracy were thinking about additional testing. Could they now conclude, he asked himself, again looking at Kim crying on shore, that it had been demonstrated that killer whales could and would kill and eat food animals not normally in their diet.

"We still need to know which whales are aggressive in the A-T pack, or are they all aggressive?" Mike noted. "While we've got the pack here we'd better get all the information we can, they may be gone tomorrow. Let's proceed."

Reed turned to Evelyn and Mario, who had brought aboard the two kennels that were just emptied and pushed them aside. "Put another two in, Mario and Ev!" he called and they immediately began to get two more kennels ready.

The pigs on board had observed the departure of Kim and they heard Kim calling and blowing the whistle. They had also heard the unhappy squealing as the pigs were dropped into the water and, from their vantage point on the *Karen Marie*, they had seen the other pigs swimming and then disappearing after some large animals in the water showed up.

They did not like what they saw and heard and were making a commotion rattling the kennels and calling with grunts and low squeals.

With Mario at the boom controls, two more kennels was lifted from the deck and guided and pushed by Evelyn toward and just over the side of the vessel. There she opened both gates and wired them open. If a pig jumped out it would land in the water. She signaled to Mario to lower the kennels and they were lowered near the water level.

The circling whales were extremely curious now about what these creatures might do next. Occasionally one of the orcas, particularly Tinga, would do a spyrise above the water surface to see what was happening on the vessels. Tinga's aggressive tendencies were tempered with concern about the safety of her group. On other occasions she had seen the surface creatures' apparent friendliness turn ugly with attempts, some successful, to kill the whales. Now, as she rose above the surface, she saw a now familiar object being lowered near the water surface. She did not know what it meant, but she waited with increasing curiosity.

On shore, Kim sat on the edge of the skiff with her head in her hands. She was losing her enthusiasm for calling the pigs to shore. But yet, she had saved one pig by calling and blowing the whistle. She looked up and saw two more another kennels being lowered to the water. "Why don't they quit?" she thought. "They know more pigs are just going to be killed and eaten." Rosy had started rooting in some nearby grass.

Evelyn noted that one pig was much heavier than the others, 200 pounds or so, and she decided to dump it first. Again, she took the long handled gaff and hooked the rear bottom of the kennel. This time the larger pig got lodged crosswise in the kennel door and did not fall out. Evelyn let the kennel go back to horizontal and, as soon as the pig shifted positions, raised the end again. This time the pig slid out and splashed into the water.

As with the others, this pig began swimming back and forth near the boat, trying to get back aboard and out of the cold water. Evelyn again turned the gaff around to push the pig toward shore with the blunt end, but, with Kim silent on shore, she suspected the pig was not likely to go.

"Hold on a minute, Ev," Reed called. "Let's see what will happen if the pig stays near the boat."

Sounds from the hydrophone speakers indicated the whales were again echo-scanning the pig. Tinga, circling with the other whales, noted that another one of the animals was swimming at the surface near the vessel. Abruptly she became impatient; she was not going to wait for this slow and helpless creature to make up its mind about swimming to shore. With rapid strokes of her tail she accelerated and grabbed the pig by the hind quarters as she zoomed past the *Karen Marie*. After a shallow dive she swiftly returned to the surface with the coughing and sputtering pig in her mouth. She had turned the pig so she held it by the hind quarters with the head facing forward. As soon as the pig caught its breath, it began to squeal loudly with the squeals echoing off the hulls of the boats and from the rocky shoreline. The sound was bloodcurdling. The whales heard it and became more excited.

Tinga released the pig at the surface and it struggled to swim with rear legs that had been damaged by the whale attack but it was still squealing. The wavy dorsal fin of Kray, the large male, pierced the water surface and the pig disappeared in one bite. Blood stained the water red where the pig had been.

The observers on the other two boats, the *Glacier Bay* and the *Vamp*, had seen all the action. Rolly and Dan were not happy that they had been left out of the planning and the events and that they had been required to just stay on the Vamp to record and take photos. Rolly, in particular, was very unhappy that they had been given no chance to show these Americans how ingenious Canadians could be.

"Buns," he waved to her to step into the cabin of the *Vamp* so the others could not hear. "I'd like to use the skiff to go out for a few minutes to take my own mini-survey."

"Well, I don't know," Buns told him. "We'd better check with the others to see what they think about that idea."

Rolly pulled out a roll of money and peeled off five one hundred dollar bills. "Now how about letting me use the skiff?"

Buns grabbed the money. "OK, let's get it in the water while the others are busy watching the whales." She was beginning to like this Rolly McAllister.

They swung the skiff, on an overhead pulley, out away from the *Vamp* and lowered it into the water.

"Do you know how to operate that outboard?" Buns asked Rolly.

"There are oars, I'm not going to use the outboard. It might disturb the whales." Rolly replied. With no float coat or preserver, he climbed down into the skiff and pushed away from the *Vamp*.

Meanwhile, observers in the four vessels saw the release of the pig by T-7 and the large male orca then take the pig.

"My God, I didn't know pigs could squeal that loud," George Maxwell said from the deck of the *Glacier Bay*. "I'm astounded. And that male took the pig in one bite!"

"T-7 knew that pig was an airbreathing animal," observed Herb Bracken, excited by the action. "That's why she released it and then she got out of the way so T-4 could eat."

"Great cooperation." Tracy noted. "But Kim is taking this very hard."

On shore Kim was sitting on the side of the skiff and crying softly, asking herself why she ever agreed to be involved in this slaughter.

"Here goes the next one!" Evelyn called to them as she lifted the gaff under the kennel shaft was swinging over the water. The pig landed with a splash in the water.

Tinga was beginning to enjoy this fun and eating. She grabbed the next pig from the surface and took it down for her pack members to tear apart and eat. There is no hostility between whales as they swam in to get a piece of the pig and all are eager for more of this feed. The pack began cruising back and forth as they wait to see what may be offered next.

"What the hell?" Mike suddenly shouted. "Rolly, what are you doing? Get back to the *Vamp!*" Thinking there would be some help needed, he told Sally "Let's get my skiff in the water." They scrambled to launch the skiff.

Rolly just waved and kept rowing into the area near the *Karen Marie* where much of the whale action had taken place. The whales were circling and scanning the skiff, expecting that more food might be presented.

Rolly stopped rowing and shouted to those in the boats: "I'm going to show you that these whales will not harm a person in the water!" And with that he jumped into the extremely cold water feet first. The wool cap he was wearing floated away. At the shock of the cold water he grabbed the side of the skiff thinking he would soon get back in.

Tinga and her pack had watched closely. They had encountered these two legged creatures before. This was not food but an opportunity to have some fun. She grabbed one of Rolly's legs and swam with him at the surface. Rolly was now screaming and coughing with water getting in his lungs. Tinga decided this one was fragile and would quickly die if left in the water. Still at the surface, she turned and took Rolly back to the skiff and released him. Rolly hung on with one arm.

Mike started the motor on this skiff and headed toward Rolly, whose muscles were ceasing to function because of the cold water. As soon as he reached Rolly he pulled him into the skiff and headed for the *Karen Marie* where he figured Dr. Remington would be the best one to help with a medical emergency. When he arrived at the boat, Reed, Mario, and Evelyn pulled Rolly aboard. Reed performed CPR while shaking his head at how foolish Rolly had been. Mario and Reed half-carried Rolly into the nearest cabin, got him out of his wet clothes and wrapped him in some towels and blankets.

Mike was still in his skiff next to the *Karen Marie*. At Mike's request, Evelyn handed one empty kennel down to Mike and then climbed into the skiff with him. Mike motored in to the beach where Kim was waiting. He and Evelyn took the kennel to shore and shoved Rosy inside. They then skidded the kennel back to the skiff, hoisted it aboard and pushed away from shore. The pig was returned to the *Karen Marie*. Kim, who had the skiff from the *Karen Marie*, pushed the skiff off, started the outboard and returned to the boat. In a few minutes she was back aboard the vessel and the skiff was hoisted and hung over the stern. Five empty cages had been put in their places. Two pigs remained, along with the Rosy the survivor.

When no more food being offered, Tinga decided it was time to leave and she called her pack to move along the southern margin of the bay to hunt additional mammals. Five pigs would not satisfy the appetites of this pack of orcas.

Mike called over to the *Glacier Bay* and the *Vamp* and requested that they, along with the *Czarina*, come alongside the *Karen Marie* to discuss the next step. When all three boats were alongside the Karen Marie, Herb Bracken didn't hesitate to speak: "Well, there sure as hell is no doubt now that they'll eat mammals which are totally foreign to them."

"That's right, Herb," Reed responded. "But we know only that one female whale, T7, and possibly the male T4, seem to be the important aggressors. Some of the whales, remember, actually seemed to remain back out of all the action. What if half of this group is not aggressive toward strange mammals?"

"By God, that's right!" Herb responded. "While we're here and that pack is hunting, we'd better run some more tests."

"I agree," George Maxwell nodded, thus giving the idea the support of the Alaska Department of Fish and Game.

Kim, fed up with the carnage, shouted, "Meaning what?"

Reed was sympathetic but firm. "Kim, we can't jump to hasty conclusions in this situation. The more data we have, the better analysis we can make to help the whales."

"Help the whales? It's the pigs who need help,." Kim replied with a scoff.

Evelyn nodded. "It does sort of seem like we're throwing live sausages to a pack of pit bulls."

"This storm isn't going to wait for anyone," Mike called. "We'd better get moving!"

"Look," Reed responded. "We have two remaining pigs. The pack is continuing around to the other side of the bay, let's release those two pigs ahead of the leaders and watch what happens. That would help us see which are the most aggressive. And we'll still have one recovered pig left for any other good ideas. But we won't have anyone calling this time."

"Good idea," Mike agreed. "Mario, we can see where the group is going, if you'll go ahead of them and drop off two pigs we can stand off in the other three boats to observe what happens. George, Herb, Cynthia, and Greg, what do you think about that idea?"

Those on the state-owned boat conferred among themselves. "Hell yes," Herb shouted. "We've got the rogue pack here and we'd better take advantage of it."

All four boats prepared to move. Anchors were lifted and engines started. The *Karen Marie* with the pigs on board moved away first, heading for the last place the A-T pack was sighted. The other three boats followed.

Mario decided to break radio silence. "We've got them in sight and it appears they may be prospecting again near some big rocks. We'll go ahead as planned."

"And we'll follow," Mike responded. "And how is Rolly doing?"

"Aw, he's OK. Just had to get him thawed out. He'll be up and around soon."

The A-T pack was patrolling along the shore and the four boats stayed about 300 yards off shore. They wanted to track the whales but not disturb their hunting. After thirty minutes Mario again got on the radio: "We're about one mile ahead of the pack and this looks like a good place to turn in for the drop. Nice cliff the other side of the shore line."

The *KM* motored in to within 100 yards of the shore. "How does this look? He radioed to the other boats.

Both Mike and Herb responded with approval. Buns in the *Vamp* just kept quiet.

With the anchor down, Mario and Evelyn immediately tied onto two kennels but left Rosy alone. The kennels were raised and the boom was swung over the water.

"Look over there," Herb nudged George as they dropped anchor. "A couple of anchored pleasure boats over near that island. Suppose we ought to tell them to stay in their boats?"

"Naw, with that storm coming they're not going to be out and about anyway."

"This should be a good location," Reed radioed. "We're dropping two items over right now so we'll be ready this time." Evelyn tipped both kennels and dumped the pigs into the water. Kim was watching from the deck of the *Karen Marie*, again with tears in her eyes.

"By God, look at that," Herb remarked to George as he watched through binoculars. "Damned if they're not speeding up. You don't suppose they've already detected those pigs in the water near the *Karen Marie*, do you?"

"I wouldn't be surprised," George replied. "They may be associating certain sounds with feeding time, especially if they really like the pigs as food."

"But Christ, a half mile away?"

"With the hearing those things have, Herb, they could hear you pass gas if this engine wasn't running," George laughed. He picked up the microphone and advised the two waiting vessels that subject's speed had increased.

The hydrophones detected click trains and other echo-scan signals several minutes before any whale dorsal fins were sighted. Then seven dorsal fins emerged from the water 200 yards away and the whales, coming toward them at what was obviously a high rate of speed, blew and inhaled. It was obvious the whales were not trying to sneak up on the two vessels or the two pigs swimming near the *Karen Marie*.

"We'd better be ready to record this time before they arrive," Mike noted. "She sneaked past us last time."

The recording gear was ready. Evelyn, Sally and Mario all kept a sharp eye open for any subsurface sign of whales. The two pigs were swimming unhappily in circles near the stern of the *Karen Marie* where they had been dumped from their kennels. The sound of echo-scans on the speakers became louder and more frequent but no whales could be seen.

"There's one!" Sally called, pointing down in the water as the black and white form of a killer whale on its side rocketed by. Almost before she could say it, the whale had appeared, passed both anchored boats and disappeared. Click trains and calls between the whales continued to be heard over the speakers.

A female killer whale rose from the water 100 feet behind the stern of the *Karen Marie* in a spyrise obviously meant to give the whale a view of both the animals in the water and the species on board the vessels. The cameras focused on her while she was still emerged.

"Smart move," Mike noted. "She's looking us over before she commits to taking more pigs near the *Karen Marie*."

"I wonder if she can hear well enough to determine from our voices if we are friend or foe." Tracy questioned.

"It's possible," Mike answered and added jokingly: "We could turn on some `friendly' music such as a Strauss waltz...."

A group of six whales appeared at the surface half the distance to shore, and about a dozen whales surfaced to blow 100 yards behind. It appeared that somehow the entire AT pack had rejoined and was there.

Reed, Kim, Mario and Evelyn were at the stern of the *Karen Marie* with cameras and camcorders at the ready, all eyes on the pigs. A rapid and loud click train came over the speakers. "Get ready," Reed urged as he turned on the camcorder and focused it on the two swimming pigs.

Much to the surprise of the now experienced observers, both swine, seemingly unhappy in the 2 foot swells, immediately turned toward shore from the *Karen Marie* and began swimming rapidly in that direction.

With a wide variety of sounds heard over the speakers, it was difficult to determine if the whales had detected the two swine swimming straight for a sand beach between two rock outcrops, now a football field away. The larger pig, weighing about 180 pounds, was a faster swimmer than the 140 pound pig, and it seemed determined to get to the beach even though the wind was kicking up 2 foot swells. Camcorders and cameras aboard all four vessels were focused on the two noses, held high, of the two animals as they swam toward shore.

"Go, go," Kim was urging them quietly as they swam.

A scytheshaped fin, traveling at a high speed, appeared and the slower pig was taken with only a squeal and a greasy slick on the water to indicate it had been there. The larger pig was now approaching the beach. The top of a dorsal fin rose above the surface, moving rapidly in the pig's direction.

As soon as the pig's cloven hoofs touched bottom, it moved ashore to kneedepth and then stopped to shake. The dorsal fin grew larger and it became apparent this was Kray, the large male, making a run at the pig on the beach. A wall of water, which could be heard on the boats even above the noise of the wind, accompanied the orca in its rush to shore. No sooner had the pig stopped shaking than the huge orca slid up onto the sand and seized the pig by the hind quarters. The pig voiced a loud, pained squeal which echoed across the bay.

With the 180 pound pig seeming like a squealing toy in the mouth of the orca, the huge black and white animal turned and with spray flying into the wind from its powerful flukes, beat its way back into deeper water and disappeared.

"Wow! Just like Patagonia!" Reed observed. "That was just like orcas I've seen filmed in Patagonia taking sea lion calves off the beach!"

Kim started to say something and then changed her mind and went to the stern of the *Karen Marie* to care for Rosy.

"That female was T7. Did you see the tag? And the bull on the beach was obviously T4." Tracy stated.

The two pigs were not seen again and it was assumed they were eaten in the subsurface. The whales had not wasted any time in taking the pigs.

The wind velocity was increasing in gusts and far to the southwest Mario could see rain showers moving their way. "The weather's going to hell in a hand basket. We'd better do whatever we're going to do and get the hell out of here to a safe anchorage. The forecast is for winds over 100 miles per hour!" he advised on the radio to Mike, Buns and Greg.

"With that kind of weather approaching we'd better forget about any more work with the subjects," Mike cautioned in return.

With the rain starting and the wind velocity increasing, they hustled to pick up all the equipment and took it into the cabins of the vessels. Everyone was resolved to the idea that it would be nearly impossible to follow the orcas in this weather and, besides, it was time to regroup and re-plan.

"Where are we going to anchor from this storm, Mario?" Mike, dripping wet, called to the *Karen Marie* as soon as the anchors were retrieved.

"This bay goes back in to the west about two more miles. There's a decent anchorage near the head of the bay and it should be good in a southwest wind. I'll lead the way."

With the *Karen Marie* leading and the *Czarina* bringing up the rear, the four vessels bucked into the southwest wind.

George called on the radio. "Say, this tub we're in doesn't have much in the way of accommodations. Can anyone put us up for the night?"

"You came to the right place," Mario responded. "This isn't the Taj Mahal, but we get by."

Within ten minutes they had reached a part of the bay sheltered by a steep cliff to the southwest backed by mountains rising almost 2,000 feet above sea level. The winds were considerably subdued but there was heavy rain.

CHAPTER 30

Corralled

W ith bumpers between, all four vessels were brought together and anchored so the occupants could move from boat to boat although in this storm they would get rain-soaked when doing so. The *Karen Marie* was the largest vessel and it was known that ample liquor was on board.

Mario loved his boat and took good care of her even though his days of using the *Karen Marie* for commercial fishing were long gone. He also wanted to be sure guests had a pleasant time when on board. With the expectation of arrivals from the other boats, Mario put on some pleasant music: Linda Ronstadt with the Nelson Riddle orchestra. Very soothing against the noise of the storm outside.

First to arrive was Buns, Dan, and Rolanda from the *Vamp*, all wearing rain gear dripping from the heavy rain. Buns said she was looking for that handsome Rolly, who was still warming up after his jump into the cold waters of the Sound and the encounter with the orca. Next Mike, Tracy, Sally, and Don came in after crossing from the *Czarina* in rain gear. They were accustomed to Alaska weather and had no problem with the wind and driving rain. Last to arrive was Herb and George and their game warden skipper from the *Glacier Bay*.

"That's a helluva blow out there," George Maxwell stated as he took off his rain gear and entered the cabin, which was crowded with thirteen people present. "And I'll bet you even have something to drink on board. Trouble with using one of the state boats is no liquor allowed."

"Hell yes we've got booze on board" Mario slapped George on the shoulder. "Mike, Tracy, and Reed did a damn good job of planning for supplies. What'll you have: vodka, Crown Royal, Balvenie Scotch, Jack Daniels, gin, you name it."

"I'll take a Crown, that should be a good way to warm up the innards."

Sally got busy as the bartender and poured a stiff whisky for George. Soon everyone in the cabin of the *Karen Marie* had a drink in hand. Even Rolly, who was now pretty well dried out but was still wrapped in towels. Buns made sure he got stiff shots of Scotch and she tossed down a couple of her own.

Evelyn had begun food preparation in the kitchen. Hamburgers were about the quickest and easiest and everyone could add their own preference for toppings. There was plenty of hamburger and bread on hand. Sally set the bottles of liquor out where everyone had access and proceeded to help Evelyn with the food prep.

Rolanda was being very quiet but after two gin and tonics she began to loosen up with joking and laughing. Herb Bracken had taken an immediate liking for Rolanda and seemed mesmerized by this beautiful black woman. He urged her to come to Anchorage so he could show her around. Dan was also invited, but with less enthusiasm.

Dan was chatting with Reed, Mike, and Tracy. "I'm convinced there is some way to communicate with the orcas just as they communicate with each other," he said as he took another sip of the Jack Daniels. "And by damn I intend to be the one to figure it out."

"Well, good luck," Tracy wished him. "But in the past ten years there have been lots of studies and it appears no one has gotten to first base on that one."

"They don't even respond when we play recordings of their own chatter," Reed pointed out.

"But perhaps they're not motivated to talk to those of us who walk around on two legs," Dan replied. "I've done research on motivational psychology and may come up with a solution." He was beginning to slur his words a bit. "But I need experience and this expedition could be just the ticket. I'm very grateful to you all for this opportunity and, by the way, I've got cash on hand to help pay for some of the studies, if you need it."

"That's good news, Dan." Mike responded. "This has been a fairly expensive undertaking and financial help is appreciated."

Game Warden Greg Wallace and Cynthia, the biologist, were both single and, by coincidence, both were prospecting for a companion. "It's wonderful that we have been brought together like this, Cynthia." Greg said as the two of them smiled at each other. "I understand you're located in Anchorage. I'm in the field quite a bit but still spend time in the city."

"When we return from this trip why don't you come over for dinner some evening?" Cynthia asked. "Just give me a call and we'll figure out something."

The Scotch and soda they were drinking made conversation easy. Without saying so, they were both looking forward to returning to the Glacier Bay for the night. Could be particularly romantic with a storm such as the one raging outside.

Along with hamburgers, Evelyn and Sally prepared canned corn, fried potatoes, and onions, and had laid out a platter with pickles, onions, olives and sliced cheese. Reed opened three bottles of a good Malbec from Argentina. Everyone had plenty to eat and drink. Kim slipped on her rain gear and went out to make sure Rosy had food and water and a cover to keep the rain from the kennel.

After everyone had eaten and had enjoyed the beverages, Mike tapped on a glass with a spoon to get attention. "Hey, everyone, would you please listen up for a few minutes. How about this plan? Tomorrow after breakfast, say eight o'clock, we'll all head in to Herring Bay and the camp we have there. We can have a meeting in the lodge and discuss what we have observed, our conclusions and what we might do next. There will be some disagreement, but everyone's ideas will be welcome."

George added "And we've got to get back to Anchorage, lots of things happening. But I'll call for a plane to pick me and Herb up at Herring Bay."

"OK," Mike continued, "We hope everyone had sufficient food and drinks and that you sleep well tonight."

Outside the storm was raging but the spot Mario had picked for the night was well-protected and there was only erratic strong wind. There was heavy driving rain that seemed to arrive in buckets.

Mario was feeling the alcohol. "Back in Oregon there was a saying about heavy rain like this, they'd say 'it's raining like a cow peeing on a flat rock'."

Wearing rain gear, those who were going to spend the night on other boats departed. Remaining on the *Karen Marie* were Reed and Kim, Mario, Evelyn and Sally. Herb and George also decided to stay, they were enjoying the alcohol and didn't want to go out in the storm. They said they'd just sleep on the couch or in a chair. Some help was required to get Rolly back to the *Vamp* but Buns said she would take very good care of him.

The next morning the major storm had moved on and there was only a slight rain. The pleasant aroma of coffee drifted out from all four boats indicating everyone was up and around. Greg and Cynthia were, for some reason, delayed in emerging from the cabin they had chosen on the *Glacier Bay*, which caused smiles for those who noticed. After a light breakfast, George and Herb crossed back to the *Glacier Bay*.

It was a little after 8 am when all four boats hoisted anchor and headed for Herring Bay with Mario leading. Mike radioed ahead to Don at the camp to tell him who was coming. He estimated two hours or so to get there.

It was about 11:30 when Don saw boats approaching. As he had been advised, it was the *Karen Marie* followed by the *Glacier Bay*, the *Vamp* and lastly, the *Czarina*. At the lodge, Don welcomed them to the camp. He had set out a nice lunch with wheat bread, sliced ham and beef, cheese, lettuce, tomatoes, onions, pickles and thinly sliced Jalapeno peppers. There was also cold beer, coffee, and tea.

After lunch when they were still gathered around the table, Mike got up first to speak. "Thanks to everyone for your help and observations in this study. We gathered some important information and we hope now to be able to proceed with what appears to be the next logical step in these studies. I'll turn it over now to Dr. Remington for his explanation."

Reed stood and addressed the group: "What we hoped to show here, and what we believe we have shown with these experiments, is that the whales will kill and eat creatures that are totally strange to them. And we showed that there are certain whales that are more aggressive than others. And thanks to Rolly, here, we have good evidence that man may not be on their regular menu. However, these are very fast and clever predators and we know it would not be wise to get in the water naked or near naked when the orcas are hunting mammals. It appears from what we have seen thus far that they will stay well away from heavily-clothed people, such as those wearing a life preserver or a float coat. But we believe we have identified a rogue whale pack, and a particular female within that pack, that is particularly aggressive. This is the pack that killed and ate a black lab dog. And we suspect they may have been involved in the disappearance of the couple from Reno on that island here in Prince William Sound. The orcas can interact with kids as they did with the kids from Anchorage a week or so ago, but that also tells us that they have no fear of many people. They may be smart enough to recognize fishermen or others who will kill them or attempt to kill them. This pack, we call it the A-T pack, has learned to recognize us on the *Czarina* and *Karen Marie* as friendly and we are able to approach closely. Within the A-T pack there is one female that is the pack leader. We call her T-7. She behaves more like what we call "transients" because these orcas patrol the open ocean and kill whale calves, seals, walruses, fish, octopus, whatever they can find out there. Most of our local packs stay quite close to land and feed mostly on fish but they will hunt, kill, and eat mammals once in a while. Now Mike will explain further."

Mike smiled at the group. "Thank you for being here, it is important to have verification of what we have been seeing. We have photos and recordings of most of the action but it is still important to have observers there. Remember, our efforts are directed to provide information so the whales will not be accused of certain actions such as attacking people. If we can provide that type of information it should save the lives of many orcas. Now, as Reed mentioned, we have narrowed the search down to the A-T pack and one particular female in that pack, T-7. We believe it will benefit all involved, the state, the feds, the fishermen but most of all the whales, if we catch and remove T-7. Now, I know that sounds harsh, but she can be taken to a wonderful facility where she will be cared for and more studies can be done. After two to three years she can be released again into the wild. It has been proven that releasing whales or dolphins back to the wild after they have been in an aquarium for a couple of years works very well. Are there any questions or comments?"

Dan Short had a question. "How are you going to get permits to capture an orca and ship it to an aquarium? Permits of that type have been banned in the US."

Mike responded: "That's one of the reasons we wanted to invite Herb of NOAA and George, Cynthia and Greg of the State of Alaska to join on this study. They have offered to provide what support they can and we believe even the hard core opposition will see the wisdom of this work and how it can benefit the whales. And now perhaps Dr. Remington will add his views. Dr. Remington, as many of you know is a dolphin specialist at Hydrosphere Aquarium in San Diego and he also teaches at Palisades University. Reed?"

"Yes, at Hydrosphere we have two of the largest pools in the world for dolphins and orcas. We have a very well-trained staff and the whales are well-cared-for. We do have room at the present time for a killer whale such as T-7. And, yes, we could definitely plan to release the whale after a couple of years of study. Questions?"

Buns now spoke up. "But you guys just use these whales to make money from the tourists. You're not interested in the whale welfare, your company wants the money, period!!"

"Don't overlook the fact that, because the whales are a big attraction, Hydrosphere is able to afford the best care for the whales." Reed answered. "We do take care of them and, believe it or not, once the whales get to know the staff they become very happy and even enjoy performing. Releasing them back to the wild is a new concept but we have proof that it works when done properly."

"What are you thinking for the next step?" Dan asked. "I would like to participate and I know Rolly and Rolanda would too, but we can't stay around here for days or weeks."

Mike now answered. "If we can get an indication the permits we need will be issued soon we would like to proceed immediately because we have a good setup here with the camp, the dock, the boats and, very importantly, the pigs. There are thirteen pigs remaining and they may be crucial in any next step."

Herb Bracken stood up. "I can tell you that there is a good possibility for a very speedy approval by NOAA. The headquarters staff is aware that orcas have been and are being killed by fishermen. Information we can develop on the whale's habitat and activity will be welcomed. And they like the idea that the orca can be released later. We may be able to get the permits in one week, believe it or not."

A plane was heard circling overhead. "That must be the Game and Fish plane I requested this morning," George announced. "So we'd better get going." He and Herb thanked everyone and George turned to Cynthia. "You're coming to Anchorage with us aren't you?"

"No, I'm going to go with Greg in the *Glacier Bay*," she replied. "We're going to do some fishing and, for me, sight-seeing. I'll be back to Anchorage in a couple of days."

With the two passengers and their gear boarded, the plane taxied briefly and then took off for Anchorage.

Mike suggested to Dan and the three sitting next to him that they should think about going out with Buns to search the Sound for more orcas. "You might find a pack that you can follow and try your communication ideas."

This seemed like a great idea to Dan and Rolly. Rolanda was not so sure it was a good idea but she would go along. Buns thought it was a great idea, more money for her boat and more time to get Rolly to appreciate her talents. There were plenty of supplies on the *Vamp* for another week or so and the four of them returned to the dock, boarded and headed out into Prince William Sound once more.

Greg and Cynthia boarded the *Glacier Bay*. They gave Don the food Greg figured they would not need prior to their return to Whittier in a couple of days. "By the way" Greg said to Don. "I've got some other fish and game matters I need to take care of in this part of the Sound. How about if I return in a couple of days and I'll watch the camp so you can go out on the *Czarina* with Mike, Tracy, and Sally?"

Don's eyes lit up. "Great idea, Greg. You get a blue ribbon for that one. That would be fantastic."

Kim, accompanied by Reed, walked out to the pig's enclosure to feed them and see how they were doing. The pigs looked fine and seemed happy to see Kim again. They had rooted all the grass from the original pen site so Don had moved it to a new well-grassed location adjacent to the first one. Rosy was obviously happy to be back with the other pigs.

Don had taken the seven empty kennels and stacked them up near the barn. Kim began crying softly when she recognized the kennels for Daisy and Petunia. "You know", she told Reed, "I don't believe I can take any more of the orcas killing and eating the pigs. I may not go out there again."

Reed hugged her. "We appreciate your feelings for the pigs, but if you think about the good we are doing you may change your mind," Reed said. "I know how you feel about the pigs but they are a food animal and we both eat pork products. Please go out this one more trip when we're trying to corner T-7. We'll take the pigs but, who knows, we may not even need them. And you are a comfort to the pigs."

Kim thought for a minute. "Well, OK, because of you, I'll go this one more time." They hugged each other and walked back to the lodge.

Mike and Reed had come up with a new plan. When they found the A-T pack again they would try to use the pigs as an enticement to get the A-T pack, or at least T-7, to enter a cove or bay by putting a pig or two in the water. If she really likes to eat them she'll come into the cove for some food and nets can be placed to prevent exit. Everyone but Kim agreed this was a good plan and it would show further the aggressive tendencies of T-4 and perhaps others. But they knew Kim did not want to see anymore pigs slaughtered.

The next three days were taken up with getting ready to search for the orcas again. Arrangements were made for aerial help to find the A-T pack. Listening, filming and recording equipment were checked out. George and Herb were contacted for their possible participation. Herb advised them that approval for capturing and transporting one of the subjects had been held up at NOAA in Washington. The environmental group named Blue War had heard about the project and started raising hell at their various locations to have the research program in the Sound stopped. However, there was optimism that cooler heads would prevail and permission would come through, perhaps in ten days or so.

Mike, Tracy and Reed, with Mario, Kim and Don participating, met at the lodge to discuss strategy. The conclusion was reached that they should proceed with their efforts with the A-T pack because they had so much current information as well as a general idea where this particular pack might be found. They also currently have pigs on hand they might be able to use, and these animals were not easy to come by in Alaska. They would find the pack and try to get them into a cove so fishing nets could be strung across the mouth of the cove and the orcas would be held as temporary prisoners. They could then isolate T-7, have her picked up by a specially-equipped boat, take her to Vancouver and then ship her by air to California. Good reasons not to delay. They radioed Herb and George with their plan using code words so the messages would not be understood by most who might hear them. They would be ready in two days and, if the spotting plane could tell them the location of the A-T pack, they could start the next phase of the study.

Carl Baker advised them that, with a day's notice, he and his plane would be available to try to locate the pack. Mario contacted his fishing friends in Cordova to locate a couple of boats with nets that could block the pack in a cove. Fortunately, there were no salmon openings for the next two weeks and the owners of two boats would be glad to participate and make some money when not fishing. Cost per boat and crew was $3,000 per day, but Mario figured they would need the two boats for only a couple of days because once the nets were set and holding the orcas in a cove, the fishermen and their boats could go back to Cordova.

Plans were made to once again get the *Karen Marie* and prepared for several days out in the Sound. Supplies and water were loaded and equipment carefully packed away. Don would be aboard the *Czarina* because that's where Sally was and, in addition, Mike and Tracy were long term friends. Fortunately, Greg had returned to the camp in the Glacier Bay and would be there to keep an eye on the lodge during their absence.

Mike got on the radio and called Carl in Anchorage to come over to the Sound for the aerial survey. Carl knew what he was looking for now and could search for the pack with the assistance of his niece, who was visiting from Seattle. He could radio to them with progress or sightings.

The next morning they were up early to a windy but sunny day and, with Don operating the four-wheeler and trailer, loaded the pigs in kennels onto the deck of the *Karen Marie* along with food and straw. They were even taking Wolfy this time because they might need all of the pigs. At 8:30 Carl flew over, dipped his wings to them and then flew out over the Sound shorelines where the whales might be found.

Both boats cast off and headed out into the Sound. Mario had suggested they go to the location where they last saw the whales, which seemed logical, but there was little chance the whales would be in that location. "But there." Mario said, "they could wait to hear from Carl."

By one o'clock both boats were anchored and waiting in a location protected from the wind. There was concern Carl might be running low on fuel and have to return to Anchorage, but then the call came in: "Subjects are located on the west side of Saima Island and are traveling north at what appears to be a slow pace. If you head for the north end of the island you should be able to intercept them."

Mike replied: "Thanks, Carl. Great information. We'll head that way now to find them. Good job."

The engines of both boats were started and Mario, with the faster boat, took the lead. He also knew the Sound better than anyone else in the group.

By 4 pm the *Karen Marie* was approaching the north end of Saima Island and everyone was watching for evidence of whale presence. Nothing was seen until Evelyn said "There they are!! Not far from shore." As the viewers watched, orcas came to the surface to exhale, breathe in, and then submerge. They counted nineteen whales and the big male had a curvy dorsal fin with a notch in the trailing edge.

"That's the A-T pack," Reed exclaimed, looking through binoculars. "Mario, call the *Czarina* and tell them we have the subjects in view. They'll be glad to hear that."

On the *Czarina* there was almost a sigh of relief that the pack had been found. Now they could do more planning. Mike radioed to Herb about the activities and he contacted George. Greg at Herring Bay was notified that Herb and George would be flying in to again board the *Glacier Bay* with him and they would then go to find the two boats following the orcas. They would bring supplies of food with them and they also would bring along another game warden to watch camp. It would not be wise to leave the camp unattended.

Once Herb and George were aboard the *Glacier Bay* and departed from herring Bay, more than two hours were required for the *Glacier Bay* to get to the vicinity of the *Czarina* and *Karen Marie*. George got on the radio. "We should be close to your location now. Any further guidance?"

"We're just near the north end of Saima Island and heading north at a fairly slow pace," Mario radioed back.

"OK, we see a couple of boats in the distance, that's either you or fishing boats," George radioed. And then after a few minutes: "That's you OK, we can see both boats. We'll fall in behind the *Czarina*."

Now there were three boats following the whales, which seemed to no one a good idea because of the noise but they could stay at a distance. At about 6 pm, Mike radioed to the other two boats: "We'll have to follow them again tonight. The *Czarina* crew will handle the shift work tonight. Why don't you take your boats into a quiet cove and anchor for the night. We'll let you know in the morning where we are and what is happening."

Tracy pulled Mike's sleeve. "Wait a minute, something is happening. They've started hunting near the entrance to that small, sharp cove to the east. Must be something there. But T-4, the bull, isn't going with them, looks like he's headed out to deeper water." She radioed the news to the other boats.

T-4 swam very deliberately near the surface, taking lots of time for breathing. Then he raised his tail and dove almost vertically. "Something different going on there," Reed noted from the *Karen Marie*. "T-4 appears to be diving for something the other whales are not hunting."

Meanwhile the pack appeared to have found a group of six harbor porpoises and killed and ate them. The group also found some type of bottom fish and were catching and feeding on them. "Takes lots of food for nineteen orcas" Mario noted. "They might eat six tons of food tonight if they can find it."

After five minutes T-4 surfaced again in the same spot and appeared to be resting there while he charged his system with oxygen. In a few minutes he dove again and appeared to go deep. "Whatever he's feeding on, there must be plenty of it because that whale will eat a few hundred pounds himself in one evening," Mike noted to those on the *Czarina*. The hydrophones were picking up lots of whale chatter and it was being recorded, but no one could connect the sounds with any particular action of the orcas.

T-7 gave what Tracy called the "departure call" and the whales once again began moving north. T-4 rose from the depth and joined the pack. There was no visible evidence to suggest what he may have been eating.

"I know a secluded cove near here," Mario radioed. "The *KM* and the *GB* can pull in there to spend the night. Tomorrow we'll join the *Czarina*. But there is no sense to three boats following the subjects, tomorrow how about one boat again mid-day and a second one for the night shift? Remember, we have only so much fuel before we have to go in for refueling at Whittier or Cordova."

"Good thinking, Mario," Mike radioed. "Let's hope we have enough fuel to complete our current studies in the next couple of days. We'll start the night shift right now and you guys can go anchor." Then he said to those on the *Czarina*: "It's doubtful they got enough to eat so they may be hungry again tomorrow."

As the night passed, Tracy radioed the other boats: "It appears we traveled about 4 miles last night and we're still going north at a slow pace. We expect something to happen though, because the group did not get much food yesterday evening. Suggest you move out to join us." Both the other boats responded.

Mike was up and had a cup of coffee as Tracy described an uneventful night. Don and Sally were not up yet. A review of maps showed several coves ahead, which could be useful for trying to corral the orcas, but there was no way to tell what course the whales might take. "Nevertheless," Mike pointed out, "There is some economic risk, but I'm thinking we had better get those fishermen from Cordova out here in the event, just in case, we can get the orcas in one of those coves."

Tracy agreed. "Yes, and let's check with Reed and Mario to see if they agree."

Mike got on the radio and called the other two boats, now on their way to join them. "What do you think of getting the two boats out of Cordova today so if we are successful in our corral plan they can do the net placement? We may lose a chance if the nets aren't there when we need them."

Both Mario and Reed agreed. It was worth the risk of the expense. Mario radioed to his friends in Cordova to come out to the approximate location that afternoon if they could make it. The owners of both boats had been waiting for the call and said they would leave within the hour.

Reed radioed to Mike: "Suggest you call Buns and have her bring her trio back to our location. Remember, they're supposed to have some dough that will come in handy for paying for the Cordova boats."

Mike radioed to the *Vamp* and requested that Buns bring her passengers to their approximate location. Buns's immediate response was that they would be on their way in minutes.

The A-T pack seemed to be waking up from their sleep mode and their speed picked up a bit but they continued their north orientation. Tracy mentioned that she thought they were looking for food.

In the next hour the *Karen Marie* caught up to the *Czarina* and took the lead, followed by the *Glacier Bay*, and even the *Vamp* had arrived. By early afternoon the two fishing boats from Cordova had joined the group so there were six boats now following the A-T pack, staying 100 to 200 yards back. Mario had explained to the fishermen that they would try to get orcas into a cove and the two fishing boats were to string nets across the mouth of the cove to essentially trap the orcas. One of the fishermen said the orcas could tear their nets all to hell but Mario assured them orcas had been trapped like this previously with little net damage. And, if a net was damaged, it would be replaced or repaired.

The orcas then changed course and turned northwest toward Montague Island, one of the larger islands in the Sound. There were abundant coves on this, the eastern shore they were following. As they approached one of the coves, several members of the pack split off and entered the cove. Watched through binoculars it appeared they caught a couple of either seals or sea lions and probably killed and ate them, the pack then resumed swimming 50 to 100 yards off shore.

"They're hunting," Tracy noted. "And likely very hungry." Mike nodded yes.

Mike got on the radio. "*KM* we suggest you loop out ahead of the group a mile or two and get into one of those coves. Let's try our plan of getting some members of the group to come in there."

"OK" Mario radioed back. The *Karen Marie* surged forward and went out and around the A-T pack. At about 2 miles away Mario steered the boat into a small cove about the size of two football field s and it had a narrow entrance. There was a sand beach and abundant trees on the hillside up and away from the water. The anchor was dropped about 50 yards inside the cove. On board, initial preparations were made to drop some pigs in the water when the orcas were approaching.

Reed was very sensitive to Kim's feelings for the pigs. "Any thoughts on which we might drop first?" he asked her.

Kim nodded yes. "The one I care least about is Wolfy, the male pig. He's not friendly and is even hostile at times."

Reed, Mario, and Evelyn got the kennel for this, the largest of the pigs, pushed over near the side of the boat. The sling for picking up the kennel was put in place. Evelyn had been looking toward the beach with binoculars and she said: "Oh, Oh! Good thing we're not planning to go ashore, there's a female grizzly at the edge of the trees and she's got two cubs."

"That's good to know," Mario replied. "She's going to be very edgy with strangers."

Kim was watching for the whales to arrive when she shouted: "Hey, looks like we've got some visitors! There's a good-sized blue boat out there." She looked with binoculars. "It appears the name is... No, that's not the name, it says Blue War."

"Oh my gosh, they've found us," Reed lamented. "I hope they don't cause trouble or interfere." He called the other boats and told them about the new visitors.

"Let's just go about our plans anyway," Mike stated. "They probably will not interfere. We have NOAA and State of Alaska people in our group." Meanwhile, the *Czarina* and the other boats continued following the A-T pack along the island's coast.

Mike radioed to the *KM*: "The pack leader is now within 300 yards of the cove mouth. Suggest you put something in the water."

On board the *KM*, Evelyn opened the gate to the kennel with the large pig and wired it open. It was obvious the pig did not want to come out. Mario lifted the kennel with the winch, Evelyn pushed it out over the water and it was lowered. The pig did not come out and Evelyn again took the gaff and tipped this kennel, which was much heavier. On the third try the pig fell out and hit the water with a large splash. The pig immediately began swimming in small circles. Evelyn pushed it out away from the boat. To the surprise of all on board, and unlike the other pigs, Wolfy turned and headed directly for shore, swimming strongly. On board the *KM* they could only watch.

"Oh, oh." Mario exclaimed. "Ev saw a grizzly there. Get your cameras ready."

After a couple of minutes of swimming, Wolfy's hoofs touched bottom and he waded in and shook some water off. The bear, downwind from the pig, had already picked up his scent and stood up, 7 feet tall, for a better view of this creature that she could smell and hear.

Wolfy wanted to get away from the water but also was hungry. He began rooting and rustling around in the brush just above the sand beach. The grizzly approached within 50 feet and stood up again, looking, listening and testing the air. Her cubs followed. Then she charged the pig and sank her teeth into Wolfy's neck and picked him up as if he was a rag doll. Wolfy was squealing loudly and the cameras were rolling aboard the KM. It appeared that the bear shook the pig and broke its neck. With the pig now dying, the bear tore open the stomach cavity and brought out the still-bleeding liver, which she fed to her cubs. Then she went after the heart.

On board the *KM*, the other twelve pigs had heard the squealing of Wolfy and suddenly became very quiet.

"Poor things," Kim noted, "they're probably petrified with fear."

Reed suddenly realized they had been watching Wolfy and the bear and they needed to get another pig or two in the water. "Mario, Ev! Let's get two pigs in the water, the pack is approaching!"

A call came from Mike: "Looks like the pack leaders are about to reach the mouth of the cove. Is everyone ready?"

"We'll be ready!" Reed responded as Mario and Evelyn lowered two pigs to the water in wired-open kennels. Evelyn dumped them out and the pigs began swimming near the boat trying to get back on board.

The A-T pack had not found good hunting the past couple of days and they were definitely on the hunt for more food. As they approached the mouth of the cove, T-7, in the lead as usual, picked up some sound of creatures in the water. As soon as she turned into the cove she scanned and noted the anchored boat and two of the creatures that were good eating swimming at the surface. Here was some good food for the pack. She signaled to the others that this could be good feeding for at least part of the pack. Ten of the pack stayed out of the cove and waited while the other nine went in to check out this possible food source. T-7 recognized the boat as a friendly one and she recognized the type of creatures in the water, which had been such good eating previously. She accelerated toward the boat and immediately took one of the pigs down. The next whale took the other pig. Evelyn and Mario got two more pigs ready to dump.

"Go ahead and dump!" Reed called as he watched T-7, with her tag still attached flash by the *KM* at high speed, obviously excited.

Mike and Tracy, Don and Sally in the *Czarina* were now at the mouth of the cove near the waiting ten whales, and could see what was happening. Mike radioed to the other boats "Now is the time to gather at the mouth of the cove. Part of the pack is in there and we want to keep them in there. Fishermen, get ready to put out your nets across the cove mouth."

Engine noise increased as the fishermen expertly began stringing nets across the mouth of the cove. The *Glacier Bay*, the *Czarina* and the *Vamp* stayed outside the cove and out of the way of the netting operation.

Tinga and the other eight whales could hear the engine and propeller noise behind them but they were focused now on the pigs as a good food source. Almost as soon as they took two creatures to eat two more would be dropped in the water. All nine whales now wanted food and were feeding heavily on the pigs.

On board the *Karen Marie*, Evelyn shouted: "There are only two pigs left, should we put them in?"

"Yes!" Reed replied. "They're still stringing the nets and we don't want any orcas to escape!"

Kim had been watching and saw her prized pigs dropped in to be slaughtered and eaten. She watched the last kennel be hoisted off the boat and the pigs dropped. She asked herself how she could ever get involved in such a scheme.

All nine whales had gotten some food from the twelve pigs although they were not full by any means.

Tinga was now aware something strange was happening. As she and the other orcas swam in the cove there were boats near the entrance and of the whales could detect two of the boats, with lots of engine noise, stringing a net across the entrance. She and the other whales circled, looking for some way to get out, but the nets were shore to shore and surface to bottom. There seemed to be nothing they could do so they continued circling.

On board the *Karen Marie*, Reed, Kim, Mario and Evelyn were ecstatic.

Their plan to capture this pack of whales had worked almost perfectly. They had part of the A-T pack trapped in the cove, including the tagged T-7. They would figure out a way to isolate her, ship her to Vancouver and then fly her to San Diego and Hydrosphere.

Sally, Don, Mike and Tracy, on board the *Czarina*, looked to the north and saw that the Blue War ship remained there but with noise from an engine powering a generator. It was obvious there were people on deck watching and taking photos. "Well, it's really something we expected," Mike noted. "We just didn't know how or when they were going to show up. They're probably going to raise a big stink and use this as a chance to stir up their supporters and raise more money."

On board the *Karen Marie* within the corral, Kim wanted to know: "How do we get this boat out of here? We've trapped ourselves too."

"No problem," Mario answered. "We'll approach the net near shore and one of the fishing boats will lower it so we can pass over the net. Easily done."

"The whales might escape, right?" Kim asked. 'And with no food they may starve."

Reed answered this time. "No, we know from experience when the orcas are enclosed like this they become quite docile and appear to accept the fact that they are captured. They could ram through the net or even jump over it, but they won't. No one knows why they seem to accept their capture, may have something to do with their group cooperation. Concerning food, orcas can go for a week or more without food when they have been feeding on salmon, as these have been."

One of the fishermen called Mario on the radio. "Looks like our job is done. Should we head back to Cordova?"

"Not quite yet," Mario responded. "I'll take the *Karen Marie* over near the net and you guys can drop the top of the net so we can cross over and get out of here. Then you can raise the net again. Once we're out of here you can head back."

Within an hour the *KM* was out of the enclosure and the two fishing boats headed back to Cordova. The whales had been corralled without any injury or problems on either side. Everyone was happy except Dan and Rolly on the *Vamp*, who still wanted their chance to communicate with the whales.

"All right," Reed told Dan by radio. "The subjects are here and you're just outside the enclosure. Go ahead and try to communicate through the net, it won't stop your sounds." He then winked at the others on the *Karen Marie* and told Dan, "Explain to the orcas what we are intending to do so they'll understand. You can also try to communicate with those outside the enclosure because they are still standing by out there waiting for those we trapped."

"OK, OK," Dan responded. "We'll see what we can do." He and Rolly were now smiling and happy but Rolanda just shook her head wondering how much longer they were going to be out here. Buns was enjoying the trip, she was making good money and having fun with "Rolly-boy."

Sally, with Don at her side, steered the *Czarina* toward the *Vamp* and Mike spoke to Dan, Rolanda and Rolly without using the radio. "Remember, this expedition was pricey and we're counting on you guys to come through with some financial help."

"Yes, yes." Dan said. "Come alongside and we'll help out right now." He went to the cabin he and Rolanda had been staying in and returned.

Sally brought the *Czarina* next to the *Vamp* and Dan reached across to Mike and handed him a large tan envelope. "Hope this helps," he told Mike. "And remember, we'd like to participate in more whale studies down the road. Keep us in mind."

"Thanks a bunch" Mike smiled. "Hope you get some reaction from the whales when you try to communicate."

The *Glacier Bay* idled up to the *Czarina* and George spoke to those on board: "That was a fantastic job of capture if I ever saw one. That was brilliant to use the pigs as a sort of bait to get and keep the orcas in the cove. The State of Alaska congratulates you for a job well done. And at virtually no cost to the state."

Herb added: "The federal people will be pleased to learn how this all came about and it will help us get a permit to remove one female orca. I'll push ahead to keep things moving in a positive direction. Oh, and I believe we have some good photos to go with a report."

George thanked everyone for their cooperation and then added "With the subjects now corralled and held in by the nets, me and Herb had best be departing. But don't you think it would be a good idea to have someone stay here near the nets to be sure there are no shenanigans attempted with the whales? The State of Alaska is willing to leave Greg, the game warden, here with the *Glacier Bay* for the next week or so. Greg has firearms in the event they are needed."

"Great idea!" Mike responded. "We definitely need some security. And some of us need to get back to civilization to take care of business back there."

"When we know the time we'll get to Herring Bay," George commented, "I'll radio ahead and have a Fish and Game plane fly over to pick up me and Herb."

When Mike and Tracy later looked in the envelope there was $10,000 in cash. "Wow!" Tracy remarked. "These Canadians are OK!"

"But we'll have to be careful how we handle it because the feds will think we're drug dealers if we deposit lots of cash," Mike smiled. "But we're clean and have nothing to hide." Then he added: "We've got to get George and Herb to the *Karen Marie* from the *Glacier Bay* if we're going to leave that vessel here with Greg as a watchdog."

Don on the *Czarina* immediately volunteered. "Set me out in the dinghy and I'll pick them up and drop them off."

Mike lowered the dinghy and Don, running the small outboard motor, went to the *Glacier Bay* and picked up the two waiting men. He dropped them off at the *Karen Marie* and returned the dinghy to the *Czarina*.

The *Karen Marie*, with Reed, Kim, Mario, Evelyn, George and Herb on board and the *Czarina*, with Sally, Don, Mike and Tracy on board, departed for Herring Bay. Within two hours they were back at the dock. As planned, the float plane arrived to pick up Herb and George and return them to Anchorage. Mike, Tracy and Reed departed for Whittier on the *Czarina*. Mario was returning to Cordova until needed further and was taking Evelyn and Sally along, much to the dislike of Don, who wanted Sally to stay at the lodge with him. "Don," she told him, "Relax, I have my own small boat at Whittier. In about two days I'll be back to visit this place again and we can have some fun." Don was smiling broadly.

Arriving at Whittier, Reed rushed to a phone to call his office in San Diego to tell them to get ready because they were likely going to be shipping a mature female orca, hopefully within the next week, and she was an intelligent one. The people at Hydrosphere were delighted. They had a great spot for a new orca and a male they thought could be used for breeding. Reed also called and spoke with his oldest boy. He told him he would soon be back in California and expected to bring along a lovely lady he was sure the boys would like.

Within the corral created with the use of fishing nets, those A-T pack orcas which were trapped were very upset. They were used to the open sound or ocean and plenty of fresh food and exciting hunting. The orcas noted that all the boats that had been near the nets departed except for two. One of those had a noise-making device which only irritated the whales. Another larger boat was further away and it made a steady noise. The whales kept circling.

Dan and Rolly, with Rolanda and Buns on board the *Vamp*, could see no response from the whales no matter what they tried: music, recorded whale sounds, people talking. Dan speculated that it might be because the orcas were penned and refused to communicate under those circumstances. But they could also get no reaction from the orcas circling a half mile offshore waiting for those trapped. After another day of trying without success, Dan told the others: "We've tried every approach I could think of and we're getting no response. Perhaps it's time to head back to Whittier, get to Anchorage and then fly back to Vancouver."

"I'm ready," Rolanda told them. "Never in my life did I think I'd spend this much time in a small boat in Alaska. Let's get back to town and get a flight scheduled."

Rolly smiled. "It's been great being out here with you two and Buns, but we'll come back again in the future for another try at communicating. I've got some good stories to tell the Orca Communication Society, I even went swimming with orcas!" He turned to Buns, "How do you feel about returning to Whittier?"

"Aw hell, Rolly, you and me was just getting acquainted. But it's true we've been out here for longer than I planned for. Let's call it quits for now, I've probably got more requests for charters waiting."

The engine on the *Vamp* was revved up and they headed back to Whittier. After arriving, Rolanda, Dan and Rolly took the train to Portage and then drove their rental car to Anchorage. From there they flew to Seattle and then caught a flight to Vancouver. Buns was very happy with the money she made and she had even taught Rolly a thing or two about love-making.

Two days later, back near the cove where the A-T pack had been corralled, Blue War members, on their ship *Compassion*, had watched all the action of the whale capture and penning. They were outraged. The boat captain, Max Baer, got the crew, and "guests" who were donors, together and explained his plan. "As you can see, all the boats but one are gone, departed. That one boat appears to have one person aboard; must be a sort of watchman. Tonight two of our best divers will dive on the net, cut an opening and release the whales. This will be a noble act." The crew and guests on the boat clapped their approval of this plan.

At 1 am it was reasonably dark and three people were getting ready to board the skiff: one was there to row and the other two were divers who would wear scuba gear and take sharp knives and shears. The three slipped quietly into the skiff and it was lowered to the water surface. No outboard would be used, only oars because they were silent. Once on the water, the skiff was rowed toward the fishing net stretched shore to shore. There wasn't much light but they could still see the top of the net. They said not a word to each other.

Tinga, extremely unhappy at being caught in a trap, sensed that something was going on when she detected this other small craft approaching in the semi-darkness. In spite of the net, she was able to watch it on sonar. She signaled to the other orcas in the corral that "Something was going on here."

The skiff arrived over the net at a point about 75 feet away from shore. Max had figured the water would be 20 or so feet deep at this point. The two scuba divers got ready and then slipped into the water. They both had headlamps, which they turned on once they were below the surface.

Tinga swam up within 50 feet of the divers she could see with the light from their head lamps. She also had scanned them with sonar. She was very curious about what they were doing.

The two divers estimated when they thought they were about 10 feet below the surface and began cutting the net down vertically, one using a knife and the other shears. They worked their way down the net, which Max had estimated would be about 25 feet total. In ten minutes the two divers had cut their way to near the bottom of the net at the bottom of the cove, but they saw that the net did not open as they hoped it would. Using hand signals to communicate, the two rose to where they had started cutting and began cutting laterally toward the center of the cove. When they had cut about 20 feet the current swept the cut net away to create an opening large enough for the largest killer whale. The two divers turned off their lights, surfaced and climbed back aboard the skiff. Within thirty minutes they were back aboard the *Compassion*.

Tinga and the other whales had observed and sensed with great interest that the net was cut and the current then swept the flap away from the cut revealing an opening. The whales waiting outside, although a half mile away, had also been sensing the drama unfold and they continued circling as they waited for their comrades. Not willing to take chances, Tinga carefully approached the opening to check it out. She swam slowly through the opening and was outside the corral. Then she turned around and swam back through the opening into the corral again. She was now satisfied it was alright for the other whales and she signaled them to join her. One at a time, all nine whales exited through the hole in the net and joined the others which has been waiting further out in the Sound. With the pack now together again, they swam rapidly away from the area toward deeper water and the open North Pacific Ocean. Tinga was leading them away from this dangerous area.

The next morning, game warden Greg in the *Glacier Bay* awoke and looked out to see what the whales were doing. He could see no whales. He then saw the hole in the net and knew what had happened. During the night someone, probably from Blue War, had cut the net and the whales had escaped. He immediately got on the radio to advise headquarters what had happened. Word spread quickly through the state offices and at NOAA. George called Mike and Tracy to tell them what had happened. They passed the word on to Reed and Kim who were staying at their home.

The news was very disheartening for all who had spent the time and effort to carry out the study of this pack. No one had the desire to start anew at this time.

Over coffee, Mike, Tracy, Reed and Kim discussed this latest turn of events. Reed explained that he thought that, even without the whales, the study of whale activities 24-7 would provide new insight into how and why the whales behaved in certain ways and what sort of actions might be expected.

Mike added "There is, of course, a possibility that the A-T pack can be spotted again and perhaps more studies done. But, let's face it, everyone involved is ready for a break and a chance to do something else."

"There's another consideration too," Tracy reminded them. "By the time all the bills are paid there isn't going to be much money left, if any."

"Hydrosphere management will be disappointed that they aren't getting an orca out of this, but they will appreciate what we have learned about the whales. I'll prepare a report that will contain good information for anyone interested, along with photos."

"Yes," Mike noted, "We have a ton of information to go through, videos, photos, sound recordings. But Reed, it is probably best if the Hydrosphere staff does much of that type of work on this. They're better trained than me or Tracy. And we're thinking of a retreat to Hawaii to get away from the orcas, the bank and the gold for a while."

"And southern California sounds good, too," Kim smiled at Reed. "We're going down there and I'm going to make some new acquaintances."

After going through and sorting all the information they had gathered, Reed and Kim checked in for their flight to Seattle and then to San Diego. The data from the studies was shipped in boxes on the same flight. There was a once-per-week direct flight from Anchorage to Hawaii and Mike and Tracy were happy to get away from Alaska for ten days.

Flying over Prince William Sound on various tourist and other flights for the next several weeks, Carl kept his eyes open for the A-T pack but he did not see them. The A-T pack had apparently disappeared. He sent an e-mail to Mike and to Reed with the observation.

After reading the e-mail, Mike discussed it with Tracy and then sent a message to Reed. "The disappearance of this pack could result in some bad news. That A-T pack remains smart and aggressive, particularly T-7. They're going to show up somewhere and I hope it doesn't mean more dogs and people disappearing."

"Yes, but there is not much we can do now," Reed replied. "I've made it back to San Diego and my boys as well as Hydrosphere and teaching. Fortunately, Kim is here with me for at least a couple of weeks before she goes back to Colorado. Of course, I'm hoping she does not return to Colorado but decides to stay for the long term. At Hydrosphere they are working on the photos and other records and may come up with something." Kim and Reed smiled at each other.

It is a year later and no one has seen the A-T pack. Most people have forgotten about the events, even the kids who were so frightened.

A small girl scout troop from Seattle had been looking forward to an outing in the San Juan Islands northwest of Seattle. For weeks they and their scoutmaster had been discussing and laying plans for this outing. They had arranged to take the Washington State Ferry to San Juan Island and rent six two-person canoes, which would hold ten Scouts and one canoe for the scoutmaster. There was great excitement when they got off the ferry and walked to the canoe rental shop. The owner explained to them that canoes were not as stable as boats and they should not try to stand up or lean over too far because they might tip over or fall out. He issued life preservers to the scouts and the scoutmaster.

Within an hour, the scouts, wearing their orange life preservers, were paddling north toward another small island where they planned to stop and have lunch before heading back to the starting point. One of the scouts happened to look behind the canoes. "Looks like something is following us," she yelled to the other scouts.

The scoutmaster looked. "Oh, it's a pod of orcas. How wonderful to see them up close like this."

The scouts stopped paddling and turned their canoes so they could look back. They saw what appeared to be a large group of whales and the largest whale had a tall dorsal fin that was wavy. The whales split into two groups, one group stayed behind the canoes and the other swiftly and silently passed the canoes near the surface. The whales seemed to be looking at the scouts and one whale even did a spyrise for a better look at the canoe occupants. The orcas then turned to rejoin the trailing group and they all disappeared from sight going south. The scoutmaster was not very concerned about the safety of the scouts and, once again, urged them start rowing toward their destination. The whales disappeared going south.

On San Juan Island, marine biologist Sean Hoyt, retired from NOAA, had purchased a point of land on the west side of the island where he could watch to the west and observe activity in and on the water. He particularly liked to keep a log of killer whale numbers and activities as they passed by. He had been getting very concerned because killer whale numbers appeared to be decreasing significantly. Perhaps something was killing them off such as *Toxoplasma gondii*, a cat parasite that was now showing up in marine mammals. The parasite was known to infect human brains in strange ways and it had now been found in dolphins off Hawaii and Oregon. It is excreted in urine and feces and finds its way into the ocean through sewage runoff. The domestic cat populations, even in Hawaii, had exploded in size and thousands of *Homo sapiens* were infected. Many didn't know they were infected but exhibited symptoms of cat craziness such as keeping twenty or more cats. Some infected people had more than fifty cats. The parasite had recently been found in dolphins offshore California near Los Angeles.

Sean was watching as usual with binoculars and spotted a pod of whales traveling south about one half mile offshore. He was astounded because this pod appeared to have more than fifteen members, more than he had seen in one pod in years. He wondered where they were going but had no way to tell. But he called his friends to tell them the news.

Near the south end of San Juan Island there are some coves with sand beaches that are popular with some of the local people. Teenage friends Sam Roberts and Merl Bowling had decided to take advantage of a warm day and go to the beach. The water was too cold for swimming but they figured they could have fun on the surface anyway in the inflatable small dingy that Sam had received for his 16th birthday.

At the beach it was a warm day and they pumped up the dinghy. No heavy clothing needed, they decided to wear just their swim suits. They could sit on the two preservers they had brought along as requested by Sam's mother. With two small oars in the craft they pushed off and began paddling out into the small bay.

Three hours later, Sam's mother became worried and urged her husband to go check on the boys. He found the dinghy and two preservers washed up on shore along with the two paddles. Clothing of the two boys were there on the sand along with the air pump, but no swim suits, nothing else. He called his wife and then the sheriff.

E N D .

Visit http://AuthorRVBailey.com to get insider information of his
next book due out, *Dɪɴᴏsᴀᴜʀs*.

Mr. Bailey ("RV") was born and raised in a small coal mining town in southern Wyoming where wildlife and insects were a constant source of interest and study. After attending the University of Wyoming and majoring in geology he was involved in various business activities, most of which were focused on locating economic deposits of gold, oil and gas, copper, uranium and coal.

He was one of the first to recognize the importance of "roll front" uranium deposits in Wyoming and elsewhere. He co-authored a 540 page textbook on uranium exploration and has written numerous articles on that subject. Important gold discoveries were made in the course of his exploration in Alaska.

While carrying out exploration for both placer and lode gold deposits he met, and joined with, a marine biologist who was studying killer whales in Prince William Sound, southern Alaska. In this study he and the biologist would be out in Prince William Sound for days at a time in a fishing boat discretely observing killer whale packs, often 24-7.

RV also enjoyed sport fishing for salmon and halibut in southern Alaska, the Seward Peninsula and Siberia. He participated as an observer aboard a commercial salmon fishing boat operating from Cordova on the eastern edge of Prince William Sound. He currently spends summers in Wyoming and winters at Port of the Islands, Florida, where he observes wildlife including manatees, fish, birds and alligators.

32151267R00285

Printed in Great Britain
by Amazon